ONE WORLD

JᵼMᵼJ

ONE WORLD: Book Three of the Iamos Trilogy
Copyright © 2023, 2025 by Lyssa Chiavari.

Published by Snowy Wings Publishing
www.snowywingspublishing.com

Cover and maps by Qamber Designs and Media.
Model photos by Mosaic Stock Photography.
Interior graphics by [adj] Millennial.
Interior formatting by Key of Heart Designs.

"Joseph (For None Can Stop the Sun)" © by RoAnna Sylver. Lyrics reprinted with permission.

ISBN (Hardcover): 978-1-946202-11-6
ISBN (Paperback): 978-1-952667-52-7

FOR THE LEOPARDS,
one last time.

DEAR READER,

The first book in The Iamos Trilogy, *Fourth World*, was published in 2015. Due to ongoing health problems, there were long gaps between the publications of each book in the series—particularly between *New World*, the previous book in the series, which was published in 2018, and this book.

Because many of you read the previous books in the series quite a long time ago and may not remember everything that happened, I have put together detailed recaps for each of the preceding books in The Iamos Trilogy. You can find these on my website at **iamosrecaps.lyssachiavari.com**. Please bear in mind that these recaps are intended for people who have already read the other books in The Iamos Trilogy, so they are full of spoilers. If you haven't read the previous books in the series, please do read those first, as this book is the conclusion of an ongoing, continuous story and cannot be understood without the foundation of the previous installments.

Thank you for reading and for all your support over the last eight years!

LYSSA CHIAVARI
2023

ONE WORLD

the iamos trilogy , book three

LYSSA CHIAVARI

Snowy Wings
PUBLISHING
TURNER, OR

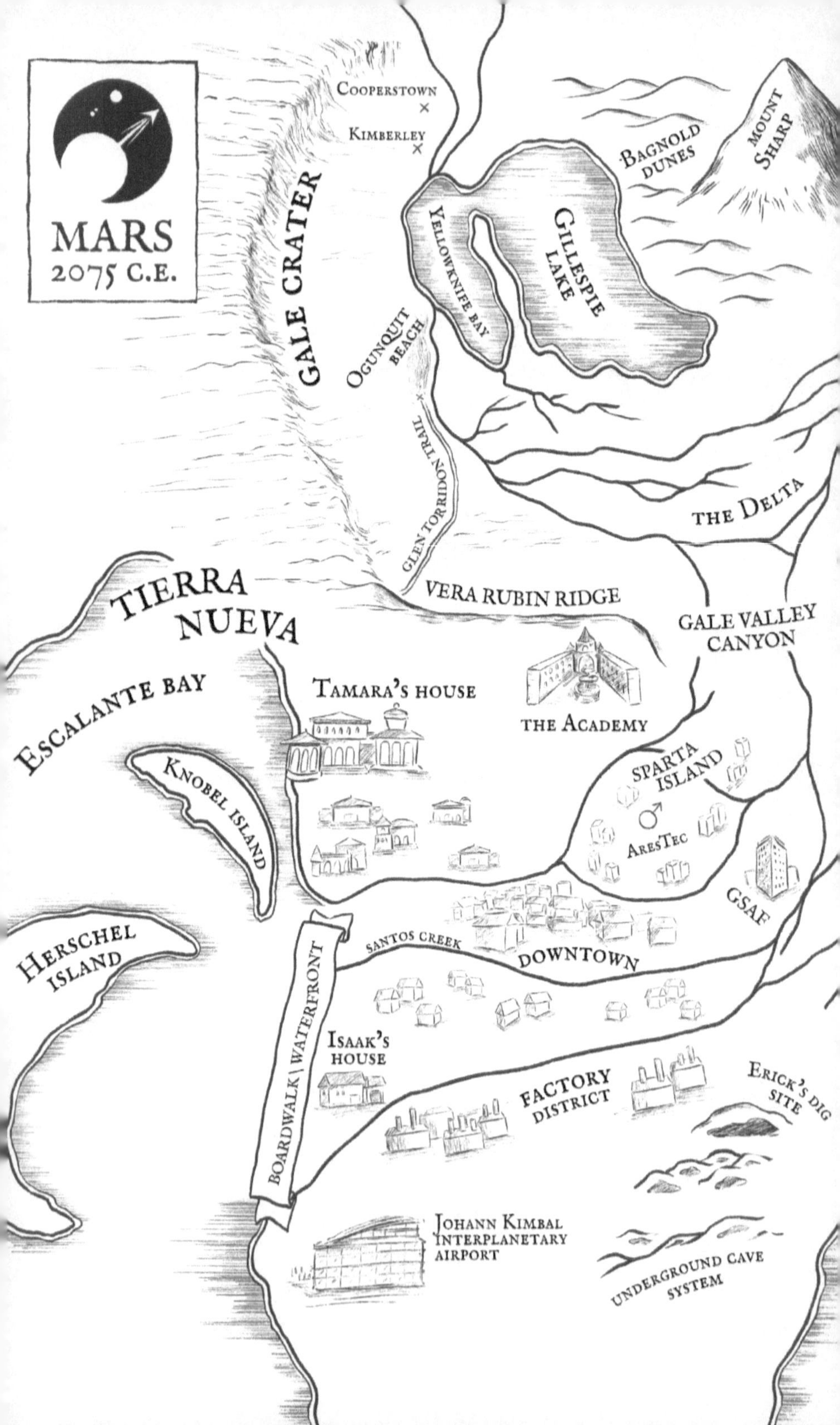

MARS
2075 C.E.
COOPERSTOWN
KIMBERLEY
GALE CRATER
YELLOWKNIFE BAY
OGUNQUIT BEACH
GILLESPIE LAKE
BAGNOLD DUNES
MOUNT SHARP
GLEN TORRIDON TRAIL
THE DELTA
VERA RUBIN RIDGE
GALE VALLEY CANYON
TIERRA NUEVA
ESCALANTE BAY
TAMARA'S HOUSE
THE ACADEMY
SPARTA ISLAND
KNOBEL ISLAND
AresTec
GSAF
HERSCHEL ISLAND
SANTOS CREEK
DOWNTOWN
BOARDWALK\WATERFRONT
ISAAK'S HOUSE
FACTORY DISTRICT
ERICK'S DIG SITE
JOHANN KIMBAL INTERPLANETARY AIRPORT
UNDERGROUND CAVE SYSTEM

DRIED LAVA PLAIN
IAMOS
S.C.D. 8378
BRIGHT HORIZON
ELYTHERIOS
HAOI IFAISTEOI
ELIIN'S OUTPOST
HOODOO CANYON
GREAT CRATER
KALDEROS IFAISTEOS
KATAI'IOS
HOPE RENEWED
ANCIENT OBSERVATORY RUINS
ANCIENT CAPITAL RUINS
UNDERGROUND CAVE SYSTEM

I SHIFTED MY WEIGHT FROM ONE FOOT TO THE OTHER AND BACK AGAIN AS we stood facing the postern. Waiting. The smooth white marble walls and floor of the pyramid's innermost chambers made the room cold, far colder than even the deepest levels of the caves. Those, at least, had channeled hot springs running through every level. The inside of the pyramid was like ice.

As I shifted again, trying to keep from shivering, *Gerouin* Melusin glanced over at me. "Stop fidgeting, Nadin," she murmured, her voice gentle but firm. I was still young then, just a few weeks before my fifth annual. The *geroi* were perhaps a bit more tolerant of my lack of impulse control in those days. That tolerance waned as I grew older and they realized I wasn't turning out to be the perfect young *gerouin* they'd imagined I'd become.

"I am sorry," I said, standing up straight, shoulders back, in what I hoped was an adequate imitation of my mother. "It's cold in here."

"All of Iamos is cold," *Geros* Antos said from my other side. It wasn't an admonishment. It was just a statement, wistful and laden with regret. It made me feel guilty nonetheless. Our resources were limited enough—artificially heating this part of the pyramid would mean using energy that was needed elsewhere. Antos was right: I could make do for a short time. The System would regulate my body temperature enough to keep me from getting *too* cold.

The postern started to quietly hum, and a soft, digitized chime came from my earpiece. "*Arrival imminent,*" the System said in my ear.

I'd been trying to mentally prepare myself for this moment for months—years—but my stomach still lurched. This was the day I'd been awaiting my entire life. The moment I'd been both anticipating and deeply dreading. The end of everything I'd ever known. The end of me as *myself*, a single entity. The start of my new life as *half* of something else, whatever that may mean. And the first step to becoming a *gerouin* in my own right.

The arrival of my partner.

I'd spent these past days wondering, worrying, wondering again: What would he be like? Would he be tall or short? Broad or slim? I knew nothing of him other than that he came from Bright Horizon.

Would he… Would he like me?

I couldn't tell if I was excited or afraid.

The grooves and joints of the archway began to glow, and I ducked my head as the light became too bright to look at. The postern's hum grew as deafening as the light was blinding; then, everything fell still.

I looked up, and three strangers looked back at me. They stood just on the other side of the postern, the stable connection between the two arches forging a doorway through space. The room they were in was the exact double of this one, creating the illusion that I was looking through a mirror, only to find a reflection on the other side that wasn't mine.

Then they stepped forward, passing through the door and entering my reality. A man, a woman, and a boy my age. His wheat-colored hair was shorn close to his scalp, and he stared at me unblinkingly with somber green eyes. I smiled hesitantly at him.

He did not smile back.

"Tibros, Clodin," Melusin said, extending her hands to clasp those of the other *geroi*. "It is good to see you. And Ceilos." She turned to look at the somber boy. Instantly, his demeanor changed, so fluidly that for a moment I found myself second-guessing the coldness that had been in his eyes when he'd materialized.

"*Degiim, Gerouin*," the boy said with a smooth smile. "And *Geros Antos*. It is good to meet you at last."

I shifted awkwardly in my place, feeling left out. He was to be my partner; shouldn't he greet me as well?

Geros Tibros glanced at me and nudged his son. "Ceilos, this is Nadin. Your partner. Say something to her."

Ceilos' eyes flashed for just a moment as he looked at the *geros*. He smiled at me, but his eyes were cold once more. "*Degiim*, Nadin," he said.

The *geroi* didn't seem to notice the venom in his tone. Clodin turned to Melusin and Antos. "We thank Hope Renewed for your hospitality. We know how tight resources are, and the burden an extra body can be on a citidome," she said.

Melusin inclined her head. "Of course. All lives are one. Your mission on Hamos is of the utmost importance. We wish you the best of fortune."

I looked at Clodin. Her narrow, angular face added to her poise.

There was nothing in her demeanor to betray any sign of nervousness or concern, though she and her partner had been chosen for a dangerous assignment. We all knew Iamos couldn't sustain us much longer. Our attempts at conservation were failing. It was time to leave.

And Tibros and Clodin were one of the six *geroi* partnerships chosen to establish colonies on the other worlds, the great splitting of our people. Two were going to Hamos, our sister planet. Four were going to Simos, the second world from the sun. These were the only two of the eight greater planets in the solar system that appeared to be able to support life. And if neither proved hospitable to our kind...

We would die.

"We will entrust Ceilos to your care, then," Tibros said matter-of-factly. "We apologize that we cannot stay longer; we must return to Bright Horizon to finish the preparations with the new *geroi*."

I swallowed. The new *geroi* of Bright Horizon were a partnership from Prosperous Future and Fertile Mountain, just past their *enilikii*. Paolin and Shiros. Only four years older than myself. They were to be the last partnership until Ceilos and I came of age. Which citidome would we rule? One here on Iamos? Or would we have to travel to a different world? I glanced over at Ceilos, but he avoided my eyes. My stomach clenched with nerves all over again.

"Farewell, Melusin, Antos, Nadin." Tibros paused before saying, "Ceilos." There was an almost undetectable hint of warning in his voice. Ceilos set his jaw.

I tried not to flinch as the postern closed behind Tibros and Clodin in a blinding flash of light. When the room grew dim again, Antos turned to Ceilos.

"Welcome to Hope Renewed. You are one of us now, Ceilos."

Ceilos looked up at him, the spark of animosity that I'd noticed between him and his father extinguished. He smiled smoothly, effortlessly, in a way that made him seem older than I knew he was.

"Thank you, *kyrios*. I hope to prove myself worthy," he said.

He followed the *geroi* out of the room, but I hovered one step behind, watching the back of his head and wondering:

What sort of person was he, this boy who could change his face as easily as one changes clothes?

PART ONE

IAMOS

S.C.D. 8378
10,942 B.C.E.

CHAPTER 1

THERE WAS NO SKY HERE. THERE WAS ONLY SMOKE. THICK, ACRID, AND dark. It squeezed my lungs until I choked on it. Not long ago—just this morning to the people here, those who had remained in this timeline, who hadn't passed through the postern and spent months on an alien world thousands of years in the future—there had been swirling clouds above, and bright, cheerful sunlight reflected from mirrors around the village. But that was gone now. All that remained was darkness, ash, and destruction.

Just like everything the *geroi* ever touched.

My eyes struggled to adjust to this dimness after the blinding sun of the Veracruz morning I had just left behind. I lay there for a moment, my body aching from the force of traveling through the postern, the impact of hitting the ground hard as the tesseract ripped shut behind me. My palms were bleeding from scrapes against the rocks as I'd collided with the cave floor.

The static had barely cleared from my eyes when I was wrenched upright by an Enforcer. His fingers dug into the bare skin on my upper arm, exposed by the short-sleeved shirt I'd put on this morning—perfect for the hot, muggy jungle where I'd been moments before, but far too lightweight for the cold air of Iamos. I tried to jerk my arm out of his grasp, but he merely held on tighter.

The old Nadin would have snapped at him for daring to touch a future *gerouin* this way. But I was no longer the same person I'd been mere months ago, and it seemed that everyone knew it.

Especially the *geroi*, who were staring at me as if I were a stranger.

All around me, there was shouting. Voices of anger, of disbelief. In the distance, I could hear screams and the crying of children. The sound turned my stomach. Straining against the Enforcer's tight grip, I looked around at the devastation. Everything was burning. Black smoke rose from the roofs of the village longhouses, and farther away, where I knew the precious crops were growing, I could see a horrific orange glow. Enforcers were everywhere, rounding up Elytherioi and herding them into huge transport vehicles. I watched in dismay as one drove past, crushing the carefully grown vegetation that the people here had fought so hard to cultivate, against impossible odds.

Behind me, the postern stood empty and dark. What had moments before been a door of light was now nothing but a stone archway. I'd done it. I may have been far too late to save the Elytherioi, but at least I'd been able to do this much. The connection to the future had been severed in time. Isaak and the others were safe.

For now.

"Nadin, what have you done?" *Gerouin* Melusin demanded, her usual hushed voice rising into an unrecognizable shrill pitch.

What had I done? If only she could begin to comprehend. I'd traveled across millennia in an attempt to save my people, only to learn that those I'd trusted most—the *geroi*, the saviors of Iamos, whom I'd spent my entire life trying to please, desperately wanting to become one of their ranks—my *parents*—had been deceiving me all along. They weren't the self-sacrificing leaders of a dying world they'd pretended to be. They were authoritarian dictators who would resort to anything to preserve their own power, even if it meant the destruction of this world and the genocide of another.

I shot a glare at her. "I've stopped you. The door is closed now. You won't be able to open it again." When we'd created the stable connection between Elytherios and Earth, the *geroi* had had the perfect opportunity to invade Earth with their army of Enforcers. But with the time postern now closed, they could do nothing. "Isaak is safe in his own time. You won't be able to harvest his DNA for your barbaric neurotoxin," I spat.

"We don't need your door," *Geros* Antos said. "And we don't need the boy, either. We've got *him*." He gestured over his shoulder to where an

Enforcer restrained Emil Hassan. I silently cursed. The Martian scientist. If only I could have gotten him through the door before it closed…

"Look at yourself," Melusin said in disgust, coming over to me and plucking a tendril of blue-black hair off my shoulder, wrinkling her nose as if she were touching something filthy. "Our planet is *dying*. The *geroi* needed you. Your people needed you. And instead of fulfilling your assignment, you ran off with a band of anarchists and allied yourself with Simoi. With aliens. You even degraded yourself enough to adopt their appearance. I trusted you, Nadin. I believed that you could be one of us. And you betrayed us."

"Better a traitor than a useful *fool*," I spat.

"That is enough," Antos interjected. Turning to the Enforcer whose fingers still dug into my arm, he said, "Take her to the transports. We have a job to finish."

"What are you going to do to them?" I asked, though I was sure I already knew the answer.

Antos leveled his gaze on me, his blue eyes locking with mine. "The same thing we do to all traitors," he said.

I swallowed. "You can't. Look around you. Surely you must see! This place… the crops, the wildlife, the vegetation—we need it, *kyrios*. We believed almost all of these species to be extinct, but here they are. Alive and thriving. And the Elytherioi's technology, their knowledge of climate restoration… You can't destroy this! We need—"

"Enough!" Melusin broke in. "What makes you think you are in any position to argue with our decisions? We have given you chance after chance. Just moments ago, I offered you yet another opportunity for redemption, and you spat in my face. You are not one of us anymore, Nadin. I realize now that you never were." Her words stung more than I would have expected, considering the rage I felt toward her and my father. "This is a hive of rebels, of anarchists who have sought to destroy the peace and unity of Iamos for decades. This place, and the people in it, must be exterminated."

"No!" I shouted.

"I *said* take her to the transports," Antos snapped, and the Enforcer dragged me away, even as I fought against him, screaming until my throat felt ragged and hot tears leaked out of my eyes.

"Nadin!" The voice came from behind me. I refused to turn my head. I refused to look at him. But he ran to catch up, stopping the Enforcer and putting his hands on my shoulders so I couldn't avoid him. "Nadin, please—"

"Don't touch me!" I recoiled from him, squeezing my eyes shut. I couldn't look at Ceilos now.

"Nadin, listen..."

"I don't want to listen to you, Ceilos. I don't want to speak to you. I don't want to look at you. You betrayed all these people, after they trusted you!"

"I didn't know about any of that!" Ceilos protested. "I didn't know anything until it was too late. The *geroi* made a deal with me the same as with you. A way to save our partnership. The anarchists were destroying Iamos—"

"You know that's a lie."

"I do now, but I didn't then. And neither did you. By the time I came to understand it, it was too late."

I wouldn't meet his eyes. I kept my stare resolutely past him, over his shoulder, to where Enforcers were rounding up *gurzas* and other large livestock and herding them onto one of the transports. "But why the whole kidnapping pretense? You and I were already working with Isaak to try to find Gitrin. We would have solved her riddle together, and that would have fulfilled my bargain with the *geroi*."

At Isaak's name, Ceilos had bristled. It was almost imperceptible, but I caught it. His tone colder now, he said, "The *geroi* felt that you weren't working fast enough. They wanted something to spur you on."

"Spare me the excuses, Ceilos. You lied to me. I told you right away about the deal the *geroi* had made with me to save our partnership. But you worked with them behind my back. You terrified me, and you kept the charade up even long after you'd arrived here. You showed up here with false bruises and a lie about being kidnapped. You could have told me the truth, but you didn't. You're not the person I thought you were."

Each sentence was like a blow, Ceilos' face falling more and more with every word. I refused to feel guilty about it. He deserved every bit of it and more. He'd betrayed us all, and now Elytherios was lost.

He dropped his hands from my shoulders, and the Enforcer pulled me away.

✦

As the Enforcer shoved me into a transport vehicle, I finally saw the cause of the explosion that had shaken the ground beneath us as Isaak, his father, and I had passed through the postern all those months before—less than an hour earlier in this timeline. A gaping hole had been blasted into the side of the mountain, the hollow caldera that Elytherios was situated within. Big enough for these vehicles to fit through, for an invading force of *geroi* and Enforcers to storm their way inside. A pit formed in my stomach as I saw animals fleeing through the opening now, trying desperately to escape the fires burning within. Orange-eyed *kerkopiths* and scaly *savra*, winged *ielak* and *kela* broken free from their pens. They were trying to escape the fires, but they'd never survive out there. The atmosphere was too thin; there wasn't enough air left for most species other than the high-altitude *gamadas*, who'd adapted to low oxygen levels long ago. Within hours, all these precious creatures would be dead.

And so would the people.

Unless...

I twisted the ring around my middle finger in agitation, the black hematite cool and hard. It was a big *unless*. If the *geroi* had been able to find Elytherios, I couldn't know that they hadn't already found the rebels' other hiding places—and if they had, then everything truly was lost.

And it was all because of Ceilos. I ground my teeth furiously. There was no way the *geroi* could have sneaked up on the Haoi Ifaisteoi without the Elytherioi knowing they were coming. They had to have used one of the vehicle posterns in Bright Horizon to instantly travel here, to the location that Ceilos had informed them of after following Isaak and me here. A surprise attack the Elytherioi could never have hoped to escape. And no way the *geroi* ever could have pulled it off without his help.

The Elytherioi had been so distrusting of me and Ceilos. They'd voted not to let us join the community. They'd said they could never trust *geroi*'s blood, and it turned out that they'd had good reason all along. I'd worked so hard to earn their trust, to prove that we could become part of their movement to save Iamos and fight against all the injustices that the Progression had wrought. But I never would have believed Ceilos was capable of doing this. My blind faith in him had now led to the destruction of the one hope Iamos had of being saved.

I had caused this. My stomach churned with revulsion. By coming here, I'd inadvertently led Ceilos and then the *geroi* directly to them. This was all my fault.

I wished I could use the time postern to go back and change this. Warn the Elytherioi. Warn myself. But I knew now that such a thing would be impossible. Changing events that had already unfolded could destroy the universe. I would have to live with the consequences of my own foolish mistake.

Or maybe I wouldn't live with them, I realized, glancing at the Enforcer. Maybe this would be how I met my end. If the *geroi* had their way, the Elytherioi would be executed—why should I be any different?

I had come so far to save Iamos. Traveled through time, across centuries, sailed through space to another planet, all with the desperate hope of saving my people. And I'd failed. What if this was where my story ended? After everything I'd gone through? Had everything I'd done been for nothing?

No. Even if Iamos truly couldn't be saved, there was hope that Mars could. I had to believe in Isaak, and in Henry, Tamara, and Scylla... in Lizeth and the Stateless... They could still save the future from the System, and if it hadn't been for me, they never would have even known the danger. I had to believe that even if I'd failed in every other way, it hadn't been for nothing.

Through the windows, I could see the Elytherioi being forced into other transport vehicles. Gitrin, Emil, Eos, Marin. The Ferre smuggler, Shuliin, and her partner, Syrin. The *plivoi* couple from Hope Renewed, Gios and Corin, who had only just escaped the *geroi* days before. They'd longed for a new life here with their unborn child, and now they'd never get a chance. Their baby would never breathe its first breath.

When I saw the woman who'd spoken to me on my first day in Elytherios—the mother who had voted to allow me to join the community when so few others had—torn away from her young children and loaded into a vehicle, I couldn't look anymore. I raised my knees into my chest, burying my face in them. Hot tears burned behind my eyes until I couldn't hold them back anymore, and they soaked through the fabric of my jeans.

✦

The ground vibrated as the convoy of transport vehicles rumbled out of the caldera and down the slopes of the mountain. The *geroi* had not said a word to me when they'd entered the vehicle. I looked down at my canvas shoes, caked in Earth mud, refusing to glance in their direction or at Ceilos, who had entered the vehicle after them. Despite my disgraced status, they wouldn't deign to group me with the other prisoners. I still rode with the *geroi*, even though I was now their prisoner rather than their equal.

No. Never their equal. Always their pawn.

The transports rolled single-file down the mountain's slope, like the ants I'd seen on Earth crawling out of their nests. The *geroi's* smaller vehicle took up the rear. At the base of the mountain, a massive plain spread as far as the eye could see, the desert broken by streaks of black—the remnants of a long-ago lava flow. Isaak and I had crossed this plain on our *gurzas* and it had taken hours, but these vehicles could travel much faster. I was sure we would bypass the canyon of rock spires and the cave systems that Isaak and I had hidden ourselves in as we'd traveled from the outskirts of Bright Horizon, trying to stay out of sight and within the oxygen pockets of the underground. There was no need for secrecy now. Traveling directly across the plain and through the valley, we'd be at the citidome by sunset.

As we crossed the lava plain, the mountain receded behind us, and the conical silhouettes of its sister volcanoes appeared on the horizon. The other transports rumbled on ahead of us, but here Antos broke the silence, holding a hand to his earpiece and ordering the vehicle to stop. At his word, the automated vehicle shuddered and stilled.

I watched him, frowning, as he swiped at the air before him. He was using a System panel, but because I no longer wore an earpiece, I couldn't see what he was doing.

Then the ground began to shake. This wasn't just the vibration of the transports' wheels. This was bigger—a lot bigger. Like the way the ground had shaken when I passed through the time postern hours— months—before. Like an explosion.

A *massive* explosion.

In the distance, fire erupted along the rim of the caldera, as though the volcano itself had awakened. Black smoke billowed out of the opening the *geroi* had blasted into the mountainside. Boulders began to tumble down the slope, dragging streams of loose red dirt along with them. Even from this far away, the noise was unbearable. I dug my fingers into my ears, but it did nothing to dampen the sound.

And then, with a deafening crash followed by an enormous cloud of debris, the top of the mountain collapsed into itself.

I stared in wordless horror, unable to tear my eyes away as smoke and plumes of dust billowed up into the sky, disappearing into the thin atmosphere. The central peak of the Haoi Ifaisteoi was now a lopsided crater. The hollow caldera that had once housed Elytherios was no more. My stomach roiled with nausea. Across from me, Ceilos stared through the window, his face frozen in shock.

It was gone. It was gone *forever* now. It could never be saved. It could never be rebuilt. There was no part of it that could be salvaged. It was no matter, a numb little voice whispered in my mind, that Isaak's father had told the media about Elytherios. There'd been no treasures for the future Martians to uncover. In a single instant, the *geroi* had destroyed them all.

At last, my voice caught up with me, and I whirled on Antos. "What have you done?" I screamed. I tried to jump to my feet, but beside me, the Enforcer wrenched me back down, pinning me hard into my seat.

Antos wouldn't meet my eyes. "Silence her," he said to the Enforcer.

The Enforcer hesitated. "*Kyrios,* she is not connected to the System. The adherence protocol..."

Melusin huffed in annoyance. "Put your hand over her mouth if need be. Just keep her quiet. We have a long journey ahead of us and I am in no mood for her nonsense."

The Enforcer reached toward me and I jerked away, baring my teeth. "I wouldn't if I were you," I hissed at him.

"Then keep your mouth shut," he hissed back.

I wanted to disobey. I wanted to scream and scream until my voice would no longer come, to vent all the rage and despair and hatred and fury and spite that welled up inside me now. I wanted to hurl invectives in my language and every Earth tongue Isaak had taught me. But what good would it do? What good would any of it do? I couldn't bring

Elytherios back. I'd held the key to time and space in my own hands just an hour before, but still there was nothing I could do. Elytherios was gone forever.

Utterly defeated, I sat back on the vehicle's bench seat, my shoulders slumped. But my eyes never left the window. I could do nothing but watch the smoking hulk of my planet's last chance for survival grow smaller and smaller in the distance.

CHAPTER 2

THE ENFORCER SHOVED ME ROUGHLY INTO THE CELL, SLAMMING THE DOOR behind me without a word. No one had spoken to me since Antos had detonated the explosives. We'd lumbered silently across the lava plain and up into the hills, past the nearly dry lake bed that Bright Horizon had been built beside, years ago when water had still flowed. Bright Horizon had been the first citidome built on Iamos, in the time of the first *geroi*, not long after the Progression. It was the city where Ceilos had been born. His parents, Tibros and Clodin, had been the ruling *geroi* of the citidome at the time of his birth. But when Shiros and Paolin had passed their evaluations, the *gerotus* had decided that Ceilos' parents would move on to the new colony on Hamos, Ascendant Dawn.

That was when Ceilos had come to live with us, in the *geroi's* villa in Hope Renewed. From that day on, he'd never returned to Bright Horizon.

Until now.

A contingent of Enforcers awaited just beyond the double-layered glass doors to the city, the airlock which kept the artificial atmosphere from escaping. This quarter of the city had been cleared of ordinary citizens. A convoy of vehicles this large could never hope to escape the *plivoi's* attention otherwise, and the riot that would surely ensue would make the one I'd seen back in Hope Renewed—a lifetime ago, it seemed—look like child's play.

The Enforcers herded the Elytherioi out of the transports and toward the pyramid. The massive stepped structure of glass and stone rose to the very top of the dome that enclosed the city. It towered over all else.

It was the administrative hub of the citidome, but it was also the place where prisoners were kept. There usually weren't this many all at once. I wondered dimly where Shiros and Paolin planned to keep them all. I supposed it didn't matter in the long run. They wouldn't be here long. It would be a matter of *disposal* rather than *storage*. That train of thought made me nauseous. I swallowed down the bile that rose into my throat and tried to block the thought out of my mind.

As the *geroi's* vehicle halted and the doors lifted open, I hesitated, looking at my mother. She watched me impassively, but for just a split second, I thought I caught a glint of something that almost looked like remorse in her eyes. When I blinked, it was gone. More than likely imagined.

She nodded to the Enforcer seated beside me, and he wrapped his iron fingers around my bruised arm once again. As he pulled me into the cold air of the citidome, gooseflesh rippling across my bare skin, I saw Ceilos watching me from beside Antos and Melusin.

He made no move to intervene.

The Enforcer dragged me to the pyramid along with the Elytherioi, but once again, I was kept apart from them, segregated even in my exile. As he hauled me past a group of detainees, I saw Gitrin, and my pulse jumped. I called out to her, but even as she turned in my direction, the Enforcer shoved his body between us and pushed me through the arched door into the building.

They brought me back to one of the inner chambers, which, unlike the shining glass exterior of the pyramid, was made entirely of stone. Here the *geroi* shielded themselves from the dangerous rays of the sun, even as they kept up the pretense of being among the people in the upper levels. The presence of the administrative offices of the *gerotus* and other members of the *patroi* caste in the upper levels had been meant to be a sign of solidarity with the common people, who lived and worked entirely aboveground, exposed to the ever-increasing solar radiation as Iamos' atmosphere thinned. But as with everything else the *geroi* did for the so-called good of Iamos, it was a farce. Safely shielded behind thick walls of white marble—appearing from the outside, through the glass, to be nothing more than a reflection—the *geroi* never once put themselves in harm's way.

It was clear that my presence here now was not for my own protection, but rather a way of hiding me from any prying eyes. A child of the *geroi* allying herself with rebels—that could never be known by any on Iamos. *Unity through fidelity*, after all. No cracks in the *geroi's* perfect façade could ever see the light of day.

Three female Enforcers waited within the stone chamber, dimly lit with blue phosphorescence. Roughly, they stripped me out of my Earth clothes and dressed me in a silver Iamoi bodysuit. I kept my fists tightly clenched, hoping they would not notice my ace ring, but they pried my hands open and took that, too. Then they turned their attention to the most egregious offense: my blue-black hair, dyed by Zero before we'd fled for the Keysteads. The women held me down, heedless of my protests, and one produced a pair of shears.

Wordlessly, they cut my hair close to the scalp, then used a razor to finish the job.

Wordlessly, I chewed my lip until it bled, and tears etched hot trails down my cheeks.

And then they brought me here. To this tiny glass cell at the highest point of the pyramid. The place on Iamos with the least protection from the sun's ultraviolet radiation, short of total banishment from the citidome.

It was here that the *geroi* kept the most dangerous threats to Iamos' society. The most remorseless criminals, whose actions could warrant only reeducation, or, in the most extreme cases, execution. The scum. The terrorists. The anarchists.

That was what I'd become, wasn't it? A rebel. A criminal. And utterly unrepentant.

I braced myself against the lone stone wall of the cell. Suddenly, I felt as though my legs couldn't support my own weight. My back against the wall, I slumped down until I was seated, resting my bare head against the frigid marble. I was shaking all over—from the cold or from shock, I couldn't say. Probably both.

From here, I could see far beyond the reaches of the dome. In the distance, the misshapen lump of the Sios Ifaisteos, the central volcano of the three sisters, stood in stark relief against the setting sun.

I couldn't help but feel that the choice of this cell in particular had been deliberate. It was a fitting way to twist the knife. The only way I could escape the sight of the ruined hulk that had once been Elytherios was to close my eyes.

I squeezed them shut, but the burning behind them didn't cease.

When Ceilos and I had been in our fifth annuals, we'd climbed to the top of the pyramid in Hope Renewed while the *plivoi* had watched from the ground below. We'd stood at the peak, high enough to be seen from every corner of the citidome. There were only two times in the lives of *geroi* that they would ever voluntarily expose themselves to that much radiation. The second was at the ceremony in which an initiated *geroi* partnership would assume command of a citidome.

The first was at the betrothal ceremony.

On that day, Ceilos and I had pledged ourselves to each other and to the people of Iamos. We'd sworn to uphold the creed of the Progression and the values of our society. And we'd vowed to work together always, to support one another, and to always do what was right for our partnership and our people. We'd sworn it then, and again that day on the shore, looking over the ruins of the ancient city, crumbled and sand-covered, his hand in mine, our fingers tightly interlaced. A promise for Iamos, and a promise for just Ceilos and me.

Those vows ate away inside me now. We'd both sworn the same oath. But which one of us had upheld it? Him, or me?

I ran a hand, numb and stiff with the cold, across my smooth, bald scalp. A scab was forming in a place where the Enforcer had nicked my skin with the razor. I picked at it until the blood ran freely down the side of my face.

We had no religion on Iamos. Though we may have at some point, since the Progression, we believed in no deities, no afterlife, no spiritual world, no divine forces shaping the cosmos. But now that I had been to Isaak's time, now that I'd seen what Martians like Mariyah believed in, now that I'd been to Veracruz and seen the pyramid in the jungle, so much like this one, and heard Professor Senghas explain what it was for, the beliefs of the Simoi who lived there, I understood.

The *geroi* had made themselves gods. They weren't parental figures to the people of the citidomes the way they painted themselves to be. It was not a relationship of nurture. The *geroi* were meant to be worshiped. The people of Isaak's time had called me a princess. But I'd been more than that. I'd been born to be a *goddess*.

But I had fallen. Now I was something else entirely.

The sky grew darker and darker until the silhouettes of the Haoi Ifaisteoi disappeared into the blackness. The sky was ablaze with stars, the thick band of galaxy. In the city far below me, lights flickered on in the insulae. The glowing golden orb of Hamos slowly rose above the horizon, larger and fuller than Earth's moon had been.

It was only then, there in the darkness, with nothing around me but stars and night, that I allowed my thoughts to turn to Isaak. *Where is he now?*

And, with a hitching breath and a lump in my stomach, the next thought:

Is he safe?

I had left Henry with all the instructions for making a second key. I had given him the data for the location and the time. But the question was: Would he do it? Would he open the second door? Or would he choose to leave Iamos in the past and stay in the comparative safety of the future?

I knew the choice would have to be his. And I couldn't fault him if he decided not to open the door. In fact, I almost hoped that he wouldn't. On Earth they were fugitives, pursued by GSAF and living in hiding. But they had Lizeth and the Stateless. It was possible, if they kept the door between our times closed, that they might make it out of this alive. But if Isaak opened the second door, he would be walking into certain death. I couldn't know that he wasn't already in the *geroi*'s clutches. And that was possibly the worst part of all: I may never know. I could die without knowing whether Isaak was safe.

I leaned my head back against the stone. It was so cold. Everything was so cold. Everything was falling apart.

I squeezed my eyes closed, and there in the darkness I thought: *Why didn't I tell him?*

I'd known what was in my heart last night. I could have told him. But I'd held it back, and now it might be too late.

Above my head, stars swirled.

CHAPTER 3

- n a d i n -

THERE WERE SOUNDS BEHIND ME IN THE CORRIDOR. I HELD PERFECTLY still, listening. Someone was coming.

A moment later, the door slid open. In the darkness, I could see only shadows. A man's voice brusquely said, "Get up."

When I hesitated, the Enforcer at the man's side yanked me to my feet. My hands were shoved into restraints, and the Enforcer kept a tight grip on my arm as we wound our way through labyrinthine corridors into the heart of the pyramid. The rooms behind the stone walls were dim, illuminated only by phosphorescence, but as the first man passed an intricate, glowing mosaic, I caught a glimpse of his features. They were different than those of the Enforcer, and of almost everyone else in this citidome. Gray eyes and gray hair, the traits of Fertile Mountain. This was *Geros* Shiros.

I'd seen him only a few times in my life. The last time had been at my betrothal ceremony. He and his partner, Paolin, had been the same age that Ceilos and I were now. Only four years had passed since then, but those years had hardened Shiros. His profile in relief showed someone who looked much older than he was.

Though I'd never been inside the pyramid of Bright Horizon, I knew where he was taking me. The deeper we descended behind the marble walls, the closer we drew to the *geroi's* inner sanctum. Bright Horizon had been the first citidome built after the Progression, and thus it was the home of the *gerotus*. This was where the leaders of the eight citidomes—two on Hamos, the rest here on Iamos—would meet in secret, traveling by postern to the capital of capitals.

I had never seen the chamber of the *gerotus*. If everything had gone as planned, after our evaluations, Ceilos and I would have undergone the initiation to become *geroi*. Our partnership would have been permanently sealed, and I would have entered these walls as their equals.

But Gitrin had seen a different path for me. I had believed I was a failure when I didn't pass my evaluation. But I knew now what the *geroi* truly were. Gitrin had known I didn't belong with them, but not because I was a failure. Because she believed I could be something more.

If only I'd understood sooner, before it was too late.

When we reached the arched doorway, Shiros stopped the Enforcer. "No further," he said.

Shiros withdrew his medallion from beneath his tunic, and the doorway opened. The Enforcer prodded me forward but remained outside.

The chamber was a perfect circle, with a domed ceiling soaring high into the pyramid above us. Against the wall opposite the door, a small but ornately carved chest sat on a pedestal. In the center of the room a round table of burnished metal stood, and sixteen chairs of woven copper surrounded it. Not long ago, there would have been more. Seats for Achillios and Eristin, lost forever to the annals of time. For the three *geroi* partnerships who had gone before them, disappearing to different parts of Simos in different time periods, their colonization missions derailed by a saboteur. Each trapped there, unable to return home, unable to let us know what had become of them. Each leaving an indelible Iamoi footprint on Earth's history. Becoming the stuff of myth. Becoming, as Isaak had called it, Atlantis.

And if things had gone differently, there would be eighteen seats now. One for me, one for Ceilos. Would we have inherited a citidome on Iamos, as Shiros and Paolin had? Would they have sent us to Hamos, to found a new citidome? Or would we have been sent to Earth, too, never to be heard from again?

Behind each of the chairs stood the *geroi*, all of them watching me impassively. My stomach twisted as I looked at them. They were each arranged according to the citidome they represented, and it reminded me disconcertingly of the GSAF Council and the members of the continental unions of Earth. The six cities of Iamos: Bright Horizon, Radiant Tomorrow, Fertile Mountain, Dauntless Spirit, Prosperous Future, and Hope Renewed. Melusin and Antos were positioned with their backs to the door. They didn't turn to look at me, and I refused to look at them.

My eyes instead fell on an empty chair beside *Geros* Tibros, representing Ascendant Dawn, one of the two cities of Hamos. The seat for *Gerouin* Clodin, Ceilos' mother, remained unoccupied. Was she still in the hospital, after this long? In my anxious state, I couldn't remember how much time had passed since the earthquake on Hamos, but it seemed that surely she should have recovered by now...

The thought fled from my mind as I saw the figure standing in the shadows behind his father.

Ceilos.

Dressed in fresh clothes and washed, with his earpiece returned, he almost looked as though he belonged here. But while the eyes of the others remained cold and distant, Ceilos' face betrayed his thoughts. He met my gaze imploringly, looking worried and distraught—

And afraid.

The same fear rose up in my chest now, despite my attempts to swallow it down.

Shiros took his place beside Paolin, and the *geroi* all seated themselves. But *Geros* Tibros remained standing. "Kneel," he commanded me.

I stood tall, rooted in place.

"I said *kneel*."

I glared at him. I refused to kneel for anyone, but especially not the *geroi*.

In two strides he was at my side. His fingernails dug into my skin as he grabbed me and shoved me down. With my hands bound, I was unable to catch my balance and I hit the ground hard, sparks flashing before my eyes as my face collided with marble with a *crack*.

When my vision cleared, I saw I'd fallen at my parents' feet. They stared at me, their expressions unreadable.

From across the table, *Gerouin* Paolin spoke. I could hardly hear her voice over the ringing in my ears. "This is not a trial, Nadin," she said. "Trials are for those whose guilt has not yet been determined. But your guilt is known to us. There can be no denial, no defense. This is a sentencing."

I struggled to catch my breath. "I thought my sentence was already being carried out," I said sarcastically.

"Guard your tongue," snapped the *geros* from Dauntless Spirit. He was an older man, one of the eldest in the room, and he looked familiar to me. After a moment, the answer came to my bleary mind. This was Ilios.

Melusin's father.

Beside him, his partner, Alusin, watched me with the cool detachment I'd seen many times before on my mother's face. Despite the difference in their coloring—Melusin's hair was an almost-white blond and her eyes a bluish violet, the traits of Dauntless Spirit, while her mother bore the traits of Bright Horizon—the resemblance was uncanny.

I had never known my grandparents. Once a partnership was initiated into the *gerotus*, the familial ties were severed. By the time I'd been born, Melusin's childhood in the villa of her parents had been nothing but a distant memory. I found myself thinking of Isaak's family, the close relationship he shared with the beloved grandfather he called *Abuelo*. How absurd the world of the *geroi* seemed in comparison. There were eighteen people in this room, but only six sets of traits among us. For the first time, the reality of what the Elytherioi had called me— "*geroi*'s blood"—truly sank in. Over the past five generations, the six bloodlines of the Progression's original *geroi* had consolidated into one.

Every person seated around this table was my own blood relative, my own kin. Yet none of them cared anything for me. I had been nothing more than a useful fool to them before. Now I was a threat. An enemy.

"The *geroi* have questions," Ilios said, "and we demand answers. How you choose to respond now determines your fate."

They could ask all the questions they wanted. They would learn nothing from me.

"Nadin," said Melusin in her soft voice, the voice that had always made me admire her as much as I feared her. "Where were you when we found you this morning? On the other side of the postern."

I looked down at the floor silently.

"Were you on Simos?"

The sole of her right boot had a ring of dirt around it, a final remnant of Elytherios on her feet. I kept my eyes on it resolutely, not opening my mouth.

"You are making things worse for yourself, Nadin," Antos warned. "Say something. What did you learn from the Simoi?"

The corners of my mouth twitched involuntarily. I'd learned everything from them. I'd learned strength, and loyalty, and friendship. I'd learned the truth about the Progression and the *geroi*, about the dangers of the System. I'd learned what had really happened to our colonies on Simos, and perhaps the ultimate fate of the Iamoi. I'd learned what made a leader.

I'd learned who I really was. I'd learned my own worth and my own potential. I'd learned to love myself.

"Speak, Nadin," said *Geros* Shiros.

I looked up at them. "I learned nothing," I said.

"Are the Simoi planning an attack on Iamos?" Alusin put in.

I started to say *no*, but then I remembered GSAF and what we'd uncovered before escaping from Lago Verde. "I don't know," I said instead.

"Do the Simoi have access to the System?"

Yes. "I don't know."

"Our patience grows thin, Nadin," Antos warned. "What did you learn of the Liberator inside the mountain?"

"I learned nothing," I said.

"We know you are lying," Tibros interjected. "The Liberator is the leader of the rebels. He is responsible for the deaths of almost a thousand of our citizens on Hamos. He is responsible for what happened to Clodin. Tell us his name."

I swallowed roughly. "I do not know who is responsible for the attack on Hamos, but I can tell you that it was no one in the mountain."

"You're lying!" Tibros shouted, his voice echoing off the vaulted ceiling. The other *geroi* stared at his sudden outburst of emotion. He'd leapt to his feet, and he stood there now, breathing heavily. Slowly, he ran a hand over his rust-colored hair, braided neatly in narrow rows from his scalp to the nape of his neck. "We've heard enough," he said, his composure regained. He crossed the room, walking over to the chest on the pedestal. He opened the lid and removed a wooden flail, its handle carved and polished, knotted twine affixing three narrow switches to the handle. A relic of the kings of our past, from long before the Progression. I recognized it from my lessons with Gitrin. My stomach curdled inside me at the sight of it.

Tibros turned to Ceilos and held out the flail to him. "Beat her. Perhaps a bit of pain will loosen her tongue."

My heart stopped.

Ceilos froze in place, his eyes round and his mouth slightly open. "But, *kyrios*," he managed after a moment, "she has not yet been sentenced by the *gerotus*."

"Indeed not," said Tibros. "This is your trial, Ceilos. Show us where your loyalties lie."

"I've already proven my loyalty to the *geroi*," Ceilos protested. "I led you to Elytherios, just as you asked."

"That proves nothing," snapped Tibros. "You accepted that mission to save your partnership. That showed only your loyalty to Nadin. Now prove your loyalty to the *geroi*." He stepped closer, pressing the flail into Ceilos' hand.

Ceilos stared down at it for a long moment. Then he walked to the pedestal, putting the flail back in the chest. "*Kyrii*, I can't—"

"Adherence protocol activate."

I gasped as Ceilos' hands flew up to the sides of his head and he buckled in on himself. *Geros* Tibros watched, emotionless, as Ceilos fell to the floor. The sound of his scream seemed to cut deep into my bones. Tibros had activated the adherence protocol against his own *son*.

Ceilos fell silent, bracing himself against the marble floor, breathing heavily. As the echoes died away, *Geros* Shiros rose to his feet, looking around at the other members of the *gerotus*. "Brothers and sisters, it seems a lesson must be learned here. As the leaders of Iamos, we of all people know that all lives are one. We know that unity must be upheld at all costs. But I question now if there is disunity among our own ranks."

"Both Nadin and Ceilos were raised in Hope Renewed," said Ilios.

"This failing falls upon the *geroi* of that citidome." He said it without a hint of remorse, condemning his own daughter without a moment's hesitation.

"It was that tutor of theirs, Gitrin," Melusin countered. She hid it well, but I heard it—the defensiveness in her tone. "She poisoned their minds, the both of them."

"You should have seen the warning signs," Tibros said.

"We warned the *gerotus* more than a year ago," said Antos. "The consensus at the time was that it was more important to use Gitrin to attempt to trap the Liberator's faction. Something, I may remind you, that we just successfully did."

"But at what cost?" Tibros argued back. "Iamos is in need of more *geroi*. More colonies must be established. But we find ourselves with no *enili*, and now Clodin—"

"Enough!" *Gerouin* Paolin jumped up from her seat, slamming her hands down on the table. All eyes in the room turned to her. "There will be order among the *geroi*. As *gerouin* of the city of cities, capital of capitals, I must insist."

The others sank back into their seats—all except Tibros. He and Paolin stared at each other for a long time, a silent power struggle seeming to play out between them. Paolin and her partner were the *geroi* of Bright Horizon, the first citidome. That gave them authority within the *gerotus*. But they were the youngest initiated members, and Tibros and Clodin had held the role before them. Despite their claims of unity, there appeared to be more problems among the *geroi* than just my own rebellion.

At last, Tibros acquiesced. Without blinking, his expressionless stare still locked on Paolin, he sat.

Paolin exhaled. "Antos, Melusin," she said coolly. A tendril of light-brown hair had escaped her tight braid. She smoothed it back. "Now is your trial. Prove your loyalty to the *geroi*. Beat her."

The gazes of the other *geroi* now turned to my parents. Antos looked quickly at Melusin, then at me, sprawled on the ground before him. "Our loyalty has not been in question," he said, his eyes never leaving me. "We should not be expected to degrade ourselves—"

Melusin stood wordlessly, striding over to the chest without hesitation. She gripped the flail tightly as she came back over to me, and her hands did not shake.

"Unity through fidelity," she said, her voice echoing across the room. Then she looked down at me. "You had your chance, Nadin," she whispered. "I gave you nothing but chances."

I ducked my head and squeezed my eyes shut, willing myself not to scream, no matter what pain awaited me.

Of course I failed.

Chapter 4

- n a d i n -

THE GLASS WALLS AND MARBLE FLOOR OF MY CELL SWAM AROUND ME, spinning and whirling. The smell of blood was overpowering, making me retch. But I had long since been emptied, so I lay there on my stomach, unmoving, as my dizziness and nausea overwhelmed me. I drifted in and out of consciousness, the throbbing pain in my shoulders drawing me back from the blissful darkness over and over again.

Maybe I would die here. Maybe I would bleed out, or they would leave me here to starve. But I hadn't given them answers. The little piece of my mind that was still lucid enough to hold a thought reminded me of that much. My secrets would die with me, and Isaak would be safe.

He had to be safe.

"Please don't open the door, Isaak," I whispered to the empty cell before the blackness closed in again.

Some time later, I became distantly aware of the cell door behind me opening, of footsteps against stone. Then she crouched before me, and I blearily looked up at her. *Gerouin* Melusin. In her hands she held a small, narrow-necked amphora. Automatically, I flinched away from her.

She did this to me.

I didn't think I spoke aloud, but as if in reply, she said, "You brought this on yourself, Nadin." When I made a derisive noise in the back of my throat, she added, "This is not a joy for me. Seeing my own child suffer in this way. Knowing that I'm the one who caused it. But you left us with no choice. Through your actions and your decisions, you gave me no alternative. I have to choose the wellbeing of this world over the wellbeing of my daughter."

I thought about Bryn and Delia, back on Mars. The way they loved Tamara, the way they protected her. And the way they'd protected me, though I was no child of theirs. The way Bryn had stood up to Joseph Condor the last time I'd seen her, risking her family's safety and security, all in defense of me, a total stranger.

I sluggishly attempted to get to my knees before slumping over again. "You think you have the right to call yourself my mother? When have you ever treated me like your daughter? When was I ever shown anything but scorn and contempt by you?"

Melusin glared at me. "I carried you in my womb!"

"Do I really even count as your daughter?" I argued back. "All the tampering that was done to me in vitro. All the genetic material injected into me to ensure that no part deviated from the norm—eye color, hair color, skin color, traits and temperaments and dispositions all modified to ensure I came out exactly the way the *geroi* wanted me to be."

"And yet you deviated anyway," Melusin said scornfully. "So much for a perfect system." She set the amphora down hard on the ground before me. "Drink."

I frowned. "What is it?"

"Water."

I looked at it. I was so thirsty, I couldn't bear it, but I still didn't trust her. "Not poison?"

"Don't be ridiculous. Drink."

I still felt hesitant, but the temptation of water was too great to resist. I managed to ease myself up on my elbows, taking the amphora and drinking deeply.

"Not too fast, unless you want to be sick again."

I scoffed. "Why should that matter to you?"

Before she could answer, there was a knock at the door. Melusin put a hand to her earpiece and ordered the door to unlock. It slid open and a man entered the cramped space, pushing a metal, wheeled cart like what I'd seen in the hospital level. As he emerged from the shadows, I recognized him.

"The medic from Hope Renewed," I slurred, setting down the empty amphora.

Melusin tugged her earlobe. "Heros is the *geroi*'s most trusted medic on the whole of Iamos."

"Why do I need a medic?" I asked. "Aren't I to be executed?"

"There is no time to train a suitable *patroin* to assume your role as Ceilos' partner, and the next partnership will not reach their *enilikii* for nearly three more years. We can't afford to wait. You are too valuable to us alive." As she spoke, Heros rummaged through the cart. "The *gerotus* has decided that you are to be reeducated."

I stared at her, my vision swimming. *Reeducated.*

I wasn't to die, but in a way, this was worse. I would still be alive, but I would no longer be myself. How could I be? The System would reprogram my every thought, assaulting my mind with conflicting information until my brain was malleable enough to manipulate. Until I no longer knew myself—until I knew only what the System provided me.

My memories would be gone. Erased.

The Elytherioi, Gitrin... My time on Mars... the friends I'd made there, everything I'd learned about myself... everything I'd learned about my world...

Isaak...

Gone. It would all be gone. As if I'd never known them.

Heros approached me, an amphora in one hand and a glass jar in another. Instinctively, I scooted away from him.

"Now, *kyrin*," he said, "your wounds require dressing."

I tried to get away, but even if my broken body had been willing to cooperate, there was nowhere to go. There was barely room in this tiny cell for all three of us. He touched me with cold hands and I hissed in pain. He withdrew a pair of shears from the reticule at his hip, and I felt him gently cutting the torn fabric away from my shoulders and upper back, peeling it painfully from my skin. Then he flushed the wounds with whatever antiseptic liquid was in the amphora. I bit down on the inside of my cheeks to keep from crying out, but my vision turned white. When the wounds were clean, he rubbed an ointment from the jar into them and withdrew some strips of cloth from the reticule to bandage them with.

"These will not require stitching," he pronounced. "She is lucky you went easy on her, *gerouin*."

I dug my fingernails into my palms incredulously. She'd gone *easy* on me?

He stood again, replacing the ointment and antiseptic in the cart and withdrawing another amphora. "Drink, *kyrin*," he said, holding it out to me. "For the pain."

I hesitated.

"*Now*, Nadin," Melusin snapped.

Reluctantly, I drank. The liquid was bitter on my tongue, and it burned my throat going down.

"When will she be well enough to begin the reeducation process?" Melusin asked.

"Not long. Possibly by morning. I need to get her down to the hospital level for a more complete evaluation."

By morning? I looked out through the glass walls at the black sky above. Hamos had already passed overhead—it had to be past midnight. Just a few more hours...

Heros reached out to me again, and I scrambled out of his reach, my back colliding painfully with the angled wall. "No," I said, my voice shaking. "I won't go."

"Nadin, my patience with you has reached its limits," Melusin warned.

I shook my head stubbornly, though I knew the gesture would be lost on Iamoi. "No."

"Heros," Melusin said. The medic tugged his earlobe and rummaged through the cart, withdrawing a syringe. He was going to sedate me.

There was nothing I could do. No way I could escape this.

If they reeducate me, I'll lose my memories of Isaak. If he comes through the door...

I wouldn't know him. If he found me, I would have no memory of him. And my reprogrammed brain would be loyal only to the *geroi*.

He'd be walking into a trap.

I tried to move away, but Melusin grabbed my arm, holding me tightly. "There is no point in struggling, Nadin," she snapped. "It's over."

"No," I whispered. No, *no, no... please...*

Heros put a cold hand on my face, steadying me, and with the other hand injected the syringe directly into my neck.

Melusin let go of my arm and I slumped against the floor, defeated. There was nothing I could do to stop this. I might never be awake again with my memories intact. Frantically, I tried to grab on to them, hold them in my mind as tightly as I could, as if that would keep them from slipping away.

That night on Mars, when Scylla and Mariyah brought me to Lal Qila. A "girls' night out."

Melusin stood up, reaching for her earpiece, saying something I couldn't understand to someone I couldn't hear.

Tamara sitting beside me on the piano bench, telling me I was normal.

"Just be calm, *kyrin*," Heros said.

The sound of music. Music I'd never been allowed to experience before during my whole life on Iamos. The songs we sang together on the beach in the UFS, my first time ever singing. The way the melody had flowed through me, rising up from inside me like uncontainable joy.

"Heros," Melusin said.

The pyramid in Mexico. Ipilchan, New Home. Achillios' message.

"There's an emergency. We're needed in the hospital level."

Elytherios, full of life. The psara nibbling on my fingers. The rain on my skin.

"But, *gerouin*, what about Kyrin Nadin?"

Gitrin telling me that I could be more than what the geroi had planned for me. Henry telling me that what made me unique was what made me strong.

"She's going to have to wait. We need a medic. You're the only one we can trust."

Isaak, putting a flower in my hair.

"She'll be fine here. If the sedative wears off before we come back for her, we can re-sedate her later. We must go now."

Isaak, telling me I had him.

The door slid open again and Melusin and Heros left me alone in the dark.

Isaak saying, "Wherever you have to go —to whatever time —I'll go with you."

But the darkness was swallowing me.

"I won't leave you. I promise."

I couldn't hold my head up any longer. It hit the floor with a dull thud.

Ceilos falling to the floor as the adherence protocol exploded inside his head.

Everything faded away.

Because he wouldn't betray me.

CHAPTER 5

- n a d i n -

MY MEMORIES SWIRL AROUND ME, BUT TRY AS I MIGHT, I CAN'T HOLD THEM.

I stare at the stars overhead, unsure where they've come from. Was I looking at them before? Didn't I close my eyes? Or have I always been here, staring silently at the night? Watching them trace their patterns across the sky, dimly registering the glowing orb of Hamos rising higher in the darkness? Something about Hamos seems important, but I can't remember what. It feels too big, too far away. Too much of a problem for me to face now. I'm trying to hold too many memories, trying to keep them all from slipping away.

Then I blink, and I realize it isn't Hamos after all. It's smaller, glowing blue-white, not the familiar golden clouds of my sister world. No, of course it isn't Hamos. It's the Earth's moon.

A breeze whispers past my face, gently lifting tendrils of my black hair. I move my fingers and they brush something loose and silty. I lie back against it and it doesn't hurt my shoulders. Was I expecting it to? Is there a reason it should? I can't recall.

I sit up and look around. I'm back on the small islet Lizeth brought us to in the UFS, lying beside the dunes where long grasses grow from the sand and saltwater laps against a small wooden dock. This afternoon, Isaak taught me how to swim. I look out at the sea now, so dark that it's almost black, save for the glow of the moon on the cresting waves. Tiny, twinkling lights on the distant horizon remind me that we aren't far from Sea-Star Island. On the air, I can still smell the remnants of the smoked meat that Henry and Isaak cooked for us tonight, and the grilled vegetables for Scylla. In spite of everything that has happened before now and everything that is to come, tonight I feel full, and more peaceful than I can remember feeling in all of my life.

Behind me comes a rustle of movement. I turn, expecting to see Isaak climbing over the top of the dune, leaving the wooden walkway to come sit beside me in the sand. That's what happened in this moment, in my memory. He'd sat beside me, and we'd talked until late into the night. Eventually, Scylla and Tamara and Henry had joined us, and we'd laughed while they'd tried to teach me their card games. Tamara had begun singing, and we'd all joined in, even though I hadn't known how. I'd never sung before, and my voice had wobbled as I'd tried to get it to match the notes of their melody. It didn't matter. My friends had helped me find my voice, and the song still sings inside me now.

But it's not Isaak who appears on the walkway. It's Gitrin.

My eyes widen in surprise. "Gitrin, what are you doing here?" I ask.

She smiles as she sinks onto the sand beside me. "I thought I might find you here."

"But... I mean... what are you *doing* here? You never came to Earth with me. You... You should still be on Iamos."

"What are you talking about, Nadin?" Gitrin looks at me in confusion. "I've been here this whole time."

I frown, looking back up at the moon to try to get my bearings while Gitrin smiles placidly beside me. Is this what could have happened, in another lifetime? Gitrin had been supposed to come with us to the future, and Emil, and... Ceilos. How would things have been different if it had all gone according to plan?

But it could never have been. Because Ceilos hadn't merely lost his grip on my hand in the explosion. He'd let go. Deliberately.

He'd been working with the *geroi* all along.

A way to save our partnership.

I squeeze my eyes shut. I won't excuse him. I can't. He should have been honest with me. We could have found another way together.

"That showed only your loyalty to Nadin. Prove your loyalty to the geroi."

"Nadin," Gitrin says slowly, shattering the sound of Ceilos' agonized scream in my ears, whisking the memory from my mind. It's quiet here, still. Those memories are distant, muted. Maybe they're the dream and this is reality. I open my eyes, turning to look at her.

"Do you remember what we spoke of all those years ago, when Ceilos first came to us?" she asks.

My brows furrow. "No."

She smiles sadly. "Anger is poison."

I snort. "You've said that hundreds of times." She repeats it every time I lose my temper, something that tends to happen at least once a day. "But I have every right to be angry with Ceilos," I add defensively. "After what he did to me, and to you. To the Elytherioi. To everyone on Iamos."

"Don't you remember?" Gitrin asks, not seeming to hear what I just said. "What you and I spoke of?"

I struggle to think. When Ceilos first came to Hope Renewed, he'd only just passed his fifth annual, and mine had still been weeks away. Those early days had been hard, but by our betrothal ceremony, things had changed. We'd shared secrets and learned to trust each other. He'd become the only person I *could* trust, apart from Gitrin. Or at least, that was what I'd thought. But the memories are such a blur now...

"Remember what I *said, alin.* On that day."

"But I *don't* remember, Gitrin! That was years ago. I was a child." I sigh in exasperation. "Can't you just tell me?"

She doesn't answer. She just looks away, out at the sea. The wind has picked up, the waves growing rougher. I start to stand but lose my footing as the ground beneath me begins to shake violently.

"What's happening?" I cry, but there's no one to answer me. Gitrin is gone.

I'm alone on the beach as the ground roils, as if I'm standing on a turbulent sea. The sky above me blazes brightly, and I jerk my head up. The light overhead isn't the Earth's moon—it's Hamos after all. Hamos in the sky, huge and bright, closer than it should be, then too far away. Small and hideous and yellow, like a too-bright star. Enormous and looming, ready to swallow me up.

There's screaming, faint and distant, making my stomach go sour as I suddenly remember my dream from when I was on Mars. Clodin, screaming...

The System's been tampered with.

She hadn't been at the *gerotus*. Why?

"This is your fault —"

There's pain in my shoulders, sharp and sudden. It burns fiercely, but my body can't move to do anything about it. I feel sluggish, heavy.

"You knew —"

Drugged.

"Kyrii, I can't —"

More screaming now, closer. Shouts of panic and alarm, terrified voices roaring over the cacophony.

"That showed only your loyalty to Nadin."

The air is aflame. Balls of fire pour down from above.

"Its orbit must have been disrupted —"

Ash is cascading around me like rain, stones and debris like hail.

"An incredibly massive piece of space debris —"

I stare up at the sky.

The fire is coming from the sky...

Voices in my ear whisper-shriek, *"Ne'haoi ifaisteoi mesau elytherios."*

My eyes flew open. This wasn't a dream. Around me, the reinforced glass of the pyramid was shaking, warping but not breaking, the joints groaning with the effort to stay together. Adrenaline coursed through my veins as my body realized the danger it was in, slicing through the haze of the sedative like a knife. I scrabbled to find something to cling to, to shield myself with, but the cell was empty, its surfaces smoothed. If the outer wall were to shatter, I would have no protection.

There was screaming. So much screaming. Outside the pyramid, far, far below me. The *plivoi* in the upper levels of the citidome. I could hear them, but I couldn't see them in the darkness. Overhead, the once-clear glass of the citidome was caked in an ever-thickening layer of gray ash. It was covering the dome from the top down and piling on the ground just outside the dome's rim. But the center was not yet covered, and through that, I could see a blinding light piercing through the darkness. It wasn't coming from the sky—it was coming from the mountains.

The Haoi Ifaisteoi had awakened.

As I watched, dumbstruck, the central volcano erupted with fire, smoke and ash billowing from the mouth. I could no longer make out the shape of the mountainside—there were only swirling clouds of black and gray punctuated by violent bursts of orange and the white-hot flicker of lightning.

It made the explosion the *geroi* had triggered earlier look like a spark from a campfire.

Seconds later, the sound reached me, a deafening thunderclap that ripped a scream from my throat involuntarily. I squeezed my eyes shut, curling in on myself, my fingernails digging into my bare scalp. But though I closed my eyes to the sight of it, there was no way I could escape the noise.

CHAPTER 6

- n a d i n -

HOURS PASSED.

I was certain it must have been past daybreak now, but the city was still as dark as night. Ash had continued to rain down until the dome was completely encased in it, and it seeped through the infinitesimal gaps between the plate joints, through the walls of the pyramid, until I was choking with it.

As the citidome grew darker and darker beneath the blanket of ash, the horrible rumbling and crashing and other sounds of the eruption outside became muffled, distant. But that just seemed to amplify the sounds from *inside* the dome—the screams and sobbing wails of the *plivoi* below me. Slowly, painfully, I managed to crawl over to the angled glass of my cell's outer wall and look down at what was happening in the city. But from this vantage point, I couldn't see much, and the darkness didn't help matters. I could make out some lanterns on the upper floors of the insulae, and occasional shadowy movement along the flat-topped roofs, but little else.

The *geroi* should have evacuated the people to the underground. At least to the levels of the *esotoi*. As it was, even sealed within the pyramid, I was struggling to breathe from the ash. It had to be much worse for the people in the city. Bright Horizon was far enough away from the Haoi Ifaisteoi that the lava should pose no threat to the city, but there were other dangers in a volcanic eruption. It wasn't safe for the people to stay aboveground. An evacuation must have been in progress. Surely they wouldn't just *leave* them—

No. Not even the *geroi* would leave an entire city of their own people to die. Right?

I couldn't bring myself to believe it.

I sat back against the marble and glanced upward, my eyes focusing and unfocusing. The blanket of ash was darker than night, without the bright glow of Hamos, the stars, and the band of galaxy to illuminate the blackness. Heros and Melusin should have come for me by now. The eruption must have distracted them. But trapped here, there was nothing I could do but wait. I wondered how many hours, or even days, I would wait here while the mountain continued to spout its fire.

My eyes focused again, and I saw it. Practically invisible in the near-darkness, a crack in the glass of the outer wall of my cell. Small and splintering. It must have happened in the earthquake. I knew it hadn't been there before.

I followed the lightning-bolt pattern of the crack down the glass with my eyes. How much structural damage had the earthquake caused to the pyramid, I wondered. Enough that the wall could be shattered? If I hit it with enough force, would it break?

But even if it did, what good would that do me? I was injured and weakened, and still dragging through the fog of the sedative Heros had given me. I didn't trust that I could scale the stepped pyramid in the best of circumstances, and certainly not now.

By the same token, though... It may be the only chance I had. If I lost my grip, I would fall to my death. But death was preferable to what the *geroi* had in store for me. And if my dying meant that I wouldn't be able to accidentally betray Isaak and the others...

I swallowed. There was no other choice. Escape or die. Either way, I couldn't let them reeducate me.

Shakily, I rose to my feet. I braced myself against the inner marble wall, taking a few deep breaths to steel myself and then choking on the ash. There was little room to stand in this cell, and not much space to get a running start. But I stubbornly backed up as far as I could, until I was against the sealed door. Then I ran the three steps across the floor and hurled my body against the glass as hard as I could.

White light and blackness flashed in front of my eyes as pain ripped through my wounded shoulder. I struggled to stay upright. Nausea roiled in my stomach. This was such an incredibly bad idea.

But once again, I pressed myself against the door and then ran forward. This time, as my body impacted the glass, I heard it splinter. I sank down to my knees, waiting a moment for my vision to clear, breathing heavily. The crack was bigger. It had spread across the width of the cell wall.

I grinned between panting breaths. I could do this. I could break the glass.

Even as I thought it, I heard the noise in the corridor. Footfalls.

No, *please*. Not *now*. Not when freedom was within my grasp.

The cell door slid open.

Ceilos stood on the other side.

CHAPTER 7

- n a d i n -

I STARED AT HIM FOR A LONG MOMENT FROM MY PLACE ON THE FLOOR. "What are you doing here?" I finally managed to ask, my words slurred from the aftereffects of the sedative and the ringing in my ears.

He glanced over his shoulder, and it was only then that I realized he was alone. He stepped into the cell, closing the door behind him, and crouched beside me. "I'm getting you out of here," he said in a hushed voice.

"What? But... how?"

He held up his medallion between forefinger and thumb. "In all the chaos, the *geroi* didn't get a chance to revoke my access. My genetic signature can still open every door in the city. It will take some time for them to notice. They have more important things on their minds right now." He looked past me, through the cracked glass and out at the ash-covered dome. "The early warning protocol malfunctioned again. No one had any idea the eruption was coming until it was too late."

"What?" I gaped at him. The same thing had happened with the earthquake that struck Ascendant Dawn. This made two times in only a matter of weeks.

The System's been tampered with.

"And there's more. *Geros Shiros*—" He broke off at a distant, echoed sound in the corridor. He waited for it to pass, then waited a breath more before speaking again, his voice lower. "Never mind. There's no time to explain. Follow me."

I hesitated. Ceilos had lied to me before. He'd betrayed the Elytherioi.

He'd led us into a trap. He'd been working with the *geroi*.

But he'd also refused the *geroi*'s orders to beat me. They'd called him a traitor for that as well. They'd used the adherence protocol against him.

I swallowed as I realized the truth of what the *geroi* had said about him. *Ceilos is loyal to me.* Everything he'd done had been for me. He'd betrayed the Elytherioi for me. And he'd betrayed the *geroi* for me as well.

I had to trust him.

I took his outstretched hand and he helped me to my feet. Swaying slightly, I hurried after him into the hallway. "But, Ceilos," I whispered, "how are we going to get out of here without the *geroi* spotting us? Even if you're offline, there are still Enforcers all over this building..."

"I'm going to show you something. Something I found as a child, when my parents were the *geroi* of this citidome."

I frowned but said nothing, following him into the shadows.

He led me along the same route that the Enforcer had brought me down the day before. The corridor was narrow and dim. Once, long ago, the way might have been lit artificially, but now the need to conserve energy was too great. These upper layers of the pyramid housed only prisoners—heating or lighting would have been a waste of resources. Natural phosphorescence illuminated the corridors just enough that, with the aid of the System, those who needed to travel this path would be able to find their way. But without my earpiece, I could barely see an arm's length in front of me.

Abruptly, Ceilos stopped walking. "There's one here," Ceilos said quietly, more to himself than me. He crouched, running his hands over the smooth marble floor. In the near darkness, I could just make out the outline of a square—a tile, fitted so tightly into the solid stone floor that the groove of it would be imperceptible to the feet that walked over it.

Ceilos fitted his thumb into a divot in one corner, and the tile popped out of joint. I realized then that it was a hatch. Ceilos opened the small, square doorway, and we peered down into a pitch-dark tunnel. A ladder mounted against the tunnel wall disappeared into the blackness.

"What is this?" I breathed.

"I don't know," Ceilos admitted. "There's a whole network of these tunnels beneath the floors of the pyramid. They wind behind the rooms of the capitol. I found them when I was a child. Before I came to Hope Renewed."

"You never told me about them."

"I'd forgotten about it by the time I came to your citidome," he said defensively.

I exhaled. There was no sense in being antagonistic toward my rescuer. But I didn't like walking blindly into what I still feared could be a trap. "The *geroi* don't know about them?"

"No one seems to, *geroi* or otherwise. They're concealed by the System. I used them as a way to test my cloaking protocol when I was still smoothing out the wrinkles in it. Clodin and Tibros never realized I was there, and I never saw another person using them."

My mind reeled as I stared down into the darkness. How could the pyramid be full of tunnels and the *geroi* not know about it? Who had put them there?

"Hurry," Ceilos said, beckoning me to the hole in the floor.

Nowhere else to go. Nothing to do but trust him.

I hesitated for just a moment more, then I eased down to the floor, swinging my legs into the tunnel and grasping the ladder. I climbed down into the shadows, and Ceilos followed, pulling the hatch closed behind him.

We were swallowed by absolute darkness. I struggled not to panic as I tried to get my bearings and failed. Without even a sliver of light, I couldn't know up from down or left from right. At least above there had been the blue phosphorescence. Now there was nothing. It was a void, a tomb.

Hearing the unsteadiness of my breathing, Ceilos grabbed my hand, a firm reassurance. "Don't worry," he said. "I've got you. I know the way."

We walked slowly, though my heart beat erratically and I wanted nothing more than to run. He'd freed me from my cell, but we were still in the pyramid, the *geroi*'s domain. I wouldn't feel safe until we were well outside of the citidome. But where would we go? What would we do? What about—

"Wait, Ceilos," I said, my breath hitching. "We can't just run away. What about the Elytherioi? We have to help them. If the *geroi* are distracted by the eruption, there might still be time to get them ou—"

Ceilos made a soft hiss, shushing me. "Someone's out there," he whispered. "Don't move."

In the silence, I could hear voices now, muffled and faint. They were coming from the other side of the wall to my left; the tunnel we were in had snaked around so we were now level with a lower floor.

Quietly, Ceilos crept forward, guiding me along with him, until we were just behind the room where the voices were coming from. I recognized them now, and my heart began beating wildly again. First came Tibros' voice, then Paolin's. And finally Antos and Melusin.

The *geroi*. We were behind the *geroi's* office. In the very heart of the pyramid.

Ceilos' grip tightened on my shaking hand, and he tried to pull me forward again, but I held back. "I want to hear what they're saying," I whispered. Their voices were muted, but I could just make out their words.

"We need our top System experts working on this problem," Tibros was saying.

"They already have been," Antos replied, his voice taut.

"Not hard enough," Paolin spat. Though I couldn't see her, I could envision the way her amber eyes flashed as she spoke, the way they had during my hearing the night before. "The stakes have obviously not been made clear. They need to understand that if we don't see results, there will be consequences. Not just for the whole of Iamos, but for them personally. There will not be leniency for any more mistakes."

"If only we hadn't lost contact with Tirios," said Melusin in a quieter tone than the others. I had to strain to hear her. "He was our foremost System expert."

I bit my lip. Tirios was the System expert who had accompanied Eristin and Achillios' colony to Simos—to Earth. The recording we'd found in Ipilchan, the archaeological site in Mexico, had explained their fate. Though they'd left Iamos less than a year ago in this timeline, they'd wound up more than five thousand years in the future. The System had been shut down by then. Tirios had attempted to return to Iamos and restart the System, but instead, he'd found the planet a deserted wasteland. He'd died, alone on a barren planet, in the nebulous time between when Iamos had become Mars. The memory of it made me sick.

Melusin said something else I couldn't quite hear. Then, Antos asked, "It's not possible that the explosion we detonated in the central mountain caused this, is it?"

Tibros made a derisive sound. "Of course not. The explosives we used were nowhere near powerful enough to reach down to the planet's core."

"This type of eruption is something the System should have delivered a warning about weeks ago—months ago," Paolin said. "The failure of the early warning protocol has already damaged two of our citidomes and cost us a *gerouin*. It cannot be allowed to continue."

Ceilos' grip on my hand wavered almost imperceptibly, and I turned my head in his direction, though I could see nothing in the darkness. Cost *us a* gerouin.

"Ceilos," I whispered. "Clodin..."

He didn't respond. Paolin's voice was growing louder as she raged. "I will not accept any more excuses. The System will be completely repaired, *correctly*, by the end of the day, or every single so-called 'expert' in this city will be thrown out of the dome and into the radiation by nightfall."

"You cannot blame our System experts," Melusin protested. "This is the Liberator's doing."

Tibros laughed scornfully. "*Everything* is the Liberator's doing."

"This time I'm not so sure," Antos interjected. "The rebels' base was inside that mountain. Yet they hadn't even begun evacuation operations. If they knew the volcano was going to erupt at any time, why would they risk the lives of their entire movement by remaining there?"

"There must be traitors among the rebels," Paolin said dismissively. "A rival faction, perhaps. One that wanted to wipe out its enemies as much as the *geroi*."

"I think it would be prudent if we held off executing the prisoners until we can get to the root of this issue," Antos said.

"Absolutely not," snapped Paolin. "This insurrection has gone on far too long. Those scum need to be made an example. Forget euthanization. I will have every one of their heads on pikes around this city. The people need to understand the consequences of defying us."

"That has never been the *geroi's* way," Antos said, the shock in his voice apparent.

"The old ways of the *geroi* have failed us. This is war, Antos."

"Paolin, think," Melusin urged. "The prisoners hold valuable information that we will not be able to recover once they're dead."

"The rebels have been sowing discord on Iamos for far too long," Paolin said over the top of Melusin, her voice rising. "Because the *geroi* have been *weak*. We allowed this to happen—*you* allowed this to happen. Smuggling in Ferre, spiriting out criminals, turning the populace against us, using the System to endanger the lives of everyone on Iamos, and now this attack on Shiros—"

I narrowed my eyes in the dark. *Attack on Shiros?*

"Paolin, you need to calm down," Tibros said, his voice firm, authoritarian. "You are the leader of this citidome. You need to act it."

"Or what?" she demanded. "You'll take it back? Is that what you mean?"

"Of course that's not what he means," Antos said.

"It is! He wants this citidome back!" Paolin shrieked. "He never wanted to give it up in the first place!"

"Come, Paolin. It's understandable for you to be upset, but you're not being rational," Tibros said.

"Hypocrite!" cried Paolin. "After your behavior during the tribunal, you have no right to tell me to be rational when my own partner has been attacked just as surely as Clodin—"

"There's no reason to think that Shiros was attacked," Melusin interrupted. "He may have simply fallen ill."

"No one on Iamos just *falls ill*," Paolin shot back. "The System regulates our body functions from birth through death. If Shiros is ill, it's because the System was sabotaged. Just like the early warning protocol. We are under attack, and you can do nothing but make impotent excuses. The *gerotus* was clearly right to doubt your loyalties. You're as treacherous as that venomous *anguis* you birthed. If you're looking for unfit leadership, Tibros," she spat, "don't cast your aspersions on me. Look no further than the *geroi* of Hope Renewed."

Antos started to protest, and even Melusin's voice rose, though I couldn't understand their response. Their voices were drowned out as

Tibros roared, "That is enough!"

A moment of uncomfortable silence passed. In a more subdued tone, Tibros said, "We will have order among the *geroi*."

Paolin, her voice cold as ice, said, "I am the *gerouin* of this city, Tibros. Not you. Have you forgotten? I am in charge here. And I will take care of the rebels. My way." I heard the slam of a door, and her footsteps heavy in the corridor opposite our passageway.

In the distance, another voice, fainter, said, "*Kyrin*, are you well? You're bleeding—"

"It's nothing," Paolin snapped, though I had to strain to hear her now. "Ash in my sinuses."

Still inside the office, Tibros said, "She's taken leave of her senses. She's not fit for duty in this state. The citidome is in chaos and this is how she responds. With paranoia and hysteria. The *gerotus* needs to take action. *Gerouin* Paolin will be removed from her post. Immediately. This city must be restored to order." He paused. "As for the other allegations... We'll deal with those in due course."

I heard the door slide open and closed again. It was quiet for a moment, long enough that I thought that the office was empty. But then I heard Antos' voice, low and somber. "Paolin is not well. Did you see?" he asked. "Her nose was bloody."

"That's how it started with Shiros," Melusin murmured in reply.

I heard the door once more, and then the room on the other side of the wall fell silent.

"Ceilos," I whispered, my voice shaking. "What's going on? What happened to Shiros? What's wrong with Paolin? And Clodin, is she...?"

"Later," he replied, tightening his grip on my hand and pulling me forward again. "Right now, we need to get out of here. Before they realize you're gone."

- n a d i n -

CEILOS GUIDED ME THROUGH THE TUNNEL IN SILENCE. I COULDN'T BE entirely sure in my disorientation, but the floor felt slightly angled in places, as though we may have been descending a gradual incline. How far did the tunnel extend? To the bottom floor of the pyramid? Or even deeper, into the underground?

Finally, Ceilos stopped walking, placing a steady hand on my shoulder to keep me from losing my balance. "It's here," he whispered. He guided my hand until it touched cool metal. Another ladder.

"Wait here," he said, brushing past me. There was the sound of his boots on the rungs, and then a sliver of blue-gray light flooded the tunnel as he opened a hatch above our heads. It was only more dim phosphorescence, but compared to the absolute void we'd been traveling through, it seemed as bright as day.

"I checked my tracker. There's no one nearby," he murmured, the shadowed form of his silhouette gesturing to his earpiece. "Come on."

I climbed up after him. He replaced the hatch and led me a short distance down another corridor. Then he stopped in front of a door with the emblem of a corbeled arch engraved upon it.

I knew what this room would be. There was one just like it in the pyramid in Hope Renewed. The administrative transport room.

As we crept inside, Ceilos cautiously sliding the door closed behind us, I stared at the postern before me. I'd seen this room once before. Not just a room like it, but this very room, though I'd never been within the pyramid of Bright Horizon before.

The day that Ceilos had come to Hope Renewed.

I'd stared through the archway on my side at Ceilos on his side, wondering what sort of person the boy who was to be my partner would be. I'd thought I'd known, once. Now I wasn't as sure.

"What are we doing here?" I asked, turning to face him.

He withdrew a posternkey from the reticule on his hip, holding it out to me. "We're escaping."

I frowned. "But where are we going to go? There's no citidome on Iamos that we could go to where the *geroi* won't be looking for us."

"Of course we can't go to another citidome," Ceilos said. "But we can go *anywhere*, Nadin. Don't you see? Any place, any time. We have the power of the time postern. We don't have to stay in this time."

I gawked at him. "What other time would we go to? We can't go forward. Iamos is dying. By the time Isaak's people came here, the planet was completely devoid of atmosphere and no trace of the Iamoi remained. We don't know how much longer the planet has left." I tried not to remember what had happened to Tirios when he'd come here, the cosmic radiation he'd been assaulted with...

"Why should we go forward? Think about it, Nadin." He took a step closer to me. "We could go back, just a few hundred years. To the time before the climate disaster, before the Progression. We could make a quiet life for ourselves, the two of us. A peaceful life."

"We can't go back in time, Ceilos," I protested.

"Why not? We know the old language thanks to our lessons with Gitrin. It would be an adjustment at first, but—"

"Have you completely lost hold of your senses?" I couldn't believe what I was hearing. "Ceilos, if we go back in time, we could alter history. We could cause a paradox that would destroy the entire universe."

"Only if we change something that wasn't meant to be changed. What if we're *supposed* to go back? Isaak traveled to our time and it didn't open any kind of cosmic rift." He looked angry now. More than that—he looked hurt.

"Ceilos," I said plaintively, "see *reason*. We have a responsibility—"

"A responsibility to whom?" he argued. "The *geroi*?"

"The *people!*" I ran a hand over my scalp in agitation. Already, the skin felt prickly with new hair growth beneath my palm. "I don't know about you, but I can't just leave our people here to die. After everything I've been through, everything I've done to try to save them? There are people here I care about, Ceilos, and I am not going to turn my back on them. We can't run away. We have to stay here and fight for them."

Ceilos folded his arms. "Do you really feel that way? Or is it just that you don't want to build a life with *me*? Would you choose differently if it were Isaak standing here?"

Fury bubbled up inside me, and I had to struggle not to shout. I couldn't risk alerting Enforcers to our presence here, but I was just so *angry*. "Isaak wouldn't even suggest it in the first place," I said coldly, my fists shaking at my side. "Think about what you're saying. The people you're asking me to abandon. What about Gitrin? She practically raised us. And think of all those people we met in Elytherios. Eos and Marin. Eliin. Gios, Corin. That mother who voted to give us sanctuary when it was placing her children in danger." A hot tear spilled from my eye, running down my face. "All the people in these citidomes whose lives are in danger every single minute because the *geroi* care more about preserving their power than the lives of their own people. You're not the only one who matters, Ceilos!"

He stared at me for a long, silent moment. Then he sighed, defeated, and reached for his earpiece. "Where do you want to go, Nadin?" Though I couldn't see it, from his hand movements, I knew he had opened a System panel. "I will enter any coordinate you ask me to. I will go with you wherever you want to go. Just tell me."

I swallowed, wiping my tears away with the back of my hand. I was still furious with him, but I needed to focus. We couldn't stay here, and as angry as I was with him, I couldn't turn his help down. If I was going to save my people, I would need any ally I could get.

And besides, I'd had an idea. I knew exactly what coordinates to tell him, knew them by heart. I had just given them to Henry two nights before. But I wouldn't need the fourth coordinate this time. Because we weren't going to travel through time—only to a place that I didn't know how to find on my own.

Ceilos entered the data I gave him. Then he placed his medallion into the posternkey, and it sprang open, unfurling. The arch before us started to hum, reacting to the key's activation.

"Wait," I said as the space between the stones began to glow. "You can't bring your earpiece with you. You have to leave it behind."

"If I take off my earpiece, we won't be able to program another key."

"We won't need to," I said firmly.

He stared at me another moment longer. Then he pulled the device from his ear and dropped it to the floor.

He held out his hand to me, and I took it.

Don't let go this time, I thought, my stomach twisting within me.

We stepped forward, into the light.

Reality ripped apart and then reassembled around me. I opened my eyes. Ceilos' hand was still in mine. We were in a tunnel I knew, one that I'd stood in before. The sandstone it was formed of was rough, variegated with brown and tan hues. We were outside Bright Horizon, several leagues south of the city. Unlike the smooth, even corridors of the citidome, this tunnel was irregularly shaped, narrowing here and widening there, the walls pockmarked and riddled with crevices and gullies. Sunlight angled in through small holes in the ceiling far above.

"We're in the right place," I said. "It's this way, down this tunnel."

But as we moved forward, I heard sounds—voices.

My pulse quickened. No. Had the *geroi* found it after all? If they had, then everything was truly lost...

I hurried to the place I remembered, alarmed that the sound of voices seemed to grow louder the closer we drew to the crevice. I had been unable to see it last time because I'd still been wearing my earpiece. It had appeared like a solid wall until Isaak had passed through it without hesitation. The System had tricked my eyes, a special cloaking protocol concealing it from anyone who wasn't meant to see it. But now, without a connection to the System, I could see the narrow opening clearly. And the voices were coming from inside.

I squeezed through, my heart in my throat. I dreaded to see what waited on the other side. Enforcers, arresting Eliin and any other rebel who might have been with her. Rounding up her *gurzas*, pillaging her store of supplies...

But there were no Enforcers here, I realized with a start, stopping short and looking around in wonder.

Eliin's outpost was bustling with activity. A dozen or more people crowded around the cavern, most of their arms laden with provisions. Some carried baskets or large amphorae, others loose stacks of folded linens or bushels of fodder. They scurried in and out of the central cave, hastily gathering supplies and carrying them through the network of hidden *vi'i* that connected the caverns of this small rebel base. In their frantic activity, none of them seemed to notice me hovering in stunned silence at the entrance, Ceilos at my shoulder.

From the passage that led to Eliin's home, a man hefted overstuffed burlap satchels over each shoulder, hurrying into one of the other tunnels. He was followed by two boys carrying amphorae that were much too big for them, taking care not to slosh their contents as they walked. They intercepted a woman and a small girl standing near the corridor leading to the cave where Eliin had kept the livestock, and together, they poured water from the amphora into a series of waterskins.

My heart leapt as I realized I recognized these children, and the woman with them. The little girl had been playing with her brothers the first time I'd seen her, and she'd nearly collided with me. I remembered now. Her name was Sasin.

"The Elytherioi!" I exclaimed, barely able to contain my amazement. Some of them had managed to escape! Had the eruption provided a distraction for them, as it had for myself and Ceilos? How many had been freed? Was there still hope for the rest of them?

At the sound of my voice, the woman and children looked up and gasped. My soaring heart fell as I saw the look of panic on their faces. I was no ally to them. Not anymore.

"Eliin!" the mother called out, her voice wavering. "Eliin, hurry!"

Her cry alerted the attention of the others. They whirled on me and Ceilos. Some of them had been carrying sharpened tools in their loads of supplies, and they quickly pointed these in our direction, while the unarmed dropped their provisions and raised their fists. The man who'd been carrying the satchels burst back into the cavern. He ran protectively over to the woman and child. He must have been the woman's partner. "*Geroi!*" he shouted.

"No, wait!" I cried as the crowd advanced to surround us. Their voices blurred together into an angry roar. I tried to raise my own to be heard over them. "We're not—" I broke off. I was not *geroi*. But what about Ceilos? He'd proven himself a traitor to the Elytherioi before. They had every right to consider him their enemy.

"Don't move," one of the men said fiercely. I held up my palms, and behind me, Ceilos did the same.

This had been a mistake. A terrible mistake. The Elytherioi would never accept me as one of them. How could I have ever thought they would?

A short woman emerged from the tunnel that I knew led to the livestock pens. The crowd parted to let her pass, though none of them lowered their weapons. I recognized her, her wild blond curls and bright-green eyes. Eliin. She had helped us once before. But then, she'd believed me to be one of them. I *was* one of them now. How could I convince her that that was the truth?

Then another person appeared from the shadows behind her, and every other thought left my mind. Tall, dark-haired, light-brown skin. Traits I'd once considered so alien that I couldn't stop staring at him, but now were so familiar to me that they made my very bones ache with relief.

He hadn't left me behind.

He *should* have left me behind. It would have been so much safer for him.

But he hadn't.

"Oh my God," he said in English, his eyes wide as he took in my appearance, and I suddenly felt so aware of my shaved head, my torn bodysuit, the blood that had soaked through the bandages Heros had wrapped around my shoulders.

He pushed past Eliin and hurried over to me as the others watched in trepidation. "Nadin, are you okay? What happened? What did they do to you?"

I couldn't respond. I wanted to run to him, to throw my arms around him. But I found I couldn't move even a single step. I felt rooted, immobile, as I stared up at him, a lump forming in the back of my throat.

"You're here," I managed at last, my voice ragged. "You came."

His mouth quirked up into an awkward grin. "Of course I came," he said. "I made you a promise."

Isaak.

He'd opened the door.

PART TWO
EARTH

2075 C.E.

Chapter 9

- t a m a r a -

EVERYTHING HAPPENED SO FAST. TOO QUICKLY TO REACT, REALLY, OTHER than to dive frantically for the medallion as it skittered across the stones. I just managed to grasp it between my fingers before it flew off the edge and was lost in the jungle.

In that fraction of a second, Nadin was gone.

I stared, dumbstruck, as she disappeared into the blinding flash of light. One moment, the corbeled arch on the pyramid's peak had been a doorway to another world and another time. Smoke had billowed through the opening, and a group of people stood on the other side. I didn't know what they were saying, couldn't understand their language, but from the anger in Nadin's voice as she'd spoken to them, I knew these weren't our allies. It had to have been the *geroi*, the rulers of her world. They'd found Elytherios and the rebels somehow. And they had an army with them.

The next moment she was gone. I heard her tell Isaak in English not to open the door again, and then she'd popped the medallion out of the key with her thumb. In the second it had taken for me to catch it, the door had closed—with Nadin on the other side. The postern stood empty now. The only sign that it had ever been anything but an ordinary archway was the acrid smoke that still hovered in the air around us.

"Nadin!" Scylla shouted, running forward as if she meant to follow her. But she couldn't. The door was shut. She just passed through, remaining here atop the pyramid with the rest of us. "Damn it!" She kicked the arch with all of her might. A few loose pebbles tumbled out of the crevices between the stones, but the arch remained silent and empty.

"She saved us, didn't she?" I murmured, turning the medallion over between my fingers. I remembered what Isaak and Nadin had told us about what had happened at the GSAF Council. How they'd learned that the *geroi* had been planning to use Isaak's DNA to create a neurotoxin to invade Earth and kill anyone who tried to stop them at no risk to themselves. If those people had been the *geroi*—and I was sure they must have been—Nadin had just prevented them from passing through into our time and conquering the planet. "Without the key, they won't be able to come back here."

"And we can't get to her," Isaak said raggedly. The emotion in his voice made my heart break for him.

"We can't just leave her with them," Scylla protested.

"But what can we do?" I asked. "She told us not to open the door again." Even if she hadn't, I knew we couldn't. The posternkey was programmed not only to a specific place, but to a specific time. If we used it again, it would rewind however many minutes had passed from when we'd opened the door just now. But this time, Nadin would no longer be with us. Isaak had told us about Emil's warning—if we tried anything like that, we risked creating a paradox. The best-case in that situation would be some kind of multiverse situation. The worst...

"Not this door," Henry said, interrupting my thoughts. We all turned to look at him.

"What did you say?" asked Isaak. He clutched the key that Nadin had pressed into his hands with white knuckles.

"Not *this* door. That's what she said, right?" When Isaak nodded, Henry grinned. That cocky, *I've-got-the-answers* grin that always used to drive us all crazy at the Academy but now made my heart start to swell with hope. He pulled an object out of his pocket, one I'd seen before. The day that all of this began, more than two annums ago, when Isaak had unearthed it at the dig site on Mars and sent us catapulting right into Joseph Condor's path. It looked almost like an earpod, but an ancient one, rusty and corroded. I knew what it was now: a System earpiece.

"What is that?" Lizeth asked, coming over to inspect the object.

"Nadin had a feeling something like this would happen," he replied. "So she gave me this last night."

Nadin knew that of everyone not affiliated with GSAF, Henry understood the most about her people's technology. But I still didn't grasp what her plan was. I got shakily to my feet, brushing off my knees, and asked, "What is it?"

"Instructions. Data points. All the stuff we need to reprogram the key." Isaak stared at him, dumbstruck, while Henry beamed. I came up beside the two of them, my grip on the medallion tight. *Reprogram* the key—make it open to a different place and a different time.

There was still a chance.

"Now you get it," Henry said, laughing at Isaak's expression. He caught my eye, holding the earpiece up to the sunlight peeking through the jungle canopy above us, and I found I couldn't hold back my own grin as hope flooded through me once more.

"Yeah," Isaak whispered. "We can make another door."

We hurried down the makeshift wooden stairs that had been erected beside the pyramid, Isaak just ahead of me, taking them two at a time. Over my shoulder, Lizeth's uncle had found his voice.

"Now, wait a moment," Professor Senghas huffed, out of breath as he tried to keep up with us. "I don't quite understand what just transpired, but I really think we need to sit down and discuss this before we make any hasty decisions."

"We don't have time," Isaak replied, almost as breathless as Senghas, his voice shaking—more with adrenaline than from the exertion of the stairs, I suspected. "We need to get to Nadin. Fast. Who knows what could be happening to her right now?"

As we reached the midpoint of the pyramid, where the stairs to the top ended at a wooden gangway leading in one direction to the pyramid's chamber and in the other to a second set of stairs stretching down to the ground, Scylla paused and put a hand out to stay Isaak. "Well, hang on. The new key will get us to a specific time, right, Henry?"

When he nodded, she said, "So we can take a sec to process all this."

"But—"

Scylla interrupted him. "It won't make any difference to Nadin. You won't be able to help her any faster if we leave now or leave a week from now. We'll still get there at the exact time she told Henry, and not a minute sooner."

"We're not going to be ready to leave right this second, anyway, Zak," Henry added. "Nadin showed me how to do it, but she said it's going to take a bit to run the calculations and reprogram the key. Not as long as it took when you built the key for coming back to Mars, because she at least had some of the data from programming that key memorized." He looked down at the earpiece, twisting it between his fingers thoughtfully. "But we're dealing with a piece of hardware that's not only several millennia old, but also, the mainframe is located on another planet. There's going to be some lag. It's probably going to take at least a few days."

Isaak looked frantic. I wasn't sure if there was going to be any reasoning with him.

Behind us, the adult members of the expedition—Professor Senghas, Professor Espinoza, and Isaak's grandfather, Professor Garcia— descended the staircase more carefully. "Isaak," Professor Garcia said calmly as he reached the gangway, "I really want to try to understand what just happened. Whoever those people on the other side of that arch were, they did not look friendly. I know you made a promise to your mother that you wouldn't do anything to endanger yourself again." Isaak's face fell at the mention of his mom, and his grandpa put a gentle hand on his shoulder. "I realize that you might not be able to keep that promise if it means doing what's right. But right now, for all intents and purposes, I'm your guardian. So I at least want to understand the situation and the risks before I let you go anywhere."

Isaak stared at him for a long moment, his shoulders slumping. "Okay," he said at last.

We descended the remaining stairs to the ground at a more subdued pace, Professor Espinoza leading us into the large tent that served as the base of operations for the dig. He excused the grad students who were working in there at the moment, and when he was finally convinced that the area was clear of any potential eavesdroppers, he closed the tent flap and turned to face us. "All right. How about a debriefing of what went on up there? Last night we were told that the time door was going to lead us to a group of refugees on ancient Mars who were ostensibly our allies. But the people we saw just now appeared hostile."

Isaak sank down into a folding chair behind a table covered with bins of backdirt. He put his elbows on his knees and rested his face in his hands. "Yeah," he said, looking up after a moment. "Elytherios—the rebel base—they..." He swallowed, not seeming to know how to go on. "They've been caught. The *geroi* found them. They captured the city. The *geroi*, they're like... the dictators of Iamos. Mars in Nadin's time."

"And they had an army with them," Lizeth said flatly.

Isaak nodded, his expression glum.

"But how did the *geroi* find them?" I asked, sinking into a chair next to Isaak. "When Nadin told us about Elytherios, it sounded like it was completely impenetrable."

"Right," said Scylla. "Inside Elysium Mons, and with those System tricks set up so that no one except the rebels could see it."

"They were betrayed." Isaak's shoulders slumped. "Ceilos betrayed them. Us. He betrayed all of us. He told the *geroi* where Elytherios was."

"Ceilos?" Scylla repeated. "Wait a minute, isn't he Nadin's fiancé?"

Isaak nodded again.

"I don't understand," I said, my mind reeling at this revelation. "Why would Ceilos do that?"

"He said the *geroi* blackmailed him into doing it. That's what he told Nadin just now, anyway."

"It doesn't matter *why* he did it," Lizeth interrupted. "The point is that we very nearly *brought* him here. Nadin told us that the people who were waiting for us were on our side. She said that the rebels would be an asset to the Stateless, and instead, they had a traitor in their midst."

"That's not Nadin's fault," Isaak said.

"You just said he was her fiancé."

"That doesn't make her responsible for his actions," I protested.

"She sacrificed herself to save us all just five minutes ago," Henry added. "If that doesn't prove her loyalty, I don't know what would."

Lizeth hesitated, seeming conflicted. "There's still that Liberator person she told us about in Xalapa," she finally said, changing tack.

"But he's not with the Elytherioi," Isaak argued.

"You don't know that. You and Nadin said yourselves that you don't know who he is. Other than a terrorist and a *psychopath*." She spat Isaak's words from the museum back at him. He opened his mouth to protest, but she cut him off, holding a hand out to silence him. "The bottom line is that working with these Iamoi rebels is not a viable option for us. I've had reservations about it ever since she dropped that whole *Liberator* bomb on us, but this thing with her fiancé is the last straw. It's not going to be safe for the Stateless to partner with people we can't trust. Our entire organization is an extremely tightly run ship. But all it takes is one weak link to bring the whole thing down. I am not going to be the one responsible for that weak link. I'm sorry about Nadin. I really am." She swallowed. "I like her. But I have to make judgment calls for the good of the whole. The Iamoi are just going to have to stay in the past."

"Lizeth," Scylla cried, "we can't just *leave* Nadin! Her life is in danger. We have to go back for her!"

"No," Lizeth said firmly. "I mean it. Nadin and the Iamoi are not my responsibility. They're not my priority. My priority is the people of Earth, and the people of Mars, who are, frankly, also people of Earth. Some alien species is not my problem."

"They're humans," Isaak argued. "They're genetically identical to us in almost every way."

"I don't care. They're not our people."

"Lizeth, that's your mother talking," Professor Senghas chided.

Lizeth whirled on him, her eyes flashing and her uneven blue ombré hair whipping around her face. "Uncle Karl, not right now."

"Yes, right now. I can tell what's going on in your head. This isn't you. You're afraid of what *she's* going to—"

"Uncle *Karl*—"

"I am not leaving Nadin!" Isaak roared over the top of them. "I made her a promise."

"And I made her one, too," Henry said, coming to stand by Isaak. "She's one of us. We're not leaving her behind. Period."

Lizeth ground her teeth, looking around the tent at the rest of us. "All right. I can see that I'm outnumbered. But what are we going to do about it?"

"I'm going back for her," said Isaak.

"You're not going alone," I said quickly. "We're all going."

"I'm not going anywhere. The Stateless need me here," Lizeth said. "And we need Henry. He can't go."

Scylla protested, "You can't—"

Lizeth cut her off. "Henry is too valuable to the Stateless. He's the one our organization went to great lengths to rescue from GSAF in the first place. We need *him*. Everyone else was just extra baggage."

Scylla's nostrils flared. "Thanks a lot," she fumed.

Lizeth glared at her. "I'm not here for your attitude. We invested a lot of time and money on that operation. Many of us risked our lives. Dante, Bruno, Zero, dozens more. And now this entire detour with Nadin has been nothing but a huge waste."

"It wasn't a waste," Professor Espinoza protested. "It produced vital knowledge for the scientific community about the origins of this cultural heritage site—"

"It's not just that," Isaak broke in, jumping to his feet. "You aren't thinking about the big picture. The bad guys potentially have access to the time postern now. Someone—I don't know if it was the Liberator or the *geroi*—deleted Gitrin's research from the System database. But whoever that was obviously kept it for themselves. That's how they were able to send Achillios and the others here." He gestured across the tent, toward where the pyramid and its postern cast a shadow across the archaeologists' camp. "Just because the door is closed now doesn't mean it's not going to open again. You were worried about us bringing a terrorist to our time, Lizeth, but he may come here himself, and we won't be prepared. Or those same dictators we just slammed the door on could open it again at any time and bring their whole army through with them. If we don't do something to stop them, we won't only be endangering the Stateless. All of Mars *and* Earth are at risk. We have to go back." He sank back down into his chair. "At least, I have to go back."

"We're not going to let you go alone, Isaak," I said.

"Okay, wait a minute," Henry said. He leaned against the table with the backdirt, crossing his arms thoughtfully. "Maybe we should let Isaak go alone."

Scylla and I both cried out in protest, but Henry held his hand up. "Listen. None of us speak Nadin's language. Isaak is the only one who does. All of us look very conspicuously *not* Iamoi, and it's going to be harder to hide four of us than one. And we don't know what's waiting for us on the other side. Nadin said the coordinates she gave me would be familiar to Isaak. But none of the rest of us have any clue what we'd be getting into." He looked at me earnestly. "I think we'd just be a liability."

Isaak rubbed the back of his neck thoughtfully. "You might be right."

Professor Garcia made a concerned sound in his throat. "I don't know if I like the idea of you going off by yourself again." He came over to Isaak, looking down at his grandson with a frown. "But by the same token, I'm not sure there's a better solution."

Isaak stared at him in surprise. "So... does that mean I can go, Abuelo?"

The older man smiled at him. "I know you care about Nadin, *mijo*. Trying to help her is the right thing to do. And you're right—as things stand, both this terrorist and the ancient Martian dictators pose a threat to our world now. You're the only one of our people who understands their civilization. I think... you're the only person for the job. And I believe your mother would say the same thing, if she knew all the facts."

Henry let out a sigh. "All right, then. It's settled. I better start working on reprogramming that key."

"And if the rest of you are going to be here a while longer, we're going to need more supplies," Professor Espinoza said. "I'll send a couple of my graduate students on a supply run."

He opened the tent flap and everyone bustled out in a flurry of activity. But I held back a moment, watching Isaak as he followed Henry out of the tent, talking quietly together about the postern.

After everything we'd gone through when Isaak had vanished the first time, now we were letting him go back again. But this time, we knew the stakes, and they were so much higher than I could have anticipated. The familiar ice-cold hand of anxiety snaked up from my stomach, clamping on to my lungs.

Deep breath. Slow breath. One, two, three.

I couldn't help but worry that we were letting him make a huge mistake.

CHAPTER 10

- h e n r y -

I SET UP SHOP IN THE PYRAMID'S CENTRAL CHAMBER. THE TOMB. IT SEEMED the most logical place. Quiet, secluded, and unlikely to be privy to the prying eyes of the other members of the archaeological dig. Espinoza had said that the tomb was restricted and most of the student workers weren't allowed to access it. I figured I'd have to trust him on that one.

It may have been quiet, but it was still creepy. A dark, small, square room, its stone walls unadorned save for the engraved words that Nadin had been able to read. The last words of the *geroi* who had colonized this small corner of the Americas.

"This was always an anomaly of a site, from the moment we discovered it," Espinoza said, flipping on the makeshift electrical lights his team had installed to illuminate the space while they worked. "That was thirty years ago now. Before that, the oldest known pyramid tomb in the Americas was at Chiapa de Corzo. That one dated to the end of the Olmec period, coinciding with the rise of the Zoque offshoot culture. It was primarily built of packed earth, not stone. The masonry here suggested a more sophisticated architectural style, but by all indications, this was an older site. And there were other anomalies as well, beyond the artifacts we found here. For instance, the tomb at Chiapa de Corzo was accessible via a shaft at the pyramid's top, not through a door in the central steppe. There was no arch at the apex, either. Although, the pyramid's structure had been so badly damaged by the elements that it's hard to say whether it had simply been destroyed, or if that architectural feature was unique to this site due to the"—he looked around the small room, seeming to be struggling with making sense of this whole thing—"*unusual* origin of the civilization here. We're going to have a lot of work in front of us now, learning how to piece together the way the Iamoi influenced the extant proto-Olmec culture of this area."

"Hm." I nodded, though I wasn't fully paying attention to what he was saying. The whole archaeology schtick had always been Isaak's thing, not mine. I didn't want to seem rude, especially after all the help he'd given us so far, but my mind was elsewhere.

Espinoza seemed to get the message. "Right," he said. "Well, I'll let you get to it, then. I have to brief my team. When my grad students learn the enormity of what they've been working on—"

I glanced over at him. "You sure that's a good idea? If GSAF gets word that this is an Iamoi site..."

Espinoza frowned. "You have a point. But I can't exactly keep it from my workers, can I?" He sighed. "On the other hand..." He rubbed his chin, then nodded to himself. "I'd better talk this over with Karl and Hector. Figure out how to proceed. I'm sure Karl's niece is going to have some opinions. Let me know if you need anything."

"Will do," I said, watching his back as he disappeared through the door. Lizeth hadn't mentioned whether Espinoza was affiliated with the Stateless. I doubted it, but he was friends with Senghas and Isaak's *abuelo*, and they both trusted him. What seemed most important to him was preserving the integrity of this site, his life's work. It didn't seem to bother him that that might mean breaking the law. Isaak's *abuelo* had mentioned before that the government could be more of a hindrance than a help when it came to protecting and preserving historic sites, and he'd also implied that skating the thin ice of legality was something most archaeologists had regular experience with. For those reasons alone, Espinoza would probably be more than inclined to cooperate with the Stateless.

I just hoped that we'd managed to be discreet enough that the student workers wouldn't be overly curious. Even if Espinoza was trustworthy, we couldn't know where all *their* loyalties lay.

I eased myself down onto the floor, sitting cross-legged and leaning back against the cool stone wall. I kept the carved words behind me, to resist the urge to keep looking at them. I couldn't let my mind wander to everything that had happened here, everything that Nadin had told us. And I didn't have time to worry about the archaeological dig, either.

I had work to do.

CHAPTER 11

- t a m a r a -

A LITTLE WHILE LATER, I SAW ISAAK DUCK INTO THE TENT THAT THE SIX OF us—well, five now, I supposed—were sharing. Hesitantly, I followed him. I found him sitting on his cot with his shoulders slumped, staring down at something in his hands. He looked absolutely miserable.

"Hey," I said, closing the tent flap behind me and coming over to him. "Are you okay?"

"I'm fine," he said, though everything in his demeanor and his voice told me that he was definitely not fine.

I sat on the cot next to him, glancing at the object he was holding. It was a blue flower, its petals drooping and turning brown on the edges.

He noticed my gaze and shrugged. "It's nothing. It's..." He sighed. "I gave this to Nadin last night. She left it behind." He turned it over in his fingers, not looking at me. "I hope she's okay. God, I really, really hope she's okay."

I watched as one of the flower's petals dropped off, drifting to the floor. "You really care about her, don't you?"

He opened his mouth to reply, seemed to change his mind, and closed it again. He did this a couple of times before laughing halfheartedly. "Ay," he muttered. "This is awkward."

"Don't let it be awkward." I put my hand on his shoulder. "You're my best friend, Isaak. You'll always be my best friend. You know you can talk to me about anything."

He finally looked at me then, giving me a half-smile. "Yeah. I know."

He took a deep breath, setting the flower on the cot beside him. "Last night, after I gave Nadin this, I... I tried to kiss her. I wish I hadn't. It was a mistake."

I blinked. That was definitely not what I would have expected. "She rejected you?" I tried to keep my voice neutral, but I could hear the surprise—more than surprise, shock—in my own voice.

"Not... exactly." He looked down at his hands again, now empty. "You know she's ace, right? She said you talked about it." When I nodded, he went on, "I think she's sex-repulsed. She definitely isn't neutral about it. She really, really doesn't like kissing."

I thought about that for a moment. It made sense, I realized, based on what Nadin had said back when she'd been staying at my moms' house. But still, there was no reason for Isaak to be beating himself up about this.

"You couldn't have known that," I pointed out.

"She told me she was asexual."

"That doesn't mean anything. You know it doesn't. Being ace doesn't automatically mean you're not going to like kissing. It doesn't even automatically mean you're sex-repulsed."

He sighed. "I should have *asked* her, though. Before I just went for it."

I chewed my lip, considering. "Was she mad at you? She didn't seem upset last night when I saw her at camp. And she seemed like she wanted to stick close to you this morning."

He shook his head. "We talked. I think it was okay. It just... keeps plaguing my mind now. On top of everything else."

"You're worried about her," I said. "It's understandable that your emotions are all over the place now because of that worry. But I know Nadin, Isaak. I know she cares about you. And the two of you talked about it. That's all you can do."

He smiled tightly and nodded.

Hesitantly, I asked, "But is that okay for you?"

"It's her choice. I'm not going to pressure her into anything."

"Of course not. I know you never would," I said. "I just meant, if you two want to pursue a relationship, it has to be fair to both of you. You're demi, and I know that's ace spectrum, but it's not the same thing as being *ace*. If Nadin is sex-repulsed—if she doesn't even like kissing—is that going to be okay for you?"

He was quiet for a long time, thinking. "Yeah. It is," he said finally. "Truly. Of course I'm attracted to her, but I'm not like..." His face, already flushed, got redder than I'd ever seen it, and he ducked his head down, wrapping his hands around the back of his neck. "*Cristo*, you know what I mean. I love Nadin." His voice was muffled, his face hidden by his elbows. He wouldn't look at me when he said that, but once he'd spoken, he seemed relieved to have gotten it out. "That's what matters to me. If she loves me, too, then I just want to be with her. I don't care about the other stuff. That's bottom priority."

I smiled at him. This was the most honest I'd ever seen Isaak get about his feelings. It made me feel protective of him, like a big sister. I supposed I *was* older than him now. I used to be a month younger, before our timelines had unsynced.

He lifted his head up, his face still red. "That's assuming she feels that way, of course. She didn't actually *say* she did."

I smirked. "She does." That much was obvious, especially after the last week. The time we'd spent together in the UFS and then here in Mexico.

He looked away, down at his shoes. "I dunno."

From outside the tent, I heard Scylla's voice yell, "I promise you, she does!"

I laughed as Isaak groaned, getting to his feet and ripping open the tent flap. Scylla was crouched just outside. "Thanks for eavesdropping," he said.

She straightened, completely unrepentant. "You're welcome," she chirped. "It's one of the many services I provide."

"You know what?" Isaak said, raking his hand through his hair as if trying to shake off this entire conversation. "I think I'm going to go see how Henry's doing. You know, with the System stuff, and... everything." He paused in the doorway and looked over his shoulder at me. "Thanks, Tamara," he said. Then he ducked through the flap.

Scylla turned to me and shook her head. "Boys," she said with a roll of her eyes.

"Tell me about it," I agreed with a laugh.

CHAPTER 12

- henry -

I HADN'T BEEN AT IT FOR VERY LONG WHEN ISAAK APPEARED IN THE doorway.

"Hey," he said, coming in to sit by me. "How goes it?" He tried to keep his tone casual, but I could tell how worried he was. He didn't like being here, not knowing what was happening to Nadin, not being able to do anything about it. I couldn't blame him. If it had been Tamara, I would have been beside myself.

"Haven't gotten very far yet," I told him. "I did manage to initialize the protocol, at least. Nadin got me started on that much last night. She was able to use her *geroi*-in-training privileges to grant access to me, so long as I have this." I held up the medallion that we'd brought with us from the museum, the one she'd used to open the time door. You needed to have one of those to use the posternkeys, she'd explained, so that only the members of the upper caste would be able to access instant travel. Couldn't have the drudges coming and going as they pleased, after all.

"Some of the commands are in English now, though," I commented. That was new. It did make things easier for me, but it was a cause for concern. It meant that GSAF was making inroads toward System functionality. "Wasn't like that the last time I was on here. The programming language was like nothing we'd ever seen before. We called it 'M-VHLL,' but I guess it was Iamoi. Or derived from it, rather."

Isaak stared at me thoughtfully. "So it's really true?" he asked after a moment. "You really worked for GSAF?"

I shrugged. "Yeah. Not exactly the crowning achievement on my résumé, but…" I trailed off, then shrugged again. "Shit happened."

He frowned. "Tamara kind of told me what went on when I was gone, but she was holding stuff back."

"She didn't want to upset you."

"I appreciate that, but I don't need to be coddled. Seriously." He gave me a look. "So just tell me what happened."

I sighed, leaning my head back against the cold stone wall. "You disappeared, and we thought GSAF took you."

"Logical conclusion, considering the fact that they were in hot pursuit of me when I made the impulse decision to open the postern to begin with," he said.

I nodded. That old wingnut Emil—David—whoever he was—had implied as much when I'd tracked him down the day after Isaak had disappeared. I hadn't realized at the time that there was any other possibility than GSAF having managed to successfully catch him and hold him. Emil had, though. Because unlike me, Emil had figured out the realities of alien civilizations and of tesseract travel through time and space. I had still been living in the simpler world, where there was just one timeline to contend with and the only existential threat came from our government overlords.

"So I started trying to hack into GSAF's network to look for evidence about what might have happened to you, where they might be holding you… assuming you were still alive." Even if I hadn't wanted to admit it, there'd always been the distinct possibility that something might have happened—accidentally or "accidentally"—that had killed Isaak and they were covering it up. But there would have been a record of that in internal incident files, so I kept searching. Anything for an answer.

"My hacks got noticed, of course," I went on. "I was cocky. Complacent. Condor had already tried to warn me off multiple times, but I just kept going. I figured the worst thing that would happen to me would be whatever had happened to you, and at least then I would know. The not knowing was the worst part." Isaak looked down at the medallion I'd set on the floor between us, his face unreadable. "But Condor had another idea. Unbeknownst to me, GSAF had been trying to gain access to the System for years at that point. They had dozens of contractors from GalaX working with them on it, but they hadn't had any luck. So Condor thought, since I kept managing to break into GSAF's network, the best of the best…" I shrugged. "Maybe I could figure out the System."

"But why did you go along with it? That's the thing I've been having trouble understanding all this time. Tamara said they blackmailed you, but I couldn't think of anything they could threaten you with that would make you of all people be willing to work with the *government*—" He broke off, staring at me for a moment. I had no clue what my face was betraying right now, but whatever it was, it must have said it all.

He smacked his palm against his forehead. "Duh. I really am stupid."

I smirked, shaking my head. "You're not stupid. I'm stupid." I'd always been stupid. There was one area of my life that had always been my weakness, my blind spot. The one thing I'd always been incredibly, unbelievably stupid about.

"*Reckless behavior can leave collateral damage,*" Condor had said. I still could feel it, vividly—the way my blood had run cold when he'd added, "*It would be unfortunate if anyone else got hurt because of you.*"

Of course he'd known exactly how to manipulate me. The only thing in the world that would make the consequences matter to me. I'd lashed out, my short temper getting the better of me, as always. But that had just left me with a trashed apartment, a busted lip, and a bruised jaw. He'd had me. He'd known it, and I'd known it. I'd agreed to go along with him, though I couldn't stand to look myself in the mirror after that. Punched out the one in my living room just to spite myself and given myself some nasty scars from the glass cuts on my fingers to serve as a constant reminder of how pathetic I really was.

I'd tried to walk away from her then, for her own safety. But as always, I'd been too weak to keep my distance forever. Even though keeping her close to me had put her in danger every minute.

Even now.

"Henry," Isaak started, but I waved him off.

"Don't even." I knew him. He was going to apologize, as if my own stupid behavior was somehow his fault. But it was never anyone's fault but my own. Isaak didn't need to beat himself up over it anymore. He'd already done that enough.

"But it *is* my fault," he argued.

"None of it is your fault."

"But if I hadn't opened the postern—"

"Nope."

"Everything you and Tamara had to—"

"No."

"I didn't even notice that you two—"

"Just drop it, Zak."

He let out a growl of frustration. "Even the System is my fault, Henry!" he snapped. "You say it's working in English now? The *geroi* were using a cranial scanner to try get the System to start translating English. That *is* my fault."

"Do you always think in English?" I interrupted.

He blinked at me. "Huh?"

"The System decrypts your thought patterns. That's what Nadin said. It was scanning your brain to analyze your thought patterns. But do you always think in English? I know you've got, like, four hundred languages in your head."

"Just eight," he said. "Well, nine, I guess, now that I've got Iamoi."

"Right. But usually, when someone's fluent in more than one language, their thoughts aren't always in just their primary language." I knew that was true of me. My mom, having lived half her life in Delhi, spoke Hindi as well as English, and my dad spoke Punjabi on top of the other two. I knew my thoughts could be a jumble of the three, even though my proficiency in Indian languages was just rudimentary. Isaak, on the other hand...

"No, they're not," he admitted. "I never really thought about it before. But it's kind of... I guess it's kind of a mess. Sometimes one thought will veer into a different language without any grammatical syntax involved. I never paid attention to it, I suppose."

I nodded. "The System was having trouble decoding your language. I think it's because 'your' language is a language no one but you speaks. And it doesn't follow any typical rules, which will confuse the System more. So basically"—I drummed my fingers against the cool stone floor next to me—"the System didn't start working in English because of you. It was because of GSAF."

He let out a long breath. In the flickering electric light, I could see relief starting to dawn on his face. "Well. That's good, at least."

"Yup." I adjusted the uncomfortable, rusted piece of metal in my ear. There was a lot of static coming through it, a side effect of the earpiece's age and corrosion. Every time I adjusted it, a wave of dizziness and nausea accompanied it. This thing was an antenna, and it was tuned to my brainwaves. That much was clear. Transmitting information in, transmitting information out. Giving my brain orders that it had no choice but to obey.

"When I worked on the System, I was interacting with it via Speculus headsets," I said. "It could only hear stuff I said out loud, but it couldn't get into my head. It wasn't like this thing."

"The Elytherioi had something similar to Speculus. Gitrin used it to program the key Nadin and I used to come here. They didn't use the System directly. That way, the *geroi* couldn't track them." He sighed. "But GSAF has earpieces now. They had a bunch of them at our meeting at Lago Verde."

"Right. And I'm sure the GalaX contractors working on it with them have had access to them for a long while now. *That's* how it managed to translate English. If they had earpieces, it was reading their thoughts. It had nothing to do with you." I turned, angling myself away from the wall to face him. "You want to blame yourself for all of this, but the reality is that most of it wasn't your fault. GSAF had already found the System and were trying to break into it for years. If you hadn't disappeared, *maybe* I wouldn't have wound up in the position I did. But maybe I still would have. It's not exactly like I wasn't already moving around in anti-government circles."

He snorted. "True."

I grinned. "Right. So you can't blame yourself. Think about the good that came out of it instead. You never would have met Nadin if you hadn't gone after the answer to that arch. You wouldn't have been able to help her and her people. And if I hadn't been in the position I was, I never would have been able to warn everyone about the System. Things suck right now, but there's still a chance that we'll be able to do some good. And if we hadn't made the choices we did, we never would have had that chance in the first place. We'd have been bystanders while both Iamos and our home were destroyed."

"Yeah. You're right."

We sat quietly for a minute. One of the electric lights flickered again. The bulb probably needed to be tightened.

"So," Isaak said, "did Nadin tell you where exactly these coordinates she gave you are going to send me?"

I started to open my mouth, but I bit it shut again. I wanted to ask him if he was sure he wanted to go by himself. If, on second thought, it might be a better idea for some—or all—of us to go with him. Everything we'd gone through was because he'd disappeared. It wasn't his fault—I'd never accuse him of that, never blame him for it—but it didn't change the fact that everything that had happened over the last two years had been because we hadn't known where he was, hadn't known whether he was safe. And now we were just going to let him go back there, with no clue as to whether we'd ever see him again?

But even as I thought it, I knew it was pointless.

"She said you'll know the place," I said. "The sandstone caves. She said there was someone there she thinks will help you."

Recognition dawned on his face. "Eliin's outpost." Then his grin melted into a frown. "But will Eliin want to help me after what happened with Elytherios?"

I glanced down at the posternkey in my lap, the odd metal trapezoid covered in engravings. "The time coordinate she gave me is the same time coordinate as the one Gitrin used for the key to Elytherios. You should arrive on Iamos the exact same moment Nadin did."

"Okay. So that means Eliin might not know about the attack yet. Assuming they haven't—" He broke off.

I quirked an eyebrow. "Assuming they haven't...?"

He shook his head. "I'm sure it's fine. It's just a risk I'm going to have to take."

I grimaced. I had a feeling that the *they* in that sentence was the *geroi*: Assuming the *geroi* haven't already raided Eliin's outpost. Assuming he wouldn't be walking directly into a trap like the one that had awaited Nadin.

I hated this. I really, *really* torquing hated this.

"Any clue how long it's going to take to get the key reprogrammed?" he asked hopefully.

I shrugged, leaning back against the stone wall again. "Based on the number of processes to run and the current lag time, I'm guessing around sixty hours."

He rubbed the back of his neck. "Damn. So, two and a half days?"

"Yeah. It's Tuesday now. It will probably be done sometime Friday evening, but I'm thinking you should probably not plan on leaving until Saturday morning. That way, you'll be fresh for... whatever." There was a lump in my throat, making me struggle to get that last word out. *Goddammit.* I swallowed it down and added, in a more even voice, "Since Nadin said it was morning when you guys left Elytherios."

"Yeah." He got to his feet, brushing the dirt off his jeans. "Sounds good. I guess I'll let you keep working."

"Okay." It wasn't exactly like I was doing anything other than waiting for this current process to end, however long that would take. But I also wasn't sure I could keep my mouth shut if he stayed in here much longer, so it was probably better for him to just leave.

I didn't look at him, instead staring at the flickering light as he disappeared through the narrow chamber opening.

When he was gone, I exhaled. I'd been second-guessing myself for hours. Was it really a good idea to let Isaak go off by himself again, after what had happened last time? But by the same token, no matter how I looked at it, I couldn't see a better solution. The rest of us blundering along with him, unable to speak the language, with no hope of picking it up the way Isaak had—the rest of us conspicuously lacking his inborn linguistic talent, not to mention the seventeen years of not just bilingualism, but... octolingualism, if that was a word—the odds were completely against us.

Nadin's only chance was if Isaak went back alone. The only hope for all of Iamos, and maybe for us too, was if Isaak went back alone.

But I still hated it right down to the depths of my core.

CHAPTER 13

- t a m a r a -

THE SUN HAD DISAPPEARED BEYOND THE TREETOPS, CASTING THE CAMP below into shadow. But up here, at the top of the pyramid, I could still see the sky. It glowed a deep magenta, the slowly sinking sun reflecting off the bottoms of the clouds, turning them vibrant shades of orange. As I'd climbed the rickety wooden staircase for a second time this evening, clinging tightly to the rough, weathered rope that they'd strung alongside the steps like a guardrail, the arch at the pyramid's peak had stood in relief against the sky. Black-on-red. Ominous. I'd turned my back to it, sinking down onto the weathered stones, the loose pebbles and moss digging into my skin. I focused my mind on the sensation, the impressions that were being etched into the backs of my thighs more deeply the longer I sat there, my bare legs exposed by the shorts I was wearing.

The sky grew darker, the noise of the Los Tuxtlas rainforest—the squawks of macaws and the chirps and chitters of small, colorful songbirds, the chattering of unseen spider monkeys and the periodic distant shriek of a howler monkey—gradually fading into the more subdued sounds of the evening. As I listened to the jungle, I suddenly noticed approaching footsteps on the stairs behind me. I glanced over my shoulder and saw Henry emerge onto the flat-topped roof of the pyramid.

"Hey," he said. "Dinner's going to be ready soon. The others weren't sure where you'd gone, but I thought I'd heard someone go by when I was finishing up"—he gestured in the direction of the chamber beneath our feet—"you know, in there."

He came over to sit next to me, leaning back against the uneven stonework of the postern. He looked out at the jungle canopy around us, into the inky shadows of branches and vines. "What are you doing up here?" he asked.

I shrugged. I wanted to tell him, but my brain was currently doing the thing where it froze up like a bricked electronic and no words would come. After a moment of struggling in vain, I opted for an easier conversation to begin with. "Professor Espinoza talked it over with Lizeth and her uncle, and they decided that they want to have us work on the dig until—" My brain hit a wall again, and I swallowed, starting over. "For the rest of the week. He told the other diggers that we're a student crew of Professor Garcia's from Berkeley."

Henry nodded. "Yeah. They told me just now when I went down. Sounds like a good idea."

"Since all of us except Lizeth have experience from working on Erick's dig back home, he figured we should be able to pull it off."

"Right. It's within the realm of plausibility."

"Yeah."

We sat quietly, Henry waiting patiently for me to say what was on my mind. I fidgeted, reaching out of habit for the red yarn bracelet on my wrist, only to find it wasn't there. Lizeth had made us all take them off back at Bruno's house. Said they were too recognizable. She'd been right, of course, but it still felt strange to be without it after wearing it for over two annums.

"Um. How goes the…" I trailed off, waving my hand vaguely in the direction of the tomb, as he'd done a moment ago.

"It's fine. It's running a process right now that's going to take a few hours. I left it and I'll check on it again before bed."

"Okay," I said. "Everything seems to be working?"

"Yeah. I'm not a huge fan of that earpiece, though," he said. "When I was working with the System before, with Speculus, it only reacted to my spoken commands and physical inputs. It wasn't interfacing directly with my brain. But with that thing"—he tapped the side of his ear, the place where the earpiece had been inserted all afternoon—"I can feel it doing stuff to my brain and body. It feels weird. Kind of makes me carsick."

I sat up ramrod straight, my heart hammering with a fresh worry, another to add to the ever-growing pile of anxieties that had sent me up the pyramid to try to calm myself down in the first place. "Is it going to hurt you?"

He quickly shook his head. "Of course not. Nadin said it would be fine."

"What if she's wrong, though? Does she actually know?"

He took my hand and threaded his fingers through mine. "There's nothing we can do but trust her."

I swallowed, trying to keep my mind focused on the firm grip of his fingers. "Yeah."

"Remember what your doctor told you to do. Ride the wave."

When Henry said my "doctor," he meant the therapist I'd started seeing after Henry had blown the whistle about the System eight months ago. That was when my anxiety had graduated from general unease and nervousness—and the fear of getting into trouble that had given me the reputation for being a goody two-shoes as a child—to full-fledged panic attacks. I didn't want to take medication if I could avoid it, so my roommate, Mariyah, had recommended a counselor at our university's health center, who worked on CBT and DBT with me. It helped to an extent, at least. But it was better if I managed to catch the panic attack *before* it started.

"I don't want to ride the stupid wave," I complained, feeling how my heart was beating, the roar in my ears, the way my stomach was twisting so hard that I thought I might throw up.

"I know you don't," he said in a soothing voice. "Do it anyway. Slow breaths. Deep breaths. Ride the wave."

I wanted to run. I wanted to run right down those stairs, through the clearing and into the jungle. Keep going until I couldn't run anymore.

Instead, I sat still, closing my eyes, focusing on just the touch of Henry's hand. His fingers were warm and strong. His grip on my hand was firm but gentle, not too tight. I kept my mind focused only on the touch. Gradually, I let it expand to more senses. The way he smelled, familiar and comforting. The fresh, damp scent of the jungle, and farther away, the smell of cooking food. The feel of the cool stone beneath me, against my back. The distant sound of voices in the campsite below, everyone congregating outside the mess tent and loading their plates up for dinner.

The things that were happening to me and to us were things I couldn't control. *Let go of the need to control. Ride the events like a wave. Ride your emotions like a wave. Up and down. Ebb and flow.*

I opened my eyes.

Henry was right there, smiling at me. "There," he said. "Feel better?"

I nodded, taking a shaky breath.

"Good." He squeezed my fingers. "Can you tell me what made you come up here now?"

"It was nothing, really. I just…" I frowned, looking up at the darkening sky. The magenta had faded into purple. The first stars were starting to peek through. Earth stars. Not the same as my view of the sky back home. "After Professor Espinoza told us what he wanted us to do, Isaak and his grandpa started talking. Just about archaeology stuff at first, but then Isaak said to his grandpa"—my eyes started to sting, and I swallowed before the lump in my throat could advance to something more—"that he had promised Celeste that he wouldn't leave again without telling her first. And now he was breaking his promise. And Lizeth said that his grandpa can't tell anyone from their family what's going on. She said that they've already got his grandma in a safe house, and that when we leave here, Professor Garcia can't go home. So now Isaak's family isn't just going to not know where Isaak is, they're not going to know where his grandparents are, either. And Lizeth couldn't say when it would be safe to let them talk to them again."

Henry grimaced. He didn't say anything, but I could tell by the look on his face that he felt the same way about it as I did.

"There's just no end to this," I said, my voice almost breaking now. "No end to it in sight. It's not just Isaak's family that's suffering. I haven't been able to talk to my moms in weeks. I didn't even get to tell them that I was safe after the bridge exploded, because they locked down the café and then when Bruno busted us out, he took away our palmtops." The Stateless had used them as decoys, luring the police west while we'd traveled south. It had kept us safe, but that meant our parents had even less of an idea of where we were or whether we were okay. "I'm sure

GSAF brought Mom and Mama in for questioning when they couldn't find me. How do I know *they're* safe? I have no way of knowing, and I don't know if I'm ever going to see them again, and—"

I couldn't finish my sentence. My vision swam now, and Henry let go of my hand, instead wrapping his right arm around me and pulling me against him. I buried my face in his chest, feeling the tears soak into the fabric of his shirt. This was all too big, all too *much*. I was so worried about everyone. My moms, and Henry's parents, and Scylla's parents. Isaak's mom and sister and his stepdad, Erick. Our friends back on Mars—what about them? Had they questioned Mariyah, too? Was Wyatt okay? What about *his* parents? Would everyone be safe? Would we ever be able to go home again?

And then on top of it, Isaak was going back to Iamos in just a few days. And this time, even though we knew where he was going, we had no way of knowing when he'd be back. *If* he would ever be back.

The *geroi*. The Liberator. Dictators and terrorists. And we were letting him walk right into their grasp.

"Henry, what are we thinking?" I said, hearing my voice reverberate through his chest. "Letting him leave again, after everything that happened before?"

"I know," he said, running his left hand through my hair, staring off into the middle distance. "It's been bothering me all day too. But I can't think of a better solution, Tam. We just have to trust him, and Nadin. She wouldn't have given me the means to make another door if she didn't believe there was at least a chance. And with things the way they are now... a chance is the best we've got."

"I would have felt better about it if it weren't for Nadin's fiancé," I muttered. "She believed he was our ally. She trusted him. But if he can't be trusted, then how can we be sure it's really safe to let Isaak go back there?"

Henry made a thoughtful noise in the back of his throat, and I sat up to look at him. "What?"

He pressed his lips together into a tight line. "When I talked to Isaak earlier, he was asking about when I was working for GSAF."

I frowned. I didn't like thinking about that time. The annum that we'd lost Henry. The annum that he'd cut off contact with me and just...

drifted away. I understood why he'd done it now, but I still didn't want to relive it.

"He said that word, *blackmail*," Henry went on. "He said you told him that GSAF had blackmailed me."

"I mean, they did, right? Joseph Condor threatened…" I gestured awkwardly at myself. I didn't like to think about *that*, either. I loved Henry more than anything. I hated that GSAF could use me to hurt him like that.

"Yeah. But then I remembered what he said earlier. About Ceilos. Nadin's fiancé. Isaak said that the *geroi* blackmailed him."

I chewed on the inside of my cheek, considering. "You think it was… something similar?"

"I mean, if it was, who am I to judge him? I did the exact same thing, Tamara. I betrayed our whole movement. I started working with the enemy. How am I any better than him?"

"Henry, you didn't—"

He waved me off. "I did. Don't bother making excuses for me."

I exhaled, my brows furrowed. I didn't want to have this argument again. Besides, if Henry was right, we had another problem now. Namely, what Isaak had told me earlier about his feelings for Nadin, and what I knew about Nadin's feelings for him.

What would happen when Isaak went back there, if Ceilos considered his betrothal to Nadin to be more than just a political arrangement? If he had feelings for Nadin, too—feelings strong enough that he'd been willing to betray the rebellion to the *geroi* for her? How far was Ceilos willing to go for her sake?

What a torquing mess.

I closed my eyes, breathing deeply and thinking about the wave again. Up and down. Ebb and flow.

"I wish we'd never let Nadin open that door," I whispered.

"Yeah," said Henry. "Me too."

CHAPTER 14

- h e n r y -

I WOKE UP TO THE SOUND OF BIRDS OVER MY HEAD. LOTS OF BIRDS. Chirping, squawking, trilling, shrieking, and all sorts of other annoying noises to announce the arrival of a new day. We didn't have birds—or any other animals, apart from the few pets only the very rich could afford to import—on Mars. Their omnipresence on Earth was a stark reminder that we were far from home.

And at the crack of dawn, I could have gone without that reminder.

But I could hear the sounds of people moving around in the campsite outside our tent, so I knew it was time to face the day. It was my own fault for staying up so late. I'd left the System protocol running overnight, letting it perform its calculations. I'd check on it later today, but for the time being, it didn't need any further input from me. It hadn't been my work on the posternkey that had kept me awake deep into the night, but rather my own swirling thoughts. My worries, my trepidations. Everything Tamara had said, everything I'd reassured her about, even as I'd felt completely unassured myself.

Not to mention the other worries that had come into my mind while I'd been initiating the protocols Nadin had left me with. For example: Isaak had said that the Elytherioi didn't use earpieces because the *geroi* would be able to track them. That meant System users with certain administrator access could pinpoint the location of other System users. The good news was that, since the *geroi* didn't exist in this day and age, we didn't have to worry about *them* noticing what I was up to. But the bad news was that I didn't know whether GSAF had the *geroi*'s full access to the System. They hadn't as of the time of Isaak and Nadin's meeting with the council two weeks ago. But Nadin had lost her medallion when we'd fled Lago Verde. And while certain functions were DNA-locked, I'd been able to override some admin access with Achillios' medallion. So if Nadin's medallion had similar override capabilities...

I had no way of knowing if my actions could lead GSAF directly to us.

Nadin had believed the risk was worth it. I would have to trust her. But it was one more thing that ate away at my mind in the dark solitude of the night.

The noise outside in the camp was louder now. The others beside me began to stir. I sat up on my cot, stretching and looking over at Tamara. She had her arm flung over her eyes in an attempt to block out the growing sunlight. Her newly dyed, now-short blond hair was sticking up at crazy angles. I smiled in spite of myself.

The zipper to the tent flap glided open with a *shwip* and Lizeth's uncle, Karl Senghas, stuck his head inside. "Up and at 'em, children," he chirped in his indescribable accent, a mixture of so many different regions that it represented none and had morphed into something all its own.

"Children?" Lizeth grumbled, sitting blearily up on her elbows. "I'm pretty sure once you hit twenty that you're not a child anymore."

"You're still just a pup," Senghas said. "Breakfast in five minutes. You'll want to be punctual—food disappears quickly when a sizable group of college students and an impending day of hard labor are involved."

We dragged ourselves out of our cots, quickly changing and hurrying out to where the rest of the camp was congregating around the mess tent. A small generator outside the tent powered a mini fridge within that stored perishables like juice and eggs. I'd been told that right after supply runs, there would be bacon as well, though the group tended to go through that pretty quickly. This morning, we had the option of toast or tortillas, a variety of semi-fresh (as of last week's supply run) local fruits, eggs fried over a portable cooktop, rice, black coffee, and orange juice.

One of the student workers glanced over his shoulder at me as we stood in line with plates in hand, the sturdy metal kind used by campers and hikers. "These are definitely the most spartan accommodations I've had on a dig so far," he confessed. "My last one was in Peru when I was an undergrad. It wasn't too far out of town, so we stayed at a hostel. Sleeping in beds, eating food we didn't have to cook for ourselves. No taking turns for kitchen duty. They even had a local woman come out to the site and make us lunch every day. Usually chicken and rice, but for the last day on site she made us *lomo saltado*." He sighed mournfully.

"That sounds nice," I said.

"What was your last dig like? José said you'd done one with Professor Garcia before." José was Espinoza's first name, I remembered.

"Yeah, it was like the one you had in Peru," I said, not wanting to give away too many details, unsure of what the other workers had been told. "We stayed in town."

"Fresh." Before he could say anything further, the line moved and he stepped up to the buffet.

Tamara and Scylla were already seated next to Isaak by the time I came over with my plate. I squeezed in next to them, ruffling Tamara's bedhead as I sat.

"Don't remind me," she groaned as her cowlick sprang back up.

"Your first time at this kind of dig in a while, eh, *mijo*?" Isaak's *abuelo* said, coming to sit across from us at the table. "I bet you're excited. Especially knowing what you know. You may be the foremost authority about the artifacts in this site now, more than Karl or José."

"But we keep that *quiet*, okay?" Lizeth warned, parking it in the chair next to mine.

The old man held his hands up disarmingly. "I remember, I remember."

Scylla was watching Isaak carefully over her plateful of fruit. Under ordinary circumstances, I knew he'd have been over the moons about being on a real archaeological excavation, but his mind was clearly elsewhere. "It's all right, Isaak," she said. "Just a few more days. Until then, try to pretend we're back at Professor G's geology dig."

At the mention of Erick, Isaak's expression grew even more dismal. I knew him well enough to know that only made him go from worrying about Nadin to worrying about his family back on Mars.

"I wonder if today we'll find evidence of your underground kingdom of little green men," I said, trying to lighten the mood. I circled my finger around my temple and whistled.

That seemed to do the trick. Isaak smirked and took a bite of egg. "Who knows?" he replied. "Maybe we'll find a relic from Atlantis."

"Either option seems equally plausible."

"At least if your tinfoil hats are adjusted correctly," Scylla added. Between us, Tamara snickered.

"Okay, everyone, I've got your assignments for today," Espinoza said, winding his way between the tables. Everyone paused their chewing to look politely at him.

"Since we've got Professor Garcia's students joining us for this week, I adjusted the trench assignments. On the northwest quadrant..."

Once we had our assignments, the group quickly finished eating and brought our dishes to the collection tub in the mess tent, where the students assigned to kitchen duty this morning would wash them with water from the nearby stream. Then we dispersed to our respective quadrants.

"Hey, you're with me," said the guy who'd stood in front of me in line at breakfast this morning. "Name's Horlando."

I nodded at him. "Henry."

"So you're at UC Berkeley right now?" Horlando asked, leading me over to where the tools were stowed, pulling out a trowel and handing it to me.

I glanced down at the rich brown dirt caked onto the tool. Nothing like the rusty silt from Erick's dig. "Yup."

"Fresh. I went to Davis for undergrad."

I nodded again, noncommittally. I'd never even been to California before. Now they'd put me with a guy who had lived there for at least four years, if not longer, and I was supposed to pretend that I lived there as well. I didn't even know if Berkeley and Davis were near each other, if I should be reacting with a "hey, neighbor" or making a crack about our schools being rivals. Better to say nothing at all.

It made me antsy that Espinoza had interspersed our fugitive group among the other members of this dig team. But by the same token, it would look suspicious if we'd stayed completely isolated from them. Horlando seemed friendly enough, but I didn't know anything about him. I had no clue whether he could be trusted. I would just have to be on my guard and talk as little as possible, and hope to high heaven that the others would do the same.

I glanced over in Scylla's direction. She was already chatting animatedly to the people in her assigned quadrant. Of course. I shouldn't have expected anything less out of our resident extrovert. Lizeth was watching her with her mouth drawn into a frown. She clearly shared my concerns. On a dig site this remote, even if people figured out our identities, the odds of anyone being able to notify the authorities without Espinoza or the other professors noticing were slim, but still...

Three more days. Just three more days.

At least we were reasonably convincing in our roles as student archaeologists. Our two months of Saturday detention had paid off, apparently, though I was a bit rusty, since two annums had passed between then and now. The basics came back to me surprisingly quickly, though. Dig with the small hand tools, saving the earth we dug up in backdirt bins to be sorted through by the lab. If you find anything—even something as small and seemingly innocuous as a fragment of pottery— switch to brush to ensure you don't damage it. Document absolutely everything on the small, cheap digital tablet Espinoza had given each of us. Generally mind-numbing, back-breaking work, but I could see Horlando and the other students were about as enthralled with it as Isaak always had been. It wasn't exactly *Indiana Jones*, but to these people, it might as well have been.

After a few hours, dripping in sweat and covered in mud, I'd about had my fill of this and was ready to take a break and go check on the System protocol running in the pyramid. I wasn't sure what excuse I could use, though. Claiming a bathroom break seemed the most plausible, but would anyone notice if I detoured in the direction of the pyramid instead of heading toward the latrine?

As I considered this, I heard a commotion over by the camp. My pulse spiked, but before I had a chance to get too alarmed, I heard Senghas' cheerful voice call out, "José, your supply scouts are back." Espinoza had sent out a group of grad students to pick up some extra food and other supplies the previous afternoon. Supposedly, there was a town not too far from the dig site, but since they hadn't set out until late in the day and the return trip would feature a good five-kilometer hike from the parking area to the camp—in the evening, when critters of a more dangerous variety than the birds still squawking overhead would be prowling—they'd stayed in town overnight.

"Oh, good." Espinoza stood from where he'd been crouching in the southeastern quadrant, brushing dirt off the knees of his cargo pants. "Hector, do you want to stand by here while I go give Leslie and Manny a hand?"

Isaak's grandfather nodded as Espinoza peeled away from the group he was working with. This seemed as good a distraction as any to excuse myself as well.

Horlando eyed me as I shook the sand out of my legs, fast asleep after crouching in the trench for hours. "You'd better not be planning on stealing all the bacon, man," he said.

"Don't worry. I'll save some for you," I replied with a smirk. "Just don't rat me out to the prof."

Horlando laughed. "I'll hold you to that."

Isaak looked up from the tidy, meticulous square he was excavating as I passed. He didn't say anything, but he shot me a look, eyebrow raised. I inclined my head in the direction of the pyramid looming over the campsite. He nodded, returning to his work.

I entered the camp quietly, hoping no one would notice my presence. The students were turned away from me as they emptied out a large ice chest of perishables and the two hiking backpacks they'd transported the rest of the supplies in. I walked quickly along the far edge of the camp, skirting the trees, and had just about cleared the corner of the pyramid when I heard Espinoza say, "Leslie, I thought you said I didn't have any mail this week."

I glanced in their direction. Leslie had been hefting two gallon jugs of milk into the minifridge, but she turned to look at the object the professor now held in his hand. "There wasn't anything in the box."

"Where did this come from, then?" He was holding a white envelope.

She shrugged. "I don't know. Maybe it was from last week's mail and I didn't notice that it was still in my backpack?"

"Maybe."

I should have taken advantage of their distraction to keep going and hurry up the steps to the chamber while no one was paying attention. But something about Espinoza's face gave me pause. I had a bad feeling about whatever was in that envelope.

He ripped the corner open with his thumb, pulling out a second envelope that had been sealed inside the first. He stared at it for a moment, then glanced up. I must not have been as sneaky as I'd thought, because he looked right at me, catching my gaze.

"Uh, Henry?" he said. "I think this is for you."

He held up the envelope. Even from this distance, I could see it had only one word written on it: My name.

Everyone was staring at me now. So much for being incognito. I came over to the mess tent, taking the envelope from Espinoza's hand. This one was unsealed. I turned it over, opening the flap and removing the piece of paper inside.

The paper was thick, a heavier stock than plain printer paper. The top of the page had been torn off. I suspected it had been a letterhead, but the letter-writer had ripped it away. One corner was jagged, leaving two black dots a millimeter or so apart. It could have been the bottom of an N, or a K, or even a W. But I couldn't shake the suspicion that it was the remnant of an X.

Below this, a note had been hastily scrawled in dark-blue ink. My eyes ran over the words over and over, my stomach curdling as their meaning sank into my brain.

"Not bad news, I hope?" Espinoza asked in a strained voice. I felt the eyes of the two grad students, Leslie and Manny, burning right into my skin. But there was nothing I could do about it. They'd seen me now. Everyone had seen me.

What utter torquing dumbasses we'd all been.

The System is online.

You've been seen. You need to be less conspicuous. Don't worry—I've overwritten the data.

I'll be in touch soon.

Be careful of anyone with Nano.

CHAPTER 15

THE HARDEST PART WAS THE WAITING. BECAUSE, OF COURSE, I COULDN'T tell the others right away. That would have drawn everyone else's attention to us. As of now, the only outsiders who knew anything about the note were the two grad students, and I was pretty sure I'd managed to convince them that the contents of the letter had held nothing more than news of a family emergency. That didn't explain how the note had gotten into their backpack unnoticed, but Espinoza had come up with a quick excuse about the hostel owner having taken down a message and tucked it into their bag, and they seemed willing enough to accept that.

Which meant I had to sit on it until later, when we got our hour-long break for lunch. Which likewise meant I had to go back to my little square of dirt in the northwest quadrant and keep digging for beads and potsherds, somehow acting like nothing was wrong, while my brain felt like it was going to explode. I shoveled dirt automatically, paying little attention to what I was doing, instead mentally running through the details of the note over and over.

Item One: *The System is online.* That wasn't exactly news. What Isaak and Nadin had seen on Lago Verde had made that fact more than apparent. Besides which, I was using it now, running the protocols to reprogram the posternkey—I'd at least managed to check on that before I had to return to my dig assignment. So the fact that the letter-writer had brought it up at all meant that something about the System being online had changed. And that was more than a little concerning.

Item Two: *You've been seen.* We'd been so damn careful, disguising our appearances and avoiding interaction with other humans like the plague. How had we managed to be spotted?

But that brought me to Item Four (skipping over the third point in the note for the time being): *Be careful of anyone with Nano.*

I'd had an uncomfortable thought yesterday when I'd been working with the System earpiece, one I hadn't dared voice to Tamara last night when she'd been so anxious. I could feel the System doing things to my body and to my brain when I wore the earpiece. And that had reminded me of Speculus Nano.

I hadn't paid much attention to the tech when they'd launched it last annum. There wasn't enough money on Earth or Mars that you could pay me to want to put that shit inside my body, and Rainier had been expecting people to pay *them* for the privilege. Yeah, right.

But I remembered what Isaak had said about the arcade back on the *Athena*, the ship we'd taken here from Mars. He'd tried to kill some time joining a raid in an MMO, and when one of the party members had wiped, she'd screamed in pain. Said it was the nanobots doing it— making her experience the pain of her video game character for one brief moment. Making the game more real.

And yesterday afternoon, I'd thought to myself: What would happen if the System wasn't just connected to you through an antenna in your ear, but through technology *inside* your body, running through your bloodstream? What if that technology could see through your eyes, hear everything you hear, and control your autonomous functions?

The System is online. Be careful of anyone with Nano.

It was enough to make me swear. Violently.

The only silver lining to the note had been Item Three: The letter-writer had overwritten the data.

That raised even more questions, though. The fact that they had access to the data meant that my hunch about the letterhead containing the remnant of an X was likely correct. It would have to be someone at GalaX. Someone who was on our side. But who could that be?

Whoever they were, they said they'd be in touch again soon. Maybe then we'd know more.

Or maybe it would just open another wormhole of mystery, knowing our luck.

Finally, noon rolled around and the smell of cooking food emanating from the mess tent drew everyone's attention away from their work and toward their growling stomachs. "All right, everybody," Espinoza called out, getting to his feet and wiping sweat from his brow. "Why don't we break here for lunch?"

I practically jumped up, a cloud of dirt rising in my wake, and left my tools in a heap on the ground. I rushed over to Isaak's quadrant. "Hey," I said, giving him a hand as he stood. When he was upright, I drew close to his ear and said in a low voice, "Grab your lunch and meet me in the tent. Let Scylla and Lizeth know. We've got a situation."

He furrowed his brows but nodded, setting his tools down much more carefully than I had and heading over to where Scylla and Lizeth were packing up their own things. Tamara was watching us fretfully from her own quadrant. She came over to me and I nonchalantly took her hand.

"What's wrong?" she whispered.

I kissed the top of her head. "I'll tell you when you've got your lunch," I muttered into her hair.

"Great," she grumbled as I pulled away. "Like I'm going to be able to eat now."

The student chefs had prepared what was apparently a supply-day treat: tacos with fresh meat—your choice of chicken or beef, or beans as a vegetarian option—guacamole, salsa, cheese, rice, sour cream, and fresh corn or flour tortillas. Once again, I found myself marveling how on Earth you could just get meat anywhere, at prices even student volunteers at an archaeological dig could afford. On Mars even *lunchmeat* had been out of the price range for everyone in our friend group except Tamara. Well, and probably Scylla. She was a vegan, but she made such a big production out of it that it gave the impression she could afford to make that choice conscientiously. Most of us ate food that came out of a can or a dry goods bag, supplemented with the produce that people like Isaak's mom had managed to bioengineer to grow in Mars' alien soil. Fresh meat and dairy were generally not in our diet, and not by choice.

I turned away from the buffet table with my plate full, scanning the area for Isaak and the others, when I saw Horlando waving at me from the table where he was sitting with a group of other college students. "Hey, Henry, come sit with us!" he called, gesturing to the empty seat at the table beside him.

I hesitated, unsure of how to respond. "Sorry, I... uh..."

He frowned. "You okay, man? You've been really quiet since earlier." Then, with a smirk, he added, "Did José catch you trying to steal the bacon?"

I snorted, the joke almost knocking me out of my funk. I tapped the side of my nose. "Nah, don't worry. Your share of the goods is safe." In a more serious voice, I said, "No, the prof intercepted me when I was heading to the latrine. I got... some bad news from back home. Some family... health stuff," I settled on.

Horlando's face fell. "Oh, no. I'm sorry. Nothing serious, I hope?"

"I think it'll be okay. Hopefully. I just need a minute. And, uh"—I glanced over at Tamara, who had emerged from the lunch line, holding her sparsely filled plate in one hand and a tin cup of water in the other—"I want to talk to my girlfriend about it. She's pretty close to the situation."

Horlando nodded. "That's rough, man. I'm sorry. Hope everything works out."

"Thanks," I said, and I meant it.

I chewed my food in silence while the others passed the note between them, frowning down at it.

"Well," Isaak said, staring at the words on the torn paper. He followed this up with a carefully chosen swear word, and a second one in Spanish.

"So what are we thinking?" Scylla asked, stirring the beans and rice together on her plate with a fork.

"GSAF has the System connected to those torquing nanobots, that's what I'm thinking," Isaak spat.

I nodded. "That's what I'm thinking, too."

"They're tracking our location with the System?" Tamara asked.

"Could be," I said. "But even if not, I'm sure the nanobots themselves have facial recognition capabilities and location trackers."

"And I'm sure the terms of service that no one reads say that law enforcement has access to the data. That's how most tech is these days,"

Lizeth agreed.

"I thought the whole reason you made us cut our hair and change our appearances was to fool the cameras," said Tamara.

"That only works at a distance, though," Lizeth said. "We avoided most people when we were traveling, but the owner of the motel in Veracruz saw Isaak."

"And we have no way of knowing if any of the students here have Nano," Scylla said. "For all we know, most of them do."

I winced, thinking about how friendly Horlando had been. I seriously doubted he was working for GSAF intentionally. He would have had no way of knowing we would be coming to this place. But if he had nanobots installed in his body, he was inadvertently giving them all the information they needed.

Or at least he would be, if whoever wrote the letter hadn't overwritten the data.

"So who sent the note?" Lizeth asked, seeming to follow my line of thinking.

"Someone who works at GalaX, if they had access to the data."

"Your moms?" Scylla suggested hopefully, looking at Tamara.

Tamara shook her head. "I mean, first of all, I don't think they would have addressed it to Henry if it were them. But more than that—Nano isn't part of my moms' division. They're at AresTec, and Speculus and Nano are made by Rainier. I think there was some talk of eventually merging Rainier with AresTec, but they were nowhere near that. Mom had a bit more info about what was going on with the Rainier acquisition than Mama did, but I don't think either of them would be able to access Speculus Nano data."

I ran my thumb over my bottom lip. "GalaX is a big company," I said. "They've probably got hundreds of thousands of employees across all of their subsidiaries. And they do contract work. There were GalaX contractors when I was at GSAF. They had the GalaX logo on their access badges. Even before that, when I was trying to hack into GSAF's network, I found some messages from IP addresses registered to GalaX."

"It could be that one of those contractors is on our side," Lizeth said. "The Stateless has hundreds of connections inside GalaX, just like we do at GSAF and the UN and within the continental unions' bureaucracy. We couldn't do the work we do if we didn't have people on the inside."

"Could you check with your mom?" Scylla asked.

"Too risky." Lizeth took a bite of her taco, wiping sour cream away from her mouth with the back of her hand while she chewed. I had to resist the urge not to chuckle at Scylla's horrified face. "The thing is," Lizeth said once she'd swallowed, "José does have a satellite phone for emergencies. That's how Uncle Karl was able to let him know we were coming. But it's not encrypted, and I don't think there's any way I could ask that question without giving something away that could be used to trace us. Just because we've got one person at GalaX able to wipe the Nano data doesn't mean that GSAF doesn't have their whole force out looking for us."

"So we're sure that this really is someone helping us," Tamara said. "It's not a trap?"

"Whoever sent that note knows where we are. If it were a trap, we wouldn't have gotten a note, we would have gotten GSAF raiding the camp," said Lizeth. She took another bite of her taco.

"We're just going to have to wait until Isaak leaves for Iamos," I said, my stomach sinking even as I said those words. "Once we get back to civilization, Lizeth will be able to reach her mom and then we can get some answers." Hopefully.

"When are you leaving?" Lizeth asked Isaak.

He looked up, seeming distracted. "Saturday morning," he said after a moment.

"Okay. Let's plan to head back to Xalapa right after he goes, then," said Lizeth. "We're lucky no one seemed to notice that Nadin is missing, but now that we've been interacting with the others, they're going to notice if Isaak is gone, too."

"The two grad students know I got a note, and Horlando does, too," I said. "They think that my parents called the hostel in town with a family emergency. If anyone asks, we can just say I had to leave because of that and Professor Garcia decided to have us all go back early instead of splitting up the group."

"Sounds like a plan." Lizeth stood, carrying her empty plate out of the tent, and the others followed suit. But I glanced over at Isaak, who'd gone unusually quiet.

"What's up?" I asked him.

Isaak rubbed the back of his neck thoughtfully. "If they don't need the System to track us with Nano—if Nano already has that capability natively—then there must be another reason the note warned us about the System being online."

I frowned. "Yeah. I had the same thought."

"If GSAF has full access to the System, that means they've got the *geroi*'s ability to manipulate the populace at their fingertips," he said. "And if they've got it connected to Nano... that means that anyone who has nanobots in their bodies could be in danger."

I exhaled, looking down at my filthy shoes and thinking about Horlando.

"Or could be a threat."

CHAPTER 16

- t a m a r a -

I COULDN'T SLEEP ON FRIDAY NIGHT. I JUST LAY THERE, STARING AT THE way the tent poles converged in the center of the canvas dome, listening to the patter of raindrops above us. The storm that had blown in that evening was going to leave the dig site a muddy mess. I supposed it wouldn't matter for me. We'd be packing our things and leaving at first light. What with the new information about the nanobots and the realization that a good number of the student diggers probably had them, we'd decided not to wait until sunup for Isaak to leave like we had on Tuesday. We didn't want to risk him being seen. Professor Espinoza said he'd set an alarm for an hour before dawn, and we could see him off then.

I hadn't been this nervous before Nadin left. But, of course, I hadn't expected her to be *leaving* then. The scenario had been completely different. We were going to open a stable connection between the two posterns, a door between times. We could go through with her, see Elytherios. Meet Gitrin and Ceilos. I'd finally be able to meet Emil, whom I'd heard so much about from Henry, Isaak, and Mama, but whom I'd never spoken to before. We'd work out a plan with the Elytherioi, and then everything would have fallen into place. An alliance between our two rebel groups that would force GSAF's hand and maybe finally spell an end to all of this and a beginning of peace.

Instead, we'd found that maybe we'd never had any hope to begin with. Elytherios had fallen. Nadin was gone. Maybe it was already too late. Maybe this was how it was going to end. The *geroi* had won in the past, and GSAF would win now.

We were sending Isaak back there with no way of knowing if he'd ever return. But we also had no way of knowing if any of us were going to survive this, either. Isaak could die in the past, but we could still die now, in the present.

Three-three-three. Focus on the sensations around me.

Three sounds: The rain. Isaak snoring. Someone moving inside the tent...

I sucked in my breath, a scream close behind, but then I felt someone take my hand, and the weight of him sitting on the edge of my cot.

"Henry," I whispered raggedly in the dark.

"It's okay," he whispered back. "It'll be okay."

I nodded, inhaling slowly through my nose, willing my heart back into its regular pace.

Three things I can feel: The cot underneath me. My sleeping bag over me. Henry's hand in mine.

I knew it was time to get up when I heard the birds. It was before daybreak, but they knew the morning was coming, despite the rain. Quietly, the five of us got up and dressed in the dark. Through the tent wall, I noticed the beam of a flashlight, and then Professor Espinoza unzipped the flap. "Morning. Are you ready, Isaak?"

We all turned to look at Isaak. In the beam of the flashlight, his face was pale, but he nodded. "Yeah. I'm ready."

Outside the tent, Isaak's grandpa waited along with Professor Senghas, the two of them wearing slickers already dripping with precipitation. Professor Senghas held a battery-operated lantern. Together, we followed Isaak up the wooden steps, slippery from the rain. I clung tightly to the guard rope. At the top, the arch looked foreboding, a misshapen hulk of rock, a darker shadow in the deep blue morning.

Henry took Isaak aside, handing him the key and the medallion and saying something to him in a low voice. Isaak nodded, and then the two bumped fists.

He turned to face the rest of us. His eyes fell on his grandpa. "Abuelo," he began. Then he trailed off, not seeming to know what to say.

Professor Garcia gave his grandson a tight smile. "It's been good to spend time with you this week, *mijo*, even if it wasn't under the best of circumstances." He put his hand on Isaak's shoulder, his eyes glistening in the light of the lantern. "I'm proud of you."

Isaak swallowed roughly. "Thanks, Abuelo." He pulled him into a hug. "*Te quiero.*"

"*Te quiero mucho, mi hijo.*"

When the two broke apart, Scylla was waiting to throw her arms around Isaak. "You be safe, okay? You have to be safe. You rescue Nadin, and the two of you come back right away, okay?"

"I'll try," Isaak laughed. "I've kind of got some other things I have to take care of there, too. The *geroi*, the Liberator, and... other stuff."

"Whatever. Just come back, got it?"

Isaak smiled. "Got it."

Lizeth patted him on the shoulder. "Take care of yourself," she said.

Then he turned to face me, and all the words I'd saved up seemed to flee my mind. I pulled him into a hug, squeezing him so tightly that he squeaked in protest. I didn't want to let go of him. With every inhaled breath, I wanted to cry, "Don't go," and with every exhale, all I could think was, "Come back." Don't disappear again. Don't leave us wondering if we'll ever see you again. Don't let another two annums pass without us knowing. *Come back come back come back come back come back...*

When I finally let go of him, he squeezed my hand reassuringly. "It'll be okay, Tam," he said, just as Henry had told me in the night. Why didn't I believe them? Why *couldn't* I believe them?

He turned away from us and pressed the medallion into the key. The arch began to hum as it had a few mornings prior. The space between the stones glowed brighter and brighter, until the door of light became blinding to look at.

It wouldn't be like it had been last time. We wouldn't be able to see what was on the other side. The door would only open for a second...

Isaak stepped forward into the light, and then he was gone. Just like Nadin.

My knees felt weak, but I refused to let them buckle. I wasn't going to break down. He'd be back. I didn't know when, but he would be back.

"Well," Henry said, stepping forward to face the rest of us as we stood silently staring at the empty arch. "Now the countdown begins. The race against the clock, if you will."

Lizeth furrowed her brows. "Sorry?"

"Oh, my bad. Didn't I mention? I took the liberty of running a couple of extra calculations. I programmed a second set of coordinates onto that posternkey." He folded his arms. "I just gave Isaak a round-trip ticket. He and Nadin will be back one month from today." He looked squarely at Lizeth. "On Mars."

She sucked in her breath, staring at him incredulously.

Scylla looked at me, then back to Henry, grinning as she realized what had just happened here. I could barely believe it myself. He'd forced the Stateless' hand.

"Well, then," she said. "We're going to have to be there to meet him, won't we?"

Henry smirked. "We've got one month. I trust we'll use our time accordingly."

PART THREE
IAMOS

S.C.D. 8378
10,942 B.C.E.

CHAPTER 17

IT'S HARD TO DESCRIBE TRAVEL BY POSTERN. HOW DOES ONE DESCRIBE THE sensation of every molecule in your body being ripped apart from its current configuration, mushed together like modeling clay, compressed tightly, hurtled across the universe, and then reassembled in a single instant that feels like an eternity?

It's uncomfortable. That's what it is. Extremely uncomfortable.

I braced myself against the familiar sandstone wall, trying to catch my breath. This was also difficult because the air here was thin and cold, nothing like the heavy mugginess of the Mexican rainforest. Compounding matters was the fact that my gravity had abruptly changed, leaving me off-kilter, like I'd just stepped off a Tilt-o-Whirl. My ears were ringing.

When I finally was able to move, I saw that I'd left a puddle on the cavern floor where I'd been standing. My clothes and hair were dripping wet from the rainstorm I'd just left behind. I hoped that it would dry quickly—an inexplicable puddle of water was bound to be noticeable to any Enforcers who passed this way, and I didn't think the same System trick that concealed the entrance to Eliin's outpost would work on something like that.

Assuming the Enforcers hadn't already found her. The corridor was quiet, nothing like the sounds of chaos that had accompanied the raid on Elytherios. That was a good sign. But that didn't necessarily mean safety. Eliin might have already been caught and arrested. Or the Enforcers could be preparing to spring a trap, lurking behind a stalagmite or hiding in a narrow crevice...

I shook the thought from my mind and zipped the posternkey into the inside pocket of my rain jacket. I couldn't afford to lose it. That was our return ticket home—not just for me, but for Nadin and the others as well. Thanks to Henry, we had one last shot.

Assuming I wasn't already too late.

Cautiously, I crept down the passage to the place where Eliin had intercepted Nadin and me weeks ago, watching for signs of anything unusual. The corridor appeared just as abandoned as it had when Nadin and I had used Gitrin's key and found our way here before.

When I reached the slot in the wall that marked the entrance to the outpost, I poked my head inside. "Eliin?" I whispered. No response came.

I squeezed through the opening, looking around. Nothing appeared to be disturbed, but still...

"Eliin?" I whispered again, a bit more loudly. Still nothing.

Several tunnels forked away from this central cavern. I remembered the one farthest on the right led to where the *gurzas* were kept, where Nadin and I had begun our journey to Elytherios. One of the others surely led to Eliin's living quarters. But which one? And where did the others lead to?

I picked one at random, peering into the shadows in to see where it led. The narrow slot curved sharply, blocking my view of the end. This place was a maze. If I couldn't find her soon, there was a good chance I'd get lost.

Once more I whispered, "Eliin—"

Behind me, a voice speaking the Iamoi language demanded, "What are you doing here?"

I practically jumped out of my skin, whirling around to face her. Eliin stood behind me, brandishing a long branch of spider weed, its tip whittled to a sharp point. She exhaled as she recognized me, lowering the makeshift spear. "*Yadlag*," she muttered. Then, taking in my sodden appearance, she said, "*Alos*, what are you doing here? Is there trouble in Elytherios?"

"Big trouble, Eliin. No Enforcers have come this way yet?"

She blanched. "No. *Alos*, what's wrong?"

I swallowed. "You might need to sit down. This is going to be a lot."

She led me down the leftmost tunnel, a narrow passage with a heavy wooden door at the end of it. Eliin opened this to reveal a small, circular cavern that had been converted to a simple dwelling. I glanced around the space as she bustled in. A clay oven for cooking, pots and pans hanging from a rope strung over it; a low, careworn table that seemed to double as a worktop, threadbare cushions surrounding it; a basin and amphora of water serving as a makeshift sink. A faded curtain covered another opening against the back wall, and I supposed this must lead to her bedroom.

She guided me over to the table, taking my rain jacket and hanging it over the oven to dry while I lowered myself onto one of the cushions. I attempted to tell her everything, but she kept interrupting me, fretting over my wet state, my strange clothes, getting caught up on little details, making me backtrack and re-explain while she brought over a pot of *sokol*, pouring me a cup. I appreciated her hospitality, but we didn't have time for formalities. Time was running out.

"Eliin, you have to listen," I urged as she poured some for herself into an earthenware mug and sat. "The *geroi* have found Elytherios."

That got her attention. She froze, cup of *sokol* halfway to her mouth. "But that's impossible," she said.

"It's true. I saw them with my own eyes. The *geroi* of Hope Renewed were leading the attack, and they had a legion of Enforcers with them. They had enormous vehicles with them, like tanks."

She blinked rapidly. "But how did you...?"

"That's what I've been trying to explain. Nadin and I were on Simos, and we'd opened a stable connection between posterns. When we saw what was happening, Nadin closed the door so they couldn't get through. Then I was able to use a separate posternkey to come here and warn you."

She looked even more confused. "But Simos—and a working postern? How—?"

"That's not important, Eliin," I said in frustration. "We have to move. The raid on Elytherios is happening *right now*, as we speak. If we're going to save the people there, we've got to act fast. There must be other rebels like you—rebels who weren't in the mountain, elsewhere on Iamos. Eos said you had a whole network of runners."

Eliin tugged her earlobe. "The Liberators."

I tried not to flinch at the codename. Eliin couldn't have known what had been going on, that someone had co-opted their movement's name to do violence. What was important now was using that network to stop the *geroi*.

She stared intently down into the earthenware mug clutched in her hands, as if the steaming liquid held all the answers. I waited while she thought. At last, she set the cup down and looked at me, tugging her earlobe. "We'll need to make preparations immediately. They will bring the prisoners to Bright Horizon. It will take them several hours. Those vehicles you saw, those were almost certainly transport vehicles. They can carry many people, but they are slow-moving. That will buy us some time."

"Do you think we can stop the *geroi*?" I asked.

"We can't stop them now. Not if the attack is already taking place, as you said." She exhaled, running a hand mottled with sun-bleached freckles through her curly blond hair. "But that doesn't mean all is lost. There's one last option—getting our people out."

"Getting them away from the *geroi*? After they've already reached Bright Horizon?"

Eliin tugged her earlobe. "There are tunnels all throughout the pyramids, through the whole underground, built in secret at the time of the citidomes' construction by the founders of our movement. Not just in Bright Horizon, but in all six cities. It's how we're able to move unseen, smuggling Ferre in, smuggling people out. Many years ago, our runners would use those tunnels to sneak prisoners out of the pyramid."

"But that many people," I protested. There had to be almost a hundred living in Elytherios. "Can we really make them all disappear?"

Her green eyes flashed. "We have to try!"

I exhaled slowly. She was right. We had to try. There was no other alternative.

Eliin squared her shoulders. It was settled. She got to her feet, knees cracking as she rose from the cushions. "I'll contact Nikos now," she said, bustling out of the kitchen.

I followed. I didn't ask who Nikos was. We didn't have time to spare on any further explanations. We had to move, before the *geroi* reached Bright Horizon. It was our only chance.

Still, even if we could assemble a team of "Liberators" in time, Eliin's plan seemed impossible. Smuggling a couple people out of the pyramid under ordinary circumstances was one thing, but a hundred high-security prisoners? They were bound to be heavily guarded, if not personally supervised by the *geroi* themselves. The only possible way that we could get a hundred people out from under the *geroi's* noses would be to distract them. But it would have to be a *huge* distraction in order for them to not notice a prison break of this magnitude. And I just didn't see how that could be possible.

Little did I know that just such a distraction was about to fall directly into our laps.

A horrible distraction.

But big enough.

CHAPTER 18

- i s a a k -

WHILE SHE BEGAN MOBILIZING THE REBELS' NETWORK OF RUNNERS, ELIIN put me to work inventorying supplies. That was an element of the rescue mission that I hadn't taken into account—this outpost could be reached by postern, but it had no postern of its own. That meant that we wouldn't be able to just teleport to safety. Any refugees that passed through here had to have enough food, water, and oxygen tanks to sustain them on a journey that could take weeks. Eliin had some of these things on hand, since her outpost had been the major stopping point for runners and refugees on their way to Elytherios. But we suddenly needed to have enough supplies for a hundred people, and Eliin had nowhere near that quantity.

I needn't have worried, though. If anything, I'd underestimated the sheer scope of the Iamoi rebels' operation. Within an hour, the outpost was a hive of activity. Rebels from all over Iamos—from outpost leaders like Eliin, to smugglers like Shuliin, to those like Gitrin who operated secretly within the citidomes themselves—descended upon the sandstone tunnels. Every other mission was on hold as news spread that the biggest population of refugees on Iamos was in danger. Everything now depended on us. If we couldn't rescue the Elytherioi, the entire rebellion would be doomed.

By early afternoon, I had inventoried so many boxes and amphorae of supplies that my head was spinning. People had been coming and going all day, each of them laden with more provisions which had needed to be sorted out so that when the refugees arrived they would be able to access them easily. Many of the runners arrived leading teams of *gurzas*, a necessity for the journey ahead of us. If we were to have any hope of outrunning the *geroi*, we'd have to travel quickly, and that meant we couldn't go on foot.

Eliin bustled past me, three heavily laden satchels draped over her arms. She added these to the pile of supplies I still had to go through. "Alos, you look exhausted," she said, taking me in with a sideways glance.

"I'm fine," I lied. The truth was, I'd barely slept the night before—barely slept for the last week, honestly. All this running we'd been doing for the last several months was catching up with me, and there was no end to it in sight.

She gave me a knowing look. "Leave me with these. The livestock need feeding. Our *gurza* herd has doubled in the last hour. Can I entrust them to you?"

I tried to keep my expression neutral, but she must have caught the relief in my eyes—not just at the prospect of being able to take a breather from the frantic packing, but also at being around *gurzas* again. Over the week we'd spent in Elytherios, I'd gotten in the habit of spending my free moments at the *gurza* pens, learning from their keepers how to care for them, the animals' gentle rumbling soothing me when I felt so overwhelmed that I might break.

Eliin smirked as I placed the lid back on the crate I'd been inventorying and scrambled to my feet. "Make sure you eat something, too," she called behind me as I disappeared down the tunnel to where the animals were kept.

I waited to get something for myself until I'd finished feeding the *gurzas*—a somewhat unpleasant process that involved tossing chunks of raw meat into the *gurza* pens from a distance and staying clear as the frenzy began. Eliin had at least spared me the process of butchering the *kela* myself; the meat was waiting in an icebox near the pens. It was fresh, likely butchered this morning, and unplucked. The *gurzas* didn't mind. They devoured it in mere seconds, feathers and all.

Once the *gurzas* had finished eating and had begun their post-meal preening, I settled down on top of a bale of some kind of dried grass that felt like hay, but was a purplish-gray color. I'd taken a piece of fruit for myself out of the provisions we'd set aside. It wasn't much, but I didn't dare take more—we'd need everything we could get. I found myself wishing I'd eaten breakfast back at the camp this morning, but it was too late to do anything about it now.

I'd recognized this fruit from our trip to Elytherios. Nadin had said it was called *naransha,* which had stood out to me because it was similar to the Mayan word for orange. Like an orange, this fruit was segmented, but there the similarities ended. Closer in shape and size to an apple, its skin was pink and covered with rubbery spikes. Gripping the stem, I pulled the *naransha* apart, and it naturally separated into star-shaped slices. The flesh inside was a pale yellow, soft like a mango rather than pulpy like an orange. I took a bite, taking care to avoid jabbing myself on the spiky skin.

I had only made it through one slice, though, when I was interrupted by the abrupt appearance of a man—older, maybe in his sixties—materializing out of thin air directly in front of me, six *gurzas* in tow.

"*Cristo!*" I exclaimed, a mouthful of fruit lodging in my throat as I inhaled. I coughed, forcing it down.

"My apologies," the man said from astride the lead *gurza.* Ancient Mars' answer to horses bore a closer resemblance to a miniature version of a Tyrannosaurus Rex than anything equestrian. The one the man was riding was black, with vibrant orange stripes across its scales.

The man raised a hand to his mouth, calling, "Eliin! Are you here?" in a booming voice. It echoed through the tunnels, and I winced, hoping no Enforcers were nearby to hear it.

Eliin appeared a moment later. "Nikos, *degiim.*" She hurried over to give the man a hand as he dismounted. His posture was tall and erect, his form muscular, and his voice, as evidenced a moment ago, forceful. Despite his age, he was clearly still one of the rebels' active runners.

"How did you manage to get so many of them...?" I stared in wonder between the man and the herd of reptiles. Several of the other runners had brought *gurzas* with them, but no more than two or three at a time.

"Years of practice and training," he replied. "You have to maintain direct body contact as you pass through the postern, or else you risk being lost in the tesseract. But *gurzas* are quite intelligent. I've managed to train my herd to hold the tails of the animal ahead of them in their mouths. And they will always follow the lead of Kodo here." He patted the *gurza's* neck.

I could attest to the intelligence of *gurzas*. When Nadin and I had become trapped in a sandstorm on the slopes of Elysium Mons, our mounts—Tuupa and Thork—had shielded us, keeping us alive until the storm had passed. I tried not to let my thoughts linger on Tuupa too long. I'd gotten attached to my little dinosaur friend on the journey to Elytherios. But with the invasion of the *geroi*, I had no way of knowing whether I'd ever see her again.

"Isaak, this is Nikos," Eliin said. "He is one of the elders of our movement. Eos' brother."

"Oh," I said in surprise. Even despite the age difference—I'd guess Nikos was about ten annums younger than Eos—I didn't see a resemblance between this man and the elder I'd met before. Not enough to be brothers, anyway. "You weren't in Elytherios," I added, unsure of what else to say.

"No, I've been overseeing the harvest in Katai'ios," he said.

"It's too dangerous for all our people to stay in one place, in case of unforeseen circumstances such as... today's events." Eliin frowned, a shadow passing over her face. "It took many years for our scientists to develop the microclimate within the volcanic caldera of the Sios Ifaisteos, to stabilize it enough for a large population to safely live there. Before that, most of the people who now live in Elytherios lived in sanctuary bases all over Iamos. One of those was Katai'ios, in the hills west of the Great Crater. Its name means *refuge* in the old language." She exhaled. "Ironic, since that's what it will be now."

"Ever since the bulk of our population moved to Elytherios, Katai'ios has been largely empty," Nikos explained. "But a remnant population remained to keep it maintained as an auxiliary base. We also grow crops there to supplement supplies for our outposts. Most of the crops grown in Elytherios were needed to feed that population, without surplus to sustain the rest of the movement."

"There are outposts like this one all over Iamos," Eliin added. "A network branching out from around the citidomes and into the hinterland, allowing our runners to travel back and forth, providing safe places for refugees to rest and resupply on their journeys."

"Elytherios has been our primary sanctuary for decades," said Nikos. "It was by far the largest, and the safest. Losing it is a harsh blow. We'll have to split up the population, spread them out among other sanctuary bases." He sighed. "I hate to break up the community this way, but we just don't have any other choice. None of the other sanctuaries are large enough to hold all of our people, and it clearly isn't safe for our whole population to be concentrated in one place now."

"We'll make it work," Eliin said.

He tugged his earlobe. "We'll have to." He looked at me. "Isaak, I would like to speak to you later. I understand there's much you have to tell us. But in the meantime, could I leave you to look after the *gurzas*?"

"Of course," I said, hurriedly setting my *naransha* aside and jumping up to take the lead animal by its harness. Nikos helped me, herding the *gurzas* toward their pen.

As I shut the gate, there was a sound in the distance, outside the caves. My head jerked involuntarily in the direction of the tunnel that led out of Eliin's outpost into the labyrinthine cave systems that Nadin and I had taken to Elytherios.

It sounded like a gunshot.

The *gurzas* began to whine softly, shifting uneasily on the sandy floor of the cave.

I saw Nikos looking in the same direction I'd been. "What was that?" I asked.

He stared down the tunnel a moment longer. "Thunder," he said at last. "A *gamada* storm must be passing overhead."

I started to nod, caught myself, and switched to the Iamoi custom of tugging my earlobe instead. But I wasn't convinced. That hadn't sounded like thunder. And I didn't think Nikos thought so, either.

Whatever it was, it was sure to be bad.

CHAPTER 19

- i s a a k -

LONG AFTER NIGHTFALL, I FOUND MYSELF IN THE LIVESTOCK CAVE AGAIN. *Gurzas* only needed to be fed once a day, and I'd done that hours ago. Most of them had settled down for sleep now. I couldn't sleep, though. Nikos had taken a contingent of scouts into Bright Horizon to survey the situation with the Elytherioi. They hadn't returned yet. There was nothing we could do now except wait and worry.

I sank down on the hay bale where I'd eaten my paltry lunch earlier and watched the animals in their enclosures. Behind me, *kela* and *ielak* milled around their pens, pecking at the crumbs of grain left over on the ground from when I'd fed them earlier. I glanced over my shoulder at them before turning back to the *gurzas*, sleeping together in pairs, their tails curled around each other's bodies, their heads resting on each other's haunches. They didn't close their eyes. I'd noticed during our journey that Tuupa hadn't seemed to have eyelids, but her pupils constricted tightly when she was sleeping. The way they slept, from their always-open eyes to the defensive posture, seemed designed to keep them constantly vigilant, watching for threats. The fact that at one point in Iamos' history, horse-sized carnivorous reptiles with teeth as long as my little finger had had threats they needed to stay alert for made me wonder just what this planet had been like before the atmosphere began to drain away. Dangerous, clearly, but it must have also been beautiful.

Not all of the *gurzas* slept now, though. The black animal Nikos had brought seemed restless. He kept his eyes focused on the tunnel leading out to the road to Elytherios, as though he could see something I couldn't. Like he knew something was going on, and he was staying alert in case he needed to spring into action. His restlessness mirrored my own, and it made me feel antsy.

I laid my head back against the wooden railing behind me, sighing. What a day it had been. What a week. After the frantic activity of this morning, the quiet that had settled in this evening had left me jittery. Now there was nothing to do but wait, and now my mind was free to start attempting to untangle this mess I found myself in.

I felt wound up tighter than a spring. There was just so *much*. My thoughts kept zigzagging back and forth between what I had just left behind—my friends back on Earth, having to figure out the meaning of that cryptic note and somehow find a way back to Mars without getting intercepted by GSAF—Abuelo, having to disappear to a safe house for God only knew how long—my family back on Mars, not knowing where I was or now where my grandparents were going to be—and what I had in front of me.

I closed my eyes, listening to rumbling and lowing of the animals around me.

Nadin, where are you? I thought in the darkness. *Are you safe?*

Even if we somehow managed to rescue the Elytherioi, that wouldn't be enough. We had to save Nadin, too. And that was going to be a tougher task. I was sure the *geroi* wouldn't be keeping her with the other imprisoned rebels. But where would she be? How would we get to her?

And more importantly, could I rely on the rebels to help me free her? They had already distrusted her due to her heritage as a *geroi*'s kid. And now, thanks to Ceilos' betrayal, that distrust would be even stronger. What would I do if they refused to help me save her?

I'd have to do it on my own. Leaving Nadin behind was a non-starter. No matter what it cost, I would have to try to save her.

I must have started to doze, because when I heard the sound, I jerked upright, my eyes snapping open.

A sound in the tunnel. Not the tunnel leading back into Eliin's outpost—the one that led outside. The one that we'd taken to Elytherios.

A distant clatter. It echoed, reverberating, distorting itself. Behind me, Nikos' *gurza* growled deep in his throat.

Another sound. Scratching. And then something like footsteps, but not quite. Their cadence was different. Something was coming, but I didn't think it was human.

I stumbled to my feet, grabbing a lantern from beside the *kela* pen and switching it on. I peered into the dark corridor, the lantern only illuminating a path about three meters in front of me. Next to useless. I felt like I should say something, announce myself to whatever lurked in the dark, but I didn't know the right word to use in Iamoi. "*Degiim*" didn't seem quite right. Finally I gave up and called "Hello?" in English.

My voice echoed off the sandstone wall. There was a moment of silence. Then I heard the scratching again, louder this time, quicker. I sucked in my breath, startled, and turned to run. But before I could move, two lumbering shadows appeared in the circle of light cast by my lantern.

Not human. Animal. Reptilian. *Gurzas.*

And not just any *gurzas.* I recognized these two.

"Tuupa!" I cried as she hurtled toward me. I dropped the lantern and she shoved her muzzle into my outstretched hands. Her blue-green scales were dry and caked in dust. I ran my hands over her face, across her forehead streaked with a band of yellow. Behind her, Thork, a gelding with brighter green scales and orange stripes, rumbled a greeting.

"How in the world did you two get here?" I asked, as though they could answer me. I didn't understand—we had left these two in Elytherios. I wasn't sure if I should be relieved or concerned by the fact that they'd somehow made it here.

Tuupa whined, nudging my shoulder with her snout. "What is it, girl?" I asked. Thork approached, nosing something that was clinging to Tuupa's back. As I came over to investigate, Tuupa lowered herself to the ground, her strong back legs supporting her as she crouched almost flat on her belly.

Clutching her saddle was a little animal that looked vaguely familiar. It had a striped tail and large ears, and it clung to the saddle with five tiny fingers on each hand. In some regards it looked almost like a ring-tailed lemur, but its raccoon-like face and rusty red fur reminded me more of a red panda. I'd seen a creature like this before—in the trees of Elytherios.

This one was barely recognizable as one of those little animals, though. Its fur was singed, and its breathing was labored. This animal had almost certainly come from Elytherios, but it was sick.

My mind raced as I tried to process this. Tuupa and Thork had been in Elytherios this morning, and this animal must have come from there as well. But it had taken us an Iamoi week to make that journey. The *gurzas* must have run, and they most likely came directly across the lava plain rather than sidetracking through the canyons to avoid detection. That trip would be faster, but it was also exposed—no pockets of oxygen the way the caves had, and no protection from the radiation all of Iamos was being cooked with thanks to its atmospheric degradation. *Gurzas* had adapted to low-oxygen environments, and their thick scales would protect them from the ultraviolet radiation. But I doubted the mammals of Elytherios had those advantages.

I opened the gate to one of the *gurza* pens and Thork and Tuupa obediently entered. There was fresh water in the trough, but they'd need to be fed, especially after the ordeal they'd had. But it would have to wait. This animal needed help, immediately.

"Eliin!" I called, down the corridor toward her living quarters. "Eliin!"

I flung the door to her kitchen open just as she pulled back the curtain leading into her bedroom. "What is it, *alos*?" she asked, wiping the sleep from her eyes with the back of her hand.

"Two of the *gurzas* from Elytherios just showed up. They were carrying this." I held up the little animal. It was clinging weakly to my shoulder.

"*Yad!*" she exclaimed, suddenly wide awake. She reached out to take the animal. "A *kerkopith*. Oh, poor thing. It needs oxygen. And it's dehydrated. *Alos*, bring me a breathing apparatus from our refugee kits."

"Can we spare one?" I asked.

She gave me a severe look. "We are not the *geroi*, thinking humans are the only creatures that matter. This species is extremely endangered. If we have any hope of keeping the native species of our world alive, we have to do our best to save every single animal. Bring me the oxygen."

I nodded, hurrying to the supply cave and pulling a child-sized breathing apparatus out of the burlap sack where I had stowed them. By the time I returned to Eliin's kitchen, she had laid the animal out on a bed of that purple-gray straw in front of the oven, and she was slowly dribbling water into its mouth from a clay amphora. When she was done with that, she took the oxygen tank and gently placed the tube over its snout. The *kerkopith* lay limp, breathing shallowly through the flexible tubing.

"Let's let him rest," Eliin said. "If he survives the night, we'll need to make sure he's safely transported along with the refugees to Katai'ios. The animal medics from Elytherios will be able to care for him better than I could."

My stomach twisted. *Assuming we can get the Elytherioi away from the geroi in the first place.*

I was about to ask her if she'd heard anything from the runners when a rattling noise distracted me. I looked up. The pots and pans that were hanging from a rope over the oven were swaying, banging gently against the sandstone wall behind them. "Eliin, what's—"

The words were ripped from my throat as the ground began to shake. I barely managed to keep my footing as the dusty floor rolled and rippled under my feet. The pots were now swaying violently, banging hard against the wall and then swinging outward again.

"Earthquake," I managed to say as I struggled to stay upright. Dirt and pebbles began to dislodge themselves from the ceiling, bouncing painfully off my head and shoulders.

Eliin's face was pale. "We can't get out. We're too deep underground," she said.

"We need to get under something," I said, remembering the earthquake drills Abuelo had conducted with me when I was a kid visiting him in California. "The table!"

Eliin scooped up the little *kerkopith* and the three of us scrambled under the low wood table, Eliin cradling the animal gently in her arms. There was a crash as the rope holding the pots gave way and they clattered to the floor. Around us, more dirt poured from the ceiling, bringing with it pebbles and larger rocks, some as big as my fist now.

Don't let the roof cave in. Do not let the roof cave in, I thought repeatedly.

There was a loud crash as something big hit the table over our heads. The wooden table splintered but did not give way.

The noise was louder now. A roar in the distance, unlike anything I'd ever heard before. Eliin shifted her position, crouching on the balls of her feet.

"What are you doing?" I yelled over the din.

She stretched out her arms, handing the frail *kerkopith* to me. "I have to see what that was," she yelled back.

"Eliin, no! It's not safe!"

"Isaak, don't you understand? Iamos is not like Hamos or Simos. Our planet is not tectonic. Only one thing could cause a quake of this large a magnitude."

Then I did understand, and adrenaline spiked through my veins. I clutched the *kerkopith* to my chest, taking care to keep its breathing tube placed correctly over its snout, ensuring that the line from the oxygen tank was not kinked. Then I crawled out after her.

Eliin's home was in shambles, shards of broken pottery laying interspersed with dust and rocks. A large boulder had dislodged from the ceiling, landing directly in the middle of the table, causing it to buckle but not break. There was now a hole in the center of the roof. But where there should have been darkness punctuated with stars, there was an odd twilight glow. As I stared, the hole lit up with a bright flash, like lightning. A deafening roar blasted my eardrums. I ducked my head back under the table, wincing from the sound. Ash began to pour in through the hole in the roof.

"Volcano," Eliin shouted, her voice barely audible over the roar. "The Haoi Ifaisteoi—"

"We have to get out of here," I yelled back. I pressed the *kerkopith* against me, pulling my shirt up to shield its face from the falling ash.

She tugged her earlobe and scurried out into the tunnel. I followed her, and she pulled the door to her dwelling tightly shut behind me. The sound was muffled now, and I could hear myself think, though my ears were ringing.

"We should be safe here. These caves are far enough from the mountains that we're not in danger from the gases or from the lava flow." She leaned back against the closed door. "But Elytherios..."

"It's okay. It's been at least eighteen hours since the *geroi* raid. There wouldn't have been anyone left in the mountain," I said, sounding more confident than I felt.

"But if the *geroi* had not come when they did, our whole population would have been in there. How could we have not known this was coming? We monitor—"

"Do you use the System?" I asked. She stared at me in confusion, and I added, "Is the way you monitor by checking the System's early warning protocols?"

She tugged her earlobe.

"The System has been sabotaged," I told her. "By someone calling himself the Liberator. He's done something to the early warning protocols. There's no way of predicting natural disasters now."

Eliin blanched. "The Liberator? But none of our runners would ever do this. *Alos*, you know that."

"I know. We don't know who he is. But we know he's not one of the rebels. He's a terrorist using your name."

"The *geroi*," she said firmly. "Trying to turn the people of Iamos against our movement."

I frowned. It was a possibility I hadn't considered before. *Could* the Liberator be an invention of the *geroi*? On the one hand, it made some sense—the *geroi* were desperate to maintain their own power at any costs, and they'd already showed that they were willing to sacrifice their own citizens to do it. And using the pretense of the Liberator had certainly worked to trick Nadin into leading them to the Elytherioi's hiding place. But one of the Liberator's attacks had injured Ceilos' mother. Would the *geroi* have voluntarily done that to one of their own?

Maybe the *geroi* really *would* stop at nothing to maintain their own power.

"Will the others be safe?" I asked. "The runners, and the people in Bright Horizon?"

She swallowed. "I'm not sure. I don't know where they are right now. We have no earpieces. There's no way to reach them."

No way to reach them. No way to know.

Nothing to do but wait here, listening to the sounds of the eruption in the distance, and worry.

Chapter 20

- i s a a k -

THE SHAKING HAD STOPPED, BUT THE ROAR CONTINUED, DISTANT AND muffled by the cavern walls but still just loud enough to wear on my frayed nerves. With nothing else to do, Eliin and I began surveying the damage to her outpost, passing the unconscious *kerkopith* between us as we worked. There was dust and debris everywhere, but structural damage was thankfully minimal, apart from the hole in her kitchen ceiling.

The bigger issue was with the animals. Terrified by the earthquake and the roar of the eruption that had followed, some of the *gurzas* had broken free of their holding pens and into the *kela* run. The ground was smeared with blood and littered with feathers. A few of the birds had managed to stay safe by hiding in their coops, but we'd lost most of the *kela* flock and many of the *ielaks* as well. I sighed, looking around at the disaster zone the livestock cave had become.

"We're missing some of the *gurzas*," I said to Eliin, taking a quick count. "Looks like... eight."

"The younger ones," Eliin assessed. "Less trained, more skittish. They'll be hiding in the tunnels. Don't worry, they'll find their way back once they realize the threat has passed."

I glanced at our remaining herd. The animals whined and paced around their enclosures; some of them had curled into defensive pairs and remained there, but their focused, dilated pupils told me they were awake and alert. Tuupa and Thork were huddled in the back of the pen I'd left them in just moments before the quake, their tails entwined. Only

Nikos' black-and-orange *gurza* seemed unfazed, standing upright, surveying the scene before him almost authoritatively. Nikos had said Kodo was the leader of his herd, and it seemed that the animal took that role seriously.

"Eliin, I didn't get a chance to feed Tuupa and Thork before the earthquake," I said. "Now our *kela* situation…" I trailed off helplessly.

"There's nothing for it. They have to be fed. I'll take the little one," she said, gently removing the sleeping *kerkopith* from my arms. I opened the icebox and removed some of the remaining chunks of meat. There was precious little left in the box now, and precious few birds remaining in the pens for the amount of *gurzas* we had to feed. If only we knew how long we'd be stuck here in a holding pattern before Nikos and his scouts returned…

Fretfully, I tossed the cold chunks to my familiar *gurza* pair. They caught it expertly, quickly ripping into the meat, devouring it in just a few bites. When the food was gone, Tuupa whined, coming over to the edge of the pen, looking at me with her unblinking yellow eyes. I ran a hand over her scaled muzzle and spoke soothingly to her. "Don't worry, girl. It'll be all right," I murmured, though the words sounded hollow to my own ears.

Tuupa whined again, and for a moment I thought she was making a comment about the unconvincingness of my lie. But then I heard it. It blended with the roar of the eruption at first, but then I realized this sound was different, louder—voices.

Lots of voices.

I left Tuupa behind, hurrying out of the livestock cave, my heart pounding. *Don't let it be Enforcers*, I thought, but the worry was short-lived. I rounded the corner and found a group of about a dozen people standing in the central hub of the outpost, a few adults surrounded by children around Celeste's age. They were filthy and exhausted, but I recognized them immediately.

Elytherioi.

"You got them," I called out, hurrying over. Nikos stood with Eliin in the center of the group, and beside him was Eos. The brothers who looked nothing alike. The lack of resemblance was even more striking now that they were standing side by side. Though they both were dark-skinned with the graying natural hair of unaltered genetics, Eos' features were narrow and angular, while Nikos' jaw was square, his nose broad and flat.

They looked up at my approach, the crowd parting to let me into the circle. "Isaak, *degiim*," Nikos said.

"*Degiim*," I replied. "How in the world did you manage…?"

"Sheer luck," Eliin said.

"If you can call something like this luck," Eos added in a more subdued tone.

"The eruption?" I asked.

Nikos tugged his earlobe. "The citidome is in chaos. There weren't enough Enforcers to deal with guarding the prisoners as well as evacuating the surface castes into the underground, so they left our people unguarded. We had to take our chances. We took the families with small children first, then we'll return for the rest."

"They were completely unguarded?" I said in disbelief. This sounded too good to be true. "Where were the *geroi*?"

"Our scouts gave us an odd report just before the eruption began," said Nikos. "Something is wrong with *Geros Shiros*. Because of that, the eruption seems to have caught them off-guard and unprepared."

"Wrong?" I repeated. "What do you mean, wrong?"

"We're not sure. It sounded like he may have been poisoned. The medics said something about a toxin."

My eyes widened. "A neurotoxin?"

"Isaak, we don't have time for this," Eos interrupted. "The *geroi* were caught off-guard, but they will be bringing in reinforcements from other citidomes soon. We have to get back to Bright Horizon and finish evacuating the rest of our people while we still have a chance."

"You're right. I'm sorry," I said, though my mind was still reeling at this new information. A *toxin*. Like the one that the *geroi* had been planning on using on us? But the medic Nadin and I had heard on the recording of the *gerotus* session had said they were going to use my DNA to make it so that it would only affect Simoi—people from Earth. How could it have been turned back on the *geroi*?

And more importantly, *who* could have done it?

The Liberator. It was the only possibility. But how could he have gotten close enough to the *geroi* to poison one of them? I found myself considering Eliin's theory once more. It would make no sense for the *geroi* to do this, these attacks first on Clodin and now Shiros. But who else would be close enough to them to be able to carry this out?

"How many more refugees should we expect?" Eliin was asking as Eos and Nikos detached from the group.

"We're not sure," Eos replied. "The other runners took advantage of the unguarded posterns to bring some groups to other outposts farther out in the network. That should take some of the burden off your resources."

"Good. We lost almost our entire *kela* flock in that earthquake."

Nikos tugged his earlobe. "If we can get meat in the city, we'll bring it."

They turned toward the crevice leading out into the sandstone tunnel. I hurried after them. "Eos, wait," I called. He paused, looking over his shoulder at me with unreadable gray eyes.

"We have to hurry," he emphasized again.

"I know. But this is important. Nadin... was she with the Elytherioi?"

He frowned but didn't respond.

Nikos looked between his brother and me. "Who is Nadin?" he asked.

"She's... my friend," I said uncertainly.

"We don't have time, Isaak," Eos repeated. "We have to get our people out."

"I know." My voice broke with frustration. "But Nadin *is* one of our people."

"She's *geroi*'s blood," said Eos.

"Don't call her that."

"It's what she is," he said.

"Not anymore!" I snapped back. "You were there. You saw us on the other side of the postern. You heard what was said. You saw her reject the *geroi* the same as I did. She risked her life by coming back here. She could have closed the door and left you all here to rot, but she didn't. She came back. More than that"—I raked an agitated hand through my hair—"if it weren't for her, I wouldn't have been able to come here and warn Eliin. This whole rescue effort could never have happened if it weren't for Nadin. She was willing to sacrifice herself because she believes in your cause. Because she cares about the Elytherioi. Because she cares about all the people of Iamos. She's more than proved her loyalty. She doesn't deserve to be lumped in with the *geroi*." I crossed my arms, planting my feet firmly, trying to keep my cool but failing. "I came back here to save her, and I'm not going to just leave her behind."

Nikos turned to Eos, brows furrowed. "Remember who Marin was, brother. If this Nadin has proven herself, even if she once was *geroi's* blood, she deserves to be counted one of us as much as Marin does."

Eos sighed, his shoulders slumping. "I know. I know this. But it's impossible, don't you see? She's *geroi's* blood, whether she chooses to be or not." He looked at me sadly. "Nadin was not with our people. The *geroi* separated her from us. They took her into the pyramid."

Nikos squeezed his eyes shut, seeming to understand something that I was missing—the reason why Eos had been acting so cagey, why he was so reticent to speak of Nadin. "We're too late."

My heart stopped in my chest. "What do you mean, too late?"

"The same scout who gave us the report about *Geros* Shiros' poisoning said that the medics were preparing a reeducation," Nikos said. "For a high-level prisoner in the pyramid. There's no one else it could have been."

"A reeducation?" I repeated. My ears were ringing, and not just because of the sound of the eruption in the distance.

"To erase her mind. Make her one of them again," Nikos explained. "I don't know if they had begun the procedure before the eruption started. But it's too late to save her, Isaak."

I swallowed. *Erase her mind.*

"Maybe there's still time," I stammered frantically. "With the eruption, and with Shiros being poisoned, maybe they didn't get a chance—"

"There's no time," Eos cut me off. "Even if Nadin's mind is still whole, we don't have time to infiltrate the pyramid. We don't have the people to spare. We have to get the others out." He looked at me imploringly. "You have to understand, Isaak. The Elytherioi have to come first. We have to let her go."

"I'm not giving up on her," I protested. "I have to get her away from them. Even if she doesn't remember me—us—any of this. I can't just leave her."

"You do what you must," Nikos said. "But we can't save both of you. If you get caught, we won't be able to help you."

I swallowed. "I understand."

The brothers watched me for just a second longer. Then they were gone, racing into the darkness with a speed that belied their age, leaving me standing alone in the tunnel.

I staggered back into the outpost, barely aware of my surroundings, my mind reeling. I had to find a way into Bright Horizon. Nikos and Eos had headed down the tunnel—could I follow them? But once I got back into the citidome, what would I do from there? I'd have to find a way into the pyramid—

"Alos."

No, if she was being reeducated, she'd be in the hospital level by now. They said a medic would perform the procedure. If the layout of Bright Horizon was similar to that of Hope Renewed, I might be able to find it— if I could remember the way that Nadin had gotten me out of the hospital and retrace the steps backwards... But how would I do it without being seen? I couldn't rely on Ceilos' cloaking protocol like we had last time.

"Alos."

That was assuming the procedure had already begun. If not, where would they hold her? In the pyramid? That put me back in the situation I was in before. How would I get in there? And how would I find her? And, again, how would I pull it off without getting caught?

"Isaak!"

I started, glancing up. Eliin was staring at me, holding the *kerkopith*. I realized after a moment that the creature was no longer sleeping—it, too, was staring at me, with wide orange eyes. Eliin had removed its oxygen tank, and it was breathing on its own.

"This little one is awake. I need you to take him and get him some more water so I can help the others prepare for the journey."

"Eliin, I can't, I need to—"

She didn't even let me finish my sentence. She dumped the half-conscious primate into my arms and bustled down the central corridor. I cursed under my breath. The *kerkopith* stared up at me.

I let out a sigh. "Fine," I said to the animal. "I'll get you a drink, but then I have to go."

With Eliin's living quarters still inaccessible, I opted to return to the livestock cave to get the water. I was partway down the tunnel when I noticed that I wasn't alone. I had not one, but two shadows tailing me. A little boy and a little girl, probably around four and six annums old.

"Can we help you feed the *kerkopith*?" the girl asked.

"I'm not going to feed him right now, just get him water," I said. "But sure." Maybe this would work to my advantage—I could leave the *kerkopith* with the kids and leave to rescue Nadin. But I was still in the same quandary as before—how would I get into Bright Horizon? And how would I find Nadin? Eos and Nikos had a major head start on me now, and I was sure the road to Bright Horizon from here would not be a straight one. There would be too much risk of the Enforcers finding them if the path was easy to find. Should I wait for the next set of runners to return, and go back with them? That was assuming they'd be returning, though—what if the next set of runners was the last one?

A woman's voice echoed down the tunnel, interrupting my thoughts. "Sasin! Enros! Where are you?" The voice was filled with barely restrained panic.

"Down here, Maetrin!" the boy called back.

A moment later, the source of the voice burst into the livestock cave. A woman, with a third kid who looked to be between these two in age following on her heels. The woman's shoulders slumping with relief. "You can't go off on your own," she scolded the children. "Not now. You have to stay with me or Phados. Like Danos here."

"But we're safe now," the girl reasoned. "And we were going to help him feed the *kerkopith*."

The woman glanced up at me, seeming to notice me for the first time. "You," she said. "Your name is... Isaak, correct? The boy from the future."

"Uh, yeah," I replied. "That's me."

"And you have returned. Does that mean there's still hope?"

She tried to keep her voice neutral, but I could still hear the undercurrent of desperation to it.

I smiled, hoping it exuded more confidence than I felt. "Yes," I said. "There's still hope. We have to get through this first. But once everyone is safe... there's still hope."

She looked so relieved her face about crumpled. She glanced down at her children, and I could see in her eyes that she was trying so hard to be strong for them, but in the current circumstances it was just about impossible. Even the smallest ray of hope now—hope that her kids could still have a future—was worth clinging to.

"I am Ierin," she said. "And these are my children, Enros, Danos, and Sasin. Thank you for everything. I look forward to... journeying with you," she said with a grin.

I exhaled. She didn't just mean the journey to Katai'ios. She meant the journey to Mars. Everyone here was relying on me. If they were going to evacuate Iamos before the atmosphere ran out, they would need me. They couldn't get there without me. I was their only hope.

But Nadin needed me, too.

Assuming it isn't already too late.

Ierin took Sasin's hands and ushered the others back into the outpost. I watched the four of them go. The *kerkopith* squirmed in my arms.

No. I wasn't going to give up. I would find Nadin, and I'd bring her back here. There was no other alternative.

If only I could figure out how.

The *kerkopith* had just finished drinking and I'd replaced the cork stopper on the waterskin when I heard voices in the corridor again. The next group of refugees. I had to hurry before the new runners left. Whoever they were, I would *make* them take me with them to Bright Horizon. I would *make* them show me how to rescue Nadin.

The *kerkopith* fidgeted as I burst back out into the outpost's hub. This group of refugees had a bigger mix of ages than the last group—some young adults, some older. I zeroed in on the runner, who I recognized as Shuliin, the Ferre smuggler from Hope Renewed. I had only taken three steps toward her, though, when the sight of two others in the group stopped me in my tracks.

"Emil!" I cried in surprise. "Gitrin!"

They whirled on me. "Contreras!" Emil barked, his voice hoarse. "What the hell are you doing back here, kid? You looked like you were on Earth the last time I saw you."

"Yeah, it's a long story." I struggled to keep my grip on the squirming primate. "We found a working postern in Mexico."

Emil grinned, his yellowed teeth glistening. "Atlantean arches. Just like I always theorized."

Gitrin's eyes flitted between Emil and I as we spoke, seeming eager to know what we were talking about but unable to understand our conversation in English. I switched back to Iamoi.

"Gitrin, I'm glad you're here. I need your help."

"Is Nadin with you?" she asked, her voice full of concern.

"No. Eos said that the *geroi* took her into the pyramid. Nikos said their spies heard a rumor that the medics were prepping someone for reeducation."

"*Yad*," Gitrin spat.

"We have to stop them," I said.

She tugged her earlobe. "We have to go back."

From halfway across the room, Shuliin heard Gitrin speak. "What did you just say?" she asked, storming over to us. The *kerkopith* squirmed again and this time managed to wriggle out of my arms, scrambling up my arm and perching on my shoulder, its tail draped over the top of my head.

"We have to go back," Gitrin repeated firmly.

Shuliin was incredulous. "We are in the process of getting people *out* of Bright Horizon. Nobody is going *back* except the runners."

"Yes, runners. We need to *be* runners," I said. "There's someone we need to get out. Someone who wasn't with the Elytherioi."

"Who?" she demanded.

"My pupil," Gitrin said.

"My friend," I said at the same time.

"What's going on?" Emil demanded.

"Absolutely not," Shuliin said. She bustled away from us, down the corridor to one of the supply caves. I raced after her, nearly bumping into Danos and Enros, their arms laden with empty waterskins. Gitrin and Emil hurried after me.

"Eliin," Shuliin said, bursting into the supply cave. Eliin looked up from the crate she was rummaging through. "These three want to go back to Bright Horizon."

"Two," I corrected. "Emil needs to stay here."

"What are you saying about me?" Emil prodded me in the side. The *kerkopith* chittered at him.

"Alos, what are you talking about?"

"Eliin, it's imperative that Isaak and I return to Bright Horizon," Gitrin said. "A life is at stake."

"The runners are getting all of our people out," Eliin said. She gingerly removed an armful of *naranshas* from the crate. The *kerkopith* squeaked and leaped off my head, diving after the fruit.

"Not everyone," I said. "The girl I was with before, Nadin—she risked her life to save us all. And now the *geroi* are going to reeducate her."

"The *geroi*'s blood?" Shuliin didn't ask so much as sneer. "Out of the question."

My pulse was pounding in my ears. I was sick of arguing, and I was going to blow my stack if I heard anyone call Nadin *geroi*'s blood one more time. I didn't need their permission. Gitrin would help me. She'd know the way. We were going to leave right now and we were going to find Nadin, come hell or high—

"Eliin!" a panicked voice rang out from the outpost hub. It sounded like Ierin. "Eliin, hurry!"

Another voice quickly followed. "*Geroi!*"

I sucked in my breath in a panic. No, *not now!* I knew it had been too good to be true, the Elytherioi being left unguarded during the eruption. It had been a trap... the *geroi* had followed them here, and now the rebellion was going to be crushed once and for all...

Eliin raced into the tunnel, leaving the crate of supplies abandoned, the *kerkopith* stuffing its cheeks with the unguarded fruit. I ran after her, bursting out into the central cavern, looking around for the swarm of Enforcers I was sure awaited us.

But there was no swarm. A group of refugee men brandished makeshift weapons, surrounding just two people.

One I recognized immediately as Ceilos.

The other...

Everything seemed to slow as I stared at her. Her clothes were ripped to shreds, the neckline of her silver bodysuit torn away revealing shoulders wrapped in muslin bandages, caked in dried blood. Her head had been shaved, the long, thick locks that she'd dyed black to disguise her identity now gone. Heavy bags under her eyes betrayed her exhaustion.

She'd been here for just twenty-four hours, and this is what they'd done to her.

"Oh my God," I heard myself saying. It was so utterly insufficient, yet it was all I could manage.

I pushed past Eliin, barely registering everyone else in the cave staring at us as I hurried over to her. "Nadin, are you okay? What happened? What did they do to you?"

Of course she wasn't okay. It was stupid to even ask. I was going to find whoever did this to her, and I was going to—

"You're here," she murmured, her voice ragged. "You came."

She looked like she was fighting back tears. I couldn't bear it.

But she knew me. Despite everything else they'd done to her, they hadn't taken away her memories. She still knew me. She'd gotten away from the *geroi* before they could erase her mind. And that meant that it was going to be okay, right? It was going to be okay.

I tried to manage a smile, tried not to let it show how angry I was for her sake. "Of course I came," I said. "I made you a promise."

It was going to be okay.

CHAPTER 21

- n a d i n -

HE'D OPENED THE DOOR. HE WAS HERE. HE WAS REAL. MY MIND KEPT repeating it over and over, like it couldn't quite accept what was here before my eyes. Isaak. Real. Solid. Not my imagination. The last several months hadn't been a dream. He was real, and he'd returned.

For me.

Slowly, my tunnel vision cleared and I became aware once more of the others surrounding us. The men hadn't lowered their makeshift weapons, but they stood frozen, looking back and forth from Ceilos to me to Isaak to Eliin. Unsure of how to respond.

Then, before I could fully register what was happening, another figure had pushed her way through the crowd, shoving past Isaak and pulling me gingerly into her arms. She took care not to touch my ravaged shoulders, but she held me protectively, maternally.

"Gitrin," I said in surprise.

"*Alin*," she murmured, and I felt my tensed muscles relax. "We weren't... too late?" She glanced at Isaak for the answer to that question, rather than addressing it to me. Just as well, since I didn't quite feel sure of my voice.

"No," Isaak said. "She remembers us."

Gitrin let out a sigh of relief. She loosened her hold on me, stepping back and looking me over, taking in my shaved scalp and my bloodied shoulders. Concern was apparent on her face. "We were told you'd been sentenced to reeducation."

I swallowed. "I was." My voice sounded rough, like my throat was coated with grit. "The *geroi* were interrupted by..." I struggled to find the words. "Everything," I managed at last.

"Nadin," Isaak said. The tone in his voice was odd, almost strangled. I glanced at him and saw his eyes were dark, his expression unreadable. "What happened to you? How did..." He trailed off. His gaze was locked on my shoulders, and I felt strangely vulnerable—almost ashamed of the state I was in, though I should be anything but.

Ceilos stepped forward. "The *geroi*," he said with disgust. "They interrogated her. She wouldn't give them answers. They didn't like that."

The crowd murmured and I felt my face grow hot. I squeezed my eyes shut, but I could still feel them staring at me, gawking at the blood-stained bandages.

"Did they learn anything?" Eliin asked. "About the Elytherioi? About our movement?"

"No," I started to say, but then I hesitated. "Not from me, at least."

Guilt washed over me as soon as the words were out of my mouth. Ceilos had saved me, and now I was throwing him to the *gamadas*. But it was true—I knew that I had told them nothing. I didn't know the same of Ceilos. I didn't believe he would. But by the same token, I hadn't believed he would betray the Elytherioi to the *geroi* in the first place. Yet he'd done just that.

At my words, the crowd turned on him. The same hostility that had met us when we'd entered the cavern returned, sharper now.

"I didn't tell them anything either!" Ceilos protested, holding his hands up defensively.

"So you say," snarled the man I'd seen when we'd entered, the three children's father. "But I note that the girl is the only one standing here with stripes on her back."

"I swear, I told them nothing," Ceilos cried, but his voice was drowned out by the roar of the crowd, closing in tighter around us. My heart beat erratically, and I felt that same roar in my ears that I'd felt the day we traveled to Mars, when the crowd had surged around us. The tunnel vision that had led to me passing out. I swallowed, trying to catch my breath before that feeling engulfed me again. Isaak noticed—he grabbed my elbow, trying to steady me.

"That is enough," Eliin shouted. The cavern fell silent. "You are all guests in my home, and I expect you to behave as such," she snapped. "This is not how we do things, and you all know it. This is not the way of the Elytherioi."

"We can't let them stay here." The voice was familiar to me. The woman it belonged to had the traits of Hope Renewed, like mine—white hair, blue eyes. Shuliin, the Ferre smuggler. "We voted that they weren't allowed to join us. They're *geroi*'s blood. We knew they couldn't be trusted, and just as we'd feared they would, they betrayed us to the *geroi*. It's because of them that Elytherios was destroyed."

"That's not true!" Isaak protested. "They…" He trailed off, glancing in my direction, and then in Ceilos', seeming unsure of what to say next.

I exhaled. It was true, if only by half.

"Nadin is innocent," Gitrin said firmly. "She bears the physical scars to prove it."

"That doesn't mean she should stay here," Shuliin countered.

"She must. I insist upon it."

From Shuliin's side, a slender woman with short, light-brown hair and amber eyes spoke up. I recognized her as Syrin, Shuliin's partner. "Should we hold a forum?" she asked.

"There's no time for that," said Eliin. "We have to evacuate our people. We are wasting precious time."

"It must be decided now," Gitrin insisted. "We must know what to do with these children before any parties leave for Katai'ios."

"They must not know about Katai'ios," Shuliin hissed.

Gitrin stared between Shuliin and Eliin for a long moment, jaw clenched, nostrils flared. Then, in a commanding voice, she said, "I invoke *shedosht*."

A gasp came from the crowd. I looked around, surprised, wondering at their reaction. *Shedosht*? It was a word in the old language. It sounded familiar to me, but I couldn't quite place it. Something Gitrin had taught in our lessons, about Iamoi customs in the time before the Progression. But what…

"Gitrin, I refuse to participate in *shedosht*," Eliin said, her voice low. "It is an ancient, barbaric custom. It goes against all of our principles."

"But the Elytherioi have used it before," Gitrin argued, her brow arched.

"Only once," Eliin countered. "Years before my time. Even you would have been but a child."

"But there is precedent for it," Shuliin interrupted, her brows drawn fiercely. "I agree with Gitrin. We must decide now. I accept her invocation of *shedosht*, and hereby volunteer as *ninvidu*."

Ninvidu—arbiter. The one with sole authority, sole judgment in the matter. Suddenly I remembered, and I knew why Eliin called it barbaric. *Shedosht* was something between a trial and a duel. More likely to pervert justice than serve it. It had been banned within the cities for more than a century because of its potential to go tragically awry. For Gitrin to have invoked it, she must be truly desperate.

I swallowed. *These are desperate times.*

Silence fell over the cave. Syrin stepped hesitantly forward, putting her hand on Shuliin's shoulder, but the smuggler shrugged it off. Her eyes were locked on Gitrin's, the two women holding each other's gazes defiantly. Waiting to see who would back down first.

At last, Eliin sighed. "Very well. But know that I am against this. Everyone here, remember—I was opposed to this."

Gitrin squared her shoulders and stepped forward. "*Ninvidu*, will you accept my testimony?"

Shuliin tugged her earlobe solemnly.

"Then I give it freely. I was there in Elytherios," Gitrin said. "I heard what was said yesterday morning when the postern to Isaak's time was opened. Just moments after the *geroi* invaded our city. Ceilos admitted to betraying us. Nadin knew nothing of his betrayal before that moment. She is wholly innocent. Moreover, she had the opportunity to save herself, but instead she chose to return from the future in order to try to help us. This is my testimony, and I swear it upon my life."

Shuliin's expression was unreadable as Gitrin concluded her speech. She inhaled somberly. "A testimony has been given," she said. "Are there any other Elytherioi present who saw these events and are willing to testify?"

She looked around the cavern. The other rebels murmured among themselves, but I knew it was in vain. None of these people were there at that moment, when the postern had been opened. None of them could testify—and I was sure none of them would.

I felt ill. Isaak's hand was still firm against my elbow, and I was grateful for it, because my legs suddenly felt as though they could not bear my weight. This was the forum all over again. The past three months seemed to have been for nothing. Why had I thought it would be a good idea to come here?

Eliin swallowed. "You are a citizen of our Elytherios, Gitrin, and your testimony is valued. But under the law of *shedosht*, there must be testimonies given by two citizens. Otherwise, it's just your word."

"Eos and Marin were there as well," Gitrin argued. "They heard what was said. Surely they will also testify."

"Marin is not here. I do not know if she will be brought here or to another outpost. And Eos went with Nikos back to Bright Horizon," Eliin said. "I don't know when they'll return. In the meantime, we will have to keep these two somewhere. I suppose back there..." She gestured toward the leftmost tunnel, to the place where her dwelling was located.

"But the hole in the ceiling," Isaak protested.

"We'll cover it," Eliin said.

"Nadin is hurt," he insisted.

"She will be comfortable there."

"But the ash—"

Eliin held up the palms of her hands dismissively. "It's the best that can be done, *alos*."

He looked at me, his face riddled with a concern that only amplified the ringing in my ears. I didn't know what they were arguing about, but at this point I didn't care. All I wanted was to sit down. The last twenty-four hours had taken their toll on me. The ache in my shoulders was worsening, undoubtedly aggravated by the bruising they had experienced when I threw myself against the cracked pyramid glass. The adrenaline from our escape was wearing off now, leaving me weak-kneed and exhausted.

"She needs help—medical treatment."

"There's nothing for it, *alos*. Without the testimony of another citizen of Elytherios—"

His grip on my elbow tightened. "But I'm a citizen," he said after a moment.

I looked up at him in surprise.

"That's right," Gitrin said quickly, relief spreading across her face. "We voted to accept him, his father, and Emil at the forum. We granted them citizenship in the event that they would not be able to return to their time."

"Shuliin, is this true?" Eliin asked.

The smuggler scowled, not responding. Syrin put her hand on Shuliin's shoulder once more, and this time Shuliin didn't brush her off. She sighed, tugging her earlobe. It was true and she knew it, whether she liked it or not.

"All right, then," Eliin said, looking at Isaak gravely. "You are new to our people, though. You must understand our ways before you try to invoke them. The laws of *shedosht* are ancient, and they are unforgiving." She frowned. "*Shedosht* requires absolute truth of testimony from two witnesses. You must be willing to stake your life on it, for if the *ninvidu* chooses to reject your testimony, your life will be forfeit."

"Isaak, don't," I stammered. "It's not worth it. I'll go along with whatever they—"

"No," he said firmly. He stepped forward, relinquishing his hold on me. Absently, I wrapped my arms about myself, my fingers finding the place where his hand had been against my elbow. "I'm fine with those conditions, because what I have to say is the truth." He looked defiantly at Shuliin. "So, she decides whether we're telling the truth?"

"Yes. The *ninvidu* is the sole arbiter of *shedosht*. The ancient law demands that she must set aside her personal feelings on the situation and weigh the evidence presented in the testimony fairly. But she alone makes that decision." The ancient law demanded neutrality, but few *ninvidus* were capable of such neutrality. By the time the practice was banned on Iamos, scores of witnesses had been executed unjustly.

"What if she decides wrong?" Isaak asked.

"There are repercussions," Shuliin said. "Should the community feel I failed in my duty of impartiality, I will be killed. It is not only your life on the line. All of us risk death through this ritual." She crossed her arms. "But for the sake of our movement and our people, I believe the risk is worth it."

I wanted to argue, to protest, but my voice would not come. It was true, the *ninvidu* risked death by participating. But by the time a *ninvidu* was found corrupt, it would be too late for those witnesses. And there were cases as well when a *ninvidu* had ruled justly, but was lynched by angry members of the community anyway. *Shedosht* amounted to nothing more than mob justice. Banning it had been one of the few good things the *geroi* had done.

"Isaak, please," I whispered. "Don't."

He either didn't hear me or chose to ignore me. Taking a deep breath, he said, "Okay. I'll do it."

I felt like the cavern floor had opened into a chasm, and I was teetering on the brink. This couldn't be happening.

Eliin sighed. "*Ninvidu*, will you accept this boy's testimony?"

Shuliin tugged her earlobe.

"Very well," said Eliin. "Go ahead, Isaak."

Isaak swallowed. "I was there when the postern was opened," he said. "On the other side. We opened a stable connection between Elytherios and a location in my time. We were hoping to plan an evacuation to the future. But when the postern was opened, we found that in the three minutes we were gone, the *geroi* had attacked. And..." He glanced at Ceilos, hesitating for just a moment, almost imperceptibly. "It's true. I heard everything that was said. Ceilos is the only one who betrayed Elytherios. Nadin is innocent. And she paid for it." He nodded toward my shoulders. "As you can see."

"Do you swear this on your life?" Shuliin asked.

"I do," he said, and my stomach sank. Isaak's fate was tied to mine now, even more than it already had been.

Eliin turned to Shuliin. "*Ninvidu*, do you accept their testimonies?"

Shuliin tugged her earlobe. "I accept."

Eliin squeezed her eyes shut. "Very well. We await your judgment."

Shuliin opened her mouth to speak, and I flinched; but Syrin stepped quickly forward just then. "A moment, please," she said. "I would like to confer with my partner before she issues her verdict."

I watched in surprise as the women detached themselves from the crowd, Syrin whispering in a voice so low I could not hear. Shuliin frowned as she spoke, crossing her arms and looking down at her feet.

My knees shook. I knew my legs would not be able to hold my body weight much longer. In the back of my mind, I kept remembering the aggression in Shuliin's voice that day in Hope Renewed. The day she was caught smuggling Ferre. Her defiance as she'd argued with the Enforcers, the riot that she had instigated among the populace. Her voice leading the crowd in the chant of "Death to the *geroi!*" And the anger on her face when Gitrin had nominated Ceilos and me for citizenship in Elytherios.

She would never accept Isaak and Gitrin's testimony. Shuliin saw me only as *geroi*'s blood, and a threat to her people. I would die, that much was certain. I'd been a fool to think I could cheat death. I knew before the hearing at the *gerotus* that that much was true. My escape from Bright Horizon had done nothing but prolong the inevitable. But now Gitrin and Isaak would die too. Why had she invoked this foolhardy, barbaric ritual? And why ever had I given Henry the means to make another key? It had been selfish. By doing so, I'd signed Isaak's death sentence. His blood now would be on my hands.

Finally, Shuliin stepped away from Syrin, returning to the center of the circle and clearing her throat. My heart beat erratically.

"This girl is *geroi*'s blood," Shuliin said. "That much is undeniable. And someone betrayed us to the *geroi*. This is also irrefutable. Keeping her with us will endanger us. It will make us even more of a target for the *geroi*. For these reasons, I oppose her joining us."

My stomach lurched.

"But, as my partner has just reminded me"—she arched a brow at Syrin—"under the laws of *shedosht*, as *ninvidu*, I must not rely on my own feelings. Nor should I consider what I think the best decision for the community would be. I must look solely at the testimony and the evidence. And..." She sighed, as though what she was about to say was against her better judgment. "The fact of the matter is that all the evidence points to their words being true. And all the evidence says that the testimony is true. The *geroi* would only cause such grievous bodily harm to one who had not betrayed us. And then there is the matter of her sentence of reeducation, which our scouts heard with their own ears. The evidence is overwhelming. And it speaks to the truth of the testimony presented here."

"So what is your verdict, then?" Gitrin asked.

Shuliin narrowed her eyes at her. "As *ninvidu*, I have no choice. Nadin has proven her loyalty to our cause. My judgment is that she is innocent and may remain among us. The other must be segregated and kept under guard until the elders return. They will advise us on what to do with him."

I stared at her in shock, my mind struggling to process what had just happened. Isaak let out a sigh of relief. He turned, grinning reassuringly at me.

Over my shoulder, Ceilos asked, "But will I not be given an opportunity to argue my case?" He managed to keep his tone level, but I could hear the undercurrent of anxiety within it. I couldn't bear to look at him. I didn't want to see what his eyes might be betraying.

"Your case has just been argued," Shuliin said. "Did you not hear? Two witnesses gave testimony against you."

"But those who testified don't know the full story," Ceilos protested. "Do I not have any recourse?"

My stomach twisted at the desperation in his voice. No, Gitrin and Isaak *didn't* know the full story. Only I did. But I could not invoke *shedosht* the way Gitrin had. There was no second witness to testify for Ceilos.

And even if there were, was I willing to stake my life to testify on his behalf? *Could* I trust that Ceilos wouldn't betray us again?

I felt faithless, knowing that the only reason I was in this place with my memories intact was because of Ceilos. If it weren't for him, I would be trapped in Bright Horizon, the System erasing more and more of me until all that remained was the *geroi*'s mindless pawn. Yet I still could not bring myself to speak for him. I hated myself for it, but my tongue felt like it was weighed down with a stone.

Shuliin's eyes flashed. "*Geroi*'s blood, you are testing my patience," she said sharply. "You should consider yourself lucky that we are waiting for the elders instead of casting you into the mountain's fire right now."

"But I can help you," Ceilos insisted. "I'm more valuable to you alive than dead."

"Nothing will be done just yet," Eliin said in a placating tone. "We will wait. In the meantime, Obios, Camos, please take Ceilos to my dwelling and keep an eye on him. And see to it that that hole in my ceiling is patched. Make sure he's comfortable. We are not the *geroi*, treating our... prisoners"—her nose wrinkled in distaste at the word—"like vermin."

She turned her attention back to me. "Isaak, Gitrin, I trust you can tend to Nadin? The rest of us need to get back to work. There is much we need to do, and we are behind now." The crowd began to disperse, while two of the men stepped forward. One of them, a bearded man with the traits of Prosperous Future, I recognized as the father of the three Elytherioi children. He gripped Ceilos firmly around his bicep.

Gitrin took my hand and gave it a reassuring squeeze. "Everything will be all right now. Come. We need to get those bandages changed, and I want to get a look at your injuries. We mustn't let them get infected. Syrin, you were in charge of our medical supplies, were you not? Would you be so kind as to share a portion of antiseptic and some bandages with our new sister? And Isaak, if you will, I need an amphora of clean water."

"Okay," he said, hurrying down the central tunnel.

Gitrin tried to guide me after him, but I felt rooted in place, watching the men trying to lead Ceilos away as he struggled.

"You have to listen to me!" he cried. "There are things you need to know." They ignored him, pulling him past me. "Wait, please—" He jerked his arm away from the man, locking eyes with me. Frantically, he whispered, "I know who the Liberator is."

"That's enough," the bearded man said, taking Ceilos' arm once more. "Save it for when the elders return."

As they guided him down the tunnel toward Eliin's home, I stared in shock, mouth agape. Had Ceilos really just said what I thought he'd said?

"Nadin, come," Gitrin urged again, pulling my hand.

"Did you hear that?" I asked, turning to her with wide eyes. "What Ceilos just said?"

Her expression grew severe. "No. But whatever it was, don't listen to him, Nadin. He cannot be trusted."

"But he said—"

"We need to take care of your injuries, *alin*. That is what's most important now."

I sighed and gave up struggling, allowing her to lead me. Gitrin was right. He couldn't be trusted.

But what if he was telling the truth? What if he really did know who the Liberator was?

What if we were making a terrible mistake?

- n a d i n -

GITRIN BROUGHT ME TO A SMALL CAVE OFF THE CENTRAL TUNNEL. IT seemed to be a supply room. The earthquake that had preceded the eruption had taken a toll on this place: what had clearly recently been neat stacks of crates had been upended into disorderly piles, and dust and debris was strewn over the top of it, caking both the boxes and the floor. In the middle of the mess, Isaak had straightened some larger crates and dusted them off, forming a makeshift bench. I sat on this, grateful to get off my feet. My dizziness had resumed, and I felt disoriented, off-kilter. Ceilos' words kept echoing in my mind. "*I know who the Liberator is.*"

Was he telling the truth?

Gitrin said he couldn't be trusted. I knew she was right. And yet... Ceilos had not yet had an opportunity to tell me what he'd learned after our return to Bright Horizon. It was clear things had changed—what we'd overheard in the *geroi*'s chamber proved that much. What if Ceilos really had learned what he claimed to?

Gitrin gingerly removed the first layer of bandages, taking care not to pull too hard when she reached areas where the blood had caked the muslin against my skin. As gentle as she was being, pain still shot through me in every place she touched. I struggled not to flinch.

A shadow appeared in the doorway and I looked up. Syrin stood there, arms laden with folded linens, fresh rolls of bandages, and two small amphorae. "This should be everything you need."

"Thank you, *alin*," Gitrin said.

Syrin set the supplies down beside me and hesitated, watching me for just a moment. I smiled up at her. "Thank you for earlier," I said.

"What do you mean?" she asked curiously.

"For talking to Shuliin. For whatever it was you said to her."

Syrin exhaled, looking away. "I... I didn't do it for you. I did it for her. She should never have agreed to be *ninvidu*." She ran a hand through her short, curly hair and frowned at Gitrin. "This decision should have been made through a vote of our people. It should not have been left to a single arbiter."

"I will not apologize for my actions," Gitrin said, her hands still working as she spoke.

"I don't suppose you will. Shuliin won't, either." Syrin folded her arms, looking annoyed. "Regardless, she agreed to it, and the laws of *shedosht* are clear. I did not wish my partner to have the blood of two of our citizens on her hands. Nor did I want her to risk her own life." She swallowed. "Though her life may still be forfeit should our people decide she made the wrong choice."

"They won't," I promised her. "I will prove my loyalty to all of you. I will do everything in my power to demonstrate to everyone that she made the right choice."

Syrin smiled tightly and tugged her earlobe.

Isaak appeared just then, carrying a large, heavy amphora of water. Syrin squeezed past him, disappearing down the tunnel.

"Sorry it took so long," Isaak said. "I'd forgotten about them." He gestured with his chin to the man following close behind him—Emil, the Martian scientist from Isaak's time. I breathed out a sigh of relief. He was safe, then.

A moment later, I noticed that perched on Emil's shoulder was, of all things, a *kerkopith* with matted fur. The creature stared at me with familiar orange eyes, and I stared back.

"Where did that come from?" I asked as Isaak set the amphora down at Gitrin's feet.

Isaak followed my gaze to the primate on Emil's shoulder. "Oh... long story. Another refugee from Elytherios. And our *gurzas* are back, too. Thork and Tuupa."

I exhaled, a strange feeling of relief coming over me. So not all the animals from Elytherios had been killed, despite the treacherous conditions outside. I wondered how many had made it to safety before the explosion, and then the eruption. Was this creature an outlier?

Isaak watched me for a long moment before crouching down in front of me. "Hey," he said, grinning awkwardly up at me. "I'm sorry if I was out of line just now."

My brows furrowed in confusion. "What do you mean?"

He rubbed the back of his neck with his right hand. "The whole *shedosht* thing. I was really worried about you. It was obvious that you needed help, and I was concerned about you being in that area of the outpost. Part of Gitrin's kitchen ceiling caved in during the earthquake. Even though they said they were going to patch the hole, I didn't want you to be in there with all that ash when you..." He trailed off, watching Gitrin remove another layer of bandages with a solemn expression on his face. "When you're not feeling your best," he finished softly.

I managed a smile, though it was difficult to concentrate on Isaak's words as Gitrin touched another sore spot. I bit the inside of my cheek to keep myself from gasping at the sharp pain that followed. "You told the truth," I said.

"Yeah. I know. I just wanted to make sure you were okay with it. That I didn't overstep any boundaries."

I bit down harder on my cheek as Gitrin reached the bottom layer of bandages. I could tell from how much blood was stuck here that my wounds must have reopened during the earthquake, and perhaps again when I tried to break the glass in my cell. There was no way Gitrin could get this off without it stinging, but it made my eyes prickle and my ears ring. "Of course not," I said.

"Good." Color flooded his cheeks. "Testifying against Ceilos... I was afraid it might be, like..." He hesitated, then said in English, "A conflict of interest or something."

"'Conflict of interest'?" I repeated. "What does that mean?" It was a phrase I hadn't heard before.

"Well, uh... because of... you know..."

Emil crouched next to Isaak, prodding him in the side with his elbow. The *kerkopith* had scurried from the man's shoulder onto the top of his head, its striped tail wrapped around his face, draped under his nose.

"What are you talking about?" he asked. "What conflict of interest?"

"Nothing," Isaak replied quickly.

Emil rolled his eyes. "In that case, what can you tell me about this thing? It attached itself to me back in the other storage room and it seems to have taken up permanent residence."

I laughed, then wondered at how strange the sound felt in my ears. I hadn't expected to ever laugh again. "That's a *kerkopith*," I said in English. "An Iamoi primate. It used to live in our forests... before." When we still had forests.

"It reminds me of a cross between a lemur and a raccoon," Isaak added.

"*Kerkopith*." Emil stroked his chin. "*Cercopithecidae*. From the Greek, *kerkopithekos*, meaning 'long-tailed ape.' From what I've heard, your language shares much in common with classical Greek. And the Greeks are where the myth of Atlantis comes from."

"The connection to Greek is how I was able to pick up the Iamoi language so quickly," Isaak said. "Modern Greek was the first language I learned as a kid besides English and Spanish, because so many people in our neighborhood spoke it. It's obvious that one of the missing Iamoi colonization parties to Earth must have ended up in the Aegean, or maybe the Mediterranean."

I struggled to follow their conversation. The fate of the lost colonists was one I had a great interest in, but I couldn't concentrate with—

Gitrin tugged once more on a bandage, and this time I hissed with pain.

"There," she said soothingly. "All done. Old bandages off." I turned my head to look at her. She was staring appraisingly at my injuries, making a tsking sound.

Isaak stood up, coming behind me to look himself. He started to gasp, but managed to strangle the sound. I knew he didn't want to upset me. But I also could imagine how bad it looked. I knew what had been done, after all. I clenched my fist, fingernails digging into the skin of my palm.

"Let's get this cleaned up," Gitrin said, forced cheerfulness in her voice.

Isaak helped her soak one of the linens with cold water from the jug, and she began to gently wipe away the caked-on blood. I tried not to focus on the pain, but it was difficult to ignore. I bit down so hard on my cheek that I tasted the metallic flavor of blood on my tongue.

The orange-eyed creature on Emil's head must have sensed something was amiss. It scampered down his arm, launching to the floor. It sniffed the air for a moment, obviously detecting the smell of blood. Then it looked up at me, balancing on its hind legs, watching me unblinkingly. I smiled in spite of myself.

Isaak saw what was happening and came back around, crouching in front of me once more. "What should we name him, Nadin?" he asked.

I blinked at him in confusion. "Name... the *kerkopith*?"

"Yeah. He's going to be with us awhile, so he needs to have a name, don't you think?"

He was clearly trying to distract me from what was going on behind me. Still—I winced as Gitrin set down the wet cloth and began to apply some kind of stinging antiseptic to the wounds—I needed the distraction.

I looked at the little animal, remembering the one I'd seen that night in Elytherios, in the clearing by the stream. It had blinked at me with wide orange eyes before racing off into the trees. I remembered the elegant way it had carried itself, the way the branches had swayed beneath its feet, how nimbly it had kept its balance. As if every movement were expertly coordinated.

"Pandat," I said.

"Pandat?" he repeated. "What does it mean?"

"It's a word in the old language. It means *dancer*." Dance was dead on Iamos, and had been for many years. Even the word for it was a relic. As with music, any form of self-expression that could be co-opted by the resistance had to be prohibited. But maybe the *plivoi* still danced, in secret. Maybe they still sang. Maybe there was still time to hear the Elytherioi's songs.

Maybe it wasn't all too late.

Isaak's mouth quirked up sideways. "I like that."

Emil jabbed him once again. "What's going on?" he demanded.

Isaak shook his head in exasperation. Switching to English, he said, "Nothing. We named the *kerkopith* Pandat."

"You named it?" Emil said, disgust apparent in his voice. "For God's sake, Contreras, it's a wild animal, not a pet."

"Yeah, well, we're rehabilitating him. We have to call him something. It's not exactly like we can let him go back to the wild right now, what with the state Iamos is in."

"I think Pandat is a fine name," said Gitrin, reaching for one of the rolls of muslin. She gently began wrapping the bandages around my shoulders. I tried not to flinch. It was less painful than when she took the old ones off, but it still hurt. "There," she said when she'd finished. She got to her feet, her knees cracking as she stood, and handed me one of the small amphorae Syrin had brought. "You should drink this now, *alin*. It will relieve the pain."

I stared at the bottle for a long moment, my insides seizing, trying not to remember the draught that Melusin had forced me to drink, the injection that Heros had given me...

"Are you okay, Nadin?" Isaak asked, looking at me with concern.

I wouldn't worry them. These were my friends. They were not trying to poison me. I removed the cork stopper and took a long swallow of the liquid inside.

"There. Hopefully it will take effect soon." Gitrin squeezed my hand, then turned to Isaak. "The draught will make her drowsy, and she needs her rest after her ordeal. Where would be a quiet, out-of-the-way place where she can sleep? Somewhere one of us can keep an eye on her."

"I've been camped out in the livestock cave," he said. "And the *gurzas* know her. Thork is loyal to her. They'll help me watch over her."

I wanted to protest. Now, of all times, I should be demonstrating my loyalty to the rebels' cause by helping them prepare for evacuation. I shouldn't just lie around doing nothing.

But even as I thought it, the drowsiness started to set in. I knew the medicine wouldn't be working this quickly—it was exhaustion. The fatigue had become nearly unbearable, and now that the adrenaline was wearing off, I found I could barely manage to stay awake.

"Come on, Nadin," Isaak said, taking my arm and helping me to my feet. He led me into the livestock cave, settling me in a corner near the back beside the *gurza* pen on a bed of fresh *seno* grass.

Within moments, I was asleep.

My dreams were a riot of color and sound, voices familiar and unfamiliar mingling into a strange chorus that ebbed and flowed like the waves of the sea. The waves I'd heard on Earth, against the beach on Sea-Star Island. The waves I'd heard on Mars, from the balcony of Tamara's home. The waves that had lapped against the boat on Yellowknife Bay.

The waves from my childhood. The distant sound of the sea that had grown ever fainter as the shore eroded, until it was gone altogether.

I rolled over, tossing in my sleep, the discomfort of my bruised shoulders leaking its way into my dream. I hadn't had a mirror here, couldn't look to see how bad the bruising was, but the expression on Isaak's face had said it all.

Couldn't look in the mirror... The mirror of clear, polished glass in Delia and Bryn's bathroom. The mirrors reflecting sun into Elytherios, filling the caldera with light as bright as day. The polished bronze looking glass in my room at the *geroi's* villa.

Turning, looking at the bruises in the reflection of the polished bronze...

Abruptly, I'm a child again. Just weeks before my fifth annual. Weeks before the betrothal ceremony. The day I'd looked through the postern into the room just like it in Bright Horizon. The day he'd come, and everything had changed.

The day I met Ceilos.

Legions of *plivoi* have brought his effects from Bright Horizon over the past several days, filling his suite in the *geroi's* villa in Hope Renewed, ensuring that his every comfort will be met. Now Ceilos has retreated there, closing his door and not reappearing for over an hour.

Antos and Melusin aren't satisfied to allow him to remain there, though. They've sent me to retrieve him, insisting that I take him on a tour of the citidome. "You must get to know each other," they've urged me. "After all, you are to be partners."

So I reluctantly stand on his threshold, trying to will myself to raise my hand and knock. I keep thinking about the coldness in his green eyes this morning, the spark of animosity I saw there. But there's nothing else I can do. I can't remain out here all day. If I retreat, the *geroi* will track me down and force me to try again. This partnership isn't something I can escape.

Finally, I swallow, take a deep breath, and knock.

No reply comes. I knock again, more loudly. This time I think I hear a noise from within, muffled. A sound of pain? Or was it my imagination?

Anxiously, I try the door. It's not locked, and slides open with ease.

Ceilos' chamber is dark, lit only by a mosaic of multicolored phosphorescence on the wall. I creep in, looking around uncertainly. He is here, isn't he?

A glimmer of movement in the next room catches my eye. Ceilos stands in front of a looking glass made of brightly polished bronze. The clasps on his silver bodysuit are undone, and he's eased himself out of one of the sleeves of the tunic, his right half facing the mirror. He runs his fingers over his side and winces, hissing in a breath. It's only then that I see it, obscured as it is by the shadows of the room. A massive bruise, purple and hideous, wrapping its way around his abdomen.

I gasp, and Ceilos whirls. "What are you doing in here?" he demands.

"I... I..." I can't find the words to respond. Ceilos quickly shoves his arm back into his sleeve and refastens the clasps on his tunic. "The *geroi* sent me to fetch you..."

"And you couldn't have knocked?"

"I did knock," I protest. "But I thought I heard a sound. I wanted to make sure you were all right."

"I am perfectly well," he snaps. The way his brows furrow across his forehead seems to dare me to challenge him. Dare me to admit what I'd seen. Dare me to ask him how it had happened.

I don't dare.

"The *geroi* thought you may be interested in a tour of Hope Renewed," I say, attempting to change the subject. "To get to know your new home."

"I should imagine it's much the same as Bright Horizon was," he replies. "Since all the citidomes were built with the same layout."

"I-I suppose so..." I stammer.

"Then if it's all the same to you, I'll abstain," Ceilos says.

He turns away from me, but I remain rooted in place. After a moment, he sighs and turns back. "What is it?"

I fix my gaze on the floor, my face burning. "What will I tell the *geroi?*"

"What does it matter?" He stares at me for a long moment. "Do you always do everything the *geroi* tell you to do?"

I wring my hands. This is a disaster. This boy is to be my partner, but his dislike of me is more than apparent. I don't know why he hates me so, when I've barely spoken a handful of sentences to him, but it's clear he does, and through no fault of my own. But Antos and Melusin will blame me, as they always do.

"What else am I supposed to do?" I ask helplessly.

Ceilos stares at me, his green eyes sharp, burning directly into me. He doesn't look like Ceilos anymore. He looks like someone—something—else entirely. Memory fades to dream fades to nightmare. My pulse jumps with fear.

Not the boy I know, but a monster.

I jerked awake, my heart pounding. I was drenched in sweat. I sat upright, breathing hard, squeezing my eyes shut, trying to collect my thoughts. The remnants of the dream were already fading. Only snatches remained in my mind. It had been about Ceilos... When Ceilos first came to Hope Renewed? It was already beginning to blur, merging together with the other nightmare I'd had just before the eruption, which stood more vividly in my memory.

"Do you remember what we spoke of all those years ago, when Ceilos first came to us?"

Had this dream told me just now? I struggled to grasp at it, but it was draining away like water through a sieve. No, Gitrin hadn't been in this dream, I knew that much. Just Ceilos, and... bruises? I frowned, trying to recall. Had that been real, or just part of my fractured nightmare? It felt familiar, but it was so hard to remember things that had happened so long ago, when I was so young.

Ceilos and I hadn't gotten along when he'd first arrived—the *geroi* had continued to remind me of that fact over the years, to my chagrin. But I could barely remember that time now; it was more of a second-hand memory, something I knew only because others reminded me of it, rather than something I recalled on my own. Something had changed between us, that much I knew. He'd become my closest friend and only confidant apart from Gitrin. It seemed impossible that we ever *had* been anything but the best of friends. It hadn't been until recently that we'd begun having... problems.

I sighed, then winced, noticing the throbbing in my shoulders. My own bruises were weeping now, after however many hours I'd just spent sleeping on this lumpy *seno* bed. The cavern was dark, and I heard no sounds of activity. Only the steady rumble of the *gurzas* breathing beside me.

I looked around, getting my bearings. It must be the middle of the night now. The *gurzas* were huddled two by two, sleeping inside their pen. I noticed two familiar beasts curled up in the corner closest to me, green scales streaked with orange and yellow. The pair who had brought us to Elytherios. I smiled softly.

A short distance away from me, Isaak lay asleep on a bale of *seno*. He'd told Gitrin that he'd stay close to me, and he'd kept his promise.

He'd kept his other promise, too. The one he'd made in the Los Tuxtlas jungle. My hand curled against my chest reflexively. It seemed like a different life.

Everyone was asleep now. But I'd slept for hours, and I was awake. I didn't think I could sleep again, not for a while yet. The hazy dream I'd jolted awake from still hung in my mind, and with it came another thought. The memory of what Ceilos had whispered when they'd taken him away.

"I know who the Liberator is."

Maybe he'd been bluffing. Maybe this was just another of his lies, like the falsehoods he'd told me, told the Elytherioi about his supposed kidnapping, when all along he'd been working for the *geroi*.

A way to save our partnership.

Shuliin had said they'd wait for the elders to return before deciding what to do with Ceilos. Had that happened while I was asleep? Or were they still not back yet? Had Ceilos' fate been decided yet?

I didn't know what they would do with him. I knew what most of the Elytherioi *wanted* to do with him, though. And I remembered what Syrin had said, that this should be up to the populace to decide.

If Ceilos really did know who the Liberator was, this might be my last chance to ask him.

That thought is what drove me to stand quietly, steadying myself against the pen fencing for a moment, waiting for the dizziness to subside. Then I crept past Isaak and into the labyrinth of tunnels.

The outpost was silent, but as I passed cavern mouths, I saw groups of people huddled together on makeshift beds like the one I'd been sleeping on. Low voices came from the central cavern, telling me that not everyone was sleeping, so I moved cautiously, hoping against hope that I would encounter no one.

Outside Eliin's dwelling, a lone guard had dozed off, his head lolling to the side. I couldn't believe he'd be sleeping while on duty, but then I reminded myself that the Elytherioi were not like the *geroi*. Their society was built on trust. They'd told us before that they didn't keep prisoners. These people weren't Enforcers. They didn't have experience with this. The man had no reason to think any of his own people would attempt to sneak past while he was sleeping. I felt guilty now. I had vowed to Syrin I'd prove my loyalty, and here I was immediately betraying that.

But I had to know. Not just for myself, but for the good of all Iamos. We would have no hope of saving our people if we didn't find whoever the Liberator was and stop him before his sabotage could cause more catastrophe. Civilians had perished in the earthquake on Hamos, and the eruption of the Sios Ifaisteos had very nearly killed everyone in Elytherios, not to mention the people in Bright Horizon. If Ceilos had information about the Liberator, I had to know.

The man didn't stir as I crept past him, gently sliding the door to Eliin's home open and slipping inside.

What once must have been Eliin's kitchen now lay in ruins, though Obios and Camos had done as Eliin asked and attempted to tidy the place up. Brush marks across the floor showed that they had swept, though a fine layer of ash still coated every surface of the room. Breathing it in made my sinuses itch uncomfortably. The table in the center of the room was splintered, damage incurred by the collapsing of the ceiling above. The hole Isaak had mentioned was now patched with what looked like the dismantled remains of a storage crate.

A curtain hung along the back of the room, and as I stood there trying to get my bearings, the curtain slid aside. Ceilos poked his head out. "Who's there?" he asked.

I quickly shushed him, mindful of the sleeping guard on the other side of the door. "It's me," I whispered.

He let out a sigh of relief. "Nadin."

I followed him back into Eliin's simple bedroom, bare apart from a bedroll and a handful of personal effects. "Do you have news?" he asked, sitting down on one side of the bed and gesturing for me to sit beside him.

"I've been asleep this whole time," I admitted. "Have the elders returned?"

"If they have, I've not been given word of it," he said. "What are you doing here?"

I hesitated. It felt so strange, Ceilos imprisoned and me here to ask him for information, rather than to help him. As he'd helped me earlier. The familiar niggling of guilt came crawling back, eating away at my mind.

"I need to ask you about what you said earlier," I said at last. "You said you know who the Liberator is."

He frowned, tugging his earlobe. "Yes." He paused. "Well, I think I do."

"The real Liberator. Not the false one you and the *geroi* invented," I clarified, a slight edge to my voice.

He looked affronted, but he shrugged it off. "Yes."

"The one responsible for the sabotage of the System."

"The same," he replied. "Bear in mind, this is just a guess. But I do believe I'm correct."

"Well? Tell me, then," I prodded.

He took a breath. "I think it's Tibros."

I stared at him in shock. "*Geros* Tibros?" I said, as if there could be any other. "Your father?"

"I know it's hard to believe, but I'm near certain of it," he replied.

I felt incredulous. "But he is one of the *geroi*! The Liberator claims to be working against the *geroi*. He's sabotaging the *geroi*'s own plans."

"I know it seems illogical, but think about it," Ceilos said. "We know it's not one of the rebels. What we've learned since finding Elytherios has shown us that. Whoever this Liberator is, he's trying to frame the rebellion. What better way to turn public sentiment against the rebellion than directing the blame for these attacks that have killed civilians toward the rebels?"

He watched me intently. "And think about it. The ways the System has been sabotaged indicates someone not just with knowledge of the System, but high-level access to it. Like one of the *geroi*."

My mind was reeling. I wasn't sure what left me unsettled, the ways that this made no sense—or the ways that, actually, it made perfect sense.

"But what makes you think it's Tibros specifically?" I asked.

"You saw how he was at the hearing," Ceilos said. "What he... did."

I looked down at my feet. "My own mother did something just as abominable."

"Yes, but only because her hand was forced. *He* forced her hand."

I thought back on the hearing, and what we'd overheard in the tunnel, reframing his words and his behavior in the light of Ceilos' theory.

"But why would Tibros do this?" I asked. "He's one of the rulers of Iamos. What more could he possibly stand to gain?"

"*One of* the rulers," Ceilos repeated. "There are still fifteen others that he has to share his power with. And there were even more before the colonists to Simos disappeared."

"You think he wants to have sole power?"

"You saw the way Paolin had to assert her dominance during the hearing. Tibros resents them, Paolin and Shiros. Bright Horizon had been his citidome. Ruler of the city of cities, capital of capitals—that had been his title. The other *geroi* made him give it up. He's been bitter since then."

"I suppose it's possible," I murmured.

"It all fits. Look at the evidence." He sat forward, urgency in his voice. "First, someone patched you into that session of the *gerotus*—who but someone with *geroi* DNA could have done that? Tibros was the one who was pushing to try to dissolve our partnership. And he's the one who gave me... the assignment, invoking the Liberator as if he was playing a game, daring us to notice. He's trying to sow discord among the *geroi*. He's been doing it for some time now. And the Liberator has been doing the same thing. It's the only possible solution. Tibros is trying to cause the *gerotus* to fall apart so that he can seize sole control."

My fingers gripped the worn, thin coverlet on Eliin's bed. This seemed so impossible, and yet the facts *did* all seem to align. But how could Tibros have managed all of this without attracting anyone's suspicion? Surely his partner would have—

His partner. Clodin. Suddenly, I remembered what we'd overheard in the hidden corridor of the pyramid. *Cost us a* gerouin.

"Ceilos, what about your mother?" I asked.

Ceilos hesitated, his face unreadable in the darkness. "Clodin is dead. I learned when we returned to Bright Horizon. When we were... separated."

I swallowed. So it was true, then. Yet another piece of evidence toward Ceilos' theory. Clodin had been wounded in the earthquake on Hamos, but Melusin had said she was expected to recover. Something had changed in the time I'd been gone, something that had led to her death. Had her injuries been more serious than the other *geroi* had realized? Or had it been something else?

Had she suspected what her partner was up to?

Quietly, I asked, "Do you think Tibros was responsible?"

"I do," Ceilos replied.

"But his own partner—"

"I believe that Tibros would be willing to eliminate anyone who poses a threat to his power," said Ceilos. "That includes all the other *geroi*. And... us, as well."

I ran a hand over my prickly scalp, trying to collect my thoughts. "The illness that *Geros Shiros* was suffering from... You don't think he could have had something to do with it?"

"I don't know," Ceilos said. "You'll note that he was quick to step in, though. Removing Paolin from power. Threatening to do the same to your parents."

"This is... horrible," I whispered. "How could Tibros do this?"

"Power corrupts," Ceilos said simply.

"But this is beyond corruption," I said. "This is... warped."

"The *geroi* are warped. That's how they are," Ceilos said. "The entire system is broken."

"I know that, Ceilos. I of all people know that." If there was one thing the last several months had taught me, it was that. I was just unprepared for the depths...

"Then why are you so stunned by this revelation?"

"You mean to say you're not?"

"I'm not," he said, a surprising lack of emotion to his voice. "I have told you for years that my father—" He broke off. "There is no love lost between my father and I."

I watched him silently. An unsettling flash of memory flitted through my mind. Of the dream. Had it been just a dream?

Bruises.

Antos and Melusin had been hard guardians. *Geroi's* children were the only children on Iamos raised by their biological parents rather than Caretakers, but that didn't mean I'd experienced parental love. They were critical, distant, dismissive. But they had never harmed me. Not before last night.

But Ceilos... Ceilos had not spoken much of his life in Bright Horizon before he'd come to Hope Renewed. All he'd ever said was that one phrase, repeated over and over. *"There is no love lost between us."* Now I found myself questioning what had transpired in the first five years of Ceilos' life. If Tibros was the monster Ceilos believed he was...

Perhaps Ceilos knew better than I ever could.

"Thank you for telling me," I finally said, my voice barely above a whisper.

"You needed to know."

I looked up at the dark stone ceiling. My eyes burned from the ash in the air. I told myself that was the only reason.

Finally, I said, "But how will we stop him?"

"You *want* to stop him?" Ceilos asked.

I stared at him, baffled. "Of course. Why wouldn't I?"

"The *geroi* are monsters. We just said as much. It would be better for all of Iamos if Tibros succeeded in destroying them all."

"But an absolute dictator surely would be much worse for the people," I said.

"Let him eliminate the other *geroi*. Then the rebels can eliminate him," Ceilos replied. "Allowing him to carry out his plans only will make it that much easier for the liberation movement."

"But, Ceilos," I protested, "in the process of trying to eliminate the other *geroi*, he's left hundreds of casualties in his wake. The colonies to Simos—the people in Ascendant Dawn—anyone who might have been killed or injured in that eruption just now... Who's to say how many more will die if he continues on in this way?"

My voice rose as I spoke, and he gestured for me to hush.

"Let's not argue about this," he said. "I just wanted you to know the truth, in case..." He trailed off, not seeming to know how to end that sentence. He cleared his throat. "You'd better go now. We can't risk anyone finding you here."

Reluctantly, I stood. I looked down at him, sitting on the end of the bedroll, for a long moment. "I'm going to do everything I can to get you out of here, Ceilos," I said.

He gave me a half-smile. "My choices were my own. If I pay the price for them, so be it."

His choices were his own, but he'd made them because of me.

I turned to go. "Still. I'll get you out of here. I promise."

I was so preoccupied with my thoughts, I didn't hear the footsteps in the tunnel until I rounded the corner and nearly collided with Isaak.

"Hey," he whispered, putting his hand on my upper arm to steady me, careful to avoid touching my shoulder. "Are you okay? I woke up and you were gone."

"I..." I didn't know where to begin. I looked up at him, my heart feeling like it was being ripped in two. I had so much that I'd wanted to tell him, so many words stored up in my heart that I'd wanted to say.

Now I felt like I couldn't. Not with Ceilos imprisoned mere meters away, and the guilt of it weighing me down like a stone. I wondered dimly if this would ever change, or if the words were destined to just die inside me, never spoken.

"I had something important that I needed to do," I said at last.

Bewilderment spread across his face. "What?"

I shook my head. "Not here. I—We need to talk. Somewhere private."

"Now?" he asked. "In the middle of the night?"

I inhaled shakily. "Yes, now. If not now..."

My eyes burned. From the ash, that's all.

"Then we may be too late."

CHAPTER 23

- i s a a k -

I LED NADIN BACK INTO THE LIVESTOCK CAVERN, HOPING THE IRREGULAR beating of my heart wasn't audible. I told myself I was being irrational, but I couldn't help my nerves. *We need to talk* never seemed to lead to good news. The words had sent my brain into a spiral of what-ifs, most of them centered around my anxieties about what had happened at the dig site the night before she'd left. I'd spent the last week reliving the embarrassment of that almost-kiss, wondering if I'd ruined things with Nadin forever. Now she'd hit me with a *we need to talk.* What else was I supposed to think?

"This way," I whispered, gesturing her through the cavern and into the tunnels beyond. Dawn wasn't far off, and I wasn't sure if someone else would come into the cavern and interrupt us. For now, the most private place we could go in the outpost would be the tunnels that forked out into the hills. The first leg of the journey Nadin and I had taken to Elytherios all those months ago.

When we were far enough into the tunnel to allow for some privacy, but still close enough for light from the livestock cavern to filter in, I turned to face her, leaning back against the rough-hewn sandstone. "What's up?" I asked, hoping the shadows were enough to disguise my expression.

Nadin swallowed. "I spoke with Ceilos," she whispered.

I exhaled. So that's what she'd been doing over there. "Nadin, Eliin's apartment isn't safe right now—"

She held up a hand, cutting me off. "I know. But it was important.

He... He knows who the Liberator is."

I stared at her. "Are you serious?"

She nodded.

I shivered. I was still wearing the clothes I'd had on in Mexico (now in sore need of a washing), but I'd taken off my rain jacket earlier in the day as the work made me overheat. Now, here in the dark tunnel, I realized it was far too cold for this thin t-shirt. "And you believe him?" I asked, running my palms over my bare arms.

"I..." She paused. "I think so. He believes that it's his father. *Geros* Tibros. He thinks that he's trying to eliminate the other *geroi* so he can take sole power, and blame it on the rebels so that the citidomes will unite behind him."

I didn't respond immediately, running that through my mind, turning it around. In a way, it did seem to fit. Eliin had been convinced that the so-called Liberator must be the *geroi*. The idea of it being a single rogue *geros* made more sense than it being the *geroi* as a whole.

"But when the Liberator commed you, we could hear Tibros talking in the *gerotus* session," I said.

"It was recorded," Nadin said. "I should have realized when GSAF found the recording, when they played it for us at Lago Verde. *Gerotus* sessions aren't ordinarily recorded by the System."

"So Tibros played you a recording and led you to believe that it was live so you wouldn't suspect him of being in two places at once?"

"And he used a System protocol to disguise his voice. I thought whoever it was sounded familiar, but I couldn't place it."

"Like the voice modulator Lizeth used for her burner figuscans," I said, the pieces coming together in my brain.

Nadin nodded. "It all makes sense. I still can't quite believe it, but the more I consider it, the harder to deny it becomes."

"We need to tell the others." I started to turn back toward the livestock cavern. "Eliin, Gitrin—"

"Wait." She reached out, grabbing my arm, but when her hand touched my bare skin, she recoiled almost like she'd been burned. I turned back, surprised at her reaction. Her hand hovered in midair, the fingers curling into themselves. Self-consciously, she looked down. "Not yet. I'm not ready to tell Gitrin yet."

"Why not?"

"Gitrin..." She still wouldn't look at me. The nerves from earlier started creeping back, a tight ball forming in the pit of my stomach. "She doesn't think I should trust Ceilos."

I watched her for a moment. "Maybe she's right," I said. "He did betray us, Nadin."

She looked up at me and her eyes flashed for a moment. Then the light died. "Ceilos..." She sighed, her hand retreating further from me, resting against the base of her throat. She looked down again. "Ceilos has reasons for what he did."

And suddenly, I knew. With that one sentence, that one look, I knew what was going on, why Nadin was being so awkward with me. Had I seriously thought that, since it had just been the two of us in my own time, everything from her life here had gone by the wayside? Unbidden, I heard my dad's voice in my head, taunting me: "*Are you sore about that Ceilos guy showing up and ruining things for you with the alien girl?*" My face grew hot with shame at the memory. I was an idiot. Such a giant torquing idiot.

The sting of this realization was quickly followed by a wave of frustration. Who was I, the Amazing Love Triangle-Man or something? Was this just something I was doomed to go through for the rest of my life? Was it the curse of being demisexual, that every girl I ever developed feelings for was going to have some other guy vying for her affection?

As soon as I thought it, I felt guilty. This was selfish of me. This reaction was completely self-centered. And I'd promised myself I wasn't going to be selfish anymore, not after what I'd put Tamara and Henry through. The world did not revolve around Isaak Contreras.

But it hurt. It hurt really, really bad.

"Yeah," I said, hoping my voice wasn't shaking. "I'm sure he did."

"Let's just keep this between us for now," Nadin said quietly, her tone unreadable.

"Okay." I leaned back against the wall again, trying to look nonchalant but mostly relying on it to keep my knees from giving out on me. "But what are we going to do about Tibros?"

"I don't know. I don't think we can do anything right now. There's no way we can return to the citidome. As Eliin said earlier, the priority has to be evacuating the Elytherioi, right?"

"Yeah," I said, eagerly pouncing on the change of subject. "We probably should head back soon, actually—the first round of refugees is going to be setting out any time."

"People are leaving already?" Nadin asked. She ran a hand over her scalp and I tried not to wince. Whoever had shaved her hair off had not done so carefully—there were little scabs visible all over her head. I'd been upset that she'd had to dye her hair when we went on the run, but if I'd known the *geroi* would do this to her to remove the evidence of her excursion to Earth, I would have protested even harder. "Did the elders return?"

"They did," I said. Unlike the first party, this last group hadn't transported in by postern. Nikos and Eos had led them in on foot, and Marin had been with them. She'd filled me in on the details. Whatever element of surprise the refugees had been granted by the eruption and the sudden, inexplicable illness of *Geros* Shiros had been lost by the time Nikos and Eos had made it back to Bright Horizon. The last remaining refugees had had to hide in a safe house waiting for the runners to return, and thanks to the stronger presence of Enforcers in the dome's upper levels, they'd no longer had access to the postern. By the time they'd made it back to Eliin's outpost, it was long after nightfall, and there was no time to lose. The elders had given the order for the people to start evacuating before dawn.

"Did they decide what to do with Ceilos, then?" Nadin asked, her tone laden with anxiety.

"Not yet," I said carefully. "They want to get the people out first. They'll take care of Ceilos after they know everyone else has been safely evacuated."

"So then I still have time."

"Time?"

"I need to talk to the elders," she said. "I have to explain... about Ceilos. To advocate for him."

"Right," I said. I could hear the hollowness in my voice. I didn't mean to, it was just happening.

"Isaak." She put her hand on my arm, and this time she didn't take it away. "He risked everything to get me out of the pyramid. I can't just turn my back on him."

"Of course," I said. "I understand. I, uh"—I swallowed—"I think they're still awake. They were with Eliin earlier. I can take you to them if you want."

She gave me a thin smile, pressing her lips tight in the semidarkness. "Thank you," she said.

Nadin withdrew her hand. The warmth of her touch dissipated quickly, leaving me feeling cold.

"Sure thing," I replied.

- n a d i n -

ISAAK SAID NOTHING AS HE BROUGHT ME BACK INTO THE OUTPOST AND through the tunnels to the place where I'd heard the voices before. It was hard to tell in the shadows, but I thought his face was red, and he seemed agitated. I knew I'd hurt him, and it made me sick inside. But I didn't know what else I could have done. Ceilos was my responsibility. I was the reason he was here now, facing a potential death sentence. I'd made him take me here, convinced this would be a place of safety, only for them to accept me and reject him.

Moreover, I was the reason for the actions that had turned the rebels against Ceilos in the first place. He'd betrayed the rebellion for *me*. He'd worked with the *geroi* to save our partnership. Every event that had led us to this place had been my doing. What other choice did I have?

But I hated seeing Isaak hurting, and knowing that once again, I was the cause for it.

A trio of older adults sat huddled together in a circle against the far wall of the central cavern, deep in hushed conversation. Eliin dozed on a stool beside them, her head lolled to the side, resting against the sandstone. As Isaak entered the cave, the whisperers looked up. I recognized Eos and Marin, but I was unfamiliar with the third man who sat with them. Their conversation halted as they noticed me, and at the silence Eliin jerked awake with a sharp intake of breath.

"It's just me," Isaak said, placing a finger over his lips. "And Nadin."

"What is it, *alii*?" Eliin asked, her words slurred with sleep. Her face was wan. She looked as though she had gotten very little rest over the last day. "Is something wrong?"

"Nothing's wrong," Isaak said, his voice low and soothing. "Nadin just wants to talk to the elders."

"So this is Nadin," said the man I didn't recognize. He inclined his head to me. "*Degiim.* I am Nikos. Eos' brother."

I inclined my head in return. He was the third elder, then. I would have to make my case to these three, but I didn't know where to start. I opened my mouth to speak. It felt dry, and the words were a struggle. "I assume you know what happened earlier," I began.

"I was against it," Eliin said; then, her drowsy mind seeming to catch up to her, she added, "Not against you specifically, Nadin. Please don't misunderstand me. But against *shedosht.* That is not our way."

"No. But it has been done before," said Nikos. Next to him, Marin shifted uncomfortably.

"I promise you that I will prove my loyalty to the rebellion," I said. "The Elytherioi will not regret this outcome." I hesitated.

"But there's something else, isn't there?" Eos asked. "You wish to speak with us about the other *geroi*'s blood. Am I right?"

I flinched at the moniker, but I tugged my earlobe. "Yes. After the *shedosht* earlier, Ceilos asked if he would be given an opportunity to testify on his own behalf."

The three looked at each other in silent conversation for a long moment. At length, Marin said, "Despite Shuliin's judgment, it's not the way of Elytherios for elders to make decisions on behalf of the community. We are leaders due to the experience and knowledge imparted us by our age. But we're not rulers."

Eos sighed. "But a decision must be made as to what to do with him, and it must be done before we can leave this place. The *geroi* will now be hunting us more relentlessly than ever before. Traveling with *geroi*'s blood just adds to that risk." Isaak started to interrupt just then, but Eos held up a hand to stay him. "We do not doubt Nadin's loyalty, young one. Your testimony and that of Gitrin's has been accepted. Not just by the *ninvidu,* but by most of us in the community. Marin and I saw what transpired when you opened the postern. Moreover, our scouts heard the *geroi*'s plans for her, and her scars are testimony in themselves." He sighed. "But the other has betrayed us once already. How are we to take him at his word that he will not betray us again?"

"Execution is against our principles," Marin said, the tone of her voice indicating that this was an argument they'd already had.

"But that does not mean we should bring him with us to Katai'ios."

"I would like to testify on his behalf," I interrupted.

The elders looked at me in surprise.

"Nadin, Ceilos' betrayal is what led to you standing here before us covered in blood and bruises." Marin's brows furrowed.

I faltered, knowing that her words were true. But I stuck my jaw out defiantly nonetheless. "Be that as it may, I still feel I need to testify. You can make of my testimony what you will. But I need to say it."

Eliin looked back and forth from the elders to Isaak to me. She rose from her stool, knees cracking. "Come, *alos*," she said to Isaak, placing her hand on his shoulder and ushering him away. "Let's give them privacy."

I looked down, chewing my lip. I hated sending Isaak away, but it was probably for the best. I didn't want him to misconstrue my words now. I didn't want him to be hurt even more by them than he'd been in that shadowy tunnel.

"All right, Nadin," Nikos said when they were gone. "Say your peace."

"Ceilos is—was—my partner. But the *geroi* were threatening to dissolve our partnership. Unbeknownst to either of us, they had begun to suspect Gitrin of having ties to the rebellion. So they sought to use my close relationship to Gitrin to try to find clues that would lead them to your base. To Elytherios."

Eos exhaled. "Gitrin had believed they might have been suspicious of her. It was incredibly risky of her to have involved you by giving you the clues to finding us. She did so without consulting any of us in the movement."

My face grew hot. The Elytherioi hadn't wanted me to find them— Gitrin had acted unilaterally, just as she had when she invoked *shedosht*. She believed that strongly in me. My heart swelled with affection toward her, but this knowledge would make proving myself to the rebellion all the more fraught.

Marin, to her credit it, jumped to my defense. "She believed that the value Nadin could bring to us would outweigh the risk," she said. "And Nadin is the one who brought us Isaak. Without him, our people would have no hope for survival."

Eos held his hand up once more. "I know, I know, *yachin*," he said. Again, I could tell I was hearing an argument they'd had before. "Go on, Nadin."

Tautly, I said, "What I didn't know when I arrived in Elytherios was that the *geroi* made a deal with Ceilos to lead them to you. A deal that would save our partnership. Everything he did, he did because of"—I paused, swallowing down the lump in my throat, the knot of discomfort this sentence caused me—"his feelings for me. He did not know the truth about the *geroi*, or the truth about the rebellion. He had believed the lies the *geroi* had told about the Liberator, and about the rebel movement being terrorists who sought to harm Iamos."

"The fabled Liberator again," Nikos remarked dryly.

I tugged my earlobe. "Ceilos believed he would be saving the people of Iamos by leading the *geroi* to you. And above all, he believed he'd be helping me. Once he spent time in Elytherios, he realized the truth. But it was already too late by then. What was done was done."

"So why should this information change our decision?" Eos asked.

"I... I only wanted to make sure you understood. His betrayal was not out of malice. He thought he was doing the right thing. He just didn't know any better."

Something changed in their faces at my words. Marin's first, then Nikos'. Eos expression remained grim, but he looked down.

"Thank you for telling us, Nadin," he said, his voice a low rumble. "We will take your words into consideration. For now, I'm sure that Eliin and Isaak are going to need your help in the livestock cave soon."

I was being dismissed. My heart sank. The elders hadn't seemed much convinced by my testimony. I'd done all I could. Now the only thing left was to wait and see. But what would it mean for Ceilos?

I turned to head back down the tunnel. As the shadows swallowed me, I heard Nikos' low voice.

"'Didn't know any better.' Those words were spoken before, too."

"The *shedosht*, now Nadin's testimony..." Marin murmured. "The past is coming back to haunt us."

"But if the same decision were made now," said Eos, "would the outcome change?"

I hovered in the darkness a moment longer, listening. But the elders did not speak again.

CHAPTER 25

- i s a a k -

NADIN WOULDN'T LOOK AT ME.

She had not, in fact, met my gaze once since she'd returned to the livestock cavern. By the time she'd trudged silently in, Eliin and I were already saddling up the *gurzas* for the first party of refugees. Avoiding my eyes, she'd asked Eliin for an assignment, and Eliin had set her to gathering oxygen tanks.

I watched her for just a moment as my fingers worked the worn leather straps, fastening them across the breast of an easygoing olive-green gelding with tan markings. I'd made a decision after Eliin and I had left her with the elders: I was going to do whatever I could to make things easier for Nadin. She'd had it hard enough. I'd resolved to put my own feelings in a box and tightly close the lid on it. I would not think about them again. I was just going to focus on being Nadin's friend—and on helping her people, as I'd sworn I would do.

The children from yesterday were watching me now, albeit much more subdued than they'd been before, due to the early hour. Priority for evacuation had been given to families with children, and that meant Ierin and Camos and their three kids would be leaving with the first group.

"Have you ever been to Katai'ios?" Danos asked me.

"I haven't," I said, testing the strap and finding it secure. "Have you?"

"No," he said glumly.

"Maetrin says it will be a good place for us to live," said Enros around a wide yawn. "Phados says it's like the citidomes, but it's made out of different-colored glass. Not just blue. He said it makes the sun shine like

168

a rainbow inside."

"I liked Elytherios. I want to go home," Sasin said. Her voice shook, and I could tell that she was on the brink of tears. Suddenly a memory of Celeste popped into my mind—not the way she was now, but the way she'd been when I left Mars the first time. Just a kindergartener. The day before I'd accidentally passed through the postern, she'd made me a drawing of myself and Abuelo as archaeologist adventurers, exploring a pyramid and finding ancient treasure. She'd wanted to cheer me up from all my problems. The same problems that had inadvertently sent me to Iamos, leaving my family with no answers as to where I'd disappeared to.

When I'd returned, Celeste had been two annums older and she'd looked at me like I was a stranger. She'd cried, saying that her friend Bianca had told her I was dead.

"If you have to go again, you'll tell us this time, right?"

"Do you want to meet your *gurza*?" I asked Sasin quickly, hoping to distract myself from my own guilt-wracked thoughts as much as I hoped to distract her from her grief.

She gave me a shaky smile and tugged her earlobe.

"You and your brothers are going to be riding Kubbla here. He's really friendly."

"He's got a horn," Sasin said warily.

I grinned, running my hand over the *gurza*'s muzzle. A nubbed horn protruded from the end of his snout. "That's just to make him *look* tough, so that other animals will leave him alone. He's too much of a baby to fight back, you see." I couldn't really account for the different skull shapes each of the *gurzas* had, or if there was any meaning behind their differing bony protrusions. They seemed to vary from individual to individual. Some had horns on either side of their heads, or on the ends of their noses as Kubbla did. Others had completely smooth, hornless skulls. Tuupa had a bony frill protruding from the back of her head that ran clear down her neck. I didn't know enough about *gurzas* to know if this was some kind of breed thing, or if it was some other genetic eccentricity I didn't understand. But I did know that Kubbla was one of the more gentle of the geldings, which was why Eliin had recommended him for the kids.

I held his reins, guiding him over to the fence. He lowered his head, and hesitantly, Sasin reached out to stroke his muzzle. Kubbla rumbled appreciatively, and Sasin beamed.

Over the kids' shoulders, Nadin was watching me. I smiled tentatively at her. She smiled back, but looked away quickly.

As I gave Enros his turn to pet the *gurza*, four figures entered the cave. The elders, along with Shuliin. Their expressions were grim. Wringing her hands, Nadin approached them. Eos gestured for Eliin to join them; then, after a moment's hesitation, he waved me over as well. I detached myself from the children and the *gurzas*.

"We've spoken to Ceilos," Nikos said as I approached.

Nadin blanched, but her voice was steady as she said, "And?"

"His testimony aligned with yours."

"Conveniently," Shuliin added. There was an edge to her words, and she looked at Nadin with narrowed eyes.

"Testimonies align when they are true," Nadin retorted.

"That was our consensus," Marin said, reaching out a hand placatingly.

Eos exhaled. He seemed agitated. "But despite the judgment of the *ninvidu*, this is too important of a decision to be left to us. The community must have a say."

"So what does that mean?" I asked.

"We will bring him with us to Katai'ios. For the time being, he will remain a prisoner." Marin wrinkled her nose distastefully at the word. "It is not the way of the Elytherioi, but we have no other choice. After we arrive and have settled everyone in, he will have the opportunity to present his case. Then the people will determine if he may earn a place among us."

"Are you sure bringing him to Katai'ios is wise?" Eliin asked. "Perhaps he should remain here with me."

"No," said Eos. "You are too close to the citidome here. Too close to the *geroi*. We need your outpost. This is not the end of our movement. We will rebuild. The runners will return, and we will need this place to maintain access to Bright Horizon."

"Katai'ios is distant from every other citidome, and it's protected by our cloaking protocols," Nikos added. "There will also be a large population there to guard him. It will be safer for everyone if he is with us there."

"But he must not know the location of Katai'ios," Shuliin said firmly. "He must not be given the opportunity to betray us again as he did before."

"How will we get him there if he's not allowed to know where it is?" I asked.

"We will take a longer route," Shuliin said. "One which is less direct, so he cannot guess where we're going. And he will be blindfolded the entire way."

Nadin frowned, but she tugged her earlobe. "This seems reasonable." She cleared her throat, adding, "And fair. Thank you for your judgment, elders."

Eos exhaled. "Time will tell if we have shown wisdom here."

I rubbed the back of my neck. "So what are our next steps?"

"We must evacuate the people here first," Nikos said. "They are our top priority. After that..."

"Who will be escorting the p—" Eliin hesitated, swallowing. "The prisoner to Katai'ios?"

"A small party will take him the route along the Kalderos Ifaisteos," Eos said. "Through the Great Crater."

"Nadin must go with that party," Shuliin said, her arms folded. "She testified for him. He is her responsibility."

"I was planning on it," Nadin said sourly.

"I'll go with them, too," I said.

"Are you sure, *alos*?" Eliin asked. "It will be a long journey, and a hard one. You could go with one of our other parties and be there in half the time."

"I'm sure." I glanced at Nadin. "I made a promise, and I'm keeping it."

She looked down, her expression unreadable.

"The three of us should also go with them," Marin said, looking between Eos and Nikos. "They are as much our responsibility as anyone's."

"No," Shuliin said. "The elders are needed in Katai'ios. And this will be a hard journey. We need to keep you safe."

"But—"

"I'll go," Nikos said firmly. Eos and Marin both opened their mouths to protest, but he silenced them with a wave of his hand. "I am a good deal younger than you, brother."

"And I will go with him," Shuliin added before anyone could object further. "I also bear responsibility, as *ninvidu*. And I am our best runner, after all," she added proudly.

"There. It's agreed," Nikos said. "You go on ahead to Katai'ios, and I will see you there."

Eos did not look happy. But at length, he tugged his earlobe. It was settled, then—Eos and Marin would travel with the other refugees, and we'd catch them up later.

Of course, it wouldn't be just the five of us. Before long, Gitrin had joined us in the livestock cavern, Emil in tow. Pandat, seeming to have decided Emil was his favorite person out of all of us, was riding on his shoulder. I could tell immediately that Gitrin was not happy about the elders' decision to bring Ceilos along, but she seemed resigned to it— and she insisted that she be included in our party. And, of course, Emil would have to stick with me, since I was the only one who could translate for him.

Shuliin's partner, Syrin, also insisted on joining us on the trip. Despite Shuliin's protests, I was glad to have her along as a buffer. She seemed to be the more level-headed of the two, and she'd proved to be a calming influence on her partner during the *shedosht*. We'd had enough conflict lately, both on Iamos and back on Earth, what with Lizeth's mercenary instinct rearing its ugly head before I left. The journey to Katai'ios was already going to be long and hard, and tempers were at a high. I hoped that Syrin's calm demeanor would help ease some of the tensions we were sure to face.

The eight of us set out the following morning, after the other groups had departed and had put a safe distance between themselves and any potential threat—be it the *geroi* finding Eliin's outpost, or the danger they all seemed to sense from Ceilos' presence within our group.

Ceilos, for his part, accepted his fate without argument. I watched him as Nikos led him out of Eliin's apartment, hands bound, Shuliin flanking them, holding a rusted scythe as a weapon should Ceilos try to pull a fast one. But he walked silently beside Nikos without any sign of protest. This meek version of Ceilos didn't jibe with the anger I'd seen in him two days prior during the *shedosht*; nor with the cocky, self-assured prince I'd met in Hope Renewed.

I thought back on my brief acquaintance with Ceilos. We'd seemed to get along fine at first, the three of us planning to work together as a team to discover the mystery of the time postern. He and Nadin had formed something of a lopsided pair. Ceilos had struck me as almost arrogant in his confidence in both his status and abilities. Nadin, meanwhile, had tried to affect an air of similar assurance, but she'd been more reserved—something I'd come to realize was rooted in her lack of self-confidence. She'd relied on Ceilos to take the lead in just about everything. But when she'd been forced to go on without him after his disappearance, she'd bloomed into someone more resilient.

And there was the rub. Something had changed after Ceilos had been kidnapped—after he'd *feigned* his own kidnapping. Ceilos and Nadin's relationship had been strained, even before she'd learned of his deception. Was it my doing? My growing feelings for Nadin fracturing both their relationship and my nascent friendship with Ceilos? Feelings I never should have allowed myself to have, knowing that she was betrothed?

No, something else had changed, something between Nadin herself and Ceilos. And it had begun before the kidnapping pretense. That day in the hospital level of the citidome, she'd been irritable, jumpy, and she'd refused to talk about her partner. After that, everything between them had seemed to change. By the time he'd reappeared in Elytherios, he'd been downright antagonistic toward me, and things had been strained between him and Nadin that whole week before we left for Mars. Something had happened between Nadin and Ceilos, something bigger than just me.

Whatever it was, I was probably never going to find out. But it weighed heavily between them, even now.

With Ceilos' hands still bound, Nikos had to help him mount Kodo. Once he was safely in the saddle, Nikos covered his eyes with a cloth blindfold. The blindfold would remain there for the next several weeks. Nadin looked away as Nikos tied the blindfold on, her expression unreadable. I frowned.

Before we left, Eliin pressed Pandat into my arms, giving the little primate a scritch between his ears with a sad smile. "You take care of him, *alos*. Make sure he has oxygen when you get out of the tunnels. The air quality is abysmal out there, and even once you're clear of the ash, the atmosphere is still far too thin for a mammal like him—or you, for that matter." She gave me a look.

"I'll watch out for him, and myself as well," I said with a laugh.

She pressed her lips together in a tight line. "I hate to send him back out after all he went through to come here. But Katai'ios will be better for him. Not as good as Elytherios was, but"—she swallowed, trying to choke back her emotions—"still. There are trees there, and it will be good for him to be back among green things."

I was curious what to expect when we reached Katai'ios. We hadn't been told much about this rebel base. It was remote, that much I knew. It wouldn't be like Elytherios, with its microclimate and reflected sunlight. There was nowhere else like that on Iamos. Based on what Enros had said, it sounded like a citidome. "*Made out of different-colored glass.*" How had the rebels managed to hide a whole citidome from the *geroi*?

We'd have to wait and find out, I supposed.

The journey in front of us was a long one. Nikos said the trip would span about three-hundred fifty leagues. Emil and I worked out the math and decided that was about eighteen hundred kilometers. The journey from Eliin's outpost to Elytherios had taken Nadin and me ten days; this trip was going to be at least double that, possibly triple.

We set out two-by-two: Emil and I rode Tuupa, and Nadin and Gitrin took Thork. Shuliin and Syrin took point, sharing a *gurza* of their own, which left Nikos and Ceilos bringing up the rear on Kodo. The black *gurza* seemed to struggle against his natural inclination to lead, but, as Nikos had said before, Kodo was well-trained and obedient to his master.

As we had when we'd journeyed to Elytherios, we began this trek in the sandstone tunnels that ran through the mountains south of Bright Horizon. This provided a much-needed buffer against the air quality. After two days, the eruption of the Sios Ifaisteos had finally subsided, the continuous roar in the distance giving way to silence but leaving behind a ringing in my ears. But despite the end of the active eruption, ash and smoke still hung thick in the air, and even here in the caves, it was enough to leave my lungs itchy and uncomfortable.

Another side effect of the eruption was that the tunnels were dark, far darker than they'd been on our previous journey. The sun was nowhere to be seen, hidden behind the blanket of volcanic material ejected into the stratosphere. It was hard to tell the difference between night and day, and I felt disoriented, never knowing what time it was, how long we'd been traveling or how soon we'd be stopping. In a lot of ways, it was like a recurring fever dream—it seemed like we'd always been going on this way, and we would continue this way forever.

With Tuupa and Thork sandwiched between our guides and guardians, there was not much else to do to pass the time besides talk. It reminded me of those days that Nadin and I had spent on our way to Elytherios, filling the hours with language, me teaching her words of English and she reciprocating with lessons on the more advanced elements of Iamoi syntax that I hadn't been able to puzzle out on my own. This time, though, we had Emil and Gitrin with us, and if the two of them had one thing in common, it was their respective unending quests for knowledge.

One day they spent hours hashing out the ins and outs of earthquakes and volcanic eruptions on a planet that lacked plate tectonics. Gitrin explained the Iamoi conceptions of thermodynamics, which did not make for easy translation. But Emil absorbed the information eagerly, scribbling into one of the dozen notebooks he'd managed to cram in his pockets, adding his own observations and interpretations in return.

Still more days were spent debating whether Iamos had been colonized by humans from Earth, or whether Earth had been colonized by humans from Iamos. This subject was Emil's true passion, and he was eager to share all the findings he'd compiled over decades of studying theories of Atlantis, the presence of "Atlantean arches"—posterns like the one we'd discovered at the Los Tuxtlas site—across the globe, and the limited archaeological evidence he'd managed to unearth along with my dad during their brief time working together. It was surreal hearing it all put together this way combined with what we knew now, and Gitrin was eager to hear what we'd learned about the survivors of Achillios' colonization party.

That subject was one that managed to bring everyone in the group together. Syrin gradually started sitting with us during meals, and even Shuliin wound up joining in, grumbling halfheartedly when Pandat crawled into her lap and began begging for bites of fruit. Everyone wanted to know what had happened to the Iamoi colonists who had disappeared. But the truth was nothing they ever would have imagined.

Emil and Gitrin found so much to talk about, it managed to fill in the gaps of the silence that hung heavily between Nadin and me. But, of course, there was one subject that we never discussed, and one voice that never joined the conversation.

Ceilos'.

I knew he had to have heard when we were talking about what we'd learned in Veracruz. If his theory was true, his father was the one who had caused the party to disappear, utilizing Nadin and Gitrin's experimental time postern design to send them into the future. When I first came to Iamos, Nadin told me that the *geroi* had rejected their research, insisting it wouldn't be viable. Had Tibros known all along that their plan would work? Had he convinced the other *geroi* to reject the research so he could take it for himself, using it to sabotage the *geroi* so he could seize sole control? Had he been the one who deleted the research from the System so that no one but he could use it?

Whatever Ceilos' thoughts were on the subject, he remained silent.

Hours blurred into days blurred into weeks. The farther from the Elysium mountains we traveled, the thinner the ash became, until at last my sinuses were no longer burning and daylight began to filter into the tunnels.

And then, finally, one morning, we reached the end of the road.

When we'd taken the route to Elytherios, we'd traveled west, emerging from the tunnels into a canyon of rock spires—hoodoos—that didn't exist in my time, having been worn away over millennia. But as the *gurzas* squeezed through the narrow crevice that marked the end of the cave system, I knew exactly where we were. I knew the journey to Katai'ios had taken us due south, because the landmarks that spread out before us most definitely still existed in the future.

As we stopped to strap on our breathing apparatuses and connect our oxygen tanks, I looked around in awe. We were on the north edge of a crater that had originated about three billion years earlier, when an enormous asteroid had impacted Mars while the planet was still young. The mountain in the center had been formed when sediment deposited in the crater by ancient waterways was then eroded. That was the theory, anyway, that we'd been taught in science class in grade school.

This was Gale Crater, with Mount Sharp rising more than five kilometers in its center. But no snow remained, even at its peak. In place of the blue-green waters of the lake and the delta, a few nearly dry water features—mere puddles from this vantage point—sat evaporating, leaving behind cracked, gray clay and iron-rich rocks that turned rust-red under the oxidizing effects of the wind. Along their banks, woody spider weeds grew, one of the only plants hardy enough to survive in the deteriorating atmosphere. The only native plant life that had survived the mass extinction of this world, originally only appearing in the warmest regions during the Martian spring, then spreading like wildfire across the planet once the MarsEpoch scientists had warmed the planet enough. They looked like gnarled black claws reaching for the sun.

Even though I'd seen countless pictures of it this way in my history and science textbooks, it was jarring to see it looking like this. Barren, dead. Like an alien planet. But I knew it like I knew the back of my hand.

We were almost home.

PART FOUR

EARTH

2075 C.E.

CHAPTER 26

- h e n r y -

IT WAS HARD NOT TO FEEL RIDICULOUSLY SMUG ABOUT THE STUNT I'D JUST pulled. Everything else aside, the expression on Lizeth's face alone had made it worth it. She seemed to think the fact that they'd busted me out of Lago Verde meant I was going to be the Stateless' personal property for the rest of my life. Now maybe she'd realize that I wasn't going to be anybody's lapdog. I supported the Stateless' mission on principle, but I wasn't about to stay here on Earth indefinitely while they bickered about how best to use me. My loyalties weren't to this planet.

Lizeth had said that the Stateless considered Mars the weakest link in the statist chains shackling both her world and mine. That if Mars was able to break away from GSAF control, the continental unions' power over Earth would also start to crumble. That power would return to the people rather than a handful of oligarchs.

So now was her chance to put her money where her mouth was. We weren't going to liberate Mars from here on Earth. And, whether she believed it or not, we weren't going to liberate Mars without the help of Nadin and her people. If the Stateless wanted my help with their mission, it was going to be on my terms. My friends and allies weren't just *extra baggage*.

"Henry, what were you *thinking*?" Lizeth snapped, her voice echoing across the treetops. Her uncle hissed at her to be quiet before she woke up the whole camp, and she scowled at him. In a lower voice, she added, "A *month*? That's next to no time!"

"That's plenty of time. Travel to Mars takes ten days. That gives us twenty extra to take care of everything else that we need to."

"We're going to need a lot more than that. I'm going to have to arrange a spacecraft, I'm going to have to get a team together, I'm going to have to clear financing with my mother—"

"You'd better get on that, then. Good thing we're heading for Xalapa as soon as we get the tent torn down."

"Henry, the Stateless had plans for you when we got you out of GSAF custody, and so far, you've done nothing but derail them."

I shrugged. "If you knew anything about my track record, you'd have known I pride myself on being a wildcard."

"Look, can we just go back to camp and start packing?" Scylla asked wearily. "In case you forgot, it's the crack of dawn, it's pouring down rain, and I want to get back to civilization and take a shower."

"Fine," Lizeth huffed, stalking down the wooden steps. When she reached the bottom, she whirled on me, hands on her hips. "No, we need to talk about this. Now."

"Can we at least go in the tent?" Scylla whined.

"I agree," Senghas said. "I don't think this is a conversation we should be having out in the open."

He was right. Despite the storm making the predawn seem darker than usual, the sky overhead was getting brighter every minute. Closer to sunrise. The rest of the camp would be waking up soon. We didn't have time to dawdle.

"You're not having it at all," Lizeth snapped. "Martians, in the tent. Professors, take five."

Senghas opened his mouth to protest, but she didn't give him the opportunity. She flung the tent flap open and marched the three of us inside, zipping it shut in her uncle's face.

"What is this," she asked when the flap was securely closed, "some kind of soft coup? After everything I've done for all of you?"

Tamara said, "I don't think that's what he—"

Lizeth ignored her. "I know you're worried about your friend, Henry, but don't you think I'm worried about all of mine, too? We risk our lives every day for the liberty of the people on this planet. Any wrong move, any step we take without tons of planning in advance, could lead to someone I care about getting killed. And now you've boxed me into a completely untenable timeline without even *discussing* it with me first?"

"I wouldn't have done it if I believed you wouldn't just abandon Isaak to rot on Iamos, same as you did with Nadin," I said.

"Henry, you're not being fair to me!" she protested.

"You're not being fair to us, either," I said. "You've already made it abundantly clear that you don't want to see Mars liberated for the good of its people—it's just a means to an end for you. I know your first loyalty is to Earth because it's your home. But it's not ours. It's not mine. My first loyalty has to be to Mars because Mars is *my* home. The only way an alliance between the Stateless and the Free Mars movement is going to work is if you treat it that way: as an alliance. You don't get to just boss me around like I'm one of your lackeys. The way you've been acting this week, you've made it patently obvious that your movement was never planning on asking for my input at all. You don't see me as an equal partner. You just wanted to use me. So now you know how that feels."

Lizeth's face grew more somber as I spoke. When I was finished, she sighed. "Okay. I understand. Obviously, we need to start listening to each other more. From now on, I'll consult you about any big decisions. But that goes both ways, right? You'll also consult me before just doing stuff behind my back?"

I nodded. "I can agree to that."

"All right, then." She fiddled with the zipper on her jacket, thinking. "That doesn't change what we're dealing with now, though. We've got a deadline, so we'll have to work fast. When we get back to Xalapa I'll get in touch with... my mother." She shuddered. "She's not going to be happy, but there's nothing else we can do. We're going to need her approval and financing for transportation to Mars. This isn't something I can run up on my personal account."

"And we'll need to formulate a game plan for once we're there," I said. "How we'll reconnect with Free Mars and get them mobilized without attracting GSAF's attention. Our home base is in Tierra Nueva, and that's where most of our supporters are as well. But that's Joseph Condor's territory, so we're going to have to be careful."

"Right." Lizeth hesitated, then added, "And we need to figure out who's coming with us and who's going to stay here and go to a safe house. We need you, Henry. But these two..." She looked at Scylla and Tamara.

"You can't just leave us behind!" Scylla exploded.

Lizeth winced, gesturing for her to lower her voice—which was pretty rich, considering she'd done the same thing ten minutes ago. Still, she wasn't wrong. People in the camp were starting to wake up, and the students in charge of breakfast were going to be heading over to the mess tent any time now. We needed to keep it quiet.

Scylla glowered. "You can't tell me that I have to stay here on Earth when the only reason I came here in the first place was to help in this fight against GSAF."

"It's nothing personal. There's just not going to be a lot of room on the ship," Lizeth explained. "We need to maximize the number of people from the Stateless we're bringing. People who can be assets to the mission, people with actual training—"

"I *am* an asset to the mission," Scylla argued. "I know that you don't get a lot of real news from Mars over here on Earth, but in case you weren't aware, I was in charge of Free Mars for a whole annum while Hank here was off being Joseph Condor's flunky and decoding the System for GSAF."

I cringed, both at the nickname—which I'd told Scylla not to use multiple times, to no avail—and at the reminder of how I'd done exactly that.

"I've done more organizing for Free Mars than he has," she went on. "I've got more connections in the group. Connections that the Stateless are going to need."

"All right, all right, fine," Lizeth said. "You can come. But what about Tamara? She's a civilian, isn't she?"

Tamara's eyes met mine. She opened her mouth, seeming to want to come up with a speech to argue for her place in the group like Scylla had but not knowing what to say.

I should have spoken up for her then, but I found myself hesitating.

Before I got a chance, Scylla leapt in. "Tamara's moms are both on the board at AresTec. They've got connections in the government, and they've got a ton of money. You said before that those are things the Stateless needs, right? And they're on our side. Mama D is the one who helped us keep the Iamoi posternkey secret from GSAF in the first place. They shielded Nadin from Joseph Condor. And they've always been one hundred percent supportive of the Free Mars movement. You need them, and you're not going to get them without Tamara. Right, Henry?"

Scylla glared at me, doubtless wondering why I wasn't leaping to my girlfriend's defense. I swallowed, clearing my throat. "Yeah. We're a package deal. All three of us have to go back to Mars or nothing. You're just going to have to make room for us." I tried not to look at Tamara, the disappointed way she stared down at her shoes.

Lizeth rolled her eyes. "Fine." She stalked over to the tent flap, ripping it open. Senghas was standing on the other side, thoroughly soaked and shivering slightly.

"Now that that's settled," he said between clenched teeth, which could have been the result of either annoyance or chill. Maybe both. On the one hand, even though it was raining, it wasn't exactly cold in the jungle in late July, but on the other hand, he was soaking wet. "Hector is getting our things packed up and moved out of José's tent. I suggest you all do the same. If you want to avoid running into the others at breakfast, we'll need to grab something light from the mess tent and get a move on. It's nearly daybreak now."

It didn't take long to get everything packed up. We'd already done most of our packing the night before, and now it was just a matter of stowing our cots and getting the tent pulled down. We'd have to split the extra weight of Isaak's and Nadin's things among the rest of us, since we couldn't just leave them here.

"I think we're about set," Lizeth said as she tightly wrapped the Velcro straps around her bedroll. "Henry, go grab us some fruit and granola bars or something from the mess tent so we can get out of here. We'll get the tent pulled down."

"Are you sure you don't need help with that?" I asked, glancing at Tamara as she silently folded the metal frame of Nadin's cot.

"You think we need a big, strong man to help us take a tent apart? We're fine. Go."

I rolled my eyes, ducking out into the predawn air. The storm was starting to subside, and the rain had lightened into a drizzle.

In the mess tent, the student volunteers had begun unloading ingredients from the minifridge and the cooler chests. One of them glanced up, and I saw it was Horlando.

"Hey, man," he said. "You on breakfast duty?"

"Uh, no," I said, shaking my head. "I, uh, I got some bad news in the night. José got a call on his satellite phone. That family emergency got more urgent, so I need to go home. Hector talked about it with the others and we decided to just head back early as a group."

"That explains all the moving around I heard in the night. Even with the rain, it made it hard to sleep," one of the other students said, covering a yawn with the back of her hand.

"I'm sorry to hear that, Henry. After you guys came all the way out here," said Horlando.

I shrugged. "Yeah, it sucks. Anyway, they told me to grab something light for everyone to eat, and then we're going to head out."

"I'll help you," Horlando said, opening a food storage locker full of dry goods and removing some trail snacks. I pulled the hem of my T-shirt out and started dumping bananas in it like a makeshift basket.

Horlando followed me back to the tent, which had by now been completely disassembled. Scylla was collecting the aluminum poles while Lizeth and Tamara folded up the canvas. I hoped Horlando might not notice Isaak's conspicuous absence or might think he was helping his grandpa with something, but a few meters away from the former tent site, he paused. In a low voice, he said, "Hey, Henry?"

"Yeah?" I asked casually.

"I, uh... I couldn't help notice that your group's been shrinking throughout the week. That Black girl who was with you when you got here, I haven't seen her since Tuesday."

My mouth opened wordlessly as I scrambled to think up a lie, but he quickly added, "No, it's okay. I'm not going to tell anyone. But, you know. This dig site. We've found a lot of weird things here. Even before I got here, the stuff in the museum. Things that don't line up with what you'd find in a typical Mesoamerican site."

I frowned, nonchalantly sticking my free hand in my pocket. Wrapping my fingers around the object inside as if to make sure it was still there, that it hadn't been lifted when I hadn't been paying attention.

I felt its metal, hard and reassuring. Still there. "So what's your point?"

He seemed to struggle to find the right words. "I just... I just wanted to say good luck, I guess."

"Good luck?"

"Yeah. I know you're not from here. None of you are. You're from..." He trailed off, gesturing at the sky. "My sister and her husband live out there, and my nephews. In Tharsis province. She's let me know what's going on there. There are..." One of the granola bars in his overly full hands slipped off the pile, and he crouched to pick it up. "There are more people supporting you than you realize, I think. So that's why I say good luck."

"Um. I think you might have a case of mistaken identity," I said. "But thanks."

He gave me a crooked smile and turned back to where Lizeth, Scylla, and Tamara were waiting, the tent now neatly packed. He handed off the trail snacks, nodded at me, and headed back to the mess tent.

"Do you have everything?" Espinoza asked as he, Senghas, and Isaak's *abuelo* came around the corner. The latter two looked ready to go, their cots strapped to their large backpacks.

I watched Horlando for just a moment longer. Then I turned to face the others.

"Yeah," I said. "We're ready to go."

CHAPTER 27

WE SPENT MOST OF THE LONG HIKE THROUGH THE JUNGLE AND CAR RIDE back to Xalapa in silence.

We'd decided the night before that, in order to minimize the number of people we interacted with and hopefully avoid running into anyone else with Nano, we would be steering clear of hotels from here on in. Therefore, Professor Senghas had offered to let us stay at his home near the museum until Lizeth could make travel arrangements for us.

With two fewer people now than when we'd gone out to the site, the Jeep was significantly less cramped this time. Isaak's grandpa sat in the front with Lizeth's uncle, with Lizeth and Scylla sitting in the center seats—pointedly avoiding each other's gazes—and Henry and me sitting in the very back.

He didn't say anything to me, but he laced his fingers through mine, holding my hand tightly most of the way back. I was trying not to be annoyed with him. I knew Henry. He couldn't help his overprotectiveness, I'd figured that out long ago. Of all the stupid decisions he'd made and things he'd done thanks to this impulse, this ranked near the least consequential. But it had still stung, the way he'd hesitated when Lizeth had suggested I stay behind. I knew what he'd been thinking. I'd be safer here on Earth. I knew it wouldn't have even crossed his mind that I wasn't useful to the mission. But I felt that way nonetheless. What *did* I have to offer the Stateless and Free Mars?

Scylla was right about my connections, and I did agree those would be helpful to everyone. But I wanted to believe that I was useful in some way, too. I believed in this cause. I wanted to fight. I didn't want to stay here and sit in some safe house without contact with anyone, without knowing whether they were safe, without being able to do anything to help. And regardless of what Lizeth thought of me, I was going to prove myself useful to the cause.

The storm that had poured rain on us in the jungle this morning followed us most of the way back to the city, but by the time we'd reached the outskirts of town, the skies were beginning to clear. As we pulled up to Professor Senghas' house, the only evidence that it had been raining here was the dark dampness of the concrete sidewalk. This whole section of town seemed to be built out of concrete, not just the sidewalks. The neighborhood was made up of block after block of almost indistinguishable townhouses, square, almost brutalist in design. The only thing that differentiated one from another was the accent of color that trimmed the gray concrete of each house, as vibrant as a tropical bird. Some were green, some yellow. Senghas', on the far end of one row and at the corner of the street, was orange. The large rectangular windows on the front of the house reflected blue sky and white clouds in their glass.

We waited until the street was devoid of traffic, both vehicle and pedestrian. Then Professor Senghas unlocked the front door and we hurried inside, each of us carrying our own bag. Senghas said he'd grab the rest of the luggage—Isaak's and Nadin's things, and the suitcases of extra stuff that we'd smuggled out of Florida but hadn't been able to carry to the dig site—out of the car later.

Once inside the townhouse, I looked around in wonder. Every square inch of wall space that wasn't taken up with windows was filled with floor-to-ceiling bookcases, these crammed full of paperbacks and hardcovers, many of them yellowed with age. They gave the whole house a musty smell, but one that was indescribably appealing.

"This has Emil's print book collection beat," said Henry as he took it all in.

Professor Senghas chuckled. "Yes, well, the thing about academia is that there is quite a bit of scholarship that still hasn't been digitized. Older works, obscure topics, books that are relevant only to certain regions, and so forth."

"I haven't been here in a long time," Professor Garcia said, looking around with his hands in his pockets. "You've added even more shelves."

"And I've added a few of your books on Olmec linguistics as well, my friend," Senghas said with a wry grin. "Any chance you'd be willing to autograph them?"

Professor Garcia laughed. "Of course, of course. Well, *muchachos*," he said, turning his attention to the rest of us, "we made it, eh?"

His voice sounded hollow as he spoke, and my heart twisted. He was trying to put on a brave face, but I knew he was worried about Isaak. All of us were, but it had to be worse for him, to have seen his grandson disappear into the door of light and not know whether he was safe from this point on.

We'll know in a month. I wasn't sure if that made it better or worse.

"For now, anyway," said Lizeth. "Now that we've got reception and encrypted internet again, I'd better get a call in to my mother and start making arrangements." She sighed. "Time to face the music," she added under her breath.

I frowned. Every time she had to call her mother, Lizeth reacted with similar dread. I wondered what kind of person Lizeth's mom was. She was wealthy, I knew that much. A lot wealthier than my own moms were. And she clearly was a hard woman. Even though she'd founded the Stateless—an anti-authoritarian organization in and of itself—it was obvious she didn't like to be disobeyed. She was used to calling the shots. Lizeth had gone rogue numerous times over the last month, and Henry had forced her hand once again. Now she'd have to face her mother's wrath. My stomach knotted in sympathy.

Lizeth shook off her grim expression and looked the three of us over. "I know we'll need some rest after the last..." She waved her hand. "Not even the last day. The last week? The last month? But we're on a time crunch, so we'll probably have to be on the move again in the morning. Take advantage of the break while we've got it. Shower, sleep, et cetera."

"Will you be leaving in the morning, too, Professor?" Scylla asked.

Isaak's grandpa nodded. "I'm assuming so. By the time Karl brought me in on this, my wife and I were already leaving Berkeley. GSAF had taken Raymond"—he glowered at the mention of Isaak's dad, who was divorced from Isaak's mom, his daughter—"into custody, and we were going to be next."

"When our retrieval operation brought in not just Henry, but all the rest of you, we knew we needed to act," Lizeth said. "We were in the process of relocating them to Colombia when the connection to the artifacts at the museum came up."

"So I came here on a brief detour before moving on to join her," Professor Garcia finished.

"Are you sure they'll be safe?" I asked Lizeth.

"Of course," she said with a roll of her eyes. "Medellín has had a flourishing underground liberty movement for decades, and there's a strong Stateless presence there. There will be plenty of people looking out for them and keeping them off GSAF's radar, don't worry." With that, she disappeared up the staircase against the far wall to go make her calls.

"Let's get the rest of you settled," Senghas said. "I'm afraid I don't have a very large house. Just two bedrooms, in fact. I reckon Hector can bunk with me."

"That leaves one bedroom for all the rest of us," Scylla said with a sigh.

"At least we've got our cots this time," I pointed out. "We won't have to sleep on the floor."

"True. Well, if I'm going to be sleeping on a cot tonight, I call dibs on the bed for a nap now," said Scylla. "But first, a shower, if that's okay, Professor?"

"Help yourself. The bathroom is at the end of the hallway upstairs."

Everyone spent the rest of the afternoon more or less in their own corners. Senghas had led Isaak's grandpa upstairs to get him settled, Lizeth staked out the guest room to make her calls in, Scylla claimed the bathroom. That left Henry and me to explore the downstairs. Besides the living room just inside the front door, there was the kitchen, a cramped dining room—which, like the living room, had been turned into a makeshift library, with just a little bistro table and a couple of chairs for sitting—and a half bathroom under the stairs with only a toilet and sink. The house was laid out in a rectangular shape, and in the center was a small courtyard, boxed in on all four sides by the walls of the house. A sliding glass door in the dining room appeared to be the only way to access it.

I drifted around the rooms downstairs, looking at the shelves filled not only with books, but also knickknacks: souvenirs from around the globe. Some of these were accompanied by holo-frames, and from those pictures I deduced that many of the places pictured weren't just places he'd visited, but places he'd lived. That would explain his accent, which had been harder for me to pinpoint than Mama's Northern Irish-half-morphed-into-American brogue.

By the time I'd finished examining all the shelves, Henry had dozed off on the couch in the living room. I watched him for a moment, a tight feeling in my chest. Everyone was tired. We all needed sleep. But I felt far too wound up to even consider it now. Finally, I went back into the dining room and slid open the door to the courtyard.

It was only a few meters square and completely tiled over. It was also pretty much empty, apart from a yucca plant in a terracotta pot. The back wall and the wall to my right were concrete; the sliding door took up a third wall; and the last was glass, letting me look into the kitchen. Windows on the second story looked down into the courtyard, and above, a tiny square of sky. I sank down onto the tiles, the dampness from the rain seeping through my shorts. I pressed my back against one of the concrete walls and stared up at the blue sky overhead. Now and then, its emptiness was broken by a passing cloud or a bird swooping over. Once I saw a distant airplane. The sounds of the city seemed muffled here. I rested my head against the concrete, trying to focus on those sounds.

When had it gotten this bad? I'd always been nervous. I'd always been anxious. But even when Isaak had been missing, it hadn't consumed my life like this. My therapist had said that sometimes anxiety got worse as you got older, with panic attacks becoming frequent when you hadn't really had them before. And, of course, stress triggered it. But I'd had no shortage of stress the past several annums. Why had it suddenly become so overwhelming?

I felt like the stress in my life was a river, gradually growing more and more full until one day, it flooded its banks. I'd gone far past the flood stage now. Stemming the flood at this point felt like a near-impossible task. Grounding exercises, breathing exercises... What good did they do? Reality was closing in on all sides around me, like the walls of this teeny-tiny courtyard.

Anticipation made it worse. When we were moving, acting, I could focus on that. It was these waiting times, knowing that something was coming, but that it wasn't here yet, that made the anxiety grow. Now it was so big, it felt like my body couldn't hold it in. Like it was pressing against my organs, my bones, my skin. Wanting to burst right out of me.

I looked up at the bright blue sky, and I felt so utterly, utterly alone.

A little while later, the patio door slid open. I turned my head to see Henry shuffling out onto the tile, pulling the door closed behind him.

"Hey," he said. "You okay?"

"Yeah," I lied.

He came over, sinking onto the tile beside me. "Are you *really* okay?"

I exhaled. "No."

He watched me for a moment. "Tamara, listen—"

I bristled. I knew this was going to be about this morning. "It's fine, honestly. I don't want to talk about it."

"No, seriously. Just... Just let me apologize."

"You don't need to apologize."

"I do. I should have stood up for you right away."

I rolled my eyes. "I can stand up for myself." Or I could if my brain didn't tend to immediately blank when I was put on the spot, anyway.

"I know you can. But I should have, too. I just... want you to be safe, and that was overriding any other concerns. All of this mess, I dragged you into it."

Here we go again. "You didn't drag me into it," I said. "I walked in of my own accord, and so did Scylla."

"All I wanted for you—all I still want—is for you to make it out of this and have your life back."

"Well, I'm not going to get that at some safe house in Medellín," I pointed out.

He sighed. "I know. Rationally, I know that. It's just hard sometimes." He was quiet for a moment, listening to the sound of traffic on the street. "I wish you hadn't canceled your summer tour."

I shook my head. He'd been on about that ever since I'd mentioned it weeks ago, back on the *Athena*. As if I would be able to even think about performing at a time like this, with everything else going on. As if I'd be able to just leave everyone I cared about behind and go prance around on a stage like nothing was wrong in the world.

Besides, I hadn't practiced anything in over a month. I hadn't even so much as sung my scales since... since the day of Joseph Condor's coup. The day that Henry had been arrested. I hadn't done my breathing exercises, I hadn't touched a single key of a piano, I hadn't even brought my Casio with me on the ship. If things ever went back to normal, I was going to have to do weeks of intensives with my instructors. I wouldn't be able to just hop back up on the stage. And at this point, with my anxiety so out of control, I wasn't sure I even wanted to. Concerts and recording studios and music videos and interviews and photo shoots— had I really been doing those things just an annum ago? It seemed like another life. It seemed stupid that I had ever even *wanted* that life, ever even enjoyed it.

And even if I wanted it again, my scumbag brain was clearly going to fight me every step of the way. What would I do if I had a panic attack on stage, with hundreds of people watching me? Before, it had been hard for me before every performance. The way things were now, it seemed impossible.

Right now, it seemed better to just forget about even trying.

Aloud, all I said was, "I had to."

"But you didn't have to. That's the thing," Henry said. "You never had to be involved in all of this. Any of it. You could have just picked your life up at any time and left this whole mess behind you."

I shifted to face him. "I would never do that. Henry, I couldn't just leave you."

He looked down, away from me. "You should have."

I put my hand on his cheek, turning his face toward mine. "I would never leave you. I *will* never leave you. I love you. And this is too important. Our whole planet is at stake. I can't just bury my head in the sand and go on as if I didn't know what I know."

He smiled, putting his hand over mine. "I know. I know all of that. But it still isn't what I want for you. So that's why..."

I rolled my eyes again. "I know. I told you, I already knew." Over his shoulder, I caught the sight of my reflection in the sheet glass wall of the kitchen. My short blond hair—several centimeters of dark roots now showing—sticking out in four different directions.

"Ugh," I groaned, turning away and putting my back against the concrete again.

"What?"

"I hate this haircut," I muttered.

"You look beautiful."

I gave him a look, even as the corners of my mouth twitched up. "Thank you. But I still hate this haircut." I sighed, running the palm of my hand over the top of my head, trying to smooth it down. "And it feels like it was completely pointless, you know? Those stupid nanobots and their facial recognition software still recognized us."

"But the humans who had those bots inside them didn't. And they might have if you hadn't cut your hair. At least whoever sent us that note was able to overwrite the data. You're safe now. That's the only important thing to me, remember?" he teased. "That you're safe."

"Yes, I remember," I laughed.

"Besides, hair grows."

"Not fast enough." I looked at him, at his own short hair. When we'd been at the Academy, he'd always had long hair, in defiance of all dress codes. But he'd cut it last annum. "Was it hard for you when you cut your hair?"

He snorted. "Not really. I didn't have my hair long because I *liked* it, per se. I just..." He paused, giving it some thought. "When you're a guy, the length of your hair is a statement, you know? I was a rebel. And I wanted people to know it. When my hair was long, it got the reaction I wanted. Especially out of my parents." He shook his head. "And then when I cut it... that was also a statement, right? I was respectable now. I fit inside the box. People would take me seriously when I told them that I had worked for GSAF and I knew the truth about them. Maybe they wouldn't just see me as some kind of troublemaker. If that makes sense."

"Do you think that worked?"

He shrugged. "It seemed to. As well as could be expected, anyway. I don't regret doing it."

"How do you think you would want to have your hair, if it didn't matter what anyone else thought of when they looked at you?"

He laughed. "You're overthinking it. I don't really care about it one way or the other. Short hair is easier maintenance, though. And I don't think I need to signal to people that I'm a rebel anymore. I'm pretty sure they're aware at this point."

"I do like your hair short," I said with a grin. "Because you can't hide your face from me the way you used to."

"Oh, yeah? You like seeing my face?"

"Duh."

He caught my hand in his, pulling me closer conspiratorially. "Say it," he whispered.

I felt my cheeks turn crimson. "I like seeing your face," I whispered back.

He laughed. "I love you when you're embarrassed," he teased, reaching up to cup his fingers under my chin.

"I love you all the time," I murmured, drawing his face down and catching his lips with mine.

That evening after dinner, I headed up the stairs to finally take my own shower and get into bed early. It was going to be a long day of traveling tomorrow, and it would be better faced with a good night's sleep.

When I reached the second floor, I saw the door to Professor Senghas' room was open. Isaak's grandpa was standing beside a small writing desk. He looked up and noticed me. I gave him a little wave, starting to head into the guest room to get my things, but he called out to me. "I've been hoping to talk to you," he said.

I quirked my head curiously, coming over to him. He closed the book he'd been writing in. I saw it was one of his own works—a book on the linguistic history of the Olmec. He must have been signing it for Professor Senghas like he'd promised he would earlier.

"I wanted to tell you that it's been good to get to know you this week," he said as I came into the room. "To spend some time with you. I've heard so much about you from Isaak over the years, so I'm glad I finally got to know you myself."

"I feel the same way," I said with a smile. "Isaak always talked about you, so it was good to meet you."

In a lower voice, he asked me, "How are you feeling, *mi hija*?"

My smile faded slightly. "How am I feeling?" I repeated in confusion.

Looking chagrined, he explained, "I've noticed you haven't seemed like you're doing well this week. Especially since we found out Isaak was going to be..." He shrugged. "Well, leaving us."

"Oh," I said, not sure how to respond.

"I know how hard it is to worry. I tried not to burden him with it before he left, but I'm very worried about Isaak. And I'm also worried about my daughter and Celestita. They've suffered much over the last few years, and they're going to suffer more before this is over."

"Yeah," I said glumly.

"But you have to have faith everything is going to be okay," Professor Garcia said. "We're all going to get through this. And we have to believe that Isaak will be coming back to us."

I nodded. "I know. I'm trying. I really am. It's just so hard."

He watched me for a moment. Then he reached under the collar of his shirt, withdrawing a beaded necklace. He pulled it over his head and held it out to me, and I saw then that it was a rosary. The oval beads were made of carnelian, a deep orange-red.

He chuckled at my bewildered expression. "I know you're not supposed to wear them, but..." He shrugged. When I continued to stare confusedly at the beads in his hand, he added, "I hope I'm not presuming. Isaak mentioned you went to the same church as him."

It was only then I realized he was offering me the rosary. "Oh!" I exclaimed, flushing. "No. I mean, yes. I am Catholic." My moms had both been raised Catholic, and they'd been married in the Church after the Third Vatican Council. They'd seen to it that I'd been baptized as a baby. "But I can't take this!" I protested. The rosary looked very old. It had to be valuable, even if only in sentiment. I couldn't take Isaak's grandfather's rosary.

"I want you to have it." He pressed the beads into my hand, closing my fingers over them. Despite having been worn close to his body, they still felt cool. "In my experience, when problems get overwhelming, people tend to turn inward when they should be turning upward," he said. "This has been a help to me many times over the years. I hope it will help you now."

I looked up at him. "Thank you, Professor Garcia."

He smiled back. "Call me 'Abuelo,'" he said.

I smiled tightly, my eyes stinging. I wondered if I'd see him again after tomorrow. If he'd be safe in Medellín. If he and Isaak would ever see each other again. So many things unknown. So many answers not yet written. I clutched the rosary tightly between my fingers.

"Thank you, Abuelo," I whispered.

- h e n r y -

THE NEXT MORNING WHEN I TRUDGED DOWN THE STAIRS, I FOUND LIZETH dozing on the sofa. At the sound of my footsteps, she jerked upright, muscles instantly tensed. Her face was wan, with dark circles under her eyes. Lack of sleep was catching up with her. She hadn't come up to the guest room last night. She'd still been on her call when everyone else had gone to bed, so she'd come down here while Scylla and Tamara had taken the double bed and I'd slept on a cot. From the look of her, I guessed she'd remained on that call most of the night.

"Hey," I said as she took me in, registered I wasn't a threat, and relaxed. "Any news?"

"Yeah," she said, her voice thick. She swallowed and cleared her throat. "My mother won't give me clearance to arrange a spacecraft unless we meet with her in person in the UFS first."

"What?" I protested. We didn't have time to afford a lengthy side trip. But more than that—Lizeth had made it clear that the Stateless had had intentions for me when they'd broken me out of Lago Verde, and I'd derailed them. Lizeth was at least willing to concede that Isaak and Nadin returning to Mars meant that we needed to be there before GSAF apprehended them. But what if her mother didn't agree? What if she considered them expendable? What if she kept me here on Earth, as much a prisoner of the Stateless as I'd been of GSAF?

"Relax," Lizeth said. "She's not going to hold you hostage. She wasn't exactly *happy* about the way things are going"—she sighed pointedly—"but she recognized at this point she has to either cooperate or lose her entire investment."

"So why's she making us go to the UFS, then?"

Lizeth chewed on her lip. "She said there's a key variable that we need to be made aware of. One that she couldn't tell me about on a call, even an encrypted one. We need to meet with her in person. Then she said she'd authorize everything."

I made a noise of annoyance in the back of my throat. This still sounded like a stalling tactic to me. But there was nothing I could do about it. If we wanted to get back to Mars, we'd have to detour to the UFS first.

Which was how we found ourselves in a car on the way to the Veracruz airport a little over an hour later. We weren't going to mess around with a boat or a seaplane like we had on our previous trip. Lizeth's mother had a private jet waiting for us. She'd also couriered over some fake identification for us and had a couple of people at the Veracruz airport on the Stateless' payroll to ensure we boarded quickly and with as few prying eyes on us as possible. Still, factoring in the hour-and-a-half drive from Xalapa to Veracruz, the nearly six-hour flight, the boarding and disembarking process, and the boat—excuse me, *yacht*—we had to take from the airport to Sea-Star Island, we didn't arrive at Lizeth's mother's house until nearly five o'clock. Whatever she wanted to meet with us about, it had better be important—it had cost us an entire day.

As the yacht came alongside the docks behind her seaside mansion, I was struck once again by Lizeth's mother's conspicuous wealth. With Bryn being an exec at AresTec and Delia being their top hardware engineer, Tamara's moms *were* wealthy. They lived in a large house in an upscale neighborhood and were comfortable enough to afford luxuries like fresh meat and produce. But they certainly didn't have a private jet at their disposal.

I'd had a growing suspicion about Lizeth's mother's source of income. Even with the United Federation of Seasteads' nearly nonexistent tax burden, there had to be more to it than that. She clearly had money that couldn't be traced. I had a feeling Lizeth's mother was dealing in cryptocurrency, something that had been banned interglobally for almost forty years. Apart from its illegality, the buy-in rate for just about any kind of crypto was astronomical, which let most people out. But for those who could afford it in the first place, if you knew what you were doing with it and invested smartly, it was a great way to gain almost limitless funds.

She seemed to be putting that bottomless money pool to good use, at least. Undermining GSAF's power was a goal that would benefit us all. But would she be willing to go along with my plan, or was this so-called "meeting" an excuse to hold me here? That was the question.

As before, Lizeth didn't want us to linger on the pier, where tourists and neighbors would notice a large group heading into her mom's home and possibly recognize us—especially if they were using drones for vids or holos, not to mention now the high probability of Nano. We waited below in the yacht's cabin, and once we had a relatively clear moment, she hustled us inside.

As we came through the back door, we were greeted by a wiry man, maybe in his mid-thirties, wearing a suit and one of those godawful cravats.

"Lizeth, good to see you and your friends had a safe trip," he said, taking in the group of us. "Ms. Perez wanted me to let you know that she had rooms made up for your guests."

"Ms. Perez being your mom, I assume?" Scylla asked, looking at Lizeth. Under her breath, she added, "Or else we're making a run for it and jumping into the sea."

"Oh, sorry." The man looked chagrined. "I'm Jay Logan. Lizeth's mother's personal assistant. She's in a meeting right now in her study. It could be quite some time, so she asked me to greet you on her behalf. Should I have Harold show you to your rooms?"

"I can bring them up later, Jay," Lizeth said quickly. "We're not going to be staying right now. I wanted to show my friends the island. Could you get Harold and have him help you bring our bags in?"

The expression on Logan's face clearly read *I'm a personal assistant, not a valet*, but he merely nodded and disappeared into another part of the house. Looking for whoever Harold was, I assumed. A butler, maybe? The home had been empty the last time we'd been here and most of the doors had been locked, so I hadn't realized that ordinarily Lizeth's mom had a full retinue of staff at her disposal. Another way her lifestyle clearly differed from the Randall-Torreses'.

Once the two men had gone out to the dock to start unloading the yacht, Lizeth gestured us quickly down a half flight of stairs to a lower level of the house.

"The staff don't know what goes on here," she whispered.

I stared at her incredulously. "Not even her assistant?"

She shook her head. "The Stateless only takes up a small amount of my mother's time. She spends the rest of it on her corporate empire. Most of the people in the Stateless don't know who's financing everything, just that it's someone from the UFS. Only my inner circle knows, really. Bruno, obviously"—Bruno was Lizeth's brother, who had sheltered us at his home in West Palm Beach when we'd escaped from Lago Verde—"and Dante and Zero. To everyone else, she's just a shadow figure. And the people who interact with her real identity don't know about the Stateless. She's done thorough background checks on everyone on her payroll, but still. The fewer people who know, the less chance she has of getting caught."

I frowned. Lizeth had mentioned before that she tended to use fake identities, disguises, and burner figuscans with voice modulators when she did work for the Stateless. That was how she'd first encountered me on an agorist chatspace on Speculus. Posing as a middle-aged white man. I'd had no clue I'd been talking to a girl my own age.

But she hadn't had a choice when we'd gone to the dig site—she'd had her uncle with her, and he'd announced their relationship to pretty much everyone in camp, so everyone there knew she was Lizeth Senghas. He'd also blabbed the full details about who we were and why we'd come to the site to Professor Espinoza. That meant that at least one more person, someone outside her inner circle, now knew both her real-life identity and her role in the Stateless.

And on top of that, Horlando had figured out who we were. I hadn't dared mention that to anyone else, but it was eating away at me now.

I could finally see why Lizeth had been so angry that the alliance with the Elytherioi had fallen through, why she felt the trip had been a waste. That trip had been unauthorized, hadn't been pre-planned, and she'd taken a huge risk by going on it.

A risk that hadn't paid off.

"Don't worry. Nobody here has Nano," she said, noticing my uneasy expression but not understanding the reason for it. "She told the staff last year that she wouldn't allow it for anyone on her payroll because a lot of her business projects have non-disclosure agreements associated with them. That's also the ostensible reason why her study is soundproofed."

She turned down a short hallway. A closed door stood at the end. Beside it, an elegant console table held a square-cut crystal vase containing a single lily, the flower's long stem artfully angled against the container's wide mouth.

"I'm just warning you all right now," Lizeth said, "my mother can be a lot."

"That's really something out of you, since you are also a lot," I said.

She rolled her eyes. "Don't say I didn't warn you."

She pressed the button on a small, square box next to the door. I noticed it had a camera on it, so Perez could see who was on the other side of the door. I wondered how many more cameras could be found throughout the house.

Through a speaker on the box, a woman's voice said, "In." The door automatically unlocked, and Lizeth opened it.

Directly across the room, seated behind a large mahogany desk, was a long, angular woman with her sleek black hair pulled into a tight bun. A man sat in a cushioned chair across from her, and he stood, turning to face us. He wore a nondescript gray suit with a pale-blue shirt under the jacket, with no tie or cravat. The man was of average height, average build—but his shaved head made him stand out, the familiar sight of it sending adrenaline slicing through my veins.

"What is he doing here?" Scylla demanded, the horror on her face matching what I knew was on mine.

"Nice to see you, too, Miss Hwang," the man said.

It was Geoff Preston.

PART FIVE
IAMOS

S.C.D. 8378
10,942 B.C.E.

Chapter 29

- n a d i n -

IT WAS HARD RIDING ONCE WE'D EMERGED FROM THE TUNNELS. THERE WAS little cover available here, leaving us completely exposed. The odds of Enforcers being out here, so far from any citidome, were slim, but we all knew that they would be searching for us more aggressively than ever. Nikos urged the *gurzas* on as fast as they could manage with two riders on their backs. Though he'd stayed in the rear within the tunnels, now his big black *gurza* took the lead, keeping the others in line as they raced down the barren slope of the Great Crater.

I'd never been to this part of Iamos in this timeline. On clear days, the peak of the Kalderos Ifaisteos was visible from the upper level of the citidome in Hope Renewed, but I'd never seen the mountain from anything but a distance. But I'd been here in Isaak's time. In the future, the crater flowed with water, and the mountain had loomed over Yellowknife Bay when we'd gone out on Bryn and Delia's boat. It felt surreal to see it this way now. I could tell by the expression on Isaak's face that he felt the same way.

We rode hard for hours, following the carved path of a dry riverbed, the sun passing from the east side of the crater to directly overhead. At last, we reached the remnant of a larger tributary, some water still remaining in the deepest portion. Nikos directed us to stop here, allowing the *gurzas* the opportunity to drink and us to rest our aching muscles after the hard ride.

I adjusted the uncomfortable tube over my face, struggling to catch my breath. The *gurzas'* physiognomy meant that they could survive in the low oxygen environment Iamos' degrading atmosphere provided. But humans—and primates like the *kerkopith*—needed higher oxygen levels, and even with the tanks we'd carried along for the journey, I felt like I was having trouble getting enough air.

I helped Gitrin climb off our *gurza's* back, and she groaned, putting her hands against her lower back and stretching. "I'm too old for this, *alin*."

"Come now, Gitrin," Nikos said with a laugh, taking Thork's reins and leading him to the water. "I'm older than you are."

"Not that much. Besides"—Gitrin adjusted her shawl primly—"the life of a scholar is not one of physical exertion."

"What's she saying?" Emil asked in English, prodding Isaak in his side with a gnarled finger.

He'd asked that question so many times that Gitrin knew what it meant without anyone translating. "I'm *old*," Gitrin said loudly in Iamoi, as if volume would make up for the language barrier.

Isaak and I shared a look, and awkwardly he translated. Emil scoffed. "She's not old," he decreed. "She's what, in her mid-fifties? Sixty, maybe? I'm seventy-five. *That's* old."

Isaak shook his head. "What is this, an age supremacy thing? Whoever's oldest wins a gold medal?"

"'Age supremacy'?" Emil repeated, an expression on his face that could only be described as *curmudgeonly*. "Contreras, you say the nuttiest things."

Gitrin waited expectantly for a translation, but Isaak held his hands up. "I'm not getting involved," he said. "I need to get Pandat something to drink." He removed the *kerkopith* from Emil's shoulder, where the animal had been perched for most of the journey, and followed Nikos to the water's edge.

I watched him go, a hollow feeling forming in the pit of my stomach as he passed Shuliin. The runner had helped Ceilos off the back of the black *gurza*, and she and Syrin stood beside him now. Guarding him. The two women spoke to each other in low voices, but Ceilos didn't respond. It had to be uncomfortable for him, being blindfolded for so long, but he hadn't complained. He'd been so quiet on this journey. He hadn't said anything to me since that night in Eliin's outpost. He hadn't spoken much to anyone, honestly. I'd seen him exchange a few words with Nikos, but he'd been nearly silent almost the entire journey.

What must he be thinking about, after all these days in the dark?

My eyes drifted between him and Isaak, the hollowness intensifying. Isaak had taken Pandat's breathing tube off and was smiling as he watched him splash through the shallow pond. The *kerkopith* scrambled up on a rock, shaking itself mightily, water droplets flying through the air. Isaak's *gurza* Tuupa had finished drinking and came up beside him, nudging her head up under his arm. He stroked her muzzle absentmindedly.

I swallowed, looking away. I knew I didn't love Ceilos. Especially after everything that had happened on Mars and on Earth. Everything that happened with... Isaak. I had a basis for comparison now, and I knew. This was more than just being asexual. My feelings for Ceilos could never be what he wanted. The love that Ceilos desired belonged to someone else.

But I felt strangely burdened by Ceilos, in a way I couldn't explain. He'd made himself an enemy of the Elytherioi, of the entire rebellion, because of his actions, but those actions had been motivated by his feelings for me. It made me feel responsible somehow. Like I had to carry some of the blame, despite the *ninvidu* declaring me absolved.

Moreover... Ceilos was our ally. If we had any hope of stopping Tibros, we needed him. I couldn't risk alienating him. This left me feeling like I was walking a delicate line in the sand, one that left me off-balance and fearing taking any wrong step.

I knew what was in my heart. I'd known it since that night in the jungle, and I longed to tell Isaak. But I also knew that until all this was over, I could not. And it made me angry. I wasn't Ceilos' property, but I may as well have been.

Things had been so much easier before, when Ceilos had merely been my partner. My best friend. Why couldn't things have stayed that way forever?

Even as I thought it, I remembered uncomfortably the feeling of his body against me, his mouth against mine. Things wouldn't have remained easy with Ceilos. This day would have come, with or without Isaak. But I still felt the loss of my old life, painful and raw.

"Is something the matter, *alin*?"

I jumped. Gitrin was watching me. I hadn't realized I'd been staring so obviously. My brain scrambled to think of an excuse. I didn't want to drag Gitrin into all of this. It was my burden alone.

"Gitrin, do you remember what you and I talked about when Ceilos first came to us?"

I'd blurted it out without thinking, just searching for some kind of distraction to get both our thoughts off Isaak.

She furrowed her brows. "What do you mean?"

My face grew hot. "It's nothing. I just—I had a dream a while ago. You were in it. You kept telling me to remember what it was we spoke of when Ceilos first came to Hope Renewed."

Gitrin frowned and looked at Ceilos, running her thumb over her lower lip. "I'm sorry, *alin*, I don't recall. But you must know that dreams don't hold greater meaning, right?" She put her hand on my shoulder and I winced. The wounds on my back had mostly healed by now, but the area was still tender. "The System regulated our dreams, kept them from being too unruly or too vivid. Off the System, dreams can be strange, even unsettling. But they mean very little. They are just our brains' way of processing information, usually in ways that seem nonsensical to our conscious minds."

I tugged my earlobe reluctantly. "You're right, Gitrin."

She smiled once more before gesturing to Emil to accompany her over to the water's edge. But I didn't follow, not yet. I was thinking. Dreams were just our brains' way of processing information, she said. But what if my brain was trying to tell me something? There was a memory there, but one that I couldn't quite reach in my waking state. What was it that my subconscious was trying to get me to remember?

Bruises.

Isaak turned to face me then, grinning behind his breathing tube and waving me over. I sighed. Whatever it was, I wouldn't remember it today. I picked my way down the rocky riverbed to the water's edge.

Chapter 30

- i s a a k -

THAT NIGHT, WE CAMPED ON THE BOTTOM OF A DRY RIVERBED, A SCAR worn into the crater's slopes by the movement of water long-since evaporated. It was the best shelter we'd have until we reached the western rim of the crater, Nikos had informed us. The temperature outside was bitterly cold, but we couldn't light a fire. For one thing, we didn't dare do so out here in the open—it would be visible from kilometers around, and we couldn't take the risk. But moreover, the air was so thin outside of the caves that any fire we lit would be next to useless for warmth. There just wasn't enough oxygen to build it up.

Instead, we huddled together, hemmed in by the *gurzas*, whose bodies helped trap the heat within our circle. Eliin had given all of us fresh clothing woven Iamoi-style, thicker and warmer than thermal underwear. Unlike the uniform silver bodysuits of the citidome, these were woven in the traditional method, with intricate colors and patterns that reminded me of the vibrant textiles of South America. I'd also brought my rain jacket from Earth along with me, and I pulled the hood on it up now, hoping to protect my face from the scouring wind. My skin felt chapped, and though I couldn't see myself, I could feel a sunburn forming. Emil, the only one here whose complexion was fairer than mine, looked like a boiled lobster. Any part of us that wasn't covered by our clothes had been scorched by the intense sun. The ash clouds from the eruption had either dissipated by now or had not traveled this far south to begin with. Out here, we were exposed in every possible way.

I leaned back against Tuupa's haunch, her tail curling around me protectively, and attempted to take a bite of my paltry meal of flatbread and dried fruit. Eating was something of a conundrum with these breathing apparatuses strapped to our faces. It quickly became a laborious process that involved taking the mask off, taking a bite, putting the mask on, chewing, repeat.

Beside me, Emil grumbled under his breath. I glanced in his direction. Pandat, as usual, was begging for scraps of his food. But Emil seemed crankier about it than usual. After he swatted the *kerkopith* away for the third time, I rolled my eyes and set my own food down.

"C'mere, little guy," I said, scooping Pandat up. "He just wants dinner." I set to unstrapping the tiny mask from Pandat's face. He'd taken to wearing this thing better than I would have expected for an animal, probably having adjusted to it when he'd had it on in Eliin's outpost before. I looked up at Emil wryly as my fingers worked. "What's your problem, anyway, old man?"

I was just teasing, but the joke made him scowl even harder. "Old man," he grumbled back.

"You're the one who said it!" I protested.

He was quiet for a long moment, looking up at the sky. I followed his gaze upward. The light from Hamos glowed down on us like a full moon.

"I've been working on my theory about precolonial Martian occupation for more than forty years now," he said, his voice low and gravelly. "And now I've seen it with my own eyes. Ancient Mars, live and in person. What I'm having right here is the experience of a lifetime." He pulled off his mask, exhaling slowly, drawing out the breath like he was blowing smoke. Then he took a bite of food and put the mask back on. "But how much longer will my life be, anyway?"

My brows furrowed. "I didn't mean to make you get all depressed. I was just ribbing you because of your age supremacy thing earlier."

He shook his head, a glimmer of the typical cantankerous Emil shining through. "This trip has been rough, kid. My body's not enjoying it at all. It's made me realize just how old I am." He swirled a finger through the dust beside him. "And more than that. My brain keeps fixating on the stuff you told us before. About the ancient Martian site on Earth. That's everything I've ever dreamed about discovering. That would be the culmination of my life's work, you know? But other scientists are making the discoveries I dreamed of making. Other scientists will get the credit."

He trailed off, and I realized that beside us, Nadin and Gitrin, who'd been having a conversation of their own as they ate, had quieted. Nadin was watching us carefully now, her face illuminated in the glow of Hamos overhead.

Emil hadn't noticed. Quietly, he said, "Now's the time when my career should be just beginning. Everything has finally come together. GSAF isn't trying to deny it anymore. They can't shut me up anymore. The world knows the truth. When we get back—if we get back—I could be leading expeditions, or teaching classes about my research."

"You still could, though," I said. "You're the one who discovered the evidence of life to begin with. That's how Henry and I found you in the first place. Everyone knows you're the expert on this. It's all over the internet." Well, all over the conspiracy websites, anyway. But still, the information was out there. Surely people would recognize...

He shook his head. "Like I said earlier—I'm seventy-five. It's too late for me now, isn't it?"

"It's not too late," said Gitrin.

I looked at her in surprise. She answered in Iamoi, but from the look on her face I could tell that she'd comprehended everything he'd said.

"What?" Emil asked.

"Gitrin, you understand?" Nadin asked in surprise.

Gitrin gave her a look. "After all these weeks of everything he and I say being translated back and forth, it would be impossible to have *not* picked up something."

She turned back to Emil. Earnestly, she said, "It's never too late to make a fresh start. You're never too old. As long as you're alive, you can still start over."

I started to translate, but Emil waved me off. "The cards are stacked against me," he told her.

"Listen," Gitrin replied firmly. "I am thirty-one of our years old." I did some quick mental math—that made her fifty-nine annums. "But for the first twenty-five years of my life," she went on, "I lived in service to the *geroi*. I did not come to the rebellion until Nadin was a child and I was already her tutor. Some may have said then that it was too late for me. That I was too rooted in my ways to start over. But it wasn't too late. And it's not too late for you, Emil. It's never too late, as long as you're breathing."

Emil sat quietly for a moment, looking down. Like Gitrin, it was clear that through their translated conversations over the last few weeks, he'd picked up some of the language. But that didn't mean he was fluent. "Okay, kid, I do need you to translate that one," he said to me after a moment. I did so, and he nodded. "That's what I thought."

Finally, he glanced at Gitrin, an odd expression on his face. "Thank you," he said. "I needed to hear that."

We ate the rest of our meal in silence, Pandat scurrying around between our feet, poking around for scraps of uneaten fruit. Emil, apparently in better spirits now, gave him a rind, and the *kerkopith* brought it over to the far corner of our encampment. I couldn't quite see his movements in the dark; it looked like he might have been digging in the packed sediment of the old riverbed, but I wasn't sure. Then he scampered back over to me, something clenched in his small, furry fist.

"What have you got there?" I asked, and he dropped the handful at my feet. Tiny pebbles, some as small as ball bearings. Black, uninteresting at first glance, but banded with stripes that shone in the light of the planet overhead.

Emil looked over my shoulder as I picked them up and smoothed them out in my palm. "Hematite," he said. "Gale Crater is abundant with it."

Hematite. I glanced over at Nadin. After eating, she'd dozed off, her head on Gitrin's shoulder. Her shaved hair was growing back in now, her scalp no longer visible through the fuzz of short white hair. But she'd carry the scars from her ordeal forever.

I tucked the pebbles into my rain jacket, zipping them into the inside pouch along with Henry's return posternkey. They'd be safe there.

We followed the path of the dried river, picking our way along what I recognized as the ancient precursor to Gale Delta. Here and there we passed areas where water still flowed at a trickle, but most of the water that had once filled this crater was long gone.

Soon we were in the shadow of Mount Sharp—which Nadin told me was called Kalderos Ifaisteos here. With the sun hidden behind the mountain during the morning hours, the air was even colder than it had been before, and a biting wind whipped across my skin. It was cold enough that Pandat, who'd been eager to explore his surroundings in the first leg of the journey, now nestled himself tightly into Emil's chest, sandwiched between the two of us on Tuupa's back.

The wind made me nervous, especially when I noticed clouds high in the upper atmosphere, and spotted buzzard-like creatures circling through them. *Gamadas.* They traveled along the air currents, favoring highly windy conditions. As scavengers with precious little to scavenge on Iamos these days, they needed these high winds to stir up any rotting material for them to feed on. They frequently advanced on coming sandstorms—to the extent that on Iamos, these were called *gamada* storms. The presence of *gamadas* here might mean a sandstorm was imminent, and that could be deadly for us.

As the sun rose overhead, Pandat squirmed out of Emil's arms and climbed onto my shoulder. He squeaked in my ear, the sound muffled through his breathing apparatus.

"I know, buddy," I said, though it felt like my voice was snatched away on the wind. "I see them." I followed his gaze to a *gamada* that had strayed from the others, flying lower than the rest. It dipped behind the peak of the mountain, disappearing from sight.

"*Gamadas* flying lower," I called to Nikos. The distant rumble of thunder punctuated my words.

Nikos grunted in reply. "We need to get over there." He gestured to the west side of the crater, taking care not to mention where we were or describe the topography in any way. Behind him on Kodo, Ceilos sat quietly, his expression grim. "There are caves there we can use for shelter."

"Let's just hope the weather holds out long enough for us to get there," Syrin said.

The rogue *gamada* appeared again, circling the mountain at an even lower altitude. Abruptly, Ceilos cried out, "Wait! Listen."

His voice croaked with disuse. I stared in surprise, and the others seemed just as taken aback by his sudden outburst after so many weeks of silence.

"What is it?" Nikos asked over his shoulder.

"I hear something. It sounds mechanical."

Nikos slowed his mount, and the other *gurzas* followed Kodo's lead. It was hard to hear anything over the noise of the wind. But then I caught it. Sure enough—a distinctly unnatural buzz.

Pandat squeaked in my ear again, and I looked at the low-flying *gamada* more carefully. And then I realized what Pandat seemed to have noticed all along. It wasn't following the pattern of the wind. It was, in fact, moving *against* the wind.

"That's not a *gamada*," I said. "It's a machine."

From astride Thork, Nadin let out a hiss. "This is ancient technology. A tracking device from before the Progression, when there was still war. The *geroi* must have activated it. It's searching for us."

I cursed.

"It's a *tirak*," Gitrin called over the roar of the wind. "They're designed to detect heat and movement. We have to get to cover, someplace sheltered enough that it won't be able to pick up our body heat."

"We'll have to risk open ground," said Shuliin. "It's the only way we'll reach the caves before that thing locks in on us."

Nikos tugged his earlobe and called out a command to the *gurzas*. With Kodo in the lead, the *gurzas* broke into a sprint, and I gripped the reins, my heart pounding. The speed these reptiles could manage was a terrifying glimpse of what they must have looked like in their days as predators, before they'd been domesticated. Whatever prey they were hunting would have never stood a chance.

The *tirak* sensed our sudden motion. It broke out of its holding pattern of circling Mount Sharp. It was heading for us now. But it was slow, slower than the *gurzas*. If we could keep this pace, we'd outrun it. But how long could the animals run at this speed, particularly with each of them laden down with two humans and all our supplies?

We streaked across the uneven ground, leaping over narrow channels and splashing through Lugh waterways that had not yet gone dry. Pandat anxiously scurried off my shoulder, clutching Emil's chest once again while Emil kept a death grip on me. I glanced back. The *tirak* was gaining. Were the *gurzas* slowing, or was it traveling faster?

The wind picked up as we neared the western slopes of the crater. I was so preoccupied with the advancing *tirak*, I hadn't noticed the change in the sky. The clouds were lowering, the real *gamadas* soaring around them. Lightning flickered in the distance. When the thunder followed, the sound was deafening.

A *gamada* storm was indeed approaching. And we were riding directly into it. But faced with a sandstorm or the *geroi*'s sentinel, I'd take the storm.

Tuupa whined beneath me, and I patted her, trying to sooth her. She wouldn't break from the herd. But all her instincts told her she should be running away from this storm, not toward it.

I glanced over my shoulder. The *tirak* was nearly on us.

We had no other choice.

Nikos spurred Kodo on again and called out his command to the *gurza* herd once more. Obediently, they hurtled forward.

The clouds were lowering. I could see, now—they weren't clouds. It was a solid wall of dust.

The wind slapped me across the face. I could hear nothing over its roar.

"There's a cave here!" Nikos shouted, his voice carried away by the howling gale.

We leapt off the *gurzas*, Nikos grabbing Ceilos' upper arm forcefully in order to keep him from falling. Nadin staggered as she dismounted Thork, colliding into me as I passed. I gripped her hand, steadying her, and the two of us raced together behind Nikos.

"This way, hurry," Shuliin barked. I could barely see the cave's entrance—it was obscured by a thick clump of spider weeds. She ushered us in, first Gitrin and Emil, tightly holding Pandat; then Syrin; then Nadin and me. Nikos and Ceilos took up the rear, and Shuliin scrambled in behind them. The cave was too small to hold the *gurzas*. This notch in the craterside was barely large enough to hold the eight of us. The *gurzas* huddled together as they'd done when Nadin and I had been caught in a storm on the road to Elytherios. They formed a tight mound, covering each other's faces with their tails and compressing themselves until they looked more like a mossy rock than a group of living creatures. This was the *gurzas*' natural instinct, the way their species had evolved to survive these harsh sandstorms in the wild.

Shuliin pulled the clump of spider weeds back over the mouth of the cave just as the wall of sand descended. Despite the small degree of shelter the cave provided, I had to squeeze my eyes closed, pulling my hood down over my face to try to block the grit from getting into my eyes, into my mouth.

Beside me, Nadin was shaking violently. Her grip on my hand only grew tighter. Instinctively, I put my arm around her, and she pressed her face against my chest. "Three," she whispered against me, her voice rough. "Three times."

My mouth formed a grim line. "Yeah," I said back, choking back a cough. This was the third time we'd endured a storm like this. And our journey wasn't over yet. How many more still faced us?

Over the howl of the wind outside, I could just make out Nikos' voice in the darkness on my other side. He spoke to Ceilos, his voice low, tone somber. "You saved us," he said.

If Ceilos replied, I couldn't hear.

CHAPTER 31

IT FELT LIKE AN ETERNITY BEFORE THE STORM FINALLY PASSED. Sandstorms were a way of life on Iamos, but I would never get used to them. We'd all known that traveling aboveground meant we risked being caught in one. I should have been more prepared for this eventuality. But I still could not stop trembling, not until the roar of the wind had finally calmed, until the storm had finally moved on.

At last, when it had been quiet long enough that we could be certain that it really had passed, Nikos rose unsteadily to his feet, stooping beneath the low ceiling of the small cave.

"We'd better scout the area," he said to Shuliin. "Find out if that *tirak* is still nearby."

Shuliin tugged her earlobe and turned to her partner. "Syrin, we'll need you to watch the *geroi*'s blood."

"No," said Nikos. Shuliin looked at him in surprise. He ran a thumb over his chin thoughtfully. "He's our charge, *ninvidu*. We'll bring him with us."

Shuliin scowled, but she helped Ceilos, his hands still tied together and his eyes still blindfolded, to his feet.

They were gone for some time, long enough that nerves began to turn sourly within my stomach. What was keeping them? Had there been Enforcers nearby? Had they been caught?

Or worse... had Ceilos betrayed us once more? That thought made my insides roil even harder. I had testified on his behalf. What if I'd been wrong? What if we were all doomed now because of my loyalty to someone who'd already proved himself untrustworthy once before?

Syrin crawled over to the entrance of the cave, pulling back the curtain of *fraouloi* in front of the opening and peering out. "We're losing the light," she said. "We'd better plan on being here overnight."

Emil prodded Isaak and he translated. Then Isaak asked, "Do you think everything's all right out there? Should we go look for them?"

"No," Syrin said, though her tone sounded less than assured. "Shuliin will want to be thorough. We can't know that the *tirak* didn't transmit our location to the *geroi* before the storm hit."

We opened our packs, withdrawing our allotted rations for our evening meal. I frowned as I looked at what was left in our rucksack. This would only last us a few more days. We had to be close to Katai'ios now—otherwise, we would be in big trouble.

I chewed on my last bit of dried *naransha* and watched as Isaak gave Pandat a drink from his waterskin. As he was replacing the stopper, a rustling came from outside. My muscles tensed, but a moment later the *fraouloi* were swept aside and Nikos entered. Even in the near-darkness, the grin on his face was visible. He was followed by Shuliin and then Ceilos—hands unbound and blindfold hanging loosely around his neck.

I looked at the others in shock. Beside me, Gitrin's brows were drawn. "What's this, then?" she asked.

"The boy has saved us again," Nikos said, still grinning.

"What happened?" Syrin asked, looking up at Shuliin. Her expression was the opposite of Nikos'—drawn into a deep scowl.

"We found the *tirak*. It had gone down in the storm, partly buried. But it was still operable," Shuliin said.

"We thought about destroying it, but I knew there'd be more. It had to have sent data to the *geroi* before it went down. These things are going to be all over Iamos."

"Is Katai'ios safe, then?" I asked, trying to keep the alarm out of my voice.

"Katai'ios is protected by a System protocol," Syrin reassured me. "Like the one that guards Eliin's outpost. To any eye on the System, and to any device that operates with the System, it will appear invisible."

"But we only have the ability to use that kind of protocol on stationary objects," Nikos said. "Until now, at least."

And then I understood. "Ceilos' cloaking protocol?" I said.

Nikos tugged his earlobe and clapped Ceilos on the shoulders. Ceilos beamed, and something taut inside me loosened. Ceilos' real smile, the one he'd only ever used around me before. Not the false one he showed to the *geroi*. Did this mean that the rebels were accepting him at last?

"I told him that I could give him access to it," Ceilos said.

Shuliin's scowl grew deeper and she sat beside Syrin, crossing her legs. "It was incredibly dangerous. That could have been a trick. It could have sent the *geroi* straight to us. It still could."

"The protocol was solid," Nikos said. "I'm no fool, Shuliin."

"It's true," I said. "Ceilos and I used his protocol many times when we were younger. The *geroi* never caught us." Until I'd found Isaak outside the dome and gone back online, at least. But that had been no fault of Ceilos' program.

"This protocol is incredible," Nikos said. "It does more than just divert the System. It can cloak an object fully in motion. We programmed the *tirak* to beam false coordinates of our movements back to the *geroi*. But even if another *tirak* comes upon us, it won't be able to find us. And when we get our runner network operational again—"

"Whenever a person who's connected to the System sees a cloaked person, the protocol supplies an artificially generated image to disguise them. The System user will see another human altogether," Ceilos explained.

"Smuggling supplies in, people out—think of the uses," Nikos said. "Running will be safer than it ever was before."

"Assuming we can trust him," Shuliin snapped.

"I'm happy for the Elytherioi scientists to analyze my program and check it for safety," Ceilos said quickly. "Truly. I want to prove myself to you. Anything I can do to help the movement, I'm happy to do it."

Syrin put her hand on Shuliin's shoulder. "It sounds like a great opportunity for us, *yachin*," she said.

"So Ceilos doesn't have to be blindfolded anymore?" Isaak asked.

"I didn't agree with that decision," Shuliin muttered.

"No," said Nikos. "But you'll recall, as *ninvidu*, you left responsibility for Ceilos in the elders' hands. I am the only elder here. And I feel that by his actions today, Ceilos has proved himself."

He sat down on the cave floor, gesturing for Ceilos to sit beside him. He rummaged through the pack and handed Ceilos his portion of flatbread and fruit.

"Well, then," Gitrin said as they chewed, trying to break the tension that simmered between Nikos and Shuliin. "You're one of us now, my boy. Does that mean we'll finally be hearing your voice again?"

Ceilos laughed, taking another bite of bread. "I have enjoyed listening to the conversations these past days, even if I didn't feel at liberty to join in."

"Since it's your first night as one of us, you should pick the discussion for tonight," Syrin said with a smile. "What do you want to talk about, Ceilos?"

He took a sip of water before speaking. "Well, there is one thing I've been wondering about." He looked at Nikos. "There are tunnels in Bright Horizon. I used them to help Nadin escape from the pyramid. They're not on the plans in the System. Were they built by the rebellion?"

Nikos tugged his earlobe, swallowing his own food and clearing his throat. "Many of the founders of our movement worked on the construction of the citidomes."

"So the rebellion goes back as far as the Progression?" I asked in surprise.

"Of course. The *geroi* would have you believe that all of Iamos were eager participants in the Progression. But the truth is, many of us fought back, even in the early days."

"'Us'," Isaak repeated. "Were you there? How long ago was the Progression?"

Nikos barked out a laugh. "I'm not quite that old, my boy. But almost." He sighed, looking out the cave's entrance into the darkness. "Marin, Eos and I are the last who remain from the second generation of our movement. Maetrin and Phados... they were the first."

"You said Eos is your brother, right?" I asked.

Nikos reached to tug his earlobe, then hesitated. "In every way that counts, at least. Eos was born after the Progression, in the city beside the lake. Where Bright Horizon would be built. He never knew his birth parents. Never knew what became of them. He was taken from them as an infant and given to the collective to raise. The—what are they called?"

"Caretakers," Shuliin said dourly.

Nikos frowned. "Yes. *Caretakers.* They raised him until he was old enough to work. Then he was apprenticed to Maetrin and Phados. My parents."

"You weren't raised by the collective?" Ceilos asked, a brow arched in surprise.

"No. I was not. When the *geroi* came to power, one of their first acts was to introduce birth control substances into the water. But back then, when the domes were still being built, it wasn't as easy to control the people as it was after everyone was moved inside. And there was more water back then, too. Maetrin and Phados were farmers. They knew where you could get water, water that wasn't tainted.

"So they had me, and they kept it a secret. The only one who knew was Eos. Their apprentice. But he was a lot more than that to them. He was only five years old when he came to them. Just a child. They loved him. And he loved them. How could you not?" He smiled wistfully. "Especially after being raised with no family of your own. They welcomed him into our family, and he was as loyal as if he'd been born to us. He always has been." He looked around at us seriously. "Eos is my brother. There can be no denying it."

"Of course not," Gitrin said in agreement. "We all know it to be true."

"How did your parents come to join the rebellion, then?" Ceilos asked.

"Yes, Nikos," Syrin said. "I've never heard this story. I've always wanted to know more about the elders of our past."

Nikos sighed. "This part of the story is not one that I enjoy reliving."

He tossed the peel of his *naransha* to Pandat, who began picking at the small pieces of fruit that remained. Isaak scooted over to where the *kerkopith* was and removed the animal's mask so he could eat.

"It was Eos who joined. Not my parents. He became involved because he wanted to protect them. Protect me. No one knew about my existence. Officially, at least. He knew that we couldn't keep living under the *geroi*'s rule. Sooner or later someone would find out about me. Eos believed the rebels could protect us.

"By the time he was *enilos*, construction on the citidome was nearing completion, and word was spreading through the community that the eugenicists had made their choices about who would be allowed to enter. And Eos knew we wouldn't be on it. We were considered *plivoi*, you see. Our only worth was in our ability to work. Our parents' farm was less than prosperous—the lake was already drying by that time, and the land was not as abundant as it had once been. Maetrin and Phados were getting older, and they'd passed their knowledge on to Eos. As far as the *geroi* were concerned, it would be better to have a young apprentice farmer who could give them more years of work than an aging partnership who would be a draw on resources."

Isaak looked up from securing Pandat's breathing apparatus. "Wait... what were they going to do to the people who didn't fit in the citidome?"

I swallowed. I knew the answer. I'd grown up knowing the answer. Why hadn't it bothered me as a child the way it did now? Why hadn't I seen how abhorrent it was? Why hadn't I cared?

"They euthanized them," I whispered.

Shuliin's eyes flashed. "Euthanasia. Such a tidy word. So clinical, so detached. They *killed* them," she corrected.

"Your parents were killed by the *geroi*?" Isaak asked in horror.

"Not exactly," Nikos said slowly. He closed his eyes. "A pair of Enforcers came to the farm. One of them spotted me. Eos held... her... off until I could get away. But Phados did not survive the altercation."

He was holding something back. I watched him thoughtfully.

"Through his connections in the early rebel movement, Eos had heard rumors about Elytherios. So after they... got out of the pyramid,

Eos brought me and Maetrin to Elytherios. It was early days, then. The microclimate was still being formed. When I was old enough, they sent me and Maetrin to Katai'ios to work the crops. Eos could have helped, I suppose, but by then he'd started running."

"He became the Liberator," Isaak said.

Nikos smiled wryly. "Indeed."

"But then how did Marin factor in?" I asked. "The three of you have known each other for a long time." And there was more to it than that. The conversation I'd overheard back at Eliin's outpost had belied something else, something deeper. Something in the Elders' past that still seemed to haunt the three of them.

Nikos exhaled. Didn't answer for a long time. In the shadows I saw that Shuliin and Syrin were watching him, Syrin's face curious, Shuliin's wary.

"Marin was one of the two Enforcers. That day at the farm."

I stared at Nikos in shock. "Marin was an *Enforcer*?" More than that— she'd been involved in their parents' death? "And yet you still trusted her?"

"She didn't know any better," Nikos said simply.

Didn't know any better. Nikos had said those words had been spoken before. But I never would have expected this.

"Having a former Enforcer within the rebellion would have been useful," Ceilos remarked.

"Indeed," said Nikos. "Smuggling prisoners out of the pyramid became much easier after Marin joined our ranks. She still had access to that part of the System, locked to her DNA. She would overwrite their records to show that the prisoner had already been reeducated or euthanized. And instead they would just... disappear." He looked at Ceilos seriously. "Marin proved her value to the rebellion. As you did today."

Ceilos smiled, sitting up a bit straighter.

"But what happened to the others?" Isaak asked. "The people in your community. The other... *plivoi.*"

He blew out a breath. "Some of them joined us. Most of them didn't. They either were given spots in the citidome, or..."

He didn't finish. He didn't need to.

Ceilos took a last bite of *naransha* and clenched the peel in his fist. "Didn't it infuriate you?"

"Of course it infuriated me. It still does," Nikos said. "That's why I'm here, boy. The *geroi* have no value for human life. They took every one of our freedoms. They turned us into slaves."

"I didn't mean the *geroi*," Ceilos said. "I meant the people. Your neighbors. They just went along with it. The ones the eugenicists slated for extermination just went meekly along to their deaths. And the ones who joined the citidomes—they just stood by while members of their own community were killed. They did nothing."

"What were they supposed to do?" said Nikos. "They couldn't stop the *geroi*."

"Of course they could have. The *plivoi* must have outnumbered the Enforcers a hundred to one. The *geroi* didn't *take* their freedoms, the people gave them away. One by one, they handed them over freely in exchange for safety."

"That's ridiculous," Shuliin said.

"Is it?" Ceilos laughed humorlessly. "The life of a slave isn't a happy one. But it's a safe one."

"That's not funny, Ceilos," Isaak said.

"It wasn't meant to be."

Isaak made a growl of frustration in the back of his throat. "I don't think the thousands of people who died through the slave trade on Earth would agree with you about slavery being *safe*. You're underestimating the role of power. The *geroi* have power. The slavers had power. The *plivoi* don't. You can't blame the victims for the actions of their oppressors."

Ceilos gritted his teeth. "It's always about Simos, isn't it?"

"Please, please," I interrupted them, holding my hands up. "I want Nikos to finish." I looked at the elder placatingly. "Please, go on."

He sighed. "There's not much else to it, honestly. I need to feed the *gurzas*." He got to his feet and brushed off his knees, joints cracking.

Shuliin followed him. "And I want to scout the area. Make sure that there are no Enforcers around." She shot Ceilos a suspicious glare. "Keep an eye on them, Syrin? Make sure they don't get into any trouble."

Syrin scoffed. "Of course."

By now, Emil was prodding Isaak hard enough to bruise, demanding a translation of the conversation. I sighed, turning to face Ceilos. "Why did you say all that? I wanted to hear the rest of Nikos' story. Now he's upset."

He leaned back against the rough wall of the cave. "I'm tired of it, Nadin. The same old narrative. Someone else is always to blame for their problems. No one takes responsibility for their own actions. They just point the finger at one another and let whatever happens happen."

"That's not true," I protested. "The Elytherioi are trying. But the deck has been stacked against them. They don't deserve the blame. Everything that's happened *is* the fault of the *geroi*. Even now, they could have used the Elytherioi scientists' discoveries to heal our planet and they're letting it die to preserve their own power. The *geroi are* to blame."

"All of Iamos is to blame. The *geroi* only have power because the people *let* them have it. Even Eos and Nikos and their little band of smugglers, calling themselves Liberators, are doing nothing of real consequence. Ironically, the only person who is making an impact is the other Liberator."

I sighed. "Tibros."

He hesitated, then tugged his earlobe. "Yes. If I'm right."

"You still think we shouldn't stop him, then?"

"Of course we should stop him. I just meant that, strategically, it might be easier if we wait."

"But think about what could happen in the meantime, Ceilos. He hasn't just been taking out other *geroi*. By disabling the early warning protocols, he's killed hundreds of innocent bystanders who were caught by natural disasters unprepared. And if we don't act fast, there's a chance more will die. Without the early warning protocol, there's no way to know what kinds of disasters could be coming. Maybe even something big enough to destroy the whole planet."

"Maybe we'd deserve it," he said.

I stared at him, aghast. "What?"

"There's a word in the old language," he said. "Do you know it? *Ypris.*"

I did know it. There was a loan word in English—if Emil's theory was right, passed down from our people to the ancients on Simos. I'd heard them use it on Earth.

Hubris.

My skin was tingling now. "Ceilos, you're scaring me."

He laughed. "Sorry. Just philosophizing out loud. You're right. We have to stop Tibros before he goes any further. And don't worry. We will. Everything will be fine."

In the back of the cave, Syrin was helping Gitrin lay out her bedroll. Ceilos turned from me, bending low to go over and offer his assistance. I watched him, frowning.

His words just now had frightened me. But what frightened me more was the part of myself that thought maybe he was right.

Chapter 32

- n a d i n -

I SIT AT THE TABLE IN GITRIN'S CLASSROOM WITH A SYSTEM PANEL OPEN, swiping through page and subpage, reviewing it all over and over. I've been sitting here long enough that my back is starting to hurt, a dull, distant ache that only registers on the edges of my mind. I'm so focused on the task before me that I don't even notice my surroundings—the table, three woven copper chairs clustered around it; the globe and other antiques dating to before the Progression that Gitrin salvaged for our history lessons; the baskets filled with black *fraouloi* that Gitrin feels the need to cultivate for whatever reason. The multicolored phosphorescent mosaics embedded into the walls around me, providing enough light to see by, the distant drip of moisture somewhere else in the caverns, everything seems to blur together in the back of my mind.

So it should be no surprise when I don't hear the door slide open, don't notice the footsteps approaching behind me. I don't realize Ceilos is here until he's been standing over my shoulder for some minutes, and it's far too late for me to conceal what I'm doing.

"What is that?" he asks, and I jump, sucking in my breath and waving the System panel away with my hand.

"Nothing," I answer quickly.

Ceilos gives me an appraising look, and I want to crawl out of my skin. I've been avoiding him for the last two weeks. Ever since that day in his chamber. He hasn't said anything to me about it, hasn't brought it up at all. If the memory weren't burned so vividly into my mind, I'd think that maybe I'd imagined the whole thing.

But his coldness toward me hasn't changed. To the *geroi*, he is smooth, polite, charming. But he puts on no such façade around me. His disdain could not be more clear. I don't know why, but it's obvious that Ceilos detests me.

The *geroi* have been unsympathetic to my plight. Last week after the evening meal, after Ceilos had left the atrium, Melusin asked me, "Well, Nadin, what do you think of your partner?"

When I'd sourly told her, "He doesn't like me," Antos and Melusin had burst into laughter. I'd stared at them in shock, my face flushing. I'd *never* heard them laugh before.

"I would think there was something wrong with him if he did," Antos had said at length, a wry smirk still pulling at the corners of his mouth.

My face had grown hotter, and I'd looked down at the silver *psara* bones lying on my platter. "I did not realize I was so offensive," I'd murmured.

Melusin had laughed again, an almost harsh sound in comparison to the typical soft, lilting tones of her speech. "That is not what we meant, Nadin. All *geroi* partnerships start this way. You will grow into each other."

"Oh," I'd replied. I didn't believe her. I didn't believe it when she said it, and I still don't. She and Antos are always in tandem. Two halves of a single whole. It's impossible to believe that such unity could have been achieved if they'd begun their partnership at odds.

I haven't told anyone of my plan yet, but I am intending to ask the *geroi* for a repartnership. Such a thing has never been done before, but the laws of the *gerotus* allow for it—a suitable *patros* from a high-ranking family would be chosen to take Ceilos' place as my partner. If Ceilos and I are so incompatible that he won't even speak to me, it seems the only solution. The *geroi* will understand. They *have* to understand.

That's what I've been telling myself, at least. But there's a part of me, deep down, that worries even this won't be a solution. What if the problem isn't Ceilos? What if it's me? What if I am incompatible with every *patros*? What if I'm incompatible with every person on Iamos?

Those fears ring in my mind now as Ceilos stares at me, eyes narrowed. "It wasn't nothing. I saw it," he says. "On the System panel. It looked like plans for a postern."

"You can't tell the *geroi!*" The words burst out of me involuntarily, and I want to clap my hands over my own mouth in horror. But it's too late. His expression is changing now, turning thoughtful.

"Maybe I won't," he says. "But you have to tell me what it is first."

I have no choice. He'll likely tell them either way, but if I stay quiet now, my fate is sealed.

"It's a project Gitrin has been working on," I begin. Technically true, though it was my idea initially. Even though no one but the *geroi* can read the System to tell if I'm lying, I've gotten in the habit of telling partial truths to everyone, to cover my tracks just in case.

"Involving postern travel?" Ceilos asks.

I tug my earlobe. "Postern travel uses tesseract technology to open a passage in three dimensions—through space. But I"—quickly, I backtrack—"I mean, Gitrin suggested that this technology may be able to be adapted to operate in four dimensions."

Ceilos blinks. "Through time?"

I tug my earlobe again. "Think about it. What if we could go back into Iamos' history and warn our ancestors about the climate disaster? Then we could prevent it. We could save Iamos."

Ceilos' brows furrow thoughtfully, and he sinks into the chair beside me. "It makes sense... theoretically."

"Gitrin and I had the System run the calculations, and it all checks out. The time postern is possible." I sigh. "But Gitrin brought our findings to the *gerotus* today, and..." I trail off.

Ceilos is quiet a moment. "They said no?"

I swallow. "They said no."

He watches me. "But you're still working on it, aren't you? Even though they told you not to?"

I open my mouth, but I can't formulate a response. Finally, I manage, "It will work. I know it will."

"Can I see it?" Ceilos asks.

I hesitate. Ceilos has spoken more to me in these past five minutes than he has the whole time he's been in Hope Renewed. Why? Is it so he can report me to the *geroi?* Does he want to see me in trouble? Or maybe he's had the same thought as me—he wants a repartnership, and if he catches me doing something forbidden, he'll have ammunition to use against me to the *gerotus*. What will become of me then?

But there's an earnest quality in his green eyes that's unlike any I've seen before. The smooth charm he uses around the *geroi* has fallen away like a mask. This feels like the first time I've ever seen the real Ceilos.

Before I can change my mind, I open the System panel again, swipe the screen a few times, and rotate it to show him.

He leans close, looking at the plans on the projected screen. He swipes, his expression growing more pensive.

"This will work," he says at last.

"Do you think so?" I ask eagerly.

"I know so." He meets my gaze, holding my eyes long enough that my face starts to get hot under his scrutiny. Then he grins, and I am taken aback. "I underestimated you," he says.

I'm not sure how to reply to that. But before I can dwell on it for too long, he gives me a conspiratorial look.

"You shared your secret with me," he says, and he brings a hand to his earpiece. "Now I want to show you something, too."

I opened my eyes slowly, dimly registering as the cave around me took the place of the cave from my dream. I wasn't in that comparatively spacious room in the *geroi*'s villa anymore. This cave was small, stuffy. Unlike the tunnels, there was not enough air trapped in here to allow us to breathe without our oxygen tanks, and the mask was digging into my face uncomfortably.

I lay on my back, staring up at the ceiling, sorting through the memory that my dreams had produced for me tonight. It was odd, the way things that had felt unimportant at the time suddenly seemed to hold so much insight. Things about why I was the way I was. Why Ceilos was the way he was. Why we'd become what we'd become.

Finally, I sat up and looked around. I no longer felt sleepy, just cramped and uncomfortable. The cave was dark, and the sky beyond the cave mouth showed that dawn was still a long way off. Isaak had agreed to take a watch with the *gurzas* so Nikos could get some sleep. So I crawled out of the cave opening to join him.

I didn't see him at first. Then, at last, I saw his silhouette seated next to the mounded hump of Tuupa and Thork's entwined bodies. His profile was illuminated by the blinding array of stars overhead.

Quietly, I came over to sit beside him. He started, letting in a sharp intake of breath; then he relaxed, recognizing me.

"What's up?" he asked.

"Couldn't sleep. Well, more like woke up and couldn't fall back asleep," I admitted. "I keep thinking about everything that happened earlier. The *tirak*, the storm. And then everything Nikos said, and... and Ceilos." I tried to keep my tone neutral.

Isaak looked away from me, staring up at the sky. "Sorry I got into it with him earlier. I probably overreacted. But what he said was not okay. It reminded me of all the crap Henry used to say when we were in school that would get me so torqued at him."

I adjusted the uncomfortable mask over my nose and mouth. What Ceilos had said had got me thinking, and that, I thought, must have been what prompted the dream. It had been a long time since I'd heard him talk that way, but as I'd dozed off to sleep, I'd realized it hadn't been the first.

"*Do you always do everything the* geroi *tell you to do?*" He'd asked me that when he first came to Hope Renewed. It had been just one of many snide comments he'd made those first days—when he spoke to me at all. But my dream had reminded me of how things had changed. What made Ceilos start looking at me differently.

It had been that day after Gitrin had presented our theory on the time postern to the *geroi* for the first time and they'd told us it was unfeasible. Melusin and Antos had forbidden me from continuing to work on it. But I'd done it anyway.

Ceilos had found out. And after that, he started treating me differently. He'd realized I wasn't just a *geroi*'s pet who did everything they told me after all. And then he'd shown me his own project: his cloaking protocol. The way he could go offline, sneak around the citidome unseen. Just a bit of harmless fun, a way for him to get out from under the *geroi*'s ever-watchful eye. When he'd shared it with me, he'd taken a risk, just as I had when I told him about the time postern. But that risk had brought us closer. We'd formed a bond of by sharing our secrets, and Ceilos had become my first true friend.

But there was more to it. Maybe it had just been a bit of fun, but we'd been working together against the *geroi* in our own little ways, hadn't we? I hadn't thought about it that way. But I realized now that he had. He'd been so angry earlier about the people who'd stood by and allowed the *geroi* to take power without pushing back. But the way he'd seen it, we weren't just standing by. The two of us had been pushing back.

But if Ceilos had felt so strongly about the *geroi*, why had he been willing to go along with Tibros' mad plan to betray the rebels? I knew that answer now, too, and it made my skin burn with shame. Because of me. Ceilos had had every reason to believe that I wanted to be a part of the *geroi*'s world. So he'd gone along with it, because it was what I wanted. Because no matter how he felt about the *geroi*, I was more important to him.

His one true friend.

Isaak was still looking at the sky, seemingly unaware of the uncomfortable turn my thoughts had taken. "It's crazy to me," he said, "how the stars here are the same as they are at home, even though everything else is so different." He chuckled softly. "You know, when I was a kid, my mom would send me to Science Camp every annum over Easter break. They'd take us out at night in the freezing cold and teach us how to recognize the constellations. The ones we can see in the spring and the ones we can see in the fall, depending on which season Easter fell in."

I watched him silently. I didn't know what *Easter* was, but it was unimportant. I wanted to hear this—this glimpse at Isaak's life before I knew him. His own childhood.

"I always had the easiest time with my boy Orion," he said, pointing at the cluster of stars my people called Oryos. "And the Big Dipper, of course." Then he trailed off, frowning. "I don't know that one, though."

He pointed, and I followed the direction with my eyes. A large star glowed on the horizon, bigger and brighter than the star we called Seirios.

"I've never seen that before, either," I said, trying to think. I hadn't often seen the sky directly, without the glass of the citidome between myself and it. But I didn't recall seeing this star when we were on our journey to Elytherios. It was new.

I suddenly found I was having trouble breathing, and it wasn't because my oxygen tank needed changing.

"*An incredibly massive piece of space debris struck Earth at that time. Possibly a comet, or an asteroid.*"

I barely registered the sound of footsteps behind us, Isaak turning to look at the approaching figure.

"*The impact was devastating to our planet.*"

How could I have forgotten? Things had been so hectic, so jumbled and confused, that Professor Senghas' words from the museum had fled from my mind. With Hamos still above us in the night sky, big and steady and bright as it always had been, the horrific memory of that tiny yellow star I'd seen on Mars had seemed like nothing more than a bad dream, a worry for a different time and a different place.

Maybe I'd just assumed that we still had time. That we could make it through everything else that was falling apart around us before it was too late. I should have known better. Of course that would be too good to be true.

"I thought I heard voices," the old man said, coming to sit beside Isaak and me. As always, the *kerkopith* was attached to him, balanced on his shoulder. "What're you doing out here, anyway?"

The Clovis impact.

"Emil," Isaak said, his voice strained, almost strangled-sounding. "I have a question."

Emil narrowed his eyes curiously. "Well, spit it out, then."

"If there was an asteroid heading for us... Like, a really, really big one..."

He swallowed. I squeezed my eyes shut. I didn't want to hear the rest of this sentence. Didn't want to hear the answer. But I knew it was coming, just as I knew what it was we were looking at in the sky overhead beyond a shadow of a doubt.

"How long before it hits would we be able to see it?"

PART SIX

EARTH

2075 C.E.

CHAPTER 33

- h e n r y -

I TENSED, POISING ON THE BALLS OF MY FEET, STARING THE MAN DOWN, MY hands involuntarily curling into fists. Instantly shifting into fight or flight mode. *Geoff Preston, here.* It should have been impossible. Lizeth had insisted that the Stateless had impenetrable security. How had GSAF managed to infiltrate them—and not just anywhere, but in the home of the organization's shadow leader?

"Wait a minute, wait a minute," Lizeth said quickly, leaping in front of me and holding her hands up, trying to disarm me before the situation escalated. "Let me explain. Mother said that she was bringing someone else to the meeting, someone who would help us figure out our next steps."

"And you didn't feel the need to share that info with me earlier? He's with GSAF!" I protested. "He was on Lago Verde the day you guys busted us out." The last time I'd seen him had been the night before everything had gone down, when I'd been locked in a pool house with an ankle monitor on my leg. He'd tried to deal with me—the System in exchange for my freedom. He'd most definitely not been on our side.

"He was on the inside the day our organization raided the island," Lizeth's mother corrected me.

"He's been working with GSAF on the System," I argued.

"As I've consistently maintained every time I've met with any of you, I am affiliated with GalaX, not GSAF," Preston said.

"Same difference!" Scylla shouted.

"If you don't *mind.*" Lizeth's mother raised her voice over the top of all of us, her tone cold. "You are guests in my home, and I want you to behave in a civilized manner. There is no need to shout." The room grew quiet at her command. I could tell by her expression that she was used to that. Used to being obeyed.

"That's better. Now, if you would all please take a seat"—she gestured to a sitting area against the far wall, made up of a couch and a few plush armchairs—"we can discuss this like adults."

I eyed Preston suspiciously but sat on the couch nevertheless. Tamara sat beside me, and Scylla beside her; Preston pushed the cushioned chair he'd been sitting on over to us, and Lizeth and her mother each perched on one of the armchairs.

"Let's start over. I am Carla Perez."

"You're the head of the Stateless," Scylla said.

She sniffed. "I am the founder, chief strategist, and primary financier of a covert organization dedicated to the principles of universal stateless governance and the deregulation of transnational commercial cooperatives."

I blinked at her. "So you're an ancap?"

She folded her arms across her chest. "I'm a liberty activist. And the rest of you are...?"

"Henry Sandhu. Also a liberty activist." I could literally *feel* Scylla preparing to argue about the *deregulating transnational commercial cooperatives* thing, so before she could speak, I quickly added, "And these are my associates, Tamara Randall-Torres and Scylla Hwang."

Scylla glowered but kept her mouth shut.

"And who is he?" Tamara asked, gesturing to Preston.

His mouth turned up at the corner. "Geoff Preston. I'm the one who sent you the note."

The room was silent for a long moment. My jaw dropped. Of all the answers I'd been expecting, that was definitely not it.

"*You* sent Henry the note?" Scylla repeated incredulously. "But you work for GSAF."

"GalaX," Preston corrected once again, sounding testy.

"But, Mr. Preston," Tamara said in a more conciliatory tone, "Isaak told us that you were the one who was in charge of the System at the meeting with the GSAF Council."

"Not by choice," Preston said. "As you'll recall, I made multiple offers to work with both the Iamoi and the Free Mars movement that would have prevented that incident. Nadin refused, and Henry did as well. So I was left with no other alternative."

Scylla blew out a frustrated breath. "But you wanted the System!"

"Will you stop interrupting him?" Lizeth said. "Give him a chance to explain."

"Okay," I said. "Start at the beginning. Who are you really?"

Preston paused before answering to smooth out the lapels of his light-gray jacket. "I'm the chief director of a non-publicly disclosed division of GalaX called ConneX."

"ConneX?" Tamara repeated. "I've never heard of that." I doubted her moms had, either. They'd tried looking into Preston when he'd first made contact with us, but they hadn't been able to learn anything.

Preston sat back in his chair, crossing his legs. "You wouldn't have. As you of all people are aware, GalaX began as an aerospace manufacturer, but it has grown to become the largest corporation on Earth. It's the parent company to dozens of subsidiary corporations: AresTec, Rainier, GalaX Habi, GalaX Air, just to name a few. ConneX is just one of those many subsidiaries. But its existence is classified, known only to some of the highest-ranking executives at GalaX and few others."

"Including Joseph Condor and the GSAF Council?" said Scylla.

"Of course."

"Get to the point, Mr. Preston," I said. "What is ConneX, exactly?"

He exhaled, looking down. I was right—he was stalling. I had a feeling I knew what he was going to say, and he knew we weren't going to like it.

"I believe you're aware of the research of Professor David Hassan."

I nodded. That was Emil's real name.

"Back in the 2030s, when GalaX was working with NASA on the MarsEpoch colonization project, Professor Hassan's team at JPL found evidence of previous sentient life on Mars. His work was discredited, but as we all now know, his theories were correct." Preston uncrossed his legs and crossed them again in the other direction. "As NASA and ESA and the other global space agencies consolidated into GSAF, they commissioned GalaX to conduct further research on the pre-modern Martian settlements. This is how we discovered the System."

The System. It all came down to the System.

"We soon deduced that what we'd discovered was an ancient computer system. So GSAF continued to work with GalaX in order to figure out what we were dealing with. And moreover, to gain access to it and hopefully restore function."

I glanced at Tamara, and past her to Scylla. They both were frowning deeply.

"I've been in charge of the team of contractors working with GSAF on this assignment for roughly the last decade. We had tight security clearances and worked under stringent non-disclosure agreements. No one was allowed to know anything about the work that was being done or even about our existence at the company. Hence why your mothers were unable to dig up any dirt on me," he said wryly to Tamara. "But it was only thanks to Mr. Sandhu's assistance that we were finally able to decode M-VHLL and gain access to the System. That we were able to recognize it for what it truly was. And for the potential that it held."

My stomach clenched. *Potential.* I knew only too well about that *potential.* And he was right. It was my fault that they'd unlocked that potential in the first place. Decoding M-VHLL—decoding the System— was squarely on my head. All because I'd agreed to work with Condor instead of fighting back. *"Reckless behavior can leave collateral damage."* No torquing kidding.

"It was at that point that GalaX made the decision to move the programmers and engineers who'd been working on the System project to a new division. ConneX."

"But what *is* ConneX?" Tamara asked. "What does it *do?*"

"Let me take a guess," I said. "System integration."

Preston arched a brow. "Nail on the head, Mr. Sandhu. ConneX researches and develops ways to implement certain System functions into existing Earth technology."

"Like Speculus Nano," Scylla said flatly.

"Which System functions are you talking about here, exactly?" Lizeth asked.

"When he ran into us at Lal Qila—me and Mariyah and Nadin—he told us a bunch of crap about how GalaX wanted to use the System to further world peace and stuff," said Scylla. "But I can't shake the feeling that it was just that. A bunch of crap."

"That was, in fact, one of ConneX's intended goals," Preston said defensively. "The interconnectivity of humans, growing to understand one another, increasing empathy... Those are all admirable goals that GalaX and ConneX are proud to support. But as a business, our primary focus is always going to be finding innovative ways to increase profit margins. That's just the nature of the beast."

"Ah," I said. "There we have it. Profit margins. You thought you could make money off the System."

Tamara looked baffled. "How?"

"Advertisers." I looked sardonically at Preston. "Am I right?"

He nodded. "System compatibility would be an incredible draw for advertisers and investors. With its ability to subliminally influence users to purchase particular goods and services—"

"Are you torquing serious here?" Scylla demanded. "With everything you know about what the System is capable of—"

Carla Perez interrupted sharply, "Let him *speak*, please."

Preston held up a placating hand. "Things have changed now, Miss Hwang. I'm merely trying to explain to you what ConneX's *intention* was. But that was months ago. I've had reservations about the viability of that option for quite some time, and that was only exacerbated after the conversations I had with Nadin. There's still too much that we don't know about the System, how it works. That was why we wanted to negotiate with Nadin, why I attempted to meet with her twice before the conference with the GSAF Council. And why I tried to appeal to your connection to her at Lago Verde, Henry. With a native user at our disposal, and the promise of more experts from Iamos to work at ConneX in the future, we could learn to use the System efficiently and beneficially without accidental harm to the userbase."

"Don't you think that brainwashing people to buy products without their consent is harmful?" Scylla demanded.

Preston looked affronted. "The user agreement for Speculus Nano opts the users into advertising."

"No one ever reads user agreements!" Scylla looked like she was about to leap out of her seat.

"Miss Hwang, look around you," Carla Perez broke in. "This

organization only exists because businesspeople like myself and Mr. Preston are willing to risk our positions, our fortunes, and, frankly, our lives on this cause. And the only reason you're here and not in a windowless cell in a maximum-security prison right now is because of us. So please show our guest some more respect."

Scylla scowled, crossing her arms and slumping down in her seat.

"Regardless," Preston said, satisfied that Scylla had been put duly in her place, "Nadin declined to negotiate, so we were left without any alternative. We had a contract with GSAF, and I couldn't stall any longer." He smoothed his jacket lapel again. "But after the incident at Lago Verde, all my reservations about the System were laid bare. It is clearly capable of causing much more damage to its users than any of us thought possible. Full integration with Speculus Nano now, when we don't understand the full risk, is a major liability for our corporation. And beyond that, from a moral standpoint, it's unethical. I can't stand behind it."

I frowned, remembering what his note had said. *The System is online. Be careful of anyone with Nano.*

"I have a feeling there's something you're not telling us, Mr. Preston," I said.

He nodded grimly.

"Unfortunately, despite my reservations, there are certain elements that have been set into motion that I can't stop now," he said. "ConneX pushed a firmware update months ago to the nanobots to make them System compatible. They've been ready for integration for some time."

He hesitated. I could tell that wasn't all, but he was reluctant to say the rest. That could only mean bad news.

"And?" I pressed.

"And, in order to apprehend the fugitives of Lago Verde—who, I have been assured, pose a dangerous threat to our democracy—the board of directors at GalaX has agreed to turn all of our resources over to GSAF. Including full access to ConneX."

Beside me, Tamara blanched. Lizeth, who'd been remarkably reserved throughout this entire conference, jumped to her feet in a fury. "You're saying that GSAF has full access to the System, and that the System is fully integrated into the nanobots?"

"Not yet. It will take them some time to sort through everything and implement it. But they will soon."

"How soon?" I asked.

"About a month. Maybe a bit less."

"Now you understand why I insisted you come here immediately," Carla Perez said. "You see that this changes everything."

"But what are we supposed to do about it?" Tamara asked. "We can't stop the System without Nadin. And we don't know if—if she—" She broke off, her eyes doing that glazed-over thing they did when her anxiety was threatening to overtake her.

"She won't be back until the end of August," I amended, sounding more confident than I felt.

"That's around when GSAF will have the System online. That may be too late," Preston said.

"We can't rely on the Martian princess," Carla Perez said. "We can't waste this chance. This is just the opportunity the Stateless has been waiting for."

"How so?" Scylla asked.

"Mars is the weakest link," Lizeth said, sinking back into her chair. "When Henry leaked the existence of the System eight months ago, it inspired a movement. That movement got derailed when Isaak returned with Nadin, and the twenty-four-hour news cycle pounced on the Martian princess. We need to get the train back on its tracks." She glanced at her mother with an arched eyebrow. "Right?"

"Precisely."

"But to do that, we need to get the word out that GSAF using the System against its citizens isn't theoretical," I said. "Before, the government still had plausible deniability. Their official position was they were merely researching the ancient tech and had no intention of using it. Now we have proof that GSAF has done everything they swore they weren't going to. But we have to get that info to the people."

I looked at Geoff Preston. He met my gaze unflinchingly but said nothing.

"Well?" I demanded.

"I gave you the information," he said. "I trust you'll know what to do with it."

I gawked at him. "I'm sorry, you're expecting *me* to be your whistleblower?"

He shrugged. "You did such a good job the first time."

"Coward!" Scylla shouted. "You mean to tell us that you know what's going on at GalaX and you're not going to do anything about it?"

"I am doing something about it."

"Oh, yeah, sure," she snapped. "You put it off on us while you keep your cushy job at ConneX, and we get to take the heat for it."

"Scylla, don't you get it?" Lizeth argued. "We need him on the inside. We need him to continue funneling information for us. And remember what his note said—the only reason GSAF hasn't found us yet is because he's overwriting the data that would lead them right to us. We can't jeopardize that."

Scylla huffed, flopping back into her seat on the couch.

I ran my thumb over my bottom lip, thinking. "We need to get back to Mars." Not just because of Isaak and Nadin. Not anymore. Now the survival of the entire Martian liberation movement—the only chance at freedom for both Mars and Earth—hinged on us getting out ahead of GSAF.

Carla Perez nodded. "Lizeth will make the arrangements and organize a strike team."

It was an order, not a request. But Lizeth nodded without protest.

"We'll need our own people, too," I said. "Not just the Stateless. We need the Free Mars movement."

I looked over at Scylla, and she grunted, still looking annoyed. "If someone gives me a way to get in touch with ProLibertate, I can let him know to have the gang ready to hit the streets."

That took care of everything except the obvious elephant in the room: How the hell were we supposed to get the leak out when GSAF had us on the run? And before it was too late to stop them?

We'd have to figure it out along the way. Preston and Lizeth's mother had made it obvious they weren't going to help us. I was beginning to see why the members of the Stateless considered Lizeth the true leader of the movement—all her mom seemed to want to do was bark out orders and demand results. But they had put us in an extremely precarious situation. If we couldn't figure something out, it would all be over. It was enough to make me want to punch something.

"Well, if that's everything..." Carla Perez started to say.

"Wait. There's just one more thing I need to know," I said. "Does GSAF have Nadin's medallion?"

Preston nodded. "Unfortunately. It was recovered in the aftermath of the Stateless raid."

"There are some things that are restricted to *geroi* DNA, but a lot of it can be overridden if the user is in possession of one of those medallions," I said.

"I know." He looked grim. "They've already made significant progress in accessing a number of functions that were previously available only to *geroi* and Enforcers because of that medallion."

"So you're saying they've got the adherence protocol."

He nodded again. "And the reeducation protocol as well."

Scylla gawked at him. "Reeducation? Like, wiping your memories and turning you into GSAF's willing slave?"

"That's the theory, yes."

"And we've got one month to stop them before they can use it on anyone who tries to get in their way," I said.

"Only people who have Nano," Tamara pointed out.

"That's over four-point-five billion active users across both worlds," Preston said. "More than half the total population of Earth and Mars combined."

I stared at him in horror.

Lizeth cursed. "There's no time to waste. We've got to get to Mars. Now."

"My dear child," Carla Perez said, getting to her feet. "That's what I've been trying to tell you."

CHAPTER 34

I KEPT STARING AT THE CANVAS PRINT OVER LIZETH'S MOM'S DESK. IT WAS the only bright spot in the room. The walls of her study were windowless, which made sense, considering the covert nature of her activities, but it was claustrophobic. It made me feel boxed in. The room was paneled in a dark wood, which made the feeling that I was trapped in an underground box even stronger, but since this room was soundproof, we needed to stay here to carry out all of our assignments.

Well, most of us, anyway.

Ms. Perez had a number of encrypted burner palmtops and Speculus headsets at her disposal. She gave those to Lizeth with instructions to start making the arrangements while she and Mr. Preston put in some public appearances, wining and dining for whatever reason he'd given GalaX and GSAF for coming to the UFS in the first place. Once her mother was gone, Lizeth set to organizing transportation for us and started contacting members of the Stateless to make up the team. Meanwhile, Scylla and Henry got on chat with ProLibertate and some of the other leaders of the Free Mars movement.

And I sat there feeling relatively useless.

I glanced around the room while my friends' voices blended together into an unintelligible hum. The carpet of the study was plush, deep-pile and a rich burgundy color. The wall across from the sitting area featured an alcove with built-in shelves, but unlike at Professor Senghas' house, these shelves held no books. There were a few industry awards that Ms. Perez's corporations had won, some carved out of frosted glass, some trimmed with gold, like trophies. In between these, a decorative, old-fashioned globe here, a minimalist statuette there. A potted plant that, it seemed to me, must have been artificial because there was no natural light to be found in this elegant prison cell.

Over Lizeth's mother's desk there was a large, unframed canvas print of an artist's rendering of Sea-Star Island, the seastead on which this mansion was located, and that was where my eye kept landing. I knew Ms. Perez also owned at least one private stead—likely more than one—but she'd chosen this resort island as her base of operations. That seemed risky to me, but Lizeth had pointed out that most of her mother's time was not spent on the rebel organization, but rather on publicly acceptable ventures. And Carla Perez struck me as the sort of woman who enjoyed others seeing her wealth.

I could see now why Lizeth was so uptight when she talked about her mother. The two of them were as different as night and day. They seemed to have radically different ideas about what their rebel group was rebelling about, too. Ms. Perez had said the Stateless was dedicated to creating a system of stateless governance; she'd talked about free markets and deregulating corporations. That was a completely different explanation than the one Lizeth had given us. She'd said the word *stateless* was a reflection of the disenfranchisement of the people on Earth, left without a voice or a vote by the global adoption of passive citizenry—which meant that only those who could afford to own property, pay taxes on it, and who didn't take the universal basic income were allowed to vote or hold office. She'd said they were fighting to take the power away from oligarchs and bureaucrats and give it back to the people. The people of Earth, who had been cut out of the political process by those with enough money to make rules they themselves were exempt from; and the people of Mars, where all offices were appointed by GSAF and an election had never even been held.

So which one was it? Maybe the two goals weren't in total conflict, but I wasn't so sure. After all, how much different would things be if the government were dissolved, but the worlds were run by megacorporations instead? If GalaX had their way, the System would still be implemented on Speculus Nano. It was just that instead of using the reeducation protocol to force citizens to comply, they'd be using those same brainwashing techniques to trick people into buying products. How much better would that be?

I sighed, looking at the picture of the island again and thinking of home. My parents had a coffee table in our living room that had a shadowbox set into the top. They'd filled it with sand from this island and shells they'd found on the beach. Among those was a sand dollar with a notch in the corner. A gift that Mom had given Mama the first time they'd met. They'd been younger then than I was now. I'd heard the story so often, I could recite it in my sleep. They hadn't started dating then; they'd only known each other for a few days, when Mom had been here on a graduation trip and Mama had been doing her gap year tech program. But Mama had kept that sand dollar. And years later, when they'd run into each other again at a MarsEpoch orientation... Mama said she'd known it could be nothing else but fate.

I smiled wistfully. We'd been here many times on vacation growing up. The only place on Earth we'd visited more was Belfast, to see my Nan and Uncle Finn, Mama's younger brother. I hadn't talked to my relatives on Earth in a while, but I suspected that GSAF had rounded them up for questioning the same as they had Isaak's. I hoped they were okay now.

"Okay, team huddle," Lizeth said, setting down her palmtop and coming back over to the sitting area. She flopped down in the chair her mother had sat in earlier. "Here's the plan. We can't take a passenger ship to Mars. At the very least, you three can't because, obviously, people will see you."

"So what do we take instead?" Scylla asked, removing her Speculus headset.

"We'll have to take a cargo ship. Unmanned, no chance of being seen."

"And that also means no artificial gravity," said Henry.

"That's okay. It's just ten days," I pointed out.

"Actually," Lizeth said, "it's going to be more than that. More like... twice that."

"*Twice* that?" Scylla repeated. "As in, almost three weeks?"

"A little under twenty days," said Lizeth. "Cargo ships travel slower. Passenger ships don't land, remember. They stay in constant orbit, and they get a gravity boost from the way they structure their routes. That cuts down on their travel time. But cargo ships actually touch down, so it's slower for them to get going."

Henry cursed. "I forgot about that. I should have factored in more time—"

Lizeth waved him off. "It doesn't matter anymore. If you hadn't forced our hand, GSAF would have. We're just going to have to make it work."

"But how are we going to get on a cargo ship?" Scylla asked.

"We're going to use a smuggling network. The people we're dealing with transport luxury goods from Earth to Mars duty-free. They said they'd be willing to sneak some duty-free humans in. You know, for a price."

Henry smirked. "Naturally."

Lizeth leaned back in her seat and kicked her shoes off. "So that's logistic number one taken care of. Logistic two is how we get from here to the smugglers' base. They operate out of a lunar storage facility. But we can't take a spacejet there. Those only are able to do low-planetary orbit, to intercept with passenger liners. So." She took a sip of water from a glass her mother had left on an end table. "We're going to have to use an RPS to get from here to the moon and then transfer to the cargo ship."

I winced. RPS. Rocket-propelled spacecraft. They were a lot less reliable than spacejets, and there were more risks associated with them. The odds of them exploding on takeoff were significantly higher, for a start. That usually didn't matter as much because their only contents were typically cargo. But this time, the cargo was going to be of the living variety.

Lizeth saw my expression and shrugged. "It's a risk we're just going to have to take. But because of that, we need to minimize the number of people who are traveling with us. That way, if something happens..." She trailed off, making a gesture with her hand. "The Stateless can go on without us."

I looked down at the floor, trying to ignore the familiar crawling sensation in my stomach—only heightened by the sensation that I was currently trapped inside an elaborate, overlarge coffin.

"Okay," Henry said. "So we know how we're going to get there. But we still have to figure out the game plan for once we actually get to

Mars."

"ProLibertate is working on getting Free Mars onto the streets as soon as the leak goes out. He's concerned about GSAF's reaction, though," Scylla said.

"I'm sorry, you call this guy by his screen name in real life?" Lizeth asked, one eyebrow raised.

Henry shrugged. "His real name is something really generic. Like, Gordon or something."

"You think Gordon is generic?"

"I dunno. Probably."

"*Anyway*," Scylla said. "GSAF has been cracking down on demonstrations. It's only gotten worse since Condor became governor. The curfew has gotten tighter, and they're enforcing it more strictly. They're basically not letting anyone outside after dark at this point. So ProL—Gordon—whoever—he's worried that GSAF will just arrest everyone and keep the movement from being able to gain any traction."

"They can't arrest everyone. Not if we have a big enough crowd," said Henry.

"It's a moot point." Lizeth took another swallow of water. "We're not going to be able to overthrow GSAF just with street protests. Those will help influence public opinion, but historically, just about every successful revolution has relied on getting the defense forces on the side of the rebels. On Earth that would usually be the army, but Mars doesn't have a standing military, right?"

Henry shook his head. "No military. No need. Not as of yet, anyway. It's not like there are neighboring enemies to contend with. There's provincial law enforcement, and then there are GSAF's agents."

"What are the odds that we can turn them against GSAF?"

He ran his thumb across his bottom lip. "We might be able to if we had Ponsford."

"Ponsford?" Lizeth repeated.

"Yeah. Kate Ponsford, the former governor. Her son, Wyatt, was a member of Free Mars. He's helped us before. Condor was able to pull off a coup, but I think that we could manage a counter-coup if we had her on our side. The only issue is, I don't know where she is. She was taken into custody the same time I was, and so was Wyatt for helping Nadin.

I'm not sure what happened after that, or where they wound up. But my guard when I was in custody said a lot of people at GSAF are not happy with the way things are going. Kate Ponsford was a popular governor. It sounds like Condor's got a small core group of loyal followers, but they don't make up the majority."

"So if we can get the Ponsfords away from GSAF, we might be able to mobilize that silent majority around Kate as the leader." Lizeth pulled her feet up onto the chair. "And you're sure that she would be willing to support our movement?"

"I think so. Like I said, Wyatt was a member of Free Mars. Beyond that, Kate declined to prosecute me for whistleblowing. And she helped Nadin try to get the time door to Iamos open on Mars, even though she hadn't been authorized to do so by the GSAF Council. That's how Joseph Condor was able to have her removed from power."

"So we can most likely count on her being an ally. It's a risk we'll have to take." Lizeth sighed. I could tell she was thinking about the last risk she'd taken in order to gain a potential ally—the Elytherioi—and how well that had worked out for us. "Okay. First order of business when we get to Mars is Kate Ponsford. I'll mobilize the Stateless intelligence branch and have them pinpoint where she's being held."

"But what do we do once we find her?" Scylla asked. "She's sure to be in maximum security."

"We get her out," Lizeth said, as if it were the simplest thing in the worlds. She slouched down in her seat, wrapping her arms around her knees. I thought about how stiffly Carla Perez had sat in that same chair, her back ramrod straight, her shoulders back. Lizeth's poor posture almost seemed like an act of rebellion in contrast. "Once that's done, we'll have the enforcement class on our side. That will help. But we'll also need militia presence on the streets."

Scylla snorted. "Good luck with that. Weapons are banned on Mars, and most countries on Earth, too."

My mouth went dry. *Militia? Weapons?*

"Through official channels," Lizeth said. "What about unofficial ones?"

"Wait a minute," I burst in. My heart was racing in my chest. "You guys can't be serious, right? You're legitimately talking about *shooting* people?"

Lizeth stared at me incredulously. "I've got news for you, princess. This is a revolution now. It's war. There are going to be casualties. That's just the way it is."

"I thought that if we got GSAF's agents on our side..."

"You think the GSAF Council is just going to roll over and let us take their planet?" Lizeth scoffed. "Even if the bulk of the enforcement class sides with Ponsford, there are going to be loyalists. You said yourselves that Joseph Condor does have a core group, even if it's a small one. And the Council will send people in from Earth if we don't get a decisive victory before they get a chance to. Actual military, not just agents. We're going to need to be ready for them."

I had tunnel vision. I blinked, trying to clear it, but of course that didn't help. I fumbled in my pocket for the rosary, squeezing the beads between my fingers so hard, it hurt.

"Hang on. I'm with Tamara on this one," Henry said. "I want this to be as bloodless as possible."

"We all *want* that," Lizeth said. "I'm just saying that it might not be possible, and we need to be prepared for the alternative."

Henry shook his head. "No. No violating the NAP."

"The NAP? The torquing non-aggression principle?" Lizeth groaned. "Henry, the government is inherently an aggressor."

"The ordinary people working for GSAF aren't, though. They're just doing their jobs."

Her eyes flashed. "They will 'do their jobs' and see us all killed. Then *they'll* have violated the NAP and we'll be too dead to fight back."

"No need to be snarky."

"We need to have a quick and decisive victory. The longer this drags out, the worse it's going to be."

"You managed it when you got us out of Lago Verde. Structural damage without human casualties."

"Well, we had time to plan that in advance, didn't we?" Lizeth snapped. "But I don't have that kind of time now, as you may recall. Between you and GSAF, I've got a deadline here."

Henry exhaled. "Okay. Point taken. I'm sorry."

Lizeth's prickliness seemed to soften at his apology.

"Let's try to make it a point that we'll avoid violence as much as we can," Scylla said.

"Agreed. But we also need to be prepared to defend ourselves if attacked," said Lizeth.

"Okay. That's fair," Henry said, though my stomach still felt tied up in a knot. "So, we've got a gameplan for what we do once the leak is out. But that doesn't solve the problem of how we get the leak out in the first place."

I sat up, eager for the change in subject. I'd given that some thought while I'd been sitting here twiddling my thumbs, and I had an idea. "I think—"

"We don't have time to worry about that right now," Lizeth said over the top of me. "We've got too many other logistics to plan for, and we have to leave in the morning. We can figure it out on the way."

"Yeah, but my—"

She acted like she didn't even hear me. "We can utilize Stateless resources once we're on Mars. Dante is organizing a team. The best of the best. They should land on Mars next Wednesday or Thursday, depending on their flight schedule. They'll be there a full ten days before we arrive, so they'll have time to get things in motion while we're still en route."

I sighed. I supposed my idea could wait.

"Dante won't be coming with us on the RPS?" Scylla asked. "I thought you two were, like, glued at the hip."

Lizeth hesitated. "No. Bruno is going to be staying on Earth to coordinate support from this side of things. That makes Dante my second-in-command for this mission. So he can't be on the RPS, just in case..." She trailed off, swallowed, and switched gears. "The RPS holds six people. We make up four. One of the smugglers will be along for the flight, in case manual override is needed, and to ensure we are safely transferred to the cargo vessel. The last seat is going to Zero."

Henry laughed incredulously. "Zero? Are you torquing kidding me? You gave Tamara shit for coming but you're bringing *Zero*? I thought you said this team was supposed to be 'the best of the best.'" He made air quotes with his fingers.

Lizeth's face clouded. "It is," she said coldly.

Henry scoffed. "Zero is a hairstylist."

"They're also a trained street medic."

"We've got street medics in Free Mars."

"Well, you're going to have one more, then," Lizeth snapped.

I watched Lizeth thoughtfully. There were three people she counted in her inner circle. Her brother was one, and the second, Dante, seemed to be her boyfriend. The third was Zero, a non-binary aesthetician with a lavender undercut and a thick southern drawl, who'd helped the group of us reshape our appearances before going on the run. If the only other two she allowed to know her secrets were that close to her personally, it followed that Zero must be, too. When we'd been back in Florida, she and Zero had had a clear rapport, and they'd called each other nicknames.

Zero was one of her best friends. And even if Henry couldn't understand it, I knew why she would want them to come.

"Lay off her," I said. "The three of us have each other. Lizeth deserves to have a trusted friend coming with her now, too. The RPS is dangerous, and she's nervous—"

Lizeth barked out a laugh. "You must be joking."

I blinked. "I'm sorry?"

Her face was red, flushed. Her voice shook a little as she snapped, "You think I'm *nervous*? Do you think that I could do what I do every day if I got nervous?"

"It's normal to be nervous," I stammered. "I get—"

"Please. We all can tell what *you* get. But I'm nothing like you."

I felt like she'd slapped me.

"Don't talk to her that way," Henry said, his voice as cold as ice.

"Okay, calm down," Scylla said, getting off the couch and physically inserting herself between the three of us. "I know everyone is stressed, and we're all tired. We've been arguing a lot over the last week. But we need to hang in there, right? If we want this to succeed. If we want to save our worlds. We can't be at each other's throats."

Henry glared at Lizeth for another long moment. He didn't look like he was going to back down.

"It's fine," I said, putting my hand on his shoulder. I didn't want to drag this out any more—or make Lizeth even more torqued off at me than she already was, for whatever reason. "It's normal to have disagreements, but we're allies. It's not going to do us any good if we aren't able to get along."

"I thought we were more than just allies," Scylla said. "I thought we were all friends."

Henry snorted. "You think everyone's your friend, Scylla."

She laughed and sat back down. "That's because everyone *is* my friend."

Lizeth exhaled. "Okay. If we're done here, I've got more calls to make. And you all do, too."

Henry and Scylla did, anyway. I still hadn't been given an assignment. I looked up at Lizeth as she stood and started to move back over to her mother's desk. "Is there anything you want me to—"

She pointedly ignored me.

Henry watched me for a minute, reaching over and squeezing my hand. Then he put his Speculus headset back on.

Hours passed, the others working furiously, fingers flying across digital membranes as they typed out messages, voices blurring together in a hum as they made calls.

I sat quietly on the couch, trying not to get in anyone's way and wondering what exactly I was doing there.

Chapter 35

- h e n r y -

THAT EVENING, LONG AFTER EVERYONE ELSE HAD GONE TO BED FOR THE night, I sneaked across the hall to the guest bedroom where Tamara was staying. Lizeth's mom had enough rooms in this mansion for everyone to get their own, and that hadn't even filled the house. It made quite the change from all the sleeping on couches, cots, and floors that we'd done over the last month.

I tapped softly on her door, just loud enough that I was pretty sure she would hear but not enough to attract anyone else's attention.

She hesitated a moment before calling, "Who is it?"

"It's your secret admirer," I whispered through the door.

"Sorry, I don't have one of those," she replied.

I waited, a smirk tugging at the corner of my mouth. A minute later, the door opened.

"Why, there's a strange man at my door," she commented to no one. "Should I let him in?"

"Better not," I said. "A pretty young lady can never be too careful these days."

She laughed, stepping aside so I could enter and closing the door behind me. I looked around the room. Much the same as mine. A large bed in the middle, made up with sheets that undoubtedly contained thread counts nearing insanity levels; a wardrobe of dark wood and a matching vanity with a large square mirror mounted over it; a picture window looking out over the sea, with heavy drapes closed over it so no passing sailors or night photographers could see in. On the bedside table, a small lamp with a square lampshade cast the room in a golden-yellow glow. It made the otherwise drab furnishings look almost cozy. Sitting on the table under the lamp was a necklace of blood-red beads I'd never seen before.

"What brings you to my parlor at this time of the night?" she asked. The question drew my eyes off the necklace and back to Tamara. She was already dressed for bed, wearing a tank top and shorts.

"Oddly enough, after several weeks of sleeping in cramped quarters with all my closest friends—and some highly irritating acquaintances—no more than an arm's length away from me, I found that I couldn't sleep in a spacious room by myself." I said it in a sarcastic tone, but it actually wasn't that far from the truth.

"I know the feeling," she said, sinking down onto the foot of her bed.

I watched her for a moment. She looked tired. "How are you doing?" I asked her.

Tamara sighed. "Could be better. Could be worse."

"I'm sorry about what happened earlier," I said.

She shrugged. "Not your fault."

"Still sorry it happened."

She ran her hand absentmindedly over the plain dark-blue bedspread. "I don't understand why Lizeth dislikes me so much. I've never been anything but nice to her. I think, anyway." She looked up at me. "Did I do something rude without realizing it?"

"Of course not. I don't think it's that she dislikes you, per se." I came over, sitting next to her. "She just seems like she mega overreacts to things she's sensitive about. She acts like she's got something to prove to... someone. I don't know who. Probably her mom."

She nodded. "I'm sure you're right. But it doesn't make it sting any less." She sighed. "She wasn't kidding, though. Her mom is... *a lot.*"

"That's an understatement. No wonder her dad lives on another island."

I sat quietly for a moment, thinking. We hadn't started having problems with Lizeth until the plan with the Iamoi had fallen through and she'd realized she was going to have to tell her mother that she'd taken an unauthorized gamble that hadn't paid off. It's what her uncle had called her out on, that day when Nadin left. Lizeth had been afraid.

Afraid to admit failure. Afraid of her mother's reaction. Carla Perez didn't seem the type who was willing to accept failure. She probably never had been, even when her kids had been little. Growing up in this household had undoubtedly been anything but easy for Lizeth, despite the wealth surrounding her. I supposed I should feel sorry for her. But taking it out on the rest of us wasn't going to win her any friends. And I didn't like the way she talked to Tamara a single bit.

"You know..." Tamara said. I glanced at her. She was smiling. "It made me happy earlier, when you said that Wyatt had helped us."

I blinked at the sudden subject change, wondering what had made her mind go there. "You don't have to ascribe any special meaning to it. He *has* helped us. If his mother is on our side, it's only because of him, and I appreciate that."

"I know. But there was a time not that long ago when you would have never considered him an ally. You would have done pretty much anything other than say something nice about him. I'm glad you guys have moved past that."

"You mean you're happy that you were right and I was wrong?"

She grinned, her cheeks flushing. "I didn't say that."

I elbowed her gently in the ribs. "You didn't have to. Why don't you gloat a little harder?"

"I'm not gloating," she laughed.

"Yes, you are. Little Miss Gloats-a-Lot." I ruffled her hair. She ducked away, smoothing it.

As hard as it was for me to admit, she wasn't wrong. I *did* consider Ponsford an ally. More than that—the bastard had grown on me. I almost kind of liked him now. Just like Tamara had always thought I would, if I hadn't been biased against him on account of his money, his blond hair, his punchable name, and... yeah, I'd admit it. His friendship with Tamara.

But I'd spent a lot of time getting to know him over the last annum. Despite our drastically differing opinions on law enforcement—as in, I felt they shouldn't exist, and he wanted to be one of the fabled Good Cops who served others out of a naive sense of civic duty—we tended to have fairly similar opinions on the role of the government. Namely, that it should have as minimal a role as possible. We'd killed more than a couple of hours brainstorming how we'd build an independent Mars, learning from the mistakes of Earth and forming a truly free society. Realistically, I knew that no matter what safeguards we put in, things would probably start going sideways five minutes after we let go of the reins. Idealistically, Wyatt believed we could make it work. And that naive idealism... it almost kind of made the guy endearing.

What had I become? Thinking of Wyatt Ponsford as *endearing*.

"Um," I said slowly, not looking at her. "Speaking of allies..." I hesitated. I hadn't told anyone, but it had been bothering me all day. The more time passed, the more I felt like someone needed to know. Even if it made them torqued at me. "You know that guy Horlando, back at the dig site? The one in my quadrant."

"Yeah. I saw him talking to you a few times this week. He seemed nice."

"Yeah, he *seemed* nice. It's just that, right before we left..." I swallowed. "He said that he knew who we were."

Tamara sucked in a breath, her eyes wide, but before she could freak out, I quickly added, "He said he's got family in Tharsis."

She still looked alarmed, but all she said was, "Oh?"

I nodded. "He said there were more people supporting us then we realize. And he wished us good luck."

Her expression instantly turned to one of relief. "Oh. That's great, then."

"You think so?"

"Yeah. I mean, isn't it? Maybe it's a good sign. Maybe he's right."

Eternal optimist. "I hope so. I've just been worried about it ever since. I didn't want to say anything to Lizeth because I knew she'd go nuclear about it. But what if I'm wrong? He *seemed* like an okay guy, but I don't actually know anything about him. What if he's the sort of person who would offer support to your face and then turn around and make a call to the feds behind your back?"

"If he were that way, we wouldn't be sitting here now. He had all week to make that call. The fact that we made it back to Xalapa in one piece and then were able to get onto the plane and over here without getting arrested at the airport..."

I smiled at her. "Yeah. I guess you're right."

"We can't let everything that's going on now turn us into the kind of people who don't trust others," she said. "We still have to believe in the fundamental good of humanity."

I quirked an eyebrow. "Do we?"

"Yes. Because the alternative is that we lose our own humanity. And I don't want that, for you or for me."

I smiled in spite of myself, reaching over and putting my hand against her face. "You could never be that type of person. You don't have it in you."

She placed her hand over mine. "And it's like I said about Wyatt. I'm glad to see you making friends."

"I already had friends. I had you and Isaak. And Scylla, too, I guess. As big of a pain in the butt as she can be."

"You need more friends than just us."

I snorted. "Why?"

She didn't answer. She just dropped her hand, and I dropped mine, and she turned away from me. I watched her. She seemed deflated, her shoulders slumped. And then I realized the answer.

In case something happens to us.

She was afraid of what had happened before, when Isaak had disappeared. When I'd gotten expelled from the Academy and decided not to finish out my diploma at the local public school. When I'd detached from reality and holed myself up in my apartment for months, leaving only to go to work. When the only thing that had kept me going had been her, fighting tooth and nail to not let me slip away.

What would I do if I lost her?

"We're all going to be okay," I murmured. She didn't look at me, but she nodded. I could tell she wasn't convinced.

I watched her for another moment longer.

"You don't sing anymore," I said finally.

That got her attention. She looked over her shoulder at me. "Yes, I do."

"You don't. Not like you used to. You used to sing all the time."

Defensively, she said, "I sang when we were on the island. Before we went to Mexico."

"We all sang then," I said, smiling wistfully. Even me, with my off-key voice. We'd come down to the beach with Isaak and Nadin and Scylla. We'd played games and sung, Tamara's voice strong, Scylla's boisterous, Isaak's reserved, Nadin's tentative. Our last few moments of everything being all right, before it had all started falling apart.

"That was just a few weeks ago," she said. "So you can't say I don't sing anymore."

I studied her. She was making excuses, but I'd noticed. That one night had been an outlier. She wasn't singing, not like she used to.

"What made you want to then, but not now?" I asked.

She turned away again, picking at the corner of the bedspread. She'd found a fray. Carla Perez would have been scandalized if she knew. The servant responsible for not replacing it the instant it had become anything but perfect would probably have been given fifty lashes.

"I was happy then."

I lay back on the bed, curling myself around to look up at her. "So, what, you're not happy here with me?"

The corners of her mouth pulled up, but she turned away again. "Shut up."

I caught her hand in mine. "What's different now?"

She pulled her hand away and was quiet for a long time. "I had hope then."

And there it was. I looked at her steadily, earnestly. "There's still hope now," I said.

"I can't feel it anymore." Her voice shook as she spoke. She squeezed her eyes closed again. "All I feel is worry. It dries my voice up. Makes it shrivel up inside me."

"Sing anyway."

"I can't—"

"You can. Sing anyway. Sing now. Don't let them take it from you," I said, almost urgently. Tamara had said she didn't want to see us losing our humanity. But she was losing her song, and that was what made her *her*. "Show them that you won't back down without a fight."

She stared at me for a long moment. I thought for sure I'd lost this argument.

Then softly, quietly, her voice barely above a whisper, she sang:

"It'll be such a beautiful morning,
Blue sky and gentle breeze,
The meantán gorm will sing joyful songs,
If only you could see.

It'll be such a terrible sunrise,
They've sworn to kill your dream.
By a tyrant's cruel and bloodied hands,
They'll take my love from me.

But sing, my love,
So all can hear
Above the cry of guns.
We'll sing for you
All through the night
For none can stop the sun."

The melody was lilting, sad, but there was an undercurrent of hope to it, too. The hope that Tamara had all but lost.

My skin broke out in goosebumps as she sang. When she trailed off, I swallowed. "Rebel song?"

She nodded.

"And you an Ulster girl?" I teased.

Her mouth quirked up. "A Catholic Ulster girl, remember. These are our songs, too."

"All right, then." I lay back, looking up at the ceiling. The bedside light created a halo of gold against the cream-colored plaster, and each facet of the little jeweled beads of Tamara's necklace cast a reflection of crimson and orange. "Sing the rest."

She did. The story of an Irish freedom fighter due to be executed for his part in an uprising, and the young woman he was supposed to marry. That he *would* marry, even if only for a brief few moments. Their love for each other, and their love for their fellow rebels. For their homeland. For liberty. For everything that I also held dear. Her voice grew stronger as the song progressed, and it filled the room, filled me. It was the most beautiful thing I'd ever heard.

It was also probably the most depressing.

When she was through, I sat up on my elbows to look at her. "Did that really happen?" I asked.

"It did. He died seven hours after their wedding. More than a hundred and fifty years ago." She wouldn't meet my eyes. She stared resolutely down at the floor. "I think about this song a lot," she whispered.

I didn't say anything. I hadn't wanted to voice aloud what I'd been thinking as she'd sung: That those lyrics were hitting awfully close to home. That they could soon be even closer. But I didn't need to. She'd already thought it.

I wanted to tell her, then. How much I loved her. How very, incredibly much I loved her. But anything I could say felt insufficient compared to the words of that song. It said everything I could never express on my own.

And she already knew.

I covered her hand with mine. "Thank you for singing, Tamara."

She smiled, but her eyes were a bit too shiny. "Thank you for asking me," she said.

We set out the next morning. The smugglers launched their RPS from an offshore launch platform in the middle of the Pacific. The location of this platform shifted regularly—not only to avoid the authorities, but also to steer clear of tropical storms and stay out of the paths of the frequent tsunamis that affected this region thanks to the tectonically active "Ring of Fire." The smugglers sent the pad's current coordinates to Lizeth, placing them in a location near the island nation of Fiji. We would fly to the airport on Viti Levu and then travel the rest of the journey by boat. Even flying private instead of commercial, between the flight and the time spent on the water, it would take us nearly two days to reach our destination—and we were already losing an extra day to the time change.

We rendezvoused with Zero in Florida before continuing onward, westward. Stopping only to refuel, never disembarking. The advantage, at least, was that the jet was much more comfortable than a cramped commercial flight. The seats were leather, spacious, more like a high-end recliner than an airplane seat. There were also couches and a bedroom in the back, so we could take turns lying down and resting. We needed that time for sleeping, or at least I did. One night in a comfortable bedroom on Sea-Star Island hadn't been enough to make up for the weeks before it, let alone to prepare for the weeks to come. I was exhausted.

When we landed, we quickly transferred from the plane to a boat. And this one was definitely a boat, not a yacht. A rusty, ancient fishing tub. Apparently, Carla Perez's luxurious accommodations had run out.

I was only able to glance briefly around at the island before we were out at sea. In some ways, it was reminiscent of where we'd just been. But the artificial islands of the United Federation of Seasteads weren't mountainous like Viti Levu, weren't covered with jungle. The waters were just as blue, though, and the sand just as white. I wondered if the water of this ocean was warm the way the Atlantic was. The oceans on Mars were cold at all times of year.

It took two hours by boat to reach our destination. The floating platform. Flat and rectangular, with a reinforced bunker at one end of the deck for those manning the launch. As long as the door was tightly shut, they'd be shielded from the heat blast caused by takeoff. The platform itself looked like one of the ones GalaX had used in the early days, when they'd been developing their reusable rockets that had traveled first to the International Space Station, then to the moon, and finally on to Mars. In fact, the closer we got to it, I realized that this *was* one of those launchpads. If I remembered right, the originals had been converted from old oil rigs. This launchpad had to have been a good fifty years old, and the rigs it had been built from even older. The smugglers must have rescued it from a junkyard.

That was less than reassuring.

Two men were waiting for us on the deck, standing beside the tall, narrow RPS, about as high as a three-story building but nowhere near as wide. The men stepped forward to greet Lizeth while the rest of us carried our things off the boat. We had weight and size restrictions for what we could bring with us onto the RPS—everything had to fit inside a small nylon bag. But that didn't matter much, since everything we'd brought with us from Mars was long gone by now. The clothes we'd been wearing since we'd escaped from Lago Verde had all been provided to us by Zero, and this time, Lizeth's mother had given us our provisions. Zero's clothes had all been lightweight, touristy things, but it would be cold on the cargo ship and even colder on Mars. I had never been the sort who liked wearing long sleeves. Even on days with near-freezing temperatures back home, I tended to prefer T-shirts, supplementing them with a hoodie only if I had to. But Perez hadn't given us much choice in the matter. We'd each been presented with two sets of long-sleeved thermal shirts, two pairs of long pants, and assorted undergarments. They fit in the bags and that was what we were bringing, end of story.

There was only one extra thing inside my personal bag apart from the clothing I'd been provided. The one small item I'd brought with me from the site at Los Tuxtlas. I'd tucked it securely into one of the pairs of socks. My insurance policy. Just in case.

When the five of us were safely aboard the platform, the boat pulled away. The captain would anchor a safe distance from the platform so the boat wouldn't be damaged by the RPS' launch. He would return for the smuggler who'd remained in the bunker once the RPS had safely disappeared.

One of the smugglers crouched now to open a bin at his feet. "I'm Ashraf," the man said as he rummaged through the bin, "and my companion is Farrell. He is the one who will be joining you on the RPS and assisting your transfer to our cargo vessel." He straightened, his arms laden with a bundle of blue and gray nylon. "Here are your flight suits to wear aboard the RPS. You can just put these on over your clothes."

"How long till takeoff?" Lizeth asked as she took the suit he'd handed her and unzipped it.

"The way our operation works takes advantage of gaps in satellite coverage. GSAF has a number of satellites up there that monitor Earth's airspace specifically to prevent activities such as our own." He gave a theatrical little bow. "But they aren't able to get total coverage. There are gaps of a few minutes every couple of hours. There's one in about thirty minutes, but it will only last three minutes. I advise we wait another hour, at which point we will have a safer ten-minute window."

"That makes sense."

We stepped into our flight suits, full-length body suits that zipped closed. They were snug, and the collar was high. Not the most comfortable thing to wear, but the tough loops attached in various places around the suit would allow the RPS' seatbelts to hold us firmly in our chairs. Travel by rocket could be very bumpy, especially when you were ascending through the atmosphere and battling Earth's intense gravity. It was crucial that we be secured to our seats.

"Hey, think of it like a ride at an amusement park," Scylla said cheerfully as she finished zipping her suit up. "Like the Drop Zone over on Knobel Island, or something."

"Yeah," Tamara said with a faint chuckle. She hated that ride.

Once we were in our flight suits, Ashraf and Farrell started getting the RPS ready for takeoff. Most of the prep work had already been done before we'd arrived. Ashraf went into the bunker and started running the automated pre-launch sequence. A hatch near the top of the tall spacecraft opened, and a metal ladder lowered automatically. We'd need to climb up into the cockpit and strap ourselves in soon.

As Farrell stood watching, his arms folded over his chest, a radio crackled to life at his side. "Chief, we got a call for our client on our encrypted channel," said the voice on the other end, which I recognized as belonging to the captain of the fishing boat.

Farrell frowned. That in and of itself told me that this was not an ordinary occurrence. And that was not a good sign.

He turned a dial on the radio, changing its frequency, and then held it to his mouth. "Go ahead," he said.

"Lizeth?" The voice was male, familiar. After a moment, I realized it was Lizeth's brother.

"Bruno, is everything okay?" she asked, taking the radio from Farrell's outstretched hand.

"*Fraid not. We've got big problems, Sis, big problems.*" His voice crackled with static. *"Uncle Karl's been arrested."*

"What?!" Lizeth snapped.

The others gasped. Zero came over to Lizeth, putting a concerned hand on her shoulder.

"Tell me what happened," Lizeth said.

"That whole dig in Mexico got raided. Espinoza's been brought in as well. Someone called in an anonymous tipoff about the site in Mexico being connected to the ancient Martians."

My heart sank. *Dammit.* Horlando. It had to have been. He'd been too friendly, too interested in our group. I'd been a torquing idiot to not take that as a red flag. I should have known better. The old Henry would have known better. When had I gotten so soft?

I grabbed the radio out of Lizeth's hand. "Is Isaak's grandpa safe? Hector Garcia?"

Annoyed, Lizeth snatched the radio back, but I could hear Bruno replying, *"Yeah, he's fine. He's in Medellín already. Our scouts in the city said everything seems quiet so far. The feds don't seem to have worked out that connection yet. They only figured out Uncle Karl had been there because he'd told the staff at the museum where he was going when he went out-of-office."*

"Like the torquing *blabbermouth* that he is," Lizeth snarled. "Are you safe? What about Dad?"

"Yeah, we're fine. Mom is sending a plane for me to ride this out in the UFS until we know what's going on. No extradition treaty and such. But Dad's staying on Conch. He's far enough removed from the Stateless that he thinks he'll be all right. And, you know. Anything to avoid interacting with Mom."

As Bruno was finishing that sentence, Ashraf yelled something from the bunker doorway. Farrell cursed. "We've got more bad news," he said, turning to us. "There's a PAA patrol boat heading straight for us."

Lizeth looked about ready to hurl the radio in her hand clear off the platform and out to sea. "How far off?"

"Not far enough. Ashraf wants to know if we should scrub."

"No, we can't. We have to get to Mars by a certain date. Nonnegotiable." She shot me a poisonous glare, conveniently forgetting that GSAF was just as much to blame for our hard deadline as I was. "Can we still make that three-minute launch window?"

Farrell grimaced. "It will be tight."

"Tight is the best shot we've got."

Farrell nodded, rushing over to the bunker to tell Ashraf the new plan.

"*Lizeth? Lizeth, what's happening?*" Bruno's voice was broken with static.

"We're taking off now," she replied.

"*Wait, there's —*" he started to say, but she shut the radio off and ran over to the bunker, handing it in to Ashraf.

Zero, Scylla, Tamara, and I hurried over to the ladder as Lizeth and Farrell raced back toward us. "Climb up and strap in," Farrell shouted. "We're launching in two minutes."

My heart was hammering in my chest as I climbed the ladder behind Scylla. The cockpit of the RPS was tiny and cramped. Six seats were positioned like a pinwheel around the circular space, back to back. Diving into one, I yanked the straps on my seat through the loops on my flight suit. I pulled them as tight as they would go, the latch clicking into place. Then I slid the lock over the clasp and squeezed my eyes shut.

I was not one much given to panic, but I could feel it now—my pounding heart, the roar in my ears. Tamara took the seat next to me, and her hands shook as she buckled herself in. When she was done, I reached over and took her hand, as much to try to calm myself as her. Her fingers were as clammy as mine.

"*All set on my end. Are you ready?*" Ashraf's voice crackled over the intercom.

Farrell pressed a button on the dash in front of him. "We're ready."

"*Okay. I'm going to launch you and then I'm abandoning ship. With luck, by the time the PAA get here, they'll find nothing but an empty platform.*"

With luck. With luck, the hastily loaded RPS wouldn't explode on takeoff. With luck, we'd make the three-minute window and GSAF's trackers wouldn't pick us up. With luck, we'd make it to the moon in one piece and not get busted at the lunar storage facility. With luck, with luck, with luck.

I hated relying on luck. It never seemed to be on my side.

"Liftoff in five... four... three... two..."

Tamara squeezed my fingers tightly, then let go. Keep your arms and legs inside the ride at all times.

"One."

The sound of an explosion ripped through my eardrums.

CHAPTER 36

- t a m a r a -

THE SOUND OF THE LIFTOFF WAS TERRIBLE. THEY'D TOLD US IN ADVANCE that we wouldn't need protection for our hearing. The bulk of the spacecraft itself, its airtight seal—strong enough to protect us from the vacuum of space—and the position of the rocket beneath us all created a noise-dampening effect. Within less than a minute, the craft would accelerate beyond the speed of sound and we would no longer be able to hear it at all. But the blast at launch was still enough to nearly make me go deaf. The only thing worse than the noise was the way the rocket shook us around, the way the force of it pressed me into my seat so hard that I felt like I would be crushed by the weight.

I gripped the handles on my seat tightly, knuckles white. Gradually, the shaking stopped, and the sound began to die down. When the cockpit had grown quiet enough that I could hear again, Ashraf's voice came over the intercom. "Liftoff looks good on my end. Everything good up there?"

"Everything stable up here," Farrell replied.

"All right, then, I'm bailing out. Best of luck to you all. Mate, I'll see you when you get back. Assuming I'm still in one piece."

The radio went dead.

Once we'd exited Earth's atmosphere, gravity lost its hold on us. We floated in our seats, only our seatbelts keeping us in place. The straps chafed uncomfortably against my neck.

There was no way to know if we were in the clear, though. This wasn't some sci-fi flick. We wouldn't know if we'd been caught by the sight of a GSAF cruiser on our tail. It wouldn't be until we reached the lunar storage facility that we'd know whether we were safe. If a GSAF retinue was waiting to arrest us, that would be it. There'd be no escape. We'd exhausted the last of our backup plans.

Long hours passed in relative silence. I watched through the porthole in front of me as the blue orb of Earth grew smaller and smaller. Back when space exploration had first begun, it would take three days to reach the moon from Earth. Now it took about twelve hours. But twelve hours felt like a lot when we'd already been stuck together for so many days, traveling from the UFS to Fiji and all the endless travel that had taken place before it. We were all exhausted, sick of each other, and had run out of conversation topics days before. Scylla doggedly tried, but all her attempts fizzled out pretty quickly, since the only other person who seemed willing to try to reciprocate was Zero.

Slowly, the RPS turned, and the view through my porthole shifted away from Earth, toward the silver orb of the moon. As the hours went by, the moon seemed to grow, from the size of my fist until it filled the entire window. The pockmarked craters on its surface, which could only be faintly seen from Earth, became more visible, expanding into enormous hills and valleys. Finally, the various ports and storage facilities—in abundance, since the moon was used as a refueling and repair station for the passenger ships that traveled in a constant loop from Earth to Mars, circling around the moon for an acceleration boost before returning to pick up more passengers—came into view.

Farrell said, "All right, we're coming into port now. I'm going to radio in, so everyone stay quiet."

I stared out my porthole. The RPS turned once more. I couldn't really feel the movement, other than the slight pull of my harness, tugging me in the direction of the turn. But the view through the window abruptly changed, and I could no longer see the spaceport, only black space and stars. As I watched, the emptiness was broken by another ship gliding by in the distance, launching from the moon. Just a freighter, I was sure. Just a freighter. I squeezed my eyes closed.

"LRX, this is *Phoenix* AE-15. How's everything looking on the ground?"

It was quiet for a long moment. Even though I knew better—I should have been breathing at a time like this, deep and slow—I held my breath, my heart pounding.

"*Phoenix* AE-15, this is LRX. You are clear to land." The voice betrayed nothing. Spaceport communications would be monitored, so of course they wouldn't. But by the same token, if we were walking into a trap, they wouldn't say, either.

"All right, we're going to be landing now. This will be far less rough than takeoff," Farrell said. "Lunar gravity is only one-sixth as powerful as Earth, between a third and half as powerful as on Mars. When we land, you will not be able to walk as normal. Any big movements will cause you to lose your balance. I'll show you how to do it once we've landed."

Henry reached over and squeezed my hand again.

"Do not talk once you've left this ship," Farrell went on. "I'll let you know when it's clear, and you'll need to move as quickly as possible. Copy?"

"Ten-four. Don't move too fast because you'll fall, but also move fast. Clear as mud," said Henry.

"Wise guy," Farrell grumbled. Henry caught my eye. He was smirking.

As the craft pulled into port, it turned again, and I could see now. The sight of the dull gray ground littered with dull gray buildings. The sky overhead was black, full of stars, the blue orb of Earth rising overhead. I felt sick to my stomach.

The ship rattled slightly as we drew closer to the surface. One of the buildings centered itself through my window, swallowing up the rest of the view. A hangar door in its roof opened automatically.

The ship shook as it entered the range of the moon's gravity. I closed my eyes again, clutched the handles on the seat tightly, and felt my body suddenly have weight again—sort of. Compared to how it had been on Earth, it was next to nothing. Far lighter even than home. But it was there. My body slowly sank down into my seat.

Then, with a silent thud, we'd landed.

We sat quietly, waiting, as the hangar door overhead closed, sealing tightly, then waited some more as this area re-pressurized, filling with oxygen. The climate-controlled cargo facility would allow us to breathe without a spacesuit, and it would prevent our bodies from being exposed to the extreme temperatures of the moon: The unsurvivable heat of the two-week-long lunar day, and the far-below-freezing temperatures of its night.

At last, the glowing light on the dashboard changed from red to green. Farrell unfastened his seatbelt and stood. His movements were exaggerated in this gravity, but he moved with ease. He'd been up here many times before.

"Wait here," he said. "I'll find out what's going on."

He pressed a button, opening the door and lowering the ladder. Then he disappeared.

When he'd been gone a moment, Scylla laughed awkwardly. "Well, this has been an experience. I've never been to the moon."

No one answered at first. My mouth was dry. Finally, Zero replied in their Southern drawl, "I've never even left Earth."

"Seriously? And your first trip off-planet was on an RPS?"

"Doin' life on hard mode," Zero said, running a hand through their short purple hair.

"Achievement unlocked," Scylla laughed.

"Shh," Lizeth hissed. "He's coming back."

Farrell climbed the ladder and stuck his head into the cockpit. "All clear."

"No GSAF?" Henry asked.

He shook his head. "At least not yet. You should move quickly just in case."

We raced to free ourselves from the straps on our suits, grabbing our stowed nylon bags from under our seats. Once upright, I realized just how weird this gravity felt. My stomach was in my throat, and for once, it wasn't because of nerves. Every movement felt exaggerated, and I understood how much practiced skill it took for Farrell to be able to move around as easily as he did.

At the bottom of the ladder, Farrell whispered, "Walk like this." He showed us an odd little shuffling step. It looked strange, but he seemed to be able to move quickly this way. We followed after him, but this movement did not come naturally. I felt incredibly off-balance. It was less like walking on a trampoline, as I'd expected, and more like walking through the ocean as sand drifted beneath your feet, and you suddenly found yourself far from shore. Everything felt in slow motion. I wondered if our twenty days of weightlessness on the ship would be easier or harder than this.

He led us into an elevator of sorts, but rather than going up and down, this one was on a horizontal track that would take us to a different part of the facility. To a bigger hangar, I realized when the car slowed and its doors opened. The cargo ship was huge, much larger than the RPS. Dull gray and somewhat worn-looking, with the words *Quasar Freight* painted in faded black letters along the side.

"Takes far less fuel to launch these here than it would on Earth," Farrell explained as he shuffled onto the dock. "We could never launch a ship this big from down there. Used to have to assemble these in space, before they built the bases here."

We followed him across the hangar, where another man was overseeing a robotic arm loading crates into the back hatch of the freighter. He must have been one of the smugglers, or working with them, at least, because Farrell approached him without hesitation.

"Got the last of our cargo here, Sarge," he said to the man.

The man nodded without looking up. "Get it aboard, then."

Farrell led us up the gangplank, through a cargo bay—loaded full to busting with crates made of metal and plastic—to a hallway that led to even more cargo bays. "The ship is automated, so you won't need to worry about controlling it yourself," he said. "But it's an older model. It's got facilities from back when they still had manned crews. It should be all stocked with the supplies you'll need for the journey."

"You're not coming with us?" Scylla asked.

"Oh, no. Get you aboard, that's what I was paid for. But you'll be fine on your own. There'll be someone from our team waiting to get you out when you reach the other side."

"Thanks, Farrell," said Zero. "It's been a long, rough day, but we do appreciate it."

"No thanks necessary. Gratuities welcome, though."

Lizeth rolled her eyes. "I'll make sure your group gets a substantial bonus."

Farrell grinned. "Well, then. I'm off. Best of luck to you."

With that, he shuffled back the way he'd come.

It wasn't long to launch. As soon as the man on the dock had finished loading the last pallet of cargo into the hold, his voice came over the intercom informing us to strap in for takeoff. There were six seats on the flight deck. We took our places, one seat standing empty, and secured the safety belts to our suits. Within moments, the enormous cargo vessel lifted out of the hangar, and we were once again in space.

Over four hundred hours of nothing to do but wait anxiously. Our trip from Mars to Earth had only been half as long, and that time, we'd at least had the various accommodations of the GalaX ship to keep our minds off our troubles. This time, we'd have no distractions.

Once we'd left the moon's orbit, everyone separated. Henry, exhausted from weeks of little sleep, had dozed off still strapped into his seat on the flight deck. I quietly left him. I needed to use the bathroom—not an easy feat in zero-gravity, but I couldn't put it off any longer—and then I wanted to change out of this uncomfortable flight suit and the clothes I had on underneath. I'd been dressed lightly back on the ground, due to the hot temperatures in the South Pacific when we'd launched, but the ship was chilly. I changed into the thermal clothing that Lizeth's mom had provided for us, grateful for the thick white socks. There was no point wearing shoes right now, so I went without.

The crew section had six bunks made up with sleeping bags that you could loosely strap yourself into in order to not drift away while sleeping. I stowed my nylon bag in a drawer at the end of my bunk, then hesitated a moment. I loosened the drawstrings of the bag and reached in, my fingers closing around the cool beads of the rosary.

Behind me, the door to the cabin opened. I quickly let go of the rosary as if it had burned me, my face flushing.

Scylla glided in with a sigh. "What's up?" I asked her.

"Zero and I wanted to snoop through all the stuff they've got in the cargo hold, but Lizeth wouldn't let us. She said we might leave fingerprints." She scoffed. "We're going to leave fingerprints all over this entire ship! By the time anyone gets to the crates, we're going to be long gone, and we'll have bigger problems on our hands than *fingerprints*. Lizeth is so paranoid."

"She's stressed out," I said. "That call from Bruno would have been really upsetting anyway, but now on top of it, she has no way to communicate with home for almost three weeks. She has no way of knowing whether her friends and family are okay, or if any of the operatives from the Stateless get intercepted on their way to Mars."

Scylla huffed. "Yeah, I know. I know it's a big deal. But she's been such a jerk lately, it's hard to cut her any slack."

She opened the drawer to her own bunk, pulling out her bag of clothes and starting to strip off her flight suit. Surreptitiously, I grabbed the rosary again, clutching it to my chest and guiding myself out the door into the hall.

I wanted to go somewhere quiet, private, and decompress. One of the cargo holds seemed the most logical place. I propelled myself along the hall, pressing a button to open the door to the closest hold. It slid open silently.

Voices greeted me. I hovered in the doorway. I recognized Lizeth speaking, and Zero's drawled responses. Their words were muffled, coming from deeper in the hold, behind one of the tightly secured stacks of crates. This must have been where Lizeth had interrupted their snooping.

I started to turn to leave—easier said than done with no gravity—but I paused when I realized that they weren't just talking. Lizeth was crying.

"Don't tell me to calm down," she said between sniffles. "There's no way Uncle Karl is going to hold up under questioning. Discretion is not his middle name. The authorities are going to figure out his connection to the Stateless, if they haven't already. Everything is going to come crashing down like a house of cards and—" She broke off with a sob.

"But getting so worked up isn't going to solve anything," Zero said gently.

"Don't you get it, Zero? It's all my fault!"

"It's not your fault."

"It *is*," she insisted. "Me and my stupid, *childish* obsession with the Atlantean Arch. I had more important things to worry about, and instead, I went off chasing a kid's daydream—"

"How was it a kid's daydream?" asked Zero. "You were right, Zee. You've been right all these years. Atlantis was real, and you got to be in the middle of its discovery." Earnestly, they added, "And you did a good thing, helping Nadin and Isaak. It was the right thing to do."

"I jeopardized the Stateless."

"Everything we do every day jeopardizes the Stateless. It's a dangerous operation. You never know how things are going to turn out. Sometimes things just happen, even with the best laid plans."

"Mother is going to kill me."

"Your mom isn't here," Zero pointed out. "And you ain't gonna see her for a looong time."

The words seemed harsh, but Zero's tone was light when they spoke, and they leaned hard on the accent at the last bit. It must have been the right thing to say, because Lizeth laughed. My mouth curled up at the sound.

"There. See? You need to chill. You let your stress get to you, and it makes you go crazy."

Lizeth sniffled. "You sound like Tamara. She said that, back at the house. That she thought I was *anxious*. Or nervous. Something like that."

"Was she wrong?"

She sniffled again. "No. I guess not. But don't let her know I said that."

Zero laughed. "Can't let anyone know Lizeth Senghas isn't perfect?"

"Shut up." She sighed. "I wish I hadn't had to hang up on Bruno like that. I hope he's okay."

"He'll be fine. He's tough." In a softly assuring voice, they added, "You can't go back, darlin'. You can only go forward. Your whole family has dedicated their lives to this cause. The sacrifice is worth it to them. All of them. So you have to just keep moving ahead. Fight the good fight."

I drifted away, and the door slid silently closed behind me.

Later, when everyone else had retreated to the cabin to sleep but my confused whirl of thoughts and adrenaline kept me wide awake, I went back to the cargo hold. I glided just inside the door, letting it close behind me, and braced myself against the pallet of crates strapped to the floor. Then I stared down at the beads in my hand, as I had dozens of times over the days since Abuelo had given them to me. Once again, I found myself at a loss.

"In my experience, when problems get overwhelming, people tend to turn inward when they should be turning upward."

I did believe in God. But the truth was, I didn't really think about it anytime except Sundays. We went to Mass every week, and I volunteered as a cantor, but it was like... I don't know. Like God was inside that church and nowhere else. Like He existed during that hour once a week, and the rest of the time, I was on my own, having to figure things out for myself and carry everything alone.

My roommate, Mariyah, she prayed a lot. Five times a day, her mat oriented toward Earth's position, the closest approximation to Mecca you could get on a foreign planet. She said praying so often kept God in the forefront of her mind. Even if she got preoccupied with other things, the reminder of the prayer times would reorient her thoughts, make her regain her focus.

But she'd had a lifetime of putting that into practice. It was easy for her. It had never been that way for me. And I was nineteen now. I had a lifetime of other habits ingrained into me. What if it was too late to start?

I looked down at the beads fanning out in a circle around my hand, their deep burgundy color, the silver chain connecting them.

Isaak's grandpa had thought this might help me. And I was desperate for help. The CBT and DBT were a good start, but I needed more than that. I needed hope right now, when things were so dire. I needed hope that someone was on our side. That someone cared about what happened to all of us. I needed to believe that in the grand scheme of things, everything was going to be okay.

"All right," I whispered. "Come on, Tamara. You can do this."

I knew that the ten little beads were *Hail Marys*. I was pretty sure that the bigger bead that went in between them was *Our Father*. But what were the three beads by the crucifix? What about the big bead that separated those from the circular sets of ten beads? And was I supposed to do something on the crucifix itself?

I had clearly failed Catholic 101. Isaak's grandpa had given me this nice gift, and I didn't even know how to use it. I felt stupid even trying.

As I stared miserably down at the beads in my hands, the door to the hallway swished open. My head jerked up, my hair rippling around my face.

Zero had glided through the door, but when they saw me here, their eyes changed, as if they wanted to hesitate, maybe turn back. Making abrupt directional switches in zero-gravity was easier said than done, though. After a moment, they chuckled awkwardly. "Sorry to bother you, Tamara," they said. "It, uh—it looks like we may have had the same idea, though." They gestured to the rosary in my hand. When I blinked in confusion, they added, "I'm not super religious or anything. But I do like to have, you know… quiet time with the Creator. When I can. It grounds me."

"Oh. Yeah?" I said, my face hot with embarrassment.

"Yeah. Should I go somewhere else?"

"Of course not," I said earnestly. "Please stay."

Zero smiled, bracing themself against the pallet until we were floating together side by side. I glanced at them sideways for a moment as they closed their eyes, seemingly as comfortable in their prayers as I was uncomfortable in mine. Why did it come so easily to other people, but not to me?

Maybe it's not about doing it right. Maybe it's about just trying.

The thought seemed to come out of nowhere, but it was comforting, and I clung to it. Getting it right seemed impossible, but trying, I could do.

I squeezed my eyes shut, clutching the beads between my fingers, feeling the hardness of them, the coolness. And in my mind, I reached out to an invisible hand that I could feel was already reaching for mine.

"Please, keep everyone safe," I whispered almost inaudibly. Win or lose, that was all I asked for.

Just keep everyone safe.

The ship hummed silently onward. Twenty days until we reached Mars.

Twenty days until everything changed forever.

PART SEVEN
IAMOS

S.C.D. 8378
10,942 B.C.E.

CHAPTER 37

- i s a a k -

THE SUN WAS RISING BEHIND US AS WE WOUND OUR WAY THROUGH THE narrow slot canyon. Our shadows walked ahead of us, elongated and distorted—strange, dark impressions that turned the *gurzas'* now-familiar silhouettes into something deformed and monstrous, like a creature out of the *leyendas* Abuelo had taught me as a kid. The sight made me uneasy.

Not that I wasn't already uneasy. Reality had made it so I could be nothing but.

We'd left Gale Crater behind, traveling into the far western reaches of what would be Aeolis province in my time. The landscape was scarred with deep, winding channels left in the porous rock by water long since evaporated. We took advantage of these to hide ourselves, though there'd been no sign of a *tirak* or anything else since the day of the *gamada* storm. Much of the land here was unfamiliar to me, and for good reason—it was not land in my time period. The path we were traveling now led directly through the Gulf of Tyrrhenum. It should have been deep underwater. But there was no sea to be found here. Just dry, sandy badlands that were raked with abrasive winds, pelting us in the face with scouring dust.

The last several days we'd ridden at a frantic pace, stopping only long enough to rest ourselves and the animals before beginning the journey again. This morning Nikos had awakened us before dawn, when Hamos was just dipping below the horizon. We had to get to Katai'ios as soon as possible. Even with Ceilos reprogramming the *tirak* to mislead the *geroi* about our whereabouts, it still wasn't safe to be traveling out in the open. But we had another threat now, one even more urgent than the possibility of capture by the *geroi*.

The Clovis impact was coming. There was no escaping that fact. It was looming over us, quite literally.

I'd asked Emil how long we had, based on the appearance of the mysterious star on the horizon. The answer had not been encouraging.

"Depends on how big it is," he'd said. The asteroid that had killed the dinosaurs was between ten and fifteen kilometers wide, and he'd estimated it wouldn't have been visible to the naked eye until maybe three days before the impact. More than three days had passed now, and the star's size in the sky had remained roughly unchanged—a fact confirmed by Emil's dutiful measurements with his pocket ruler, recorded hourly in one of his myriad paper notebooks. Emil's overpreparedness and analog-only policy had paid off once again.

The good news: We still had time.

The not-so-good news: We didn't know how *much* time.

The bad news: The longer it took, the bigger that meant the object was. And the bigger the object was, the more screwed we would be when it got to us.

"Now, bear in mind, kid," Emil had tried to reassure me, "this is just an estimate. We don't know what that thing is. If it's an object with a high albedo like a comet, we've got more wiggle room."

That had *not* reassured me, in particular because I didn't even know what an albedo was. Something to do with reflectiveness and brightness, I gathered. The star didn't seem to have a tail, so I was doubtful that it was a comet. But what *was* it, then?

"An incredibly massive piece of space debris —"

I tried to block Senghas' voice out of my mind. It had sounded so abstract when he'd described it, so detached from reality. Even though I'd known it was a possibility, I think deep down I hadn't actually believed we were really in danger from the impact. Even though I knew we were in the ballpark time-wise, what would the odds have been that it would happen right *now*?

The odds were terrible, but apparently my luck was even worse.

The threat posed by the ominous star in the sky had motivated Nikos and the others to get us to Katai'ios as fast as possible. The argument between Shuliin and Nikos about whether Ceilos should be allowed to see the route to the outpost had gone by the wayside, and so had the meandering sidetrack we'd been taking to reach it. All that mattered now was getting to Katai'ios and figuring out a plan to get the Iamoi evacuated as quickly as possible. Time was not on our side.

As the sun rose higher, the canyon mouth began to widen. We'd been descending deeper and deeper as we'd traversed the canyon, and now sheer cliff faces soared on either side of us, at least half a kilometer high at this depth.

"It's just around the next bend," Nikos said.

My knuckles tensed in anticipation as I gripped Tuupa's reins. She rumbled beneath me, glancing over her shoulder with her yellow reptilian eyes.

Then we turned the corner, and I sucked in my breath. Even with what Enros had told me, I wasn't quite prepared for the sight of a patchwork citidome nestled in an alcove of the canyon. When I'd seen Hope Renewed for the first time, with its smooth honeycomb of blue glass, it had reminded me of a greenhouse. But this... The closest comparison to this was a Tiffany lamp, a colorful mosaic, a work of art. The glass that it was built out of was multicolored and brilliant—not just blue, but green, red, yellow, intermingled with perfectly clear pieces. Sunlight shone through it and reflected off the red stone of the canyon walls, creating a beautiful stained glass effect.

"Amazing," Ceilos said from where he sat behind Nikos on Kodo's back. "A hidden citidome."

"How in the world were you able to build this?" Nadin asked.

"Our people salvaged glass from the ancient cities abandoned by the *geroi* after the Progression," Nikos said. "We also helped ourselves to discarded glass created during the process of building Bright Horizon."

"Incredible," said Ceilos. "It would have been no easy matter to smuggle this much glass out without being noticed. It just goes to show once again how much the *patroi* have underestimated the rebellion's determination."

Nikos didn't respond, but I saw the way he beamed with pride, sitting a little taller in the saddle.

We approached the entrance, and Nikos swung his leg over Kodo's head and dismounted. There was a handwheel with metal spokes mounted to the door, and he turned it with a grunt. With some effort, the dogs spun loose and the door opened. Like the *geroi's* citidomes, Katai'ios was built with an airlock entrance—a door to the outside world that we would enter and seal tightly behind us. The airlock would then stabilize, and we could enter the rest of the citidome safely, without the precious recycled oxygen that the rebels had hoarded over decades escaping.

Nikos sealed the outer door, and we waited for a breathless moment. "It's safe now," he decreed at last, pulling the oxygen mask off his face. The rest of us followed suit, gratefully inhaling air that didn't come out of a tank.

When the inner door opened, we saw that we'd been expected. A bearded man waited just inside. He looked familiar, and I recognized him after another moment—he was the father of the three children I'd encountered in Eliin's outpost.

"*Degiim,* Camos," Nikos said, striding forward. "It's good to see you made it here safely."

"And you. We've been anxious for your arrival."

I slid off Tuupa's back and looked around in wonder. Katai'ios was nothing like the only other citidome I'd seen, Hope Renewed. The aboveground portion of Hope Renewed was highly urbanized, with adobe apartment buildings crammed tightly together, outdoor marketplaces bustling with people, and the central pyramid looming over everything, reminding the populace that the watchful eye of the *geroi* saw all.

Katai'ios, on the other hand, was like a rural landscape in a snow globe. A short distance away, I saw a cluster of longhouses like the ones in the village of Elytherios, and behind those an orchard of *naransha* trees. The rest of the dome was dominated by fields of grain: The tall, purple grasses that we'd used to feed the *kela* and *ielak* in Eliin's outpost, which Nadin had told me was called *seno*; a golden-brown grain called *psenik* that resembled barley; and in the distance, a green maize-like plant that I'd seen growing in the fields of Elytherios. Nikos had said this outpost was used primarily for agriculture, to supplement the supplies needed by the rebellion beyond what could be grown in Elytherios, but I still was taken aback by the sheer scope of it.

And I was surprised, considering everything I had to be anxious about now, how much I felt my body relaxing at the sight of this place. Growing things truly were good for the soul. For the first time, I thought I might understand what had drawn my mom to botany.

I turned to give Emil a hand out of the saddle. Once Emil's feet were on solid ground, Pandat scurried off his shoulder. Before I could react, the *kerkopith* had disappeared into the *seno* grass, making a beeline for the orchard and its trees full of fruit.

"Did the other refugee parties make it here safely?" Nikos asked, drawing my attention away from Pandat.

Camos tugged his earlobe. "You're the last party we were expecting. Well"—he hesitated—"in a manner of speaking."

Something in his tone made Nikos frown. "What do you mean by that?"

"It's nothing urgent," Camos hedged, but there was an air of falseness to his voice. "You need to rest first. You must be exhausted from your travels."

Nikos put his hand on Camos' shoulder. "We have no time to rest. Not yet. There are important things we must speak of. You clearly have something weighing on your mind, and we do as well." He looked around, craning his head toward the longhouses. "Where is my brother?"

"That's what I mean to explain," Camos said. "Almost as soon as we arrived in Katai'ios we received urgent word from the citidomes. The situation there has deteriorated greatly."

Shuliin jumped out of the saddle, coming up beside Nikos and planting her feet shoulder-width apart. "How so?"

"More of the *geroi* have fallen ill. Many more."

"A disease in the citidomes?" Syrin asked. The gold flecks in her eyes flashed with worry.

"Not exactly. Thus far it has only affected *geroi* and... some of the *geroi*'s blood as well." Camos glanced anxiously in the direction of Nadin and Ceilos. "Our intelligence has indicated that they may have been deliberately poisoned."

"The *geroi*'s blood... Even the children?" Nadin slid off Thork's back behind Gitrin, her brows drawn. She caught my eye, explaining, "There are three partnerships not yet of age. The youngest are... very young."

Camos tugged his earlobe grimly. "If word is to be believed, yes. Even the children. The onset is sudden and symptoms progress rapidly. It appears to be attacking their nervous systems, and it has not been responding to the medics' treatments."

I sucked in a breath. "Attacking their nervous systems?" I repeated. "The neurotoxin. It has to be."

Nikos shot me a look over his shoulder. "We heard rumors of such a possibility before we left Bright Horizon, but at that time only *Geros Shiros* was affected."

"*Geros* Shiros is dead," said Camos. "And *Gerouin* Paolin soon after him. That much we can confirm. Beyond them, we cannot say."

Beside me, Nadin grew unnaturally still. "My—" she began, but she broke off abruptly, clearing her throat. "The *geroi* of Hope Renewed?" She was trying to keep her expression neutral, but her eyes revealed her conflicted emotions. My exposure to Nadin's parents had been limited— the one and only time I'd seen them in person, it had been at the head of an army determined to destroy us all. And I knew what had happened after that. Who had been responsible for the scars on Nadin's shoulders. The *geroi* were monsters, and no one knew that more than Nadin.

But they were still her parents. And in spite of everything, I could see the tension reflected in her eyes. She didn't want to care. But she did.

I moved to take a step toward her, but Ceilos turned just then, taking Nadin's hand and squeezing it. She glanced up at him, face unreadable. I looked away.

"I don't know. The only *geros* I can say for sure is not infected is Tibros."

Ceilos looked up, Nadin's hand still in his. "Tibros? You're certain?"

Camos tugged his earlobe again. "Tibros has seized control of the *gerotus*. He's declared a state of emergency in all the citidomes on both Iamos and Hamos."

Nadin caught my eye, and I nodded slightly. Tibros had not yet fallen ill. Tibros had taken control of the citidomes. Ceilos had been right about his father. And that meant he was likely right about the rest, too. Tibros was the Liberator. But what did we do about it?

"We do not know what the toxin is or how it's being administered. But the fact that it is only affecting the *geroi* indicates this is some kind of coordinated attack, and that implicates our movement." Nikos' expression was grim.

"Just like the sabotage of the early warning protocol," I said.

"The false Liberator is trying to frame the Elytherioi," Ceilos remarked.

"The Enforcers are cracking down on even the slightest rumor of seditious behavior," said Camos. "A number of our safehouses were raided and those within taken into custody. Our movement is in danger of falling apart. We had to act quickly. There was no time to wait for you."

"Of course," Nikos said.

"Eos and Marin...?" I asked.

"They left with a group of runners yesterday for Dauntless Spirit. Marin's... skills... were required in order to get our people out."

Nikos turned back to Kodo and began rummaging through the few supplies remaining in his saddle pack. "I have to go after them," he said.

"Wait, Nikos," I protested. "There's no time—we have *other issues*." I added this last part under my breath. The situation in the citidomes was dire, but it would do us no good to waste precious time trying to resolve that problem when the greater threat in the skies overhead could vaporize us all in an instant.

Nikos froze, staring into his saddle pack for so long that I wasn't sure he'd heard me. Then he exhaled. "Ask your scientist how long he expects we have."

I turned to Emil, translating Nikos' question.

Emil folded his arms, chewing on the inside of his cheek thoughtfully. "Depends," he said. "There are too many variables that I just don't know. The size of the thing, its speed, its trajectory. I can't calculate that on my own with just a ruler and a pad of paper. We need instruments." He exhaled. "But my best guess is that we've got at least a week."

I relayed this back to Nikos, and he tugged his earlobe. "Then we can spare one day." I opened my mouth to protest, but he waved me off. "One day, Isaak. That is final. We have to get our people out before we can make any other plans." He turned to Shuliin. "Will you come?"

She grinned. "Of course. The Liberator needs his best runner."

He tugged his earlobe again, turning to face us all. "We will be back by this evening. Then we will resolve everything. In the meantime, there are things to do here. Take some time this morning to rest and recover your strength. Then Camos will give you assignments around Katai'ios to fill the rest of your day."

I tried not to groan. Seriously? We'd been traveling for weeks, and I was bone exhausted. Nikos had insisted we could spare one day, but he wouldn't let us take that day off? But one look at Nikos' expression told me there'd be no room for argument.

Camos glanced warily at Ceilos, still standing beside Nadin. "Nikos, what of the *geroi*'s blood? Should I not confine him to one of the longhouses, place him under guard?"

Nikos gave Ceilos an appraising glance. "The boy proved himself on our journey. He is valuable to our movement."

Ceilos stood a little taller at Nikos' words.

"And during the harvest time, all available hands are needed," Nikos went on. "Keep him under supervision, but give him an assignment in the field."

Camos hesitated, but he tugged his earlobe nonetheless. "Very well. But first, you all must eat. Come this way."

We followed Camos down a path between the crops that led toward the longhouses. As we approached the cluster of buildings, I noticed a few smoke trails drifting up to the top of the dome where an exhaust vent would capture them, recycling whatever oxygen it took in and expelling the pollutants into the outer air. I could smell the scent of cooking meat even from here, and my stomach growled.

A few steps in front of me, Nadin wrapped her arms around her own stomach. I watched her wistfully, a smile tugging at the corner of my mouth. She was a pro at concealing her emotions even under the best of circumstances, and whenever situations got tough, she would expertly project that feigned detachment she'd cultivated over a lifetime as a *gerouin*-in-training. But over the last several months, I'd started to notice the little ways she let her feelings show.

If only I could talk to her more openly about everything that was going on. It felt like we hadn't had a moment to ourselves since the night we'd spotted the star. Despite the image she was projecting, I knew Nadin. I knew that the stress would be eating away at her. I wanted to help ease some of that burden, but I didn't know how. Things had been so much easier before, when it was the two of us on the road to Elytherios. The two of us on Mars, on Earth. Now things were so much more complicated, and I didn't know what to do about it.

As we walked, we passed an area where sheaves of the harvested grain lay stacked in piles, each baled tightly with twine. From out of the pile, Pandat suddenly bounded toward me, scrambling up my leg like a tree trunk and perching on my shoulder.

"And what have you been up to?" I asked him, scrunching my nose as he draped his striped tail across my upper lip.

As if in reply, he opened his fist and thrust it into my face, revealing what he'd pilfered now. A handful of baling twine and some fine wire.

I rolled my eyes. "Pandat, we're not here to make trouble—" I began, but then I paused, considering the items in the *kerkopith*'s hand, and what I had in my pocket.

"I'll take that," I said, taking the scraps and slipping them inside my jacket. "You know what, Pandat? You just gave me an idea."

CHAPTER 38

- n a d i n -

AFTER WE'D EATEN, CAMOS PUT US TO WORK. ISAAK, WHO'D SHOWN AN affinity for the animals in Elytherios and again in Eliin's outpost, was sent to the livestock pens; and, of course, Emil went with him—though the old man's proficiency in our language was improving, he still required an interpreter much of the time. Gitrin and I would join a group already in the field, assigned to follow the harvesters and gather the cut stalks of *psenik*, binding them into sheaves. And Ceilos was assigned to the group who would go after us, gathering our bound sheaves and hauling them to the outbuildings where the grain was stored.

I knew Nikos believed that assigning us tasks, keeping us busy, would keep our minds off the worrying object we'd spotted in the sky. But I could not help but be uneasy. It felt absurd that we should be harvesting grain, storing up food for the future, when it was entirely possible the planet would be destroyed within a week. But by the same token, we couldn't panic the other Elytherioi yet—not when we had no plan in place. If Professor Senghas' so-called Clovis impact was imminent, it wouldn't be just the rebels who needed to be evacuated. All eight citidomes would have to be. The only alternative was death. But in order to evacuate the citidomes, we would have to contend with the *geroi*. What was left of them, at least.

We'd have to contend with *Geros Tibros*. The Liberator.

I had no idea how we were going to manage such a feat, and manage it within a *week*. Nikos believed that the other elders could help us devise a plan, but I just didn't see how.

"Come, *alin*," Gitrin said, putting a reassuring arm around my back. "There is nothing we can do for now. Worry will solve nothing. Fear will only paralyze us. Tomorrow's problems will be for tomorrow. Today, we will focus on the task we've been given."

I wanted to argue with her, to snap some response back, but my mind was a blank. She was right. Until Nikos returned, there was nothing to do but focus on the task we'd been assigned. We would harvest the crops, even if doing so seemed pointless and futile.

As our group dispersed, Syrin and Shuliin held back. I glanced over my shoulder back at them. Syrin held Shuliin's hands tightly between hers, her face drawn with worry. They said a few things to each other in low voices. Saying goodbye. I started to turn away, but then Shuliin's voice rose just enough that I could make out what she said.

"*Oesi yachin mou*," she murmured. It was a phrase from the old language, one that just didn't quite carry over into the new standard language quite as well. Maybe there wasn't as much use for it in the language of the Progression. It was a promise of eternal love. I smiled tightly. Shuliin was usually so gruff, but she was different around her partner. I could see that much.

They kissed briefly and then parted, and Shuliin hurried to join Nikos where he stood waiting, a posternkey in his hand. As Elytherios had, Katai'ios possessed a postern, stolen from the citidomes or constructed in secret. I'd seen it behind the longhouses. They'd use this to travel to Dauntless Spirit. Nikos said they'd return by tonight. But what if something went wrong?

As Gitrin and I walked in the direction of the fields, I heard Syrin call breathlessly after us.

"Nadin, wait," she said as she caught us up. "I'm with you."

Gitrin smiled, extending her other arm to Syrin. "It will be good to have another familiar face with us."

"Keep our mind off things," Syrin agreed, trailing her fingers unconsciously over her lips.

"You must be worried about your partner," I said, watching her.

Syrin gave a wan smile and tugged her earlobe. "All the time. It's not easy being partnered with a runner. I know that her work is critical to our movement. After all, I wouldn't be here at all if a runner hadn't smuggled my parents out. Runners keep the rebellion alive. But it's still frightening."

"You grew up in Elytherios? Did you ever leave the caldera?" I asked her.

"Yes, a few times, to help out in the outposts as needed. But I've never been to the citidomes. I would be terrified of going there." She glanced over her shoulder again. "Shuliin's made of stronger stuff than I am."

Gitrin squeezed her arm. "You don't give yourself enough credit. You're stronger than you know."

I heard voices ahead, and then we came upon the rest of our group. Most of them were strangers to me, but I recognized Ierin, and the *plivoin* from Hope Renewed, Corin. It had been weeks since I'd last seen her, and I noticed that her belly was swollen now, her pregnancy beginning to show. She sat on an upturned basket, and one of the other workers handed her the cut stalks of *psenik*. She laughed self-deprecatingly as the three of us approached.

"I told them that I'm perfectly capable of bending and lifting myself," she said. "I'm not that far along yet. But they insisted."

Gitrin made a *tsking* noise. "She needs to stay active, you know."

"That's what I told them," Ierin said with a laugh. "But a new life is a wonder, even among those of us who have never needed Ferre. There's not enough of it here on Iamos."

With a sick turn of my stomach, I remembered Camos' news from the citidomes. The neurotoxin hadn't just affected the adults, the current *geroi*. It had been unleashed on their children as well. The youngest was Achillios' and Eristin's daughter. They'd left her with the *geroi* of Radiant Tomorrow when they'd left for their doomed colonization of Simos. She was less than two years old, younger even than Sasin. What kind of monster would poison a child?

One who knew that any *geroi's* blood, even a child, was a threat to his power.

Gitrin hadn't noticed the way my face had fallen. "It will do Corin no good to be coddled. Honestly, all of you," she chided.

"Come, Gitrin. Everyone wants to pamper the new mother," Ierin said, handing each of us a roll of baling twine. "Let them have their fun."

"How are you feeling, anyway, Corin?" Syrin asked, crouching to gather a bundle of stalks in her arms.

"Better than I had been," Corin admitted. Her braided white hair slipped over her shoulder as she wrapped the twine around and around the *psenik*. "Of course, the timing of the worst of my sickness coincided with Elyth—with—with the incident." She glanced in my direction before adding hurriedly, "I could barely keep food down on the journey. But it's better now."

I nudged Gitrin with my elbow. "Sickness? Corin has been ill?"

"Pregnancy sickness," Gitrin whispered. "It's common in the first few months. It usually passes by the time the baby is visible."

"Oh," I said, feeling sick to my stomach myself. This was not a subject I'd ever thought about. As with the... urges of desire... I suppose I'd always thought it was something beneath me. Something for unrefined *plivoi*. Even the knowledge that at some point I would have been expected to carry a future *geros* or *gerouin* had seemed like nothing but a distant, abstract concept, something not worthy of my consideration. But I'd learned the hard way that day in Gitrin's classroom with Ceilos that what I'd assumed was normal for *geroi*—the lack of interest in carnal pleasures, and everything else that came with it—was, in fact, only normal for me.

But it is normal, I reminded myself. Being back on Iamos, I felt like the confidence I'd gained on Mars was starting to slip away. The assurance that I was, indeed, normal. Not the same as everyone else, but still normal. I looked down at my bare right hand as if searching for the black hematite ring Scylla had given me. But it was gone. Lost, like so much else, to the *geroi*.

"Is something wrong, Nadin?" Syrin asked, peering at me with an expression of concern in her amber eyes.

My face grew hot. "I..." I glanced down at the lopsided bundle of stalks in my hands, the poor job I'd done binding it. I swallowed. "I was just thinking. I have... no interest in motherhood."

Syrin gave me a crooked grin. "Neither do I. One of the perks of being samelove."

I smiled back tightly. "Syrin... Has anyone ever thought it odd that you and Shuliin are samelove?"

"Of course not," she said. "We're not alone. Many people on Iamos are. There were a few others in Elytherios. They were men, though. I was lucky that Shuliin came to us and that we were close to the same age." She quirked her head at me. "Why do you ask?"

I exhaled. "Some desire those of a different gender. Others desire those of the same. But… would you think it abnormal if you met someone who desired no one? Of any gender?"

She furrowed her brows. "Someone who experienced no attraction?"

I tugged my earlobe.

She gave this some consideration. "I don't think that would be abnormal," she said at last.

I felt some weight lift. "Really?"

She pulled her twine taut and deftly worked it into a knot between her fingers. "To me, it seems similar to how I am. I'm sure others would feel the same way if it were explained to them." She tossed her bundle into the pile with the others.

I smiled, relieved. Maybe it wasn't so different here from how it had been on Mars after all.

Normal.

We spent the rest of the morning working together, periods of conversation interspersed with periods of companionable quiet. When we'd finish binding the stalks in one area, we'd gather our things and move to the next, leaving the bundles behind for the next workers to carry to the storehouses. Surprised as I was to admit it, perhaps Nikos had been right to have us do this. The ability to busy myself with a physical task had done wonders for my nerves.

We had just finished the sheaving in our third station and were preparing to move on when Camos and Ceilos came upon us.

"We're catching you up, *yachin,*" Camos said teasingly to Ierin as he scooped up a bale. "You'd better pick up the pace."

Ierin made some remark back to him, but I didn't hear it. Ceilos had stopped at my feet, hefting two heavy bundles upon each shoulder, and as they spoke, he shot me a grin—the easy, unforced grin I used to say was meant only for me. Back in the days when the only people we'd had who we could trust were each other. Now that grin made my stomach twist uncomfortably. Maybe because of the thoughts I'd been having all morning—the memories of that day things between us had begun to fall apart, and the realization I'd had that had changed everything. That I was different.

I'd been afraid to let anyone here know I was different. But I wondered now if that fear had been misplaced. What if it had all just been a misunderstanding?

As Ceilos and Camos walked away, Syrin watched me for a long moment.

"Nadin," she said after a pause, "tell me. What was it like growing up in the citidome?" When I gave her an odd look, she added quickly, "Remember, I've not been there."

"You could ask Corin," I hedged. "She grew up in Hope Renewed, same as me."

"I want to know too, though," Corin said. "We all know, or most of us at least, what it was like growing up among the *plivoi*. But what was it like to be a *patroin*? What was it like in the underground?" She swallowed. "What... was it like in the *geroi*'s villa?"

I looked around hesitantly, and found that all the others had ceased their sheaving and were watching me with curiosity written across their faces. The only one who looked away now was Gitrin. She stared sadly down at her own hands as she tightly bound the stalks.

Gitrin knew. But she was the only other one here who did.

I sighed. Where to begin?

"It was lonely," I said finally.

"Lonely?" Corin asked with a curious quirk of her head. "In the home of your own parents? Since the *geroi* are the only people on Iamos— outside of the Elytherioi—who raise their own children, I assumed..."

I worked the rough twine between my fingers for a moment. "The *geroi* are not like other parents. Not like Ierin, for example," I added, trying to lighten the mood. She smiled tightly, but her brows were still furrowed.

"The *geroi* were hardly present in my life. I would see them at the evening meal, and that was usually the only time. When I did see them, they were very distant. Detached. Cold." I stared down at the stalks of grain piled at my feet, but I wasn't really focusing on them. "There was no love in our home. Antos and Melusin at least seemed to grasp that this was a deficiency, because they were always telling me things had to be this way. They couldn't treat me any differently than the people in the citidome they were responsible for. They couldn't show me preferential treatment. They had obligations, and those obligations were mine as well. I understood. Or I thought I did, at least." I twisted the twine in my hands again. "I believed them, you know. Believed they were doing what was best for everyone. Believed that they had our people's best interests at heart." I'd been foolish for doing so. A *useful fool.*

I reached for a fistful of *psenik*, wrapping twine around the middle of the stalks. "Other *geroi*'s children had it far worse than I did. I know this. Antos and Melusin were distant and detached, but they weren't outright cruel. Other children..." I swallowed. *Bruises.* "Other children didn't have it even that lucky. But still. It was very lonely."

"But you had *patroi* children to play with, didn't you?" Syrin asked.

I shook my head out of habit and then checked myself. "No," I said. "The *geroi* keep their children apart, even from the upper castes. We can't be believed to be showing favor to anyone within the citidomes. Friendships might lead to that sort of favor. The only person I had in my life was Gitrin." I glanced over at her. She was still staring down at her hands. Her face was in profile, turned slightly away, but I saw it. Her eyes were glistening. I swallowed down the lump in my throat. "Until Ceilos came. Ordinarily, betrothed partners don't live in the same citidome until their final year before their *enilikii.* But because Ceilos' parents were establishing the colony at Ascendant Dawn, he was sent to us early." My fingers were struggling to form the knot. I gave up and let the twine go slack between my fingers. "It was good for me. But maybe better for him. He hadn't even had the benefit of a caring tutor as I had with Gitrin. He really had been alone."

The others were silent for a long while after I finished, staring at me with unreadable faces. Finally, Corin spoke.

"I'm sorry, Nadin," she said softly. "I... I misjudged you. The sort of life you led. We all assumed the *geroi* led a life of privilege, of comfort. But it seems you had it no better than the rest of us. As bad as it was being raised by the Caretakers, at least we *plivoi* have each other. Our friends in the Carehomes, our neighbors in the insulae. I can't imagine being entirely alone like that."

Ierin made a tutting noise with her tongue. "It's not good for children to be raised that way. Completely isolated." She finished her knot, cutting the excess twine with her blade and moving on to the next pile of stalks. "Isolation can do things to a person's mind. Mood disorders, anger issues. Low self-esteem, or the other end of the spectrum—narcissism, self-centeredness. Even cognitive problems. It's no wonder the *geroi* are the way they are, if they all were raised this way." She looked up at me, holding my eyes earnestly. "I am grateful that fate allowed Ceilos to come to you at a younger age. It was better for the both of you. And I am grateful you had Gitrin as a stabilizing influence in your lives."

Gitrin still didn't turn to face us, but I saw the way the tension in her shoulders eased, the way the corners of her mouth turned up.

"And you're here now," Syrin added. "You're still young, and you've got us. You've got Isaak. We'll make sure you never have to be alone again."

My eyes stung, but I blinked the tears away. "Thank you," I whispered, and I meant it. "Thank you all."

At last, the work was finished for the day. The harvesters had finished cutting the *psenik*, we had finished binding it, and all our sheaves had been carried to the storehouses. The smell of cooking food was wafting from the village, and we followed it. My muscles ached, though the work of today had been far less grueling than the hard riding of our journey to Katai'ios. But the physical exhaustion served to slow my frantic thoughts to a more manageable pace, and for that I was grateful.

As in Elytherios, tables were arranged in a circle in the midst of the longhouses, to allow the community an opportunity to sit together and converse while they ate. But there were far fewer tables here than there'd been in the caldera—and far fewer people, too. It was only now as I saw how small this village was that I realized how thoroughly the Elytherioi had been dispersed. Nikos had said there was not room in any of the outposts to house the entire community the way they'd been in Elytherios. Everything truly had changed forever when the *geroi* invaded. I wondered sadly how many friendships, how many extended families had been separated.

And I wondered how, with the rebellion now spread across Iamos in small outposts rather than together in one place, we were going to manage to evacuate all of them before it was too late.

"Nadin!" I turned at the sound of my name and saw Isaak already seated at one of the tables, Emil beside him with the *kerkopith*, as always, perched on his shoulder.

I came over to join them. Isaak looked as exhausted as I felt, his skin sallow and deep circles etched into the skin below his eyes. There were little pieces of *seno* stuck to his clothing, and even a bit in his hair. But he was smiling.

"How'd your day go?" he asked me.

"It went well," I said truthfully. In spite of everything, I was glad I'd had the opportunity to get to know Corin, Ierin and Syrin better. "What about you? You look tired."

Isaak laughed. "It shows, huh? They've got a lot more animals here than I'd bargained for. But their *kela* and *ielak* flocks are robust, which is a relief. We lost so many at Eliin's outpost in the eruption."

As he spoke, Emil nudged him in the side. Isaak swatted his hand away in annoyance. As I quirked my head in confusion, Emil rolled his eyes.

"Fine. I'm going to see how Gitrin is doing," Emil said, getting to his feet with a noisy cracking of his knees.

"What was that about?" I asked, watching Emil shuffle away with a bemused smile on my face. Emil and Gitrin were having an easier time communicating without interpretation, it was true, but they'd still been largely sticking close to Isaak and me. What would entice Emil to go off on his own?

When I glanced back at Isaak, I saw his face had reddened. "Emil's just being pushy," he said, seeming chagrined. "During our downtime today, he helped me with a little project. I suppose I might as well give it to you now."

He unzipped his jacket and withdrew something from his pocket. He handed it to me, and I stared down in confusion. It was a small circlet of braided twine, with a few shards of black rock wrapped with wire attached at intervals. A crude piece of jewelry?

"What is this?" I asked.

"I know it's kind of lame, and it might not even fit you," he said. "But those pebbles are hematite. I know the *geroi* took away your ace ring, so…" He shrugged, his face growing even more flushed. "I thought you might like a new one. Such as it is."

I stared down at the handmade ring a moment longer, the sound of the conversations around us seeming to grow ever more distant. There was a stinging behind my eyes.

"Maybe it was a bad idea—" he started to say, but I shook my head and slipped the ring onto the middle finger of my right hand. It was a bit on the loose side, but that was probably for the best, since the uneven fragments of hematite would have dug into my skin had it been any tighter.

"Do you like it?" Isaak asked.

I swallowed down the lump in my throat and nodded.

He gave me a lopsided grin. "Good. I'm glad."

"Thank you, Isaak," I murmured. "Thank you so much."

There was the sound of raised voices, and the two of us looked up. Camos' group was entering the camp now, talking boisterously and laughing. From among them, Ceilos caught my eye. He started to detach from the group, but Camos stayed him, clapping his hand on Ceilos' shoulder.

"You worked hard today. I underestimated you," Camos said.

"We all did," Syrin commented, walking past with a plate of food. "He never complained once on our entire journey to Katai'ios, even though he was bound and blindfolded. He learned to rely on his ears, and because of that he noticed the *tirak* long before we did. Before it would have been too late. We never would have made it here without him."

Ceilos was beaming from ear to ear.

"Gitrin was right to sponsor you both for citizenship," Ierin said, joining her partner and squeezing his hand. "I'm glad that both of you are with us. If it came to a forum again, I would be proud to stand for both of you once more."

The others murmured their agreement, and Ceilos caught my eye, still grinning. With my left hand, I squeezed my new ring between my fingers. After this afternoon, after what Ierin and Corin and Syrin had said in the fields, I'd once again been thinking about everything in a new light—why I was the way I was, why Ceilos was the way he was, why we'd become what we'd become. Even now, at what could be the end, the Elytherioi were offering him a chance at a fresh start. I needed to as well.

It was time to tell Ceilos the truth.

I asked Ceilos to meet me somewhere private, somewhere we could talk quietly without interruption. After the evening meal, we excused ourselves from the group and he led me back into the fields, to where the *seno* was still waiting to be harvested, its soft tufts stretching toward the colored glass above. The light that trickled into the dome was fading, leaving us in an odd, multicolored twilight.

Ceilos pushed through the swaying grass into a clearing of sorts, where we were shielded by the tall *seno* all around us but would have room to breathe. He turned to face me, a grin tugging at the corners of his lips. "What's all this, then?" he asked. "A clandestine meeting?"

"Not exactly," I said, my cheeks hot. Ceilos was happy—it was written all over his face—and suddenly I felt anxious. I was afraid that what I had to tell him now was going to spoil his good mood, ruin the contentment we'd found in this place. And what if doing so was pointless? If that star we'd seen really was what we feared, weren't there more important things we needed to worry about than my feelings? And if we were too late—if everything would be over in a week's time anyway—was it selfish of me to tell him this now? Maybe it would be better to just take this to my grave...

The thought made me feel sick. But no. Even if this was the end, Ceilos needed to know. And I needed to be honest. If this *was* the end, I wanted to have no regrets. I wanted to go out knowing I had truly been myself, and I was no longer living a lie.

"Ceilos," I said. "I... I wanted to talk about what happened before. That night in our old classroom."

The grin on his face faded. He looked wary now. My stomach flip-flopped.

"What about it?" he asked.

"I wanted to tell you the truth about what happened that day. You asked me..." I paused and attempted to swallow, but my mouth was too dry. "You asked me why I didn't... *want* you. And I didn't have an answer then. But in the time I was on Mars, I learned the answer. I learned the truth about myself."

He looked away. In the semidarkness, I couldn't see what his face was saying. "And what is the truth?" he asked, his tone unreadable.

I gripped the rough stones of my new ring tightly. "I learned that I am asexual. That means someone who doesn't experience sexual attraction... someone who doesn't feel..." I tried to describe it in our language. We didn't have words for this the way they did in English. "Desire," I settled on, though I knew that wasn't entirely it. But for me, it was true, so it would do.

"Doesn't feel desire?" he repeated incredulously.

I tugged my earlobe. "I've never felt it," I said. "I thought that was normal for *geroi*, for *patroi*, but our conversation that night and... and everything else that happened"—I hurried on, trying not to relive it— "made me realize that wasn't the case. The revulsion I felt when I saw the *plivoi* in the marketplace, that wasn't something most other people feel. And I realized that I have never felt desire."

"Not for me." His face was still shadowed.

"Not for *anyone*," I said emphatically. "And when I realized this, I thought there must be something wrong. But on Mars, I learned that it's a real thing. It's called asexuality. And it's normal. It's not common, but it's normal."

He was quiet for a long moment, and I watched him, my heartbeat seeming frozen, breath not coming. Waiting for his reaction. Waiting for him to say he understood. That it explained so much. That he supported me. That he was glad I told him.

He still wasn't answering. Why wasn't he answering?

"You..." He took a ragged breath. "You expect me to believe this?"

My heart sank. "Of course I expect you to believe it. It's true."

"True?" His voice raised in volume, breaking on the word. He took another breath. "You know, I always thought that you were a poor liar. But apparently I was wrong."

I stared at him, aghast. "Ceilos, why would I lie about something like this?"

"You'd say anything to keep me from realizing the truth, apparently," he snapped.

I blinked repeatedly. "This *is* the truth!"

He turned to face me, took a step closer. I wanted to flinch away, but I stood my ground. He had to know that I was telling the truth.

He held my gaze, scrutinizing my face. Then he sighed. "You really believe it," he said.

"What are you talking about?" I demanded. "Of course I believe it. It's the *truth*."

"There is no such thing as 'asexuality'!" he snapped.

"Yes, there is. On Mars I met others—"

"What you're describing isn't real, Nadin," he insisted. "Those Martians, those *aliens*—they were trying to poison your mind with alien ideas. But Iamoi aren't like that. You have to know. Iamoi aren't like that."

My temper flared up inside me. "Yes, we are. And do you know how I know that? Because I *am*." I stamped my foot on the ground in frustration. "I know it to be true, because I know myself. Honestly—" I floundered for words, desperately fixating on what Syrin had said this afternoon, my earlier confidence draining out of me like water from a sieve. "Samelove is known and accepted on Iamos. Syrin and Shuliin are a samelove partnership. Why should this be any different?"

Ceilos scoffed. "Samelove," he said derisively. "Samelove only exists among the *plivoi*. The *geroi* introduced samelove into their genetics specifically to limit population growth. It doesn't occur naturally."

"That's not true," I protested. "On Mars I met people who were samelove. My friend Tamara's parents—"

"On Mars, on Mars, on Mars," he spat. "Again with the aliens. They are not Iamoi, Nadin. This is not the Iamoi way. And if this—this *asexuality* were real, if it were a genuine inherent trait, the *geroi* would have introduced it to the *plivoi*. It would have been a better way to limit population growth than samelove. But they did not, because it isn't real." His voice was cold, each word cutting into me like a sharpened blade. "And even if it were real, it never would have occurred in a *gerouin*. Our genetics are thoroughly honed, every detail of us—from our physical appearance to our temperament to our genetic predisposition to disease—every bit is engineered to be absolutely perfect. What you say you are, you could never be. The *geroi* never would have allowed it."

The sun had dipped behind the cliffs, leaving Katai'ios in darkness. I was glad for it. I could barely see Ceilos' face now, but I was grateful he couldn't see mine. Hot tears were burning a trail down my cheeks.

"This is just another lie, another excuse," he snarled. "Maybe you even believe it, but it's not true. It's not who you are. The truth of the matter is that you do experience desire—for Isaak."

I swallowed, my throat sticky. "I do not desire Isaak," I said, entirely truthful.

"You expect me to believe that?" Ceilos scoffed. "You're honestly going to tell me that you don't love Isaak?"

I stood silently in the darkness for a long moment, trying to hold myself together. "I do love Isaak," I said, and the words sounded strange in my own ears. How many times I'd thought them. How I'd longed to say them out loud, but I never thought I'd be able to. And now I was saying them here, like this. Not telling Isaak. Not saying them with love in my heart. Saying them to Ceilos, angrily. Defensively. I hated it. I hated everything about this. Why had I ever thought this would be the right thing to do?

"I knew it," Ceilos said, his voice thick, heavy. "I knew you—"

"But I don't *desire* Isaak," I interrupted loudly, almost shouting over the top of him. "He knows that, and he accepts it. And if you want to know the truth, it's this." I was shaking, my fists clenched tightly at my sides. "I would never have fallen in love with Isaak if you hadn't treated me the way you did. I loved you, Ceilos, for who you were. Who I thought you were, at least. But you didn't love me for who I am. You wanted me to become someone I could never be. You want to change me, even now. You deny that I could ever be who I say I am. But Isaak accepts me the way I am. That's why I love him. And why I don't love you anymore."

I couldn't see his reaction. His face was a silhouette in profile, looking away from me, into the mass of *seno* grass surrounding us.

"All you needed to say was that you loved him," he murmured. "I knew it all along. I didn't need the rest of your lies."

I wanted to scream. But there was no point. Nothing I could say would make him understand. I had told him the truth, but I couldn't force him to believe it if he refused.

"Leave me," he said in a strained voice. "I need to compose myself."

I started to turn to go, but then I paused, glancing back over my shoulder. "Before I do, there's one thing I want to know." Something that had been bothering me for months. A question I already knew the answer to, but one I still had to ask.

"That day in Elytherios, when we were just about to enter the postern... why did you let go of my hand?"

Silence. It lasted so long I thought he wasn't going to answer. But just as I began to turn again, he said it.

"I wanted to see if you'd come back."

I squeezed my eyes shut, a fresh round of tears burning behind them—tears of anger, this time, rather than the shame and frustration that had coursed down my cheeks minutes ago.

I didn't respond. I just stormed away, leaving Ceilos there in the dark.

CHAPTER 39

- i s a a k -

I LOOKED UP AT THE SOUND OF RAISED VOICES COMING FROM THE FIELDS. Beside me, Tuupa growled, a low sound rumbling from deep within her. I peered into the darkness, looking for the source, but the torchlight here was too dim to see much farther than a couple meters away.

I'd retreated to the *gurza* pens after dinner. I wasn't sure where Nadin had gone—she'd disappeared after Emil had roped me into translating the finer points of a conversation he and Gitrin were having about Martian evolutionary biology, which had been an adventure considering I didn't really understand the terms they were using, even in English—and I'd needed to find a calm, quiet place to decompress. I was still bone tired after our journey and stressed about... everything. Back on Mars, when I'd needed to calm myself after a long, stressful day, I would go to Escalante Bay, where the lapping waves would relax my soul. On Iamos, I'd found the same stillness among the *gurzas*. It seemed strange to be so soothed by the kinds of creatures they used to make horror flix about back in the day. But I connected with them, somehow. I had right away, on the road to Elytherios.

Another shout. I frowned. Mostly everyone in Katai'ios was still sitting around the firepit chatting amongst themselves, or else they'd retired to the longhouses to rest after the day's labors. I patted Tuupa's muzzle reassuringly until her growling subsided, then detached myself, taking a few steps toward the darkened rows of crops. The sun had set quickly thanks to the sheer cliffs around the dome, and Katai'ios had become almost pitch dark in what felt like the blink of an eye. Gios,

Corin's partner who'd been assigned to the livestock with me this afternoon, had come through about fifteen minutes ago to light the torches scattered around the village, and we'd spoken briefly. But I hadn't seen hide nor hair of anyone else.

My muscles tensed as I heard the sound of footsteps pounding on the ground. Running in this direction. A moment later, a figure burst out of the tall purple grass, careening into me hard. I managed to keep my footing, balancing the person. She recoiled, staring at me with wild blue eyes. Then the two of us recognized each other.

"Isaak," she cried, her voice ragged with emotion. She gripped my jacket tightly.

"Nadin? Are you okay?"

She stared at me a moment longer, her face seeming to crumple in slow motion before my eyes. Then she hurled herself against my chest, her shoulders shaking with sobs.

"What's wrong?" I asked in alarm. Had that been her voice I'd heard shouting in the field? What had she been doing out there this late?

"Ceilos," she said between hitched breaths.

I put my hands on her shoulders, my brows drawing together in concern. "Did he hurt you?"

She shook her head, then hesitated. "Not... physically," she finally said, her voice still thick with tears.

I managed to guide her over to a bench near the pens. One of the torches was burning beside it, so we could see each other a bit better. We sat side by side, Nadin's knees drawn up in front of her, her face buried in them, crying herself out. I felt awkward sitting there next to her, like I should be doing more to comfort her, but the mention of Ceilos had thrown a wall up between us. I wasn't sure where the boundary line was, but I didn't want to cross it.

"I told him," she finally said between her sobs. "I told him the truth. About being asexual. I told him the truth, but he didn't believe me. He was angry. He said it's not real. He said I was lying because—" She broke off abruptly, a new wave of sobs washing over her.

I watched her in the flickering torchlight. Her hair had grown back in now, short and white and curly. The flames made it glow orange.

"Why wouldn't he believe me? Why did he—*mock* me like this?

Doesn't he care how hurtful it is?"

My stomach contorted inside me. I wanted to tell her how much I understood. Because I did. It was exactly how my dad had reacted when I'd come out to him. When I'd realized I was demisexual, I'd been so proud and relieved when I'd found a word that explained my experiences. When I'd realized I was normal. But Dad had just laughed. And then the mocking had begun.

If I told her about that, would she feel better, knowing she wasn't alone in this? That, just as she wasn't alone in being ace, she wasn't alone in experiencing aphobia? Or would it make her feel worse? I didn't know what to say. My tongue felt like lead.

"I want to go back. I want to go h—" I swore she was going to say *home*, but she changed course. Maybe she did think of it that way, but she knew it wasn't quite home. Not yet. "I want to go back to the future," she amended, "where I could be myself and I had friends and nobody said these things to me."

No. I couldn't tell her. I couldn't bring myself to say that there were people in the future who were like Ceilos. That I'd met them. That I was related to one. She'd been lucky in that she'd only encountered affirming people thus far. What she'd gone through I wouldn't wish on anyone. I knew all too well how humiliating it was, how dehumanizing it was. For people to doubt your identity, to brush it off as a product of your imagination. If someone close to you, someone you trusted, denied who you were at your core, how could you ever feel comfortable in your own skin ever again? I couldn't bring myself to tell her that this might not be the last time it happened.

"I miss Scylla," she sobbed. "And Mariyah. I miss Tamara and I miss Henry. I miss Delia and Bryn and Wyatt and Kate."

"I know," I said quietly. "I miss them too. But there are people here you love. Like Gitrin."

"Yes. And Syrin. She believed me. She said she didn't think it was odd. It's just torquing Ceilos!" she yelled in English. Her use of Martian slang took me aback.

"He makes me so angry, Isaak. So, so angry." She lifted her head from her knees for a moment, meeting my eyes fiercely. "I finally asked him. I finally asked him why he let go of my hand when we were leaving

Elytherios. All those months I was terrified something horrible had happened to him and Gitrin and Emil. That they'd been caught in the tesseract, that they'd been killed. *Months* I worried about them. And you know what he told me?" Her hand clenched into a fist at her side. "He told me he wanted to see if I'd come back. He was *testing* me. Like I was some faithless *anguis*."

She slammed her feet down onto the ground, no longer crying. "He made me so *angry* when we were in Elytherios. The way he was acting, from the very night he arrived there. The jealousy, the possessiveness. The way he tried to mark me like an animal whenever you were around. Like I was his property. It made me so angry I wanted to never speak to him again. But then he'd turn around and be so kind, I'd think maybe I'd imagined it. Maybe I was being too harsh toward him. Maybe things would be different now. Time and time and time again I would give him these chances."

I swallowed. This sounded familiar, too. I'd heard those exact words before—out of my mom, every time she'd try to break it off with Dad and then wind up taking him back. It felt weird now, hearing them out of Nadin. When I was a kid and I'd hear Mom saying these things, I hadn't understood. I wanted to kick myself, now, for what I'd said to her when I'd heard my parents talking when we returned to Mars. When I'd asked her why she hadn't given Dad another chance. What a ridiculous thing to have asked. She'd given him way too many chances already. Why did it take hearing those words out of Nadin's mouth for me to see it?

Because I'd been a kid then. I hadn't understood. Words like *manipulation* and *emotional abuse* were just that—words. She'd done a good job of shielding me from the reality behind those words. But I could see it now.

"I don't want to keep going through this," Nadin said, raw emotion creeping back into her voice. "I want him out of my life. But I don't know *how*, Isaak. With everything going on now, we're stuck together for the foreseeable future. And beyond that, I feel like we're *bound* to each other. I... I can't explain it. I feel *beholden* to him."

I frowned. "What do you mean?"

"Because he freed me from Bright Horizon. He got me away from the *geroi*, prevented the reeducation. He risked his life to bring me here, and he very nearly lost his life because of the *shedosht*—which he never would have gone through if I hadn't brought him here. I feel like I have to be responsible for him." She shook her head furiously. "But I don't *want* it anymore. I don't want this obligation anymore, this responsibility I feel for him."

"You don't actually have a responsibility to him, Nadin," I said. "I don't think you have to worry about the Elytherioi sending him to the guillotine or whatever anymore. Today proved that. He's got people in the rebellion who will vouch for him now, like Nikos and Camos. What happens to Ceilos from here on in is his responsibility, and you don't have to feel guilty about that. He's his own person. You're your own person. If he isn't willing to respect your identity and your choices, you don't have any obligation to keep him in your life."

She swallowed. "That all sounds very logical and reasonable, but I just don't see how that can work in practice with everything that's going on now. I... it's not the right time."

I inhaled slowly, looking over at the *gurzas* in the flickering torchlight. Most of them were curled up asleep, but Tuupa was awake still, watching me. She could sense our agitation and she was staring at me, her pupils narrowed to slits.

"If you always wait for the right time, it will never come," I said finally. "No time is ever going to be the right time. And honestly, with that thing in the sky overhead"—I swallowed—"it feels more important than ever that you make the most of the life you've got." *However much we have left of it.*

I kicked a pebble on the ground with my foot. "You don't deserve to be going through this. And you shouldn't have to keep going through it. I don't like seeing you suffer like this, Nadin."

She didn't answer for a long time. Finally, I chanced a glance her way. She'd drawn her knees up into her chest again, but now she rested her chin on top of them instead of hiding her face. Tears were flowing freely down her cheeks again.

"Ceilos isn't the one I love," she whispered. "Ceilos isn't the one I want to be with."

I turned, angling slightly to face her. That was all she needed. She pitched forward, barreling into me, burying her face in the place where my neck met my shoulder.

"Why does he hold me this way?" she sobbed. "Why can't he let me go? Am I never going to be free?"

I tightened my arms around her, trying to swallow the lump in my throat. I loved her so much. I wanted to do everything for her. I wanted this to go away. I wanted her to be happy again. I wanted to see her smile again, hear her laugh again—see her uninhibited by this burden again. I wanted to confront Ceilos, make him answer for what he was putting her through. But I also feared that doing that would only make the situation worse, make things harder for her. That it would somehow be making things about myself again instead of about Nadin. I just didn't know what to do. Who could tell me what to do? What was the appropriate response here? What would be right by Nadin? What would be right by *me*?

I had no answers. I was at a complete loss. I realized, with a sick turn of my stomach, that the one person in my life who might understand this, the one person I knew who had gone through anything remotely similar, the one who could probably advise me best was Erick. The stepdad I'd never wanted, who'd said I reminded him of himself and driven me to such irrational, immature anger in response. But he'd been right. He really had been right. About everything. More and more, I found myself missing him, wishing I could talk to him. Wishing I could go back in time and give him another chance. But I knew more than anyone that I couldn't. And the odds were pretty much unbeatable that I would never see him again. Funny how those things go.

I was on my own here. And I had no answers. There was nothing I could do but be here for Nadin, and hope that that was the right thing to do.

So we sat quietly, my arms around her, until her tears were dry and the torch beside us had burned down low.

We walked back to the village awkwardly, arms' length apart from each other. She didn't say anything to me, and I didn't say anything to her. I don't think either of us *knew* what to say.

It didn't matter. There wasn't time for that, anyway. There were more pressing matters to worry about. We'd heard the commotion from the longhouses, and I could see them now, clustered around the large firepit in the center of the village. A small group of people I was unfamiliar with, and alongside them Eos, Nikos, and Marin.

The elders had returned.

CHAPTER 40

- n a d i n -

THEY USHERED US INTO ONE OF THE LONGHOUSES, EOS, MARIN, AND NIKOS.
Two rows of beds lined the walls. This, Nikos told us, had long been his
dwelling, along with the other permanent residents of Katai'ios. But the
others weren't here now. They'd gone to the citidomes. We'd have this
place to ourselves.

"There are things you've been needing to tell us," Eos said as Nikos
closed the door. His eyes were fixed on Isaak. "Things you tried to tell us
the day of the eruption. I told you then that there was no time. But it
seems that we've run out of time for anything else."

I looked around the room. They'd brought Isaak, Gitrin, Emil and me
here... and Ceilos. I'd been avoiding looking at him this entire time. Now I
chanced a glance in his direction. His expression was pleasantly neutral,
fixed on the elders. No sign of his earlier outrage was visible now. I felt
completely out of sorts still, and I was certain it showed in my
demeanor. But there was not a single crack in Ceilos' perfect composure.
It was as if nothing had happened. I suddenly found myself questioning
whether that entire exchange had even occurred, or if I'd been imagining
the venom that had been in his words.

No. I couldn't let myself forget. I couldn't just keep slipping back into
the pattern of assuming any conflict between us was my imagination—
or worse, my own doing. My *fault*. Something had to change.

"Nikos told us of the new star you spotted on your journey here,"
Marin said. "So when night fell in Dauntless Spirit, we looked for it
ourselves. And we discovered something very strange. Those in our

movement who do not use earpieces were able to see it. But those who were connected to the System could not. The System was *preventing* them from being able to see it."

"Which raises the question, what is it that we're not supposed to be seeing?" Eos asked. He looked at Isaak archly. "My brother tells us that you know that answer."

Isaak sighed, running a hand through his hair. "When we were on Earth, a scientist there told us about a catastrophic astronomical event that took place twelve thousand years before my time. We calculated that this coincides with... now. The time we are in on Iamos."

"So you're saying that this new star is on a collision course with Iamos?" Eos asked brusquely.

Isaak swallowed. "Not exactly."

I squeezed my eyes shut. I didn't want to hear what came next.

"The orientation of the solar system is... different in my time," Isaak began. "Hamos is not in the position it's in currently. It's... very far from where it is currently, in fact. Something must have impacted it. Something very big. Big enough to disrupt its orbit. Debris from the collision reached as far as Earth—as Simos," he amended. "The debris was severe enough that it caused Simos to fall into a global ice age that lasted thirteen hundred years."

"If such an impact were to occur now, it would not only devastate Hamos," Gitrin said, her voice grim. "The debris from the collision would wipe out all life on Iamos."

Marin sat down on the edge of one of the beds, exhaling. "This is something that should have triggered the early warning protocol months ago. Like the earthquake outside Ascendant Dawn, and the eruption that destroyed Elytherios."

"The early warning protocol has been sabotaged," Ceilos said flatly.

"By the so-called Liberator," said Gitrin, frowning.

"By my father," Ceilos corrected. "*Geros Tibros.*"

Gitrin stared at him with such shock that I felt guilty for not having warned her sooner. Behind her, the three elders looked at each other, alarm written on their faces. "You're certain?"

"As certain as I can be," Ceilos admitted. "His behavior has become erratic. Camos told us that he has seized control of the citidomes. I believe that he invented the Liberator persona to sow discord in the cities. Disaster requires response. Chaos requires a strong leader to bring order. By sabotaging the System, Tibros orchestrated a situation through which he could assume power."

Nikos ran a hand over his jaw. "Logical. And he is one of the only ones who has not yet fallen ill." He arched a brow, eying Ceilos. "Then he is the one who has poisoned the other *geroi?*"

"I believe so."

"This is what I tried to tell you on the day of the eruption," Isaak said. "Nadin and I heard a recording from a *gerotus* session where they discussed developing a neurotoxin—something that attacks a person's nervous system. They were planning on using it on the Simoi, to try to wipe out the population and colonize that planet. Now suddenly the *geroi* seem like they're being poisoned by their own toxin."

"That same *gerotus* session is the one that the so-called Liberator patched you and Isaak in on, right?" Ceilos turned, addressing the question directly to me. His expression was neutral, his voice casual. But my stomach still curdled inside me. I could still hear the hateful words he'd hurled at me an hour before. They paralyzed my voice in my throat.

I swallowed, struggling to manage a response. "Yes."

"More breadcrumbs," Ceilos said, turning back to the elders. I gripped the ring Isaak had made me tightly, trying to regain the rhythm of my breathing.

"At that point, the entire *gerotus* suspected Nadin was in league with the rebels. By sending them that message, by making them aware of the neurotoxin, Tibros knew he was making the rebellion aware of the toxin as well. Then when the *geroi* began falling ill with it, the rebels would take the blame. More chaos, more discord. Yet another way to consolidate his own power."

Nikos made a thoughtful sound in the back of his throat. "But he may have gotten himself in over his head. He sabotaged the early warning protocol in order to create chaos, but didn't consider that while the protocol was disabled something larger than earthquakes or eruptions might occur. This new star has the potential to wipe out our entire populace."

"If it actually *is* what Isaak thinks," Eos pointed out. "It could be something else entirely. A supernova, perhaps. Or a particularly bright object in the asteroid belt. Perhaps the System is concealing it for a different reason. We may be worrying ourselves for nothing, at a time when the rebellion needs all our attention. If Tibros is truly to blame for all this, then he is a powerful enemy. Our entire movement is at risk. If the star turns out to be nothing, we'll have wasted important time—crucial time—on folly."

"But if it *is* the Clovis impact," Isaak argued, "then we're wasting precious time that we need to be spending on evacuating the populace."

"How can we know for sure?" Marin asked. "All our instruments rely on the System. If the System is malfunctioning..."

Emil cleared his throat then, and the others looked at him in surprise. "Now, I've only been able to follow about a third of this conversation," he said in English, "but I have a suggestion. I've got years of practice reading analog data, running calculations. I used to work for NASA, remember," he added proudly. "If you could get me access to a telescope, I might be able to give you the answers you need." He smiled almost smugly, his arms crossed. Then he prodded Isaak in the side. "Well, go on, tell them."

Isaak dutifully translated.

"Hmm," Gitrin said when Isaak was through. "Telescopes are a relic of the past. We have not relied on them for centuries. And you would need a large one—a powerful one."

"What about the celestial observatory in the ruins of Thalash'a?" Ceilos asked.

My heart squeezed at the mention of Thalash'a. The ancient capital, near where Hope Renewed was built. As when Ceilos had locked eyes with me a moment ago, it happened involuntarily, so intense that it caught me off guard—the flood of emotions that I wouldn't have expected. A rush of anger, shame, grief. The ruins by the sea. The home of one of my most cherished memories for almost half my life. Suddenly everything was much more complicated.

Was this how things were going to be from now on? Memories that once brought me joy would now bring me pain?

Beside me, Gitrin made a thoughtful sound in the back of her throat. "That's a long shot." She looked up at the others. "It's said there was a lighthouse in Thalash'a, beyond the dry coastline. It was on an island originally, but the sea has long since receded. By the time the capital was evacuated, the island was accessible by foot."

"I said telescope, not lighthouse," Emil protested. He looked at Isaak. "That's what she said, right?"

"Let her finish," Isaak replied with a roll of his eyes.

Gitrin smiled patiently. "When our people began using satellite technology and the System to perform astronomical observations, the telescope was no longer needed. Because of its location on the headland overlooking the sea, the building that had housed the observatory was ultimately converted into a lighthouse. But none of the historical sources knew what had become of the telescope. Some believed it must have been disassembled for parts. But others theorized that it still remained within the lighthouse building, intact but merely disused."

"Do you think the telescope could still be there after all this time?" Nikos asked. "And more importantly, would it be operational?"

"That is difficult to determine, on both counts. The observatory was already centuries old at the time the capital was evacuated. Even the lighthouse had been abandoned as the sea receded away from the island." Gitrin exhaled. "Whether it's still functional is anyone's guess. But at this point, I fear we have few alternatives. It can't hurt to try."

Marin frowned thoughtfully. "If the telescope is there and Emil is able to use it... and if he discovers that the new star is the... *Clovis* object"— she stuttered over the foreign word—"what then? We won't be able remain here." She leveled her gaze on me. "When you left us, you were planning on making a treaty between the people of Isaak's time and our people, to allow us to evacuate safely to Isaak's time. Were you successful?"

Isaak and I glanced at each other. The truth was, we'd been an utter failure.

I opened my mouth hesitantly, trying to find the words to explain the bad news. But before I could speak, Isaak reached into his jacket pocket and withdrew a posternkey. The same key I had pressed into his hands the day I returned to Iamos. The one I'd taught Henry how to reprogram. The key that had brought Isaak back here.

"This key will bring us to my time," he said.

My eyes widened. He hadn't told me he had this. Had Henry given him a return key? But what about GSAF?

He was bluffing. He had to be.

But his bluff paid off. Satisfied, Marin tugged her earlobe, and Nikos stepped forward. "Evacuating both Iamos and Hamos will be a risky mission. The *geroi*—what remains of them, at least—will be opposed to us at every turn. If Tibros is, as we fear, the one posing as the Liberator, he is a dangerous enemy to contend with. We will have to plan carefully, and we're running out of time."

"We can't make any plans until we know for certain that this new star is what Isaak says it is," Eos said. "A party must leave for the ancient observatory first thing in the morning."

"Ceilos will lead us," Nikos said.

Eos froze, something in his face changing. "The *geroi*'s blood? I don't know if that's wise."

"Ceilos has proven himself, brother," Nikos said.

"We agreed that we would leave this choice up to our people," Eos replied. "We'd have to call a forum, and there's no time for that. Surely Gitrin—"

"The *ninvidu* ruled that the elders must make this decision," Nikos interrupted. "I believe that we should follow her judgment. As you say, there's no time for a forum. We need Ceilos' knowledge."

"Nikos, Eos," Marin said in a soothing tone, inserting herself between the brothers. "There's no need—"

"Why are you pushing this, Nikos?" Eos demanded, ignoring her.

"Because of Maetrin," Nikos snapped. "Maetrin taught us to trust those who had proven their trustworthiness, regardless of their past. She testified for Marin in the *shedosht*, despite what had happened to Phados. Have you forgotten already? The years have hardened you, brother."

Marin still stood between them, concern etched into her face.

Eos cleared his throat, breaking the tension. He looked down at Marin, his expression pained. "What do you think, *yachin*?" he asked in a low voice. "I'll abide by your decision."

Marin exhaled shakily, glancing around the longhouse. Her eyes fell on Ceilos for a long moment. She took another breath and sighed. "I agree with Nikos," she said. "I was given a chance, and I believe I proved myself. Nikos says the boy deserves that chance. He knows him better than you or I. He... he says he sees what you and Maetrin saw in me." She squeezed her eyes shut. "So I will choose to trust him."

Eos was quiet for a long moment, his expression grim. Finally, he tugged his earlobe. "Very well. Ceilos will lead the party to the ancient observatory."

Ceilos grinned. "I won't let you down," he said.

I looked down quietly. This morning I would have been happy for him. But now I couldn't bring myself to celebrate. Ceilos leading our group would mean more time spent with him. Isaak had said I didn't have to keep him in my life, but fate kept insisting on throwing us together. I couldn't escape the oppressive feeling that I truly was never going to be free of him.

Nikos didn't notice my downcast expression. "All right," he said, his voice taking on the authoritative quality it seemed naturally inclined toward. "Our party will leave first thing in the morning. Emil will come with us, Isaak and Nadin to translate—Gitrin, what about you?"

"History is my passion. I wouldn't miss a chance to see one of the great cities of our past." Gitrin smiled, casting a glance in Emil's direction. "And I am interested to see our astronomer do his calculations."

"Right." Nikos tugged his earlobe. "We'd best get to our beds now. We've had a long journey behind us, and there's still more ahead."

I tossed and turned for hours, the comfortable bed in the women's longhouse jarring after weeks of sleeping on the ground. But in truth, the bed was not the reason I could not sleep. My thoughts tormented me. Over and over his words burned into me like acid.

"What you're describing isn't real, Nadin."

"What you say you are, you could never be. The geroi never would have allowed it."

Hot tears streaked down my face. I wrapped my fingers tightly around my ring, the uneven surface of the stones biting into my skin.

The *geroi* had planned many things for me. But I'd deviated anyway. *"So much for a perfect system,"* Melusin had said. They'd called me a fool. Now Ceilos had as much as called me an abomination. What if they were right? I had always been doomed to be an utter failure as a *gerouin*. Gitrin had believed I could be something more. But maybe she was wrong. Maybe I was nothing more than a freak and a disappointment to everyone around me.

In the bed beside me, I heard Gitrin lightly snoring. I rolled over on my side, turning away from her.

Why had I thought it would be a good idea to tell him I was asexual? If I had kept it to myself, if I had just swallowed my feelings, everything would still be fine between us. We could have gone on as we always had. I should never have told him. I should never have said anything that night in Gitrin's classroom. I should have just kept going on being what people expected me to be. An obedient *gerouin*. A useful fool. A body for Ceilos to desire. A vessel to incubate the next generation of *geroi*.

A girl whose anger poisoned her from the inside out.

What was the point in knowing who I really was? These answers hadn't brought me peace. They'd only brought me misery.

We were to return to the ancient capital tomorrow. Why did it have to be that place?

I tried to block it, but my mind kept drawing me back into it, the memory playing over and over in my mind. It had been the one day in my life when I'd been the most free. I'd never experienced anything like it before, and wouldn't for many more years. Not until I left the citidome and traveled to Elytherios. No—not until I traveled to the future. It had been the first and only time I'd felt completely liberated from the constrictive world of the *geroi*. And Ceilos had given it to me. He'd shared his secret with me, and for a few blissful hours, we were free. And I'd known then—I would never ask for a repartnership. He and I would be the best of partners, because he was the only person I could trust. We were alone in this world, but we were alone together. And that had made everything all right.

I squeezed my eyes closed, the burning behind them painful now. I didn't want to remember. But remembering was all my mind could let me do.

✦

I can hear the sea.

When I was very young, you could still hear the sound of the waves from the upper levels of the citidome. But it's been years since the last time I heard it.

But I can hear it now.

Yesterday was my fifth annual. Ceilos had reached his a few weeks ago; despite the precise timing of Melusin's and Clodin's pregnancies, there was still a slight difference between our ages. But the ceremony couldn't be conducted until the date of my annual. The whole city had come together, the *patroi*, *esotoi*, and *plivoi*. The higher castes had emerged from the safety of the underground, all united as one people as Ceilos and I ascended to the very peak of the stepped pyramid. All had watched as *Geros* Antos and *Gerouin* Melusin had presented the people with the next generation of *geroi*. Ceilos and I had pledged our loyalty to the people of Iamos, swearing to serve faithfully and to hold the creed of the Progression in our hearts: *All lives are one.* We'd sworn to uphold our partnership, and Antos and Melusin had sealed our betrothal.

We're partners now, Ceilos and me. Just a few weeks ago, that had seemed a fate worse than death. But things are different now. Things changed after I shared my secret with him. Because Ceilos had a secret, too. One he'd never shared with anyone. But he shared it with me, because I shared mine with him.

He's built a System protocol—one that lets you go wherever you want without being traced by the *geroi*. It makes the System think you're somewhere different than you really are. After he showed it to me, he told me he was going to take me somewhere special after my annual. A gift just for me. But I never imagined it would be this.

When we were on top of the pyramid, I could see farther than I'd ever seen before. Clear out over the valley, beyond the dried shoreline. I could see the ocean, far in the distance.

And now we're here. We've sneaked out of the citidome now, creeping down the hills to the ruins. I knew they were here, but I've never seen them before. Not like this. Crumbling buildings, centuries old, half buried in rusty sand carried by *gamada* storms. Their decay has been helped along by raiders, smugglers who sneak out of the citidomes and steal things from the ruins to sell on the black market. I'm nervous that we might encounter one now, but Ceilos isn't afraid. I'm becoming more and more certain that Ceilos isn't afraid of anything.

Awestruck, we make our way down abandoned alleyways. Ceilos climbs up on a toppled pillar of marble, riddled with cracks. He reaches his hand to me, and I take it. He pulls me up on top of the pillar and I laugh. It's so strange to imagine that just a hundred years ago, before the Progression, this was the center of life on this part of Iamos. A bustling city... before the atmosphere began to drain away. Before the sea began to disappear.

"I want to see the ocean," I say. "Can we reach it?"

"I think we can," Ceilos says. "It didn't look far from here when we were atop the pyramid yesterday."

Gleefully, we scramble over ruins, ducking through partially collapsed archways, following the sound of the waves. It's not far now. The sea is near. The sea.

We squeeze through an alley and emerge between two ramshackle buildings, and suddenly, without warning, there it is. It is far from us, farther than Ceilos thought—I don't think we can walk to it and still make it back to Hope Renewed before Antos and Melusin notice we're gone. I won't be able to feel the water against my skin. But it's still there. I can see it. I can see the waves lapping against the eroded shore. It still exists. The sea.

Abruptly, I notice tears stinging my eyes. I sniffle, then notice the smell of the salt on the air I breathe in. The atmosphere is fading, but there's still air to breathe. For this moment, the sea still exists, the air still exists. For this moment, I can pretend that I don't have to live my life in a tiny glass dome, breathing recycled oxygen. I can pretend that I don't have to return to the *geroi*'s dark underground villa, to my parents' disapproval and a life of rigorous obligation. I can pretend that there's no one in the world except me.

And Ceilos. My friend. My partner.

I turn to him now, smiling wide, my heart full. "Thank you for bringing me here," I say.

He smiles and takes my hand in his, squeezing it tightly. "Yesterday we promised we would be loyal partners, faithful to Iamos and to the Progression," he says. "But that was just for the *geroi*, right?"

I quirk my head at him curiously, my heart falling slightly. "Was it?"

He tugs his earlobe with his free hand. "I want to make a promise that's just for you. I won't just be your partner for the *geroi*. I'll be your partner for real." He smiles, his expression slightly anxious. "Will you promise the same thing?"

I grin, tugging my own earlobe. "I promise. Partners for real."

He holds my hand tightly as we watch the waves crest in the distance.

Partners for real.

A promise for Iamos, and a promise for just Ceilos and me. We'd both sworn the same oath. But which one of us had upheld it? Him, or me?

I lay awake, tossing and turning, and hours passed.

CHAPTER 41

- i s a a k -

WE GATHERED AROUND THE POSTERN BEHIND THE LONGHOUSES THE NEXT morning. Before sunrise, Nikos and I had saddled Kodo, Tuupa and Thork, packing them with provisions. We didn't know whether we'd find any posterns in the capital ruins, so we had to plan for a potential return trip. I was told that Thalash'a was a day's ride southeast of Katai'ios, not far. We would use Katai'ios' postern to get there; with luck, Emil would be able to get the readings he needed; and we'd return to the outpost late tonight.

Despite the good night's rest I'd gotten, sleeping in a bed for the first time since we left the hotel in Xalapa, I felt fatigued and braindead as we congregated around the arch. I was not looking forward to more traveling, but we had no other choice. We had to go, and as quickly as possible.

As I leaned on Tuupa for support, Nikos handed me a breathing apparatus. Great. One day's reprieve, and we were back to canned air.

Beside me, Nadin looked wan, heavy bags under her eyes. As exhausted as I was, she looked like she hadn't slept at all.

"Hey," I said in a low voice, nudging her gently. "How are you feeling?"

She opened her mouth, but froze before replying. She exhaled heavily and busied herself with strapping the breathing apparatus onto her face. "Fine."

I frowned, glancing in Ceilos' direction. He stood in front of the postern, holding the posternkey he and Gitrin had programmed while

Nikos and I prepped the *gurzas* this morning. Nadin hadn't looked at him—it was more that she was pointedly *not* looking at him. "You don't have to talk to him," I told her. "Stick close to me or Gitrin."

She nodded, but she didn't appear any less miserable. Once again, I found myself feeling useless, wishing I had a better idea of what to do. If there even *was* anything I could do.

I made a click of my tongue and Tuupa lowered her belly to the ground so Emil could mount. Emil was devoid of Pandat for once—he'd left the *kerkopith* in Gios' care, something Pandat had been none too pleased about, but was necessary for the animal's safety. Once Emil was safely settled, I climbed into the saddle in front of him.

Nikos finished strapping his breathing apparatus to his face and took the posternkey from Ceilos' outstretched hand. The posterns were designed so that only the upper castes could operate them. Only someone in possession of a medallion like the one Nadin had lost in the raid on Lago Verde could open them. But as with the postern technology itself, the Elytherioi had found a way around this, either through thievery or through bootlegging. There was a snap, and the trapezoidal object in Nikos' hands began to unfurl. As the device opened, fold after fold, the archway began to hum. Light glowed between the stacked stones that formed the postern's shape, growing brighter. The colored glass of the dome that stood behind the postern disappeared as the arch filled with light. It was a door between space and time. A door of light.

"All right, everyone," he said, looking around at the five of us. "Hold on tightly."

The others mounted their *gurzas* in the same arrangement we'd used on the journey to Katai'ios—Nadin and Gitrin on Thork, Nikos and Ceilos on Kodo. The animals obediently took each other's tails in their mouths as I'd seen them do back at Eliin's outpost. Kodo took the lead, tall and proud as always.

The humming grew louder, the postern impossibly bright to look at.

Nikos dug his heels into Kodo's side and the *gurzas* bounded forward, into the light.

I was getting better at postern travel. Or maybe it was just the fact that I was on *gurza*-back this time instead of having to rely on my own two feet. Emil's fingers were clenched into my sides in a death grip, but I felt relatively steady myself, though my eyes still struggled to focus after staring into the blinding glow of the postern.

As I blinked away the light residue, I looked around to get my bearings. "Whoa," I breathed.

There was sand everywhere. That was the first thing I noticed. But then I realized that half-buried in that sand were the collapsed ruins of dozens of buildings. Stone pillars that had once supported heavy rooftops now lay tumbled and broken. Other, smaller buildings that had once been made of mud-brick were crumbled down nearly to their foundations.

"Thalash'a. The ancient capital," Nadin said quietly from the back of Thork. "It's fallen even further to ruin in four years' time."

"Incredible," Emil breathed. "An entire city, completely deserted in its heyday. Abandoned to the elements, so that all who come after can only wonder what caused its inhabitants to leave it behind. Like Tikal, eh, Contreras?"

I nodded without entirely registering what he'd said. My eyes had been scanning the hills surrounding us, and after a minute I realized I'd recognized the familiar shape. Realized that, despite having never seen ruins like this before, I'd stood on this very spot. Quite recently, in fact. I'd been here every time I took the ferry over to where Tamara had her music lessons. And again, just a couple months ago, on the night I'd picked Tamara up for our disastrous first—and only—date.

This was Herschel Island.

I scanned the horizon, my brain reorienting as I placed familiar landmarks dotting the otherwise entirely alien landscape. That flat bluff to the north, striated with black streaks, was Vera Rubin Ridge. It towered behind where the Academy had been built in my time. To the east, the hills that divided the peninsula, Tierra Nueva on one side and Curiosity Bay on the other. Erick's dig site had been in those hills, which meant... I scanned the horizon, and I saw it. There. Peeking between the hills, a glimmer of blue glass. There was Hope Renewed.

Nadin had said the ancient capital had been located on the coast, and west of Hope Renewed. Hope Renewed—the underground portion of which I'd stumbled into haphazardly while fleeing the factory district. Why hadn't I connected the dots before? Thalash'a was on the site of what would become Tierra Nueva. Buried under twelve thousand years of sand and devastated by impact craters—how much of this was still here in my time, waiting to be discovered?

The ruins of the ancient Iamoi capital had been right under our feet the whole time, and we hadn't even thought to look.

I marveled at the ruins surrounding us now. Herschel Island was in Escalante Bay, only a short ferry ride from Tierra Nueva. Within easy walking distance had there been no water in the way. But the bay was dry in this timeline. Nadin had said when she was a child she could still hear the waves, but if there was sea remaining now, it was far to the west of us. What remained was a valley, gently sloping down far below us, dotted with the remnants of buildings.

The changing coastline had clearly been gradual, ongoing for many years before this city was ultimately abandoned. In the valley below us, I could see newer buildings, less dilapidated than the ones farther inland, although still crumbling and buried in sand. The city had moved westward, following the changing shoreline, and the inhabitants of the island had likewise built eastward. But they didn't quite meet. There was a gap in the middle of the valley, a bare patch on the edges of the newer construction that seemed incongruous in its emptiness.

"After the Progression, the *geroi* forcibly evacuated this city," Gitrin explained. "Building had continued even as the coastline receded, filling in the empty space left behind by the evaporating sea. They were still building until the day the *geroi* forced them to stop."

We turned away from the valley and toward the hill ascending gently behind us. Herschel Island seemed pretty flat in my timeline, but that was when looking at it from a landscape full of water. Without the presence of Escalante Bay, the island appeared more like a flat-topped butte.

"The lighthouse is on a headland on the southwest part of the island. If it's still intact," Ceilos said.

Nikos nudged Kodo into motion and the other *gurzas* followed him, picking their way between partially collapsed buildings and over piles of sand that their taloned feet sank deeply into. It didn't seem like we'd climbed that high until I glanced back over my shoulder and saw the ruins we'd started at far below us, near the valley that marked the ancient shoreline. But there was still no sign of the lighthouse. If it was still standing, it would tower over everything else on the landscape. But from the slope of the mountain and surrounded by ruined buildings, our view of the top was obscured.

Then, as we reached the end of an alley where two three-story insulae had collapsed into each other, I finally saw it. That had to be it—there was nothing that could be but the lighthouse.

It was unlike any lighthouse I'd seen in my own time, though. The lighthouses on Escalante Bay were dull, nondescript towers, straight and narrow and square. There were, of course, the holos I'd seen online of historic lighthouses, especially those in the northeast of America and in places like Britain. Picturesque round towers, usually with a little cottage beside them. But neither of those images of what a lighthouse was fit with what loomed over us now.

This tower was stepped, like a ziggurat that someone had stretched out like a potter stretching clay. Each steppe was taller and narrower than the one below it. At the peak, a roof of some kind of burnished metal winked in the sunlight. But whatever light had once stood at the top as a beacon to sailors in the sea below had long since gone out.

"Amazing," Emil said over my shoulder. "That design—it's incredibly similar to the Pharos of Alexandria."

"The pharaohs?" I repeated.

"Pharos, you ninny," Emil barked. "The great lighthouse, one of the seven wonders of the ancient world."

"Oh, right," I said, feeling foolish. I loved archaeology, but I had to admit I was more interested in Mesoamerica than Egypt. But of course I'd heard of the ancient lighthouse that had collapsed in a series of earthquakes in the middle ages. I never knew what it looked like, though. I'd never been interested enough to research it.

"This style of architecture is found all over the globe," Emil was saying. "Stepped pyramids, ziggurats. Found in South America, Africa, the ancient Near East. It's incredible to think of the influence the Atlanteans—the Iamoi, I mean—had on the people of Earth."

I frowned. Each place the "Atlanteans" had touched was a place that a party of colonists had disappeared to. All thanks to Tibros—the Liberator.

Emil kept talking as we rode the *gurzas* the rest of the way up the slope toward the lighthouse, though I was only half listening. The closer we got to it, the more I was able to appreciate just how tall this building was. Unfortunately, I was also able to see that it had fallen to much the same disrepair as the rest of the city. The wind had dislodged much of the stone masonry that encased the outer walls. But, though weather-worn, the bones of the structure seemed to still be sturdy. It was fortunate that it had been built out of stone rather than adobe the way many of the buildings in the capital were. It would hold up better to time.

Of course, nothing was impervious. The Pharos lighthouse Emil had mentioned was proof of that. A few good earthquakes had been enough to send it crumbling down to the bottom of the sea. If ruins of the celestial observatory remained on Herschel Island, they'd been long destroyed and completely buried by the time my people arrived. It was a sobering thought. Even something as sturdy as this lighthouse appeared couldn't hold up to ten thousand years of wind and...

We crested the hill and my thoughts died within me. Things hadn't held up as well as they'd appeared.

Though the tower of the lighthouse was indeed still intact, the bottom level of the ziggurat—the wide, rectangular building that the tower rose from—was in shambles. The roof had caved in, support pillars toppled. Thick black spider weeds had grown around the building, choking it like a brier hedge out of a fairy tale.

And how we were going to get to the lighthouse was beyond me. Because the cliffside itself had crumbled.

The fierce eroding winds had been too much for the narrow headland that jutted out from the crescent-shaped landmass that formed Herschel Island. Now a chasm had erupted between the mainland we now stood on and the headland that held the lighthouse, at least five meters wide.

Nikos growled and dismounted from Kodo, approaching the edge and peering down. "The entire cliffside has separated. This fissure reaches all the way to the old seafloor." He knelt, brushing away sand and picking up a larger piece of debris. He inspected this. "The rock here is porous," he said. "The elements have worn it away to almost nothing. The headland the lighthouse is on won't bear its weight much longer. The whole thing could collapse at any time."

I slid off Tuupa's back, coming over to look myself. "Is it safe for us to go inside?" I asked.

"Assuming we can even get over there," said Ceilos.

"Would the *gurzas* be able to jump this gap?" Nadin asked.

"*Gurzas* aren't jumpers," Nikos said. "And they couldn't climb something this steep."

"So you're saying we've made it this far, but we might have to turn back?" Emil asked. He seemed to be following the conversation well enough, although the giant chasm at our feet made for a good context clue. He made a noise of annoyance. "Why didn't they program the space door to deposit us on *that* side?"

"We didn't know the exact coordinates," Gitrin pointed out. "And if we'd guessed wrong..." She stared pointedly at something on the cliff face on the lighthouse side, about twenty meters below us. I followed her gaze, my pulse jumping in alarm as I noticed the bleached white against the rust red rock. Bones. Human bones. A skull, crushed in on the side. Someone—a looter, no doubt—had tried to vault this gap. And failed.

I swallowed roughly.

"If there's not a postern inside that building, we also would have been trapped on the other side," Nadin said.

"There's nothing for it. We'll have to find a way across—but a smarter way than what he attempted," Nikos added, gesturing to the broken body on the rocks. "If only we could construct some sort of bridge."

I glanced around at the ruins of the city, trying to find anything that we could put together to build a bridge. But what would be both long enough and strong enough to support our weight?

I turned, my eyes falling on a column standing near the gash. It was one of the few in the area that had not collapsed. I gauged it mentally. It looked like it might be taller than the gap was wide. But could we topple it without it breaking? And bridge the gap without it falling inside?

"What about that?" I asked.

Emil scoffed. "That thing must weigh at least two tons. How are we supposed to move it?"

Nikos moved over to the pillar, testing it with his hands. "The *gurzas* are strong. If we can position it just right..."

"But will it be safe?" Gitrin asked.

Nikos hesitated. "There's no way we'll know unless we try," he said at last.

It felt like an eternity, time we couldn't afford to waste. But eventually we managed to get the heavy packs of provisions unloaded from the *gurzas'* backs. Nikos had a long rope in his supply kit, and he used this to create a crude pulley around the base of the column. He then hitched the long end of the rope to each of the *gurzas'* saddles in turn and led them into position parallel to the gash in the rock.

"When I give the signal, all of you push," he said. The five of us huddled together behind the column.

"All right... now."

He whistled, and Kodo lurched forward, Tuupa and Thork behind him. The rope strained with their effort. I shoved my body against the hard stone of the column with all of my might, jostling against the bodies of the others as we pushed. It seemed like nothing was happening—but then, all at once, the column swayed, rocking back and forth in place.

"Keep going!" Nikos called.

I grunted with the effort, but I could feel it now. Just a little more...

With a terrifying *crack*, the thick pillar of solid stone careened forward. I winced, part of me wanting to close my eyes. But I needed to know where it landed.

For a horrible instant, it looked like we'd gauged wrong. The column was going to miss the other side—it was going to plummet straight down into the chasm, and we'd have lost our final chance.

But then it hit. BAM.

An enormous cloud of dust flew up around the column. I squeezed my eyes shut now, but the grit still found its way in, itching, burning. I coughed as it found its way into my breathing apparatus.

But when the dust cleared, I could see. We'd gotten it just right. The column had toppled forward and slightly to the right, bridging the chasm at an angle, but firmly situated on both sides.

Nikos came over to the column, testing it with his weight. "It's sturdy for now," he said. "But it could shift. Someone will need to stay on this side to make sure it doesn't slip." Kodo nudged him as he spoke, and he reached a hand out absently, stroking the animal's muzzle. "The *gurzas* mind me. The rest of you go on. I'll wait for you here."

Ceilos stepped forward. "I'll go first," he said. "Just in case."

"The wind will be dangerous," Nikos warned. "Go on your hands and knees. Lower your center of gravity."

Ceilos tugged his earlobe, awkwardly scrambling up onto the smooth, sand-blasted stone. As Nikos advised, he crawled forward slowly, hugging the column and shimmying forward. It felt like it took forever, but at last he reached the other side.

"It's safe," he called. "The rest of you can come."

"I'll go right behind you, Emil," I said. "Be careful."

"Of course I'll be careful," Emil snapped. "When have I ever been anything but?"

I smirked in spite of myself. It was true—when he'd come through the postern to Iamos in the first place, he'd been more prepared than me. He'd brought an oxygen tank, for a start.

Once he was firmly balanced on the column, I crawled up behind him, praying that the weight of both of us would not cause the pillar to shift. But though he insisted he would be fine, Emil was the oldest of all of us. I couldn't risk him losing his balance and falling. If nothing else, we needed him. And I had to admit, the cantankerous old man had grown on me.

The wind rose as we crawled out over the chasm. Though I gripped the stone firmly, the strength of the wind hitting us made me feel like my balance was more precarious than I knew that it was. I chanced a peek over the side and my stomach lurched up into my throat. It was a long way down. A long, long way down. I squeezed my eyes shut, but that just made images of the sun-bleached skeleton on the cliff below us flash through my mind.

Slowly, achingly slowly, we inched our way across. By the time I scrambled off the column on the other side and got to my feet, my muscles were shaking, from fear more than anything. My stomach wouldn't settle for a long time, I was certain. And the adrenaline coursing through my veins didn't cease until Nadin, crawling behind Gitrin as I had with Emil, rose to her feet.

"I'll wait here for you," Nikos called from across the chasm.

"Well, let's get it over with, then," Emil said, turning to the ruined hulk of a building in front of us. "I want to see that telescope."

We clambered over sand and rocks, through a jagged, tangled thicket of spider weeds that had taken root near the entrance of the building. The door, a sliding type like most of the ones I'd seen on Iamos, had collapsed halfway off its track. With a grunt, Ceilos leveraged his shoulder against it and shoved it the rest of the way open. I ducked through the low opening, half buried in the debris of innumerable *gamada* storms that had pelted the peninsula since the city's abandonment.

The inside of the observatory looked even worse than the outside. Sand had piled up everywhere through the partially caved-in roof. Despite the inaccessibility of the building, it was obvious that looters had been through here many times, probably before the chasm separating the headland from the mainland had been formed. It appeared that anything not bolted down had been taken. The interior of the main wing of the observatory was stark in its emptiness.

"Based on what we could see from the outside, I'm guessing the telescope itself will be in the tower," Emil said. "If it's anything like the early optical telescopes from Earth, it will operate using mirrors built into that structure."

"Assuming they're still intact," I said, looking around doubtfully. "If looters made it here, they might have trashed the tower, too."

We passed through a door from the debris-filled main wing into a narrow corridor. At the end of this, a door stood tightly closed.

"Is this the entrance to the tower?" Nadin asked.

Emil looked up through the hole in the roof at the structure looming above us. "It must be. The tower is directly over us."

"The door is sealed. That may be a good sign," Gitrin said.

But as we approached the door, I saw why it was sealed and let out a sigh. An intricate lock had been bolted to the door—with a familiar round divot in the center. Deep scratches and gouges in the stone around it indicated that many robbers had attempted to pry the lock opened and failed.

"It needs a medallion to open," said Nadin.

"And we left the medallion with Nikos," I said in frustration. One of us would have to crawl back over to get it from him and then crawl back. The thought made me sick to my stomach. Apart from the danger, we were also wasting time. The sun was already directly overhead. We still had to find the telescope, use it, analyze the data, and then get back across the chasm, ride back to Katai'ios...

"I still have my medallion," Ceilos said.

Nadin and I both turned in unison, staring at him in shock. He withdrew the medal from beneath the collar of his silver bodysuit.

"The coin!" Emil exclaimed.

"You told me to leave my earpiece behind," he said, holding Nadin's eyes. "But not my medallion."

She looked down. "Of course," she said.

Ceilos stepped forward, removing the medallion from around his neck and pressing it into the divot in the lock. It clicked into place, and the lock unfurled the way a posternkey did, opening like a flower, into an unrecognizable geometric shape. I heard the sound of pins turning on the other side of the door. Then the lock fell away. Ceilos retrieved his medallion and then moved to open the door. It took another forceful shove the way the broken outer door had, but with a shrill scraping sound the door slid open.

The room on the other side of the door was rectangular, matching the shape of the ziggurat tower, and far dimmer than the rest of the observatory. Where above us the sky had been visible in the other room, in here we found ourselves in near darkness.

"The lens of the telescope was protected by a metal shield," Gitrin said. "It must still be intact."

"That's good news," Emil said.

A squared spiral staircase led up, winding its way around the inner walls of the tower. Cautiously, we began to climb.

When we reached the second level of the ziggurat, we found a platform elevated in the center of the tower. I peered through the shadows at the strange, dark shapes that stretched up from the platform into the heights of the tower above. As my eyes adjusted, I recognized some of the shapes as gears, other moving parts. And flat discs that after a moment I realized must be the mirrors Emil said would be required to make an optical telescope of this size work.

"Yes, very good news," he murmured under his breath, taking it all in. "If these parts are in working order..."

He trailed off as we came around a corner. The walls tapered in once more—the third level of the ziggurat. Here, another platform was suspended between the stairs, accessible by a gangplank. In the center of this platform stood some kind of a console, and beside the console, a lever.

"This must be it," Emil breathed. "That lever should open the protective shield over the lens. Providing nothing's been damaged, at least."

"Only one way to find out," I said. I moved forward, shoving against the lever with all my might. It wouldn't budge.

I cursed. "It's jammed," I said.

"There's sure to be sand in the gears," Ceilos said. He came up beside me, hefting his own weight against the lever. With a horrific scrape, it moved a few centimeters. "Come on," he said, looking directly at me. "Help me push."

I hesitated a moment, then nodded. Ceilos and I leaned against the lever together, shoving as hard as we could. The gears groaned, scraped, shrieked. Nadin slammed her hands over her ears and winced. It sounded like nails on a chalkboard, but the gears were turning. As the lever inched forward, light began to pour in overhead.

The shield was opening.

As abruptly as the toppling column outside, the lever gave way. The gears turned, the wheels on the panels of the shield spun. The shield swung open wide, and then with a heavy thud, shuddered to a stop.

"There. The lens is exposed. Now let's see what this thing can do," Emil said. He looked down into the console, then turned to Gitrin. "Can you make heads or tails of this?" he asked her.

She peered into the console beside him. "These are markings indicating the right ascension and declination," she told him.

"Excellent," Emil said. "Then would you be so kind as to point it to..." He pulled his notebook out of his jacket pocket and flipped through the pages where he'd been scribbling his notes over the last several days. He read off some coordinates, then glanced from his notebook to me. "I may have picked up some Iamoi over the last few weeks, but I'm not advanced enough to translate that. We need to be sure we're accurate," he told me. "Could you...?"

I quickly translated. Gitrin tugged her earlobe and peered back down at the console, pressing some buttons and flipping a few switches. This caused more grinding out of the gears, and shrill squeaking as the mirrors suspended above and below us moved into different positions.

"There," she said when the machinations had ceased.

Emil eagerly returned to the console, looking down at it. He frowned. Looked up, as if the giant lens at the top of the tower would tell him something. Looked down again. Flipped to a fresh page in his notebook and scribbled some notes down furiously.

The next while was spent with Emil barking out coordinates, me translating them to Gitrin, Gitrin reorienting the telescope, and Emil scribbling down more notes. The more he scribbled, the deeper the furrow of his brow grew. I didn't like that look, not one bit. But I was afraid to do anything more than obediently translate. Emil looked like he was in the kind of mood where he might get into a brawl with me, like he had with Henry back in Tierra Nueva.

"Well," he said at last, straightening and looking wearily at me. The timbre of that *well* was enough to freeze my blood in my veins.

"Well?" I repeated.

"It's not good news. None of it is good news. But it's a great deal more complicated than I was expecting."

My heart sank. "So it is the Clovis impact?" I asked.

"Possibly. We have no way of knowing if this particular event is what caused the Younger Dryas climate episode." He ran a hand through his wild shock of white hair. "I'll start with the straightforward part. That star we spotted in the sky a few days ago is in fact an object consistent with the typical characteristics of a dwarf planet, of approximately the same mass and diameter as Ceres. This is not the asteroid that wiped out the dinosaurs. This is much, much larger. We're not talking mass-extinction levels. We're talking complete obliteration of whatever it impacts."

"And its trajectory?" Gitrin asked.

Emil's face was grim. "This dwarf planet appears to be in an extremely elliptical orbit. And, as we feared, the trajectory of its orbit puts it on an exact collision path with the other planet that shares an orbit with this one."

"With Hamos," Nadin said. Her voice was flat, absolutely no inflection in it. Numb.

"Hamos," Emil repeated, nodding thoughtfully. "That's the part where things get complicated. Contreras"—he turned to me—"that moon that we've been seeing. The planet in the binary orbit with Mars in this timeline. You're positive it's Venus?"

I blinked at him. "Yeah. I mean... yeah?" I glanced at Nadin. The same confusion I felt was written across her face. "The System translated *Venus* as *Hamos* when I first started talking to Nadin and Ceilos. And in their language, the word for *Earth* is *Simos*—'second world'. What else would it be?"

"Hmm." He raked a hand through his hair again, gave me some more coordinates to give to Gitrin. She inputted them and he stared down into the console once more. "Yes, that's Mercury. Everything is as it should be there. And Earth is right too. But *this* planet is all wrong." He straightened, crossing his arms. "For a start, it has far too much mass to be Venus."

"It must lose some of its mass when the dwarf planet collides with it, right?" I asked. "I mean, you said it yourself. This is beyond the Chicxulub asteroid."

"Yeah, but that's another thing I have a problem with." His free hand went from picking at his scalp to picking at his stubbly chin. "An impact of the scale required to shift a planet's whole orbit, occurring this close to Mars...? The damage to this planet wouldn't be limited to the superficial damage evident in our time period. It would absolutely obliterate Mars." He flipped through some more pages in his notebook. "This data is not lining up. Based on the size and velocity of the oncoming object, the impact will most certainly account for the loss of mass to Venus, and for its pole reversal—the reason it rotates 'backward,' in layman's terms. But its orbital shift—that's impossible. The orbit would shift, that's without a doubt, but not to this extreme. It would be closer to Earth, but there's no way it would be shifted all the way between Earth and Mercury."

"But it did," I protested. "We know it did. It's *there* in our time. How would it get there if this impact doesn't cause it?"

"I don't know. None of this makes any sense. Mars shouldn't even *exist* in this form in our time if this impact occurs where it does. Venus should not be in the orbital path that it is in our time. But both those things are true."

As he spoke, something in Nadin's eyes suddenly shifted. "Of course," she interrupted, speaking English. "Both those things are true. Both those things are true, right?" she said, taking a step closer to me.

"Uh, yeah?" I said, bewildered.

"Which means something has to change."

Emil took in a sharp breath. "I see what you're saying."

"You do?" I asked. I didn't. I was completely lost.

"You said it yourself, kid. Back in the Elysium Mons caldera," Emil said. "You asked what if the people here didn't disappear—what if they came forward?"

"Yeah, but what does that have to do with—"

"Think about it," Nadin said. "What if the impact isn't what causes Hamos to move away from Mars? What if *we* move it? If we move the entire impact itself? If we could create a large enough tesseract to contain the impact, we could move both Hamos and the planetoid to an area of open space. Far enough away from Iamos that this planet won't be destroyed."

My jaw dropped involuntarily. "Is that possible?"

"It must be possible," Nadin said, "because it *happened*."

"But why not just move the planetoid away before it collides with Hamos?" Gitrin asked.

"That would be changing events that have occurred in the existent timeline," said Emil. "We know this impact occurred—the evidence is everywhere, from the fact that Venus is in a different orbit in our time, to the fact that its mass has decreased and its rotation has changed in our time, to the physical evidence of debris from the collision impacting Earth during the Younger Dryas period. But we also know it couldn't have occurred here, because the lack of physical damage to Mars proves it." He nodded to himself. "It's the only solution."

"But is such a thing possible?" Gitrin asked. "How can we build a postern large enough to move an entire planet?"

"The satellites," Nadin said eagerly. "The ones that monitor our worlds, that are supposed to activate the early warning protocol. If we could reprogram them into a giant postern network..."

"But how would we do this?" Gitrin asked. "It would take incredible knowledge of the System."

"I could do it," Ceilos spoke up.

"That's right," Nadin said. "Ceilos knows the System better than anyone. He was able to build his cloaking protocol on his own when he was only five."

"But how will we manage such a thing without the *geroi* finding out?" Gitrin asked.

"You won't," an unfamiliar voice broke in from the shadows. We froze. My eyes caught Nadin's in time to see the color drain from her face, an unmistakable look of panic washing over her.

A man stepped forward, one I'd only seen once before. That day in the jungle, on the other side of the postern. With an army at his back. This time he was alone, or at least he seemed to be. But it didn't matter. In his hand he held an object, unfamiliar in shape, yet instantly recognizable as a weapon—pointed directly at us. With two members of our group elderly and the rest of us unarmed, there would be no fighting back. He had us cornered.

Geros Antos.

"It's already far too late for that," he said.

I FELT AS THOUGH I WERE FROZEN IN PLACE. THIS COULDN'T BE happening—not here, not now. Not when things were so dire, when we had so little time to spare. How could he have found us? How could he have known we'd been here?

I found myself swiveling to glare at Ceilos before I'd even registered what I was doing. Ceilos threw his hands up defensively. "It wasn't me!" he protested, knowing exactly what my glare implied.

Antos took a step closer, and my eyes locked once more on the weapon in his hand, my heartbeat staggering within me. A pulse blaster. Like the *tirak*, this was ancient technology—technology the *geroi* had claimed to have destroyed long ago. Technology they'd called barbaric. One press of a button and a beam of pure energy powerful enough to stop a person's heart would be unleashed on the target. I should have known they'd never destroy something that could one day be useful to them.

"It was, though. In a way," Antos said. "You used your medallion to open the lock on the door. It triggered an alarm. When I saw whose medallion had opened it... I had to come right away." He looked at us solemnly. "Don't worry. I disabled the alarm before anyone else noticed."

"Why would you do that?" I asked. Despite my best efforts, I could hear the way my voice shook.

"Because I need to know the truth." He gestured around the dusty space. "You are fugitives of the *geroi*. You knew your lives would be forfeit if we ever found you. And yet you risked coming here. *Here*, of all places. A celestial observatory, sealed for decades. A place of historical significance, locked away by the *geroi* after the Progression, that has no value to any but historians and looters. A place that the rebellion should have no interest in, no need to access." He took another step closer, his voice growing dark. "Not unless there was something that needed to be seen that could not be seen otherwise. Because, for example, the early warning protocol has been sabotaged. Because our satellites, reliant on the System, could not detect it."

"You know," Ceilos said. "Clearly you do."

"I have my suspicions." He lowered his weapon. "I want to see what you've seen. Can I trust you to be civil?"

I swallowed hard. "You're the only one here who's armed."

The corners of his mouth tugged up slightly. "A necessary precaution. I'm sure you'll understand. If you'd be so good as to show me what you've seen through this telescope?"

Beside me, Isaak cleared his throat. "Emil, what are the coordinates again?" Emil gave them to Isaak, and Gitrin entered them into the console.

"You won't be able to see it with your earpiece in," Ceilos said as the mirrors finished swinging and the gears ground into silence. "To anyone connected to the System, it's invisible."

Antos' brows furrowed. "Interesting. But not unexpected." He slowly raised his hand to his ear, and after a moment's hesitation, removed the earpiece.

He did his best to keep his expression steady, but I saw it flit across his face—the pain caused by disconnecting from the System, possibly for the first time, after a lifetime on it. I knew the symptoms. Dizziness, nausea. A stabbing headache. The first time I'd done it, it had even given me a fever. But he took a deep breath and proceeded as if he were unaffected.

He peered into the console for a long moment, his lips pressed together in a line. Finally, he straightened. "How long do we have?" he asked.

Isaak translated the question to Emil.

"Until impact? Probably around a month. But in practicality, far less than that," Emil said. "The gravity of the object as it approaches the binary planet system of Iamos and Hamos will start wreaking havoc, and their gravity will likely cause it to start breaking apart as well. Minor impacts before the final one will still be enough to cause destruction and mass casualties. If they're substantial enough, it could even expel what little atmosphere is left on Iamos. The people here will likely be dead within a week if no action is taken. And the window of opportunity to take action is very rapidly closing."

Isaak translated this. As he spoke, Antos' face grew darker and darker. When Isaak had finished, Antos sighed and looked at me. My pulse jumped as his blue eyes settled on mine. He'd been born in Hope Renewed, as I had. One of the only *geroi* who had ever inherited the citidome his parents had ruled. Our shared traits had never been something I could see as a source of comfort, though. His blue eyes had never been anything but cold. But there was something else in them now, something unfamiliar. Something I'd never seen.

Remorse.

For some reason, this was more frightening to me than the anger they'd held the last time I'd seen him.

"Nadin," he said. "You tried to tell us back in the caldera, and again during your hearing. We silenced you. But now I recognize that this was foolish. The fact that you came here tells me that the rebels were caught as off-guard by this development as we were. You told us that the person who sabotaged the System was not anyone in the mountain, but we refused to believe you. But I see the truth now. I am sorry."

"Sorry?" I repeated, the fear inside me shifting into something else, an emotion just as ugly. It was more than anger. It was rage. "I risked my life for the good of Iamos. I begged you to see reason—to honor your oath to protect the people on this world—and instead you had me silenced and beaten. Do you suppose a simple apology is enough for that?"

"Of course not," he said, seeming chagrined.

"There will never be apology enough. *Never*," I spat. "Forgiveness is not an option."

"I would not expect it," Antos said. "But would you accept a truce? For the good of Iamos. Because I have seen with my eyes now." He gestured to the console. "There is no hope for our people if we do not work together."

My breathing was heavy, labored behind the mask of my breathing apparatus. The thought of working with the *geroi*—even just one of them—made bile rise up in my throat. My father had been silent when his partner beat me bloody on the order of the *gerotus*. He could have protested. She could have protested. But they'd been too cowardly to push back. Just as they'd been too cowardly to listen to what I'd tried to warn them in Elytherios. I hated both of them. I hated them all.

But he was right. There was no hope without him. I knew it. I despised it. But I knew it to be true.

"All right," I said.

Over my shoulder, Gitrin gasped. "Nadin, think," she whispered. "An alliance between our movement and the *geroi*, the very people who have hunted us down and slaughtered our people for decades—think what this would mean."

"And think what it means for me, Gitrin," Antos replied dryly. "These are desperate times."

"I agree with Nadin," Ceilos said. "We have no other choice. Especially with that in play." He gestured to the pulse blaster in Antos' hand.

"I knew I could count on you to see reason," Antos said. "Now. This plan of yours, to shift the location of Hamos and the impact. Tell me about it."

My voice still shaking from residual adrenaline, I explained. That Isaak had not come from Simos in our time period—he'd come from the future, using the theoretical time postern that the *geroi* had discredited. That I had been to the future as well. I explained what I'd learned about the fate of Hamos and Iamos in the future, and the concept of the paradox, and how changing history could cause the universe to implode. And finally, hesitantly, I told him how I'd learned, inadvertently, what had happened to the parties of colonists we'd sent to Simos, and what Tirios had found here when he'd returned to Iamos in the future.

A dead planet. Abandoned, or extinct. Our only two possible options.

Antos' frown had deepened as I'd been speaking, and he let out a sigh. "We're in an impossible situation," he said. "Made all the more dire by the terrorist who's been playing us all for fools. The Liberator has had control over Iamos for far longer than we've given him credit for," he said. "I've had my doubts that he is truly one of the rebels for some time, and particularly after the eruption of the Sios Ifaisteos. If they were behind the sabotage of the early warning protocol, they would have known that the eruption was imminent. And the need to access this observatory to see the rogue planetoid only confirms it. It must be someone in the citidomes, but who I cannot begin to guess."

"One of the *geroi*," Ceilos said quietly.

Antos froze, turning on him with an odd expression. "It cannot be. The Liberator has attacked the *geroi* themselves."

"We'd heard as much," Gitrin said. "But we weren't certain what the circumstances were."

"Critical," Antos replied grimly. He stared down at the weapon in his hands for a long moment. "You have been honest with me, Nadin. I suppose I should be honest with you as well." He looked up at me. "Almost all of the *geroi* are dead."

I let out a long, slow breath. *Dead.* It was only to be expected after the news Camos had given us. But still, it seemed impossible to believe. The *geroi*, who'd seemed to be the backbone of Iamos for my entire life... all dead. Yet, as evil as they were, the alternative—a lone dictator with absolute power, one with so little regard for human life that he'd kill thousands to get his way—was even worse.

"They've been poisoned with their own neurotoxin," Isaak said, an edge to his voice.

"No," Antos said. "We never developed such a toxin. It was still only a theory. Heros had planned to extract DNA from you or the astronomer." He gestured to Emil. "But he never got the chance. There is no neurotoxin."

I stared at Antos in confusion. "But if the toxin doesn't exist, how have the *geroi* been poisoned? The symptoms they're exhibiting mimic that of—"

"I know they do," he said. "But the medics have run every test known to our people. There's been no trace of any poison in the bodies of those who have succumbed."

"Could the System be interfering with the test results?" Isaak asked. "Like the early warning protocol preventing people from seeing the dwarf planet?"

"It's possible," Antos admitted. "But that still wouldn't explain how such a toxin is being administered in the first place. We've tightened security, we've isolated the remaining *geroi*, and yet they still fall ill. And no one is affected except the *geroi* themselves."

Suddenly the answer was as clear as day. "It's a System protocol," I said slowly.

Antos stared at me. "What?"

"The toxin. It's not a toxin at all," I said. "It's a System protocol. The Liberator is a master of the System, right? He's created a System protocol to attack the *geroi*'s nervous systems. That's how they're falling ill."

Antos' eyes widened as he took this in. "Of course. Of course. That's the only explanation."

Ceilos took a step forward. "Antos, how many of the *geroi* still live?"

"Very few. The toxin... the protocol... has attacked each *geros* and *gerouin* by partnership. All who remain are..." He swallowed, seeming to struggle to get the words out. "Alusin and Ilios of Dauntless Spirit, myself and Melusin of Hope Renewed, and Tibros of Ascendant Dawn."

"That's it?" I asked. My brain was still struggling to reconcile this. Of the sixteen people who'd gazed impassively at me as I lay sprawled on the floor, all but five were dead now.

Antos tugged his earlobe. "And the *geroi* of Dauntless Spirit are gravely ill. Melusin and I have been... awaiting the onset of the symptoms. That is why I've been so determined to find answers, as quickly as possible. Before it's too late."

"Don't you see the obvious?" Ceilos said. "Does it not occur to you that if you and Melusin die, the only *geros* remaining will be Tibros?"

"Well, assuming he doesn't succumb before us..." Antos trailed off. "What are you saying?"

"Tibros," Ceilos replied, sounding exasperated.

"You believe that the so-called Liberator is *Geros* Tibros?" Antos asked incredulously.

"I know it seems hard to believe," I said, "but consider the facts. The Liberator has access to the highest levels of the System. Access only those with *geroi* DNA can obtain. He had knowledge of the planned neurotoxin, enough to program a System protocol that mimics its symptoms. And he had knowledge of Gitrin's and my plans for the time postern, something that no one knew of besides ourselves and the *geroi*."

"Tibros wants total control of Iamos," Ceilos said. "He's systematically eradicating all who stand in the way of his sole authority."

Antos took a few shaky breaths, considering. "It seems impossible to believe, and yet... It also seems the only solution." After a moment, he tugged his earlobe decisively. "Tibros must be stopped. And quickly. The window of opportunity to stop the cataclysm is closing rapidly, as the astronomer said."

"So what do we do?" Isaak asked.

"We must return to Hope Renewed. The first matter of business will be to get all surviving *geroi* disconnected from the System as quickly as possible. There may still be time for Ilios and Alusin to recover. Then we must take Tibros into custody and remove his System access as well, before he can perform any further mayhem."

"He won't go without a fight," Ceilos warned.

"I am disconnected from the System now," Antos said. "And to this point, the System has been his greatest weapon. He won't be able to use it against me, and he won't be able to trace me. I will mobilize the Enforcers." He spoke with authority, with total confidence in his plan. But I feared he may be misguided in that confidence. If the Enforcers were loyal to Tibros...

"In the meantime, Ceilos must begin his work on creating the satellite postern network immediately," Antos was saying, not noticing the doubt on my face. "Time is of the essence."

"But won't Tibros notice if Ceilos reappears on the System?" Isaak asked.

A cocky smile formed on Ceilos' face. "Not with my cloaking protocol on our side."

Antos tugged his earlobe. "All right, then. No time to waste."

We took the *gurzas*. Getting Nikos to agree to our plan took quite a bit of convincing, but when all was said and done, he realized we had no choice in the matter. The survival of every Iamoi was dependent on our success. The *geroi* and the rebels would have to work together.

Nikos drove the *gurzas* onward as quickly as they could manage, though we were slowed by the weight of an extra person. The sun was beginning to set by the time we reached the hills, the dome of Hope Renewed towering over us. My stomach turned as I stared up at the blue glass reflecting the glare of the sun. I glanced over my shoulder at Isaak. This was the place where we'd met, all those months ago. Where I'd spotted him collapsed outside the dome, without a breathing apparatus, completely exposed. Where he'd accidentally blundered to by passing through a time postern. Where the trajectory of both our lives had changed forever.

Nikos turned the *gurzas* away from the dome, angling us downward. We couldn't enter at city level. We'd be spotted in an instant. We'd have to go in through the underground.

"What I'm about to show you could spell the end of the rebellion," he said gruffly as we dismounted the *gurzas*.

"The end of the rebellion is as certain as the end of the *geroi* if we don't stop the rogue planetoid," Antos said.

Nikos tugged his earlobe grimly and gestured us behind a large boulder. There, a narrow crevice was cut deep into the side of the hill.

"This is ordinarily guarded by System protocols," Nikos said. "Invisible to any who wear an earpiece."

Beside me, Isaak's breath hitched. I glanced at him curiously.

"This is it, isn't it?" he whispered. He said it not to me, but to Emil.

In the shadows, I saw Emil nod slowly. "Yes," the old man replied.

"This is the cave I found that day I was escaping from GSAF," Isaak explained at last. "The tunnel that led me to the postern."

"If we continued down this passage, we would ultimately connect with the Vi'in Exelishin," Nikos said. "But there's another way."

He crouched in the semidarkness. Some natural phosphorescence, though less bright than the mosaics inlaid on the main *vi'in*, lit his movements just enough for me to see. He pressed the floor, and there was a click. A hatch opened in his hands.

"Just like the tunnels in the pyramid in Bright Horizon," Ceilos said in surprise.

Nikos tugged his earlobe. "Our network is everywhere," he replied.

We climbed down a ladder into the dark. Unlike those in the pyramid, these tunnels weren't cold—as I descended the ladder, I could feel steam around me. I wiped my forehead with the back of my hand. Where were we?

Nikos rummaged through his satchel, producing a handheld lantern like the ones Eliin used in her outpost. "A runner's best friend," he said. "Light in the darkness."

I took a step forward and heard a splash. I looked down at my feet, and then I realized where we were. The underground levels were heated by hot springs that had been channeled to flow under the floor. I could see now, the way the floor sloped down to where a stream of running water flowed. I'd known these tunnels were here, but it had never occurred to me that they'd be large enough for a person to stand upright in. All this time, the rebel network had been moving around right beneath our feet.

"Careful," Nikos said. "That water will burn you if you touch it. Stay as close to the wall as you can."

We followed the passage deeper into the mountain. Above, we could hear footsteps and the voices of people on the Vi'in Exelishin. This was the level of the *patroi*, and this *vi'in* one of the busiest in Hope Renewed's underground.

The sound of running water grew louder, rushing. I knew what this would be. In the center of the *vi'in*, a large fountain stood, one of the sources of the hot water that was transported in from far away. The water flowed from a postern into a large basin underneath, then drained into the tunnels below the floor. Here the passage split; the rightmost fork sloped sharply, descending toward the lowest level of the underground.

"This is as close to the *geroi*'s villa as we can go," Nikos said. We'd decided that Antos' and Melusin's villa would be the safest place to serve as our base of operations—unlike the pyramid, it was secluded and off-limits to any but the *geroi* themselves. "Beyond this point, the tunnels fill with water. Even if you could swim that far, you'd be scalded to death in short order. If you want to go that way, you'll have to go the rest of the way aboveground." He folded his arms.

"'You'?" I repeated. "Aren't you coming with us?"

"Forgive me if I don't trust the *geros* quite that far yet," he said, eying

Antos.

"Nikos has a point," Ceilos said. "If anything goes awry in our plan, it will be safer if our entire group isn't together."

"Hmm," Antos said, running a thumb over his chin. "You may be right."

"I don't like the idea of splitting up," Gitrin said.

"Think about it, though, Gitrin," Ceilos said. "Before we can do anything else, we must win Melusin over to our side. As of now, she's still connected to the System. If she sees outsiders, she may react badly. It will do us no good to alert Tibros to what's going on."

I sighed. "He's right. And if we do get caught, the rebellion will still have a chance if some of you are free to warn the people."

Isaak stepped forward. "If you're going, Nadin, I'm going with you."

I couldn't look at him. I didn't want to separate from him—I was terrified of it, in fact. But as much as I hated to admit it, Ceilos was right. We had to be prepared for the worst possible outcome. "You have to stay with Emil. We need him, and he doesn't speak Iamoi well enough to get by without a translator."

Isaak swallowed. I knew he could see the sense in this, but he didn't like it. Neither did I. The thought of returning to the *geroi*'s villa filled me with dread. I'd barely escaped from this place with my life, and now I was returning to it voluntarily. Every fiber in me cried out in protest. But there was no other choice.

"We won't be gone long," Antos said confidently. "Wait here. We'll return for you within the hour."

I looked around the villa with a disorienting sense of surreality. It seemed impossible that everything should look the same as it always had. Not when so much else had changed. But the subterranean palace was as unchanged as ever. Colorful phosphorescent mosaics were laid into the floor, artificial constellations into the ceiling high above the atrium. A warm-water fountain burbled in the center, surrounded by tables and woven copper chairs, delicate sculptures and urns holding decorative *fraouloi*. The villa had been built in the style of the ancient palace in the capital ruins we'd just left behind us, a perfect mirror in permanent darkness, deep below the mountain. Far from the surface, where the depleting atmosphere would leave us exposed to ultraviolet radiation.

I had not returned to this place since the day I'd figured out Gitrin's clue that would lead us to Elytherios. At that time, I'd had no intention of betraying the *geroi*. As far as I'd known then, the *geroi* were who I'd always believed them to be. The noble protectors of Iamos. In my mind, it had been the rebels who were the forces of evil, the ones who needed to be stopped. I'd believed they'd kidnapped Ceilos, and Gitrin as well. But I'd been played for a fool. The *geroi* had been the ones manipulating me.

And Tibros had been manipulating them. How neatly he'd strung all of us along.

"This way," Antos said, ushering us through the atrium to where the living quarters were located. The *geroi*'s villa was arranged in a rectangle, with four separate wings. In the center, the atrium served as the place where we would eat together, often the only time Ceilos and I would see the *geroi* the entire day. The front wing held the more public spaces, such as the classroom where Gitrin had tutored Ceilos and me. The west wing was where my apartments were located, and the east where Ceilos' were found. The north wing was the *geroi*'s sanctum. Their private chambers. I'd never set foot within.

But this was where Antos ushered us now. I looked around the space in wonder. This front room seemed to serve as a second office of sorts. A smaller version of the round table from the *gerotus* chamber was situated in the center. Behind it, a postern stood.

"To allow us to quickly reach the pyramid or the *gerotus* in Bright Horizon," Antos said, noticing the direction of my gaze. "Now, Ceilos. You said there's a way we can throw Tibros off our scent?"

Ceilos tugged his earlobe. "With my cloaking protocol. I can activate one of my decoy earpieces and it will show him that you're in a different place than where you are. I lost one in Bright Horizon"—he tossed a wry look in my direction—"but there are more hidden in my rooms. I'll go get one."

He slipped back out into the atrium. I watched him go, my stomach twisting inside me. He was doing it again. Acting as if nothing was wrong. As if our argument last night had been nothing but my imagination. And I could feel the automatic way my mind was trying to dismiss this, go along with his act. Nothing had happened. I was blowing things out of proportion. Ceilos didn't *really* mean what he'd said. I was misremembering. I was making something out of nothing. The anger I'd seen in his eyes, the hatred and bitterness, had just been reflections of my own flaws of character. How long had this been going on? My excuse-making for Ceilos' unacceptable behavior? My dismissing of his bouts of temper, his jealousy and possessiveness, as products of my own imagination? Or worse, my own *fault*?

"It seems I underestimated you," Antos said, breaking my reverie. "Both of you."

"What?" I asked.

Antos gave a half-hearted smirk. "Don't think I hadn't noticed the way you would sometimes disappear from the System. The day you were outside the dome, your location showed you here when you were there. We knew you were doing something, but we didn't think..." He paused, cleared his throat. Trying to think of a delicate way to phrase this. One that didn't involve calling me a *fool*, the way Melusin had to the *gerotus*. "I didn't believe you were capable of outright treachery. Melusin and I believed Gitrin had given you this protocol. That it had come from the Liberator. That she was attempting to influence you. I certainly wouldn't have thought *Ceilos* was capable of such a thing, let alone that he'd developed it himself."

I sighed, looking down at the floor. "It seems there was much happening on Iamos that you were unaware of."

The prominence in his throat twitched slightly. "You needn't remind me." He moved over to the round table in the center of the room, setting the pulse blaster down on it and leaning his weight against the table. "But of all the deceptions, none fooled me more than Tibros. He fooled all of us, to our utter ruin."

"I don't think anyone suspected Tibros. Except Ceilos," I said.

Antos tugged his earlobe. "He knows the man better than anyone, I suppose. But I do feel responsibility. I've known for years that Tibros is an angry man. His short temper on the *gerotus* floor was a clue, but..." He exhaled heavily, taking a few steps away from the table. "Ceilos did his best to hide it when he first came to us, but I could tell that Tibros had laid hands on the boy. And yet I did nothing. What could I do, after all? He ranked above me in the *gerotus*. And I doubt very much that the other *geroi* would have much cared, regardless.

"Still," he went on, not really looking at me. Caught up in his own memories. "I am surprised he's managed to pull off such an elaborate scheme. He's never struck me as a man who can help but keep his heart on his sleeve. His fits of temper are not well-disguised. And I never would have believed he would be so proficient with the System as to be able to pull off such sophisticated hacks. He's always relied on System experts to do the work for him. But I suppose that would all be part of the deception..."

I didn't hear the rest of what Antos was saying. Time had seemed to freeze. Or maybe it was just me who was frozen.

It was strange, the way events unfolded. The way one thing led to another. If I had heard those words two days ago, I never would have made the connection. If it hadn't been for the hateful things he'd said to me last night, I would have just continued on as I always had. Blindfolded. Unable to see what was happening right in front of me. What had been happening all along.

"Do you remember what we spoke of all those years ago...?"

I did remember. I remembered now.

Gitrin looks up as I storm into the classroom, slamming the sliding door hard behind me. "What's the matter?" she asks in surprise.

"The *geroi* wanted me to show Ceilos around the citidome, but he refused."

My tutor waves away the System panel she'd had open and gestures for me to sit across from her in the woven copper chair I sit in for lessons. It used to be just the two of us, one across from the other, engaged in deep discussions that lasted for hours and never quite felt like lessons in the traditional sense of the word. But now there's a second seat across from Gitrin's, beside mine. It's empty now, but it won't be tomorrow. Things are never going to be the same.

"Perhaps he's too tired. It's been a long day," Gitrin says.

"Perhaps he's a surly, antisocial *utz'os*," I spit.

Gitrin makes a disapproving sound with her tongue, though I can see the corners of her mouth curling up involuntarily. "Temper, Nadin."

"I don't understand why he's being so rude to me!" I exclaim. "He wouldn't even look at me this morning when he arrived. He greeted the *geroi*, but he completely ignored me until *Geros* Tibros all but forced him to acknowledge my presence."

"Hmm." Gitrin adjusts the embroidered shawl that she wears about her shoulders, but says nothing more.

"The last day he has done nothing but avoid me, or look condescendingly at me, all the while oiling Antos and Melusin so smoothly that they can speak nothing but praise about him. How am I to be partners with someone who belittles me, who treats me like a nuisance, like an insect buzzing at his ears?" My eyes begin to burn as I speak, tears of anger and frustration building up inside them.

"Nadin," Gitrin says carefully, "much has changed these last several days. I know you've felt it. You've been tense and full of worry."

"Yes, worry that my partner wouldn't like me. And see how right I was to be worried," I mutter.

She ignores my words and goes on smoothly, "Does it not occur to you that perhaps Ceilos would feel the same? His life has been uprooted even more than yours. He had to leave his home, and his parents have left Iamos entirely."

"Why should he be angry with me, though?" I ask. "I'm not to blame for any of that."

"That boy has a lot of anger inside him. Especially for such a young age. If he can't find a way to release that anger, it will destroy him." She looks at me seriously. "Anger is poison, Nadin," she says, "of a particularly insidious sort. It eats away at you slowly. If you let it fester inside you, it will destroy you."

"*Anger is poison.*" Gitrin said it all the time. I'd thought it was directed at me, at my short temper, at my high emotionality. But I wasn't the only angry person in the underground. There was someone else whose anger had grown a great deal more poisonous than mine. He was just good at disguising it. Hiding it behind a mask that he could slip on and off at will.

It took high-level access to the System in order to pull off the types of hacks the Liberator had—the kind only achieved by *geroi* DNA.

Something Ceilos and I both had flowing through our veins.

It took knowledge of the research Gitrin and I had done on the time postern in order to hijack the Simoi colonists' posternkeys and send them to other time periods. Something Ceilos had, because I'd given it to him.

It took deep, complex knowledge of the System to not only sabotage the early warning protocol, but replace it with a cloaking protocol—one that wouldn't just disable the warnings, but disguise visible omens of calamity like the glow of the rogue planetoid in the sky. A cloaking protocol like the one Ceilos had designed to let us go offline, to sneak around without the *geroi* catching us.

And it took anger to be willing to destroy so many lives.

"That boy has a lot of anger in him."

Anger. That was what my subconscious had been trying to remind me through my dream. The key connection that I'd already made in the back of my mind, even as my waking self could never have conceived it. Ceilos had anger in him. Anger toward the *geroi*. Toward his parents. And particularly toward his abuser, *Geros* Tibros... the man he had framed as a terrorist.

What sort of person was he, this boy who could change his face as easily as one changes clothes?

The door slid open once more. Ceilos stood in the doorway, holding the decoy earpieces. Antos straightened, smiling, and started toward him.

"Antos, stop," I cried, my voice unsteady. He turned to me in alarm. He was close to where Ceilos stood now, beside the round table. Too close. "Don't get any closer to him. Ceilos—Ceilos is the Liberator."

Even as I said the words, it was too late. Ceilos lunged forward, dropping the decoy earpieces and making a wild grab for the weapon on the table. Antos' response was quick, but he'd been caught off his guard, withdrawal from the System dulling his reflexes. They both reached the pulse blaster at the same time, grasping for it. Grappling. The two scuffled for one brief, horrible moment, their movements slowing before my eyes, as if they were underwater.

There was a bright, blinding flash of light as the weapon discharged. Antos crumpled.

"Phados!" I screamed. I rushed forward, kneeling beside *Geros* Antos, turning him onto his back. His hand fell across my lap. The fingertips were red, like they'd been burned. His lips, too. Scorched by the electricity. But he was breathing. He still had a pulse, but it was faint, erratic.

I looked wildly up at Ceilos. He stood still, holding the blaster in his hands, his expression unreadable.

"Why?" The question tore out of me like a screech.

He smiled. He *smiled*.

"You finally see me," Ceilos said.

"What?" I asked, my voice trembling.

"The two of us have been weaving quite the twisted tapestry," he said. "Spinning round each other, warp and weft, sometimes passing just a hair's breadth apart, but never quite... connecting."

The Liberator's words to me on the comm, back when all of this had started. His voice had sounded familiar to me, but distorted. Ceilos had tried to get me to believe that it had been *Geros* Tibros' voice I'd heard passing through a voice modulator. But of course it hadn't been. It had been a voice I'd known far more intimately, and still I'd been blind to it.

"I'd wondered how long it was going to take you to see. All the hints I'd left you. The clues, more and more brazen, more and more blatant. I even used your own time postern to eliminate four *geroi* partnerships. I thought for sure that when you learned that, you'd recognize me. But still you didn't see." He smiled again. "All I wanted from you, Nadin—all I'd wanted all along—was for you to see me."

"But *why*, Ceilos?" I demanded.

"The *geroi* are an abomination. They deserved to pay for their crimes against our people. Iamos deserved better rulers."

I swallowed down the bile that was burning my throat. "Like you?"

"Like *us*," he hissed back. "Don't you see? Everything I did— everything I ever did—was for us. For our partnership. I thought you'd understand that. I thought you believed it, too. You pushed back against the *geroi*. You're the only person I ever knew who did. And that made you the only person worth saving. Everything would have been perfect. Until *Isaak* came. Until Isaak poisoned you against me."

"He didn't—"

"I don't want any more of your lies!" Ceilos roared. On the floor beside me, Antos twitched. I felt for his pulse again. It was growing weaker. Ceilos' gaze flicked over the *geros'* body impassively. "Not the way I'd meant for him to go," Ceilos said. "It was much more fitting for all the *geroi* to die from the barbaric neurotoxin they'd devised. *Ypris.*" He chuckled. "But it will serve my purposes. I had to stop him before he managed to get Melusin disconnected from the System." He looked up at me again. "And I had to stop *you*, too. I can't let you interfere any more. I can't let you move Hamos. I can't let you prevent this cataclysm."

I stared at him in confusion, horror. "But Ceilos, don't you understand? It *has* to be moved, or it will create a paradox. The entire universe could be destroyed."

"But that's what I want. Don't *you* understand?" His voice was so emotionless. It made the weight of his words all the more terrible. "It isn't enough for just the *geroi* to die. Not anymore. I see now. You've opened my eyes. You did it yourself, Nadin. You and your beloved Isaak. I see now that there's not one thing in this universe worth saving. So I will unmake it."

"You can't do this, Ceilos," I begged. "Think about everyone else! Think about Nikos—"

"Nikos." Ceilos snorted. "Our wise rebel elder. How quick he was to discard his own principles, to take the power that the *ninvidu* had granted him. Just this once—it's an emergency—that's how it always starts."

"Then think about Camos and Ierin. They believed in you. They said they'd stand for you at a forum! Think about everyone, please. You're—"

"What? I'm not the only one that matters? You said that before. But the truth is, Nadin, I *am* the only one that matters. Because I will singlehandedly be the universe's undoing."

Keeping the weapon trained on me, he rummaged through his reticule with his left hand, withdrawing a posternkey. He snapped it open with his thumb. Behind him, the postern began to glow, emitting a low hum.

"The others will stop you," I said desperately.

"Hmm. Maybe. Or maybe not. After all—I know where they are, and they don't know who I am." He smirked. "But it doesn't matter either way. Even if they do stop me—even if this universe survives—I've still won. You see, I took the liberty of adding an extra protocol to the System before we left Bright Horizon. One that I'm sure your friends on *Mars* will enjoy."

"What?"

There was a noise outside, in the atrium. I barely registered it.

"The protocol will activate on an unspecified date after your return from the future. Anyone who's connected to the System at that time will be affected." He smirked. "I'd meant my little prank only for GSAF—for anyone who would try to use our people's technology against us. But then I heard you and Isaak speaking on the journey to Katai'ios about the note he'd received. About the so-called nanobots. You were worried about them, about what the note meant."

A crash came from the other side of the door. Voices echoed off the high cavern ceiling.

"You were right to worry," Ceilos said. "As soon as the System connects to the nanobots, every one of those *aliens* will be infected with the same neurotoxin that I've used on the *geroi*."

I couldn't breathe. The room was spinning.

"*Gamoak*, Nadin." Ceilos tossed the pulse blaster toward me. It skittered across the floor, landing near *Geros* Antos' feet. "Thanks for the memories." He stepped forward, disappearing into the light.

A moment later, the door to the *geroi*'s chambers slammed open. A team of Enforcers burst in, surrounding me, shouting. Someone yanked me away from Antos' prone form.

"She shot him! She shot *Geros* Antos."

I should have protested, said it wasn't me. The real culprit was getting away. But it was too late—Ceilos was gone. All trace of him had disappeared. And the only other witness to the crime lay dying at my feet.

"He's still breathing! Get him to the hospital level!"

I couldn't speak, could barely move. I didn't resist as they bound my hands. The Liberator had been two steps ahead of us all the way. I'd been a fool, and now it was far too late to do anything about it. It was over. We were lost.

As the Enforcers dragged me out of the *geroi*'s chambers, one thought echoed over and over in my mind, drowning out all other sound.

Even if, somehow, we managed to stop Ceilos from destroying the universe...

Everyone in the future was going to die.

PART EIGHT
MARS

2075 C.E.

CHAPTER 43

- h e n r y -

"HENRY."

The sound of my name cut through the fog of my dream. Dimly, I became aware of someone prodding me in my side.

"Henry," the voice said again, and I grunted, opening my eyes. Lizeth was hovering next to my bunk. Her black ponytail fanned out around her, the stark white fluorescent lighting behind her head casting her in quasi-silhouette.

"What?" I grunted.

"We're going to be landing in about an hour. I need to get back on deck and listen for any communication from our guy on the ground. Can you round up the others?" she said. "Everyone needs to get all their stuff out of here and make sure there's no trace of us left anywhere on the ship. Make the bunks up how we found them, make sure everything in the bathroom gets packed or trashed, the whole nine yards. Bring your stuff up front so as soon as we land, we can get out of here." She held up her gray nylon bag. "I took care of mine already."

"Okay," I said, rubbing my eyes. She pushed away. Without her form blocking them, the bright overhead lights hit me full in the face. I winced. "What time is it going to be when we land?"

"Around four in the afternoon in Tierra Nueva. Thursday, August twenty-second," she said, disappearing from the cabin.

Four in the afternoon. Time had lost all meaning after nearly three weeks in space. The view through the windows was always dark, the fluorescent lighting in the ship always too bright. I hadn't done much interplanetary travel in my life—just a few visits to India growing up—but I would never take the artificial gravity and timed lighting on the passenger ships for granted again.

I still felt hazy as I unstrapped myself from the sleeping bag and pushed myself out of my bunk. I must have been really deeply asleep when Lizeth poked me awake. I knew I'd been dreaming something, but now it was fuzzy. Something about Isaak. It hadn't felt quite like a dream—more like a memory I'd forgotten, that was already slipping away again. Something I'd overheard him asking Senghas about back at the museum, when they were looking at that underwater model of the solar system. I'd only heard a snatch of it then, so it was odd that I'd be thinking of it now. *Clover?* No, that wasn't it. *Jarvis?* That was closer. It had sounded like a name. But that still wasn't right.

I sighed. Whatever it had been, it had drained from my memory once more. It probably wasn't important. Some obscure archaeological detail that no one but Zak would care about.

I glanced out the small porthole at the end of the row of bunks. For most of the journey there'd been nothing but a sea of black visible, but now the window was taken up by the huge orb of Mars: rust-red with patches of green, punctuated by masses of blue ocean and laced over with streaks of white clouds.

I zipped the sleeping bag closed, rolling it up and strapping it the way it had been when we first launched. Then I maneuvered myself around to the drawer at the foot of my bunk, checking it to make sure everything was still inside my nylon bag, that nothing had come out during the trip. I felt for the rolled-up pair of socks at the bottom of the bag, my hand closing around the small, hard object within. Still there.

I looked around the cabin. No one else here. No one was in the bathroom with its incredibly awkward vacuum-powered toilet, either. I shot it a dirty look as I checked to make sure the room was clear of any trash. Another thing I would never take for granted again: plumbing. The portable toilets in the latrine area at Los Tuxtlas had been more tolerable. Even the bathing situation at the dig—solar-powered portable showers, using tanks filled with creek water—had been a dream compared to the sponge-baths and squeeze-bottle hair washes on this ship. It was no wonder most of these cargo vessels were automated now.

This was a job I couldn't see very many people wanting to do long-term.

I floated across the hall, guiding myself with handholds mounted along the walls. There hadn't been much in terms of crew entertainment left on this ship, since it had been stripped when it was converted to run on autopilot. But there was one stationary bike in the old rec room that seemed to have been overlooked. We'd all been taking turns using it, partly out of boredom and partly out of necessity. After almost three weeks of weightlessness, our bodies would have a hard time returning to gravity, even the comparatively easy gravity on Mars. Any kind of exercise that we could do up here would give our hearts and muscles a bit of help when we got back on the ground.

When I entered the rec room, Scylla was using the bike. Zero was hovering in front of her, upside down, their legs crossed. I couldn't tell if they were attempting to do a weightless yoga stretch, or if they were just comfortable in that position.

"Hey," I said, floating over to the pair. "Lizeth said we're going to be landing in an hour."

"Thank *God*," Scylla bellowed, abruptly ceasing her pedaling and shoving herself off the bike. She did a slow-motion backflip, feet hitting the ceiling, and then propelled herself upright again.

Zero laughed. "What, you aren't going to miss doing that?" they asked, still upside down.

"Nope. That novelty wore about three days into the trip."

"Lizeth said to get your bags out of the cabin and bring them up front." I looked around the rec room. "Tamara not with you?"

Scylla shook her head. "I haven't seen her since breakfast. Or lunch. Whatever it was." She made a face that made her opinion about the meals on this ship clear. The prepackaged provisions the smugglers had provided us weren't exactly gourmet fare. They hadn't been up to Scylla's vegan specifications, either, but beggars couldn't be choosers.

Zero started twisting themself around to face upright again. Everyone's hair had grown out somewhat on this trip, and Zero's was no exception. Their once-fuchsia undercut had faded into an ashy color, long and curly on top, with the shaved sides now a short and prickly brown. The longer part swirled around as they turned, creating the impression of a Kewpie doll. "I'd check Bay Two in the cargo hold," they said.

I furrowed my brows as Zero and Scylla glided out of the rec room. Grabbing on to a handhold, I pulled myself along the hallway out of the crew area and into the cargo area. I'd pretty much stayed out of this section of the ship for the duration of the trip. Scylla had been curious what was inside all the shipping containers, but I doubted it was anything interesting. Most of it was probably just raw material for manufacturing.

Sure enough, though, Zero was right that this was where Tamara was. I wasn't sure what she was doing in here, but when I opened the door marked with a two and stuck my head in, I heard her, though her voice was muffled. It took a moment for me to realize what I was hearing.

She was singing.

My heart soared inside me at the sound. Her voice was soft, barely above a whisper, but the tune didn't sound sad like the one she'd sung before we left Earth. This one had a more optimistic quality to it. I found myself thanking whatever deity was listening that she'd found her voice again.

I came around the corner of one of the pallets of crates strapped to the floor and saw her hovering there, her head down and her eyes closed.

"*Sing a new song —*"

"Hey."

She jerked. If we'd had gravity, I'd have said she jumped, but even without it she still managed to flail around wildly in the air. She'd been holding something in her hands, but she quickly shoved it behind her back. It looked like that weird red necklace I'd seen back in her room in the UFS.

"Sorry, I didn't mean to startle you," I said. "We're going to be landing soon. Lizeth wants everyone to get all their stuff together and come up front so that we're buckled in when descent starts."

"Oh, okay," she said, flustered. "Coming."

I grinned. She was so damn cute when she was embarrassed.

She pushed herself away from the crates, starting to maneuver herself out of the hold. But I stayed her, grabbing on to the tough ratchet strap holding the crates to the floor, using it to balance myself as I put my hand on her shoulder.

"Hey," I said in a low voice. "I'm glad to hear you singing again."

Her face, already flushed, turned deep crimson. "That wasn't really…"

"It sounded like it was. And it was good to hear."

She smiled awkwardly, and I gave her a quick kiss on the cheek. We floated our way out of the cargo bay.

The closer we got to Mars, the more radio chatter began to filter over the speakers on the flight deck. Spacejets and passenger liners made up the bulk of it, since any ship carrying passengers had a human crew on board, even if the ship was running on autopilot. Other sounds came not from the radio but from the console of the ship itself, long beeps and digital static. It reminded me of the sound of a dial-up modem that I'd heard in my History of Tech class my first year at the Academy. This would be the ship communicating with the automated air traffic control unit on the ground.

We were going to be landing at Johann Kimbal Interplanetary Airport, the sprawling facility on the outskirts of Tierra Nueva we'd flown out from more than two months ago. The south end of the complex had landing areas for larger spacecraft like this one, as well as runways for cargo jets and warehouses for temporary storage as freight was shipped in and shipped out. Tierra Nueva was the largest city in the province and one of the biggest industrial regions on Mars. Manufacturing had been outsourced here decades ago—a convenient source of greenhouse gases to sustain our artificial atmosphere, and a convenient way to get those same emissions off Earth, where they'd been causing more harm than good. Just about everything from clothing and shoes to electronics to even cars was made here, which meant that there was a shit ton of goods needing to be shipped offplanet every single day. Because of that, the cargo facilities were even bigger than the commercial airport, and freight was coming in and out almost constantly. Growing up in the factory district near the airport, I'd become accustomed to the nonstop roar of jets and spaceships taking off and landing.

We sat in a holding pattern, back in our flight suits and strapped into our seats, for what felt like an endless amount of time. Now that we were at the finish line, everything seemed like it was crawling. But at last, a voice came over the radio saying, "QF-42, *do you copy?*"

That was us. QF—Quasar Freight, the company that owned this tub. This must be our so-called man on the ground, because ordinarily an automated ship like this one wouldn't get a radio ping. Lizeth pressed a button on the console in front of her. "Copy."

"You are clear for landing. Bringing you in now."

The ship moved so smoothly that the motion was almost imperceptible, but through the window in front of me I could see the orb of Mars growing larger, individual features on the planet below becoming more visible. Olympus Mons, in Tharsis Province, cut through the clouds, its staggering height more than twice that of Everest back on Earth. We sailed over it, our target west of the mountain. The ship began to shake as we entered Mars' atmosphere. My body suddenly had weight again, and I gripped the handles as I jolted down into my seat.

Then the ship steadied, the vibration tapering off as we descended further into the atmosphere. Tamara exhaled deeply. Behind us, Scylla let out a whoop, clapping her hands. "We made it, guys! We're almost home."

"Don't get too excited yet," Lizeth said. "We need to be on our toes. I won't breathe easy until we're out of the airport and have rendezvoused with Dante."

While we were still spacebound, the Stateless operatives should have landed and made contact with ProLibertate—Gordon—whoever he was. With luck, they'd have made some progress on tracking down where the Ponsfords were being held and maybe even have a game plan in place for getting them out. But we'd have no way of knowing until we were able to reconnect with them ourselves.

Through the window, the features on the ground were growing larger and more clear. We passed over Mount Sharp and the Bagnold Dunes, the little towns of Kimberley and Cooperstown just dots on the landscape. At the foot of the mountain lay Gillespie Lake, the main tributary for the network of intersecting rivers that formed the Gale Delta.

I remembered a trip to Earth I took with my parents when I was younger, probably close to ten annums ago. The water levels had been higher then, and as we'd passed over the delta on the spacejet, I'd thought the twisting blue lines—punctuated by sandy islands, dotted with native spider weeds and desert sagebrush from Earth that had managed to adapt to the Martian climate—looked like an intricate Chinese knot. Now it was apparent how much the water levels had dropped. Several of the smaller channels appeared to be almost completely dry.

Nadin had been right. We'd overestimated our ability to build and keep a world artificially. We needed her people. We needed the Iamoi scientists. They understood this planet better than we could ever hope to. This was not Earth, but we'd tried to make it a second Earth all the same. What we needed was to treat it as what it really was. Mars. Iamos. The Elytherioi's climate-renewing technology was going to be our best chance at making this planet livable—for all of us.

A scar was visible in the south side of the crater, one that the early colonists had blasted in order to allow the rivers to flow south to the sea. The highway from Tierra Nueva to Copertino, near the Elysium mountain range, ran through this artificial canyon. The cars on the road looked like ants crawling in a line. As we descended, the ship followed the highway's trajectory, and within seconds we were over Tierra Nueva. The city appeared dull and gray from here, but to the west, Escalante Bay was as blue as a sapphire.

We passed through a cloud of haze from the factory district, and then the airport was below us. My safety harness dug into my neck and bruised my chest as the ship rocked and rattled, preparing for its final descent. The retrorockets fired with a jolt, forcing the ship to decelerate, slowing it before it collided with the ground.

And then, with a bone-shaking thud, we touched down.

We were home. We were back on Mars.

I started unclasping all of the straps running through my flight suit, but Lizeth held her hand up. "Hold on. Wait for clearance."

I rolled my eyes and continued undeterred. "We're on the ground now, Lizeth. We can unbuckle our seatbelts at least."

A few more minutes passed. Eventually the others started undoing their belts as well. Scylla got out of her seat, walking over to the window and looking out. "Are you sure we were supposed to wait for someone?"

she asked.

"That's what Farrell said. And somebody radioed us up there."

"Maybe he cut and ran," Zero suggested.

Lizeth frowned. "Okay. Bring your things and let's see if we can figure out what's going on."

I grabbed the nylon bag with my personal effects from under my seat, pulling the drawstrings apart and slinging them over my shoulders like the straps of a backpack. As Lizeth opened the door to the flight deck, I heard a bang on the far end of the ship. One of the cargo doors opening.

"Oh, good, there—" Tamara started, but she broke off at the sound of heavy footsteps rushing toward us. Whoever it was, they weren't walking to meet us—they were running.

Not a good sign.

I tensed on the balls of my feet. But there was no escape route. There was nowhere for us to go. We were cornered here.

The inner door to Bay Four opened, and a man in worker's coveralls appeared, out of breath. "Quick," he panted. "GSAF is here."

For one awful second, everything was absolutely still.

"Move!" Lizeth shouted, and the five of us raced after the man.

He hurried us through the hold and down the ramp onto the unloading dock. The dock was a jumble of forklifts and pallets of crates, rusty barrels and huge shipping containers. It was like a maze, but he guided us deftly through it.

A delivery truck was parked a short distance away. He beckoned us toward it. The roll-up door on the back of the truck was open, and we clambered inside. He yanked the overhead cord down and whirled away. In his haste, the door didn't shut completely. The crooked angle it closed at left us about a hand's breadth of light streaming through the bottom on one side.

Lizeth scrambled over on her stomach, peering out through the gap. Scylla, not to be outdone, scuttled over beside her.

"Don't put your face too close to the opening," Lizeth warned.

"No, really?" Scylla retorted.

"Can you see anything?" asked Tamara.

"A bunch of cars just pulled up to where the ship was docked," Scylla whispered. "They're talking to that worker. Oh, *crap*," she hissed, "it's

Joseph Condor."

My stomach sank. Of course it torquing was.

"How did he find us already?" Tamara's voice was taut in the darkness.

"Can you hear what they're saying?" Zero asked.

"No. They're too far away. They're going into the ship."

A few moments passed. I could hear nothing but the sound of everyone's breathing, shaky and uneven, and my own pounding heartbeat in my ears. Then there were more wheels on pavement, doors slamming.

"Some more suits just pulled up," whispered Scylla.

"They're fanning out," Lizeth said. "Dammit, they're doing a search."

I cursed under my breath. And we were stuck here like sitting ducks. We couldn't do anything but wait for them to come across this truck, open the door, and find us.

Lizeth crawled away from the opening. "Move to the back," she whispered.

I scoffed. "What good's that going to do? You think they won't see us in the back?"

"Just do it."

I sighed and started shuffling backward. As I did, my hand landed on something. It lit up at my touch.

"What is that?" Tamara whispered.

I picked it up, turning it over in my hand. A tablet. It must belong to the shipping company.

Voices were approaching. Scylla, undaunted, was still positioned by the open gap. She whispered, almost too low to hear, "They're over by the containers."

I recognized the voice as it grew closer. It was definitely Joseph Condor's. That voice haunted my nightmares.

"Our source said they would be on that ship. They must have been there."

"Maybe the source got the freighter identification wrong," a second voice said. "I don't see how they could have gotten away so quickly."

"Was there any evidence that there had been people on board?"

"Any waste would have been jettisoned to burn up on entry. That's standard procedure," the second voice admitted. "The bunks had sleeping bags in them, but that doesn't necessarily mean anything. Those could have been left behind when the ship was retrofitted. There was a stationary bike that hadn't been scuttled."

"They were there," Condor insisted. "Which means they're around here somewhere. I want every available agent out here searching. Have provincial police bring in K-9s to sniff them out. And let them know to be on the lookout for them in the Tierra Nueva metro area."

"Yes, sir." There was a familiar chime as he turned on the message record function on a palmtop. "Put out an A.P.B. for four individuals wanted by GSAF for questioning. Names and descriptions as follows: Arun 'Henry' Sandhu, male, twenty years of age, South Asian ethnicity. Priscilla Hwang, female, twenty-one, East Asian. Tamara Randall-Torres, female, nineteen, mixed Caucasian and Hispanic. Lizeth Senghas, female, twenty, mixed—"

Lizeth made a strangled noise in the back of her throat. I grimaced. So they knew, then. The connection between Lizeth and us had been made—which meant her connection to the Stateless was likely now known as well. Someone from the dig site must have spilled the beans. It had to have been Horlando. That was the only thing that made sense. But how would he have known when and how we were traveling to Mars, down to the identification of the ship?

"Our source indicated they may have one other person traveling with them, but that person's identity is not known. It's likely the fifth person would have been either Isaak Contreras, male, seventeen, Hispanic; or Nadin of Iamos, female, seventeen, appears Black. List them as persons of interest as well. Weights, heights, and other identifying features can be found in our database." The chime sounded again as message recording stopped.

As the man was dictating this message, I ran my fingers over the silky digital membrane of the tablet I'd found. It lit up again at my touch.

"What are you doing?" Lizeth whispered.

"Excuse me," I whispered back, quickly swiping across the screen a few times. "What exactly put me on the Stateless' radar in the first place?" My eyes moved over the display. Password so easy a baboon could guess it, two-factor authentication disabled. With a few quick swipes, I was inside the facility's security system.

"We need to get this facility locked down," Condor said. "Keep all other freighters in a holding pattern. No more vehicles in or out. I need—"

His words were cut off by the sound of a klaxon blaring in one of the nearby warehouses. That should get their attention.

Over the sound of the siren, I heard someone shout, "Warehouse Five!"

"They must have broken in and triggered the alarm. Get over there, quick!" Condor bellowed.

Scylla scrambled away from the opening as a group of men rushed by, their black-trousered legs visible for a brief instant as they ran past the truck. She crawled back over and peeked out again once they'd passed.

"Are we clear?" I asked.

"They all went in the warehouse."

"Do you see anyone else nearby?"

"No."

"Then let's get the hell out of here," I said. With a few more swipes across the tablet's screen, I was in the truck's self-drive app. In seconds, the truck was in motion. I crawled over to the opening next to Scylla and looked out. In the commotion of the warehouse alarm, no one seemed to have noticed the truck had started moving.

"How do we get out of the airport if they've got it locked down?" Tamara asked.

"Don't worry, I'm on it. I disabled the security at the front gate when I set the warehouse alarm off."

Zero let out a shaky chuckle. "Well. I'd say your investment in renowned hacker Henry Sandhu has paid off, Zee."

"Damn right it has," I agreed.

The sound of the alarm klaxon grew fainter in the distance as the delivery truck rolled out of the cargo facility and onto the street beyond, into Tierra Nueva.

CHAPTER 44

- t a m a r a -

WE ABANDONED THE TRUCK ON THE SIDE OF THE ROAD NOT FAR FROM THE airport. It wouldn't take long for GSAF to figure out they'd been tricked, and the truck would be easily traceable. We stripped off our flight suits, leaving them in a heap in the back of the truck. Our plain thermal clothing would blend in more easily if we were spotted by a random passerby.

"Where are we going to go?" Scylla asked as we hurried down the sidewalk, glancing around to make sure no one was nearby. Lizeth had arranged for the Stateless to rent a place for us to stay before we left. But we hadn't counted on GSAF finding out that we were back on Mars this quickly. Even a relatively secluded vacation rental reserved with fake identification seemed too dangerous now.

"And now that I'm a known associate, I can't risk interacting with any of the Stateless operatives, either," Lizeth said. She cursed under her breath.

"But we were supposed to meet up with Dante at eight," Zero reminded her. "What do we do about that?"

"I don't know," Lizeth said. When Zero looked at her in surprise, she snapped again, "I don't know! I didn't plan for this contingency! We've always been so damn careful. I blew it with that trip to Mexico. I acted on impulse, and look where it torquing got us."

"You think your uncle cracked under questioning?" Scylla asked.

"He must have."

Scylla looked unconvinced. "I know he's dithery, but he's also principled. He seems the type who would refuse to answer anything, on pain of death. Probably using those exact words, frankly."

"How else could GSAF have figured out my identity, though?"

"Someone from the dig site," Henry said glumly.

Lizeth looked at him quizzically, but I cut them off. "It can't have been," I said. Henry was still blaming himself, assuming the leak came from Horlando, but I didn't buy it. "No one from the dig site knew our plans. You heard Joseph Condor. He knew which ship we were on, what date and time it was landing, who was going to be on it. No one we met in Mexico would have known any of that."

"Then the only alternative is that someone from the Stateless is a spy," Lizeth said, her voice numb.

"Maybe the explanation is simpler than that," I said. "Maybe it was the smugglers."

"Yeah," said Scylla. "Maybe that PAA patrol boat caught up with Ashraf after all."

Lizeth frowned thoughtfully. "Maybe. I didn't give them any of our real names, but..."

"It wouldn't have been hard to figure out. Especially after that call you got from Bruno before takeoff," Henry pointed out. "Ashraf, Farrell, and the captain of that fishing boat all heard it."

"Yeah," said Lizeth.

"Right. So don't beat yourself up anymore," Zero said. "In the meantime, we need to figure out a game plan. Where are we going to go?"

"You can go to the rendezvous with Dante," Lizeth said. "You're still off their radar, for the time being at least. We can take advantage of that. Use one of your burner I.D.s to rent a car. Let Dante know what's going on, and find out what info he has."

"Sure. But what about the rest of you?"

"I've got an idea," Henry said. We all looked at him. "If you want to disappear in this town, there's an easy way to do it. It won't be pleasant, but..."

"Nothing about the last two months has been," said Lizeth. "Let's hear it."

✦

He led us through the back alleys of the factory district, taking care to avoid any areas with people or security cameras. "Down here," he said, guiding us down the steep embankment beside Armstrong Slough, one of the dozens of tributaries of the Aeolis River that snaked its way through town. The slough ran under D Street, and from down here I could see the underside of the bridge was covered with graffiti. Soggy old boxes, rusty cans, plastic bottles, and all other sorts of detritus littered the ground underneath. Nearby, a shopping cart was turned on its side, precariously close to the water. It looked like people had been camping here recently, but whoever it had been was gone now.

"You want us to stay here?" Scylla asked, wincing as she looked at the mess around us.

Henry shrugged. "If you want to be invisible, become one of the people society doesn't want to look at."

Once we were settled, Zero left. They'd need to walk back to the airport to rent a car, and by the time they took care of that, it would be almost time to meet up with Dante. Hopefully they would have some answers for us when they returned.

"Assuming that Dante and your buddy Gordon have managed to make progress with intel gathering, we should hopefully have an idea about where GSAF is keeping Kate Ponsford soon. Then we can formulate a plan for how to get her out. That's step one," Lizeth said.

"Right. But we need more than that," Henry added. "If we want to stop Joseph Condor, we have to have the public on our side, too."

"And that brings us back to what Geoff Preston told us about Nano," Scylla said.

"I wish he hadn't left that on us," Henry said. "It's going to be a lot harder for us to get the word out if we're having to stay in hiding. Last time I had Wyatt get me in touch with Nancy Ramirez." Nancy Ramirez was the host of a popular VR cast on Speculus. "But we had the element of surprise then. Condor's watching for us now, Wyatt's who knows where, and I have no way of getting in touch with Ramirez without drawing GSAF right to us."

I stared at the dirty water in the slough, chewing on my lip. I hadn't even tried to share my idea after what had happened back on Sea-Star Island. But we were out of options now.

"Maybe there's another way of getting the word out," I said quietly.

Henry looked at me. "What are you thinking?"

"You know how Preston said that ConneX was pushing the System compatibility to the nanobots in a firmware update?" I looked down at my fingernails. There was already red dirt under the nails of my right hand. "What if we could do something similar? Push an update to people's devices that gave them an alert about it?"

"We'd need Preston to do that, and he already said he wasn't going to give us more help than what he already has," said Lizeth.

"Not to the nanobots. To another device. Like a palmtop."

Realization dawned on Henry's face. "You mean have Mama D push an update to the A-Tops?"

"Yeah."

Lizeth looked confused. Scylla folded her arms smugly. "Yeah, remember how you thought Tamara didn't have any use to us? One of her moms is the lead developer at AresTec."

Lizeth ignored Scylla's barb. Turning to me, she asked, "You think she'd be able to pull something like that off?"

"I think so. But I would have to talk to her about it to know for sure."

"We need to arrange a meeting," Lizeth said, sounding decisive for the first time in hours.

"But that's going to be tough with GSAF watching all our known associates," Henry said.

I looked down at the water again. Brackish, slow-moving. The water level in the slough was low. That shopping cart would be underwater if it was as full as it had been a few annums ago.

"I have an idea about that, too," I said.

My plan was risky, but at this point, the only options we had left were risky ones. Which is how I found myself in Zero's rental car the following afternoon.

We'd spent the previous evening and most of the morning in bursts of activity and planning followed by long hours of quiet worrying. Zero had been able to rent the car and meet with Dante with seemingly no problem. They said no one appeared to be following them, and the meeting hadn't been broken up by police or GSAF suits.

That was the good news.

Unfortunately, Dante hadn't had much else to report. The Stateless operatives had managed to connect with Free Mars, but in the ten days they'd been here, they hadn't been able to find any information on where they were keeping Kate Ponsford, or Wyatt for that matter. The most they'd been able to learn was that GSAF had a secret facility, which ProLibertate had determined was referred to as the Underground. But no one knew what it was, where it was located, or if it even actually existed or was just a rumor.

There was really only one thing that they'd been able to determine for certain, and that was that the Senghas' cover was definitely blown. There were arrest warrants out for all of them. Carla Perez, Bruno, and even Lizeth's dad had been forced to retreat to one of the family's private seasteads within the UFS, which had no extradition treaty. They were safe for now, but they would not be able to travel to a NAEU or PAA country without being immediately taken into custody.

We had to reach my moms. Lizeth may not have been able to cultivate the connections we needed, but I knew they had them. It was just a matter of speaking to them without attracting GSAF's attention.

That's where my plan came in. Condor's spies would undoubtedly report back to him if anyone they didn't recognize contacted my moms, or if they did anything out of the ordinary. But if it was someone they already spoke to regularly, someone that they also were watching, that would be more likely to escape their attention.

Someone like Isaak's stepdad, for example.

He'd stayed in touch with my family during the months Isaak was missing, even though Isaak's mom had cut off contact with us. Scylla had been able to use him to facilitate that first meeting with Isaak after his return from Iamos, though she'd been able to reach him at the university where he was her academic adviser. But now Scylla couldn't set foot on campus without being immediately taken into custody.

But there was another way we could reach him. Because there was one person, out of all of our families, that I was pretty sure it wouldn't have occurred to GSAF to watch.

Early on Thursday afternoon, Zero came to pick me up in their rental car. Since the rendezvous wouldn't be able to take place until after two o'clock, they'd spent the morning putting together supplies for the second part of the plan. Warm clothes and hiking boots, sleeping bags and trail food, purchased from a variety of different stores using cards with different names on them. They'd also brought us some fast food for breakfast. It was greasy, and it sat in my stomach now like a ball of lead. But despite my twisted-up insides, I didn't feel the overwhelming urge to run that had become my constant companion over the last few months. I was nervous, but nowhere near as anxious as I'd been on Earth. Abuelo's method seemed to be working. It made me feel confident, like I'd finally turned a corner. Like maybe I had broken free of this cycle I'd been stuck in, and I could go back to my old life—a worrywart, yeah, but not constantly consumed by panic. I truly hoped so.

"So, where are we going?" Zero asked as I followed them to where the car was parked.

"I'll give you directions," I said. I knew that self-driving rental cars stored the destinations you selected through the map function, but not if you drove the car yourself or entered directions manually. Hopefully that would work to our advantage if GSAF went through the rental company's records.

They entered the directions I gave them—left from D Street to Water Street, right onto San Marcos, and so forth. Then they pressed the start button, and the car turned on, signaling to the other vehicles nearby that it would be entering traffic.

"You sure you want to do this alone?" Zero asked as the car drove over the bridge the others were still waiting beneath.

I nodded. "A group of us will attract attention. And we need to avoid being seen with you, since you're still off GSAF's radar. Besides"—I shrugged—"she knows me."

"And a whole bunch of other people know you, pop princess."

"I've gotten good at blending in in crowds. And anyway," I said, gesturing to myself, "that's what this is for." I'd put on one of the hats Zero had bought—a bit warm for this time of day in August-II, though it would have been good last night when we'd been huddled under that bridge with outdoor temperatures near freezing—and some overlarge sunglasses as well. I glanced at my reflection in the rearview mirror and tried not to wince. "I've, uh, never had my hair like this before, either."

Zero chuckled. "Not a fan?"

"Oh, no, it's nothing to do with your cut," I stammered quickly, remembering that Zero was the one who'd styled my hair this way in the first place. "It looked really good when you first did it. I've just had trouble maintaining it since then."

They held up their hands. "No worries, hon. No offense taken. I should have warned you with your hair type that this cut might be hard to manage. We were just so pressed for time. I noticed when I was working with it that your hair is straight in the front, but it's curly in the back. It had been so long before that the weight was keeping it in line. Now without that, it's got a mind of its own. We could tame it with heat tools, but..." They trailed off and I laughed. It's not exactly like I would have had access to tools, electricity, or time over the last two months.

"My hair does the same thing if I don't keep it really short. Runs in my family." They sat back, watching through the window as the car turned smoothly onto Water Street. We were leaving the factory district now. We passed a row of apartment buildings, tall and boxy, all of them almost identical. "Do you have a parent with curly hair?"

I nodded. "Yeah, Mama does." She had copper-red hair, curly and wild. Mom's hair, meanwhile, was stick straight, but she'd worn it short for most of my life.

"You have two moms, right?" Zero asked. "Are they both your biological parents?"

"Yeah."

"Is one of them trans?" They flushed. "If you don't mind my asking. Sorry, I'm nosy."

"No, no, it's fine." It was a question I'd gotten many times throughout my life. I was used to it by now. "They're both cis. They did that treatment that turns an egg into a sperm."

Zero whistled. "They *do* have money."

I let out a chuckle of embarrassment. They did have money, but I didn't really like talking about it. "Not *that* much," I hedged. "You'll notice I don't have any siblings."

My face must have betrayed something, because Zero smiled reassuringly and put a hand on my shoulder. "You'll see your mamas again soon. I'm sure this is going to work."

I smiled back. "I hope so."

"It's a good plan. Don't second guess yourself."

The car turned onto San Marcos Street, which ran parallel to Santos Creek. The creek served as the unofficial division between the north and south sides of town. South of the creek, the buildings were older, having been built during Tierra Nueva's first incarnation as a manufacturing hub. Before AresTec had moved into the area and transformed the city into a tech haven and tourist destination. As we moved westward, we entered a neighborhood made up mostly of duplexes. A neighborhood I'd visited many times growing up.

We came around a curve, and then I could see the school. Ellen Ochoa Elementary. Incredibly to me, the school year was already in session. It would have started on Wednesday—two days ago, if I had my dates right. We'd used up the entire two-month off-session on our little Earth misadventure. I felt a pang in my chest, but I tried to ignore it. It would have been move-in day for me at Herschel on Monday. Mariyah and I had been planning to room together again this year. I'd texted her periodically during the trip over on the *Athena*, but once I lost my palmtop, I lost my ability to communicate with the outside world, too.

I wondered if Mariyah was okay. I was sure GSAF must have questioned her when I went missing. Had she been worried? Was she still wondering where I was? I knew I must have missed dozens of messages from the school, too. Had they kept my spot for the dorm? How long would they hold it once they realized I wasn't going to be showing up for the semester? How much time could pass before they dropped me as a student? I'd probably need remedial classes by the time I went back...

If I ever went back.

I couldn't think about that now. I had more important things to do.

"That the place?" Zero asked as we drew closer to the school. The pickup/drop-off lane was full of cars, as was the parking lot. Most of the kids at this school were too young to legally ride in a self-driving car unsupervised, so parents and other relatives were swarming the area, waiting for the last bell to ring and the kids to start pouring out of their classrooms. The sight of the crowd made me antsy. On the one hand, this many people, all of whom would be focused on their own children, meant that I would most likely slip by unnoticed. Even though I was relatively well-known on Mars as a singer, after two months on the run—barely sleeping, barely eating, with my long dark hair now short and blond—I doubted anyone would recognize me, especially in an incongruous place like this.

On the other hand, there were sure to be at least a few people in this crowd with nanobots. Even if the people themselves didn't notice me, the tech within them would. And based on what Geoff Preston had said, that tech would recognize me, too. I could only hope he was continuing to overwrite data that showed our locations.

"Yeah. Drop me off out front and then drive around the neighborhood. So the car doesn't log the stop. Check back in twenty minutes."

"Are you *sure* you want to do this alone?"

I swallowed. "Yeah. I have to."

The key to not standing out, I decided, was to walk with purpose. Everyone here was here for a reason—picking up their kid, or their sibling, or meeting with a teacher. And I had a reason, too. I needed to look like I belonged here.

Zero paused the car at the tail end of the drop-off line, and I hopped out, following the throng of parents through the school gates. I kept my gaze forward, not making eye contact with anyone, and followed the familiar path I'd taken with Isaak several times before. Back when we were at the Academy, I came along with him sometimes when his mom was working late and couldn't come down here herself.

To pick up his little sister, Celeste.

Celeste was our best shot. The one person out of any of our families that GSAF was most likely not going to be watching. Because why would they suspect an eight-year-old girl? But if she could get her stepdad to give my moms a message, then we might just have a chance. Otherwise, it was only a matter of time before GSAF caught up with us, and this time there'd be no getting away from them.

Celeste's after-school program had met in the cafeteria the last time I was here, over two annums ago, and it looked like that was still the case. A sign hung on the wall on the walkway just outside, the word *Bridge* printed in large, block letters, with an arrow pointing in the direction of the cafeteria. I didn't want to just loiter in the hallway, though, in case a teacher saw me and started asking questions. But I definitely couldn't risk actually going into the cafeteria, either.

Along the walkway, the school had planted bitterbrush in thick clusters. Cold-tolerant desert sagebrush like these tended to do better in Mars' arid climate than other Earth plants, and these had grown tall enough to form a thick screen. I felt like an absolute creeper—and I knew if anyone saw me here, they'd definitely think I was a predator—but I couldn't think of a better solution. I ducked into a clump of brush across from a couple drinking fountains, and I waited.

Within minutes, I heard the electronic chimes of the school bell, and the sound of voices as kids began pouring out of their classrooms. I shrank back into the brush, praying no one would see me. Praying that Celeste would come this way on her way to Bridge. Praying that she'd be alone when she came by.

Please. Please. Please.

Minutes passed. A dozen or more kids streamed by in the direction of the cafeteria, but I didn't recognize any of them.

The school got quieter. The cacophony of voices simmered down to a soft buzz, punctuated now and then by a distant shriek or squeal. My legs started to ache from holding this crouching position for so long.

I'd missed her. I knew it. She'd taken another route to the cafeteria. She was already inside by now, and I'd have no hope of catching her. Our last best chance at getting a message to my moms was gone. What was I going to tell the others? Lizeth would never let me live it down. And what were we going to do now?

Just as I was getting ready to emerge from the sagebrush and head back to tell Zero of my failure, I heard the soft sound of footsteps on concrete. Moving slowly, trudging almost. I peeked between the olive-green leaves of the bitterbrush and my heart leapt. She was looking down at her feet, but I recognized her. And she was alone.

"Celeste," I whispered as loudly as I dared. She jumped, startled, and looked around. I straightened, waving to her from behind the bush.

She stared at me in confusion for a moment. I pulled off the huge sunglasses covering my face, and she gasped. "Tamara!" She looked past me into the sagebrush, as if expecting someone else to be lurking in the bushes here with me. "Is Zak with you?" she asked.

I felt a pang, but hoped I managed to keep my face neutral. "I'm by myself right now. I need to talk to you, but it's important that nobody see or hear us."

Celeste nodded, looking back and forth around the empty hallway, and then gestured me over to her. Surreptitiously, she opened the door to the darkened classroom next to the drinking fountains.

I followed her in and she shut the door. She started to reach for the light switch, but I stayed her. "We don't want anyone to know we're in here."

"Oh, right," she said. I glanced around at the classroom, dimly lit by the windows along one wall. Instead of desks, the room had two long tables with chairs surrounding them. In the middle of the tables were plastic bins—one holding plastic tambourines, another holding cheap plastic recorders. On the far wall, an upright piano stood. Automatically I walked over to it, glancing down at the keys. Despite the surface scratches in the ivory, it was in surprisingly good shape for being in an elementary school classroom.

"The music room," Celeste explained. "The fourth and fifth graders in Bridge have homework hour in here. The music teacher goes home after lunch and she leaves it unlocked so Bridge can use it. But homework hour won't start until after snack, so we have a little bit." She shifted uncomfortably. "But I need to go soon or I'll get a tardy."

"I'll be fast," I promised.

"Where's Isaak?" Celeste asked. "Is he okay?"

I hesitated, unsure how to answer that. "I..."

She frowned and nodded. "He's not here, is he? He went back there."

I swallowed. "Yeah. He and Nadin had some things they needed to take care of." At her glum expression, I quickly added, "But don't worry—they're coming back soon. It's not like last time, when we didn't know where he was or if he was ever coming back. He's got a key to bring him home this time. He and Nadin will be back in just a few days." Tuesday morning. And with any luck, this nightmare might be over soon, and Isaak could actually go home instead of having to join us on the run.

Celeste let out a sigh. I couldn't tell if it was one of relief or resignation. "Are the rest of you all right?"

"We are for now. But we have to stay in hiding for a while longer. No one can know you saw me, okay?"

"I promise," Celeste said, holding up three fingers. I smiled in spite of myself at the gesture.

"Is your mom still friends with Joseph Condor?"

Celeste made a face. "Yeah. She says he helped us when Isaak was missing. I don't like him, though. I agree with Zak. I think he's creepy. Dad doesn't like him, either. He didn't like Isaak going to Earth with him. He had a feeling something like this was going to happen."

At first I thought she meant Raymond, her biological father, and wondered how she would have gotten a chance to hear his opinion on any of this. As far as I was aware, Raymond was still on Earth and under heavy surveillance. But after a moment, I realized she meant Erick. I suppose it made sense—she'd only been six when her mom and Erick got together, and Raymond had disappeared when she was so young that she had never really known him. Erick was more of a dad to her than Raymond ever had been.

"Do you think I could give you a message to give Erick—your dad?" I asked.

"If you want to stay, you can talk to him yourself," Celeste suggested. "He's picking me up after Bridge today."

I was sorely tempted. It would be good to see a familiar face after so much time in isolation. But I knew I couldn't risk it. "I can't wait that long. I'm sorry."

"That's okay. I can give him your message."

I smiled. "Thank you. Ask him to please get in touch with one of my moms. He needs to not let Joseph Condor know. And you both need to not let your mom know, because she might tell Condor."

She stood ramrod straight and nodded, as if I'd tasked her with a top-secret mission. I suppose I had. "Right," she said matter-of-factly.

"Have him tell them that they need to go to our boat on Sunday morning at nine o'clock. Can you remember that?"

Celeste gave me a look that clearly read, *Duh*. "It's not that much to remember."

I grinned. "I guess you're right. I'm glad to see you, Celeste."

She stared at me for a minute, then came over to the piano where I was still standing and threw her arms around me in a hug. It had been so long since I'd seen her, Isaak's little sister. She'd just been a baby five minutes ago, and now she was almost as tall as I was. "I'm glad to see you too, Tamara," she said.

We left the music room in the same darkened state as we'd found it, and she headed down the hallway toward Bridge. She paused for just a moment, looking over her shoulder at me. Then she was gone.

I stood there a moment longer, watching the space where she'd been, and unconsciously reached into my pocket, feeling for the rosary beads that had become as much my security item as the red yarn bracelet had once been. I realized, kicking myself, that I should have told Celeste that her grandparents were safe, should have given her some sort of message about them. I honestly should have given her this rosary—after all, it was Celeste's family heirloom, not mine. But no. He'd wanted me to have it. Besides, it would be hard for her to hide anything like that from her mother, and if her mother found out, it might wind up getting back to GSAF. I would just have to trust that soon they'd be able to be reunited, face to face.

Cautiously, I left Ellen Ochoa Elementary School behind.

CHAPTER 45

- h e n r y -

I HAD TO HAND IT TO TAMARA—USING ISAAK'S KID SISTER TO DELIVER THE message wasn't something I would have thought of, but it seemed to have gone off without a hitch. If everything went according to plan, we'd be meeting with her moms in a little over twenty-four hours.

But to get to that point, there were several other moving parts that had to go off without a hitch as well. First of all, it was agreed upon that any of us actually meeting Tamara's moms at their boat at Yellowknife Bay would be too risky. There was a good chance GSAF might intercept the message and be waiting there for us. Even if they didn't, Yellowknife Bay—the estuary for the Murray River and gateway between Gillespie Lake and the rest of the delta—would be crawling with boaters, especially on a weekend this close to Martian summer. We'd been spotted when we took Nadin out on the boat back in May. We weren't going to take that chance again.

Instead, when Bryn and Delia arrived at their boat, they would find a note waiting for them, hand-delivered by Dante: "*Let's have a picnic.*" Tamara had selected the wording—she knew they'd know what it meant. South of Kimberley and Cooperstown, there was a small cove off the river: Ogunquit Beach. Growing up, when her family would take the boat out, they'd usually stop there to have a picnic before heading back. It took about three hours to sail from Yellowknife Bay to Ogunquit Beach. With luck, we'd be meeting them just before noon on Saturday.

Ogunquit Beach had a number of advantages going for it, primary of which being that it was secluded. It wasn't accessible by car, and it was far enough south of Yellowknife Bay that it didn't get a lot of boat traffic. But it was also within walking distance of Tierra Nueva. Hiking the Glen Torridon Trail over Vera Rubin Ridge, we'd be able to reach the beach within a day. That was good, since Lizeth was adamant that none of us set foot in Zero's rental car again.

"The important thing in planning any kind of operation is to diffuse the variables as much as possible," Lizeth decreed as we sat under the bridge that evening. "GSAF is going to be looking for patterns. If they see the same car going to the same place, or picking up the same people, or going to multiple places of interest. That's why we have to break it down into as many moving pieces as possible, to make it harder for them to pick out patterns. Zero going to different stores, using different cards. Dante going to Yellowknife Bay instead of Zero. The two of them avoiding being spotted in the same location, or using the same cars. When you're dealing with an entity that's overly centralized like GSAF, it's easy to overwhelm them with highly decentralized activities. But that requires organization. We've got to plan everything out in advance, down to the most minute detail. That's how we pull off something like the Lago Verde operation."

"Yeah, yeah, and I threw a spanner in the works, got it," I grumbled.

To my surprise, though, Lizeth didn't take the bait. She just sighed, tossing a stick into the slough. "It's okay. We can make it work. We have to."

We spent another night camped out under the bridge, taking turns keeping watch for police or anyone else who might wander too close, and listening for drones overhead. The next morning, we set out, carrying the supplies Zero had gathered for us the day before. Transforming our appearance from a gang of runaway teens to an innocent group of weekend hikers was just a matter of a change of clothes and judicious use of the public restrooms at the Glen Torridon Recreation Area at the foot of Vera Rubin Ridge.

I emerged from the bathroom to find Scylla sitting under the picnic shelter just outside, slathering sunscreen on the back of her neck. "The others will be out soon," she said. "I've been surveying the area. A couple hikers started down the trail about five minutes ago, but otherwise it's been clear."

"We ought to give them a bit of a head start before we head out," I said. "The last thing we need is to catch them up on the trail."

"I don't think we will. I heard them mention they were going to try to do the whole trail before dark. They didn't even glance in my direction. They're probably halfway up the ridge by now."

I nodded, turning to read the sign posted beside the picnic shelter, which displayed a map of the route we'd be taking. The trail itself began in the hills on the north end of Tierra Nueva and followed the Murray River as far as Bradbury Landing, about a thirty-kilometer trek. The sign advised that only experienced thru-hikers should attempt that distance in a single day. But we were only looking at going about half that far, detouring down to Ogunquit Beach sixteen kilometers in.

I glanced up at the flat-topped ridge towering over us. It was about as tall as a twenty-story building, but the trail guide posted below the map assured us that it would be a gradual incline to the top. We'd continue along the ridge for some distance before descending toward the delta.

"You know, I've lived in Tierra Nueva for half my life and I've never actually hiked this ridge," Scylla commented as she watched me read the sign. "It's really popular with rock collectors, though, because of all the hematite. That ace ring I got for Nadin was made out of locally sourced stone. I've got one like it somewhere. I got it at a craft fair on campus." She shrugged. "I've never been all that big on jewelry, though."

Lizeth and Tamara emerged from the bathroom just then. Tamara was wearing a pink baseball cap that covered the stark stripe of roots that had grown out on her bleached hair. "Did you guys put sunscreen on?" Scylla asked, holding out the bottle.

"I don't usually burn," Lizeth said as Tamara reached for the bottle.

"You can still get skin cancer," Scylla warned, and Lizeth rolled her eyes.

"You're worse than my mother. '*Wear sunscreen, eat your veggies.*'" She paused, then added, "Actually, my mother never said any of those things."

Scylla laughed, and after a moment, Lizeth laughed too. Maybe we were finally starting to see her human side.

We set out along the rocky trail. Growing up, I'd often heard people who were used to Earth's climate complaining about it being cold on Mars, but I tended to run hot. We'd spent way too much time in the tropics on Earth, and as we climbed the gradual slope of the ridge, I found myself glad to be back home where the temperature was much more reasonable. The sun was bright overhead and the day cloudless, but the brisk breeze helped keep me cool. It smelled almost nostalgic, the tangy scent of the nearby sea mingling with the distant acrid smell of factory exhaust.

The side of the ridge was striped with variegated color, dark grays and blacks popping vividly next to rust red and dirt brown. The ridge had been studied exhaustively before colonization efforts even began, due to the metals and minerals it was comprised of. There had been some interest in mining it, but the provincial government had insisted that it instead be preserved. There was a limit on the size and quantity of rocks that could be removed from the area—though, since the trail wasn't staffed, that wasn't strictly enforced.

As we drew closer to the top of the ridge, I started noticing flat-faced rocks with squiggles and lines in them. They looked like they'd been engraved, but I knew that they were the remnants of primordial fossils, exposed by the weather. We'd been told the fossils were of primitive organisms, but that was before we knew about Iamos. Now I wondered if these were creatures that Nadin would be able to name.

Then we reached the top of the slope, and we were on the apex of the ridge. From here the city spread out before us, nestled between hills to the north and east and the vibrant blue of Escalante Bay to the west. Behind us, the mammoth impact crater we now called Gale Valley stretched as far as the eye could see, the five-kilometer irregular mound of Mount Sharp sloping gently out of the center, its peak capped with thin stripes of white snow, almost completely melted as the summer months approached. At its feet lay the bays, rivers and canals of the delta, winding their way around the dark gray sands of the Bagnold Dunes.

"Wow," Scylla said as she took it all in. "That's a view. I can't believe I've never come up here before!"

"We're definitely not on Earth," Lizeth said.

I glanced back at Tamara as she gazed down at Tierra Nueva silently.

I followed the direction of her eyes into the hills along the coast, knowing she was searching for her moms' house. But we couldn't quite see it from here. Beyond, in the bay, the two crescent-moon shapes of Herschel Island and Knobel Island were just visible at the horizon's edge, another reminder of everything she'd left behind. Everything she'd sacrificed. For Mars and for Iamos. For her friends.

For me.

"It's like another life," she said softly.

I took her hand and squeezed it. "You'll get that life back. I promise."

She smiled faintly at me. "You know, standing here, I actually feel like it's possible."

We hiked until my calves were sore and I definitely had shin splints. Then we continued to hike some more. The trail showed off the rugged beauty of Mars' desert landscape, I'd grant the Aeolis tourist bureau that. I could see why the outdoorsy types would enjoy this sort of thing. But it was definitely not my cup of tea.

Around four in the afternoon, we came to a fork in the path. A sun-weathered sign indicated Ogunquit Beach with a downward-angled arrow, leading down a notch in the rock formations around us. I would be glad to leave behind the more open part of the trail. Being on top of Vera Rubin Ridge had been beautiful, but we'd been totally exposed. I'd been terrified a drone would pass overhead, whether a GSAF one deliberately searching for us or an amateur photographer who'd catch us unintentionally. But we'd be in the clear now—there were plenty of rocky overhangs on the path down to the beach that could shield us from overhead view.

"There's a campground a little farther up the trail," Tamara said, "but I'm assuming we're going to want to avoid that?"

"Definitely," Lizeth said.

"If we go off the trail, there are some caves in this area. They're pretty small, and technically off-limits. But they're probably our safest bet for tonight," Tamara said.

Fortunately, we wouldn't have to worry about wildlife out here. The only creatures that had gotten a foothold on Mars thus far were insects like mosquitoes, and without much to feed on outside of the cities, they hadn't spread too far beyond urban centers. Our biggest concern out here would be the threat of other humans.

Tamara led us down the trail a little way; then, looking around to reorient herself with the area, she guided us off the path. "I think there's one just down here," she said, more to herself than anyone. "Yeah. Here we go."

I couldn't see anything at first, apart from some leggy stands of spider weeds growing out of a small, scraggly bunch of sagebrush. Then Tamara pushed one of the prickly black weeds aside, and a narrow slot appeared in the rocks like an ancient doorway. Maybe that wasn't too far off the mark. The cave was too small and primitive to have been anything the *geroi* had had something to do with. But we had no way of knowing whether this cave might once have been used by the Iamoi rebels. My skin crawled as I realized that maybe others had been in this cave before—maybe people I knew. Maybe Isaak.

"Tuesday," I whispered under my breath. We'd know soon. We'd know if he was safe. If he'd survived. But how much time would have passed for him by the time he came back through the door? Just four months ago, Isaak had returned to our time to find us all strangers. Two annums had passed for us in what had only been a month to him. What if this time the reverse happened? I had no way of knowing what had happened in the past. If he'd been imprisoned, and if not killed, then held for years. What if, after only being gone for a month of our time, Isaak came back to us as an old man? I wasn't sure if that would be better or worse than him not coming back at all.

Time travel sucks.

The cave at least provided some shelter, as well as shielding us from the prying eyes of other people. We didn't dare light a fire and attract attention, so we'd need all the extra warmth we could get when the sun went down and the temperature dropped. We at least had warm clothing and sleeping bags now, unlike our first night back. We had a few disposable heat packs as well, though those never lasted too long. Still, it was better than nothing.

As we had the last two nights, we set up a watch schedule, so that someone would always be awake and on guard just in case. We portioned out some of the trail food Zero had rounded up for us, and ate in subdued silence.

The sun disappeared behind the hills, painting the sky with fire that reflected off the Murray River below us. The stars began to show against a purple backdrop that darkened into near blackness. These stars were familiar, unlike the ones on Earth. Regardless of the circumstances, this day had reminded me that it was good to be home. My parents may have been from Earth, but I was Martian, through and through.

My watch shift was before dawn, so I tried to go to sleep early, without much success. I'd feel like I wouldn't be able to sleep at all, then doze off for a couple minutes only to jerk awake with the vestiges of some weird dream or another hanging on the edge of my mind, leaving me uneasy.

Around two AM I sat up, deciding I'd had enough of attempting to sleep on this rocky ground. I looked around, my eyes adjusting to the dim. Tamara was sitting near the mouth of the cave, keeping her watch. Through a gap in the spider weeds only about as wide as my hand, you could see down to the beach without being seen in return.

Gingerly, I made my way over to sit beside her, careful not to disturb Scylla or Lizeth. Her face was lit by starlight, streaming through a jagged hole worn into the rock by the elements. Overhead, I could just make out the thin sliver of Phobos, the larger of our two moons—big enough to see, but not enough to cast much light. Not like the moon on Earth had been.

"Hey," she said as I sank down onto the dirt beside her. "What's up?"

"Can't sleep. I figured my watch would be starting soon anyway, so I might as well quit trying. Have you seen anything?"

She shook her head. "It sounded like a drone went over a while ago, a big one. Not a tourist. But it's been at least an hour. Nothing since then."

She moved her hand, and I heard a delicate tinkle. I glanced down and saw she'd been holding that weird beaded necklace in her lap. "I've seen you carrying that for a few weeks now," I commented.

"Isaak's grandpa gave it to me. It's a rosary," she said, holding it up.

I recognized it now—the cross on the end of it. Isaak's mom had one hanging from the rearview mirror of her sedan. I didn't really know much about Catholic stuff, but I was pretty sure it was some kind of prayer beads.

"He thought it might help with my... you know. My issues."

I nodded. "Has it?"

She looked down at the red beads, wrapped around her hand. "I think so. Honestly, I think it has. At first I felt awkward about it, but the more I do it, the more it seems like it's helping. I don't feel as constantly panicked as I had been." Eagerly, she turned to face me. "You're supposed to say certain prayers on them, but I didn't know which ones to do. But then I thought, maybe I don't have to do it exactly right. And then I remembered the psalms I would sing when I was a cantor at church, and I thought, I may not know all the exact right prayers, but I know these songs." She grinned. "My therapist always tried to get me to do meditation, but I could never get it. I could never get my brain to *stop* long enough for it to make a difference. But this is kind of like meditation, you know? And having the beads in my hand gives me something concrete to focus on, like touch grounding. So it's like..." She trailed off, looking down. Even in the almost darkness, I could see the flush on her face. "Sorry. You probably think this sounds stupid."

I took her hands in mine, closing my fingers around hers, feeling the cool beads between them.

"No. I don't think it's stupid. I'm glad you've found something that's working for you." In some ways I envied her. My parents, with their conglomeration of religious backgrounds, always seemed more at peace than I did. It had been that way even when I was a kid. They had somehow managed to reconcile their families' disparate faiths—my dad being a Sikh, and my biracial mom being raised with both Hindu and Christian traditions—and they were willing to believe in something I just couldn't bring myself to. Couldn't find a place for in my known universe, even if I tried. That, the older I got, I was ever more convinced I never would.

But if Tamara wanted it... if that brought her peace... I wasn't going to begrudge her that. More than anyone I knew, she needed that peace.

Smiling, she set the rosary down on the ground next to her and leaned into me.

"I'm happy you're feeling less anxious now," I murmured into her hair. "I worry about you."

"I don't want you worrying about me." Her voice reverberated in my chest.

"And I don't want you worrying about me."

"Well, then. I guess we're at an impasse, aren't we?"

I smirked. Apparently we were.

We sat in the mouth of the cave, watching, listening, until Tamara finally dozed off against my shoulder. The stars winked overhead, pinpricks of light reflected in the ripples of the river.

Chapter 46

- t a m a r a -

THE SOUND STARTLED ME AWAKE. I JERKED UPRIGHT, LOOKING AROUND. The sun hadn't risen yet, but the sky was lighter, most of the stars gone. It would be daybreak soon.

Henry's arm tightened around me as I listened to the rumble growing louder. "What is that?" I asked, my voice still thick with sleep.

"Helicopter. And a few more drones have gone over."

My mouth went dry. "Do you think they've found us?"

"No. But I think they're looking for us."

Someone must have seen us on the trail. Scylla had been sure those thru-hikers hadn't noticed her, but maybe they had. Or, more likely, their nanobots had.

As the helicopter drew closer, the sound became deafening. Behind us in the darkness, Scylla and Lizeth scrambled awake. Henry nudged me back further into the cave, but he remained at the mouth, watching through the hole in the ceiling over the opening.

"They sound like they're right on top of us." Scylla had to shout in order to be heard.

"Dammit, Henry, get away from there," Lizeth yelled.

He ignored her. As the helicopter passed over, I saw a search spotlight comb over the beach, and then move over the rocky path leading back up to the trail. But the light didn't reach the cave. After a minute, the sound began to fade away. They hadn't seen us.

When it was finally quiet again, Henry turned to face the three of us. Outside, the sun was just beginning to peek over the hills, turning the sky a lighter shade of blue.

"Well," Henry said. "Good morning."

After a hotly whispered conference, we decided to remain in the cave for now. We didn't know if GSAF had actually managed to track us to the Glen Torridon Trail, or if the helicopter had just been part of a routine search over the greater region. Regardless, there was still a chance my moms were coming, and we had to be here to intercept them if they did. We wouldn't get another chance if we weren't able to meet them today.

A few more drones passed overhead over the next several hours, and in the distance we could hear the helicopter continuing its sweep of the area. But it didn't fly directly over us again. I decided to take that as a good sign.

We took turns keeping watch at the mouth of the cave. Around midmorning, Lizeth doled out a few of the remaining protein bars that Zero had bought for us.

"Is that it?" Scylla grumbled.

"It's going to have to be. I'm trying to keep us on a tight ration. We've got no way of knowing how long these provisions are going to need to last us, and we didn't have a whole lot to start with."

I sat at the mouth of the cave for another turn at watch, chewing on the rubbery bar and watching the breeze rustle the black fronds of the spider weed. It had been quiet for a few hours now. Most pleasure boaters on the delta didn't come down this far, but I was a bit concerned by the total lack of movement on the river today. It was a weekend, and the weather was good. I would have expected to have seen at least *one* boat by now. The lack of activity had me worried that GSAF might have closed the river. That would be a twofold problem: it would mean my moms wouldn't have a way to get to us, but it would also mean that GSAF really had figured out that we were nearby. Had Erick's message been intercepted? Had I been seen at Celeste's school on Thursday?

As I crumpled up the wrapper to my protein bar and tossed it into my backpack with the growing pile of trash we'd accumulated on this trip, I heard the telltale sound of a motor. Of water churning faintly in the distance. A boat was approaching.

Scylla looked up. "Do you hear that? Do you think it's your moms?"

I held my finger to my lips. "It's too early." Even if everything went according to plan, they wouldn't be here until close to noon. I couldn't be sure of the exact time, since none of us had our palmtops, but the sun wasn't overhead yet.

Henry clambered over to me, peering through the gap in the spider weeds. A moment later, the boat came into view, immediately recognizable by its black and white paint.

Henry swore. "Police."

"Both of you get back here," Lizeth ordered. "As far back as you can get. Nobody move, and nobody make a sound."

Henry and I scrambled back. From this vantage point, I couldn't see anything now. Just sun streaming between the branches of the spider weeds. I squeezed my eyes shut, praying. *Let them keep going. Don't let them stop here.*

But already I heard the sound of the motor shutting off, the thud of somebody jumping onto the small jetty and mooring the boat to it, the *splish-splash* of water lapping against the hull, the boat fighting against inertia as the rope dragged it to a stop.

"They're searching the beach," Henry whispered.

The four of us huddled together as still as we could be, holding our breaths. Scylla, wedged between Lizeth and me, held on to my arm. My heart was beating in my ears. I wanted to reach into my pocket and squeeze my rosary beads, but I didn't dare move, so I sat stock still and tried to focus on the hard ground beneath me, the warm bodies surrounding me. Anything but the sound of voices down at the beach, which only seemed to be getting louder.

"No footprints," one of them said. "I don't think anyone's been down here in a few days."

"They might not have come down as far as the beach. There are a few runoff canyons and some caves in this area. We probably ought to check those."

They knew about the caves. My heart pounded even harder. *Please may they not know about this one, God, don't let them look in this one...*

"There are some tracks up here by the path." The voice was much closer now, far too close.

"That's not really a surprise, though. This is a heavy-use trail."

I could hear them. Their footsteps on the ridge outside. They were too close. They were going to find us. Scylla dug her fingernails painfully into my upper arm.

Then a shout came from down by the water.

"Say again?" one of the nearby voices called.

"Code Four," the voice down by the river repeated, louder this time. "The suspects have been spotted over in Curiosity Bay. They're calling us back in."

"You've got to be torquing kidding me," one of the voices on the ridge grumbled.

"Are you sure?" the other one called back.

"Captain said they'd been positively identified."

I breathed out a silent sigh of relief. Geoff Preston must have manipulated the data.

I could hear the sound of the two men's footsteps trudging down the trail back to the beach now. "This isn't what I signed up for when I joined the force," the first one complained. "Chasing a bunch of kids around the province just because they got on the governor's bad side."

"Condor's paranoid," the second man said. "I think because he knows nobody likes him."

The first man laughed. "Of course nobody likes him. He's creepy."

Their voices faded as they moved farther away from the cave. Finally, I heard the telltale sound of the boat's engine turning on, the churning of the water as it moved away from the jetty. Lizeth crawled over to the mouth of the cave, peeking through the gap in the spider weeds. "They're heading back upriver," she said.

Scylla finally released my arm. "So what do we do now?"

"Do you think there's still a chance your moms might come?" Lizeth asked.

"The police might have had the river closed, but they're probably going to reopen it now," I answered. "If they got the message, they'll come."

"All right, then. We wait."

After the police boat left, hours passed in unnerving silence. Not long after the police had searched the beach, we heard the helicopter go over again, but at a much higher elevation and moving quickly. When I peeked out through the weeds, I saw the chopper disappear over the hills at the valley's edge, heading east. Curiosity Bay was on the other side of the peninsula, a college town much smaller than Tierra Nueva. But it was near the dig site where Isaak first uncovered the Iamoi relics that sent us all catapulting down this path in the first place. Nadin's citidome had been located in the hills between the factory district of Tierra Nueva and Curiosity Bay over ten thousand years ago. It was logical for them to assume we might be trying to get into the ruins again, especially if they thought Isaak or Nadin were with us.

Soon, the cramped quarters of the cave were getting to me. I longed to get out and stretch my legs, go down to the beach and soak my feet in the river. The day was warming up and it was making the small space stuffy and unpleasant. But Lizeth ordered us not to move until we knew it was safe to do so.

Well after noon—the sun had already passed over the hole in the roof and into the west, behind us—I heard the sound of another motor on the river.

"A boat's coming," Scylla said from her watch position at the mouth of the cave.

I held my breath. *Not another police boat.* It could be nothing. It could just be weekenders on a pleasure craft, now that the river had been reopened. It could be...

Scylla put her hands over her eyes like binoculars, as if that would somehow help her see better. She let out a relieved sigh. "It's the *Merrow's Jewel!*"

I lurched to my feet, not quite able to stand upright in the cave, and started to rush forward. Lizeth grabbed my ankle. "Wait until we've got eyes on them!" she hissed. "It could still be a trap."

I shook my foot free of her grasp and came over to where Scylla was watching. There it was, familiar as my own house, making my insides ache. A white bowrider with blue trim, the name painted on the side in a tidy blue cursive. And the two women on deck I could pick out of a crowd of a million. One tall, curvy, her shock of curls as bright as a copper penny and her grin as blinding as the sun. The other short and tan, her slender form and angular jaw making her able to pull off with much greater success the short blond pixie cut I'd tried to emulate.

Once again Lizeth tried to stop me, but I shoved past her, barreling out through the weeds and between the sagebrush, scrambling down the steep embankment in a cloud of dust. I crossed the rusty sand of the beach in three bounds and collided with them as they leapt out of the boat without a care.

"Mom! Mama!" I cried as I crashed into them.

"Tamara, baby," they cried back, their voices mingling, their arms wrapping around me in a tangle. I realized after a moment I was shaking like a leaf, the relief of finally being in my mothers' arms after all these months making the stress drain out of me like a sieve, leaving me empty and weak.

Mom pulled back, taking in my appearance, her expression growing more alarmed as she stared. I knew I'd lost weight since this adventure began, but since I didn't have my old clothes—or even the clothes Zero had given me in Florida—anymore, I wasn't sure how much. I hadn't taken a proper shower in more than three weeks, and I could feel the bags under my eyes even if I couldn't see them.

"Honey," she said, seeming at a loss. She ran her fingers through my limp, partially grown out hair. "I don't think asking if you're okay is sufficient."

I swallowed down a lump, my eyes burning. "I'm okay."

"You're okay *now*," Mama corrected fiercely. "You weren't okay before, but you are now, Pufferfish. We're going to take care of you. And the rest of you, too," she called, looking over my shoulder. I turned to see Henry, Scylla and Lizeth picking their way down the path to the beach. "You don't have to run anymore."

Chapter 47

- h e n r y -

"YOU DON'T KNOW HOW GLAD WE ARE TO SEE YOU," SCYLLA SAID, hurrying over to where Tamara stood sandwiched between her parents.

Bryn took a step closer to us, but she kept Tamara's hand clasped firmly in hers. "We're a bit later than planned, and we're sorry for that," she said.

"It wasn't your fault. The cops were here earlier," I explained, "so we figured they'd closed the river."

"The guards were *here*? On Ogunquit Beach?" Delia repeated in alarm.

"Yeah. They didn't see us, though. They got called back before they managed to find us in that cave."

Bryn let out a sigh. The anxious expression on her face mirrored the one I'd seen on Tamara's so many times before. "Thank God."

"Right. That's a relief." A cloud passed over Delia's face for just a moment; then, slipping back into her normal cheery demeanor, she asked, "And how are you, loves? You're otherwise safe?" She glanced past my shoulder at where Lizeth was hanging back. "Ah, here! And there's a face I've never seen before."

"Uh, hi. I'm Lizeth." She seemed awkward, uncomfortable. A stark contrast from the cocky, in-control girl who'd busted us out of Lago Verde. She'd been on her home turf, then, and surrounded by her people. And it was more than apparent now that she was no longer either of those things.

She was also watching Tamara's moms, and the way that they were

"

showering their daughter with affection, with an expression that almost made me feel sorry for her. But Delia, in her typical Mama D fashion, let go of Tamara then, coming over to Lizeth and herding her closer to the group with an arm around her shoulder.

"Lizeth is the one who got us back here," Tamara explained.

"Thank you for that," Bryn said earnestly, and Lizeth flushed.

"But we're missing a few. Where are Isaak and Nadin?" Delia asked.

Scylla sighed. "They went back to Iamos."

Delia froze mid-step, exchanging a look with Bryn. "Well," Bryn said, exhaling. "It sounds like we've got a lot to catch up on. Why don't you tell us over lunch?"

"Lunch?" Lizeth repeated in confusion.

"You said you wanted a picnic," said Delia.

"That was just a code, though. To bring you here. We can't actually—"

"Have you looked at yourselves in the mirror lately?" Bryn interrupted. "If there's one thing you could do with, it's lunch."

"But we can't risk being seen," Lizeth protested. "If they spot us, GSAF could—"

"I'd like to see them try." Delia's voice was firm and left no room for argument.

"They won't come back here," Bryn added. "Not for a while yet. It will take them hours to get over to Curiosity Bay and figure out that you're not there. Eat, fill us in on what's going on, and we'll figure out where to go from here."

We spread out a picnic blanket on a secluded part of the beach, sheltered by large rocks and covered by brush and weeds. Bryn opened a basket they'd brought, loaded with sandwiches and bottles of water. After days of nothing but convenience store food and trail mix, anything would have been a treat. And they'd brought sandwiches with lunchmeat in them. That made it even better.

"The guards gave us a bit of trouble upriver," Delia said as we started to tuck into our food, "but it worked out in our favor."

"What happened?" Tamara asked, curled cross-legged between her mothers.

"When we got to Yellowknife Bay this morning, we knew there would be trouble. GSAF had the marina closed off and *Governor Condor*"—Delia's voice dripped with contempt—"was using it as a bloody base of operations."

"You saw Joseph Condor?" Scylla asked.

Bryn nodded. "But like D said, it worked out in our favor. He demanded to know what we were doing there, of course, and we told him that we'd heard the news on the police scanner—that you'd been spotted on the Glen Torridon Trail." She took a sip of water, wiping her mouth with the back of her hand. "And we told him that since the trail was closed on the Tierra Nueva side, we were heading up to Bradbury Landing to see if we could find out anything there."

"He gave us his typical shite," Delia added. "And we argued that we had a right to know where our daughter was. And of course he argued right back, '*You don't have any rights, Tamara's a legal adult,*' so on and so forth. Of course, we were petrified because Erick had told us you wanted us to get to the boat by nine. We weren't sure if you had been planning on meeting us there yourself, or if whatever you'd planned for us there would lead to you getting caught. We reckoned you hadn't been caught yet, what with all the search parties Condor was still sending out. But we didn't know if you'd be walking into a trap."

"Then around eleven o'clock, we heard them saying that you'd actually been spotted in Curiosity Bay," Bryn said. "We didn't know what to make of that, because Erick's message had definitely told us to come here. But they were adamant that you'd been positively identified over there."

"Your man Condor was not best pleased," Delia added. "He got red as a tomato, ordering everyone to come back and all available agents and provincial officers to head east. And when he saw us standing there listening..." She whistled.

"What did he say?" Tamara asked.

"It's not fit for polite company," said Bryn with a sniff. "But the gist is that he ordered us not to set foot in Curiosity Bay. He'd have officers stationed along the highway and at the maglev station, and if they caught hide or hair of us, he would have us arrested."

I snorted. "What for?"

"'Interfering with an active investigation,' I believe is how he put it.

But it basically boiled down to 'because I said so.'" Bryn took another sip of water.

Scylla rolled her eyes. "No wonder those cops said no one likes him."

"That will work to our advantage, at least," said Lizeth.

Swallowing a bite of sandwich, Delia said, "So once they cleared out and reopened the marina, Bryn and I decided to just check the *Merrow's Jewel* anyway. I don't know if they hadn't searched our boat, or if they missed it, or if they saw it and thought it was old. But this was in the cuddy." She pulled a small scrap of paper out of her pocket, containing the message Dante had left for them. "So we reckoned we might as well go see if it meant what we thought it did." She smiled. "And here we are."

"And you're sure you weren't followed?" Lizeth asked with a frown. "No trackers on your boat?"

"Nobody paid us even a second glance. They were absolutely convinced they'd found you over in Curiosity Bay. Don't ask me why, when you're clearly right here." She shuddered. "And apparently only meters away from getting caught."

"There's a good reason for it," I said. "We've got somebody on the inside."

Bryn quirked an eyebrow. "Well, now. Do tell."

So we told them, taking it in turns, about Geoff Preston. That involved backtracking, of course, to what had happened on Lago Verde, and everything that had happened since then. Our escape to the UFS, our detour to Mexico to try to make contact with the Iamoi rebels. What had happened when we opened the postern, and then building the second door so Isaak could go find Nadin. The return key I'd programmed for them, leaving us with a tight deadline to return here. And finally, the note we'd received from Geoff Preston, and the information he'd given us on Sea-Star Island.

"Jaysus," Delia said when we were done.

"ConneX, huh?" Bryn said. "I suppose that would explain why we couldn't find anything out about him when he made contact with you before. But still..." She let out a long breath, sweeping her hair back with her hand. "I can't believe not a single one of my connections at GalaX knew this was going on."

"I can't believe GalaX has fallen this far," Delia muttered. "It's not the same company I started at, that's for sure."

"I'm sorry, Mama," Tamara said. "I know how close you were with Mr. Kimbal. It must be hard to see his legacy being tarnished this way."

Delia snorted. "I wouldn't go that far, Pufferfish. Mr. Kimbal was my friend, but I have no illusions about him. I worked too closely with him. Yes, he was my hero. Yes, I liked him. Yes, he was good to me all my years at GalaX. But he was a total nutter." She laughed at Tamara's scandalized expression and leaned over to ruffle her hair. "But the difference between Mr. Kimbal and the current breed is that Mr. Kimbal made no secret about the fact that he was doing everything for his own purposes, and knew he could get away with it because he had—pardon my French—'fuck you' money. Most other billionaires of his day, and this continues to modern times, they were far more dangerous."

I crossed my arms. "Because they made believe that they were interested in noble causes and in the good of humanity. That's always their M.O. 'Create a more interconnected society, one that fosters understanding.' 'Promote equity.' 'Cure a virus.' You name a societal ill, they pretend they care about it. But all their solutions just coincidentally involved giving themselves more and more power and giving the people less and less."

"Until we're in the situation we're in now," Lizeth muttered darkly. "Where no one has a say in what the government does or doesn't do... except those same billionaires and the monopolies they control."

"But we're going to change all that," Scylla said. She looked back and forth between Bryn and Delia. "Right?"

"Of course, love," Delia said firmly. A beat of silence passed, and she added, "I, uh, I'm just not quite sure how."

Lizeth cleared her throat quietly. I looked at her in surprise. Almost hesitantly, she said, "Tamara has an idea. Right, Tamara?"

Tamara's eyebrows rose halfway up her forehead, but she quickly said, "Uh, yeah. I do." She looked at Delia. "We have to get the word out there about the System being connected to Speculus Nano. In a way that guarantees almost everyone in the world will know about it. Before it's too late. So I was thinking... an A-Top OS message?"

Delia nodded her head slowly. "Push an update that sends an emergency alert to all devices."

"Do you think that would be viable?" Tamara asked hopefully.

"Close to eighty percent of A-Top users have automatic updates enabled," Delia said. "All of them will receive the message. Word will spread to the rest very quickly."

"It's a good idea, Tam," Bryn said, putting an arm around her daughter. "A-Tops are the most widely used palmtop on both Mars and Earth. There's no better way to ensure that the population finds out. Even the news couldn't get the word spread this quickly." Tamara grinned, her face flushing.

"I have to ask, though," I said, feeling bad to be raining on the parade. But we needed to work out every contingency. "Is that risking your jobs, if you do this?"

"To hell with our jobs!" Delia barked.

Bryn gave a firm nod. "This is more important. Truly."

"All right," Lizeth said, crumpling the brown paper her sandwich had been wrapped in and tossing it into the basket. "We need to get back to town."

"With us," Delia said, her tone leaving no room for argument.

"It's too dangerous—" Lizeth started to protest, but Delia cut her off.

"There's not going to be any plausible deniability once this A-Top update gets pushed. GSAF's going to know exactly who did it, and they're going to know how we found out. There's not going to be any more hiding once this is done."

Lizeth exhaled slowly. "It's really go time, isn't it?"

"This is our last stand," I said. "For both Free Mars and for the Stateless."

"So you're going to need a good base," Bryn said. "What better place than a fortified island?"

Lizeth pressed her lips together tightly. "Like a seastead?"

"Like Sparta Island," said Delia. "The AresTec campus is closed on the weekend... but we just so happen to have the keys. It'll be nice and private."

Bryn smiled crookedly. "Our jobs are toast, anyway. Might as well go out in a blaze of glory."

"Right, then," Delia said, getting to her feet and brushing her knees off. "We'd better leg it. I'm going to be up to ninety getting that update pushed, and the rest of you have work to do, too. The sooner we get back to Tierra Nueva, the better."

CHAPTER 48

IT WAS NIGHTFALL BY THE TIME WE MADE IT BACK TO TIERRA NUEVA. THE trip back had been excruciating, every long hour spent with the knowledge that any moment now, we could be intercepted. On the river back to Yellowknife Bay. Getting from the *Merrow's Jewel* to Mom and Mama's car. Driving on the freeway through the valley, through the canyon, southward into the city. My nerves were a wreck, but somehow I managed not to have a panic attack.

I hadn't had one since we'd left the moon, actually. I'd had moments of nervousness, even fear, but not panic in close to a month. I was trying not to get my hopes up, but I thought it was a good sign. Maybe it meant what I hoped with all my heart that it did—that Abuelo's gift had cured me. That I wasn't going to have to deal with this anymore. That I could get my life back.

Well, assuming we made it through all this in one piece.

Despite the hours it took, the time we spent traveling didn't go to waste. Mama had unfolded her portable deskpad while we were on the boat, and she'd begun working on the update patch as the bowrider sailed upriver. Meanwhile, Mom had given Lizeth access to her encrypted work palmtop, the one that AresTec had them use for dealing with confidential material, and Lizeth had used this to get the message out to Dante and the other Stateless operatives who had come to Mars: *Be on the corner of Water Street and San Marcos by 5:30.* An AresTec bus would pick them up. These commuter buses had a twofold advantage to them—they would look inconspicuous when they arrived at Sparta

Island, more than if a bunch of cars filtered into the parking lot; and they were camera-free, owing to the number of NDA contracts AresTec handled and the fact that employees often worked while using the bus.

And finally, Mom had given Henry her own deskpad, unlocking it with a scan of her thumbprint and an additional scan of her retina, then passing it to him. "No turning back now," she'd said. "Here you go, Henry. The one thing you were desperate for those annums Isaak was gone. I should have given them to you then, but I'd never believed…"

Henry had narrowed his eyes, scrolling through the app she'd opened, quickly scanning the data. "AresTec security keys?"

"The highest level. Those should unlock what you weren't able to before." Mom had shaken her head and exhaled. "You can get into GSAF's classified servers now. Find this so-called Underground. Find Kate."

Henry had gotten to work. With Mom's security keys, it hadn't taken long. Just before the *Merrow's Jewel* docked in Yellowknife Bay, he'd looked up, holding my gaze, his expression unreadable.

"Bingo," he'd said.

The bus hadn't yet arrived when our car pulled into Parking Garage B, a subterranean parking complex located underneath the Hamilton Building, where development on the A-Tops took place. Mama said she'd wait here for the others while Mom got the rest of us safely inside.

I'd been to the AresTec campus on Sparta Island hundreds of times in my life. It was inevitable, when both my moms worked here. I'd even been here at night, and on days when it was closed, when the complex was largely deserted. But it always made me uneasy, and even more so now. We spoke in low voices, but the sounds still echoed noisily off the cavernous ceiling of the garage, and as the five of us hurried over to the elevator leading up into the building above—Mom once again gaining access via her fingerprint and retinal scans—the sounds of our footsteps seemed thunderous.

But I didn't need to worry. There really was no one here. Mama ensured her entire team always got the weekend off. We had the building to ourselves.

Mom unlocked one of the boardrooms on the second floor and flipped the light switch. The large room featured a table in an S-shape, with plastic chairs positioned around it. An enormous holo display that took up a whole wall displayed a pic of MIT computer scientist Margaret Hamilton, whom the building had been named after, standing beside a stack of hand-coded guidance software as tall as she was. The wall perpendicular to the holo display was completely taken up with windows, mirrored to prevent anyone from seeing inside. No one would know we were here.

Through the window, AresTec tower, the tall central building of the campus, was lit up in myriad neon colors. The tallest building in Tierra Nueva, it stood as a beacon over the city. A reminder of what—at least in GalaX's eyes—had brought everyone here. Across the river, the shorter dual towers of the GSAF building offered an alternative viewpoint. The capitol and Sparta Island seemed to face off against each other in an uneasy truce. A truce that would be broken any minute now.

"You all are going to need to eat," Mom said, brushing her hair back from her forehead. "But I can't exactly put in a catering order. We're just going to have to take whatever we can find in the kitchen. Tam, honey, can you help me?"

Each of the buildings in the AresTec campus had its own eating area, in addition to the larger, full-service cafeteria in the center of the complex. In the Hamilton kitchen, cellophane-wrapped breakfast pastries made up the bulk of our findings, but in the refrigerator we also found some withered locally grown crudites, packets of powdered ranch dressing, crackers, and some individually packaged cheese sticks—a luxury item shipped from Earth, but one that AresTec always managed to find room for in the budget.

When we made it back to the boardroom, I saw that the bus had arrived. About two dozen people now crowded around the S-shaped table. Mama was leaning against one end of the table, chatting with a blonde in her late thirties that I'd met a few times before. I couldn't remember her real name now, but her screen name was *Wine&Liberty*. She'd been one of the first members of the Free Mars movement. A short distance away from Mama and W&L, Lizeth was having an intense conversation with Dante and Zero. Zero had taken advantage of their free time during the days we were on the Glen Torridon Trail to re-dye their hair, which was now a vibrant purple once more, their undercut crisp and fresh.

I breathed out a sigh of relief at the sight of them. Everyone had made it here in one piece. How long we all would *stay* in one piece, I couldn't say, especially considering the plan Henry and Lizeth had cooked up. But for now, we were all okay.

Please let us stay okay.

As Mom and I dispensed our meager food offerings, mostly everyone took a seat. Henry and Lizeth, though, remained standing beside the central curve of the S, where a pyramidal display was installed in the middle of the table. Henry cleared his throat. Everyone turned their attention to him.

Showtime.

I nibbled on a small, withered carrot while Henry filled the others in on what we'd told Mom and Mama a few hours before: What had happened on Earth, what we'd learned from Geoff Preston. The fact that GSAF had connected the System to Speculus Nano and their plans for using it to control the populace and crush both the Stateless and the Free Mars movement. And Mama's plan to alert all A-Top users on Earth and Mars via an OS update.

"That's where we come in," Lizeth said from beside Henry. "When the word gets out, we have to move fast. We need to get as many people out on the street as possible. The populace is going to be angry when they realize that GSAF broke their word, that they've jeopardized the lives of every Nano user on both worlds. We need to capitalize on the momentum of their anger."

"We've got organizers in every province on Mars," ProLibertate said from where he sat beside Wine&Liberty. "We can have them standing by."

"This is our best—and possibly our last—chance at severing GSAF's ties to this planet," Lizeth said. "Joseph Condor's position as governor is tenuous. He's unpopular, and many people view his deposition of Kate Ponsford as illegitimate. Including key members of the enforcement class. This is the moment both the Stateless and Free Mars have been waiting for."

Henry nodded. "Kate Ponsford is a major ally to our movement. She was also a governor with high approval ratings, and despite being an appointed official rather than an elected one, she's the one that most people consider the rightful governor. We believe that most of the populace—and, crucially, the enforcement class—would rally behind her. But a major stumbling block for us up until this point has been that we didn't know where GSAF is holding her." He folded his arms, inclining his head toward Mom. "But thanks to new intelligence we acquired earlier tonight, I can now confirm that we've found GSAF's secret base."

Lizeth switched on the pyramidal display in the center of the S-shaped table. A 3-D map of the peninsula appeared. "Contacts from Free Mars learned GSAF has been holding Kate Ponsford in a top-secret facility codenamed the Underground. But up until now, we didn't know what the Underground was, or, more importantly, *where* it was. But thanks to Bryn's security clearance and Henry's hacking skills, we've got that intel now," Lizeth said, folding her arms and glancing at Henry. He tapped the screen, zooming into the hills to the east of Tierra Nueva.

"It's the subterranean ruins of the Iamoi city known as Hope Renewed," Henry said.

Murmurs of surprise rippled around the room. I'd had the same reaction an hour ago. It was something I never would have thought of, but upon reflection, I'd realized it made perfect sense. What better place for GSAF to conduct secret operations out of the public's eye than a place they'd kept hidden from the citizens for decades?

"So now we know where they are," ProLibertate said, "but how are we going to get them out?"

"Our plan is twofold," Lizeth said, and I looked down, taking another bite of carrot. It was still cold from the refrigerator. "When the update pushes, GSAF will go into damage control. Their focus is going to be on getting the protesters off the street, suppressing dissent. They'll be distracted. In the meanwhile, a small strike team will use that distraction to infiltrate the Underground and make contact with Kate Ponsford."

"A coup d'état, then?" Wine&Liberty asked, a brow arched behind her large-framed glasses.

"A countercoup," Lizeth corrected. "Taking back the control Joseph Condor seized for himself."

"But what good will that do us?" ProLibertate asked. "We'll still be in the same position we were in before. Not a democracy. Just a colony."

"Not this time. We're going to make it clear to Ponsford that the only way we're getting her out is if she's willing to work with Free Mars, and that means dissolving all ties with GSAF," Henry said.

"Do you think she'll go for that?" W&L asked. "And more importantly, will GSAF go for it?"

"They won't have a choice," Lizeth said. "When this A-Top update pushes, they're going to have more important things to worry about than their wayward colony. There are billions of Speculus Nano users on Earth, and the Stateless is going to be right there ensuring that they won't be able to shut everyone up this time. The house of cards the UN and the continental unions have built is about to come tumbling down. GSAF will just be the first to fall."

ProLibertate let out a long breath. "I still think it's a long shot. But it's the best shot we've got. What do you need us to do?"

"We've just got a few hours to get the wheels in motion before the update pushes," said Henry. "We need to be ready to go by morning."

I concentrated on the crunching of the carrot inside my mouth as I chewed.

"Lizeth and I will be leading the strike team," Henry said, "along with Dante and Brandon. We're relying on the rest of you to keep GSAF's eyes trained on Tierra Nueva. To divert as many resources away from the Underground as possible. Your job—those of you out on the street—will be to keep them distracted. Be as disruptive as you can without physically endangering yourselves. Keep GSAF's eye focused on you and we'll move in."

"But be careful," Lizeth warned. "GSAF's got a warrant out for our arrest—at minimum, for Henry, me, Scylla, Tamara. Most likely others. And anyone they perceive as organizers, they'll try to target you first. Keep on your toes. If you see cops on the ground, keep as far from them as you can."

Crunch, crunch. The carrot was flavorless on my tongue. Lizeth was forgetting that the cops seeing us was an important component to this plan's success. GSAF could not be allowed to suspect that Henry was anywhere near the Underground. Scylla and I needed to be visible, so that GSAF would know we were here and assume Henry and Lizeth were too. Close enough that they'd see us, but far enough away that they couldn't get us.

"Use the power of the crowd," Lizeth went on. "If anyone tries to arrest one of ours, interfere as much as safely possible. Make sure that the Free Mars people are aware that we're not complying."

"Pfft," ProLibertate snorted. "Noncompliance is my middle name."

"I'll hold you to that." Lizeth smirked.

"Okay, guys," Scylla said, "we've got one night to organize the biggest demonstration we've ever held. We need boots on the ground in every province. I'm going to send out a message to the Free Mars listserv, but we need to contact everyone we possibly can. Your friends, your family, your neighbor down the block. As many people as can be on the street first thing in the morning, we need them there."

"We'd better get on it, then," Wine&Liberty replied.

People started pulling out their palmtops, fingers flying across digital membrane. Still standing by the pyramidal display, Henry and Lizeth drew Dante and Brandon into a quiet conference. The strike team. I'd never seen Brandon before, a lanky, brown-haired man who looked to be in his mid-twenties, but I remembered the name. He'd been one of the Stateless operatives who'd helped Henry, Isaak, and Nadin escape from Lago Verde. One of Lizeth's *best-of-the-best*.

The carrot was a mushy lump in my mouth by now. My stomach did not seem too keen on letting me swallow it, though. Noticing my eyes on him, Henry glanced up and smiled tightly at me for just a second before looking back at Lizeth.

Thunk.

I jumped as Zero slapped a small box down on the table in front of me. In my surprise, the carrot went down my throat involuntarily.

I coughed. "What is this?" I asked when I'd finally managed to clear my windpipe. The package had a French brand name and prominently featured an image of a woman with shiny brown hair.

"Best box dye on the market," they replied. "Not my top choice, but it'll do in a pinch."

"But why—"

"Darlin', your roots have grown out clear down to your ears. And I know you hate the blond. So let's fix it."

I blinked in confusion. "But... aren't there more important things to worry about than my hair?"

"Like what? You and I don't have any calls to make. What should we do instead? Sit around being anxious all night? Tell you what, you can sit around and be anxious while I get this color in your hair." I continued to stare at them, and they leaned their weight against the table, looking down at me earnestly. "Listen, Tamara. Even when things have gone to hell, you have to maintain some degree of normalcy. It's the only way to survive in a situation like this. And hair is my business for a reason. Call this my self-care. If you don't want to do it for yourself, do it for me."

I glanced over at Henry and Lizeth again. They were deep in conversation with the others still. Zero was right. There wasn't much I could do right now other than sit around and worry. Having my hair back to normal might make me feel more like myself again. And maybe that's what I needed to get through this. To maintain that degree of normalcy that Zero was talking about. "Okay," I said. "There are showers in the staff gym."

They grinned. "Lead the way," they said.

A little over an hour later, Zero and I made our way back toward the boardroom, only to find Lizeth and Dante standing together in the hallway just outside the door.

"Is everything okay?" I asked, furrowing my brows with concern.

"Yeah, everything's fine. I just needed a breather," Lizeth said. She hesitated, then glanced at Dante.

"Oh, right," he said after a quick beat. "Hey, Zero, could you help me with something? Uh, in there." He gestured at the closed boardroom doors.

"Of course," Zero replied quickly, detaching themself from me and slipping back into the room after Dante.

"What's up?" I asked, watching Lizeth curiously.

She exhaled, leaning against one of the sleek metal columns that punctuated the space. "Look, Tamara," she began. "I just... I just wanted to say you've done good. Your idea for reaching out to your moms, and the help they've been able to give us... we never could have done it without them. Without you."

My face flushed. Whatever I might have been expecting her to say, it certainly wasn't that.

"Um, thanks," I started, but she interrupted.

"There's more. I... I wanted to apologize. For the way I acted on Earth. Especially back at my mother's house. When you said that you also get... nervous."

"No, I'm sorry," I said quickly. "I didn't mean to imply anything by that. Getting nervous is normal."

"Getting *nervous* is normal," Lizeth said. "But that's not what I get. And I know it's more than that for you, too." She sighed, locking her dark eyes with mine. "You were right. We are alike, you and me. More than I would have liked to admit." She crossed her arms, resting the back of her head against the steel column. "It started when I was, I don't know, ten or twelve. My mother... I'm sure you can tell she doesn't have a lot of patience. And zero tolerance for failure. Anything less than perfect is not good enough for her. Anything less than a perfect score on tests in school. Anything other than a perfect performance at a piano recital. Anything less than perfect behavior out of me and Bruno whenever she'd bring us along to any of her business functions."

I watched her fretfully, but I didn't say anything.

"I started having the panic attacks because I was afraid of not being perfect. But my mother saw the panic attacks themselves as a failure on my part. So it was just a vicious cycle. The more I felt like I was failing, the worse they got, but then I'd feel like a failure for having them... around and around we go. Bruno's a couple years older than me and he saw what was going on. He told Dad, and that was when Dad decided to have me and Bruno come live with him on Conch. The panic attacks got better after that, but they didn't stop." She smirked wryly. "I just got really good at hiding them."

"Lizeth," I breathed. "I'm so sor—"

She held a hand up. "No. Seriously. I don't need that. I just wanted to tell you. I... I know it wasn't right for me to lash out at you like I did. But I just couldn't wrap my brain around it. The life you had is the life I always thought maybe I could have had if my mother was different. I mean, look at the similarities. The money, the piano recitals, the private education.

Our lives were formed with the same building blocks, but your moms are… everything my mother isn't." She swallowed. "You've had everything I wanted, everything that I always told myself would have made my life better. But you still have… these. And maybe I was mad about that. Because it showed me that even if your life is perfect, you can still have problems. And that wasn't something I wanted to face. But that's a me problem, not a you problem."

"It's not a *you* problem, Lizeth," I said earnestly. I didn't try to say I was sorry again, but my tone must have still conveyed it, because she shook her head.

"No, I don't want your pity," she said.

"It's not pity."

She rolled her eyes. "Fine. I don't want your sympathy or whatever. I just… I just wanted to apologize." She exhaled. "So, are we good?"

I smiled and nodded. "Yeah, we're good."

She smiled tightly back. "Good." She straightened, turning to head back into the board room. "Oh, if you're looking for Henry," she said, turning back for a moment, "he's out there for some ungodly reason." She gestured down the hall to the door leading out to the second floor outlook, a terraced area where AresTec employees could sit to get some fresh air throughout the day. "Don't ask me why. It's torquing freezing out there."

I slipped out the door to the terrace. Sure enough, Henry was leaning against the railing, looking out over the east side of the river, beyond the outskirts of Tierra Nueva to the crater-pocked foothills where Erick's dig site had been located. To where the ruins of Hope Renewed lay buried, the labyrinthine caves of the city's underground twisting and turning beneath kilometers of solid rock.

To where Joseph Condor's secret lair awaited.

"Hey," Henry said, turning his head at my approach. He took in my appearance as I joined him at the rail, lifting a tendril of chin-length brown hair between his fingers and smiling knowingly. "There you are."

"Yeah," I said self-consciously. "Zero's been busy." Silence hung between us, heavy and tentative. I could feel the weight of it. Of the words I couldn't bring myself to say, but that I'd have to say soon.

Before the sun rose, he'd be gone.

I cleared my throat. "What, uh..." I faltered, cleared it again. "What have you been up to?"

"Out here? Oh, nothing. Just navel gazing." He chuckled at my confused expression. "In a weird way, it feels like my whole life has been building toward this moment. And not just mine. My whole family's, honestly."

I quirked my head. "What do you mean?"

He sighed. "Remember what you said that night at Lizeth's mom's house? 'These are our songs,' you said." He turned away from me, looking back out over the river. The lights of the city sparkled in the reflections on the water. "I've realized, they're mine too. Look at my family. Take my grandpa, the white one. My mom's dad. He was in the United States Army, died by a sniper's rifle while fighting a war for the NAEU. A war I'd have opposed with every fiber of my being. A war to bring the world together... by force." His hand clenched into a fist, unclenched. "Did my grandpa feel the same way I do? Did he fight because he had no other choice? Or did he *believe* in the continental unions? I'll never know. He died when my mom was just twelve years old, so I can't exactly ask him, can I?"

I frowned, but I didn't interrupt. His eyes had lost their focus. He wasn't looking at the river anymore.

"So Nani took Mom back to India. Her parents had gone back years before, and with Grandpa Henry dead, why should she stay? I'm sure Nani thought it would be safer, to be back there with family. But it wasn't. My dad, he lost *both* his parents to political violence. Got shipped out of Punjab to live with relatives in Delhi. The orphan boy, the girl without a dad. The ones who survived, trying to make a future together. Where could they go to raise their family without the threat of violence? Mars. A new planet. A safe planet. A world without war, without castes, without sects. A world that doesn't care if you're Sikh or Hindu." He glanced at me sideways. "If you're Irish or English." The breeze ruffled his hair, stirred small waves out on the river, fracturing the reflections of the neon lights. "But here we are all the same," he said finally.

I swallowed. My eyes burned. Why was he saying all this? Why was he putting words to all my darkest fears, the fears I'd carried inside of me for over two annums now?

Deep down, from the moment Isaak had disappeared, I'd known one thing with absolute certainty. No matter how much I'd tried to talk myself out of it, I'd never been able to shake it. And Henry seemed to have accepted it, seemed resigned to it now.

One of us was going to die. Maybe all of us. There was no escaping it, was there?

This was the core of my terror. The thing that had given me nightmares for annums, had ratcheted up my anxiety, made me afraid to let him out of my sight. To let him go anywhere that I couldn't be there with him, to protect him.

But I couldn't go with him now. I *couldn't* protect him. Henry was walking straight into the lion's den, and there was nothing I could do to stop it.

One of us is going to die.

What will I do if it's him?

Mama's family had lived through the Troubles. They'd carried the scars of that violence through generations. And they'd carried the songs. History books said the Troubles were a thing of the past. But Henry was right. The Troubles had followed us here.

I hadn't noticed that Henry had turned away from the river again, that he was facing me now. The eastern sky was just starting to lighten, casting a blue tint against the contours of his face. The sun was coming. Before we knew it, it would be dawn.

He had to go.

He cupped his fingers under my chin, lifting my face to his gently, resting his forehead against mine. Softly, barely audibly, he sang.

"But sing, my love,
So all can hear
Above the cry of guns."

The tears that had been burning my eyes spilled over now, leaving a hot trail on my cheeks. I choked back a sob. But I sang the rest. Even though I felt like the words were thorns piercing me from the inside out, leaving my heart bloody and raw, I sang it.

For him.

For Henry.

"I'll sing for you
All through the night
For none can stop the sun."

CHAPTER 49

- h e n r y -

WE CREPT THROUGH THE SEMI-DARKNESS, THE GROUND ROCKY AND UNEVEN
under our feet. We had to move slowly, watching our every step
carefully to make sure that neither of us tripped. If one of us stumbled
over a rock, it could trigger a cascade of dust that the drones that passed
periodically overhead would be certain to notice. We couldn't afford a
fatal mistake like that.

Our plan was simple. It was also clinically insane. Almost a full annum
ago, Emil Hassan had disappeared, following in Isaak's footsteps quite
literally. Unbeknownst to any of us, he'd been working with Delia,
reconstructing the posternkey Isaak had used from the 3-D scans she'd
taken of the device, believing that Emil could find our missing friend by
following him through the time door back to ancient Mars. The old crank
had figured it out well before any of us even had a clue.

Before Emil had left, he'd given Delia a hand-drawn map. The cave
tunnel that Isaak had used to gain access to the ruins of the ancient
Iamoi city in the hills had been discovered by GSAF and blocked off more
than two annums ago. But Emil had told Mama D that GSAF only knew
about a fraction of the tunnels that he'd discovered during his two
decades of surreptitiously studying the ruins of Hope Renewed. He'd
used a different one of these tunnels to gain access, and not only had he
not gotten caught, but GSAF hadn't even realized he'd been there.

So we were using his map now to try the same thing. To sneak in
without GSAF's knowledge, and retrieve someone who had disappeared
inside the ancient city.

But even though we had Emil's map, getting in wouldn't be that simple. The foothills east of Tierra Nueva were much more heavily secured than they'd been at the time of Isaak's disappearance. Now they were even more locked down than they'd been when had Emil followed after Isaak. That was where Dante, Brandon, and their team would come in. Just as they had back on Earth when they'd broken us out of Lago Verde, they were going to create a distraction.

Halfway between Tierra Nueva and Curiosity Bay, there was a canyon in the hills where GSAF had excavated what they called on their schematics the "front entrance" to Hope Renewed. Wyatt, under his mother's orders, had brought Nadin there three months earlier, and that act had been what had led the GSAF Council to authorize removing Kate Ponsford from power. Dante and Brandon were going to feign an attack on that front entrance, and Brandon would disable the security drones just as he'd done on Earth. With every reason to believe that the base was under the same kind of attack Lago Verde had experienced in July, the Stateless team would, as Dante put it, "lead GSAF on a merry chase." While the Underground's security was focused on the front entrance, Lizeth and I would sneak in through one of Emil's hidden tunnels.

That was the plan, at least. It seemed impossible to me, but Lizeth was confident that we would pull it off without a hitch. She had good reason to be optimistic, I supposed. After all, the Stateless had an impeccable track record. And they had every detail calculated with precision. We had data that indicated when drones passed over each area, so we'd know when it was safe to move and when we needed to duck into hiding among the boulders and spider weeds lining the hillside. We knew each drone's flight path, which allowed us to mark out the safest route toward the best tunnel entrance on Emil's map. And thanks to Bryn's credentials giving me access to GSAF's schematics, we knew what to expect once inside the facility.

The timeline was equally precise. The A-Top update would be pushed at six AM. GSAF would know within minutes that someone had leaked classified information, and more than likely their rush to internally investigate the leak would reveal my own overnight hacks into their system. They'd know whose credentials had been used to facilitate the hacks, which would paint a target on Bryn's back. We had to be ready to move fast, to catch them before they had a chance to get their feet under them. So at 6:05 precisely, Dante and Brandon would launch their distraction. With luck, we'd be inside before GSAF knew what had hit them.

With luck. Good old luck, back to haunt me once more.

Lizeth paused for a moment on the rocky slope, pushing up the cuff of her black hoodie to once again check the watch strapped on her wrist. "Drone incoming in one minute."

"Got it," I said, and we ducked into a prickly clump of spider weeds. Lizeth had outfitted us with the same uniform the Stateless operatives had worn for the Lago Verde operation: all-black clothing, including a black hoodie and black bandanas to conceal our faces. The sweatshirt Lizeth was wearing was somewhat faded, with the seven-pointed star that served as the Stateless' emblem screen printed on the back. A bit of an audacious move, advertising the Stateless like that; but, of course, Lizeth was known for her audacity. She had the hood of the sweatshirt pulled up, and with the bandana, the only part of her face that was visible was the eyes. Here in the darkness we'd be indistinguishable from the black spider weeds around us, invisible to the drone.

Now we waited. The thorns of the spider weeds around us snagged on my clothes, and the object in my pocket—the one I'd carried with me since leaving the site in Los Tuxtlas, just in case—dug uncomfortably into my hip. But still I held my breath, not moving. Once the drone had passed overhead, we'd scuttle out, claw our way forward another thirty meters or so to the next concealed area on the slope, and repeat the process.

The air around us was still in the way it always managed to get just before daybreak. I glanced through the branches of the bush. The sky overhead was growing lighter, a faded blue-green now. Sunrise was coming.

None can stop the sun.

The memory of her last kiss was still like a ghost on my lips. I didn't like leaving her alone, even though I knew she wasn't really—her moms and the others were with her. They'd protect her. They'd take care of her. But I still hated this. In some ways, what she was doing was more dangerous than what Lizeth and I were doing. So that we could remain out of sight, Tamara's assignment was to be as visible as possible—to make sure GSAF knew they were there, so they'd assume that I was there with them. She needed to keep GSAF's eye trained on Tierra Nueva so they wouldn't see what was going on under their nose until it was too late. But she also needed to manage to avoid getting arrested. It was going to be tough to square that circle, be visible enough that the plan would work but also distant enough to stay out of harm's way.

Through the shadows, Lizeth was watching me. "You worrying about Tamara?" she asked. I could hear the smirk in her voice.

"Yeah," I said, annoyed at her tone. "You worrying about Dante?"

Maybe that was a step too far. Despite Scylla's protestations otherwise, Lizeth wasn't our friend—she was just our ally, and an uneasy one most of the time. I didn't get her personal relationships, but I didn't need to. They weren't any of my business. But I was as galled by the humor in her voice just now as I'd been taken aback by her stoicism an hour earlier. The way she and Dante had parted after we left Sparta Island had struck me. She'd caught his gaze, holding it for a minute, and said, "Hey—be careful, okay?" He'd smiled and said, "You too." And that had been it. At the time, I knew what she would have said if I'd commented on it: "We do this sort of thing every day."

She just seemed like she only had two settings: torqued off or emotionlessly authoritative. Apparently that applied among her loved ones as well as her acquaintances. I supposed that was just Lizeth. Love her or hate her, but there was no changing her. I should have kept my mouth shut.

But she surprised me now. I'd expected my comment to make her chafe, the way hers made me. Expected a snapped reply and a charged tension between us for the rest of the mission. Instead she hesitated, and through the morning twilight I could see the corners of her eyes crease, the tentative smile concealed behind her bandana visible in them. "Yeah," she said. "I am."

She knew she'd knocked the wind out of my sails, but I wasn't going to hand her that victory. "Well, then," I said, adjusting my own mask. "We're on the same page."

The telltale buzz of propellers was approaching. We held still, not even breathing.

The drone passed over without hesitation. It hadn't spotted us.

As soon as the sound of propellers had died down, we scrambled out from the spider weeds, picking our way farther up the slope. We continued this way, advancing only briefly before ducking into hiding again, for almost an hour as the sun poked its way above the western hills. At this time of year, in late spring, the sun was rising earlier each morning. By the time we reached our destination, we wouldn't be able to rely on shadows to conceal us. We'd need Brandon to disable the drones to manage the final stretch.

We were getting close to the cliff face when Lizeth checked her watch again. "It should be around here..." she murmured. "There." She pointed. To the naked eye, it looked like just another uneven patch of the columnar basalt that made up the foothills here. But the nature of columnar basalt was that it was easy to miss crevices and openings in the rock face between those columns. According to Emil's map, an opening would be found behind the spider weeds that grew along the finger-shaped formations just ahead of us, only just large enough to crawl through. Small, obscured, easy to miss. As of an annum ago, Emil believed that this opening had still been undetected by GSAF. Would that still be the case?

Only one way to find out.

The opening was about a hundred meters from where we now sheltered in another clump of spider weeds, but an open patch of dirt separated us from it. No obvious crevices, boulders, or patches of brush we could duck beneath or behind.

"We'll wait here until Brandon disables the drones," Lizeth said. "Then we run for it."

"And if there are any non-drone guards up in those hills that we're missing?" I asked.

She shrugged. "We take our chances."

The seconds were ticking down on the digital watch face. 6:04:37.

I heard the faint buzz of propellers approaching once more. Another drone was coming. It was just about overhead when the seconds ticked to 58... 59... 00.

Boom.

Right on schedule, the sound of an explosion shook the hills, making a shower of loose debris come cascading down. Just meters from us, the drone hit the ground with a crash, then slid down the slope, coming to a rest on a basalt shelf a short distance below us.

"All right," Lizeth said, scrambling to her feet, "move."

We raced forward, sprinting for the basalt fingers as quickly as we could manage. Lizeth tore away at the spiky branches of spider weed, its thorns no match for her thick black gloves. Sure enough, just as Emil had indicated on his map—a small hole in the cliffside, only about as tall as my waist. We'd be able to crawl though, but only just. Emil's notes indicated that the tunnel was safely traversable. I could only hope that this was still the case.

"Come on," Lizeth said, getting down on her hands and knees and scrabbling into the hole. Nothing to do but follow her.

The tunnel was tight, and maneuvering my broad shoulders through the gap took some effort. But somehow I managed. After the early morning light, it took a couple minutes for my eyes to adjust to the near-total darkness. By the time they finally did, I noticed the tunnel was starting to widen. Lizeth, with her small, narrow frame had managed to scamper ahead of me much more quickly, and she disappeared into the shadows.

"Careful," she whispered from up ahead of me. "It drops."

Sure enough, a short distance ahead, the tunnel ended in an abrupt drop down to a lower shelf. I managed to shimmy my body around and slide out feet first. Across the room from me, Lizeth switched on the flashlight she'd been carrying in her backpack.

"This area seems to be clear," she whispered. She pulled the bandana away from her face, leaving it bunched around her neck.

As I jumped from the shelf down onto the floor, something crunched under my feet. I bent down, picking up whatever it was I'd stepped on. A piece of pottery.

My eyes adjusted further to the light, aided by Lizeth's flashlight and the dim glow of some kind of phosphorescence embedded into the walls. We seemed to have landed in someone's kitchen. Based on what Nadin had said about the organization of her citidome, the upper layers of the Underground would be made up of the dwellings of the *esotoi*, the middle caste of Iamoi society. Those members of the professional class, rather than laborers, whose positions afforded them a slightly higher position in society, and thus made them important enough to warrant living quarters in the safer tunnels beneath the surface of the dome—but not as deep in the bedrock as the *patroi*, whose lavish villas could be found in the lower levels, as far from the ultraviolet radiation as they could get.

"Nadin said the *esotoi* lived in apartments like the insulae in the dome, only underground," I whispered to Lizeth. "This must be one of those apartment buildings."

"So we're in the upper levels," Lizeth murmured.

"Emil's map confirmed as much."

"And your intel says that Kate Ponsford and her family are being held in the lower levels?"

I nodded. "The very bottom. The *geroi's* villa."

"How many floors down?" she asked.

"Five, I think."

She cursed. "The question is, how are we going to get down there without them spotting us?"

"You said we'd figure that out as we went along," I reminded her.

Lizeth sighed, picking her way over the debris to where a sliding door must have once been found. Thousands of years of water moving its way through the caves, dripping and pooling, had taken its toll on this place. Stalagmites had shoved their way up from the ground, reaching their way toward stalactites that trailed down like rocky icicles. The caves' growth had upended what pieces of furniture had not rotted away. We squeezed our way through two rocky protrusions that partially blocked the door.

Voices echoed through the corridors—surely GSAF's reaction to Dante and Brandon's diversion. They sounded far away, but still, we needed to be careful. Lizeth flicked the flashlight off.

"Come on," she whispered, making her way through the renewed darkness toward the apartment exit.

I followed after her, bracing my hand for just an instant against a part of the wall that had been sheltered from the water that had reshaped the rest of this space. The original phosphorescence mosaic that had been embedded here still slightly glowed, a faint, dim blue. But my fingers rested on something that felt different. I moved my hand through the shadows, testing it to be sure. Here, chalky stone... But here...

"Henry," Lizeth whispered, looking at me over her shoulder. "What are you doing?"

"Come here," I said. "Put your hand on this."

"Feels like someone carved something into the rock," she said, running her fingers over the uneven surface. "It almost feels like... letters."

"Yeah," I said. "Letters."

Letters carved into the wall of the twelve thousand-year-old underground ruins on an alien planet.

Roman letters. English.

H-E-N-

Lizeth turned the flashlight back on again, illuminating the engraving. "This is impossible," she breathed.

"So I wasn't imagining it, then," I said.

She shook her head. I hadn't imagined what was carved here on the wall. The lettering was shaky, like the hand that had carved it was unfamiliar with these shapes. But it was here, indisputably.

HENRY.

CHAPTER 50

- t a m a r a -

"GSAF LIED! GSAF LIED!"

The voices echoed around the park, reverberating off the walls of the tall buildings across the street. Reverberating from the dual towers of the GSAF administrative center itself.

The update had pushed at six AM as planned. Minutes later, we'd been on the street. I'd thought we'd be the first ones out, but there had already been a thick crowd of people clustered in the riverfront park by the time we made it across the bridge from Sparta Island, and it had only grown since then. The first time we'd ever held a protest, way back when Isaak had first disappeared, when the only people who'd seemed to care he was missing had been Henry, Scylla, and me, we'd gathered in the riverfront park and been told by GSAF that we couldn't demonstrate there. But I didn't think people cared much for the rules anymore.

Within an hour, there had to have been at least a thousand people in the park. This was way, way more than the people on Scylla's listserv, and way more than we could have texted and messaged and cajoled into coming the night before. These were people who saw the notification on their palmtops this morning while they were getting ready for work, getting ready for school. This was organic.

And these people were *torqued*.

Scylla was standing on top of a picnic table now, trying to gain some extra height over the crowd as she led them in the chant with a megaphone. Visible, but safely buffered by the hundreds of bodies surrounding her. But even though I knew from what had happened on the Glen Torridon Trail that we were wanted by GSAF, the cops I'd seen loitering on the sidewalks around the park hadn't seemed overly interested in making an arrest. In fact, they didn't seem overly interested in doing anything at all, other than maintaining a nominal presence.

Officers like these ones had said no one liked Condor, and that he was creepy. And surely officers like these ones—maybe even these men and women themselves—had Nano. Maybe their inaction now meant they agreed with us. Maybe they were taking our side. Maybe, even though Lizeth had scoffed at the mere suggestion, this wasn't going to be some kind of bloody revolution. Maybe good would prevail without anyone having to die.

I could hope, right?

I reached into my pocket and squeezed the rosary beads. Yeah, I could hope.

The chant had changed now. The crowd had had their fill of "GSAF lied." Now they were shouting, "*Joseph Condor must resign! Joseph Condor must resign!*"

Where *was* Joseph Condor, anyway? He'd been quick to shut down our other demonstrations, and he'd been enforcing a strict prohibition on large gatherings since becoming governor. But we'd seen no sign of him today. Involuntarily, my eyes flicked eastward, over the river, to the hills.

Just because Condor hasn't shown up here yet doesn't mean anything's wrong, I told myself. But the later it got without Condor putting in an appearance, the harder it got for me to convince myself of that.

One of us is going to die.

What will I do if it's him?

"Tamara!"

The voice jarred my mind away from that unwanted thought. I looked up, and after a moment I noticed the brightly patterned hijab on the girl pushing her way through the crowd, squeezing over to me.

"Mariyah!" I cried, rushing to her and throwing my arms around her. It had been three months since I'd seen my roommate, one of my dearest friends. The last time had been at move-out, when we turned our keys in to the resident assistant on duty.

"Are you okay?" she asked, squeezing me tightly. "I haven't heard from you in so long—the last time was right after you landed in Florida. Then my texts stopped delivering, and then I saw on the news that you were *missing*, and GSAF said that you were a suspect in a *terrorist attack*, and then—"

My eyebrows flew up my forehead. "Seriously?"

"I knew that was total garbage, but that's how Condor was spinning it." She glared at a nearby poster that one of the protesters was brandishing. I followed her gaze. Someone had affixed a pic of Condor's face to it, and drawn devil horns on top of it. The word LIAR was printed in sloppy handwriting beside it. Turning back to me, she said, "But what really happened? And how did you get back here? And where's—" She stopped short, looking around and noticing the conspicuous absences of most of my usual entourage: Henry, Isaak, and Nadin. She exhaled, grimacing. "Never mind. What matters is you're here, and I'm going to support you. What do you need?"

I shrugged. "Your voice."

She nodded. "That I can do. And I can be extra noisy for you, if it would help." She slung the backpack she was wearing over one shoulder and pulled out an airhorn. "Shall we make it obnoxious?"

I grinned. "Your obnoxiousness will be greatly appreciated."

"Oh, one more thing," Mariyah said, rummaging through the backpack once more. She withdrew what looked like a clump of red string. After a moment, I recognized it as a handmade bracelet of braided red yarn. The symbol for Free Mars that Scylla had devised more than two annums ago.

"This is for you," she said, pressing the bracelet into my hand.

From her spot on the picnic table, Scylla noticed Mariyah and began frantically waving her over. A moment later, Mariyah had scrambled up on the table beside her, shouting her own chants into the megaphone and punctuating them with the airhorn for added effect. I watched them a minute longer, trying to blink away the stinging behind my eyes. Then I knotted the yarn bracelet around my left wrist with my right hand.

"Hey, Tam." Zero came up beside me as I tied off the knot, huffing, a heavy tote of water bottles over each shoulder. "Would you mind?" Quickly, I moved to take one of the bags from them. "Thanks. I'm going to bring these around, make sure everyone stays hydrated, and let them know about the medic tent." They gestured over to the marquee that we'd set up at the corner of the Sparta Island Bridge. The AresTec logo was emblazoned on the flaps, since Mama had fished it out of storage for us. AresTec used it when they participated in trade shows or hosted other outdoor events, but we'd commandeered it as a place the demonstrators could use to get out of the sun or receive medical treatment if needed.

"I'll help," I said, eager for something to do to keep my mind from wandering.

Pushing our way through the throngs of people was no easy task, considering how tightly packed everyone was. Some people were shouting along with Scylla's guided chants; others stood quietly, waving signs or holding up palmtops, recording vids of the protest. Many had tied red yarn around their wrists in solidarity with the Free Mars movement. I was amazed by the diversity of the people here. When Free Mars first started, it was a mismatched alliance of gawky teens looking for answers about our missing friend and socially awkward middle-aged libertarians with a grudge against GSAF. Somehow it had turned into something far beyond that. These were ordinary Martians here now. Parents held young children on their shoulders, the kids yelling chants along with the rest of the crowd. Elderly men and women, their faces wrinkled and their hair gray, waved flags from their home countries on Earth.

I was nearly out of bottles when I encountered the Latino couple in their late thirties. "Oh, no, thank you, we're fine," the woman started to say, but then her arm shot out, gripping my wrist. "Wait!" she exclaimed. "You're T-RT!"

I tried not to wince at the nickname—one my publicist at Griffin Records had devised, since my real name was "so long," but one I'd never been overly fond of. "Yeah," I said, feeling the heat rush into my face.

I was strategizing a way to make my escape from this overly zealous fan, but then the woman said, "My brother met you in Mexico," and my feet became rooted in place.

"Are—" I stared from her to her husband to the two boys standing between them. I'd guess they were middle school-age, possibly twins. "Are you Horlando's sister?"

She nodded. "Yasmine. We live up in Tharsis Province, but we brought the boys down this weekend to go to the amusement park on Knobel Island. School starts a couple weeks later up there than it does in Aeolis," she added sheepishly, "so we thought this would be a good time to go and avoid the crowds. But then that A-Top update pushed this morning, and we knew we couldn't go back yet."

"We saw the crowd out here through our hotel window," one of the brothers told me eagerly, gesturing to a high-rise hotel across the street, "so we decided to help out."

"We've had enough of GSAF," the other boy added, his brows drawn angrily.

I had to struggle not to grin at their earnestness. Turning back to Yasmine, I asked, "Is Horlando okay? I heard the dig site got raided."

She nodded. "They only brought the students in for questioning, but they didn't hold them. I heard his professor got arrested, though. I don't know if he's been released yet."

Horlando hadn't been the one who'd alerted GSAF about us, then. The opposite, in fact—he'd lied to GSAF in order to protect us. Henry's fears had been misplaced, just as I suspected.

But if Horlando was innocent, then who was the real informant?

Before I could say anything else, the sound of a shout interrupted us. Not the raised voice of a chant, but a shout of anger. I jerked around, the fury in their tones sending my adrenaline involuntarily pumping. The two guys I'd given water two just a minute before were now shoving each other.

"I said back *off*, man," one of them, a tall, heavyset twenty-something, yelled.

"*You* back off," shouted the other.

"Whoa, whoa!" Yasmine's husband exclaimed, inserting himself between the two. "Come on, guys. There's no call for this."

"Mind your own torquing business," the taller one snarled.

"No, seriously," Zero said, hurrying over and joining Yasmine's husband in physically separating the two. "I don't know what you're arguing about, but this isn't the place for that. Work it out among yourselves or head home."

"It was his fault," the tall one argued. "He's being unreasonable."

"I don't care. Work it out among yourselves," Zero repeated, "or leave."

The tall man rubbed his nose with the back of his hand, trailing a dark red smear down his face.

"Hey," I said, coming over and looking up at him. "You're bleeding. Do you need medical assistance? If you come to our tent—"

"I don't torquing need anything," he snapped. "I'm out of here." He stormed off.

"What was that about?" I asked the other young man.

"None of your business," the man said coldly. He followed after his friend.

I stared after them, my surprise and alarm starting to twist into something else in the pit of my gut. Something I didn't want to name, didn't want to face, but that I recognized all too well.

"Don't let it get to you," Zero said, watching my expression. "This kind of thing happens. Just keep moving. Don't dwell on it."

With a tight smile at Yasmine and her family, I followed after Zero. But we'd only made it a few steps before another scuffle broke out just in front of us. This time it was too close, and I didn't have time to react, didn't have time to get out of the way. One second I was upright, and the next, a body collided with mine, a teenage girl, still kicking and snarling at the person who'd shoved her. We went down, but I didn't hit the ground—we were packed too tightly, and I hit the body of the person behind me.

Too close.

I suddenly remembered the warnings the management at Griffin had given me about being careful at large shows, safety precautions in place to avoid stampede events. Events where people were crushed to death because they were packed too close together.

We're too close we're too close

No, it's fine, we're in a park, there's room to spread out, people can move into the street —

But they're not spreading out we're too close bodies crushing no air

"Back off!" the girl who'd collided with me screamed at the person who'd shoved her, ignorant to the domino effect of bodies their argument had caused. I tried to get my footing but couldn't quite manage it.

Breathe.

I can't breathe

"Hey!" Scylla's voice roared over the megaphone. "Who lit that fire? Put that torquing fire out, are you nuts? No, put that flag down—"

At the word *fire*, the crowd compressed tighter, squeezing me, crushing me. I couldn't breathe. I couldn't *breathe.*

Run.

I can't *run.*

Run run run run run

Trapped

"Give her some goddamn *air!*" Zero shouted, shoving their way through the crowd, pushing us apart. Helping the woman I'd collided with to her feet, gripping my arm tightly. "All y'all are too close together! Spread out!" they commanded. At their word, the tight compression of the crowd around us loosened. But I still couldn't breathe. I tried to catch my breath, but the air was coming in too fast. I was hyperventilating.

"Come on," Zero said, their hold on my arm still tight. They guided me to the medic tent. By the time I sank down onto an empty cot, I was in tears, still struggling to breathe, the inside of my ears a roar and the inside of my mind a blur of white static.

"Slow breaths, Tamara," Zero said, crouching in front of me. "Slower than that. Come on. Deep breaths. Slow."

"I can't breathe," I sobbed.

"You can. Just give it a try."

"No. I can't. Henry's gone."

The words surprised me, yet I knew as soon as I blurted them out that that was what this was really about. The incident in the park might have been what triggered it, what set it off, but that wasn't what it was *about.*

"He's coming back," Zero said firmly.

"No, he's not. He's never coming back. I'm never going to see him again."

"That's not true," said Zero. "Come on, Tamara. Breathe. You gotta be strong for him."

"I'm not strong!" I was trying to breathe, but I couldn't. The air tore right out of me along with the sobs. I knew it now. I wasn't strong. I was weak. I was an absolute failure. I'd told him I was better, and I'd actually believed it. What, had I thought I'd been miraculously cured? I should have known better. I was never going to be cured of this. I was never going to be healed. This demon was going to hound my footsteps until the day I died.

"I can't handle anything. I'm not strong enough. Look how *weak* I am!" I yanked Isaak's grandfather's rosary out of my pocket and flung it away from myself. "I'm worthless. I can't handle anything. I can't do anything. I was so *stupid*, thinking I could beat this as easily as that. I should have known. I'm never going to get better. I'm never going to be of any help to anyone, because one thing goes wrong and I shut down in a panic attack. I'm worthless!" My voice broke on the word, the sobs back even stronger.

Zero remained crouched in front of me, watching me, brows furrowed, as I cried myself out. Eventually the sobs gave way to regular tears, and finally sniffles. My breathing slowed. The attack was passing.

I inhaled shakily. "I'm sorry," I said at last.

"Hon, there's no need to apologize," Zero said fervently.

I shook my head. "I thought I'd beaten it. I haven't had one in almost a month. I thought they were gone. How stupid was that?"

Zero sighed, glancing over at where the rosary beads lay on the ground a short distance away. "Remember what I said last night?" they asked. "Even when things have gone to hell, you have to maintain some degree of normalcy."

"Yeah," I said. "But I can't just—"

"You know what the secret to getting through a world-shattering event without completely breaking down is? Taking care of yourself," Zero interrupted me. "Even when something as big as this is going on, you can't just run on fumes. You've got to make time to take care of yourself. I don't mean just getting the necessities of eating and drinking and sleeping, though those are important too, and you haven't even been doing that much."

I looked down sheepishly. They were right. I hadn't slept last night, had barely eaten since the picnic yesterday afternoon.

"But you have to take care of the rest of you, too," they went on. "You need that downtime, that quiet time, that time for grounding yourself. Vegging out. Meditating, praying, listening to music, *making* music in your case—you have to do those things in order to maintain the strength to do what you need to do. You have to take care of yourself if you want to take care of others. You've been neglecting yourself, Tamara. You've been neglecting yourself for months, and it's showing. Your body is keeping the score."

They squeezed my hand, looking up at me. "But you also have to remember to cut yourself some slack. No matter how good of a job you do at grounding and self-care, you're probably still going to have panic attacks sometimes. It's just one of those things. But you can't treat them like some kind of personal failing. They're not some kind of reflection on you as a person, your worth as a person. Having them doesn't mean you've somehow failed. And you know," they added, hesitant now, "if you decide you want to start taking medication for it, that also doesn't mean you've failed."

I exhaled, a humorless laugh making my breath hitch. "What, are you psychic now?" It was true. I hadn't wanted to take medication for it because I'd felt like that would make me even more of a failure, not being able to manage it on my own. But I hadn't told anyone that. Not Henry, not even my moms.

"It's a pretty common sentiment. One shared by a good friend of ours, in fact." They gave me a tight smile. "I'll tell you what I told her. There's nothing wrong with not wanting to take medication, for any reason. It's your body, and you've got a right to make your own medical decisions. But there's also nothing *wrong* with taking it, and you shouldn't feel stigmatized for it. You have to decide what's best for you, whatever that may be."

They pushed themself to their feet. "Just be gentle with yourself, okay, hon? Your brain is rough enough on you as it is." They crouched again, scooping up the carnelian beads from the ground and bringing them back over to me. They pressed them into my hands. "One more thing. You have to hold on to your faith. No matter what happens to any of us, no matter what the outcome is, you can't lose that. You've got to keep your faith."

My eyes were stinging again. I closed my hand around the rosary.

"Thanks, Zero," I murmured. "You know... I see now why Lizeth said you were the best of the best street medics."

Zero grinned. "I'll wear that as a badge of honor," they said. "Now lie down for a little bit. See if you can get some rest. Your body needs it."

I nodded, laying back on the cot. I was out almost as soon as I closed my eyes.

I wasn't asleep long—twenty minutes at most—but even that small amount of sleep did wonders. I felt a lot better as I drifted awake. At least, until I heard Zero's murmured voice, Mariyah's low responses, and what they were talking about.

"We managed to get it out before it spread, but way more cops have been rolling in since then. And they brought in that big tank thing they use for riots," Mariyah was saying.

"Great," Zero muttered. "What was the idiot who set it trying to do?"

"They got a hold of one of the flags from outside the GSAF building and they were going to light it on fire."

Zero exhaled. "Well, I can't say I'm exactly opposed to that on principle, but talk about crap timing. I thought for a minute we were going to have a stampede on our hands. Those girls and their catfight had already managed to knock Tamara clean off her feet at that point, and she'd brought a couple other people down with her. Then Scylla goes and yells 'fire' in a crowded theater..."

"Sorry," Mariyah said sheepishly. "It startled her. She's been trying to keep things orderly, at least for the first half of the day. We all know that once things start getting destructive, that's when the cops start coming down harder. Based on how things have been the last several months, Scylla was afraid that anything like that would get the protest shut down."

"And we can't risk that happening until the strike team gets back," Zero said. "We need to keep this going as long as possible, for their sake."

"Yeah, Scylla told me," Mariyah said. "Oh, looks like you've got a customer."

I opened my eyes blearily, raising myself on my elbows as one of the other street medics guided in a teenage boy, his head tilted slightly back and his hand clamped over his nose, pinching his nostrils shut.

"Another nosebleed?" Zero said, jumping up and running over to the patient coming in the door.

"Yeah, and I ran out of tissue out there," the medic said. "Can you take care of him? I'm going to grab a few more packs and get back out there."

"Sure thing," said Zero. They guided the boy over to one of the empty cots across from me and handed him a box of tissue. "Hang tight here until it stops."

"Do you usually have this many nosebleeds in one day?" Mariyah asked when Zero came back over to her.

"No, never. At least, not in a place where there hasn't been a massive bar fight."

"Yeah, but there have been a lot of fights today, too," Mariyah pointed out.

Zero grunted, running a thumb over their chin. "Yeah. This is really weird. There are always scuffles at a demonstration this big, but this many? And all among people who are on the same side. This isn't a case where there have been counter-protesters trying to stir shit."

"It's almost like there's something in the water," Mariyah commented.

"Could GSAF have done something?" I asked, my voice sticky.

Zero glanced in my direction, noticing I was awake for the first time, giving me a smile and inclining their head. "It's possible, but I'm not sure what—"

They broke off at the roar of the crowd outside. The steady chanting, clapping and whistling had changed timbre, quickly evolving into angry yelling.

"Now what?" Mariyah asked, going over to the tent opening and starting to look out. She nearly collided with Scylla as she burst into the medic tent.

"High alert," Scylla said breathlessly. "Guess who just showed up."

"I DON'T UNDERSTAND," LIZETH SAID FROM HER PLACE BESIDE ME, STARING dumbfounded at the carving in the rock. "Where did this come from? Joseph Condor and his psychotic obsession with you?"

"Maybe," I said. But I didn't think so. This engraving did not look recent. Its edges had been smoothed by the passage of time.

"I mean, how else could this have gotten here?" Lizeth asked.

"I can think of a couple ways," I said. And their names were Nadin and Isaak. But what would the purpose of this have been? Why carve my name into the wall? And why here, in this spot? In some random apartment on the *esotoi* levels?

One way to find out. What had Nadin done when she found the Iamoi writing in the tomb in Mexico?

I reached into my pocket and fished out the object I'd carried with me since the day we left Los Tuxtlas.

Lizeth narrowed her eyes. "Henry, is that...?"

"Yup," I said.

A System earpiece.

"Where did you get that?" she asked.

"I brought it with me from Earth," I said. "You know, just in case." I'd felt a little bad about swiping one of Professor Espinoza's artifacts, but I'd figured our odds of needing it would be greater than his. And considering GSAF had raided the site a few days later, it's not exactly like this thing ever would have made it into a museum.

She made a noise in the back of her throat. "If I'd known you'd taken that, I never would have let you keep it. Especially not after what Geoff Preston told us about what GSAF is doing with the System."

"Hence why I didn't tell you," I said, slipping the earpiece into my ear. The typical disorientation followed, as it had whenever I'd used this earpiece, but it was followed by something else, something... sharper. I rubbed my temple with my left hand. "Well, let's see if this does anything." With my right hand, I reached up and touched the carving.

"*System protocol initiated.*" I didn't exactly *hear* the words, but I understood them. And then, a second later, I did hear something.

Nadin's voice in my ear.

"What?" Lizeth said at my expression, her own face clouding with concern. "What's wrong?"

"Hang on," I said, still listening.

When Nadin's voice had faded out, I stood still for a moment, my hand still on the carved wall in shock. Finally, I swallowed, lowering my hand, removing the earpiece from my ear.

"What is it?" Lizeth demanded.

"Nadin left us a message."

"How could she know we'd be here?"

I shook my head. "I don't know." How indeed—how could she know we'd be *here*, in this spot? How could she have known that this place, just where she'd carved my name, would be sheltered from the water that had caused so much damage to the rest of the apartment?

And how could she know exactly what we needed to know?

"What did the message say?" Lizeth asked.

"She told us the way to get to Kate Ponsford," I said.

According to Nadin's message, there were tunnels near here, ones that GSAF wouldn't know about. "To keep these levels habitable, we channeled hot water under the floors, through subterranean tunnels," her disembodied voice had explained. "The tunnels are empty now. The water is gone. The rebellion used them to access the whole of the Underground. You can do the same."

"She said there's an entrance near here," I told Lizeth. "Turn the flashlight on the floor."

Lizeth glanced around warily, but the apartments of the *esotoi* seemed to be abandoned. The sound of distant voices still echoed periodically through the corridor, but they seemed far off. Hesitantly, Lizeth switched the flashlight on, sweeping it back and forth across the floor.

I sighed, watching the beam of light move back and forth. "I don't know how we're supposed to see anything under all this," I said. Dust, rocks, sand, rubble, all manner of debris littered the floor of the passage. It was clear that GSAF didn't have much use for this part of the Underground. If this area got frequent traffic, they would have cleared it.

"Wait, this might be something," Lizeth said. She moved closer, following the flashlight's beam to where dust seemed to be gathering in a seam on the floor.

"Yeah. Let's give it a try," I said. I crouched beside her, looking for some kind of way to open the hatch. I pressed in on a divot in one corner, and the opposite side of the panel popped up with a loud scrape. I winced, and we froze, listening. The corridor remained quiet.

The two of us together managed to pry the ancient panel loose, revealing an opening in the floor just large enough for a person. Lizeth shone her flashlight down the hole. The remains of a corroded ladder lay toppled on the ground just below us. It must have been mounted to the wall here once, but it had rusted clean through.

"Nothing to do but jump," Lizeth said.

"Careful not to land on that. The last thing one of us needs is a broken ankle," I said.

Lizeth swung her lithe body down through the hole, managing to avoid hitting the ladder. She dragged it out of the way to give me clearance to squeeze my own body through and drop down to the floor.

As I landed with a *thunk*, Lizeth looked around the space with the flashlight. "And this will lead us straight down to the level we need?"

"That's what Nadin said."

She frowned. "You're sure it was actually Nadin and not a trap?"

I shrugged. "I don't know how it could have been a trap. GSAF couldn't have known we were coming, or that we'd be getting in through that entrance." At least, I didn't think so. It would have taken a lot of conjecture on their parts. But by the same token, how could Nadin have known either? To be able to set up that System protocol...

"There's only one way to find out," I said finally.

Lizeth nodded, and we started down the tunnel.

"I still can't believe this," she said in a low voice, aiming the flashlight up at the corbeled ceiling. "These kinds of tunnels are like the ones in the pyramids in Egypt. Whenever Mother would take Bruno and me to the Middle East for a work trip, she'd let us tour the pyramids. The Great Pyramid, the Red Pyramid, the Bent Pyramid. I just..." She let out a laugh, in a tone I'd never heard out of Lizeth before. "This is really it, isn't it? These are the ruins of Atlantis."

I smirked. "Sometimes I forget that weirdo I met on Speculus, wanting to know about the Atlantean coin, was actually you."

She looked sheepish. "When I was a kid, I always used to dream of discovering Atlantis. Buried under the sea somewhere. Just waiting to be found. I dreamed of what its ruins would look like. I never would have imagined this." She looked down at the sloping channel in the middle of the floor, where water must have once flowed. "Or that it wasn't actually under the sea, for that matter. Who would have believed that Atlantis was actually on another planet..."

"This is the first time I've ever seen the resemblance between you and your uncle, I think," I commented wryly.

She ignored me, still caught up in her daydream. "They said that Atlantis was a utopian society. Scholars like Plato. They said that the Atlanteans had advanced technology, of course. But it was more than that. Everyone who lived in Atlantis lived like equals. That's what the legend said." She kicked a pebble with her black sneaker. "But that Atlantis never existed, did it? Not in Nadin's time, at least."

I eyed Lizeth in surprise. She sounded wistful and sad. Surprisingly vulnerable. Maybe she wasn't actually made out of stone.

"Maybe it still can," I said. "Maybe Atlantis is waiting for you to build it. For all of us."

She thought about that for a moment. Then she flashed me a grin, revealing her crooked eye tooth. "I like that idea."

We followed the tunnel as it snaked around, descending sharply in some places in what must have once formed rushing waterfalls of boiling hot water. In other places the tunnel forked off, but Nadin had told me if I kept right at every intersection, we'd eventually wind up where we needed to go.

Now and then we could hear voices around us, above us. We were coming into the areas GSAF had adopted as their base. Every so often we passed under what had once been one of the various fountains throughout the city that Nadin had told us all about, that night at Tamara's moms' house, when Scylla had eagerly pressed her for every detail about the Iamoi civilization, about life here in ancient times. Each of these fountains featured a postern where the water would be transported in; it would then drop down through a grate, filling these channels and heating the entire cave system. Some of the grates were blocked with debris now, but many of them were clear, and through these we could hear the voices of the GSAF agents on the floors above us. We'd turned off the flashlight in these places, moving slowly and silently. We had no way of knowing how sound carried in this place.

"We're getting close," I whispered to Lizeth after we passed through the fourth intersection. "Once we make it through the next one, it'll just be a matter of—"

"Shh," she hissed quietly. "Listen."

"I don't know why I even stayed on duty," a man's voice was saying. He sounded irritated. "I've got Nano installed, you know? Condor's insisted for eight months that nothing like this was going to happen, and then it turns around and happens."

"You should have known better," another voice said in reply. "When you've been in this business as long as I have, you learn that whenever the higher-ups deny an accusation, the accusation is true. If it was false, they'd just ignore it."

"That's kind of cynical," said the first man.

"It's the truth," the second man replied, the shrug obvious in his voice.

"What are you two doing just standing around?" a third voice broke in. My muscles tensed involuntarily. *Condor.*

"It's our scheduled break, sir," the older man answered.

"We don't have time for scheduled breaks," Condor snapped. "I need all hands searching the facility. We're on high alert."

"The report said the entrance wasn't breached," the first man said. "That the facility is secure."

"The *main* entrance wasn't breached," Condor corrected. "That doesn't mean the facility is secure. No breaks when we're on high alert. Move out."

"Yes, sir," the two agents said, their voices followed by the sound of retreating footsteps.

"Useless," Condor spat once the agents were gone.

"Do you really think it's possible that the facility's been breached?" a new voice asked, sounding dubious. I recognized the speaker. Geoff Preston.

"The Stateless don't just go for the front door and then run away when they can't get in," Condor replied. "This cave system stretches for eight hundred twenty-seven square kilometers. We've only surveyed a fraction of it. There could be dozens of unknown points of entry. Stateless operatives firebombing the entrance and then retreating smacks of a diversion."

"But why would they want to get in here in the first place?" Preston reasoned. "And how do we even know it was the Stateless who carried out this attack, and not just Free Mars protesters trying to make a point?"

"It was the Stateless," Condor insisted. "Our source indicated that the Stateless sent a number of operatives to Mars over the last month. And now we know why."

"I'm glad you're confident, Mr. Condor," Preston said. "Because I'm beginning to question the quality of your informant's tips. After all, GSAF raided that archaeological dig in Mexico and found nothing. Likewise, you intercepted that cargo ship three days ago and also found nothing. How do we know GSAF hasn't been chasing a ghost?"

"Your own Nano data placed the leaders of both the Stateless and the Free Mars movement in Curiosity Bay yesterday morning, Preston," Condor said. "Unless you're telling me your tech's facial recognition capabilities are less reliable that you'd led us to believe?"

"Of course not," Preston replied quickly. "But no matter how reliable it is, all facial recognition technology is capable of producing false positives—"

Condor laughed. "No. Not this time. They've been evading us so far, but we're closing in. Once we've cut the head off, the beast will fall. That should be the end of this nuisance of an insurrection." There was a moment of silence. "And then, of course," Condor added, "there will be the investigation. How this information about ConneX was leaked to the public."

"Someone at AresTec, clearly," Preston said dismissively. "After all, considering how the leak was disseminated—"

"We know someone at AresTec disseminated the leak," Condor countered. "And I'm sure I know who. But I don't think that the person who pushed this A-Top update was the one who initially accessed the ConneX data. After all, as you've repeatedly reminded me, most employees at GalaX don't even know ConneX exists. No, I'm convinced that the source of this leak was someone at ConneX."

"Mr. Condor, I assure you that all of my people have been thoroughly vetted." For the first time, Preston's tone had lost some of its confidence, its easiness. It was almost imperceptible, but for the first time, Preston sounded nervous.

"Hmm," Condor said in reply. "Well, I heard a rumor about a visitor that Carla Perez had at Sea-Star Island recently, and I think I know who that visitor is. Our informant does, too. Ah, here he is."

The sound of footsteps overhead. Then a man's voice. "Hello, Mr. Condor. And Mr. Preston. Nice to see you again." Lizeth frowned when she heard it, her black eyebrows drawing together tightly.

"So you *are* acquainted," Condor said. "I thought as much. Is this him?"

"It's him," the newcomer replied.

"I've never seen this man before," Preston said. "But he could know me from any number of sources. A business magazine, a news interview—"

"It's possible." Condor sounded unconvinced. "That's what you would say, isn't it, though? So you'll forgive me if I decide to play it safe. Agent Paulson, if you'd be so kind to show our friend to the Basement?"

The Basement. That was what the schematics I'd pulled from GSAF's files last night had called the lowest level of the Underground, where the Ponsfords were currently being held.

"Joseph—" Preston protested, but Condor cut him off.

"Now, now. No need to make a fuss. You'll be comfortable. After all, it was once a palace."

The sound of scuffling footsteps came from overhead, the sound of a slamming door. "Well, that's one conundrum solved," Condor said as the echoes faded. "It's no wonder Sandhu and Senghas have managed to stay out ahead of us, if they've had someone helping them from the inside. I have no doubt in my mind that he was responsible for yesterday's incident. The group of them turning up in Curiosity Bay would have been a long shot. I shouldn't have taken the bait." A moment of silence. I could picture Condor's icy blue eyes, his dry smirk. "You've been very helpful, Mr. Logan."

Logan. Why did I know that name? One glance at Lizeth's horrified expression made the connection come rushing back to me.

Carla Perez's assistant.

She'd insisted that her staff knew nothing about her role in the Stateless. That her home was secure and her staff thoroughly vetted. But apparently she'd been overconfident. There'd been a GSAF spy in her home the entire time.

"Happy to serve the NAEU, Mr. Condor," Logan replied.

A slight slapping sound as Condor clapped his hand on Logan's shoulder. "The NAEU and GSAF owe you a debt of gratitude. If weren't for you, we'd still have no identification on who was behind these terror groups." He made a *tsking* sound. "Incredible," he said. "The best and brightest minds the two worlds have to offer against a group of teenagers, and yet they've managed to continually outsmart us. It's like a damn after-school special. But it ends now. We're closing in on them. And if this Lizeth Senghas is the head of the snake, like you seem to think she is—"

"She is, sir. Her mother thinks she's in charge of the whole operation, but Lizeth is the one really pulling the strings."

"And she's here in Tierra Nueva. I'm certain of that much. Now that Preston isn't going to be tweaking the Nano surveillance data to send us on any further wild goose chases, we'll have her soon. And Sandhu too. It's only a matter of time." My stomach curdled at his tone.

More footsteps overhead. "Agent Kim," Condor said, acknowledging the newcomer. "What's our status?"

"Our trackers still are working on intercepting the attackers."

"How have they not caught them yet?" Condor demanded. "We're boxed in by sheer cliffs on all sides!"

"Sir, all our tech went down."

"Do our agents' legs not work? Their eyes? They don't need tech to chase down a group of hooligans."

"They're still working on it, sir," Agent Kim said, sounding tense. "But there's more. We've got an incident in Tierra Nueva. The protesters—"

"I'm sick to my back teeth of protesters," Condor spat. "I've already made it clear that I want that riot shut down, *immediately*. This is not Kate Ponsford's government anymore. Use force. Break them up, now."

The man hesitated. "Sir, I'm not sure if that would be best for optics right now... Considering that they're protesting perceived government force against them in the form of the System..."

"I don't give a damn what they perceive. Break the riot up, now."

"Yes, sir."

A beat passed. "Why are you still standing here?"

"I had one more report to make, sir. The protesters appear to be led by Sandhu's rebels—"

"Sandhu? He's been spotted?" Condor's tone changed from anger and annoyance to almost delight. Goosebumps rippled across my arms. The man was completely unhinged.

"The reports on that are unclear," said Agent Kim. "Tamara Randall-Torres and Priscilla Hwang both have been positively identified, though."

"Then Sandhu must be there. I know him. If you want to find him, look no further than glued to T-RT's side." I hated the way he said that nickname. The way everyone pronounced it. Like *Tart*. It was disgusting. He spat out a humorless laugh. "I'd call him her lap dog, except she's too spineless to take advantage of it."

More footsteps. Agent Kim said, "Where are you going, sir?"

"I'm coming with you to Tierra Nueva. To reconnect with my dear old friend, Mr. Sandhu."

Stay out of his way, Tamara. You've got to stay out of his way. I couldn't get to her in time. Couldn't protect her this time. I'd known that when I set out on this mission. I knew she was going to be painting a target on her back. But the knowledge that he was heading straight for her and there was nothing I could do about it still clawed away at my insides.

"I want the rest of our agents to continue searching for the Stateless terrorists, both inside the Underground and in the hills. I'm still unconvinced that this facility is secure."

"Yes, sir."

"Mr. Logan, Agent Paulson will arrange for someone to get you back to your hotel."

"What about my payment?" Logan asked.

"Don't worry, we'll see to it that you're well compensated," Condor replied.

His voice faded as the door overhead closed.

Lizeth and I stood in silence, hearing nothing but the sound of our own breathing. Minutes passed. We seemed to be alone.

"Goddammit," Lizeth finally whispered. "God*dammit.*"

"Lizeth—"

"I've been beating myself up for weeks. I was positive that this was somehow my fault. Somehow, something I'd done had gotten us caught. That detour to Mexico, my Atlantis obsession—something had made me reckless, and that was how we got found out. It had to be my fault. Of course it did. But no. It was *Mother's*—"

Her voice fractured on the word. She laughed, quietly but almost hysterically.

"It was Mother's fault. It was Mother who was too complacent. Too lackadaisical. It was Mother who didn't notice what was going on right under her nose."

"You know what else she didn't notice?" I said. Lizeth's eyes flicked to me in the darkness. "She didn't notice that Jay Logan was right. Your mother isn't the real leader of the Stateless. It's you. Her ineptitude just proved that."

She was quiet for a long moment. Thinking. Finally, she let out a shaky breath. "Well. If I'm the leader, I guess I better do some leading. We need to get moving. After all, we've got an extra prisoner to break out of the Underground now, don't we?"

CHAPTER 52

- t a m a r a -

"WHAT DO WE DO?" I ASKED, QUICKLY SWINGING MY LEGS OVER THE SIDE OF the cot and jumping to my feet.

"We can't stay here, that's for sure," Scylla said. "We're sitting ducks in here. This has officially gone from the 'be as visible as possible' phase of the plan to the 'don't get caught' phase."

"Use the crowd," Zero said. "There's safety in numbers."

"Come on." Mariyah lifted up the back corner of the tent, on the side that didn't open directly onto the street. Scylla and I hurried after her.

"You coming?" Scylla asked Zero.

They shook their head. "Medic's duty is to go down with the hospital. Besides, I haven't been I.D.'ed yet. You three go."

The street was blockaded with the riot-control tanks that GSAF had brought in over the last annum for suppressing the demonstrations that had grown after Henry had blown the whistle the first time. Agents in padded armor were spilling out of the vehicles now. On the steps to the GSAF building, wearing his typical suit, cravat, and mirrored sunglasses, stood Joseph Condor.

What did it mean that Condor was here? Had our plan been a success, then? Had we managed to distract GSAF from what was happening in the hills, training Condor's eye here on Tierra Nueva? Or had Henry and Lizeth already been apprehended, and Condor was just here to finish the job?

I could feel the way my heart started beating off-kilter as we pressed our way back into the throng of people, the way my breath started turning shallow. Returning to the crowd this soon after my panic attack was not a good idea, but I didn't have a choice now. Self-care was going to have to take a backseat to survival.

As we made our way deeper into the thickly packed park, I could hear Joseph Condor addressing the crowd through a loudspeaker. "This is an illegal gathering," his voice boomed.

"Yeah, well you're an illegal governor!" someone on my right shouted back at him.

"I repeat, this is an illegal gathering. Disperse immediately."

"Go to hell!" another voice yelled.

Across the park, I recognized ProLibertate's voice over Scylla's megaphone, reprising the chant from earlier again: "*Joseph Condor must resign! Joseph Condor must resign!*"

The crowd around us erupted with the refrain, the sound of their unified voices deafening.

"If you do not disperse voluntarily," Condor said, turning the volume on his loudspeaker up, "nonlethal force will be deployed against you."

"We'll show you some nonlethal force!" someone shouted, and then I saw a body break away from the crowd, rushing toward the armored vehicle parked closest to the bridge. Dozens of people rushed forward after them, and they swarmed past the agents, throwing themselves against the vehicle, rocking the tank on its wheels. I realized with shock that they were trying to shove the tank over the side of the guardrail and into the river.

There was an enormous *boom* as the agents fired a water cannon into the crowd. But far from dispersing the protesters, this action just seemed to enrage them. Even more people raced forward, rushing the agents themselves. The Tierra Nueva P.D. officers, who thus far had stayed out of the conflict, raced into the fray now, hurrying to assist the GSAF agents. The agents raised enormous shields to try to block their bodies. Someone swung a sign that was mounted to a broom handle like it was a baseball bat, and it collided with one of the shields with a *crack*. Another figure spun around, the front of their shirt covered in blood that seemed to be flowing from their nose.

There was another *bang* as this time teargas was fired into the crowd, but still people continued to surge forward, attacking the agents and officers.

From his place on the GSAF building steps, Condor's hand was raised, seeming to hover in midair, swiping back and forth across an invisible surface.

"What's he doing?" Mariyah yelled.

I didn't understand for a moment. Not until I saw that his other hand was to his ear. He'd inserted an Iamoi earpiece.

He was using the System.

By the time I realized what was happening, it was way too late.

Of course, it had always been too late, hadn't it?

With a swipe of his hand, Condor activated the adherence protocol.

Around us, hundreds of people fell to their knees screaming. Not just Free Mars supporters—the adherence protocol was indiscriminate. Recognizing none of these people as Iamoi Enforcers, it knocked several of the police officers down, same as the protesters. If I'd thought the sound of the angry chanting earlier had been loud, that had been nothing compared to the sound of these painful screams. Those who didn't have Nano looked on in shock, falling to their own knees, trying to offer assistance, trying to understand what was going on here, why their friends had dropped like rocks around them.

"He did it!" ProLibertate shouted over the megaphone, feedback screeching across the park over his shrill words. "He just did exactly what Henry Sandhu warned us he would! He's using the System against the people!"

If Condor had thought this would help him regain control of the crowd, he'd grossly miscalculated. This had just fed the fire of the people's rage. Now even more people raced forward, the street erupting in a violent brawl. The tank began shaking on its wheels once more, swaying more and more violently, tipping—

CRASH.

The tank pitched over the side of the bridge, bringing part of the metal guardrail along with it. A moment later, it hit the water with an enormous splash. Emboldened by their success, they charged forward. With nothing else to do, the agents fell back. Condor had disappeared inside the GSAF building. With members of the crowd hot on their heels, the agents followed, barricading the door.

Lizeth had been right. This wasn't a protest anymore. This was an insurrection.

I was barely aware of what was going on, though. Bodies littered the ground around us. Nadin had said that the adherence protocol produced sharp pain in the heads of the victims that lasted several seconds, but then it stopped. It was enough to break up a riot, to enforce compliance. But while many people had shakily gotten back to their feet when the protocol stopped assaulting them with pain, many more were still on the ground, breathing heavily. Some seemed to have lost consciousness entirely.

I knelt beside a young woman with blond hair streaked pink, trying to shake her awake. But she was unresponsive. Blood flowed out of her right nostril.

"What's going on?" the brunette with her cried. "Why isn't she waking up?" She pushed me aside, shaking her friend herself. "Monica, come on! Wake up!"

Distantly, I heard sirens in the background. More police? No, the timbre was different. Ambulance. It was clear that we needed more than just the street medicine that Zero and their fellow medics could provide. But I wasn't sure there were enough ambulances in Tierra Nueva for the amount of people lying on the ground now.

What's going on here?

It was the System. It had to be. But nothing Nadin had ever described to us about it even remotely resembled this. Was this caused by the fact that these people were connected to the System through nanobots instead of earpieces?

"Fall back!" I heard someone yelling. "Fall back!"

"Tamara," Scylla called from where she knelt beside another fallen Nano user. She pointed, and I saw Mama rushing toward me.

Another screech of feedback ricocheted across the park as ProLibertate turned the megaphone on once more. "More GSAF agents are inbound! Anyone who can walk, fall back to Sparta Island! Medical assistance is on the way, but anyone who can walk, I repeat, fall back to Sparta Island!"

Mama reached my side. "Come on, love, we have to go."

"I can't just leave them!" I protested, gesturing to Monica and her friend.

"The paramedics are on the way, but we can't let Condor get you or Scylla. If he does, he'll know Henry and Lizeth aren't here. Remember the plan, Tam. Everyone's relying on you."

I swallowed hard, looking frantically at the dried blood caking on Monica's shirt, in her hair, turning the colorful pink streaks a nauseating brown. All these people—how could I just leave them?

But I wasn't a doctor, or a nurse, or even a street medic like Zero. Whatever was wrong with all these people, I didn't know how to help them. And I knew for sure, after what had just happened, that they wouldn't get help if Condor had his way. We needed Kate. And that meant we needed the plan to succeed.

I squeezed my eyes shut for just a moment. Then I took Mama's hand and she helped me to my feet. "Help is coming for your friend," I said to the brunette, but she didn't seem to hear me. Would she be okay?

Would any of us be okay? Right now, it didn't feel that way.

Mama's hand still clutching mine, we raced across the bridge to Sparta Island.

CHAPTER 53

NADIN HAD WARNED ME THAT THE TUNNELS GOT SMALLER IN THE LOWER levels, that we wouldn't be able to walk through them. She'd said they'd been blocked in her time by the water, that the rebellion had not been able to get into the lower levels through these tunnels because of it. The water had drained now, apart from some puddles here or there that had accumulated from the condensation dripping in the caverns above; but that didn't make navigating them any easier. We had to crawl on our hands and knees, and even then, it was a tight squeeze.

It took hours to make it the grueling last third of the way down into the bottom level of the Underground. According to Lizeth's watch, it was after six o'clock as we scrabbled down the final slope. Factoring in the debris we'd had to clear to get through some of the blocked passages, our need to move slowly so as not to attract attention from the agents above, and our all-too-human need for breaks, for water, for food—it had taken us twelve hours to circumnavigate the entirety of this underground city from top to bottom. Which meant that, once we got the Ponsfords and Geoff Preston, it would take twelve more hours, if not longer, to get back out. Time we couldn't afford, considering that Condor had left for Tierra Nueva almost six hours ago and hadn't, as far as we knew, returned.

And we had somewhere else we needed to be by seven o'clock tomorrow morning. I suspected Lizeth had forgotten, but it had been in the forefront of my mind since the cargo ship had landed on Thursday. The clock had run out. If we wanted to get to them before Condor did, we had to be there on that beach. But we'd be cutting it close. Real close.

Then there was the other concern—would the protest survive a full twenty-four hours, possibly even more than that? Would Condor still believe that I was there somewhere, hidden in the crowd, or had he figured out by now that we'd deceived him? Was he already back in the Underground, ready to apprehend us as soon as we emerged from this tunnel?

Was Tamara safe?

"This it?" Lizeth asked, gesturing to a grate in the ceiling just ahead.

"That's it," I said.

"Then let's get out of here," she murmured.

We positioned ourselves under the grate that Nadin had told me about. The tunnel here was only a little over a meter high, but we managed to get ourselves into a crouching position, hands raised, and shoved the grate up.

With a scrape, it gave way.

Lizeth looked around the empty room in confusion. We were in a square depression, about a meter deep, with a floor that sloped downward on all four sides toward the grate. It almost looked like a small, shallow swimming pool.

"Where are we?" Lizeth asked.

"The *geroi*'s bathroom," I said dryly.

"Seriously?"

"Dead serious. Come on. The Ponsfords should be just through here."

GSAF's fingerprints were all over this space. While the level of the *esotoi* had remained in ruins, its sliding doors falling off their tracks, debris and the remnants of people's belongings still cluttering the space, here the rooms had been cleared, replaced with modern, Earth-based furnishings. Including replacing the sliding doors with doors with hinges.

The door to this bathroom was locked from the inside—the prisoners could not have gotten in here, but we could get out. Lizeth glanced at me, her hand on the doorknob. I nodded.

The door swung open. Four people sat on the other side, crowded around a small metal table, eating the meager dinner that GSAF had provided them: Kate Ponsford and her husband, Oliver; my erstwhile nemesis, Wyatt; and Geoff Preston.

"Henry!" Wyatt cried in surprise, jumping to his feet. I gestured for him to be quiet, and he ducked his head sheepishly. "Sorry. But what are you doing here?"

"We're here to bust you out," said Lizeth.

Quickly, with the same practiced skill she'd used when informing me that they were breaking me out of Lago Verde two months ago, Lizeth explained who she was, what was going on topside—and what we needed out of Kate.

For her part, the woman listened quietly, not interrupting, nodding her head thoughtfully. "That matches with what Mr. Preston told us after he... joined our party earlier." She gave Preston a wry smile. "But it's a big risk."

"Do it, Mom," Wyatt said without hesitation. "It's not like we're ever getting out of here otherwise. If GSAF was planning on bringing you to Earth for a fair trial, they would have done it months ago."

"I'll need a palmtop," Kate said. "If we're going to do this correctly, I'll have to make some calls. Get people into position. And we'll—"

The door flew open then, a suited agent on the other side, a gun pointed directly at us. It took me a moment to recognize him as an agent, though, from his bedraggled appearance. Drops of reddish brown stained the white of his undershirt, the light color of his cravat. Though it looked like he'd attempted to clean himself up a bit, smears on his face indicated the blood had come from his nose.

"Everyone on your feet, hands up, now," he barked. His gun hand was shaking. Nerves? GSAF would have to be really scraping the bottom of the barrel for agents if they'd put someone afraid of confrontation in charge of a group of high-risk prisoners. "I knew I was hearing voices that I shouldn't have. I don't know how you two got in here, but this ends now."

I felt frozen in place, but the gun left us no room for argument, especially not with the way his hand was shaking. One wrong move and he might set it off. Slowly I stood, raising my hands, trying to think, trying to calculate. We were screwed now. How were we going to get out of this one?

"Jack, are you okay?" Wyatt asked, addressing the agent. Leave it to Ponsford to have made friends with his jailer. "What's with the blood?"

"It's nothing, all right?" the man snapped. "Back off, Wyatt."

"I don't think it's nothing. You're shaking. Are you sick?"

"I said I'm fine!" the agent shouted back, his voice loud. It echoed off the ceiling. I winced at his volume. To my shock, the agent winced too. He lowered his weapon, putting a hand to his head.

"Jack?" Wyatt said.

The man crumpled to his knees, the gun hitting the stone floor, skittering away from him. Lightning-fast, Lizeth broke away from the group, racing forward and snatching the gun off the ground.

"What just happened?" Oliver Ponsford asked. "Is he having a heart attack?"

"It doesn't matter," Lizeth said. "Now's our chance. Come on."

"We can't just leave him," Wyatt said, running over to the agent's side and rolling the man over onto his back. Blood streamed from his right nostril. "Oh my God. Jack?" The agent didn't respond. Wyatt placed his ear against the man's chest, listening. "Breathing sounds normal. Heart rate, too."

"What's wrong with him, then?" Kate asked.

"It doesn't *matter*," Lizeth snapped again. "We have to go."

"This man has Nano," Preston said.

I stared at him in shock. "How do you know that?"

"Because the System is causing this."

"And how do you know *that*?" I demanded.

"The bloody noses, the muscle tremor... this is what happened to the *geroi*. And if this man is sick"—he swallowed—"then I fear that this is happening all over the province. All over the worlds." In a lower voice, he added, "Just as she warned."

As I gawked at him, Wyatt said, "We need to call for help."

"Are you insane?" Lizeth demanded.

"No," Wyatt said fiercely. "You want the GSAF agents to side with my mom? You help them now. Then they'll see who's really on their side. Because I can guarantee that Condor is doing nothing to help them. If this is really the System, then he *caused* this. Everyone working for GSAF right now needs to see that."

"Hold on," I interrupted, still staring at Preston. "How do you know what happened to the *geroi* in Nadin's time? And what do you mean, *she warned?*"

Preston's expression was grim. "ConneX is the foremost authority on the System, remember. And the System recorded everything it ever saw."

I clenched my fist, furious. Preston had been holding out on us. Even during the meeting with Carla Perez, when he'd claimed to be laying all his cards on the table, he'd been keeping this secret. And this secret could cost millions of lives. He'd known this. Someone had *warned* him about this danger. But he'd done nothing to stop it. *Why?* Why, when he knew how deadly this could get, had he expected me to be the one who blew the whistle?

Things weren't adding up, and it was making alarm bells ring deafeningly in my head. We'd trusted Preston, but I saw now that this might have been an enormous mistake.

Who was Geoff Preston, really?

"If you know what happened to the *geroi*," I said, "then what else do you know? What else are you not telling us?"

He looked at me solemnly, unblinking. "You might not want to know."

Chapter 54

- t a m a r a -

I SAT ON A CUSHIONED BENCH IN THE FIRST-FLOOR LOUNGE OF THE Hamilton building, my knees up in my chest, my fingers working the beads of the rosary, hearing the way the chain tinkled as the beads brushed against each other. Through the window it was dark. The lights of downtown across the river were just as bright as they always were. But this wasn't a normal night. The world was ending.

Falling back to Sparta Island had seemed like a good idea at the time. The park was too close to the GSAF building, and the island was an easily defensible space. By blockading the bridge, we could keep GSAF out.

What we hadn't counted on was that now GSAF could keep us *in*. That hadn't seemed to matter at first—after all, we were just trying to buy time and keep GSAF distracted until Henry and Lizeth returned with Kate. Even as more GSAF agents rolled up, stationing themselves on the west side of our barricade, I didn't see any reason to worry.

But we hadn't been counting on people continuing to get sick.

From what we'd been able to figure out, the symptoms started with delirium. This affected people in different ways, with some just becoming disoriented, others impulsive or irrational. Many became antagonistic, aggressive. The surprising number of fights that had broken out during the protest, the impulsive fire-setters, the way people had rushed at the GSAF agents without a second thought, shoving the tank into the river—everything made sudden sense in the light of this illness.

Then came the headaches, the nosebleeds. The twitching muscles, the sweating, the constricted pupils. The loss of consciousness. What we were seeing now.

And then...

I squeezed the rosary beads, burying my face in my knees.

Are you there, God? Are you there with us through this?

We'd thought the adherence protocol had done this. It made sense. What else could have caused so many people to collapse all at the same time? But if the adherence protocol had done this, then new people wouldn't have gotten sick hours later. They wouldn't be continuing to get sick as hours passed, as day shifted to night. But more and more people were getting sick every hour.

And it wasn't just people who'd been at the protest who were falling ill. Mom had been glued to her palmtop, making calls, trying to get medical aid brought in to the island by helicopter. But there was little aid to be had.

"People are sick all over the province," she'd told us when she hung up her from her last call, her expression grim. "The hospitals are swamped. There aren't enough doctors. Even if there were, the doctors are getting sick too."

"It wasn't the adherence protocol that did this, then," I'd said, my stomach churning inside me.

"No. But it's something to do with the nanobots," Mom had said. "Only people with Nano are getting sick."

"Which means it's the System," Scylla had growled. "The System is doing this. And they just pushed it out to the entire populace without any regard for safety."

"Are people on Earth getting sick, too?" Zero had asked.

"I don't know," Mom had said, "but I'm assuming so, yes."

"I don't understand why Geoff Preston hasn't hit the kill switch on this," I'd said. "He's been manipulating the data. As soon as people started getting sick, why didn't he turn off the System connectivity?"

"He doesn't have Nano himself, does he?" Scylla had asked. "What if he's sick?"

"There's a worse possibility to consider," Mariyah had said. "What if he's been caught?"

The thought had made adrenaline spike through my veins. If Preston had been caught, then what about Lizeth and Henry? What if they'd been caught too?

If they'd been caught, we were done for. All of us were done for. But maybe we would be, anyway. Trapped here on this island, with so many sick people, and more and more getting sick every hour...

"You're T-RT," a small voice said.

Startled, I looked up. A little girl, around Celeste's age, stood in front of me holding a candy bar from the vending machine. She had the same warm brown skin as Mariyah... as Henry. Her black hair was pulled back in a ponytail. I quickly plastered on my *public appearances* face, the one I used for meet-and-greets and interviews. "Yeah," I said.

"My sister's your biggest fan," she said. "I used to say it was me, but now she's sick so I told her she can be."

"That was generous of you," I told her. "What's your name?"

"Kirti. My sister's name is Geeta."

"Is your sister here?" I asked.

"Yeah. She's..." Kirti pointed. I swallowed. She was gesturing in the direction of the boardroom we'd commandeered for extra hospital space, where Zero and their fellow medics were doing the best they could for people afflicted with a disease we had no idea how to treat.

Now she's sick. As terrible as it would be, I'd been hoping maybe she was sick with something else. Something ordinary. But of course not. Even kids weren't going to be spared from this nightmare. If their parents had let them put Nano in their bodies, they were as doomed as the adults. I wanted to throw up.

"Do you want to meet her?" Kirti asked.

"Of course," I said.

The meeting table and chairs in the boardroom had been shoved up against the wall, clearing the floor to make room for the people in rows there on the thin yoga mats Zero had requisitioned from the AresTec gym. We'd used up our few cots long ago, and the yoga mats were better than the floor.

"Geeta," Kirti said, running over to the corner where a girl of around twelve lay. A woman who must have been the girls' mother sat on the floor beside her. "Look who I found!"

The girl was still conscious, at least. A pile of wadded up tissue was on the floor beside her. She struggled up onto her elbows. Around her wrist I saw she'd tied a bracelet of braided red yarn. Like mine. "T-RT!" she said, grinning at the sight of me.

"Hey, Geeta," I said, crouching down beside her. "How are you feeling?"

"My head hurts," she said. "But the other bad stuff…" She glanced at the young woman lying a few meters away. "I'm okay apart from the headache," she amended.

"That's good," I said earnestly.

"The woman who came through before said doctors might be coming soon," the girls' mother said in a low voice. "Do you know if they're still coming?"

"They're coming," I said. I had no way of knowing if that was true. But I had to believe it. I had to believe it for all these people.

"Could you sing something for Geeta?" Kirti asked. "Her favorite song is 'A Thousand Words.'"

I glanced around the sickroom. "I don't want to bother everyone else…"

"I don't think you'd bother anyone," Zero said. I turned my head in surprise. They were kneeling beside one of the other patients a short distance away, a bottle of acetaminophen—one of the only painkillers we could use, since it wasn't a blood thinner—in their hands. "It would be comforting. And it's something special. Something only you can do," they added meaningfully.

Geeta looked at me imploringly. "Please?"

I swallowed. "Okay," I said.

I closed my eyes for just a moment, hearing the keys in my mind, the way they had echoed through the music room at home as I'd written those first few tentative notes. It had been off my first album, released just after I graduated from the Academy, and most of the songs on that album weren't ones I'd written. But Adam, my manager, had told me that the label wanted something personal to round the album out. A love song. So I'd sat there in front of the piano, feeling like an utter fraud. The only so-called romantic *experience* I'd had in my life at that point had been one disastrous kiss with Isaak that had only taught me that I *didn't* have feelings for him.

But for some reason, I'd kept thinking about someone else, someone I hadn't realized at that point that I *did* have feelings for. Someone who'd disappeared out of my life almost as completely as Isaak, leaving me feeling adrift and alone.

I opened my eyes and began to sing.

"Every time I turn around, it's almost like you're there..."

Geeta grinned, and I smiled awkwardly back at her.

"I keep trying to move on, but no one can compare..."

This was painful. Singing this song was painful. He was gone again now. He might not return. But I kept going anyway. Geeta's smile kept me going. This kid with her red yarn bracelet and a pile of bloody tissue lying around her.

There wasn't much I could do right now. Not many ways that I could help. But I could do this.

"If I had a thousand words, I'd tell it all to you..."

Suddenly I realized that there was a reason I was here, part of this movement. More than I had after speaking to Lizeth last night, more than I had by being a decoy during the protest earlier—I was convinced that I belonged here, too. Because I had something I could contribute, something I could never have done from a safe house in Colombia. Something, like Zero had said, that only I could do.

Sing anyway. Show them that you won't back down without a fight.

Around the room, others who were still awake sat up, and several of them sang along, their voices strengthening mine, carrying me through the refrain.

"Do I love you after all? The truth is..."

"I doooo," Geeta crooned, and everyone in the room laughed.

Zero met my eyes. I saw theirs were shining, like mine were. But they gave me a thumbs up and a grin.

The laughter in the room died down, and through the silence that followed came the sound of approaching helicopter blades. Loud. Close.

"The doctors?" Geeta's mother asked, the hope in her voice palpable.

"I'm sure it must be," I said. "I'll go check."

I hurried out into the hall, down toward the door to the first-floor terrace. The sound of the helicopter grew louder with each step. It *must* be the paramedics Mom had called for. It had to be. They'd said they'd send a copter as soon as one was available. They'd know how to help these people. They had to—

I flung the door open. Over the river, the sky was lightening, a greenish-blue in the predawn. Tuesday morning. Something was supposed to happen on Tuesday, wasn't it? My mind was being torn in so many directions, I couldn't...

I stepped out on the terrace and the thought fled from my mind. It didn't matter that it was Tuesday. And there would be no help. It was over.

A double-propellered transport copter emblazoned with the GSAF crest was touching down on the landing pad on the roof of the Kilby building, just across from Hamilton. Agents in tactical gear spilled out of the doors, rushing across the roof, down the stairs into the building.

In a facility as large as the AresTec campus, there were plenty of places to hide. It might take them a while to find us. But on this island, cut off from the mainland, with more agents stationed just on the other side of our barricade, there was nowhere to run. There'd be no evading Joseph Condor this time. We'd made it farther than anyone could have expected, but we were out of options now.

It was over.

GSAF had won.

PART NINE

IAMOS

S.C.D. 8378
10,942 B.C.E.

CHAPTER 55

- i s a a k -

I HATED THIS. I HATED JUST STANDING AROUND HERE, WAITING IN THE dark. I hated not knowing what was going on out there. I hated feeling so useless. I hated being separated from Nadin like this. Yeah, she wasn't alone—she was with Antos and Ceilos—but neither of them had exactly proven themselves reliable in the past. And I didn't like that she'd had to go off with Ceilos after what he'd done to her last night. It was bad enough that we'd been forced to bring him along to the ruins of Thalash'a, but having to be in close quarters with him now was bound to be painful for her.

I hated this. I hated all of it.

"How long do you think we're going to have to wait?" I asked. Antos had said they'd be back for us within an hour. It seemed like it had been more than that, but I had no way of knowing how much time had elapsed here in the dark like this. Maybe it just felt like it had been a long time because of my own impatience.

"I don't know, but I don't feel comfortable staying here much longer," Nikos said. "We need to get back to Katai'ios. They need to be apprised of what's going on here."

"We have to wait for Nadin," Gitrin insisted. "If we make a wrong move before they've succeeded in apprehending Tibros, we could jeopardize everything."

Nikos harrumphed gruffly, annoyed.

"Do you hear that?" Emil interrupted in English.

I frowned, listening. Over the sound of the rushing water pouring in from the fountain overhead, it sounded like...

"Yeah," I said. "Someone yelling?"

And footfalls. I could hear them now—heavy footfalls, irregular.

"I don't like this," Gitrin said. "It could be nothing, but..."

She trailed off as the voices got closer, sucked in her breath as she recognized one of them. A girl's voice.

No, please. Please...

"Isaak!" the voice cried out suddenly, and I knew it had to be her. Nadin. *Dammit!* They'd been caught! But how?

"Isaak, listen to me!" she screamed in English. "Ceilos is the Liberator! He's going to use the neurotoxin on the people in the future!"

"Silence!" a male voice bellowed in Iamoi. Nadin screamed again, and then her voice cut off abruptly. I sucked in my breath. Enforcers. It had to be.

"What's going on?" Gitrin whispered as the voices died out, as the footsteps faded away.

"What did she say?" Nikos asked. "Something about Ceilos?"

I struggled to get my breath, the tunnel seeming to swirl around me. Her words echoed over and over in my mind. He'd played us. He'd played us all like a torquing fiddle. "We've got to get out of here," I said. "Ceilos betrayed us again. Tibros isn't the Liberator—Ceilos is."

"What?" Nikos snapped.

"And he knows where we are," Gitrin said.

"We have to get out of these tunnels. Now," I said urgently. "Before he finds us." And then we had to try to find a way to stop him, and rescue Nadin, and get a warning to the future before the neurotoxin spread to my time, and...

"We have to get word out to the citidomes," Nikos said. "And to the rebellion. If Nadin's been captured, then—"

I swallowed hard, nodding.

If Nadin had been captured, then the plan to use the satellite postern network to move Hamos was dead in the water.

Which meant that if we didn't get both Iamos and Hamos evacuated before the rogue planetoid got into range...

Both worlds would be destroyed.

CHAPTER 56

- n a d i n -

MY VOICE WAS HOARSE FROM SCREAMING AS THEY DRAGGED ME INTO THE hospital level, my throat raw. But the important thing was that Isaak must have heard me. He *must* have heard me. I refused to accept the possibility that he might not have heard me, because the only alternative in that case was destruction.

He *had* to have heard me.

The Enforcers had closed off this entire floor, blockaded it to prevent entry by any unauthorized persons. I was certain the glass walls and sliding doors must be blackened for privacy, as they'd been months before when I'd found Isaak outside the dome and they'd brought him and me here to treat us for exposure. But that blackening was a System trick, just like everything else in this city. To me now, with no earpiece, the glass was perfectly clear, each room open and exposed. Most of the rooms were dim save for the blue phosphorescence embedded in the single rock wall of each, but I could see that the beds were taken up by figures that lay as still as death.

This wasn't a hospital. Not anymore. It had become a morgue.

Gerouin Melusin emerged from the second door on my left, one of the only illuminated rooms on this floor. Through the glass I could that two medics were in the room as well, bent over a body on a hospital bed; though their lack of reaction told me that the System was obscuring their view into the hallway. Melusin pushed the door swiftly closed behind her, leaving them there, taking in the sight before her with furrowed brows. Me, in my stained and torn bodysuit, the new growth of thick white curls on my head wild and bushy. My hands bound, an Enforcer gripping my upper arm tightly. Then her eyes tore away from me to the medics pushing past her, moving quickly. To the body on the gurney they rolled swiftly down the hallway, the angry red blisters around his mouth, on his fingertips.

When she saw her partner's body there on the gurney, his chest no longer rising and falling, his eyes staring vacantly up at the ceiling, Melusin's composure didn't waver.

It *shattered*.

The noise that tore out of my mother's throat was inhuman. The shriek was closer to the piercing hunting cry of a *gamada* than the voice I'd come to know her by, soft and cool as the dripping of water.

"What happened?" she demanded, her violet eyes still locked on Antos' body as the medics wheeled past her, not looking away until they'd disappeared into one of the rooms at the end of the hall.

"She shot him, *kyrin*. With this." The Enforcer extended the blaster that Ceilos had tossed carelessly at my feet before disappearing through the postern.

"It wasn't me!" I protested. "You have to listen to me, Melusin. I know who the Liberator—"

"Silence!" Melusin screeched. "I don't want to hear a single word out of her poisonous lips! You cover her mouth and you keep it covered, Enforcer, or mark me, you will live to regret it."

"Yes, *kyrin*," the Enforcer said, clamping his hand over my face. I struggled, jerking my head to and fro, but his grip was like iron.

"Your little rebellion is over, Nadin, do you understand me?" Melusin hissed. "I will not be letting you out of my sight again. Until the moment my heart stops, you will not leave my sight."

She hurried after the medics down the hall, and the Enforcer dragged me after her, past the rows of darkened rooms containing the bodies of dead *geroi*. Room after room of Ceilos' victims, each neatly assassinated one after another while he'd been on the back of a *gurza* riding the long route to Katai'ios. His protocol hadn't required any intervention on his part. Once he'd triggered it, it had done its job, killing one human being after another. All part of Ceilos' hideous plan to bring all of Iamos under his rule. *Our* rule. The mere thought of it made me want to vomit.

The *geroi* had been monsters. Ceilos had been right about that much, and I couldn't allow myself to forget it. But two wrongs did not make a right. And Ceilos' vengeance had extended to more than just the guilty parties, but to their *children* as well. That wasn't justice. Those children had done nothing except stand in his way. A means to an end, a means to ensure that no one could pose a threat to the legitimacy of his sole rule.

Except me. He hadn't counted on that much. I could still stop him. But imprisoned like this, I just couldn't see *how*.

As the Enforcer pulled me into the room on the end, I saw the medics had attached a cranial scanner to Antos' head, that there was an inhalator over his face. They were trying, desperately now, to restart his heart. But it was too late. I knew it was. He'd still been alive when we left the *geroi*'s villa, but his breathing had since stopped. There had never been any hope—I'd known that. There'd been no saving him. Though the burst of electricity had not been a direct hit to his heart, preventing an instant death, the damage to his organs would have been too intense for him to survive.

But still, they tried. Because to stop now would be admitting defeat. Admitting that they'd lost one more *geroi*.

Melusin was standing over his prone form, her face contorted into a grimace. She watched as the medics worked for another fruitless minute. Wordlessly, she reached under the cranial scanner, closing his eyelids with her hand. Then she squeezed her own eyes shut, exhaling.

"Blue eyes," she said quietly. She turned, looking directly at me. The Enforcer still kept his hand clamped over my mouth preventing me from responding.

"Antos grew up in this citidome," she said to me. "He was the first *geros* in three generations to take over the city ruled by his parents. You knew that. But maybe you didn't know what that did to him. His father died young for a *geros*. An accident while outside the citidome walls, while pursuing one of your precious rebels, trying to root out their lair." Her voice was laced with venom. "After he died, his partner, Antos' mother, stepped down. As is the law for *geroi* who are too aged for a repartnership, who are beyond childbearing years."

I stared at Antos' prone body, the medics still working dauntlessly to revive him. If they heard what Melusin was saying to me now, they didn't react. Maybe she was using the System to block our words from their ears. Or maybe they were so used to deferring to the *geroi* in all things that they'd learned to stop listening on their own.

"You know what the people are told when one of the *geroi* steps down. That they are resettled in another citidome, a member of the *patroi* caste, and they disappear quietly from public life. But that isn't the truth." She stared at me, unflinching. Unblinking. "When one partner dies, the other is euthanized. So as not to be a burden on our resources. For the good of Iamos."

I struggled to swallow with the Enforcer's hand clamped over my mouth. I didn't know how to react to this information. Didn't know how she *wanted* me to react.

"It *broke* Antos," Melusin said, her lip curled almost into a sneer. "He and I had been living here, in Hope Renewed. Our final year before our *enilikii*. He changed after that. We aren't supposed to have familial ties, aren't supposed to favor our parents or our children. All lives are one. But Antos couldn't help himself. He was too soft."

I wanted to look away, but in the Enforcer's grip I couldn't move, couldn't even turn my head. *Soft?* I could not reconcile Melusin's vision of Antos as a soft man with my lived experience of him as nothing but a hard one.

The geroi are warped. That's how they are.

Melusin sighed, glancing over her shoulder at Antos' body once more. "All your life, you've sought my approval. I always considered it a bit of an irony. If you'd sought Antos', he'd have given it in a heartbeat." She gestured to the Enforcer holding me. "You're dismissed," she told him.

He hesitated for a surprised moment, then released his grip on me, inclining his head to Melusin and placing three fingers across his brow. "*Kyrin*," he said.

My mother held my gaze until the man had disappeared from the room, the door sliding closed behind him.

"I didn't kill him," I finally said, quietly but firmly.

Melusin didn't respond for a long moment. In the silence, there was nothing but the sound of the two medics' breathing, of the mechanical noises of the inhalator vainly trying to inject oxygen into *Geros* Antos' dead lungs.

"I never believed you did," Melusin said. "You don't have it in you. You're just like your father. Soft."

CHAPTER 57

- i s a a k -

WE RODE THE GURZAS HARD ALL THE WAY BACK TO KATAI'IOS. WE DIDN'T bother with the route through Gale Crater this time—there was no need to take the long way around now. We cut directly across the dried bay, straight up into the Hesperia Plains, Kodo, Tuupa, and Thork thundering through the dust. It had been well after nightfall when we'd left Hope Renewed, and the too-bright star in the sky, the dwarf planet, had loomed over us the whole ride, spurring us on. We reached Katai'ios shortly after sunrise. I couldn't help but notice, though I tried not to call attention to it, that the star was visible even during the daylight hours now.

Closer. Ever closer.

"We must call a forum," Nikos said, his breath short as he dismounted Kodo. "The others must know everything. I acted on my own before, and that was a foolish mistake that could have cost us everything."

"You couldn't have known," I told him, pausing to help Gitrin and then Emil off Thork's back.

"I was afraid the group would make a mistake," Nikos muttered, as if he hadn't heard me. "That they would behave in a prejudiced way, as their parents and grandparents had toward Marin thirty years ago, and it would cost us the life of someone valuable. And instead I played directly into the hands of a traitor."

"Nikos," Gitrin said, louder and more firmly than I'd spoken. He glanced at her, seeming to snap back to reality. "You mustn't blame yourself. Ceilos is a master of manipulation. He has been from the time he was a child. What's important now is that we resolve this."

He exhaled. "You're right. We have to evacuate our people—"

"And the people in the citidomes," Gitrin added. Nikos tugged his earlobe.

"More importantly, we have to find a way to deflect that planetoid," Emil said gruffly. "If we can't correct the position of the planets before the impact wipes out both Mars and Venus, it won't matter how many people we evacuate. The universe will rip itself apart."

"We have to get Nadin away from the Enforcers," I said emphatically. "And somehow we have to get access to the System and reprogram those satellites to form the space postern network."

"First matters first," Nikos said. "We call a forum, and we begin evacuation. I will tell the people of your successful mission to the future, and that the time has come for us to leave this place."

I winced. *Our successful mission to the future.* Our mission had been anything but successful. I'd been bluffing night before last, and my bluff hadn't paid off. I'd made them a promise with greater confidence than I actually had. The truth was, I didn't know what was going to be waiting for us when we returned to Mars. Things had been bordering on disastrous when I'd left. Joseph Condor had taken over the governorship and practically instituted a dictatorship. GSAF had made it abundantly clear that the Iamoi wouldn't be welcome. And we'd gotten that note, "Be careful of anyone with Nano."

"The thing is," I began hesitantly, "I'm not so sure now… that going to the future is a good idea."

"What? But Isaak, you said—" Nikos protested.

"The girl yelled something to Contreras in English," Emil broke in. "She said that Ceilos had sent the neurotoxin to the future. That changes things."

Nikos growled thoughtfully. "We know now that the so-called neurotoxin is a System protocol. None of our people will have earpieces, and we can warn those from the citidome that they must leave their earpieces behind."

"Yeah, but…" I frowned. *The System is online. Be careful of anyone with Nano.* "I don't want to send people forward blindly without knowing what the situation is. I'd figured we'd have time to send another test party…"

"But we do have time," Emil said.

"There is no time now," Nikos protested. "The rogue planetoid draws closer by the hour."

"There is no time *now*," Emil repeated. "But we'll have time in the future, just like how Contreras only left us in Elytherios for three minutes but was gone for two months."

"He has a valid point," Gitrin said.

I felt like the floor was dropping out from under me. Who *knew* how long it would take to secure the future so that it would be safe for the Iamoi? If I left now, I could be gone for months—all the while, with Nadin trapped here, arrested by Enforcers, at the whims of whichever *geroi* now remained—and Ceilos—the Liberator—

"I can't leave now, Emil," I said emphatically. "I have to help Nadin."

"Who says it has to be you?" Emil scoffed. "What, do you think I'm incapable of doing my part?"

I blinked. "You'd go, Emil?"

"I will go with him," Gitrin said. "We will check on the situation, make sure it's safe. When we return, we can open a stable postern connection and evacuate our people."

I stared at the two of them. I hated to send them forward into an unknown future, but by the same token, I couldn't leave now.

"It's settled," Nikos said before I could respond. "Make the arrangements. And I will call a forum. Come, Isaak," he said, looking at me. "Stable the *gurzas*, and then meet me at the longhouses. There's no time to waste."

Gitrin and Emil were still working on their key when we left, using Henry's coordinates and programming a return time for themselves of two minutes after their departure time. But we didn't have time to wait for them. We didn't have another minute to lose. We'd held the forum, and the rebels of Katai'ios were in agreement: The only way we had a chance of deflecting the impact in time was to take matters into our own hands. Ceilos had nearly bested us. He'd succeeded in killing off most of the *geroi*, and when the last one fell, he'd be poised to take over—unless we got out ahead of him. The power of the Enforcers was in the System.

Likewise, Ceilos' power was in the System. The only way to break their hold on the citidomes was by removing that power.

We had to get the people off the System.

The runners quickly mobilized. A small contingent moved out to the other outposts, warning the remaining Elytherioi and calling the runners into action in the citidomes. The rest of the citizens began gathering their personal effects and as many supplies as they could carry. Whatever they could bring would be coming with them to the future. Even in the best of circumstances—even if, through some miracle of God, Emil and Gitrin returned with the news that it was safe for the Iamoi to come forward to Mars—adding an extra eight million people, as Nadin had estimated the current population of Iamos to be, would be an impossible strain on the resources of our colonized world. The harvest we'd just completed in Katai'ios wouldn't go to waste. That food would help sustain the people in the new world.

As for me, I'd be joining the runners. I wasn't going to leave Nadin—and this time, Shuliin agreed with me.

"They won't keep her in Hope Renewed," she said, slinging the straps of her rucksack over her shoulders. "Our intelligence stated that the remaining *geroi*—whoever's left of them—had congregated in Bright Horizon. This is where Tibros was administering all the citidomes from. He may not be the so-called Liberator, but Tibros is still a threat. And we can be certain that the Enforcers will be bringing Nadin to him."

"So we have to manage to find her, get her away from Tibros, figure out a way to access the System and program the space posterns, and do all of that while staying one step ahead of Ceilos, who could be pretty much anywhere in any time period at this moment," I said.

"Sound easy," Syrin said, hurrying over to join us. I noticed she also had a pack strapped to her back.

"*Yachin*, what are you doing?" Shuliin asked. "You should be helping the others prepare for evacuation."

"Not this time," Syrin said firmly. "Do you think I could leave Iamos without knowing whether you're safe? What would I do if I reached the future and found that you're not there? That you never arrive?"

"It's too dangerous—" Shuliin began, but Syrin cut her off.

"No. Wherever you go, I'm going."

Shuliin stared at her for a long minute, her blue eyes sharp. But finally, she sighed and tugged her earlobe.

"All right," she said. "We will mobilize our network in Bright Horizon. And then we take to the streets. This isn't about staying hidden. Not anymore."

Syrin took Shuliin's hand and squeezed it. "No more running. No more operating in the shadows. The time has come for us to fight."

CHAPTER 58

WE DID NOT REMAIN IN HOPE RENEWED. IT HAD BECOME, AS MELUSIN informed me, a place for the dead.

The bodies of all the deceased *geroi*, and all the *geroi*'s blood who'd become victims by virtue not of their actions but of their lineage, had been brought here, as I'd suspected when I first entered the hospital level. Heros and his team were running System scans on them, searching for any sign, *anything* that could explain their mysterious deaths. But they would never find anything. Not while they were relying on the System. It would be hidden from them, just like the rogue planetoid drawing ever closer to Hamos was invisible to their eyes.

Those who were still living, those who still had hope, had remained in Bright Horizon, where Heros was trying new System protocols and any other type of curative he could develop. But each had failed, one by one. His latest failure was the reason why Melusin had been in the hospital level at the time of my father's murder in the first place: escorting the bodies of *Geros* Ilios and *Gerouin* Alusin to their resting place among the other fallen *geroi*.

Only two *geroi* remained now: Melusin and Tibros. Ceilos had nearly won. But there was still a slim chance, and it was a chance we had to take. "I will not just lie down and die," Melusin had said when I'd told her the truth of what had happened to Antos, the truth about the toxin.

She'd removed her earpiece. I could see on her face the pain it had caused her, was still causing her. The sweat on her forehead, the way her eyes periodically lost their focus for a moment. But she continued undaunted, not letting her poise waver even for a moment. Her face held the same cool detachment as it had held the day she gave me my assignment in the villa in Hope Renewed, to spy on Isaak in exchange for a chance at a reevaluation. A chance to become a *gerouin* like her. The same cool detachment it had held when I saw her standing on the other side of the postern in Elytherios and learned that Ceilos had betrayed us.

The same cool detachment as it had held when she withdrew the flail from the carved wooden chest and said, "Unity through fidelity," before beating me bloody.

I flinched at the memory, inhaling deeply, squeezing my eyes closed. I could not think about this now. There was never to be forgiveness between us. There could not be. But we had a common enemy, and I was in desperate need of allies. The alternative was the destruction of the universe.

Now, all that mattered was that we had to warn Tibros. With only two *geroi* remaining, we needed him on our side. So, putting my feelings aside, I followed Melusin through the postern to Bright Horizon.

We emerged in the same chamber that Ceilos and I had used when we escaped from the pyramid weeks before. The sight of it made me antsy. I did not know where Ceilos had disappeared to when he left me in Antos' and Melusin's villa. He could be anywhere. He could be here now, hiding just out of sight, in the tunnels beneath the floor, behind the walls. Watching us. I didn't know what he planned next, but I knew that he was going to try to stop us.

"Tibros has holed himself up in the *gerotus* chamber," Melusin said, her voice echoing through the cold, dim hallways of the pyramid. "It's the only place he thinks is safe from the poison. No one can enter save those with *geroi* DNA."

"But Ceilos has *geroi* DNA," I said anxiously.

She tugged her earlobe. "But I don't believe he will try to enter the *gerotus* chamber. Not yet, at least. Not while Tibros is still connected to the System. His neurotoxin protocol is a far more efficient way to kill."

My palms were sweaty by the time we reached the door to the *gerotus* chamber, my stomach roiling with nausea at the thought of entering that room again. My shoulders, though healed by now, cried out with the memory of pain as Melusin removed her medallion and held it to the door, as it registered her genetic signature and slid open.

Tibros sat at the circular table, surrounded by empty chairs. All that remained of the *geroi*. He was in a sorry state. His silver bodysuit was disheveled, stained, unbuttoned at the collar. It appeared as though he hadn't changed it in days, nor had he bathed himself in some time. His rust-colored hair was falling out of its once tidy braids in messy tendrils.

"There you are," he snapped when he saw Melusin. "Where have you been? You disappeared off the System tracker over an hour ago, and Antos hours before that. What have the two of you been playing at?"

"Antos is dead," Melusin said, all hint of the emotion that had ripped out of her when she'd seen his dying body gone as if it had never been.

Tibros spat out a curse. "The toxin?"

"Not this time." She looked over her shoulder, beckoning me into the room. Slowly, as if my feet were weighted down by stones, I moved forward into the chamber.

"You," Tibros growled. At the sight of me, he leapt to his feet, knocking the chair he'd been sitting in to the floor with a clatter that echoed off the domed ceiling, making me wince. "You've caught her, then. Murderer. Treacherous *anguis!*"

"Nadin is not responsible," Melusin said.

Tibros scoffed loudly, shrilly. "No, perhaps not directly. But the rebels—"

"The murderer is your son." Melusin's voice was sharp, uncharacteristically loud.

Tibros gawked at her in disbelief. "Impossible."

"It's true, *kyrios*," I said. "The toxin is a System protocol developed by Ceilos. It's imperative that you remove your earpiece—"

Tibros cut me off with another bark of derisive laughter. "Do you think me a fool? If I disconnect from the System, it will be all the easier for the rebels to eliminate me."

"There is no possible way for the rebels to reach you here within this chamber," Melusin said. "But if you remain on the System, then you guarantee your own demise. The toxin is a System protocol. Ceilos is the murderer. Think rationally, Tibros, for once in your life. Clodin was the first victim. And you will be the last."

"Clodin died from her injuries in the earthquake," Tibros protested.

"An earthquake that you were unprepared for," I argued. "Because the early warning protocol was sabotaged. *Ceilos* sabotaged it. He wanted to hurt you. He wanted to destroy the *geroi* as a whole, but more than anything, he wanted to hurt you." *The way you hurt him. Blood for blood.*

Blood.

"I will not stand here any longer listening to this *nonsense*," Tibros roared. Blood began pouring from his nose as he shouted. It streamed out of his right nostril, dripping down onto the bodysuit, staining it crimson. I'd heard Melusin say that Paolin's nose had been bloody, and that was also how it had started with Shiros—

The neurotoxin.

"Melusin, this girl has played you for a fool, the way she always has," Tibros was yelling, not even reacting to the flow of blood dripping down his face. "But I won't stand for it any longer." He raised his hand to his earpiece. What he planned to do, I could not say—just then, Melusin threw the door to the chamber open once more.

"Call for Heros," she barked to the Enforcers on the other side. "Tell him to have a sedative at the ready. In the meantime, remove *Geros* Tibros' earpiece immediately. We may still be early enough for his body to recover on its own."

Enforcers flooded into the chamber. Tibros shouted, protested, grabbed for his earpiece, fought the Enforcers desperately in a bid to keep it. Blood sprayed across the table as he frantically struggled, then fell, slumped, as one of the Enforcers managed to pull the device from his ear.

Melusin watched as they dragged Tibros away, her expression unreadable as her eyes flicked over the blood-streaked table, the upended chair on the floor.

"Do you think they got him off the System in time?" I asked, my voice sounding loud to my ears in the quiet left behind after the struggle.

"I don't know," said Melusin. "I don't know how this protocol operates, or how much damage it inflicts upon the body's nervous system before symptoms begin to show. I don't know if that damage is reversible once the protocol is disconnected. And I can tell from my own body's reaction to removing my earpiece that his immune system will be weakened without the System. Only time will tell, I suppose."

She turned briskly, striding out the door. "But time is something we don't have. We have two million people to evacuate from Hamos, and a satellite network to reprogram."

"But, *Gerouin*, how are we going to program the satellite network into a postern if you can't connect to the System?" I asked.

"We'll have to interface directly with the satellite network's control panel," Melusin said. "On Hamos."

She led me down the hallway to the *geroi*'s office, the room I'd heard her and Antos speaking to Tibros and Paolin in before. With another flick of her medallion, the door slid open. "We'd best be prepared—" she began, but broke off midsentence.

"*Gerouin?*" I asked in confusion. I followed her gaze and saw she was staring at an open panel on the wall. I could see that when this panel was closed, it would blend seamlessly with the marble wall; but open, it revealed a small cupboard, just large enough to hold a small rack that glowed with a flickering blue light. Some kind of charging station.

Then I realized what the rack held.

A pulse blaster. Like the one that Antos had carried earlier. The one that Ceilos had shot him with, and then tossed to the ground at my feet, attempting to frame me for murder. But though there was only one weapon charging on the rack, I could see, clearly, an empty slot where a second should have been.

"He's been here," Melusin growled.

Someone had taken the other blaster.

CHAPTER 59

- i s a a k -

THE CITIDOME HAD ERUPTED INTO PANDEMONIUM.

There wasn't time to go about this in a dignified manner. That much was obvious. With almost all the *geroi* dead, with Nadin betrayed and likely held prisoner within the pyramid, and with a cold-blooded murderer doing his damnedest to bring about the end of the universe, it wasn't just that we didn't have time to play nice—it was that our best chance for survival was to incite utter chaos. Distracted Enforcers meant the odds of getting into the pyramid and finding Nadin would be higher. And most of all, it meant that no Iamoi would be caught unawares. We couldn't risk anyone being left behind. This was going to be a one-way journey. We needed everyone to know about it.

Which meant that we didn't exactly go about informing the populace tactfully. Our method of information dissemination was yelling in the marketplace like street proselytizers shouting about Armageddon and eternal damnation. Only this time, the threat was not the byproduct of an overactive imagination. It was all too real.

Syrin stood at the end of a row of street vendors, calling, "Take out your earpieces!"

Eliin, who'd abandoned her outpost in the sandstone caves and hurried to Bright Horizon as soon as the news had reached her, stopped a caretaker leading a group of children through the square. "This is urgent," she begged. "Please, you must listen."

Shuliin, whose powerful voice had incited a riot in Hope Renewed on my second day on Iamos, clambered to the top of a stone postern that pumped water into the public fountain in the middle of the plaza. She cupped her hands around her mouth and bellowed, "The early warning protocol has been sabotaged! We are all in danger! Take out your earpieces and look to the sky!"

At first, everyone just stared at us in bewilderment and mild annoyance.

That is, until the first person tried it.

"*Yadlag!*" they screeched, pointing up through the blue glass of the dome. The haze from the eruption of the Sios Ifaisteos had long since evaporated, and the sky was clear. Even now, even in the day, you could see it. There was no escaping it anymore. You could see it.

It was the end of the world.

And the people reacted accordingly.

CHAPTER 60

- n a d i n -

MELUSIN TURNED ON HER HEEL AND RAN. I HAD NEVER SEEN MY MOTHER move this quickly, and I knew, deep in the pit of my stomach, that there was a reason for her haste, and it was bound to be bad. I paused for just an instant, staring at the second pulse blaster still on the rack. Impulsively, I grabbed it, and then I ran after Melusin as fast as I could keep up.

She took the elevator leading from the pyramid down to the levels of the *esotoi*, where, as in Hope Renewed, the hospital of Bright Horizon was located. It took only a few minutes for us to reach our destination, but we were still too late. Through the clear glass walls—unobscured to our System-free eyes as the glass in Hope Renewed had been to me last night—I could see it was too late. Melusin flung open the third door on the right. Tibros lay motionless on the bed, as still as if he were asleep. But instantly I could see that the *geros* was not sleeping.

Because slumped over the top of him lay another body.

Medic *Heros*.

Melusin raced over to the bed, turning Heros over. As Antos' had been, Heros' lips were red, scorched with burn marks, and his fingertips matched. On the bed, Tibros' still body displayed the same symptoms.

"Are they...?" I breathed.

Melusin tugged her earlobe grimly. "They're dead."

My heartbeat staggered erratically. *He's here.* Ceilos was here. He was following us. He knew what we were doing. How would we have any hope of programming the posterns to move Hamos? He had control of

489

the System. He was following our every move, unseen. He'd always been one step ahead of us. There was no reason to think that would ever change. He'd won. Everything we were doing to try to stop him was futile.

"We have to leave for Hamos immediately," Melusin said.

"But, *gerouin*, Ceilos is still out there," I protested. "He's got a weapon. How can we—"

"I am not going to give in to him," Melusin snapped. "Until I draw my last breath, I will carry on." She looked at me, unflinching, but her tone softened. "We will continue with the plan to evacuate Hamos. We will not just sit around and wait for Ceilos to murder us."

"*Kyrin!*" I jumped at the new voice, whirling as an Enforcer hurried into the room. He took in the sight before him, aghast.

"Where were you?" Melusin demanded. "Why were there no Enforcers watching the *geros*?"

"*Kyrin*, there is an emergency in the citidome. All Enforcers were called to the upper levels," the man said. "The rebels are leading the *plivoi* in an uprising."

I sucked in my breath. *The rebels.* The Elytherioi. Had Isaak heard me, then? Had he managed to warn them?

"I have no time to deal with that," Melusin said. "Nadin and I must leave for Hamos at once."

"But, *kyrin*, the people are removing their earpieces. We cannot use the adherence protocol—"

"Then figure something else out."

The man sighed. "Yes, *kyrin*."

"In the meantime, I must coordinate an evacuation," Melusin said. "Tell your forces to prepare for incoming refugees from Hamos."

"Refugees from Hamos? *Now?*" the Enforcer protested. "How many?"

"We're evacuating the entire planet within the next six hours," Melusin told him.

"*Kyrin*, we cannot deal with this and the uprising together," exclaimed the Enforcer.

"You're going to have to make it work," Melusin said. "We're out of time and out of options." She looked at me. "Did you bring the pulse blaster?" she asked.

I held it up anxiously.

"Good," she said. "Hold on to it. Don't let it out of your grasp for even a moment." She effortlessly smoothed a strand of white-blond hair back into its braid. Dignified as ever, even at the end of the world.

"Come now," she said. "We have no time to waste."

Chapter 61

- i s a a k -

SOMETHING THAT HAD BECOME PAINFULLY, FRUSTRATINGLY CLEAR TO ME IN the midst of all this was that Ceilos had been right. It was disgusting to even think such a thing, but there was no denying it. He'd been right. All it would have taken to overthrow the *geroi* would have been for everyone to remove their earpieces. Maybe things had been different before, in the early days when technology like the *tiraks* and pulse blasters were commonplace. But now, the only weapon the Enforcers had to use against them was the System. Without the System, the Enforcers had no power over them.

The riot had spun out of control. The Enforcers were powerless to stop it, but I quickly realized that so were we. *Plivoi* were desperately trying to break into the underground levels, swarming the entrances, using makeshift battering rams to try to break down the barriers the Enforcers had erected. To my left, a blinding flash of light caught my eye. I whirled just in time to see one of the giant vehicle posterns illuminate and then fall dark. In a split second, a chain of people, clinging tightly to each other, had disappeared into the void.

"Where did those people go?" I demanded of a man beside me in the crowd.

"To Simos!" he replied. "If someone can get their hands on another key, I'm going with them! Better to take our chances with the natives than to die here!"

I stared at him, aghast. Atlanteans. Fleeing the cataclysm, the destruction of their great civilization. What was that old quote from

Plato? "*In a single day and night of misfortune...*"

"Isaak, look!" Shuliin shouted over the din, jarring me back to reality. "The pyramid!"

Sure enough, the Enforcers who had been guarding the entrance had been driven back by the crowd. Waves of people burst in through the opening in the glass, streaming toward the elevators that led down into the lower levels.

I couldn't worry about the people who had disappeared through the postern now. I had one job, and I had to remain focused on it.

"Go!" Shuliin called, waving me toward the pyramid.

Without hesitation, I raced forward, propelled by the crowd. Into the stepped pyramid, through its glass doors and into its hidden core of thick white marble. Into the domain of the *geroi*, and whatever else was hiding behind these walls. But unlike the rest of the *plivoi*, I didn't head for the entrances to the underground. I didn't need to go down. I needed to go up—to the levels where the prisoners were kept.

I had to find Nadin before it was too late.

CHAPTER 62

- n a d i n -

I HAD NEVER SEEN HAMOS BEFORE. TRUE, I'D SEEN RECORDINGS OF IT through the System, but that was nothing like actually *being* here. Something in me always wanted to see things with my own eyes. Not through the filter of blue glass, not through the artificial eyes of the System. It was what had led me outside the dome on that day, my *enilikin*. The day I'd met Isaak. The day everything changed.

Now I was seeing Hamos with my own eyes for the first time, and for what would undoubtedly be the last, too.

Its golden clouds, its landscapes of molten rock. Terraformation efforts had done little to make the atmosphere less toxic, but the tight seal of the citidomes had offered protection for the people who lived here. It had been a poor substitute for Iamos, but for a brief, idealistic time, we'd believed we could make it work.

Of course, that had always been a fantasy.

Melusin had ordered the citidomes evacuated, the two cities of Ascendant Dawn and Courageous Sky. And then we'd retreated here. To watch, and wait.

From this vantage point, I could see the dome of Courageous Sky. The glass had seemed green in the afternoon light. By evening, it had shifted to a pinkish hue. Strange how the colors behaved differently here.

We were outside the cities, in the System relay station. This had been one of the first buildings constructed on Hamos, a beacon that allowed it to communicate with the System more quickly, with less interference from Hamos' magnetic field. The relay station was elevated on a tower, at a height that raised it above the nearby mountains, giving it a clear signal to both cities on the planet. The lower levels of the station housed the many working components, the so-called mainframe that Henry had spoken of when he told me of his time decoding the System. On the top level, a bank of analog monitors and System controls reached waist-high around the whole of the single room, and above these, windows gave us a clear view of the planet around us.

Melusin had been working diligently at the console, long hours passing in silence. As a *gerouin*, she had full, unrestricted access to the System. At least, as unrestricted as she could manage with Ceilos' tricks at play. The System still refused to recognize the existence of the dwarf planet, which meant we were operating blind. "I'm no System expert," she said. "But my best subject was always calculations. Figures. This much I can do."

While the Enforcers in the cities had evacuated the populace, Melusin had worked on her figures. She'd visually calculated the position of the dwarf planet, brightly glowing even through the thick cloud cover on Hamos. From there, she'd worked out the position the satellites would need to take in order to fully encircle Hamos. She'd calculated how close the planetoid needed to be in order to be trapped, pulled into the postern by Hamos' gravity. And finally, she'd calculated when she needed to activate the postern by visually determining the planetoid's azimuth.

As she worked on these calculations, I monitored the System's life readings on the planet. Slowly, the numbers had ticked down. It had taken hours for the Enforcers to clear the cities, hours for Melusin to run her calculations. The sun had set, turning the golden clouds to a deep bloody hue. The relay station had grown dark along with the sky, the only lights in here coming from the screens of the consoles around us. As always, the need to conserve resources outweighed the need for artificial lighting, and this station was never meant to be manned.

My nerves crawled within me. Ceilos had to have known what we were doing. He had to have heard us. He'd managed to assassinate Tibros and Heros in just the few minutes we'd been away from them. He'd been following me, I knew it. But he'd had yet to appear on Hamos.

There had been no reported incidents in the evacuation, no further mysterious deaths. Had he had a change of heart? Or was he simply biding his time? As the hours passed, my nerves grew ever more taut. I couldn't escape the sensation that he was here, right now. Watching me.

Melusin exhaled, rubbing the bridge of her nose between her fingers. The light through the windows cast a deep crimson glow across her face. "It's almost time," she murmured. "What's our evacuation status?"

"The System shows twenty lifeforms remaining between the two cities," I said. "The Enforcers are checking for any last stragglers that may remain."

Melusin tugged her earlobe, sighed again, leaned back in her chair and closed her eyes. "Of all the things I envisioned for my life, this certainly was not one of them. A cataclysm eradicating our planet, tearing everything we'd ever worked for apart. The *geroi* destroyed. My world in tatters at my feet." She paused, then added softly, "My partner and both my parents dead in the span of a single day. Without even a moment to spare to grieve any of them."

I frowned, unsure of how to respond. Melusin had never expressed candor with me before. A year ago, I would have been honored beyond words at this woman I'd strived so hard to emulate my entire life speaking to me like an equal. But now all I felt was wary unease.

She opened her eyes, sitting up and looking at me. "Your partnership with Ceilos was supposed to mark a beginning. A new generation for Iamos. Even as our world was ending, there was hope for a new beginning."

"On Simos?" I asked quietly. I knew the answer. The *geroi*'s plan for eliminating the perceived threat of the humans who already lived on Simos. The neurotoxin. Little had they known it wasn't the Simoi they needed to fear. The true threat had come from within.

Melusin tugged her earlobe. "A new world for all of us. And new *geroi*. It would have been your time soon. A new partnership was expected to be born by next summer. It should have been your daughter with Ceilos, partnered with Shiros' and Paolin's son."

My stomach, already tight with nerves, now curdled. The thought of it—the thought that I would have been expected to bear a child before my next annual—was like a punch to the gut. This hadn't even occurred to me, I realized with a jolt. How had it never occurred to me? How single-minded I'd been in my desperation to pass my evaluation. I had never truly thought about what would happen after I became a *gerouin*. It always seemed like an ending point: I would reach it, and my parents would finally respect me and treat me as an equal. What happened after that point was something I had never cared to envision. Maybe, subconsciously, I'd dreaded it so much that I'd blocked it from my mind. Or maybe I was just naive.

It had been on Ceilos' mind. That much had been obvious since that night in Gitrin's classroom. But I knew now I could never have brought myself to it. I could never have faked it to fit in. No matter how desperately I wanted to be accepted by the *geroi*, sooner or later I would have been revealed for the fraud that I was.

Oblivious to my discomfort, Melusin chuckled softly. She was still caught in her own reverie. "Even though the familial ties would have been severed upon your initiation, I have to confess..." She smiled, her eyes unfocused. "I was secretly looking forward to seeing my granddaughter."

I stared at her for a long moment, struggling to see her features in the dark, suddenly recalling the resemblance between *Gerouin* Alusin and the woman before me. Despite the genetic manipulation Melusin had undergone, altering her appearance, that resemblance was still there. Mother and child. Undeniable. How much of Melusin's face was on mine? How much of Alusin, of Melusin, would have been in that hypothetical granddaughter that Melusin was now envisioning?

Once, I'd wanted nothing more than to be just like her. Now I hoped that there wasn't a single drop of her within me.

"Melusin," I said at last, breaking the silence. I squeezed my hand shut, feeling the irregular stones of the ring Isaak had made me dig into my skin. "I need to tell you something. When I was in the future, I learned something about myself." I swallowed, remembering Ceilos' rage, his white-hot fury. His denial. His insistence that I was lying. His refusal to believe the truth. "I am asexual."

In the reflected light of the console screen, I saw her furrow her brows, looking at me in confusion. I explained. Once again. I told her what I'd told Ceilos. I stumbled over the words, trying to find a way to define it in our language. I wondered how many times I would have to do this. Would this be the last? Would the rogue planetoid ensure I would never have a need? Or would we survive, only for me to have to go through this over and over again, explaining and educating and enduring question after intrusive question?

When I had finished explaining, Melusin sat quietly for a long moment. I braced myself for the anger Ceilos had shown, or perhaps for denial.

But finally, she just sighed, and I realized she was going to give me something new. Disappointment.

"I should have suspected," she said, sounding resigned. "You were always different, Nadin. In more ways than one."

It was quiet for a long moment, the two of us trying to process each other's words. In the silence, the *beep* from the console was loud, unmistakable. I looked down.

"A new lifeform," I said. The Enforcers were gone from the citidomes. There had been only two blips on the screen moments before. Now there were three. Fresh adrenaline coursed through my veins as I saw the coordinates for the third lifeform. "It's here. In the relay station."

He was here.

Ceilos was here.

There was no escape.

Melusin jumped to her feet, leaning over my shoulder, swiping the screen a few times to display the lifeform's exact position. "On level three," she said.

"Don't go," I said.

"No," Melusin said. "I won't just cower here waiting for my fate. I will meet him head on."

"*Gerouin*, please," I begged, rising from my chair after her. My voice was shaking.

"Lock the door and hold on to the pulse blaster. Don't be afraid to use it," she said, disappearing into the stairwell.

I squeezed my eyes shut, struggling to swallow. I didn't move, didn't bother to lock the door after her. It was hopeless. I already knew it. I already knew where Ceilos was, and it wasn't on level three. I knew Ceilos and his tricks too well.

And I'd already heard him breathing.

"Nadin."

I opened my eyes.

He was here.

"You know, I thought you were going to make this harder for me," Ceilos said, stepping out of the shadows. I didn't know how long he'd been here, lurking in the darkness. Had he heard what I'd said to Melusin? Had it kindled his fury once again? I gripped the blaster tightly, my knuckles aching, my hands sweating as I raised it, aiming it at him. At his chest. A *direct hit to the heart.* An instant kill. Not a painful, protracted process like what Antos had endured.

"Did you think I wasn't going to realize what your plan was?" he asked. "Melusin knew that without the System, the only way I would be able to reach her was in person. She thought she'd laid the perfect trap for me, locking yourselves in here and monitoring for vital signals. But you should have remembered that I could mask those, Nadin. You should have known that I could trick Melusin as easily as the rest of the *geroi.* So easy to fool a mind reliant on the System."

He cocked his head at me, a silhouette in the darkness. He was looking at the blaster, undoubtedly noticing the way that my hands shook as I pointed it toward him. "Or did you think it was simply a matter of you shooting me first? But you won't shoot me, Nadin. I know you. You don't have it in you. You won't shoot me."

"Don't come any closer," I said. My voice shook as hard as my hands.

"Nadin," Ceilos implored. "We can still fix this. You and me together. We can make this go away. We can save the universe. Move the site of the impact. We'll be heroes. We can lead our people to the future together. We can even ensure our people are always safe. I'll let GSAF know I've got the cure for the neurotoxin and they'll be only too glad to cooperate."

My hands wavered, ever so slightly. I knew I shouldn't believe a word he was saying, yet I still found myself murmuring, "There's a cure?"

He chuckled. "Of course there's a cure. You don't think I'd initiate a protocol like this without a way to reverse it? Too many opportunities for error there." He took a step forward, splaying his hands placatingly. "I'll give it to you, Nadin. I'll give you the cure. I'll give you anything you ask for. Just come with me."

"I can't, Ceilos."

Another step forward.

"But you're not pulling the trigger," he pointed out.

I *needed* to pull the trigger. For all the lives he'd destroyed on Iamos, all the lives he planned to destroy. I knew he had no intention of stopping this cataclysm. Even if I promised to go with him right now, I would never be able to live up to the fantasy version of myself he'd built up in his head. His jealousy would always win out. And he knew, now. The way to get his revenge. As long as Ceilos was still breathing, he'd always have a way to get his revenge. I needed to pull the trigger.

But I couldn't. No matter how hard I tried, I just could not do it.

He took another step. Too close. He could take the weapon from me now, and then...

I didn't see her until it was too late to react. Another figure melting out from the shadows, with a weapon of her own. Not a pulse blaster. There'd been only one remaining, and I had it. So Melusin had brought something else with her. Something more ancient, but just as deadly.

A bronze dagger, withdrawn from the ceremonial chest in the *gerotus* chamber before we'd left Bright Horizon. Because she'd always known I'd be too soft to do what I needed to do.

The blade slid between Ceilos' ribs with a sickening wet *shwip*. I don't know why I expected such a brutal act to be noisy, brash. Not so *quiet* in its utter deadliness.

Ceilos' breath was driven out of him in a gurgling gasp. Behind him, Melusin grunted as she withdrew the blade.

Ceilos crumpled at my feet.

I dropped to my knees, the pulse blaster falling out of my hands as I did so. Distantly, I heard sobbing. Then I realized with a jolt that the sound was coming out of me.

There was blood everywhere. Even in the darkness I could see it. It spread out around his body in an enormous black pool.

"Nadin," he said. His voice was full of liquid. He coughed and blood sputtered from his lips. And suddenly, he was no longer the monster, the murderer, the liar whose words brought nothing but pain. He was just Ceilos. My partner. My best friend.

The boy who'd never existed, except in my own mind.

"Ceilos, please," I begged him. His breath sounded awful. He was dying. He was dying right here in front of me. "Please—the cure for the neurotoxin. Please..."

He struggled to swallow, gave up, smiled tightly up at me. The glow from the console reflected his green eyes, but the light behind them was fading.

"If I give it to you," he murmured, "will you remember me fondly?"

My own breathing was ragged, heaving. I stared down at him, unable to look away. My mind replaying years of abuse, of lies and deceit. Of the atrocities he'd succeeded in committing and the further ones he'd attempted. Of the blood on his hands. How could he ever think I would think of him fondly? I'd thought he was my partner, my only true friend, but it all had been a lie. Our entire life together had been nothing but a lie. I would never be able to think of Ceilos again without remembering this devastation and betrayal. I would never be able to forget everything he'd taken from me. I'd never be able to forgive him for all the lives he'd destroyed. I'd never be able to feel anything but hatred for this boy that I'd once believed I loved.

"Do you remember what we spoke of all those years ago, when Ceilos first came to us?"

Yes, I did. I did remember now.

"That boy has a lot of anger in him."

I swallowed, blinking back tears.

And anger is poison.

I wouldn't let him poison me any longer.

"Of course I will," I lied.

He closed his eyes, a slight smile on his bloodied lips. He weakly reached for my hand, drawing it to the place his medallion rested against his throat. As I took the engraved medal between my fingers, his hand slumped away.

"But how do I access it?" I asked him. "How do I get to the data?"

He didn't answer.

"Ceilos?" I shook him. No response. I shook him harder. "Ceilos?"

His eyelids didn't flutter. No breath came from his lips.

Tears were pouring out of my eyes now, anger and grief and rage and frustration.

"He's gone, Nadin," Melusin said.

"But how will I get the cure?" I cried.

"There's no time for that." She gestured out the window, at the bright light in the sky. "The rogue planetoid is almost in range. You have to go."

I stared at her in confusion. "I have to go?" I repeated. "But what about you?"

She smiled grimly through the shadows. "I have to flip the switch, remember? It can't be automated."

Her words hit me like a blow. Though Ceilos was gone, all his sabotage still remained.

And Melusin knew this. She'd known it when she brought me here. I had been too foolish to put the pieces together myself. Melusin had known this would be a suicide mission.

"It's all right," she said. Her voice was soft, as I'd always remembered it. Like the sound of cool, dripping water in the caverns. "The time of the *geroi* is over. The time of the Progression is over. It's up to you, now. To lead our people into the future."

She helped me to my feet. Gingerly, she placed Ceilos' medallion around my neck, and then pressed a posternkey into my hands. She gestured me to the stairwell. The postern stood at the bottom of the tower.

There would be no coming back here.

"Go," she said, turning away from me, focusing her attention on the console in front of her. Its screen lit her face, as poised and dignified as ever.

My legs shook beneath me. But I took one step, and then another. They shook but they did not buckle.

"One more thing," Melusin said as I slipped into the stairwell. I glanced back at her. She didn't meet my gaze.

"Always remember... I am proud of you, my daughter."

Chapter 63

- n a d i n -

I DON'T KNOW HOW LONG I SAT THERE, NUMB, CAKED IN BLOOD THAT wasn't my own and bile that was. I barely recognized my surroundings, barely registered where I was. I just sat there on the cold marble floor, my hand at my throat, on Ceilos' medallion hanging around my neck, staring through the glass. Staring up at the sky.

It was so quiet here. Too quiet. I'd never heard it this quiet. In the night sky, Hamos shone so bright. The rogue planetoid shone even brighter. They drew ever closer together, trapped in an inexorable dance. Here and there, little fragments of light seemed to break away from the planetoid, like sparks from a campfire. They lit up the night sky, streaks of stardust breaking up the more distant band of galaxy behind. I heard sounds, far away, shattering the quiet. *Boom. Boom.* But they seemed detached from reality. They couldn't be real.

Then another sound, closer. Footsteps, heavy, echoing off the marble. Coming my way. I didn't turn my head. Didn't look to see who was coming. My eyes were fixed on Hamos. On the dwarf planet. On the little sparks crackling between them.

"Nadin!"

The voice was familiar. It cut through the fog in my head. I knew that voice.

"Nadin!"

A moment later, he barreled into me, snapping me back to reality. Isaak.

"Oh my God," he said. He was on his knees, crouched beside me, his arms around me. "I've been looking for you for hours. I searched this place high and low. They said you were here, but I couldn't find you."

"I wasn't here," I said, still feeling disoriented.

"Where were you, then?" he asked.

I pointed numbly up at the sky. At Hamos. At the planetoid, so close to it. So close.

The postern had deposited me here, on the ground floor at the entrance of the pyramid in Bright Horizon. There should have been people here, Enforcers, *patroi*. I should have seen lights in the city around me, in the insulae, in the marketplace. But it was dark. Quiet. Abandoned. Nobody here but me, staring up at the sky.

And now Isaak.

"Where is everyone?" I asked.

"It's a long story," he said. "I'll explain later. For now, we have to get out of here. It's not safe aboveground. Emil said the planetoid is going to start breaking up as it approaches Hamos. The impacts will hit Iamos. They'll hit the citidomes. Remember, by my time..."

Everything was gone. Decimated by impact craters. Buried in the sand. As if we'd never existed.

"I want to see it happen," I said.

Isaak stared at me in horror. "What?"

I shook my head. "No," I said. I pointed at the sky again. "Watch."

He looked at me in confusion, then followed my gaze up. Up to the stars overhead, through the clear glass of the pyramid, through the blue tint of the dome. Hamos shone so bright. The rogue planetoid shone even brighter. Until suddenly, something even brighter filled the sky. Something enormous, blinding. Overpowering. I couldn't look anymore, and I squeezed my eyes closed, ducking my head. Isaak pulled me against him, ducking his own head down, his face pressed into my short white curls.

And then it was gone. Spots were dancing in front of my eyes as I opened them again, but when my vision cleared, I saw it was gone.

The dwarf planet was gone.

Hamos was gone.

Melusin was gone.

Ceilos was gone.

Gone. Gone. Gone.

My shoulders were shaking. Isaak held me. We didn't speak.

At last, we stood, Isaak helping me gain my footing.

"Come on," he said. "We can't stay here. It's not safe."

He unzipped his jacket, the one he'd brought with him from Earth. He reached inside, withdrawing a posternkey from the interior pocket.

Yes. He was right. It was as Melusin had said. It was time to lead our people into the future.

And our friends were waiting for us.

We made our way into the marble interior of the pyramid, to the postern room. It was silent. Utterly silent. We were alone.

As I slid the door open, my foot brushed against something metallic. I glanced down. In the light of the blue phosphorescence, I recognized it. A discarded earpiece. They littered the floor around the pyramid.

I bent down, picking this one up, turning it over between my fingers.

Isaak, standing by the stone arch in the center of the room, glanced over his shoulder at me. "What are you doing, Nadin? We need to hurry."

"Just one moment," I said. Then I inserted the earpiece into my ear.

"Nadin, stop!" Isaak exclaimed, rushing over to my side. "What if the neurotoxin—"

I waved him away. Gingerly, I lifted Ceilos' medallion from its place at my throat, squeezing it tightly.

"System protocol initiated."

I sucked in a breath. Swallowed. Removed the earpiece, slipped it into my reticule.

"If I give it to you, will you remember me fondly?"

He couldn't have programmed this System protocol after I'd asked him for it. Melusin's blade had been too swift, his death too immediate. He had programmed this before. He'd believed I would go with him. After everything that had happened, he still had held on to that delusion. He still had believed I was the version of myself that had only ever existed in his mind. The version who could love him when the real me never could.

Just as the version of him that I'd loved had never been real.

"What?" Isaak asked, confused. "What is it?"

"I have the cure," I told him.

PART TEN
MARS

2075 C.E.

Chapter 64

- i s a a k -

MY LEGS BUCKLED AS OUR ATOMS REASSEMBLED, OUR FEET, WHICH seconds before had been on a firm marble floor, now sinking into uneven sand. My eyes struggled to focus at the abrupt shift from the dark inner pyramid to the blinding sunlight that enveloped us now. Beside me, Nadin staggered, trying to keep her balance, and I squeezed her hand tightly. Slowly, our eyes adjusted, and we were able to take in the sight around us. The sound of the waves lapping against the shore. The briny smell of the water.

We were at Escalante Bay, in the secluded cove that I had often retreated to for solitude. But we weren't alone now.

"Hey," Henry said. "You made it."

The breath of relief I started to let out was immediately frozen by the sight of the man standing next to Henry. Though his suit was dusty and disheveled, there was no mistaking him. He was recognizable by his shaved head alone.

Geoff Preston.

"What's he doing here?" I demanded.

Henry held his hands up. "Relax. He's on our side."

I stared for a long moment, my brain sluggishly attempting to process that. "*What?*"

Henry snorted. "Yeah. Floored me, too. We've got a lot of catching up to do, but the short version is that Preston is our letter-sending friend."

I blinked, looking back and forth between Preston and Henry. "*Cristo,*" was all I could manage to say. I didn't know what all had been going on here, but I realized belatedly that they looked as bad as I knew Nadin and I did. Clothes filthy, faces smudged, appearing that they hadn't slept in days.

"I'm relieved to see you're all right, Henry," Nadin said. "But where is everybody else? Tamara and Scylla and Lizeth?"

Henry sighed, folding his arms. "Well, let's see. Right now, Lizeth is on her way downtown with Kate Ponsford and Wyatt and a whole big group of GSAF agents and cops and basically half the enforcement class, and if all goes well, we'll get there just in time to witness a countercoup of epic proportions."

My jaw dropped. "Are you serious?"

"A lot of shit has gone down in just a month," Henry said. "You don't even know the half of it. I'll fill you in on the way. We need to get down there ASAP. But first, we wanted to talk to Nadin." He nudged Preston, and the man stepped forward, looking uncharacteristically sheepish.

"Tell her," Henry said. "Everything you told me."

Preston nodded, inhaled. "Nadin, I'm afraid I haven't been entirely honest with you," he said. Beside me, Nadin frowned. "The first time we spoke, back at Lal Qila... It wasn't the first time I'd met you. Well, in a manner of speaking."

Nadin's brows were drawn. "What do you mean?" she asked.

"As you surmised from our previous meeting, I've been working on the System for quite some time now. What I never told anyone before now is this: Over an annum ago—while Henry was still working at GSAF, not long after he'd helped us make sufficient headway decoding M-VHLL that we were able to begin accessing the System with earpieces—I inadvertently activated a System protocol. That System protocol contained a recorded message. From you, Nadin. You were speaking directly to me. In English."

Nadin's frown had only grown deeper as he spoke. Now she looked at me, and the alarm in her eyes was apparent.

"But how is that possible?" she asked. "I've never recorded any such message. I never programmed that protocol."

"Nonetheless, it's what happened," Preston insisted. "You told me who you were. That you and I hadn't met yet, but that we would soon. You told me what was going to happen, and what you needed me to do in order to get to that point. In order for events that had already unfolded to not be altered, I needed to play my part—down to the letter. Keep working with GSAF, keep working with ConneX on the nanobots despite my growing moral objections. And you told me not to speak to anyone about this except you."

"That's why you kept trying to talk to me alone," Nadin breathed.

Preston nodded. "At first, I didn't know what to believe. It seemed so impossible. But when events started to play out just as you'd said they would, I knew it had to be true. And so I knew I had to play my part." He looked down at the rusty sand beneath our feet. "I hope you'll forgive me for the harm I caused. I believe you'll understand when I say I truly had no other choice."

This was insane. I gawked at Henry. He shrugged. "Same reaction I had," he said.

Nadin turned away, looking out at the bay behind us. The waves breaking against the rocks. In the distance, the buildings on Herschel Island. I remembered how different things had been when we'd stood there just a few days ago, looking out at the dried valley where the sea had once been, and where it was again now. Thinking about the ruins of Thalash'a on that island. The lighthouse, the observatory, ultimately toppled from the headland, buried by the sands. Now drowned under a hundred meters of water.

"Mr. Preston," she said, turning back to face him. "In this recording, did I tell you anything about a neurotoxin?"

"You told me you had the cure," he said. "Is it true?"

She squeezed the medallion around her neck, as she had before we'd left Bright Horizon. I didn't know where she'd gotten it, just as I didn't know whose blood now stained her bodysuit. Those seemed like questions for another time.

"It's true," she said. "I have it now."

"Then we need to get downtown fast," Henry said. "There are a lot of sick people who need your help, Nadin."

They started to turn to go, Nadin hurrying after them, but I called out, "Hold on."

Henry stopped, looking over his shoulder in surprise.

"What time is it?" I asked him.

He checked. "Seven-oh-four."

"Give it another minute," I told him. "We're waiting on one more thing."

Before they'd left Katai'ios, Emil and Gitrin had made a copy of my key, the one Henry had given me. But they'd made a small change to his coordinates. They'd programmed their duplicate key with an arrival time of five minutes after Nadin and I were supposed to return. I'd told them that if I made it here, I would wait for them. If I wasn't there on the beach when they arrived, they'd know we hadn't made it.

But we were here, and we were waiting for them when they materialized in the same place Nadin and I had arrived five minutes earlier.

And now we were in Preston's self-driving car, everyone hurriedly trying to explain what was going on to one another. Henry trying to tell me what had transpired in the month I'd been gone, how they'd gone from being on the run from GSAF to leading an outright revolution. In the backseat I could hear Nadin, speaking in halting Iamoi, telling Gitrin what had happened on Hamos, but I only caught snatches of it.

There was no time to tell the full story, anyway. It didn't take long for the car to reach the bridge over Santos Creek, and from there we had to continue on foot. Traffic was entirely stopped. The shriek of sirens filled the streets, and overhead the deafening roar of chopper blades. Downtown was a warzone.

"What are all those sounds?" Nadin shouted as we climbed out of the car.

"Ambulances," Henry said back. "Trying to help the sick people."

"I have to activate the cure protocol," Nadin said, reaching for her reticule.

"Wait," Preston said, reaching out a hand to stay her. "Wait until we get to the capitol. The people need to see you do this, Nadin. They have to know the Iamoi are on their side. It's the only way they'll accept your people."

Nadin stared at him, aghast. But then she nodded. She understood. She'd been raised by the *geroi*, after all. She of all people understood the importance of appearances.

We raced down the street, weaving between stopped cars, sidestepping heaps of litter all over the ground—bottles of water, filthy rags, abandoned signs, bags and purses that clearly belonged to people but had been left for whatever reason. What had happened here?

We reached the entrance to the riverfront park just in time to see the standoff begin. Dozens of agents and police officers, all dressed in riot gear, with helmets and shields, lined the steps of the GSAF building and the sidewalk in front of it. They didn't seem to notice us—their attention was trained on the bridge to Sparta Island. This had been blockaded with traffic pylons and parked cars. But between the obstacles, we saw other agents dragging a crowd of people in ordinary street clothes. The people were struggling, trying to fight back, but they were restrained.

And then the leader of this second group of agents emerged from the blockade, and my muscles tensed. Joseph Condor. Just behind him were two agents restraining girls I recognized: Tamara and Scylla.

"Tamara!" Henry shouted, rushing forward.

"Don't move!" one of the agents on our side of the bridge ordered, holding out his shield to block Henry.

"What's the meaning of this?" Condor barked, taking in the sight of the agents waiting on the other side of the blockade.

"This ends now, Mr. Condor," a woman's voice said over a loudspeaker. "You're under arrest." I turned in surprise. On the steps to the GSAF building stood a blond woman in a neat suit. After a moment, I recognized her as Wyatt's mom. Kate Ponsford. Standing beside her, dressed in the same all-black outfit she'd worn that day on Lago Verde, was Lizeth, her arms folded defiantly.

"You have no authority to arrest me!" Condor shouted. "I am the officially appointed governor of Aeolis Province."

"Aeolis Province no longer recognizes the authority of GSAF on the planet Mars," said Kate.

"You have no legal right to do that!" snapped Condor.

"GSAF never had a legal right to this planet to begin with," Kate replied. "This planet was already claimed long before we arrived here." She turned, gesturing to the group of us standing behind the agents. "Isn't that right, Nadin?"

Nadin looked around in bewilderment as the crowd turned to stare at her. Then the agents parted, giving us a clear route to the capitol steps. Kate beckoned to her, and, hesitantly, Nadin moved forward. I noticed, now that the shields of the agents were no longer obstructing our view, that there was a crowd of civilians in front of the steps, watching all the proceedings. Their Speculus headsets told me that these weren't just ordinary Tierra Nuevans. These were journalists.

The revolution was being broadcast to every Speculus set, deskpad, and palmtop on both worlds.

"Nadin," Kate said, reaching her hand out to Nadin as she approached, as if this entire thing had been rehearsed. "Will the Iamoi work with our people in charting a new course for this world?"

Nadin glanced around again. I could tell she still felt out of sorts, but I knew Nadin. Whatever challenge she had to face, she'd face it head on. She squared her shoulders, slipping back into her practiced *gerouin*-in-training demeanor. "Of course," she said, her voice somber, a weight to her words. This was it. The alliance between our people and the Iamoi that she'd fought for all this time. With this alliance, everyone on Iamos would be saved.

"But first," she went on, "I have something important I need to do." She took the medallion from around her neck, held it up for everyone to see. "You see, I have the cure to the neurotoxin. The toxin that Joseph Condor unleashed on your people by illicitly connecting your nanobots to the System."

Gasps rippled around the crowd. Hands holding palmtops raised, trying to get recordings of the action. She'd said just what they needed to hear. There'd be no way Condor could spin this to keep his power now. His reign of terror was over.

Nadin reached into her reticule, withdrawing the earpiece she'd brought with her from Iamos. She slipped it into her ear.

"System protocol initiate," she said.

And just like that, it was done.

The officers on our side of the bridge rushed forward, quickly detaining Joseph Condor and the agents who had been loyal to him. He didn't even try to fight. Just like everyone else, he knew that it was over.

Freed from their restraints, Scylla and Tamara ran over to us, Tamara colliding against Henry and Scylla crashing into me, nearly knocking me over with the force of her hug.

"You're back! You saved Nadin," she bellowed, clutching me tightly. "I can't believe it! You did it! You saved everyone, Isaak!"

I laughed, trying to extricate myself from her grip. "I didn't really do anything," I said. "It was all Nadin, honestly."

"But because of this, two worlds will be saved," Gitrin said, coming over and giving me a hug herself, albeit far more gentle than Scylla's had been. "The Iamoi will be able to evacuate to the future. Our people will finally be free."

"Yeah, well," I said sheepishly, rubbing my hand across the back of my neck. "I have to admit, I wasn't too worried. I didn't want to say anything earlier just in case, but I already knew it was going to work out."

Gitrin looked at me quizzically. Beside her, Emil laughed. He'd figured it out. Just like always, Emil had figured it out.

"How could you have known that?" Gitrin asked.

I grinned, looking up at the sky, bright blue overhead. This whole thing felt surreal. But it really was over, wasn't it? We were safe. We were all safe now. And we were going to stay that way.

"Because you came back and told me yourself."

CHAPTER 65

- n a d i n -

I CAME AWAKE SLOWLY, DISTANTLY REGISTERING THE SOUND OF VOICES IN another room. I opened my eyes, turned over in the bed, a wave of disorientation flooding over me. Gradually, I remembered where I was. How I'd gotten to be here.

I sat up, looking around the room. I was in the guest room at Bryn and Delia's house. "My" room, when I'd been here before. And where I'd be staying for the immediate future. Until we got everything figured out. Until I knew where *home* was going to be.

But I was home, wasn't I? Even if this house itself wasn't going to be my permanent dwelling. Iamos was gone. Thousands of years in the past. There was only Mars now. Mars was my home. In a lot of ways, it had been since I'd first come here. After all, this was where I'd truly found myself.

I went over to the window looking out over the bay. In the distance, Herschel Island twinkled with lights. A lighthouse stood on the headland, as another had done millennia before. I sighed, turning away, walking to the bathroom. I had changed into the clothes Tamara had bought for me before, that Bryn and Delia had kept for me after Joseph Condor had brought us to Earth. I'd tossed my silver bodysuit, covered in blood and bile, into a pile in the corner. I wanted to never see it again. But it would have to be cleaned, because I still had need of it. One more thing I had to do.

But that was not a worry for tonight. Tonight, people were celebrating. The cure had worked. The sick people in the hospitals all over Mars and Earth, the ones crowded into the AresTec campus, the ones desperately waiting for someone to help them, for a miracle to occur... They'd been healed. The nanobots which had been assaulting their nervous systems turned around and began healing them instead.

For some, it had been too late. I knew that, and it was one more thing that I could never forgive Ceilos for. Yet more blood on his hands. But most had been able to be saved. I'd seen Tamara joyfully embracing two little girls crossing the Sparta Island bridge this afternoon, and a small degree of relief had flooded over me. For the first time, I had really understood that the Liberator was gone. He would never terrorize this planet again.

After it was all over, after Kate and I had finished our dozenth press conference and told the people that we'd be taking no more questions today, we'd all come back to Bryn and Delia's house. I'd soon grown too tired to stay awake, and they'd urged me up here to sleep. But I could hear voices downstairs now. I opened the door, heading down to join them.

There was music pouring out of one of the rooms at the bottom of the stairs. This was where Tamara's piano was, the place where she'd first introduced me to music. The place where she'd first told me what asexuality was. The place where she'd helped me find myself.

I peeked my head in now. She sat at the bench, her fingers running over the keys swiftly. Henry sat beside her, and the two of them were singing, Tamara's voice melodious, Henry's loud and boisterous. He laughed as Tamara misplaced one of her fingers and the piano produced a sour note. "That was your fault," Tamara protested, giggling and elbowing him in the ribs.

"I take no responsibility," Henry retorted, putting his arm over her shoulders and pulling her tight against him.

I smiled to myself and moved away, following the sound of voices into the next room. There, a large group of people was congregated. Scylla stood with Mariyah and Wyatt beside a table loaded with finger foods. Delia and Bryn were talking to Emil and a couple I'd met earlier in the day, before I'd gone up to sleep. I'd never met the woman before, but I'd seen the man once. He was Isaak's stepfather, Erick, and this woman was Isaak's mother.

I didn't think I'd ever seen Isaak so relieved as he was when he'd been reunited with them today, and with his younger sister, Celeste. I looked around now and spotted him with his sister on one of the room's two couches, talking animatedly. The little girl looked up at him raptly, absorbing whatever story he was telling with a huge grin on her face. On the other sofa, Lizeth was dozing against Dante's chest, and Zero looked on in wry amusement, sipping a hot drink out of a mug.

The door to the veranda was open, and I noticed Gitrin standing alone against the railing. Quietly, I moved across the room and slipped out onto the veranda beside her.

"*Alin*," she said, looking up and noticing my presence. She reached her arm out to me, and I came to her, letting her wrap me in an embrace. We stood together, quietly looking at the dark bay for a long while.

"Everyone's talking about it, Isaak tells me," she said at last. "How you saved the worlds from the neurotoxin. And you've saved Iamos, too. But you don't seem in a celebratory mood."

I smiled tightly. "I'm just fatigued."

Gitrin was unconvinced. I could see it in her eyes. "Tell me the truth, *alin*," she said.

I sighed, leaning against the railing. Taking the medallion between my fingers, turning it over and over. "I just have been wondering... why." Why everything. Why Ceilos had been the way he was. Why we'd become what we'd become.

"He was a sick person, Nadin," Gitrin said sadly. "He had a sickness of the mind that the System, for all its regulations, could never cure. Maybe he was born with it, after all those generations of inbreeding among the *geroi*. But I think he grew into it. I think this system, this society that our people created did this to him. The world of the *geroi* was never a healthy place for a child to grow, even in the early days of the Progression. It could only ever have ended one way." She sighed. "But one thing is true. You are the only person he ever cared about, even in his warped way. That's a terrible burden to have to bear, *alin*, to have been loved by a monster. I'm sorry you must carry it."

I exhaled, tucking the medallion under my shirt. "I've been loved by many who are not monstrous. That will give me strength."

The breeze picked up. We silently watched the lights from Herschel

Island reflect across the waves.

"Hey."

At the sound of Isaak's voice, I turned. He stood in the open doorway, smiling hesitantly at me and Gitrin.

Gitrin squeezed my shoulder, detaching herself from me and going back into the house. Isaak came over to join me at the railing.

"You feeling any better?" he asked me.

"I am now," I said, grateful for his presence.

He watched me for a long moment. "Have you figured out what you're going to do yet?"

There were many things that I needed to do. But I knew what he was talking about. We'd begun this discussion with Geoff Preston earlier. It had been weighing heavily on both of our minds ever since.

"I'll have to go back," I said. Back in time. Back to Iamos. One last time. The System protocol that Preston had unlocked. The other one, in the levels of the *esotoi*, that had been left for Henry. Other things, things that had never made sense to me before, that suddenly came together in the light of Preston's information. The deletion of the time postern specs from the System. The dream I'd had in Gitrin's classroom, the nightmare that had pointed me toward Elytherios—so unusual, for a mind regulated by the System. So obvious, now, that it had been a System protocol.

And most of all, the key. The key that Isaak had found buried in the hills outside Tierra Nueva, the ancient device with Delia's maker mark inscribed on it. The key that included a System protocol that only I could see.

Breadcrumbs I'd left for myself.

Because that's what all of it meant. What all of it had to mean. It was true that the Liberator had been dogging my steps this whole time, watching my every move. But someone else had been watching me, too. Looking out for me, and for the future.

Me.

"There are things that need to be set in motion," I said. And only I could do it.

"Are you sure you don't want me to go with you?" Isaak asked. "It seems dangerous to go alone."

"No. I'll be fine. I know I will."

Everything would work out. We had proof of that. The proof was right here, right now. In this moment. The fact that the universe was still here. That I was still breathing. That we all were.

"After all," I pointed out. "It all happened, didn't it?"

He smiled. "Yeah. I guess it did."

EPILOGUE
MARTIAN REPUBLIC

Tierra Nueva, Aeolis State
Thalash'a, Iamos Nimenos

Martian Civic Year (M.C.) 14
S.C.D. 15,294
2077 C.E.

It was crazy to me, the way that time passed. It had already been almost a whole year. Not an annum—that was the old dating convention, the one we'd agreed not to use anymore, though old habits died hard. A Martian year. A year where Earth no longer dictated to us the way things had to be.

Everything had changed when Nadin and I returned from Iamos. The movement that Henry had begun with Free Mars way back when I first disappeared had finally come to fruition. The revelation that GSAF had turned an untested alien technology on its own citizens in an attempt to control them—and the tragedy of the neurotoxin that followed, which ultimately claimed the lives of over ten thousand people—had led to the ultimate collapse of the entire agency. The Global Space and Astronautics Federation had been dissolved by the UN, and Mars had been granted its independence.

Joseph Condor had been returned to Earth to stand trial before the UN. Considering that his actions had been implicitly sanctioned by the GSAF Council and the UN itself, I found it kind of rich that they'd turned him into their scapegoat. But I shouldn't have been surprised. Henry had been right all along, hadn't he? Those kinds of people will do anything to protect their own power. All that mattered to me was that he would never bother any of us on Mars again.

In the meantime, we had a lot of work ahead of us, building a new world for ourselves. A world that would learn from the mistakes of our home planets—both Earth and Iamos. The Iamoi, together with the colonists from Earth, both vowed together that we would never let anything like GSAF or the *geroi* happen again.

When everything had been stabilized, Gitrin and Emil traveled back in time, to two minutes after they'd left Katai'ios. Just as I'd known they would. I already knew what had happened twelve thousand years ago. I'd been there. The whole population had come forward to our time, arriving six months after Nadin and I returned to the future. We were ready for them, with resources prepared to help them settle in to their new homes. The Iamoi were given the entire continent of Cimmeria, but many of them chose instead to live in the areas where the Earth colonists had settled, close to the historic Iamoi sites that had been their family homes thousands of years before. A large population of Iamoi now lived in Tierra Nueva—Thalash'a, to the Iamoi. The Aeolis State Charter, written by a joint committee of Earth colonists and Iamoi, mandated that the Iamoi would have an equal number of seats in our state government as Earth colonists. It ensured that people of Iamoi descent would always have a voice in shaping our home together.

That wasn't the only way the Iamoi were helping to shape the new world. The climate scientists from Elytherios had been invaluable in ensuring that our terraformation would be completed the right way. The cycle of drought that we'd started to slip into using Earth-based terraformation techniques was something the Iamoi scientists knew how to correct. Using their revivification techniques, the Martian atmosphere had begun to stabilize, and this last winter had ushered in our rainiest year on record.

All that rain had been greatly appreciated by the animals at the Curiosity Bay Wildlife Refuge, the newly established preserve that Nikos had founded, and where he served as head *gurza* keeper. There, the many animals that had escaped or been rescued from Elytherios before the eruption of the Sios Ifaisteos had room to roam free, and—the biologists at the Refuge hoped—reproduce. It was their hope that with enough time, the native species of Mars would eventually return to stable populations.

I had to admit, I was a little sorry that I wasn't able to keep Tuupa for myself as a pet. But I knew she and Thork would be happier at the refuge. And so was Pandat, who still scampered up onto my shoulder every time I came to visit.

The farmers from Katai'ios had also been an enormous help to my own family. My mom still worked as a botanist, though now she worked for the Aeolis State government instead of GSAF. And, with the aid of native Martian plants to work with, her genetically engineered crops were coming out healthier than ever.

Mom had a lot more to be happy about besides just the health of her crops, though. Our whole family was together now. It wasn't just that I was home again. My grandparents had come to join us, too. After leaving Medellín, they had chosen not to return to Berkeley. Instead, Abuelo had taken a teaching position at Kimbal University, in its newly formed archaeology department. I'd enrolled there after graduating from the Academy (although I'd done my last term in a home study program, since I was now three annums behind my original cohort), and now I was finally fulfilling my dream since childhood. I was studying to be an archaeologist. But I wasn't going to be doing my fieldwork on Earth. There was a great need, now, to research the history of my own planet's past, to learn more about Iamos before the time of the Progression, and I was eager to be a part of it.

Among my professors at Kimbal University were José Espinoza, one of the leading authorities of Earth-based Iamoi archaeology, and Gitrin, a professor of Iamoi history. Professor Emil Hassan had also been offered a position at the school, but he'd turned it down for now. Credited as the first person of Earth descent to have discovered the existence of the Iamoi civilization, Emil was busy leading an archaeological dig of his own—studying the history of Thalash'a, the ancient Iamoi capital. Between that, publishing the first book collecting his studies, and his various speaking engagements at academic institutions around the globe, he insisted that he was too busy for a regular teaching position.

In all the instability left in the wake of GSAF's departure from Mars, many of the Earth-based manufacturers and corporations that had been established on the planet wound up withdrawing. But it wasn't entirely bad news. That void was filled by Martian-based companies, such as the newly formed Sea-Star Industries, established by our own Delia and Bryn Randall-Torres. True, they'd lost their positions at AresTec. But the silver lining had come soon after, when GalaX—collapsing internally after the ConneX fiasco—decided to sell AresTec off to the highest bidder, which just so happened to be Sea-Star Industries. Delia and Bryn were able to ensure that all their employees kept their jobs. Delia had even managed to find a place in the R&D department for Geoff Preston, though she made it clear that his previous positions on user privacy were not going to be acceptable under her watch.

Not everyone we knew from Earth came to Mars, though. After his release from custody upon GSAF's implosion, my dad had opted to stay on Earth. He had a number of media corporations on Earth wanting to film Speculus docudramas about his time on Iamos, and they'd offered him, as he put it, "some sweet cash" in exchange. It had stung a little, to be honest, though I shouldn't have been surprised. Dad had always valued himself over any of the rest of us. Celeste hadn't taken it as badly as I'd feared. After all, she reminded me, we *had* a dad now. We had Erick.

And yeah. I was enjoying, after all this time, finally getting to know him. I'd been wrong about my stepdad after all. He wasn't a tool. He was actually pretty stellar.

And we had one more link to Earth, too. A few weeks after the revolution, Lizeth, Zero, and the other members of the Stateless had returned to Earth. Even though all the Senghases, including Lizeth's uncle Karl, had been offered asylum on Mars, they'd opted not to take it. "Earth still needs us," Lizeth had told us. "Mars is your home, but Earth is ours." I'd been worried to see them go, to be honest. Even though the continental unions were currently in shambles, with their identities known, it seemed incredibly dangerous for them to go back there. After they'd left Mars, they'd seemed to disappear. No one knew what had become of any of them. But one day, Henry had gotten an encrypted message on Speculus from an account with a burner figuscan. The message had read, "*Atlantis is waiting.*" The message had no meaning to me, but Henry had been thrilled. Every now and again, he repeated it to himself. Whatever it meant, it had made Henry confident that Lizeth and the other members of the Stateless were just fine.

So life on Mars settled into something of a regular pattern. Things were different now than they'd been before. But it was a good kind of different.

And there were plenty of things to celebrate. Like today. I smiled to myself, checking my pocket, feeling the small box I'd tucked in there earlier.

Yeah. Today was going to be a good day.

I stood on the shore, looking out over the waves. As I'd done hundreds of times at this point. But this time, it was different. This day was different. Because it was my annual. One year ago... seven thousand years ago... twelve thousand annums ago... longer ago than time could recall, I had gone outside the dome and seen the desert wasteland that Iamos had become. I'd known, deep inside me, that within a year, Iamos would be gone. But I'd sworn *I* wouldn't be. I'd vowed that no matter what, my *enilikin* would not be my last annual.

And I'd been right.

Much had changed over the last year. But it seemed nothing had changed more than I had.

I hadn't told Isaak or anyone else about what had happened when I'd traveled back in time. When I'd implemented the System protocol that would give Geoff Preston my message. When I'd sneaked into the *esotoi* apartment in Hope Renewed, scratched Henry's name into the wall, and concealed it with a System protocol so the occupants wouldn't see it. When I'd planted Delia's 3-D printed posternkey into the sand, where Isaak would unearth it thousands of years later.

Before I'd left, I'd had one last thing I wanted to do. Something just for me.

I'd gone outside the citidome. And I'd waited.

And sure enough, I'd seen her. I'd seen the small, fragile girl sneaking out of the dome, hoping to catch a glimpse of what could have been her final sunset. I watched her as the wind raked over the dust, snatching tendrils of her white hair out of her braid. Watched the stiff, awkward way she'd tucked it back in.

She looked so lonely, I'd realized. And I had been. I'd been lonely that day. I'd been lonely my whole life.

But I'd seen something else in that other me, standing outside the dome. Something that I hadn't known was there. Something that was waiting to be woken up inside me.

Strength.

Once I'd returned—once every person from Iamos had been evacuated to the future, once every supply we could salvage and animal we could find had been carried forward in time, once every contingency had been planned for and every breadcrumb had been planted—the System had been shut down. Permanently. It would never destroy another life on this planet again.

The early months after the evacuation had been hard. Finding my place in this new world, this world without the *geroi*, felt impossible at times. After everything that had happened, there was a strong part of me that wanted nothing more than to just disappear, to hide away from the rest of the world. But I knew that I couldn't. My people needed me. Melusin had entrusted the care of our people into my hands. Back in Elytherios, an eternity ago, Gitrin had said she believed I could be a real leader—not the kind the *geroi* had tried to mold me into, but the kind that the Iamoi had really needed.

It was difficult at first. Though many Iamoi actually did look to me as a leader, there were still many others who were wary of me because of my connection to the *geroi*. I had to prove myself to them, every single day, just as I'd done with the Elytherioi. If I was honest, despite how far I'd come, I still doubted sometimes whether I was up to the task. What was my role supposed to be? How was I ever going to learn how to live the rest of my life, when everything I'd ever known had been taken from me?

I'd begun by serving on the State Charter Committee, along with the elders of Elytherios, Kate and some of her advisers, and Henry, Scylla, and Wyatt representing the Free Mars movement. It had taken months to craft the charter, to create an arrangement that would benefit both our people and the Martians who lived here. But we weren't starting from scratch. There were others here, and even though the members of the State Charter Committee had vowed that the new government would learn from the mistakes of Earth's past, that the indigenous population of Mars would be integral parts of the planet from the very beginning, the fact was, there were people here who weren't Iamoi, and they were here to stay. Their ways were different from ours, and we were going to have to learn to adapt to their world while still staying true to our own heritage, our own culture.

Many of our people—like Eliin, Syrin and Shuliin, Gios and Corin, Ierin and Camos and their children—had decided to start over on the continent Isaak's people called Cimmeria, near where the citidome of Radiant Tomorrow had once stood. Even Eos and Marin had eventually gone there, though Nikos had remained behind. But I had no desire to go to Cimmeria. Tierra Nueva had become my home. It was more than just the fact that these hills, that mountain, this bay had been the place where I'd grown up millennia before. It was the people who were here. The people that I loved. Gitrin had remained here, teaching at the university in Curiosity Bay and working closely with Emil on his studies of Iamoi history. Bryn and Delia were here, Tamara and Henry and Scylla. Wyatt, Mariyah, and everyone I'd come to know and love in this timeline, they all were here. I couldn't leave this place.

So I had to do my best to learn how to be *me* in this new world. The *geroi* had considered my education to be over, but the truth was, it was only just beginning.

"Hey! Nadin!"

I looked up at the sound of my name being called. I'd almost forgotten the reason I was here. But I grinned as I saw Scylla walking across the beach toward me. Behind her, farther up the sand near the boardwalk, Tamara and Henry had spread out a blanket, weighing it down with stones. Mariyah was pulling food out of a basket and setting it out on the blanket. And beyond them—

"Come on, birthday girl," Scylla said as she drew near. "You're missing your own party!"

"I'm coming," I said. "I just... need a minute."

She followed my gaze, her eyes landing on the tall figure making his way down the steps from the boardwalk toward us. "Ah," Scylla said, mirth audible in her voice. "Sure thing. Take your time."

She scampered back over to where the rest of our friends were setting up the picnic. I remained on the shore, watching awkwardly as Isaak made his way over to me.

One more person I'd come to know and love in this timeline.

Over the last year, Isaak and I had grown closer, yet there had always remained a distance between us, something I hadn't quite been able to define. During my time living in Bryn and Delia's house, they'd noticed my frequent nightmares, my increasing anxiety. They'd recommended a doctor to me, a woman that Tamara knew. Her medicine was Earth-based, but she understood ailments of the mind better than we had on Iamos. She'd taught me about PTSD, about emotional abuse. About gaslighting. Working with her was hard, and it had seemed to get worse before it got better. But it *had* gotten better. Finally. The nightmares were starting to fade. The constant fear I'd felt before was finally starting to fade.

During this whole time, Isaak had been gentle with me, tender, but still he'd kept his distance. My doctor explained that he was giving me space. The room I needed for recovery. And I had needed that room. It had been crucial for my healing. But I was finding more and more these days that I was ready to close that distance. That I no longer wanted space. I wanted closeness.

I just needed to figure out how to tell him.

"Hey," I said, coming up beside Nadin. The breeze was crisp, and it played with wisps of Nadin's hair, fanning them out behind her, bringing them around and making them dance across her face. Her hair had grown out over the last year, now reaching to almost her shoulders in wild white coils. Her smile had returned, too. She was looking like herself again. Finally, after everything she'd been through. "What're you up to?"

She smiled, shrugging. "Just thinking. Remembering, maybe. A lot has changed since my last annual."

"Yeah," I said, unsure of how to respond. Not wanting to remind her of the things she'd been running from in her mind for the last year. Awkwardly, I attempted to change the subject. "Since it's your birthday, I got you something." I reached into my pocket, pulling out the box I'd been carrying. I handed it to her.

She looked down curiously, tugging at the end of the ribbon I'd wrapped around the box. It fell away. She lifted the lid, revealing a small, jeweled blue flower inside.

"It's for your hair," I explained. Celeste had helped me pick it out. She'd thought that it would bring out the blue in Nadin's eyes. I'd found that Celeste actually had pretty good advice. I guess I'd been wrong to call her an annoying kid for all those annums.

Nadin bit her lip, running her finger over the jewels. "Like the flower in Mexico," she said at last.

She remembered, then. "Yeah," I said.

She drew it out of the box, turning it over, trying to figure out the clip mechanic. "Here," I said, taking it from her, gently tucking it into her hair behind her right ear, cognizant the whole time of the fact that we'd done this all before.

I drew back, smiling down at her. "Really pretty," I murmured.

She looked at me for a long moment, the wind off the bay whipping tendrils of white hair around her face. Then, hesitantly, she reached out, drawing my face closer to hers. My breath hitched as she turned her face up, her lips gently brushing mine for just an instant. It only lasted a moment, but it filled me completely.

"What was that about?" I asked in surprise as she pulled away. "I thought you didn't like kissing."

"I don't," she admitted.

"Then why...?"

"Because you didn't ask me to." She looked up at me unflinchingly. "You understand me completely, and you don't try to change me. You don't try to push my boundaries. You respect me. And that's why I love you."

My lips were still tingling. "You... do?"

She nodded shyly. "I've waited a long time to tell you that. Since that night in the jungle. When you gave me the flower. I knew it then, but with everything that happened after... I had to be sure."

I swallowed, feeling off-kilter. "And you're sure now?"

"I am."

"Good. Because I am, too."

I pulled her into my arms and she rested her head against my chest. Every piece of me felt so, so alive.

"Partners are supposed to be equals," she said softly, her voice reverberating through me. "Even on Iamos, even under the *geroi*, that's how it was meant to be. But it was never that way for me. Ceilos was always in control, and he knew it. But you and I..."

She trailed off, seeming to struggle with her words. My arms tightened around her. "I'd say we're equals, right?" I said.

She nodded, looking back up with her blue eyes glistening. "I know you'll never ask me for more than what I am comfortable giving. Whatever I give you, I choose to, freely. Because... *oesi yacunos mou.*"

She pressed her forehead against mine, just a glimmer of the damp of her eyelashes brushing against my cheeks. When she stepped back, she was Nadin again—not the Nadin I'd first met on Iamos so long ago, whose stony exterior was marred with cracks of insecurity and self-doubt. My Nadin. Confident, fearless, and unapologetically herself.

"You know," I said, a grin pulling at the corners of my lips, "you've changed."

She smiled back. "Maybe I just figured out who I really was all along."

Higher up on the beach, our friends were calling. Beckoning us to join them.

The past was behind us now, and this time there would be no returning to it. From now on—for Mars, for Earth, for Iamos—there was only the future, and no way of knowing what that held.

Nadin reached out her hand, and I took it. Together, we walked forward, into the sun.

GLOSSARY

The New Standardized Language used on Iamos during Nadin's time was adopted after the Progression. This universal language, to be used across the entire planet, uses a standardized suffix format for all nouns. This format is as follows: masculine nouns end in -*os*; feminine nouns end in -*in*; plural nouns are gender-neutral and end in -*i*.

Prior to the Progression, a number of different regional dialects existed on Iamos as on Earth. These are referred to collectively as the old language. Some words from the old language use the Standardized suffixes (such as *Elytherios*, *Katai'ios*, etc.), but others do not, as each dialect had its own unique grammatical structure.

ALOS/ALIN – an affectionate term for a child

ANNUAL – birthdate

DEGIIM – greetings

ELYTHERIOS – an old language word meaning "freedom"

ENILIKIN – a person's ninth annual (almost seventeen in Earth years), signifying the transition from childhood to adulthood. A person who is now an adult is called an *enilin* or *enilos*.

ESOTOI – the middle caste of the Iamoi, who work alongside both patroi and plivoi

FRAOULOI – known in Isaak's time as the "spider weed"; a resilient, woody black plant that can grow in almost any condition

GEROI – the governors of a citidome (singular: *gerouin* [feminine], *geros* [masculine])

GEROTUS – the united governing body of all *geroi* on Iamos and Hamos

HAMOS – Venus

HAOI IFAISTEOI – "The Three Mountains"; the Iamoi's name for the three Martian shield volcanoes we know as Elysium Mons, Hecates Tholus, and Albor Tholus

IAMOS – Mars

IELAK – a type of fowl raised for meat

KALDEROS IFAISTEOS – "Crater Mountain" – the mountain on Mars we know as Aeolis Mons or Mount Sharp

KATAI'IOS – an old language word meaning "refuge"

KELA – a type of fowl raised for meat

KERKOPITH – a long-tailed primate

KYRIOS/KYRIN – a formal term of address, its closest English equivalent being "lord" or "lady"

PATROI – the most prestigious caste of the Iamoi

PLIVOI – the lowest caste of the Iamoi, considered to be the "drudges"

PSARA – fish

S.C.D. – "System Collective Date"; the annual-count system of the Iamoi, dating back to when the System estimates human civilization first arose on Iamos

SIOS IFAISTEOS – "Second Mountain" – the mountain on Mars we know as Elysium Mons

SIMOS – Earth

THALASH'A – the ancient name for the ruined capital on the coast near Hope Renewed citidome

UTZ'OS – an old language curse word

VI'IN/VI'I – road, path, way

YACUNOS/YACHIN – beloved, sweetheart (romantic connotation)

YAD/YADLAG – an old language curse word

YPRIS – hubris

Acknowledgments

I've noticed that debut novels tend to have ridiculously long acknowledgments, as the author is excited about the new experience and wants to thank everyone from their third grade teacher to the barista at their local coffee shop. In my case, this is the last book in this series and my longest acknowledgments section. That's because the list of people who have helped me has just grown longer and longer as time goes on. Getting through this last book was such a challenge as I struggled with my health over the last five years since the release of *New World*, so I really want to make sure I thank everyone. If I forget someone, I place the blame entirely on brain fog.

First and foremost, I need to thank a very special group of kids. Kids I met more than ten years ago, who are, unbelievably to me, in their teens and twenties now. You were the inspiration for The Iamos Trilogy. Saying goodbye to you all was the hardest thing I've ever done. Truth is, I couldn't really say goodbye. Not until I wrote you this story. You wondered what life might have been like on ancient Mars, when there was still water, and what life might be like in the future when we're there. Maybe when you're there yourself. Those questions were the start of everything. I hope that if any of you have read this story, that it was something you enjoyed, and something that might have inspired you to live your own adventures. To the Leopards, thank you all.

To Selenia: You encouraged me when I first came up with this story and your encouragement kept me going. Both of us came up with the ideas for our debut series together, and now both of us have complete trilogies, and that is something that's so special to me. I am so thankful for your friendship!

To Pan Z: Once again you saved my bacon with this book. You have a way of helping me figure out exactly the solutions I need for whatever story, be it a sci-fi, a western, or a Baba Yaga *isekai* (coming soon to a bookseller near you). Thank you for letting me rant at you, for enduring my panic attacks over the story, for brainstorming with me, and for basically letting me scream my way into a solution. Also, thank you for *The Legend of Barbie: Breath of the Wild Horse Rescue*. It needed to be mentioned.

Thank you as well to all the rest of my people in #writing: In particular C.G., as well as R.S.G, J.T., C.A., F.M., A.R.P., R.M., L.H., D.C., T.E.E., R.A.S., S.R.C., T.H.R., S.G., V.H.Y., and 6. (I know you said I didn't need to include you, but I'm doing it anyway. Ha.) They didn't want to be named, but they helped me brainstorm so much of this series as well as giving me some amazing ideas for new series to come, so they have to get a shoutout. I appreciate you all!

To RoAnna: Thank you for *everything*—for cheering me on as I was writing the book, for messaging me all your thoughts as you read it and encouraging me about the story, for writing Tamara's rebel song, and for crafting an all-new and unique piece of music to go with this important moment from Irish history. It fit beautifully with that part of Tamara and Henry's story, too, and I'm so honored that your words are a part of The Iamos Trilogy. CLEAN LIVIN'.

To Brenda: You know how I have trouble with mushy stuff. But I guess I'm feeling mushy today? There are so many things I want to thank you for, and here are some in no particular order: yarn crafts, spoonie stuff, being a shoulder to cry on and a level head to give advice, keeping me from drowning in publishing work, listening to me yell about *Zelda* horses (now you know you can blame Pan for that), and, of course, supporting my writing. Thank you for being there from the beginning as a beta reader for *Fourth World*, and for being one of my closest friends.

To everyone who helped me get this book into the shape it needed to be—my editors Amy McNulty and Rose Anne Roper; Najla Qamber and the rest of the Qamber Designs team, who created the covers for the series and drew the maps; Nikki Prudden, for designing the emblems that appear across the series; Meagan Davis and Jorge Bravo, who were the faces of Nadin and Isaak; Elise Marion and her team at Mosaic Stock Photography, for arranging the photoshoot; and Esther Hadassah, for all your help holding the business together over the years—thank you all so much.

Thank you to *Ama-gi Magazine* for publishing the first cornerstone of The Iamos Trilogy, my short story "The Choice." That gave me the confidence that this series would work and that I should continue on with it, and here we are now!

Claudie Arseneault and Dove Cooper, thank you for your enthusiasm for The Iamos Trilogy and your endless boosting—it helped the series so much more than you realize, and I really appreciate it and you. A second, double thank you to Claudie for the Aro and Ace Database, and to Dahlia Adler at LGBTQReads: these two resources have been invaluable for introducing more readers to the series, for which I am eternally grateful, and they are also wonderful resources for helping queer people find themselves in fiction. Thanks also to Lauren Jankowski, for all your hard work on Asexual Artists and supporting the creative endeavors of the ace community.

Thank you to Julie Bihn and the #TimeTravelAuthors on Mastodon for your support and helping me cross the finish line with this book.

Thank you to my good friend and sorority sister Courtney Barker for sharing your experiences working on archaeological digs in Belize and Peru.

Big thanks to friends who have been so supportive of my writing, the series, and just being awesome in general: Emily Davies, Dida Shepard, Mary Fan, Heather Wallwork, Karen Teal, Chris Kanther, Intisar Khanani, Jaylee James, Danny Bryn, Joyce Ch'ng, George Donnelly, Jon Garett, Richard Walsh, and many more.

Thank you to everyone at Snowy Wings Publishing for being so amazing. I am so proud of how far we've come, and can't wait to see how far we go!

All my wonderful supporters on Patreon, thank you. You have hung in there and supported my writing month after month, year after year, and I can't tell you how much I appreciate it.

To everyone who has ever written me an email or message telling me that you enjoyed the series, I want you to know how greatly I appreciate it. I have saved all those very special messages and they keep me going on the hard days.

To my family, thank you so much for your love and support. And a special shout-out to my sister, who wanted to see Henry and Tamara finally be able to be together and have some Moments™ in this book—I hope you're happy!

To anyone who has ever read and enjoyed the series, thank you so much for seeing it through, and for your patience over the years, waiting for the end of the story. Iamos was able to exist because of you.

Finally, thank You to God. I spent eighteen months in the dark, until I finally turned around and saw You'd been waiting there the whole time, ready to hand me my joy back. I just had to receive it.

BOOKS BY LYSSA CHIAVARI

the iamos trilogy

Book One: *Fourth World*
Book Two: *New World*
Book Three: *One World*

Different Worlds – An Iamos Novella

other novels

Cheerleaders from Planet X

anthologies

Perchance to Dream: Classic Tales from the Bard's World in New Skins

Magic at Midnight: A YA Fairytale Anthology